Of Days Gone By

Patrick MJ Lozon

Dedicated to my wife and family,

for all of their support.

Table of Contents

Lost Dreams

Chapter 1

The planet of Ishaida is home to remnants of a once thriving colony with a vibrant population, full of hope, ambition, and dreams. Its great surface cities now lay abandoned, barren derelicts, empty of life. Towering skyscrapers stand as battered skeletons, stripped to crumbling concrete and rusted steel, victims of the ceaseless winds and unrelenting heat and cold. What little of humanity that is left has retreated under the protection of the first domed cities and a vast network of underground tunnels.

Ishaida is dying. It has been four-hundred-and-twelve years since the 'great reversal'. The terra-forming project had failed and no one truly understood why, or how. The planet had been an investment poised with unlimited promise. Two light-years off the Cauputain trade highway with a 90% TFP index (Terra-Forming Potential), it was to be *the* stop for starfarers traveling the two-hundred light-year round trip from the Earth to the second great epicenter of humanity - the Cauputain Cluster system. There are few habitable planets within an economical 'route adjustment' distance.

Ishaida would have truly prospered.

On the eve of the last terra-forming plant shutdown, the decision had been made. The trade route was adjusted a full two degrees in order for it to cross the Kennedy system, and the planet of Jefferson, adding a significant seven light-years to the trip. At that moment, five million colonists lost everything, their investments, their livelihood, their future. Those that were able to leave Ishaida did, in one frantic migration of desperation. Left behind were the unlucky; 1.5 million destitute souls fearful of the future that lay ahead.

When the storms began and the atmosphere burned in their throats, most retreated into the domed cities of their origin. Others refused, defying the crowded living conditions, defying Ishaida to yield her worst upon them.

And she did.

The storms were only the beginning. With an atmosphere no longer conditioned by an array of working terra-forming plants, it began its long and violent path of destabilization. Earthquakes shook the planet's crust, and oceans condensed and froze during the night only to slowly boil away during the day. This was a sequence of imbalance that wrenched at the very core of the planet and brought with it unrelenting years of tectonic turmoil.

It had been four-hundred-and-twelve years since the last terra-forming plant had shut down. It had been four-hundred-and-twelve years of violent change, but now it seemed, the worst was over. Ishaida had quieted into a slow progressing death. In the evenings, she would bring on only gentle tremors, complaining in her futility.

Of the twelve domed cities that had been erected during the initial years of colonization, only seven had survived the last four centuries. The others remained empty hulks, mass burial grounds; a testament to man's arrogance of the powers of Ishaida's anger.

The vital links between the cities were maintained through a collection of specially constructed all-terrain transport vehicles. These cargo-hauling transports traveled from city to city, providing needed supplies, shuttling critical resources. The people that manned these transports were a peculiar lot, brave enough to face Ishaida at her worst, with little to rely on but their wit, antiquated technology and sheer will. Whole families would live out their lives on these transports. After centuries and through multiple generations, these 'Porters' had developed their own unique culture, very distinct from their dome-dwelling brethren. The Porters had a strict code of ethics to live by, and deviation was not tolerated. There were but few exceptions.

* * *

Chapter 2

April grabbed the hand of her father as he pulled her out of the axle maintenance tube. They were both covered in grease. She had drawn her long black hair into a tight ponytail, but the slimy black mess left no prisoners. It was matted into her hair, pulling it tight to her scalp.

"You tighten the main pinion down?"

"Yes, and I torqued it, too." She shot back, brows turned in annoyance.

He laughed at her. *So damned full of spunk. Already a bloody know-it-all. But she had the gift alright.* "And look at you, full of grease, how ya ever gonna get yourself a boy lookin' like that?"

She grabbed up the torque wrench, which lay on the floor of the tube, and tightened down the last pinion, ignoring his comments.

"Well?"

"Well, what?"

"You're not forgetting the dance are ya?"

"Not interested." She pulled at the wrench, it slipped and she bashed her knuckles on the pinion bracket.

"Damn it!"

"Ow, now that must've hurt. Here, let me see."

"I'm fine."

"Now, my little lady. S'nuff. Lemmee check it."

She held up her throbbing, bleeding hand, secretly glad he was there.

"Ya gotta gash here, nothing serious though. Let's get it cleaned up. We don't want it infected."

He dabbed at her hand gingerly, wiping away the grease with a sohol pad. "We'll get ya fixed up as good as new." He winked. "So, you don't want to go I take it?"

"No. Not really." She remembered the stories about the rape gangs in the cities and shivered.

"What's a matter, baby?"

"Dad, those stories about the cities, are they all true?"

"Which ones?" He gave her cut a quick spray of plasti-skin.

"You know the gangs and such..."

"Probably." He looked at her.

She could feel his eyes burning right through her like he could read her mind.

Maybe he could.

"Don't you worry. You'll be safe. We have our own guards posted when we have these port bay functions. We haven't had a problem in years. Besides, you should be getting out to see all those other Porter boys. Mix it up some. You might find you might even get to like one of them."

"No, I want to rebuild this differential before we go back out."

He hesitated. "Fine, suit yourself. Let your sisters have all the fun then." He turned to head up the ladder.

"Dad."

"Yeah?" He turned back, hearing something more in her voice than he expected.

"Do they know?"

"They know you're a McThurn, and that's good enough. Listen, baby girl, you get out from under that layer of grease you're always hiding under you may just find you are the prettiest catch this side of Ishaida, hell of ALL the Porter girls, and ya better mark my words on that."

She laughed. "You're just saying that."

"Oh yeah? Why don't you get into that pretty dress Grandmum made you and you'll see for yourself." He grinned like a Cheshire cat. "Remember, you're a McThurn all the way through. You were raised a McThurn, that makes you a McThurn."

"Even if Elsie say's I'm…"

"Whoa there," he cut her off. "You tell Elsie I'll tan her hide if I ever catch her saying anything." His face was already turning red.

"No Dad, it was just talk between us, no one else." She might be a bitch sometimes, but April didn't want the wrath of God coming down on her about this. Dad tended to get a little too upset about some things.

"It better be. You nevermind what Elsie says, anyway. Her mouth flaps a little too unchecked sometimes."

"I know. I'm just different, is all."

"Sokay, you know. Different is good. Keeps us all from going insane, 'specially on the road."

"I guess. Hey, don't you rain down on Elsie, OK?"

He only stared at her.

"Well?"

"I'm the Captain of this here vessel, Missy."

"You want this differential fixed or not?" She smiled coyly.

His stern look melted away into a grin. "Alright, you can have it your way. If I ever catch her flappin' 'bout that she's in for a load of trouble, though. And you think about goin' OK? You might just have fun." He started up the ladder. "If you get that done by 05:00," he called down to her, "you can come with me to the upper level. We have a hitcher signed up this run."

April felt her heart race a bit and fought down the sudden wave of excitement.

The upper level. She'd rarely been through much of any of the domed cities, especially not there. The uppers were secured for the well-to-do, reserved for off-worlders, government electives, and dignitaries - the 'high society' of Ishaida.

She gave the wrench a pull, feeling it click in her hands. Of course, she would have the differential rebuilt by then.

* * *

Domed city Monsoona was typical. The corridors stunk of sweat and stale air. Makeshift compartments littered every spare centimeter of space, leaving little room to negotiate through the narrow walkways.

April kept close to her father as they pushed their way through the busy crowd. She glanced up, seeing a ceiling that was once a transparent gridwork now patched haphazardly in all manners. Bright, cold, white stars pierced through the pieces of transparent quartz.

They ducked into a small room, labeled 'Port Office'.

A gray, thin man with a skeleton face and dark recessed eyes stared back at them. Thin lips drew taut.

"Transport Identification?"

"The SeaClear," replied her father, succinctly. "A101-593."

"Manifest?"

"Here," he handed him the card. The clerk inserted it into the mod reader and pulled up the information. "Very good, Captain. As always, you have everything in order." The thin man cracked a twisted, ugly smile showing rotten brown teeth.

"I see you have your son with you."

She could feel his pale eyes on her. She could only imagine him closer, the smell of his rancid breath on her.

"My daughter you mean."

"Oh! Well, my apologies miss." He winked at her, again a smile of rotten brown teeth.

"We have a hitcher request I'm told," her father stated casually.

"Yeah." He tapped at the mod briefly. "He left instructions that he is staying at the HildeGrande. Off-worlder with strange ideas." An eyebrow went up. "He's requested to go to the Germain TFP. I understand that he's been here for some time. Seems no one is taking his request seriously."

"Does he have money?"

"Oh yes, good credit insomuch as it seems. Here, you'll need this temporary pass to get up there." He handed her father a small orange card. "Don't lose it. It expires in three hours, so you have enough time to get there and back."

"I see. Good day, Sir."

"Good day to you Captain, and you little miss." He winked at her again.

She stared back at him icily. *Asshole.*

The HildeGrande was one of the last few surviving hotels of Ishaida, set aside to impress off-worlders upon their arrival. Unfortunately, like everything else, it was falling apart. But it was essential to maintain a positive image, regardless.

About two-hundred years ago, some lobbyists on Earth, on behalf of Ishaida, had managed to convince the government, and therefore the internationals, to allot trade allowances and allocate an annual quota of startrader landings. The frequency of visits were few but very beneficial to the suffering population.

The standard of living had improved tenfold compared to the early years of the great reversal.

The hotel clerk recognized her father at once. "Captain McThurn, it is truly a pleasure to see you."

"I understand we have a visitor."

"Yes. A young man of study it seems. Very interested in visiting the TFPs I understand. Please, have a seat in the lobby and I'll ring him."

The lobby was dark, smelled of old cigars and sour booze. As April sat down in the chair, she sank into the plush pillows.

"Wow. This is comfortable."

Her dad smiled. "We could use a few of those on the SeaClear."

"Stinks in here."

"Actually, this hotel has very good air quality, compared to the tunnels."

"You've been down there too, in the tunnels?"

April had heard the rumors of the tunnels, overcrowded, filthy, and dangerous.

"Yeah. And I guarantee it is not a place for a young lady."

"Captain," interrupted the clerk, "may I present to you, Mr. Branton Gordon."

He stood up and shook hands. The off-worlder was a touch more than lean, on the thin side, with a bony frame that peaked out with sharp edges through loose fitting clothes. Brown hair flowed back from a sharp-featured face which matched his brown eyes.

If it wasn't for his extreme thinness, he'd be quite handsome, thought April.

"I understand you will be able to provide me transportation to the Germain TFP?"

The Captain nodded. "Have a seat."

It seemed more of a direct command than a polite suggestion.

"You'd better have a good reason to go out there and a good amount of credit at your disposal."

Branton squirmed a bit under the directness of the Captain, finding it hard to locate a soft spot in the oversized cushioned chair.

"Of course, it is part of my research. I plan to find out what went wrong here."

The Captain laughed. "Hear that April, he wants to find out what went wrong. Well, why don't you just ask anyone around here, they'll tell ya sure as sweet. The damned TFPs couldn't do the job. Simple."

"Well, actually, Sir... er... Captain. I have some very interesting evidence I managed to obtain from my grandfather. Some archived information, memory mods from the TFP project."

"Really, can't say I recall any Gordons on the project."

"My grandfather was an engineer. He was on temporary placement for six months or so, about a year before the problems were noticed."

"And?"

"Well, I don't know just yet. I need access to the TFP control systems to make sense of the data."

"Of course you do. You realize the TFPs are shut up tight as a drum. They have sentinel-bots running around them, ready to burn your legs off if you get too close."

"I have clearance." He held up a ruby-red card, the old mod type.

"You sure it will work?"

"I bought it directly from Anard-Bueller."

The clerk turned his head to face them from behind the counter, ears perked.

"Young man, there are some places on Ishaida that mentioning that name will get your throat cut."

Branton cleared his throat, face a little paler than before. "Sure. Got it."

"Alright then, glad to meet you." Her father shook his hand firmly. "We'll need to sort out terms first. Oh, by the way, this is my chief engineer and daughter, April."

Branton reached out to shake her hand. April was amazed at the softness of his palms.

"Now what?" he asked, a bit desperately.

April smiled inwardly. He was obviously thinking we were walking away from this deal, too.

"I'll have my daughter send you our price to the hotel here. If you find our offer agreeable, acknowledge it with full payment details, and show up at port 34, by 18:00 tomorrow. Our transport's the SeaClear. We leave on time, all the time. You miss the ride, we keep the fee."

The walk back was just as crowded. April's dad said nothing all the way to the port, so April followed suit, satisfied to stare at the ancient, eroding remnants of the city.

* * *

April just finished pumping the water into the starboard tanks when Branton showed up. She was covered in so much dirt and grease he didn't recognize her.

"So you made it, I see," she stated flatly.

He stepped back a second, startled.

April giggled. "Yeah, it's me. Had a bit of a lower suspension problem this morning. Been working on it most of the day. Guess I look the part."

"Yes. I'm sorry... Could you direct me to the passenger entrance?"

"Sure." She dropped the hose and headed to the hatch.

"You know, I've heard of these monstrosities, but I never thought I'd see one. They are absolutely huge."

She glanced back, realized he was talking about the SeaClear. "They have to be, considering the freight we haul. We usually hook up to about 30 cars. We could do more, but we don't want to strain the old girl." She patted the SeaClear's polished hull.

"She's 81 meters from front to back, or as my dad says, bow to stern." But they were already in the shadows between the massive tires, making it hard to fathom the true size of the vehicle.

"Independent suspension over 35 axles, and strapped to each wheel is a 1100 hp motor, powered by a 250 MW fusion power supply in the rear." April slapped the inner airlock hull. "Now this baby has some serious torque!" She turned with a broad smile, white teeth a glowing contrast to a blackened, filthy face. Branton smiled sheepishly. "I see you are really into the mechanical aspect of these vehicles – ah - very commendable."

A crease furrowed through April's filthy brow. "Hey, she's my baby. I can feel every piece of this machine when she's running, every little part, every cog of every gear, every motor stator. She's alive you know. She's over four-hundred years old and still running strong. Built to last. She'll outlast me, my children, and my children's children."

"What if I were to tell you that one day we won't need these vehicles anymore and that Ishaida will become habitable again, and you won't need to live within these tin cans, or underground, like so many rats?"

April laughed. "I'd say you're crazy. Listen, buddy, you're not the first one who said they could bring Ishaida back. Nobody believes that bullshit talk anymore, no one. What makes you so damned sure of yourself?"

"Now April, that's not a polite way to treat our guest," interrupted the Captain. "Welcome aboard, son." He motioned to April's younger brother of 11, "Ty, escort Branton to the guest quarters."

"April, clean up your language, and don't you have the water tanks to fill?"

"All done."

"Double-checked all the cars?"

"All 23."

"Alright, go clean yourself up then. I want you on deck when we pull out – no way you're setting foot up there looking like that."

"Can I drive her, Dad?"

"We'll see."

April rushed to her cabin, stripping off pieces of her grimy clothes in the process. She was down to her undergarments by the time she reached her room. She grabbed her best deck uniform and rushed to the showers, and in the process, almost collided with Branton.

He looked her up and then down, wide-eyed.

April saw something more than curiosity in his gaze.

"Like what you see off-worlder. Get a good look, 'cause that's all you're gonna get."

Branton was speechless. The young woman in front of him did not seem to be the same greasy urchin that met him at the door. Scantily clad, she revealed the fine assets of an exceptionally well built young lady. Realizing he was staring, his face turned a bright crimson.

"Sorry, I..."

"Nevermind, out of the way." She pushed him to the side with surprising ease. "This ain't no public peep show." With an alluring wiggle, she headed down the hall and into the shower.

Branton watched her. *Was that on purpose?*

April tended to enjoy her showers, but she had to cut this one short. The grease and dirt quickly washed away, revealing pearl-white skin underneath and bright black hair. She dressed quickly, then stepped to the mirror to inspect her reflection closely. *Nothing wrong there. In a dress, she would make Elsie look like a dog. She had a much better shape. Elsie was too damned lazy.*

She had seen how Branton had looked at her. It made her feel good like she had power over him in a way.

It was kinda of fun.

Lights signaled down the corridor. They were getting ready to leave. She had to get up there.

* * *

The deck was lit in the soft hues of yellows, greens and reds from all the readouts and displays on the walls and overhead. The large monitor glowed eerily, presenting the darkened image of the port exit tunnel. All the members of the McThurn crew number one were seated, except, of course, for April, who arrived late.

The Captain waved her to the front to sit in the co-navigation seat beside him. "Bout time. Started thinking you weren't going to make it."

"I'm here aren't I?"

She ran a scan over the many visual displays, everything in the green. "Need to watch the temps on the differential I just rebuilt."

"Why, you miss something?" He chuckled.

The transport was rolling now, with all her cars in tow, creaking and squealing loudly in protest.

"Check car 4 will you – she feels a bit sluggish. I didn't like the look on the brakes, either."

April pulled up the graphic for the car, showing the readings from the hundreds of sensors strategically located, measuring almost every relevant piece of information one would want to know. A half-dozen of the sensors were glowing red.

"I thought you had Jim fix the sensors on this one?"

They were already gaining speed. The deck was bouncing rudely as the air chassis control struggled to compensate.

"Wish they'd fix up this damn ramp, bloody mess," grumbled the Captain. "And no, Jim had to retool car 22. Besides, he went to the dance last night. You didn't."

April bit down on her bottom lip. It was a bad habit she had. She should learn to stop doing it. One bump and she'd have a scar for sure.

"I'll raise up the hydraulic pressure a bit on 4. That should tighten'er up. Can't tell about the brakes though – sensor's gone."

Her dad just grunted with a nod.

"Pour her on Daddy'o," she cheered as the transport pulled out into the bright sunlight.

"Need a status. You guys sleeping back there?" He yelled back at the crew.

They started ringing through their checklists as they had thousands of times before. April had sat in those back seats since she was five years old. A tedious job, but someone had to do it.

"Got a brake locking up on 14," yelled Ty.

April was on it. In a second, she had the car brake system disengaged. Temperatures were already near critical on the rotors.

"A little slow on that, Ty." She yelled back slightly irritated.

"Just keep your eyes on the readouts, and nevermind yelling at your crew. You want to be Captain one day, you learn to keep a level head," stated her dad sternly.

"Approaching 150 km marker now," she stated, avoiding his stern glance.

"Ok. We're looking good. Vibration dampers reading nominal. Good job on that differential." He took a second to glance over and smile at her. "Let's put her up to 200 K, shall we?"

He tapped the horizon scanner controls. Aerials deployed up from the top of the transport. April watched as the display lit up with multiple hues of green as the image of the upcoming horizon superimposed over the hard yellow lines of the aging highway system, merging feeds from overhead satellites.

Her dad ran the checks over the environmental sensor array. "Nice and clear. Looks like she's cooling off out there, down to 120c outside. Maybe we should open a window."

April ignored her dad's quirky sense of humor, maintaining a flat tone. "Tire temps all in the green. Solar cells are charging up nicely."

"Straight run for the next 45 minutes. Then we turn." He pulled up the navigation display. "Here," pointing a finger, "the main road to the Germain TFP."

"How old is that road?"

"Doubt anyone has been down it in the last 50 years. Expect it will be a bumpy ride. Our birds in the sky show everything is still intact, though."

"What's that?" April pointed to a black line in the road within 20 km of the TFP.

"A ripple I think. Can't tell how big it is, probably a good 10 meters high. The SeaClear could climb over that, but we'll have to be careful."

April knew what a ripple was – slang for a fault line, possibly the edge of a tectonic plate. Strange they would build a TFP so close.

"I can get the buggy and run our visitor out in that. It's only a few K," suggested April.

"No. Jim will do it."

"Why can't I do it? I've never seen the inside of a TFP before. Please?"

He double-checked the laser guidance, avoiding her eyes.

"It's dangerous out there. You can't know what you'll run into. There might be scrapies out there."

"I'll be armed. I can handle scrapies – you know I can."

He shook his head, still avoiding her gaze, intent on checking the reams of instrument data.

"I want to see these TFPs. Besides, he might need some help getting something running. Jim doesn't know anything about that stuff."

"And you do, don't you? Being a genius by scoring high on some tests is a lot different than thinking quickly in a dangerous situation."

"Well, you trained me. I should be able to handle anything by now."

He leaned back in his chair and slowly wiped his face with his hands. "Fine. You can go but not alone. Jim can follow you in the other buggy. This is dangerous territory, and I don't like leaving the SeaClear sitting still very long. You have a window no more than three hours tops. That's it, then we move. If Branton doesn't like it, we leave him."

April was already up and heading to the back.

"While you're at it, find out what he is really up to."

* * *

The trip to reach the Germain TFP lasted two-and-a-half days, long enough for April to learn more about the off-worlder and why he was willing to pay so much to risk his life.

"You really think you can turn that TFP back on? They're bloody well over nine-hundred years old now. Something is bound to be broken, or worn out, or something."

"Look," he tossed a crumpled heap of yellowed diagrams at her. "The specs: every part engineered for ten-thousand years of service, with a plant robotics machine shop that is capable of fabricating almost any replacement part required."

"What about the damned earthquakes. I showed you that fault line."

He laughed, pulling his eyes from the mass of notes to finally look at her. "Your dad says you're practically a genius with machines. He's never seen anyone come close to do what you can do."

April leaned back in the cot, arching her back suggestively as she played with her hair. "That much is true."

"You don't seem like it, the way you talk." He said off-handedly, eyes again turning to burrow into his notes.

"Just give me all the mods and crap you have there." She sat up, irritated that he so quickly diverted his attention from her. "What do you know anyway, pencil–neck?"

"Hey," he half-laughed, "I'm more than just a pencil-neck. I can read these specs. Look." He pointed to a mass of congruent lines. "Redundant systems. Nine in all. Not one, not two, but nine systems."

"Bullshit." She moved in and pulled the diagram away from him. "These are all Trinary systems. Look, three sets of control channels for this, whatever it is. Well, actually, it looks like a temperature monitoring circuit off the main CO_2 vent. Nine systems my ass."

Branton didn't say anything, just watched her quietly.

April suddenly realized just how close they were in this cramped cabin. She pulled her hair back and eased back to the door.

"Just out of curiosity, how old are you anyway?"

"16. 16 and ¾ to be precise. Old enough."

He laughed again. "Old enough for what?"

She glared at him. *Why had she said that anyway? Damn it! Old enough for what, right. Stupid.*

"Just give me everything you got on this TFP. I'll need some time to study before we get there."

"Knock yourself out. I only know the control systems. That's all I need to know to figure this thing out anyway."

"Figure out what?"

He peered back at her with a sheepish grin. "Wouldn't you like to know?"

"Yes," she replied with her most authoritative tone. "Considering we are going out into a very hostile environment, risking the lives of everyone on this transport by having the SeaClear stopped and ripe for scrapies. You don't understand the danger you are putting yourself - and us - into, do you?"

His face had grown a little paler under the dim light, and his lips a little bluer. "You really shouldn't know anyway." He turned back to his desk, dismissing her.

"Too late for that." She grabbed his arm. "You got me studying schematics now, and I'm your ride to where you're going. Fess up."

He turned his chair with a grating squeak and leaned against the wall, letting out a long breath.

"OK. You really want to know. Here you go. I believe that the Ishaida TFP program was sabotaged and I have the evidence," he held up the mod chips in his hand, "right here. I just need to verify it before I publish it as my thesis."

"Those old mod chips can hold anything. Just a bunch of fabricated data."

"With Anard-Bueller encryption keys? Not a chance. These babies are the real deal. And don't you worry. This sabotage wasn't done by a bunch of amateurs. This was the work of a real genius. Chaotic equations – elegant like the iterations of the Mandelbrot set. I've figured it all out, right down to the worms they released in the control systems. Reverse engineering, right back to basic ones and zeros. It's taken me over three years to figure it all out – and that's only because I have these." He held up the aged mods once again.

"So, let's say they're real. So what? I've done my own reading. The TFP systems were scanned thousands of times for possible contaminates, rogue programs, viruses, and bugs. They found nothing."

"Yes, because this was an inside job."

April felt a little weak in the knees. An inside job. She hadn't thought about that. *There were always the rumors, but who took them seriously?* She moved back into the room and sunk down onto the cot, her mind spinning.

"That's right, an inside job. You see, the other part of the puzzle was motive. Anard-Bueller lost an unfathomable amount of money on this deal. Who would suspect them? You just had to root a little deeper, past all those holding companies. Billions and billions of dollars are hard to hide, even in a corporation as big as Anard-Bueller. Things have changed in four-hundred years. A lot of the info that was locked down back then is now part of public record. I have the smoking gun and the motive."

"Why didn't you contact the law on this?"

"Yeah, right," he laughed. "They'd lock me up and throw away the key. The corporations own everything, you know that - everything. You can't go after them or you get squashed. Hell, they toss away whole worlds in the blink of an eye."

April looked away. *She'd seen loss herself. Broken images of her mother raced through her mind. Her face was unclear, lacking features. She had disappeared, just left her. She had been what, four or five? Just a baby scrounging through the wreckage of a mangled city. How many people had died for the sake of profit?*

"April."

She looked up, and he could see the pain in her eyes.

"Oh, look, I'm sorry. I can't imagine what everyone here has gone through..."

"Nobody does, you know," April said, near tears. "The media is locked up tight around here. Ishaida is out of bounds."

"When I was younger, I grew up in a five-by-five shed under a pile of rubble. We ate rations we found from a nearby emergency center that had been buried from an earthquake. There wasn't much left, but it was enough for us. So every day you get to eat your four-hundred-year-old ration and wonder if you're going to live to the next day."

"I didn't know."

"Yeah, you thought I was a freeborn Porter, didn't you? Well, I wasn't. I was born out here, in hell, where exposure will kill you in seconds, if not minutes. My mother, somehow, kept us alive. Never knew my father though. My mom told me he had been killed trying to get food for us."

She reached over to the wall and pulled back the shield to the cabin window. The window was small, no bigger than a dinner plate. "Look out there, you see those pillars, those tall shadows?"

"Yes." He winced at the bright light.

"Those tall buildings had a nickname, called them skyscrapers. That's what's left of the first surface city of Ishaida - NewParis. There may be a few people living there, still. We call them scrapies. That's what I was, a scrapie - barely alive, scrounging for food. Scrapies had it the worst of all. The domed cities were too far away to make it, and the DD's wouldn't let you in, anyway."

"DD's?"

"Dome-dwellers, the last of Ishaida's civilized population, barring us out of their stinking cities."

"And the scrapies, they just leave them out there to die?"

"Don't feel too sorry for them, now. The ones left are mostly animals. Cannibals. Kill you and eat you. But to tell you the truth, no one really knows how many scrapies are still alive out there. They used to hit the transports pretty regular. Not anymore, not for a long time. Some say they're all dead now."

"And how did you make it here?"

"After my mom died, I decided to go to the domed cities. She had told me stories of them, about the kind people, and the food, and that you were safe there. I was only four or five then. I didn't know what to do. So I left my little shelter and I walked. The McThurns found me on the highway at sunset. Lucky for me. I would have been dead within the hour of exposure. The winds had already started up." She glanced at him, saw the pity in his eyes, and she hated it. "No one other than my family knows about this. No one."

"Why?"

"Because transports don't stop for scrapies. Ever. It's code. Scrapie kids are sent out to lure Porters in. Old trick. Lost more than a few Porters that way. The Porters would hoist my stepdad in front of a tribunal if they ever heard of it. And I would be a disgrace."

"That's ridiculous. It's uncivilized."

"That's just the way it is. It's called survival I guess. Just keep your trap shut, OK?"

"Sure." He nodded. "No one will ever know from me."

"Why the hell did I even tell you?" She stated, annoyed with herself. "I don't even know you."

"'Cause of my boyish charm." He laughed.

"Right." She crumpled the sheets under her arm. "I'll take a look at these. If what you say is true, then we're going to do more than run a few tests. I'm going to turn'em back on, all seven of them."

Branton's face turned a bit pale again. "You mean it, don't you?"

"Sure. They're just machines and I have a knack for machines, electronics to mechanics. You think you can find these worms – can you remove them?"

"Well, I guess. Sure. I should be able to isolate..."

"Can you flush them or not?"

"Yes."

"Then get writing your little programs. The clock is ticking. While you're at it, I'm going to get some sleep."

* * *

Chapter 3

Captain Oranis McThurn called over the com-link. "Jim, You at 15 yet?"

"No Dad, one more car. Be there in a minute."

"Check the brakes on axle 7 as well, will ya? She's reading pretty hot."

The transport rocked to port as it dipped down into a large hole.

"Holy shit, Dad!" Rang an irritated voice over the com. "Can't you keep her steady? I banged my head. There's not much room down here you know!"

Oranis chuckled, careful to mute the com. Yes, he knew, he'd been crawling through those access ways since he was a baby. The SeaClear had been owned and operated by the McThurns for almost 15 generations now. A long time. He knew every causeway, every maintenance hatch, every loose fitting, and the cause of every rattle.

He scanned instrumentation and yelled back at Elsie to adjust the coolant flow through zone six. The transports were mechanical behemoths, as complicated as a starship with 10 times the moving parts. *It was amazing they were able to keep these beasts running past 10 years much less four-hundred.* He kept a close eye on the horizon display. Running this many tonne at 200 K meant you had little time to react to a hazard. SeaClear's suspension, as hardy as it was, could only take so much abuse.

He remembered the time his father had hung up all 10 axels on a concrete abutment of a collapsed road. It took them days to get unhooked, pull off the lead car – or the 'tank' as it's called, and repair the suspension enough for them to limp back to Monsoona. It had been a costly repair, and his dad, nor his granddad, was too happy about it.

All it takes is a split second.

He eased the SeaClear around the collapsed high rise on the 707. They were in the remains of the old city of NewParis. The derelicts of massive buildings cast dark shadows across the highway.

The city always made him uneasy. He had seen firsthand what scrapies could do to a transport. Strip her down to a skeleton in a few days, leaving nothing – and nobody.

That had been many years ago, now. How they had survived so long was a miracle. The last few quakes had to have done them in, broke the seals of their makeshift quarters, killed what remained of them. Four centuries ago, they had refused to immigrate back to the domes, choosing to take their chances out here. They were once proud, accomplished men and women, now they were just animals. Just as well they were dead.

The SeaClear snaked around the last curve of the old 707 as Oranis guided her onto the 501. It would be clear driving now to their turnoff, which remained many miles ahead. Each city's location was carefully planned, far away from the minimum required distance from each TFP. Radiant gases and static charges often built up around the plants when they were discharging causing uncontrolled bursts of lightning and unstable local weather.

But that was when they were running so many centuries ago.

He adjusted the trim, careful to compensate with the hydraulic dampers in the process. Every car simultaneously lowered its profile, suspensions adjusted, wheels moved out to a wider stance for high speed.

With a flick of his finger, the motors whined out higher revolutions, pulling the tremendous weight of each massive car up to speed in synchronized precision.

"Taking axle 7 off-line," announced Jim. "Looks like we're getting air in here somewhere."

Oranis flipped over to the external monitor and watched as the set of wheels raised up and tucked themselves close into the sides of the car. It was best practice to pull up matching pairs, keep the weight distribution and load handling even.

"Permission to go outside?"

"Negative. Going too fast."

"I got the local panel up. She's reading the same as the main, looks like it anyway. What the hell are we hauling in here? We're near our limit on weight. Can't lose another pair that's for sure."

"Manifest says iron ore. The DD's are doing some smelting."

"Recommend we raise the hydraulic pressure up to 30,000," suggested Jim.

Oranis thought about it for a moment. The hydraulic channels that ran through the frame of each car were used to stiffen up the structure in the case of heavier loads. Each car, because of its large dimensions, had to have some flex built into it. It was a simple engineering principle: what is too rigid to bend, breaks.

"OK, but no more than that. We can live with the central axles being overloaded a bit. Ease her up real slow, those hydraulics are old."

"Understood."

"Captain?"

Elsie was calling him from the back. "What do you have there, daughter?"

"Some flickering in the ballast pumps on car 23 again. I thought April fixed that."

"So did I."

He switched over to the main intercom. "April got a yellow for you."

A few moments later April answered back sleepily. "Yeah?"

"23's ballast pumps are acting up again."

"It's just a sensor short. Nothing wrong with the pumps. I checked them."

"Sure about that?"

"Yes. I double-checked them. The short's in the sensor line somewhere. I didn't have the sniffer, so I couldn't locate it. Why don't you ask Jim or Ty where they left it?"

"Forget it, Sis!" Yelled Jim through the intercom. "I haven't touched it in months. Last time I saw it, you had it!"

"Hey, keep it down. I'll have Ty look for it when his rounds come up."

"Dad, I need to talk with you when you're done your shift," stated April, thinking more clearly, now that she was wide awake.

"Why?"

"It's about our visitor."

He could see Elsie's ears perk up through the reflection off the main deck mirror.

"This doesn't concern you, Elsie," he shot out hoarsely.

"Flip to channel 10 and lock it, April. Now, what is this about?"

"The TFPs, Dad. It's about the TFPs. We can restart them. I know how."

Oranis sat back in his chair and took a very deep breath.

"Did you hear me?" She asked.

Another breath. "Oh yeah, I heard you loud and clear," he acknowledged. "Get dressed and meet me in the mess."

He called up Jim to take the deck. It was a long wait.

* * *

"You aren't serious, are you?" Oranis asked.

"I can do it," April said, excitedly. "I studied the schematics. These things are simple to operate. Everything is automated. All I need to do is sequence the startup, the robots do the rest."

"These machines haven't been fired up in four centuries. Something is bound to break or already be broken," he refuted.

"Don't worry about that. The pre-stage tests will expose any problems, and there's literally an army of robots at each major center. They can manufacture anything that needs to be repaired. Besides, whatever the problems are, they will be minor. These things were built to run forever."

"Look, even if you can get these things started back up, who's to say that's the right thing to do? And it's dangerous. Anard-Bueller will have their henchmen down here within the year. They'll be looking for blood." Oranis's forehead was crinkled, exposing his worry.

"Who's going to tell? We get three or four traders per year landing here, and they don't give a damn what's going on. You really think they'll be here within a year? Ten years, maybe, once our atmosphere starts changing back."

"But Hun, you can't just turn these things back on. There are repercussions to doing something like this. You need an army of geologists and… well, scientists of all kinds to monitor the planet and adjust those damn things. Don't you remember the quakes?"

"'Course I do. They happened *after* they were turned off. I read the whole terra-forming history of Ishaida. The process is very gradual, not like the rapid destabilization that occurred after."

Oranis was not convinced. "We can't push this planet through that again. The TFPs failed, they had to turn them off."

"Why are you holding onto that myth? They were lying to you, to all of us. The TFPs were working, Ishaida was transforming until someone cracked into their control systems. Like I said, Branton has the proof – and the cure."

Oranis snatched at his coffee cup as it bounced and nearly tipped off the small table. "No, you cannot turn those things back on. I forbid it. This is not a decision that you and I can just make. Understand?"

April jumped up and threw her arms into the air. "Aargh! Why not? Why can't we just make the decision ourselves? It's our planet! It's my planet!"

"Then tell me this; are you sure? Can you be absolutely sure you are not putting anyone in danger when you turn them on? Are you sure this Branton character is right about his theory? Think, girl. Think."

April stared down at her father. *'Course he was right, he was always right.* "Fine," she grumbled, turning away. "But what if this is true? Then what?"

"Then we tell the DD's, and we tell the Porters, let them decide. Simple."

"Great, our future as dictated by committee."

Her dad laughed. "If only you knew."

* * *

The Germain TFP loomed on the horizon. They were still 160 km away, but the fabricated mountain reached high into the wispy, red skies.

April watched through the small porthole from car 23, feeling her palms grow hot. She was nervous for some reason. She turned away, eyes intent on a small display as she guided the sniffer along the main conduit. *Elsie's bitching about a damn short. Bloody things have been shorting out for 50 years, but she has to have it fixed right now.*

There! A blip. A crossed pair, maybe? Continuity was there, but she was getting higher than normal induction. The problem was in another circuit. Every time it shorted, it would induce a current, giving an error reading on the panel. She had seen this too many times before. The SeaClear was getting old. All her cars needed to be rewired. Why they hadn't used optics for all of these secondary channels was beyond her. She had read somewhere the engineers had specified standard cabling for durability, but she doubted that. It was money. The cheaper the better. Like everything else on this planet – everything except for the TFPs. She followed the other circuit and eventually traced down the source. Bare wire crossing over a sharp-edged rivet. She bound it with heat-shrink tape.

"Ty, you getting a clear reading on your panel?"

"Yeah, Sis. Looks good. You found it."

"'Course. Can't help it, I'm good."

Ty laughed through the intercom. "Well, since you're so good, why don't you step outside and fix axel 7 on car 15?"

"I said I'm good, not stupid. Besides, the sun is setting. The winds are getting up."

Ty whistled. "You're telling me. I'm reading 210 km winds over the deck right now."

April could hear it, too. It was trying to force itself through every facet of the aging hull, pushing and creaking from everywhere. It was creepy. A shiver ran up her spine.

She brought up the atmosphere stats on the main panel. Everything was tight, save a minute negative leak on the main bay door. Still sounds like it's leaking from every rivet.

She pulled a balloon out from behind the panel, blew it up, tied it, and let it loose. Eventually, it would get sucked out the bay door, the balloon would burst, and the goop inside would harden and seal in seconds. No more leak.

"Ty, talk to me. It's spooky back here."

"An old-timer like you? I didn't think anything spooked you."

"Hey, I'm only a couple years older than you, you know, 'sides, it's the wind I hate."

"Mom says to check the hydraulics on each car as you come up. The wind is wreaking havoc on the pumps."

The car jerked sideways, one side momentarily airborne. April caught herself, just avoiding splitting her head open on the bulkhead. Hydraulic pumps whined as the suspension readjusted itself.

"No shit. Better tell Mom to slow'er down, I almost cracked my skull open."

"I hear you, Hun." It was her stepmom, Lavenue, this time. "We're dropping down to 160. If it gets any worse, we may need to go to lockdown."

"Are you sure?"

Another gust pounded the car, metallic screeches echoed down the open hatchways eerily.

Lockdown was no fun.

It wasn't the first time. They would bring the SeaClear to a halt and fire the pile drivers into the ground, anchoring each car with four high tension cables. Usually at least one pile driver would fail, and they'd have one car, hopefully not too close to the tank, twisting around in the wind. All they could do was sit there and wait for it to end.

"Well, Mom, if we're locking down, I'm coming back up to the tank."

"Car 10 has a problem. Pump just failed. Get up there April, quick, before we lose it."

She ran, squirmed, crawled and ran again, ignoring the screeching, scraping sounds echoing around her. Ahead, through the open hatch, she could see car 10. Its deck floor was bouncing crazily.

"Mom," she yelled, nearly out of breath. "Car 10's bouncing too much. I can't fix anything like that."

"April, there's no other way, you've got to go in. I'm turning into the wind, should calm down some."

"I'll do it." It was Jim. His voice was raspy. Not enough sleep. It wasn't his shift.

"No, I got it, Jim. I'll figure it out."

She was at the bladder now. Ahead the deck of car 10 jumped up and down in synch with the titanic forces of the wind outside. She jumped and grabbed for the rail. Instantly she was on her knees with metal grating viciously bashing into her kneecaps.

She pulled herself up using the rail, trying to get in synch with the violent movements around her. The main panel was just ahead. All she had to do was reroute to the secondary pump. *Why hadn't they designed this to be done from the control deck?*

She jammed her feet under a cross-brace and reached for the panel controls. The bouncing made her fingers dance all over the panel. *Be quick. One jab at a time. Wait for a quiet spot.*

The second jab, the hydraulics menu was up.

Something gave out below the car with a savage bang. Whistling started. Shrill and sharp.

Jab, one more time.

The secondary pump started with a sharp grinding noise. The suspension controls began to compensate, and the bouncing began to level out. In seconds, it had settled to a rough vibration, but the shrill whistle was turning into a scream.

Another leak. No time for a balloon this time.

April ran down the 10's deck way, at the halfway point she could already feel her lungs burning for air. Behind her echoed shrill voices of someone screaming at her through the intercom. She reached car 9 and slammed the control panel. The hatch slammed shut so hard it almost took her arm off. She slid down on the deck into a crouch. Every muscle in her body hurt, even her eyes. Compared to car 10 car 9 was serene. The buffeting winds from the hell outside seemed muffled, tamed.

It took her a second to realize Ty was calling for her on the intercom. It took the next second for her to recognize the sound of running footsteps coming closer - her brother, Jim, barely a car away.

She just sat there and laughed.

He reached her, out a breath and visibly shaking. "What the hell are you laughing at?" He yelled, relieved but irritated. "I thought you were a goner."

"Well, I'm not am I?" She said, still unable to stop her laughing. She went to stand up, but her legs were too shaky. Her knees were bleeding.

Jim grabbed her. "Just a little too close for comfort." He said, offering a wink of encouragement.

"Hah, you know I'd be fine. It's just a low pressure area, not like being out in space or something."

He flipped the intercom switch. "We're OK. Coming up. Standby for lockdown."

By the time they set foot in the tank they had rolled to a stop, and the deck pile guns were already firing. A tired, haggard looking Oranis was up and overseeing the operation. Everyone was tense and excited. It had been years since they had needed to go to a full lockdown.

The deck shuddered as the pile guns fired. The sounds of the blasts reverberated up the hull of the transport in deafening waves. Pulse after pulse surged, then ultimately faded, to a comparative quiet.

"Well?" Oranis asked. Chancy, April's oldest sister, was checking over the cars. "Retracting. Two cables didn't hold, one on 10 and one on 19. Resetting 10 for deployment, firing now."

The deck shook again.

"10 locked in."

"Resetting 19... Reset. Firing 19."

Nothing.

Oranis looked over to Chancy. "Reroute to the backup firing circuit."

Chancy ran her fingers over the controls. "Rerouted to backup," she stated, thin-lipped and pale.

"OK. Work this time baby. Resetting 19... We're reset... firing."

The deck shook this time.

"Retracting, yep, it's holding," she announced with a wide grin.

Oranis laughed and slung his arm around his wife, Lavenue. Smiles all around.

They were locked down now. All they had to do was ride out the storm.

* * *

Branton was in the main corridor looking a little paler than usual.

"What's going on?" He stammered.

"Just a bit of Ishaida's nasty side showing. She's kicking up a wind out there, and we've had to do a lockdown," replied Chancy.

"What do you mean, lockdown?"

"We drop the suspension of each car down to its lowest profile, roll out the skid plates to their maximum extension so they block the wind from getting under our belly, and fire anchors into the ground to tie each car down and keep the lot of us from blowing away."

"Just how powerful are these winds out here?"

"Oh, well it depends, just start with your meanest hurricane on Earth and go up. What's a category 5 – 230 kmh or somewhere around there? Actually, these speeds may be closer to an F5 tornado on the Fujita scale. Winds have been known to go beyond 450 kmh. The good thing is the atmosphere is not nearly as dense as it was four-hundred years ago. But we also get tornados here too, localized cyclonic funnels within the storm. If one of those hit us, the odds are we won't survive it."

Something banged on the side of the tank, shifting the car slightly.
"What the hell!"

"Just debris. Don't worry, the hull can take it."

"And if our anchors give out?"

April piped up at the chance to explain. "There are four per car. If two give out on the same side, we may have a problem. One car can cause a cascade of failures. Then the whole transport starts to roll. Probably break every bone in your body and you die horribly." She smiled at him, watching the remaining color drain from his already pale face.

"You're kidding, right?"

She couldn't hold the smile much longer. The truth was no longer amusing. "No. Fact is we've lost our share of transports to weather like this. About 15 years ago, the Carolina was caught up in one of these windstorms. She was locked down, the satellites showed the winds peaking at about 350 kmh. No problem, until something changed in the storm. Wind speed suddenly shifted above 400 kmh. Some of the anchors let go. In less than a minute, the whole transport broke loose. The hitches can't take that type of stress, so the cars broke apart. We found the tank a day later, completely buried in sand and everyone inside dead. The human body is just not built to survive that."

"So you really don't know about this storm then," he said, looking up and down the corridor. "This could be it."

"Doubt it," April said, nonchalantly. "This is just a small breeze. Mom pulled her over to play it safe. Plus, we're pointing into the wind."

She looked around quickly, mentally inspected each corner of the inside hall. The wind was reaching a shrill shriek outside. Strange moans filled the corridors. The tank vibrated violently, just for a second. April grabbed the rail. When she looked back at Branton, he had a crooked smile pasted on his whitened face.

"Small breeze you say. You don't look so confident now." He was taunting her, although he looked like he was going to be sick.

"So. I don't like the wind," she shot back defensively. "And yes, this could be the one. Feel better? My Uncle Graham's transport, the StarGrazer was also hit by a tornado. Ishaida can get pretty rough out here."

Something fell in the mess, ringing like so many pots and pans. Someone was cursing, probably Oranda, the assigned cook for the shift.

"So I can tell," stated Branton glumly. "Well? What happened to the StarGrazer?"

"I told you, already. You don't survive a tornado on Ishaida." She pushed past him, feeling angry at herself for being so transparent. He folded back against the wall, giving little resistance.

"Oh yeah, if you hear the siren, get to the main deck as fast as you can and buckle in," she yelled back, not bothering to slow her pace. She wanted to get to her cabin. Her anger had already given way to exhaustion, her arms felt like lead weights, the muscles in her legs burned, and her knees ached.

* * *

The storm lasted for two days. They were less than an hour from the Germain TFP, and all they could do was wait. Being a McThurn, you learned to keep busy. Captain Oranis's list never shortened. There was always something to do, to fix, to rebuild or to clean. He even had Branton working.

April smiled, amused at the gangly, slightly uncoordinated student of the sciences as he fought with a small bolt on some part he was assigned to take apart and clean.

In a way, it was a relief to stay busy. It kept your mind from wondering, from thinking about the raging forces of the storm outside, about what could happen. April's dad was a good Captain, like his father before him. They all trusted him, knew he would get them through this, no matter what. So it was business as usual, and you tended to get used to the screeching winds, and the strange moans that emanated from every facet of the SeaClear.

And so, when the end finally came and the winds ceased, it was almost unnoticed. Well, for some anyway, but not for April. She kept an eye on the satellite imagery religiously throughout. She knew when it was going to break, and she was already putting together a mental checklist of what she had to do. They wouldn't start up immediately, as there were a lot of inspections to be done before they released the anchors. Standard protocol had to be followed to ensure the transport was capable of getting mobile before it was released. If some repair work had to be done, it had to be completed before they let go, just in case another storm came up in the meantime. One thing was certain: they had to do an outside inspection. Captain Oranis put the task lists together for everyone – everyone but April. As chief mechanic, she made her own lists, and she didn't need any assignments. Her inspections were thorough, and her procedures, when she bothered to publish them, had made her a well-known name amongst the Porters.

"I need Jim to prep the rovers."

"Yep. On his list first thing. And don't be thinking you're going out there alone."

"And who is it this time?"

"Why me, of course. Jim's in charge of coordinating everything this time. I'm just a fifth wheel now."

"OK, Captain, but don't worry, I'll put you to work."

He winked at her and flashed a quick silly-looking smile. "I'll meet you on the rover deck, just gotta grab my gun."

April shook her head. There wasn't anyone out here, especially now, just after a storm. Oranis was cautious to the point of being paranoid.

The rovers were tube framed 4x4s with a large transparent bubble mounted mid-frame to house a driver and a passenger, not very large, but quick and agile. April had modified them, beefed up the suspension and raised up the power to the wheels, and of course, at her dad's request, added some mobile armament.

Jim had them checked over and prepped. He was tinkering with the ramp when she arrived.

"Bloody thing has some sand in it or something, won't go all the way down."

April peered out the portal. "It's good enough, it's only a few centimeters from the ground. I'll look at it when we dock."

"Sis, don't forget to check axle 7 over on car 15. She's near the limit on weight."

"Top of my list."

"Gotta get back, Dad's got me on prep-lead."

"I heard high-roller. Next thing you know, you'll be running the show," she teased.

Jim just smiled and started out. "Oh yeah, who's going with you?"

"Right behind you."

He turned in surprise. "Oh, you surprised me, Captain."

"Aren't you supposed to be on deck, son?"

"'Course, just heading up there now."

"Good, debrief me when I get back in. I want to see if you missed anything." He winked.

They both jumped in the rover.

"Don't forget your helmet, Captain," April nodded at the headgear behind them. She triggered the remote switch to run the air pumps. The atmosphere inside the car equalized to the outside. The bay door retracted exposing a sunny desert landscape.

"She's hot out there, about 85c," Oranis stated.

"Let's hope we don't have to stay out there too long, then."

She rammed it into gear and the rover leapt off the ramp and into the loose sand, wheels throwing fountains of crystalline silica up into the air.

"Whoa. You crazy or something?"

"Hey, I'm in charge now, Captain. Sit back and enjoy the ride."

They swung around and started bouncing down the long snaking transport of the SeaClear, her monstrous cars loomed up on their right like a black wall.

"We'll get to the end and move up systematically, one car at a time. Here's your list."

She shoved over an electronic clipboard. "Oh yeah, we'll be walking for a large part of it. What side d'ya want, the sun or the shade?"

"No matter, my dear. Sure this list is complete?"

"'Course. You just make sure you do a thorough job. I'll leave you the car, since you're so old and all." She laughed.

"Jim," Oranis paged. "We're coming up on car 23 now. No surprises so far. Keep this channel open for us, and keep an eye on the satellite imagery."

"Roger. Will let you know if anything comes up."

"If you see any danger, get underneath the car and make your way to me. Here's your gun." He handed over a holstered hand blaster.

"Is this really necessary?"

"Yep."

She blew out a long breath to stress her annoyance. He ignored her dramatic behavior.

The rover rolled to a stop and they got out. April could feel the heat through the soles of her feet. The suit's cooling system was already whirring away. She held out her checklist in the bright sunlight. This was going to be a long day.

The hours clicked by slowly. The sun was in late afternoon position, but everything shimmered in the heat and all but the shade directly under the cars had evaporated. Come night the temperatures would plummet, and frost would cover everything, but that was many hours away.

She had reached car 15 and started to inspect the problem axle. Her dad was behind by one car. "Dad, need some tools out of the rover. Looks like we have a sheared line."

"Be there in a moment."

April, now standing high on the catwalk of the car, took a moment to look out at the horizon, a shimmering line of sand, devoid of any signs of life. Directly ahead lay the Germain TFP. It was the size of a mountain, casting a vast shadow over the desert plain. It stood there, an alien abhorrence, an intruder to this desert world.

From the TFP she could see a line of bent and rusted pipes tracing up through the rolling hills of sand. They were remnants of light towers following along an ancient highway, mostly buried in the shifting sands. A few miles away from the TFP a jagged black line cut across rising up in the distance, turning into a pronounced ridge.

The fault. Why would they build so close to a known fault? They had to know what they were doing...

"The TFPs are bigger than you imagined, aren't they?"

She turned to see her dad, toolbox in hand. "Yeah, they are amazing. The cost to build something like that must have been enormous."

"Don't you worry about that. Anard-Bueller has already made back any of its losses. It may have taken a few years, but the companies will never lose in the end."

"Branton says he has the financial records that prove Anard-Bueller was paid off."

"Just keep that under your hat. People that talk against the Company have a way of disappearing."

"Look around, Dad. This is what's left of Ishaida. The company has long since left us. You know where all those people disappear to? It's here – they send them right here – the end of the humanity's plight."

"Yeah, I know, I know."

"Why don't you keep going on the inspection, while I fix this? We need to get this done while we still have light," she offered.

"No problem. Once I hit the tank, I'll come back around and meet you."

"Alright."

By sunset, the last car had been checked, with only a few minor problems found.

The tank fired up with a venomous growl. Lights glared angrily upon the surrounding sands.

Tomorrow they would be at the TFP.

* * *

The ship had descended from the skies using the latest in cloaking technologies. It was a unique design, built for a particular reason. It had only one pilot, a trained professional on a singular mission. The aging equipment at the Ishaida spaceport didn't even pick up on the vessel's arrival, not that anyone would have been watching since very few ships ever landed there anyway.

Miles below the silently descending stealth ship lay the Germain TFP and a transport called the SeaClear, which was just at that moment slowly coming to a stop. On board, the McThurn family worked through the logistics of planning the turn of the massive ground transport, which would require the SeaClear to navigate through the rough terrain.

April and Branton were waiting in the rover, watching the ramp drop all too slowly.

"Jim, we're heading out."

"No you don't," came the vigorous reply.

"Captain said that you are to wait for my say. I do the security."

"We're just going to spin around a bit. Promise, I'll wait for you."

The ramp was still a meter off the ground when she jammed the small 4x4 into gear and pressed the accelerator to the floor. The vehicle launched from its berth, leaving a blue haze of burned tires in its wake. Above them, the small but deadly craft fired its payload of tracer missiles. They reached the stationary transport in mere seconds and exploded. Molten metal launched high into the air as the ancient behemoth disintegrated into a wall of heat and fire. Cars successively exploded, their hulls ripping open in a savage crescendo. In milliseconds, the SeaClear was gone.

The roaring wall of flame hit April's rover, flipping it end over end countless times. Pieces of the SeaClear razed through the small vehicle, tearing holes and searing through its interior as they passed. The rover finally settled, upside down, and well away from the burning remains of the SeaClear.

April had been knocked unconscious. When she came to, she was disoriented and in pain. Branton lay prone beside her, also still tied to his harness and suspended in mid-air. They were upside down, she realized, fighting her way out of the fogginess. She pulled her hands off the roof and found them sticky, black.

Her blood? Was she bleeding?

She could feel the panic come and fought it down. *No, she was in one piece. Nothing broken. It was Branton!*

Under the wavering light of the fire, she could see the young man's right leg had been severely cut just below his knee. He was bleeding out slowly.

The cold night air was already blowing in through the splintered vehicle, enough for a light layer of frost to seep onto the broken plexiglass.

She had to get him down. She had to get them out of the rover, now!

She fought down another wave of panic. A cold calm settled over her. Her limbs moved with mechanical precision. She pulled out her utility knife and cut away at the harness. Once he was out, she tied a tourniquet around his leg using part of the same harness. Only then, did she notice the scene behind her; the burning remains of the SeaClear.

The remains of the transport lay like a snake splayed open on the desert floor, insides burning white hot. She could see far out in the distance, large chunks of sizzling, glowing metal, other more massive pieces thrown clear by the force of the explosion. The fires burning inside the cars danced eerily in the night, throwing a reddish-orange glow on everything.

She scrambled for footing then started running to where the tank should be.

Someone might have survived. They might be calling for her.

The closer she came, the more she could feel the heat searing through her suit. She scanned the surroundings, searching desperately for someone, finding it hard to see through tears that blurred her vision.

"Dad. Dad, are you there? Tell me you're out there."

Her legs crumbled under her and she fell, her blood covered gloves buried deep in the sand.

Her stomach heaved.

No. Get hold of yourself. Vomiting in this suit will kill you. It's no use. No one is answering. No one survived this. Even if they were thrown, they would have died from exposure by now.

She lay there and cried. The tears dripped onto the faceplate of her helmet. She wanted to reach up, to wipe them from her eyes, to clear her nose, but she couldn't.

Stop. You have to stop. You'll get in trouble out here. It was her mother's voice she heard - her real mother, of years gone by. *Branton needs your help. Get to the TFP. Get to safety.*

Safety. Branton. TFP.

She stumbled to her feet and started back to the rover.

Time is the enemy now. Need to get to the TFP before the real cold sets in. The only hope of survival now. They had to get into the TFP, and only Branton knew how.

He lay where she had left him, the firelight glinting off his suit revealed a slight rise and fall of his chest.

Still breathing, still alive.

She inspected the rover, then grabbed hold and yanked with all of her strength. The lightweight vehicle rolled back over easily, bouncing on its oversized tires. She cleared away the debris of the smashed globe and checked the control panel. The power supply was OK. A quick glance underneath showed a sheared piece of tubular frame and a bent front tie rod.

But it's drivable, thank God.

She heaved Branton back onto his seat and used a lightweight emergency blanket to tie him down so he wouldn't fly off. Every few minutes he would moan in pain.

The small control panel revealed a full charge on the batteries. She hit the lights, but only one came on. Regardless, it was enough to see by. She gave one last look at the SeaClear before turning the rover toward the TFP.

She would grieve later. For now, they had to survive.

They reached the fault line in minutes. It was just a pile of rubble and the 4x4 climbed up and over it effortlessly. April fought with the wheel, the bent tie rod was making it difficult to steer. She could feel her arms burning. Straight ahead lay the TFP entrance. She accelerated as much as she dared. With every bounce, the steering wheel snapped back savagely. The first entrance was blocked by a security gate. She didn't bother to stop. The lightweight fencing gave way without difficulty, a victim of years of rust and decay.

The second gate was not passable, made of alloy bars more than 30 centimeters thick, it seemed impenetrable. "Branton," she screamed. "Branton, wake up. I need your passkey. We need to get into the TFP now!" She locked up the wheels and the vehicle slid sideways, stopping less than a meter from the entrance verification console.

Branton finally stirred, eyes then opened in a fixed gaze. She could tell he was in shock.

"Tell me the passkey. We need to get inside, now! If you want to live, tell me how to get inside!"

He fumbled with his left hand toward a front pocket in his suit. April opened up the pocket and pulled out a blue card. He nodded at her, giving a weak half-smile.

Not knowing exactly what to do with the card, she approached the console. It was featureless. She waved the card in front of it. Instantly a small square, inlaid within the face of the console, lit up green. Ahead the massive gate started to open, glinting of rust and blackened metal in her headlight. It towered above them, imposing and impenetrable, until now.

Not wasting a second, she was back in the rover and cleared the gate in a cloud of dust. The entrance into the building lay ahead. A small robot stood brazenly at the door. As she drove up, the mechanical man pulled the door open and gestured to her to come in. She didn't bother to get out of the rover, instead, she drove right through.

A secondary set of doors awaited them. It was a built-in airlock system. Her helmet fogged over as warm air filled up the airlock. She wiped at her visor, only to leave it smeared with blood – Branton's blood. A second mechanical man waved them through.

She drove the rover through to the center of the room and let it roll to a stop. They were situated within a very large anteroom, a massive receiving area constructed for the sole purpose of impressing any and all visitors. Everything presented on an imposing scale. Above, a tear-shaped ceiling stared down at them, embedded with ornate carvings and golden symbols. A large brown granite desk ran the length of the interior wall, somewhat similar to what one would see in a hotel. All throughout the area different types of glossy granite lined the walls and floor, revealing intricate composite layers of designs and shapes.

April could not spare the time to be impressed. Her enviro-sensors readout panel on her arm was blank with telltale cracks that revealed the story.

Broken. No way to tell if the air was any good. Only one way to know.

She tore off her gloves, yanked off her helmet with a quick defiant twist, and took a deep breath of warm, stale, somewhat oily smelling air.

Safe, they'd made it.

She reached over and unscrewed Branton's helmet. She hadn't noticed before, but it had a large crack in the transparent ceramic and it must have been leaking.

"Branton, can you hear me? We made it in. I'm going to look at your leg now, OK?"

She reached under her seat and yanked out the first aid kit. Unlike a standard kit, this one was well stocked with the latest equipment and medicine. She had seen to that personally. She pulled out a hypodermic and administered a shot for pain, then proceeded to use the surgical laser to cauterize the wound. The flesh had already turned black where the night air had infiltrated and frozen it.

She laid out a plastic operating sheet on the floor, in front of the light of the rover, and systematically inventoried the tools she needed. Luckily, the kit had a couple quarts of sim-blood. She activated the bags to bring them up to body temperature and linked them together for a supply. As gently as possible, she pulled him out of the seat and positioned him onto the sheet, careful to keep the tourniquet from working loose. His face held a frozen grimace of pain, and his body lay limp as if the last of his life was seeping from him.

Assessing what to do next took a moment. She was not a doctor and had minimal practical experience with this kind of thing. It became clear what she needed to do, however: cut back the dying flesh, suture the compromised artery, and stitch up the wound.

Easier said than done.

She stepped back, caught her breath that she hadn't realized she'd been holding. Her stomach was flipping and she felt like getting sick. She had seen this done a dozen times in her emergency field medicine vids, but this was not the same. If she made a mistake, Branton would die.

Stick it out, you have to do it.

The operation went quickly. The laser made a clean cut and left a pink cauterized wound. She closed off the artery, and then proceeded to stitch up the wound, just like she remembered on the medical services training video. A spray of plasti-skin served as a protectant and closed her work up neatly. When she was through, she set up the blood infusion, and medicinal drip, then covered him up with a survival blanket. His breathing was raspy but steady.

Exhausted, she sat down in the rover's seat and in moments fell fast asleep.

* * *

Branton came to a few hours later. He called for her, weakly, but it was enough. She woke from a troubled sleep.

"How are you doing?"

"My leg."

"I fixed it the best I could, but I'm not a medic, you understand?"

He nodded, but his eyes seemed glassy, and she doubted he comprehended her. It was clear he was still in shock.

"Don't worry, I know those Earth doctors can get you fixed up when you get home." She tried a weak smile.

He coughed then mumbled something about the cold. She tucked the blanket closer and adjusted the auto-heat. He coughed again. This time a spot of blood appeared on his lips.

Something else was wrong, very wrong.

She gave him a drink from the thermos she pulled from the rover, tweaking the warming strip to bring the water to a boil. As he slowly drank, a sip at a time, she could see the warmth slowly returning some color to him.

"I don't think I'm going to make it, April." Again, a harsh cough. "I have pain inside. A lot of pain."

She dug through the supplies. "Here I have some painkillers, they should help." She fed him two pills.

"And I thought it was the storm that would kill me. What happened?"

"I don't know. The SeaClear was hit – annihilated. Nothing would have done that from within. It had to be external, but I didn't see anything out there."

He coughed again. "Listen," his words bubbled out. "This had to be because of me, because of what I know. I'm really sorry."

More coughs came on, blood splattered from his mouth, and his body wracked itself in a set of convulsions. April pulled him close. "Branton! Don't you leave me, Branton! Hang on," she cried.

It finally subsided, leaving him breathless and sapped. "I can't hold on. I can't." He reached up and cupped her face in his hand. "Promise me you'll start them up. You can save Ishaida."

He closed his eyes.

She shook him frantically. "Branton, I can't do this by myself. I can't clean that virus. I can't start the TFPs. Do you hear me, Branton?"

"Pocket," he whispered. "Red mod."

He opened his eyes, reached out and ran a shaky hand through her hair. "You are so beautiful. Not a bad way to die."

"Branton, you have to hang on," she pleaded.

He tensed up again - another convulsion. She pulled him tight until he stopped, but this time he didn't come back. She knew he was gone but dared not look. She just sat there and rocked him, crying.

Her tears eventually ran dry, as she knew they would. But her tears had done little to drain the pain, the grief that wracked through her body like a sharpened blade.

Thundering steps brought a shadow upon her, and she looked up into the green eyes of a mechanical monstrosity. It watched her with curiosity, head tilted askew. The security 'bot's body was covered in layers of dust which covered its once shiny exoskeleton. Years of neglect and inattention showed throughout with scrapes, scratches, and dents, many of which must have been afflicted by armor-piercing rounds, most likely from a desperate scrapie. One component stood out, clean and smooth from constant use – its plasma blaster. At least it remained retracted.

"He died," she said. "Someone killed him – out there," she pointed.

The 'bot's eyes followed the direction of her pointing but for a moment, and its green eyes returned to her.

"Whoever it is, they might come for me. Will you protect me? That's your job isn't it?"

The creature only stared back, refusing even the remotest sign of understanding.

April knew what she had to do from her talks with Branton. She had to go to the control room, and that was one direction – up. She laid Branton down gently and pulled the emergency blanket over him. The emergency bag made a handy knapsack, which she proceeded to fill with anything left that was useful, including her thermos, which she gave a shake to see what water was left within.

Almost empty, she'd have to find water. Branton had told her the place had emergency stations located throughout. She'd just have to find one.

She all but ignored the mechanical 'bot, satisfied that he would do nothing to harm – or help her.

Once ready, she turned back to the mech. "Which way to the elevators? Do you understand my question?"

He reached a massive arm out to point to the rear section of the atrium, to a lobby past the long receiving desk and then nodded slowly.

"Thanks." She promptly turned and headed in that direction.

* * *

Chapter 4

Porters are a strange bunch, fiercely independent, obsessively reclusive, yet they watch over each other very closely.

Porter dispatch had caught the fiery remains a few hours after the disaster. The image of the SeaClear's burning hulk was very clear from the eye-in-the-sky miles above the surface. They relayed the news to the nearest possible help.

The closest transport was the TriggerFix, owned by the Sequin family. It was three days away at average speed.

"We'll be there in two," Captain Ishbar Sequin stated to dispatch with stubborn determination. The transport dropped her cars and altered course, leaving behind the Sequin's very livelihood to Ishaida's neglectful care.

When a transport is in trouble, the closest one will always come to help. That is the code.

* * *

The closed doors of the elevator lay directly in front of her. A fine layer of dust lay over everything. *Would this ancient machine still work? Should she try it? What if it fails? The control room was on the highest floor, and she certainly wasn't up to climbing it. No, it will not fail. The engineers built this to last.*

She pressed the call button and the doors opened, not so smoothly and with enough noise, but they opened. She stepped in, and with a slight hesitation, pressed the button for the top floor, skimming a trace of dust off with her finger. Behind her imprint, the button glowed green and the doors ground closed in a protesting shriek.

The elevator shot upward, making April feel slightly dizzy and heavy. In no more than a minute it reached the top, slowing and stopping fast enough to turn her stomach slightly. The doors opened to reveal a gridwork walkway towering far above a complex maze of pipes and steel. A brisk wind blew across the deck and gave her a chill. She refastened the top of her suit to block out the cold and stepped out.

She stared down through the gridwork into darkness. Flickering lights far below helped provide her an inkling of just how high she was. Her legs suddenly felt weak, forcing her to drop down onto the catwalk.

So far down. It had to be a kilometer.

Looking up there was at least another kilometer to go. She sat there and marveled at the sheer size of the plant surrounding her.

To see this thing working. It would be amazing. Yes, sure she had promised her father. But that was before they had killed him, killed her family, killed Branton, and almost killed her. They had to pay. They didn't want these machines started for some unknown reason. She would change that now. It was time for the truth.

She pulled herself up and headed across the catwalk, fighting the urge to look down. The walkway turned back into a closed section. To the right, a door led to a labeled emergency center, and April let out a sigh of relief.

Water.

Water, like many other parts of the terra-forming, was a critical ingredient. The TFPs were strategically located to ensure access to the network of underground channels that honeycombed through Ishaida's subsurface. These would become future underground rivers once the poles melted again. It was always easier to utilize the planet's water resources than manufacture them. Some of the mysteries of why this site was chosen were becoming clearer to April. The engineers could build a plant to survive an earthquake much easier than create the incredible supply of water needed to seed the skies above.

She topped up her thermos after taking a few healthy drinks and searched the room for anything useful. A wall mounted tablet brought up a directory and map, showing the way to the control deck. She quickly memorized the directions and started on her way with renewed confidence.

A second set of elevators, a long walk, and she finally arrived. This door was locked, but the card afforded by Branton provided the key. It opened to an expansive room, which had walls sloping up to a point, similar to the inside of a pyramid. Conduits and lines of all shapes and sizes slung down and buried themselves into the walls, which were populated with arrays of monitors. Everything, for the most part, had been switched off, save for a few key displays showing the vital statistics of the automatic building control systems. She knew from here she could effectively start the whole plant, every machine, every system.

A large cushioned seat, from a collection of six, looked invitingly comfortable after her long hike. She eased her sore body into the chair and felt the strain seep from her body.

These were the primary system control workstations. Looking all too inviting, she passed her fingers along the console, which instantly sprung to life in a dance of color. Surrounding her from all sides, monitors blinked on displaying symbols in streaming chains and video feeds of various sections of the plant.

The streaming chains of symbols caught her eye. She understood the garble, unconsciously, like it was a second language to her. Her fingers flew across the console with deftness intention. Programs were initiated. She waited patiently as each system worked its way to a new wait state, from idle to a standby called 'pre-stage ready'. Before she could realize, all the primary systems were blinking in a ready to start state.

If Branton was right, she would find out now. She pulled the red mod from her suit pocket and held it in her hand. It felt warm and heavy. *Perhaps there was more to this thing than just a storage key. Now or never.*

She inserted the red mod and watched. A new stream of symbols flowed from the multiple arrays of displays, churning and flipping, rolling out statuses as the numerous programs fought for processing time.

It's performing its self-diagnosis.

Alarms rang out, error messages blasted out quarantine signals. The cleansing program performed rituals of sound and color. More and more monitors flashed alive. Wave after wave of the banks of monitors began to sing their hieroglyphic song. Beyond the control center, distributed throughout the plant, processors initiated and exchanged a language of ones and zeros.

April watched with excitement. But how long would it take? How many programs, how many instructions were buried in the recesses of this gargantuan machine?

Her stomach growled. She was starving. She ate the last bit of protein bar she had brought with her in the suit from the SeaClear. It would not hold the hunger pains off for long, she knew. Maybe there were rations somewhere.

Satisfied that the programs were far from ending, she decided to go on a discovery search to find something edible. She checked the cafeterias, the vending machines, the storage lockers, but they all lay bare and empty, unused for centuries. She returned to the control room, defeated, feeling very weak and scared. She could survive up to 40 days without food, at least she had water.

Maybe they wouldn't reach her in time. She struck the idea from her mind.

No. Stay positive. Stay alive. They will come.

Uncountable hours passed. Patterns danced on the monitors, weaving from one programmed stage to another. A digital war was occurring in the depth of its circuitry, a virus against an antivirus simultaneously working against one another as the system strived to renew itself into a modified ready state.

Every time she dozed off an alarm would signal, prompting for her input, which usually required a simple 'Yes' or 'No'. She would refer to the online system manuals and dig out some cryptic reference, or have to double-check a memory area's contents. It was painstaking.

She lost track of time. Hunger pangs gave way to a low twisting ache, which she fought to counter with drinks of water, in between long naps. Two days later the displays faded to a quiet calm, and the once blurring stream of activity had surrendered to an unsettling quiet. Systems were staged and ready. The central console display waited on standby, with a single status blinking, beckoning.

READY.

It was done. The virus was purged, and all systems were pre-staged to initiate.

She could feel her heart pounding in her ears. With a few keystrokes, she was about to change Ishaida forever.

It was time to reclaim her home.

She acknowledged the state, and via the elegant yet straightforward graphical display, started all systems.

Below, in the bowels of the ancient machine, smaller machines sprang to life and began to systematically and precisely fulfill their pre-dispositioned functions. The fusion reactors fired up, pumping power through the plant's primary circuits, bringing life to more components of the plant, waking countless machines in the process.

She watched the monitors begin a dance once again. The plant was coming to life all around her. April giggled and watched as bands of colored lights announced the activation of thousands of components. Every once in a while, the lights would dim, just momentarily, as if something gigantic was sucking up every watt of power available. She could hear the machines below, reverberating in a low bass that permeated right through to the control deck, her chair, and into her bones.

Miles above the TFP, its sister satellite woke up. A blanket, only microns thick, began to spiral out, slowly forming a gigantic mirror, which would, once wholly unfurled, use the passive energy of the Ishaida's sun to melt the polar caps.

Underground, spreading out like a web from the main TFP, miles and miles of tubes slowly filled with a cocktail of manufactured atmosphere. External vents opened, and the gases shot upward, sometimes pushing through many yards of sand, to whistle out into the open air forming a brazen fountain.

Throughout the plant armies of robots scoured over the equipment, cleaning, inspecting, repairing. April watched it all from the monitors, slightly amused at the sheer simplicity of such complexity. She switched to the outside monitors and noticed the skies were already starting to darken, then panned down to view a strangely speckled ground.

Snow. It was snowing! Once the clouds became thick enough, the heat wouldn't be able to radiate away. The snow would turn to rain – soon, very soon.

A bolt of lightning flashed between the clouds, an indication of differing atmospheric charges – a common occurrence around a TFP. Something else caught her eye, a small plume of dust in the distance. She brought the tiny spec into focus.

A Porter tank. Help was coming.

April had guessed that help would be on the way. How long it would take them, she had no idea. She knew the code the Porters lived by. It had been burned into her mind by her father, day after day. The code was the dirt on the ground, the sun in the sky. It was an unbreakable way of life, an expected set of rules one had to follow, no matter what.

She watched the transport for a while. It didn't seem that far, but that was deceiving. She mentally calculated its arrival time to be at least another three to four hours.

She wiped a tear from her eye. She was going to make it.

* * *

"Bring her about," commanded Captain Ishbar. The TriggerFix turned into the last sand dune, climbing up at almost full acceleration, massive wheels churning up tons of sand.

It wouldn't do to get stuck now. The Sequins were buckled down as the gigantic machine flew up into the air and successively crashed back down onto the latter side of the dune.

"Pa, we got sumtin' ahead. Dunno what it is, never seen it before."

Ishbar unbuckled, straddled down the narrow steps to the control deck, and peered over his son's shoulder to look at the image from the satellite feed.

"Aye, I can say, boy, I've never seen the likes of it 'tither. But I's heard of it no less. She's a bit of a miracle. Boy, we need to get out of this sand, quick, before we hit that snow."

Billy looked up at his father in surprise.

"You did 'ere me right, ease up on the throttle a bit there, Mary, me girl!"

A young girl with crimson-strawberry hair that reached down to her hips had already taken the hint and was busily passing the Doppler over the area, simultaneously superimposing the satellite scans with archived transportation grids. "It's 70 degrees to starboard, Captain, little more than a mile ahead."

Ishbar glanced at the imagery. "Can't see her, lassie."

"It's there, just under less than a meter of sand."

"Billy, waste no time, we need a hard surface and fast."

The clouds were already approaching from the northeast, ominously dense and foreboding.

The TriggerFix flew over the last dune and then adjusted its course to follow the valley between the hills.

"Got'er, Captain."

"This is the old freeway leading directly to the TFP," added Mary. "Should be a straight run from here."

"And our ETA is?"

"I'm guessing, 12 minutes."

"Aye. Good work, your guess is better than most men's by my cipherin'."

Mary smiled proudly.

"Tensen, Mog, Taron, get yer' butts over to the rover bay. Mary, go tell yer' mom to be ready, and get the rest of those emergency supplies to the med bay."

They all looked at him for a second. They had nearly forgotten the reason why they had come – this was a rescue mission. People had died ahead.

"Well don't just sit there, git!" urged Ishbar fervently. "By God, we may save a life yet."

"Wind's pickin' up, she's getting a bit slushy, not responding too well."

"That's wet fer ya, water's a habit of making things slippery."

Ishbar eased down into the copilot's chair, taking the time to buckle in. He flipped the intercom. "Boys, lock'n load, and bolt on the straddle guns. We may have some unfriendlies ahead, or we may not and they be long gone."

"Pa, looks like she's coming down hard on us and it's changed now – it's not snow no more."

"Aye, she's turning to rain. Outside temps are climbing like crazy."

The TriggerFix slid sideways a bit, and Billy fought with the controls to right her.

"Ease up on the throttle some more, we're running in soup right now. No use rolling her over at this stage, is it?"

Billy glanced over, tight-lipped and white-faced. "No, Sir."

Ishbar flipped the intercom again. "Boys, you make sure you keep those safeties on until we know the situation. We don't want to be killing any McThurns. No shootin' unless I say, got it?"

"Aye," answered Tensen, the oldest. "Taken care of."

"Standby to deploy, we're closing in on the SeaClear now. Lots of wreckage, so be careful. Remember the grid we talked about. She's wet out there, so take your time or you might miss something."

"Pa," clicked the intercom. It was Mog. "This rain, it's just water, right?"

"Yeah, just water, son. Nothin' more. But those bright flashing bolts, well that is another story, that is intense electricity. That'll kill ya, so don't be gettin' out unless I OK it, just like we planned."

"Aye."

"Don't ya worry Mog, just follow the plan, you'll be OK. Tensen keep an eye out there for ya brother."

"No worries, Captain. We've our end covered, you just keep Billy from drivin' over us now." A short bit of laughter followed. It stopped as the TriggerFix slid to a stop.

"Run'er out, boys."

The ramps dropped, and the bay doors flew open. The rovers roared out into the harsh night, their lights barely cutting through the heavy rain.

"Billy, got all their signals?"

"Yep, and we got a cam on each rover. Pictures aren't the best though. Want me to change to infrared?"

"No. It's good enough. I see well enough. Damn, look at that."

The picture was coming through alright, a murky image of death. "She's been split open like a tin can."

"Got something over here." It was an excited voice of Mog. The focus sharpened on the sandy floor as the rover moved close.

"Hold it, Mog. By God boy, you put those brakes on, now!"

"But Pa, I think it's somebody."

"Tensen!"

"Yeah, movin' in. Mog, turn over there and start scanning."

Tensen wired in his image. It was as Ishbar had feared.

"I think I'm going to be sick, Dad," complained Billy, suddenly green.

"Look away boy, you needn't see this."

"I think I recognize her, at least what's left. I think it's Elsie McThurn. You remember her pa."

"Aye, a sweet girl. A bloody shame."

"Boys, just check to see if there is a sealed car remaining, I'm a-feared we have only a burial detail to attend to here."

"Pa, maybe not, see those lights on over at Germain?"

It was hard to make out in the rain, but the lights were on over there.

"Aye, then we will go there next."

"And then?"

"And then we hope the bloody security 'bots are long rusted away, 'course."

"Yeah, right," nodded Billy. "But not bloody likely."

Their small reconnaissance team took a little less than an hour. Once the rovers were reloaded, the group assembled back on the main deck.

Ishbar could see it clearly on all their faces. It was unsettling for them – all of them. Maureen Sequin, Ishbar's wife, led a small prayer in respect to the dead.

Grim-faced, Ishbar ordered Billy to proceed on. Secretly, he hoped they would find someone inside, anyone, but he doubted they were able to get through the TFP security.

The TriggerFix arrived at Germain with all turrets and cannon ready, just in case. They were all surprised to see the secondary gates wide open. There were no security 'bots to be seen.

"What do we do, Captain?"

"Will we fit through?" asked Ishbar.

"Just..."

"Then ahead, my boy, ahead."

Billy guided the TriggerFix tank up as close to the main TFP entrance as he dared, leery of overhanging balconies above. They could see the primary entrance through the monitors, the small 'bot standing guard, and the imprint of tracks, protected from the rain by the entrance overhang, which led directly in through the doors.

Ishbar and Tensen had already donned their suits.

"Don't you worry now, we'll be careful." Worried looks were coming from all directions. Maureen grabbed him, and gave him a long kiss, then pulled back to allow him to drop on his helmet.

Tensen gave a half-smile to his tearful young bride of less than three weeks. She was a Touloose, a genuinely nice girl, good blood from a prosperous family.

Ishbar glanced around, flipped on his external microphone. "Stopped ya damned squawking everyone. This is a rescue mission, not a funeral. Girls, you stand ready in case we find someone. May be near dehydration, or near death. We'll be countin' on you."

Determined nods came back. "You can count on us, Pa," replied Mary confidently.

Ishbar reached over and tussled the mass of red hair. "Good."

He checked his supplies, including the enviro-bag he had in his side pocket. They'd be putting any survivors into it to transport them between the TFP and the tank if they found anyone that is.

They stepped inside the lock and closed the door.

In a minute, they were both outside, in the rain, facing a 'bot that showed no sign of movement.

"Maybe it's dead," offered Tensen.

"Don't count on it. If it points anything at us, blast it."

Ishbar stepped ahead. This time the 'bot did move. Tensen was ready, but Ishbar grabbed his arm. The 'bot grabbed the sizeable polished handle of the door and pulled. The door swung open.

"Merely a door 'bot it seems," Tensen chuckled.

The door closed behind them as they stepped into a dark room. Ishbar could feel his suit clamming up to him. "Pressure's returning. By God, if this old bugger ain't still workin'."

Tensen checked the enviro-scanner on his wrist, its readout was reflected back under the light from his helmet.

"Roger on that one. We've got air." He reached to untwist his helmet.

"Just wait 'till we're inside. Don't forget your common sense, boy. You're still in an airlock, and the inside door ain't open as yet."

On cue, another 'bot opened the door ahead. The two walked into the almost empty anteroom.

"There's a rover in here!" blurted Tensen and dashed ahead.

"Who's that in front, on the floor?"

Tensen bent down, peeled off his glove and folded back the blanket. A thin young man lay there as if he was sleeping. He felt for a pulse on his neck. "He's dead, Pa."

"Last McThurn, I guess."

"Funny, I knew Oranis. This don't look like any of his boys. Look at this, that leg's been attended and wrapped. Little tough to do that yourself, I would hazard."

"Guess we have someone else here, then."

"I guess you're right."

A low hum started. It was coming from the back of the room. The lights of the anteroom flickered on from centuries of slumber. The odd light shorted out with a loud pop.

Ishbar squinted, letting his eyes adjust. "Seems our arrival has been noticed."

To the left of them, another light flashed on, accompanied by a friendly 'ping'. This one was inset on the wall, in the form of an arrow pointing down.

"Elevator," added Ishbar.

"Someone is coming down to see us, Pa."

"Pull your safety off, Tensen."

They marched to the elevator door, Ishbar had his blaster hip level, ready if needed. Another 'ping' as the elevator signaled its arrival. The dusty stainless steel doors slid open with a slight scraping sound. Inside stood a girl, no more than 16, leaning against the side wall, her eyes heavy, and features drawn.

"Hello, there. You must be my rescuers," she stated, putting on a slight, mocking smile. "Welcome to the Germain TFP. I truly hope you have got some food on you. I am literally starving."

"Hello, April," Tensen said smiling ear to ear. "I'm glad you made it."

She straightened up and wearily sauntered out, stepping through the two of them. "That's right, Tensen. I made it! Me and only me." She turned quickly and almost fell.

Ishbar stepped ahead and grabbed her. "Thank you, Captain. I'm afraid I feel a bit weak. Probably blood pressure or something."

He looked at her carefully. Her face revealed darkened red-lidded eyes, streaked cheeks.

She has seen too much, this girl. Too much suffering for a young heart.

"You know, you got my dad's eyes," she said, slightly choking out the last word. She turned away, but Ishbar pulled her close, he could feel her sob through the thick padding of his suit.

"Maureen, stand ready, we have a survivor."

* * *

She had fallen asleep during the transfer. Not much to see in a dark survival bag. She woke up in the med center, an intravenous drip connected to her arm. An older lady was busy doing something beside her, bustling about.

"How long?"

"Oh, I'm sorry my dear, did I wake you?"

Kind eyes looked down at her. Soft, caring, loving eyes.

"How long have I been out?"

"Less than a day, dear. It's alright, you know. You need your strength."

April sat up. "I need to get back. I need to contact the McThurns."

"Of course, we're on our way to Languana. We've already arranged for your cousins to meet you. So you know the McThurns of the ShadowLink?"

"Yes, I know them. The Captain is my uncle."

"Oh well, don't worry dear. We take care of our own here. We'll make sure you have a home. If you don't want to join your cousins, I'm sure other families would certainly welcome you in."

"No, my Uncle will do fine. Thank you, Mrs. Sequin."

"It's Maureen, please call me Maureen." An awkward moment passed.

"You know dear, I'm – we all are, very, very sorry for what happened to your family. Our hearts go out to you. I can only imagine what you are feeling inside."

"It's OK," April looked down, not wanting to bear her soul to anyone. "I'm OK now. I'll get through this."

Maureen reached out and touched her cheek, smiling warmly. "If you need anyone to talk to..."

"Thanks," she said, forcing herself to smile.

"Ishbar has some questions for you, of course, about what happened and such. I told him to wait until I thought you were ready. How do you feel, are you up to talking to him?"

"'Course. I'll tell him what I know, but that's all."

"OK then, I'll call him down. If you find it to be too much, you tell him so, he'll give you the time you need. I otta know. I trained the old rascal."

She left the room, leaving April to her thoughts.

What will she tell him? The truth? What would he do? Would he demand they return, that she shut it back off? Maybe she should wait.

Ishbar stood in the doorway. With his suit off, he looked a little less imposing, a little gentler in nature.

"Hello, Captain."

"I wish we could have seen each other in better circumstances, April."

"Yeah."

"Need to know what 'appened out there. Every bit a detail, dear, every little bit."

She sat up. "You see the SeaClear?" she asked, something reflecting a splinter of hope came across her face.

"Yes, but there were no survivors, dear. No one but you."

She nodded, feeling it crash down into her chest. For a moment, she felt like she couldn't breathe. Like her diaphragm was frozen open, unable to draw in a breath. She bit down on her lip, hard, and tasted the coppery blood. The pain helped. She breathed in.

"What happened?"

She lay back down, temporarily too weak to speak.

"Are you OK? Want me to call Maureen?"

"I don't know, for sure."

"Was it something you were carrying, some type of internal malfunction? You were chief mechanic, weren't you?"

"Yes. No, it wasn't anything internal. Nothing we haul could have done that kind of damage, nothing."

Ishbar nodded, but he had to ask, he had to be sure. If there was some kind of engineering flaw, even after four centuries of service, the transports had to be repaired. "What was your manifest?"

"It was the same old stuff we've been hauling for years. Some ore, mostly food and perishables, some mining equipment. Nothing unstable or capable of exploding. That much I know."

"I see, so you believe this was external. Was it the TFP 'bots, or maybe scrapies?"

"No."

He stood there quietly. *She knew the answer, she just wasn't telling.*

She sat up, then pushed herself to her feet, ignoring her sore muscles. "Had to be a ship." She finally said, staring him straight in the eye. "We were hit, on purpose."

"I already checked with the DD's. There's been no sign of any vessels even close to Ishaida."

"The Dome-Dweller's technology can't pick up a cloaked company ship."

Ishbar took a moment, taking in a deep breath. Something bigger was going on here, to wipe out a transport – why? Why would the company care about a measly Ishaida transport?

"OK. Explain this to me, then. Why are you pullin' in the Company on this?"

"I can't. It'll put you in danger as well. I just can't."

Ishbar tapped his fingers on the wall, just a little harder than normal. "OK. You won't tell me what killed your family, fine. Why's that TFP crankin' out atmosphere then? Tell me that, at least."

She remained quiet.

"Did ya turn it on or not?"

She hesitated. *This was all going wrong. This was her family. All the Porters were her family - they had a right to know. It was the code.*

"Yes." She stated defiantly, her face a tight mask, heart pounding in her chest.

Ishbar almost fell backward into the corridor. It might have been the bump they had just hit, or something more.

"Did you just say you turned on the Germain TFP?"

"Yes."

"Why?"

"Because I know why it failed. I know why they all failed, and I have the fix."

Ishbar stepped all the way into the room and slid the door shut behind him. "You realize what you are saying, do you? This kind of decision's not yours to make."

"Oh well," she half-laughed, sarcastically, "it's done now, ain't it? Germain's pumping out air, and I'm not stopping it. And I put the security 'bots back online, too. Triggered to go on as soon as I left. No one's getting back in, I promise you that. Not even Anard-Bueller."

"I don't think you know what you've done here."

"Disagree with me, but don't patronize me. I think I know damn well what I've done. I understand more than anyone on this planet the repercussions of turning on that TFP. I ran all the simulations. Germain is just the first, and it's not the last."

"Ya cannot! Ya cannot continue to start those infernal machines. Look at what they've done to us already!" His hands were clenched on the door frame, ever tightening.

April could see the anger dancing in his eyes. "No. You are wrong. This has happened because we turned them off! You just don't know enough about it, so you are relying on past superstition."

She sat back on the cot, let out a breath and tried to calm down, but she could not fight that feeling of utter despair. Ishbar reminded her of her dad. She remembered him just before it happened, that silly grin and wink he always did. She traced the lines on the floor decking with her eyes, not wanting to look back at Ishbar. "I'm not wrong." A tear crept down her cheek. "You just don't get it. My family died because the company wants to keep the TFPs off because they don't want the truth out there that their failure was engineered – it was supposed to happen."

Ishbar reached over and gently tilted her face up, which had been hidden in a mass of hair.

She was crying. Damn it. Why'd she have to cry?

"You have proof of what you're saying, do ya?"

"Yes. Check the wreckage of the SeaClear for isotopes. Nothing we were carrying could have done that. We were bombed, from above. As for the TFP, all you need to see is out there – it's running ain't it?" She turned away, looking out through the small cabin portal, Germain was a dark storm on the horizon, a mass of clouds. "They didn't kill me, though. And they will pay."

"Look, you can pardon me if I don' quite believe ya. But I know what I know. The TFPs, they ran fer most of three centuries they did, and then they shut down, and then came the great reversal. The whole system, she went out of balance. They couldn't bring it back. They tried everything, that much I've 'erd. That 'tis what I know."

She pulled the aged mod from her pocket. "The off-worlder that you found lying in front of my rover, his name is - or was - Branton Gordon. He was an engineering student from Earth who was going for his masters. He brought this with him. This is the evidence the programming was tampered with."

He reached for it, but she pulled it away. "Stays with me. It's proof. You see, this mod was handed down for generations in his family. Turns out Branton's great-grandfather was temporarily assigned to Ishaida as an engineer. He knew about the virus, and on this mod is the cure."

"The cure?"

"The antivirus. It cleans the control system. It works. I watched it purge the malware. I was there, in the control room when it did it."

"This's a bit of a pill to swallow, my dear. You're a saying that Ishaida can be resurrected again, only this time, all the way?"

"Yes, I'm saying that. There was a virus in the TFP control system. This program removed it. No more lies from the companies. But we need to move fast. Whoever blew up the SeaClear will be back. Once he sees that the Germain TFP is online, he'll know he didn't succeed. He'll want to finish what he started."

"He?"

"He, she, them, I don't know - the Company."

"Just outta curiosity then, 'spose I ask the obvious? What's to stop the Company from just blasting the TFPs?"

"Exposure, publicity, suspicion, it's easier to kill a couple people, make it look like an accident rather than destroy something they may want to resurrect someday. A TFP cost billions to build, billions and billions. You never know, maybe Anard-Bueller's agreement with Soho-Beher may go sour and the profit fades. Jefferson becomes too expensive. Ishaida is just a pawn of the company's whim, that much I am sure."

"Aye. But we're not. Not anymore. Our families, our generations, 'ave paid the price for this planet in blood." Ishbar's face was flushed with anger. "She's ours now. All of her, including these bloody damn TFPs. You 'ave to be sure about this though, absolutely sure."

April nodded her head. *No, she wasn't absolutely sure, you can't be that sure about anything. Maybe the process will reverse again, maybe the virus isn't destroyed. But she was sure as she could be.*

"Then, April McThurn, 'tis time to call together the Porters. We put you into hiding when we turn on these blasted machines for good. You must realize my girl, if we go down this road, there may be more bloodshed, more dying. It'll be us payin' the price of this small revolution we are startin' here. Understand that. Know that 'tis going to happen and more people may die."

April turned to gaze out the portal. A glimmer of light on the horizon. Soon the sun will rise. The snow and ice will melt to rain.

"I've already paid in full."

"Have ya, love? Perhaps you don't realize what you still have left. You have plenty more you can lose. Better you make this decision knowin' that, understanding that. Better you consider this now than later."

"I'm not backing down now. I'm not letting my family die in vain. I'm starting those TFPs."

He looked at her hard. "So be it." He stated flatly. "I'll tell you now, I'll do everything in my power to make sure the Porters are behind ya. The Sequins will back you up, as well as the McThurns, that much you know. The others, though, they may need a bit more convincing. It'll be you that'll sway their decision in the end. Time you should spend to think about what you should say."

April looked down at the white sheet on the bed, avoiding the Captain's probing eyes. "You call them together. I'll do the rest."

"Very well. You are a rare breed of a woman, and a brave one at that." He slid open the door. Cool air rushed into the stuffy cabin. "I can only hope you are right about this. If ya are, this will save us, this will save Ishaida." Then he was gone.

Through the small port window, April watched the billowing clouds outside. Every once in a while, a colossal lightning bolt would jump from the sky to the ground in a flash of angry white.

I hope I'm right, too.

* * *

Chapter 5

P orters have their ways of sending word out.
Of course, arranging a get together of all the Porters at any one city was all but impossible. There was simply not enough room to do such a thing. Communications had to be coordinated to connect all Porters – in transit, or docked, all around the planet.

Porters were supporting a precisely timed network of arrivals and departures, a logistical challenge to keep goods flowing between the cities. The Porter dispatch centers in each city had worked out a number of secure encrypted messaging protocols over the centuries not trusting what could be siphoned off the public satellites for anyone to access – including any corporate eavesdroppers.

The invitation was sent out. Anyone who wanted to meet April face-to-face, to ask her questions were to make their way to the city of Languana. It was there her presentation to the rest of the Porters would be sent over the secure channels, to every transport, everywhere.

Certain Porters, some self-elected, others of respectful nominated positions, had chosen to be present. The trick was not alerting the DDs that something abnormal was occurring. Transports met in mid-course to exchange personnel, others came in for unscheduled maintenance, which in turn, adjusted other transports in due course to assume new routes. This all took time.

April hated the waiting. Six days at dock, on top of the eight days it had taken to reach Languana in the first place. TriggerFix had docked for extended maintenance, which seemed very plausible, due to their intensive rescue efforts. What was worse was that April had not been allowed to leave the transport since they had arrived, not even to step outside in the bay. As for actually doing something of value, they had stuck her inside to do the menial work that her sisters had so enjoyed and she hated. TriggerFix had her own mechanic staff, and they preferred she'd not get involved.

News travels fast, even down into the network of tunnels below the domed cities. Word of the Germain TFP was spreading, as well as what had happened to the SeaClear. At every port bay, people talked in hushed tones. Words were exchanged quietly, as the citizens of Ishaida didn't want it to spread to the wrong ears, to reach the Company.

The Mayors learned of it as well. Little happened in the corridors, tunnels, and bays of the cities that they did not eventually learn of. Their request to attend April's speech was taken very seriously by the Porter leadership. The meeting was set for the next day.

Ishbar came to tell April the news.

"It's about time. I've been waiting here too damned long. I've had enough of this waiting."

"Are you ready?"

She produced her stack of notes from her multiple attempts at drafting a speech and threw the small pile onto her cabin bed. "Sort of."

"I see. Just speak from the heart, that's all you need to do."

"And the politics, the questions?"

"You leave that up to me, now lassie. I'm a part of the Porter council you know. We'll be taking the questions first, when we need you to answer, we'll ask you direct. No need to worry about some jack-off in the crowd. OK?"

"Thanks."

"You'll do fine," he put his hand lightly upon her shoulder. "How about the other things. How are you doing with them?" His voice had dropped a little quieter, a little gentler.

Does he even give a damn? What could he do anyway, he can't bring them back.

"I'm fine, really. I'm OK."

"Maureen tells me you been having trouble sleeping."

That much was true. The nightmares wouldn't leave her alone. Every time she closed her eyes all she could see was Branton looking at her in that stone cold gaze, or her father waving goodbye at her from the deck, giving her that wink of his. It was hard to believe they're gone.

"Just some dreams, I'm OK. Really."

"If you ever need to talk..."

"Yes, yes I know. Thanks. I'd just rather not. Not yet, anyway."

"You'll be glad to know the ShadowLink has arrived. Your uncle Zed will be over shortly to see you."

"Can you tell him that I'll go over after the meeting? I'd rather have some time to myself, before, I just want to make this speech is perfect."

"Of course, I'm sure he'll understand."

"Well, if you'll excuse me." She hinted.

"I'll come fer ya around 08:00 tomorrow."

"Thanks." She eased the door shut, literally pushing him back out of the small room. She needed time to think, to review what it was she wanted to say. She grabbed the paper and pen and looked at her words. They stared back without meaning or form. Memories flooded back. Smiling faces of Elsie, Chancy, Jim, and Ty.

Gone. They're all gone.

Tears stained the paper. She wiped them away, but they smeared the ink.

Lavenue would have helped her with this. She was good at this kind of thing. She had a knack for helping her sort things out in her head, get things figured out. She might not have been her real mom, but she was the next best thing.

She fell asleep, the pad still resting on her lap, all but a few words written.

* * *

"Alright, let's bring this to order." The council judge cracked the small gavel onto the makeshift bench of overlapped tables.

"We meet this day to discuss something of tremendous importance and urgency, and of grave sorrow." The old man let the last word sit for a moment as he gulped down the last of his water. "In addition to every Porter receiving this telecast, we have also welcomed the Mayors of each of the domed cities." A murmur rose up from the crowd.

"As this matter has significance for all of Ishaida, it seems only reasonable to involve them. That being said, I'd like to have us all pray for a moment, recognize the loss of our brothers and sisters of the SeaClear: the McThurn family."

A minute of silence prevailed, a moment in time representing far too many lives.

The council judge interrupted the lengthy silence. "May God save their souls." He slammed the gavel down with a finality. "Let us get to the heart of the matter."

"Captain Ishbar Sequin, you are the appointed guardian of the young lady, April McThurn?"

"In the matter of this hearing, yes, as the officially-appointed guardian in the matter of her family, no."

"I see. And April McThurn," he turned a graying, emotionless face upon her, "do you accept Captain Ishbar's sponsorship and guidance for this hearing?"

"Yes, I do," she stated, trying not to squirm under the stare of so many eyes.

"Very well, as this is a public hearing and is not, at this time, a judicial matter. No charges will be laid, and no activities are as recognized to be criminal in nature. You, April McThurn, are granted amnesty for any infraction in turn for your honest and total statement. Do you understand?"

"Yes, but I have not broken any law."

The old judge cleared his throat. "Regardless, young lady." He turned to Ishbar. "Captain Sequin, please outline the nature of this hearing."

"Very good, Sir." He cleared his throat. "Some 'you may already 'ave heard, and many of you 'ave already seen that the Germain TFP has been turned back on."

Murmurs from the crowd raised in volume, but the judge suppressed it with a raise of his hand.

"This lassie," Ishbar pointed over to April, "has undeniable evidence the TFPs were sabotaged. This crime took place more'n four centuries ago. 'Twas a virus that had been loaded into each of the TFP's control systems, 'twas this virus, accordin' to her, 'tis the cause of the great reversal."

A wall of muted undecipherable noise rose up from the crowd.

"And who would have done this alleged sabotage?" asked an angry voice over one of the few monitors facing the bench of Porters.

Ishbar knew the voice and the man behind it, the mayor of NewBerlin. "My good Mayor Talbot, you slip in the word allegedly so smoothly. One would think you to accept nary a fact I've just stated. Facts are as they is, and the virus is out of the Germain TFP. Behold, she runs."

The judge interrupted. "Perhaps, Captain Sequin, you should continue with your statement. May I remind everyone to refrain from interrupting the Captain until he has completed. Mark me, I will remove those who refuse to cooperate," warned the judge.

"Aye, your honor-ship. I'd like to point out, for clarification's sake, that young Ms. April McThurn witnessed the purge of the virus 'erself, as she is indeed one with the gift of machinery and 'lectronics alike, as many of you would attest. But I also bring to you more troublin' evidence that the loss of the SeaClear was not caused by accident. She was destroyed by explosive, morn' likely by one or more missiles."

Again raised murmurs from the crowd. To destroy a complete Porter transport was unthinkable.

"Some of you here can only ask why, why perform such evil? 'Tis simple really: they were not aimin' to kill a family of Porters. No. They were trying to stop an off-worlder, a young man named Branton Gordon from reaching the Germain TFP, from clearin' the virus from the control systems."

"And where is this off-worlder?"

"Mr. Gordon also perished in the bombing."

"And what of this evidence?"

"I've collected samples from the wreckage." Ishbar handed over a small mod to the judge. "The radiation signature does not lie. Truth is clear in these readings. 'Twas at least one small tactile nuclear missile, likely two. I also had my daughter, Mary Beth, analyze the blast pattern. Evidence supports ignition just above the transport."

He cleared his throat again.

"Ms. April McThurn and Mr. Gordon had just left the SeaClear on a rover mere seconds before the explosion. Unfortunately, they were still too close. Branton was injured badly. April managed to get them both to the Germain TFP, but Branton did not survive. Our April decided her family would not die in vain, so she used the mods Branton had given her, and she started the TFP."

The crowd rose to their feet, throwing out questions of all kinds, the noise level was deafening. The judge struck his gavel repeatedly and futilely.

Ishbar held up his hands to bring quiet and order back. "Aye, this is difficult news to accept. But facts stand on their own, I say. I'd like to ask April to say a few words on this to us all. I ask each of you to tone it down, and listen instead of jabbering on." He gestured to April to join him at the small podium.

She walked up, feeling their eyes upon her. The glare of overhead lights kept the faces of the crowd as blurry shadows. In a way, it helped. She pulled her crumpled papers from her pocket and smoothed it out on the podium, hands shaking. Her stomach burned and her palms were sweaty. She felt like throwing up.

Hold it together.

The crowd quieted to an utter silence, awaiting her words.

"Ladies and gentlemen of Ishaida," she said, then nervously cleared her throat. "My family, the McThurns, did not die because of an accident. They were killed."

She hesitated a moment, fought back a sudden surge of emotion.

"But they will not die in vain because I have the proof. Proof that the virus that was impregnated into the TFP control systems was done so on purpose and that such a deed required detailed knowledge. This is the kind of knowledge that only system engineers would have access to. System engineers working for a Company. Branton spent three years studying this failure. He insisted it was designed to cause a slow and eventual reversal in the terra-forming process. It was designed to make it appear as if the whole system was failing. I believe him. I've seen the source code he analyzed. The question, I'm sure on everyone's mind is: Why would a Company do this? If it was Anard-Bueller, why would they do this and lose their investment? Or just maybe it was another Company at work? We may not ever know precisely why, but I would deduce there was profit in it, plain and simple."

She took a breath and returned to her crumpled papers.

"I've read through Branton's notes he had left behind. He had also discovered that a large amount of money had been exchanged directly proceeding the years of the reversal. This evidence is available on Earth as a matter of public record, and the other party involved, according to his research, was Soho-Beher. That was all he was able to find out. And ever since his research, he has suspected he's been followed."

"For those who doubt me, I can tell you I knew Mr. Brant Gordon personally. I spent time with him and got to know him very well. He was an honest and competent software engineer. He was only interested in the truth. He had nothing to gain by coming here. He wrote the cleansing routines to repair the TFP control systems, the ones I installed. I monitored them as they scraped through the software libraries. I will state, for the record, that these programs did find and purge multiple viruses located within the Germain TFP's control system."

She shuffled her papers, checking over to make sure she didn't miss anything.

Damn it, she should have written down more.

She took a deep breath, feeling a little calmer and noticed her hands had stopped shaking.

"We were all fooled into thinking the Ishaida project was a failure with an indeterminable cause. It was not. We have a chance here, before any Company arrives, to right this injustice. Ishaida is not lost. We can start the remaining TFPs. We can bring this planet back. It is time to reclaim our home."

She stared through the lights, trying to catch the eyes of the onlookers but couldn't. She folded her crumpled papers and tucked them back into her pocket. Then the questions started.

"Hold it." Ishbar held up his hands. "Questions to me only, as I am the appointed. Thank you, April." He motioned her to sit down in his abandoned chair on the small, elevated stage. "I'll open it to the floor, as long as ya take turns and act civil."

"If this is true, why haven't we heard of this, or found evidence of this before?"

"You know as well as I, ain't the first secret kept from us."

"This is just gibberish. The TFPs failed, plain and simple," argued another, gruffly.

"Aye, failed you say. That they did. Question is, was it arranged, or was it just a terrible miscalculation?"

"More importantly, what," interjected the judge, "is the cost to Ishaida if we resurrect the TFPs?"

Eyes again turned to April.

Ishbar eyed her carefully, "You have an idea, young lady?"

"I'm no astro-geologist, or whatever you call it. I just fix machines, but I ran the simulations. The cost is that Ishaida is successfully terra-formed."

The judge clarified. "Forgive my vagueness, I would like to determine what we can expect here such as storms, shifts in the magnetic field, quakes. What's going to happen?"

Ishbar turned his attention to the crowd. "Well, after four centuries, this may be a lost art. Does anyone know enough to help us out?"

A voice on the monitor crackled through. "Yes, I may be of some help."

This time, it was the Mayor of AlphaRosetta. "I had studied in this field when I was on Earth, as part of the Ishaida mentorship program."

A few snickers came from the back of the crowd. Earth had stepped up to help the native Ishaidans, but minimally, of course. A few chosen young people had been invited to attend Earth universities, with the provision that they had to return to Ishaida once their education was complete. If one failed to return, once apprehended, one would spend the rest of his/her life in prison.

"I, too, was curious why the Ishaida project failed. I did my own in-depth research on this topic, as many have before me. What I found were incomplete data, contradictory statements, and misleading conjectures. For such a high profile failure in the field, there seemed a definite lack of sufficient research into the cause of the failure. I must concede, however, that the records of four centuries ago are sparse and incomplete. In any case, if the TFPs are turned back on, the first and most dramatic effect will be the reintroduction of a denser atmosphere. The carbon dioxide greenhouse effect will start to contain the heat during the night. The direct sunlight during the day would be dispersed, effectively cooling the daily temperatures. Cyclonic storms will begin to traverse the skies, and rain will fall for some time. The rain, at first, will be created artificially and fed by the TFPs' ion conversion engines. The very dirt we walk upon is the fuel for these machines. If you look through the sat-images, you'll see the army of 'bots already mining away near Germain. You see, the TFP's ionic conversion centers break apart the sand and gravel material to their basic molecules. They manufacture water and many other essential molecules. But this is only the beginning. A substantial part of the oceans and lakes of four centuries ago, if it has not all sublimated into space, is now located at the poles, and it will once again melt. Torrents of water will fill the low lying areas, following old tributaries created during the first great melt."

"Are our cities in danger?"

"No. I don't believe so. Sites were selected for the cities with these considerations in mind, but things have changed in four centuries. Rivers may wind through areas where they did not before. I'm not completely sure."

"And the plants? Tell us about the greening of the hills," asked a young man, face flushed with excitement.

"Yes, but I'm not sure of the actual trigger when this will happen. Once we hit a certain mean temperature maybe the TFPs will begin reseeding. We'll see the barren deserts turn green with algae, then more complex forms of plant life will be introduced."

"The question, however," interrupted the judge, "are there any dangers?"

"Well, I suppose so, to the Porters especially. The storms we have now are ferocious but lack key elements – water and density. Heavier moisture-laden air can be very destructive. I suspect our cities, aged and in disrepair, may suffer more damage with an increase in this harsh weather. We may see more quakes as well, and possibly some of the dormant volcanoes on the North Ridge will wake up. I'm not completely sure."

"I remember," stated an old man in the crowd. "I was the chief librarian for many years, and I've seen the archives from the original project. You can bet on the storms, that much I know."

"Do we want to do this?" added the judge.

"Well now," interrupted Ishbar. "Ain't this a pretty picture. The little lady here finds out that the Companies all but abandoned us, leaving Ishaida to rot, and you gents are sitting there wondering if we should be doing this. Look around ya – what have we got to lose!"

Heads nodded, voices tumbled over the crowd, angry, defiant.

"Of course, we turn the rest of these damned TFPs on! The real problem is keeping this quiet and keeping our national heroine, April McThurn, safe so she can get the job done, that's my thinkin'," offered another especially passionate Porter from the floor.

"I believe this needs to go through the Porter council for ratification before we go charging ahead doing anything," retorted the Judge.

Ishbar cleared his throat as loud and indignantly as possible. "Aye, the council needs to consider. Meantime April is in danger from a professional killer. You saw what lengths they'll stoop to. She's the last McThurn of the SeaClear, or did you already ferget?"

"And what would you want us to do?" asked the Judge.

"Call the vote, and call it now. No need to wait." Ishbar had the agreement of the crowd this time.

"We'll have to have a closed…"

"Bullshit. No closed session. Open vote, let the people see. This is too important." Ishbar was almost yelling, his face was flushed with excitement.

The crowd roared, and a chant started by someone: "Vote, vote, vote…"

"Alright, alright," conceded the judge. "We'll do the vote now."

"And what about us?" questioned one the mayors via the remote connection. "We should also be part of this vote as well."

"Yes. We do have precedence for that. I'll do the roll call, and when I call your name, you cast your vote. The question is simple, turn on the remaining TFPs - or not."

The Judge began going through the council list, each time logging the oral response. Not everyone was in agreement.

Ishbar glanced over to April. She gave him a nervous smile.

The votes came in. The majority were aligned with Ishbar. Once the voting had completed a brief few minutes passed as the Judge and his aide tallied up and verified the results.

He slammed the gavel down, rudely awakening one of the sleeping mayors. "It is decided then. April McThurn, by order of the council of the Porters, you shall proceed with the activation of the remaining TFPs. It is my ruling that you shall start immediately. It is also my ruling that all Porters are now bound to you, to protect and guard you against any hostile or ill-intentioned parties that wish to interfere with your assigned task. Do you understand, my lady?"

Again, all eyes were upon her. "Yes, but I could use some help. Other people should know what to do, just in case."

"Of course, I will personally assign you some aides. The best and the brightest we can find, however many you need."

"Fourteen, two per TFP."

"Done."

"I can't waste any time. I'll need a tank dedicated to getting me to each TFP."

"And possibly," added Ishbar, "some decoys would be wise."

"Captain Ishbar Sequin," ordered the Judge. "You will be in charge of the logistics of this operation. You have all the resources of the Porters at your disposal."

"I express my thanks." He nodded reverently.

"Then this meeting is now adjourned, and this matter is settled. We reconvene again when all the TFPs are operational."

He closed the meeting with the sharp crack of his gavel.

* * *

Chapter 6

M arcus Delgany eased down into the pilot's chair and listened as the air slowly hissed out of the cushion.

It was time to call in.

He brought up the communications console with a flip of his index finger, quickly raced through the encrypting sequence and engaged the link.

"Tyranus port 1, this is Captain Scour, over."

"Captain, please standby. Base command has requested an update."

Marcus chuckled. *Base command his ass. Uncle CEO wanted to talk.*

He pulled the sanitary container from under his sink and yanked it apart. The aroma of tobacco filled the small cockpit. The cigarettes, although highly illegal, were easy to come by on Earth. Not so easy out here in the colonies. He lit up, waiting patiently for the other party to get on the line.

He could wait. He had nothing else to do out here in space, light-years from home.

How far away was he? One tiny, unanticipated accident could set this ship drifting forever. How did those traders keep their heads?

"Hello, Captain Scour."

"Not too often I have the pleasure of talking to the base commander himself," Marcus commented dryly.

Beady brown eyes stared back at him from a pasty, white face, bones sharp and angled.

How old was this fossil of a man anyway? Kept alive by every artificial operation money can buy.

"Cut the crap, Marcus. What the hell am I paying you for? Just remind me." The old man's voice carried a bit more viciousness than normal.

"Alright, what's the problem now? I did what you asked."

"Did you? Why don't you explain to me why four of the seven TFPs on Ishaida have been activated then?"

"What the hell do you mean? I terminated the target. I did my job."

The old man looked away, hastily tapped on something out of scope. "Here, look at this – it's an image from the freighter Spartacus taken 38 hours ago when it passed by Ishaida."

Ishaida hung in the starry blackness, bright with the reflected light of its sun. The small brown ball revealed a haze of clouds tracing across different lines of latitude. He studied the image for a moment and was able to discern the epicenters of each of the cloudy streams.

Sure enough, TFPs, at least four of them, running full tilt.

"Right, looks like you have yourself a problem."

"No, you have the problem. You want your money, and I want the job done."

"And what would you have me do?"

"My intelligence sources inform me this is the work of a single girl – a survivor of your poor marksmanship apparently. Turn around and finish what you started. By the time you get there, I suspect they'll be firing up the last of them, so you'll know where to start."

"Won't this look a bit too obvious?"

"I'll worry about what things look like. It's time for a message."

"And the TFPs, do you expect me to shut them down too? Hey, I don't have a clue..."

"You don't worry about the TFPs. I'll take care of that detail. I want all the people with the knowledge of those infernal machines permanently expunged from Ishaida."

"That sounds like more than one girl."

"Everyone who knows."

"My rate is by the head. This will definitely get expensive."

"Do it. And this time, no survivors."

The old man's skeleton face faded to black as the link dropped.

He sat back and reflected on the conversation. All of them. By the time he was done, he could retire. He blew smoke rings toward the cabin's ceiling, watched as they dissipated, sucked into the whirring filters. Easing back in the seat, he could feel a comfortable rush of the nicotine.

Ishaida could wait until after he finished his smoke.

* * *

The ceiling soared five meters above, coffered with a deep finish of dark walnut finish which continued along support beams. On the walls, wood panels dressed with ornate carvings stretched their full length, richly engrained with a matching dark walnut. In the center of the theatre-sized room was the stone fireplace, dressed out by a collection of leather couches huddled around it. Within a large worn, leather-bound wheelchair the Old Man sat, bent over in front of a slowly dying fire, adjusting a burning ember with a brass poker.

The room was filled with the aroma of cherry.

The Old Man eyed his visitor carefully, then slowly, and quite unsteadily rose to his feet in order to shuffle his wheelchair over slightly.

"So you can walk."

The Old Man smiled. "Now that my boy, is a secret between you and me." He slipped down into his chair exhaling relief. "My day's exercise is complete. I'm not as young as I used to be." He reached down to massage his calf, calming a muscle spasm.

The young man sat down across from him, noiselessly, with the litheness of a cat.

"I appreciate you coming on such short notice."

"It's truly my pleasure. We rarely see each other it seems."

"Yes, business is slow, more civilized, not requiring your special talents. That is a good thing, Mr. Montigue."

Cruez Montigue nodded, quietly agreeing. "And so, it seems things have taken a turn for the worst."

The Old Man jerked the chair up close to the fire, a gray hand latched onto the brass poker. He jabbed at the embers furiously. "You remember her, Cruez, don't you?"

"You mean your niece. Of course, seems only yesterday."

"A year. A year ago, last Saturday." He gave it another jab. The fire crackled, spitting out red sparks.

"I had plans for her. She was the last of the Bueller line, excepting me, of course. The very last. I do believe you know, Mr. Montigue, that I am dying."

"No, I didn't." His eyes were wide with surprise. "Not you. I'm sure your medical staff can..."

"My medical staff!" he pounded a fist on his chair. "They've kept this fossil body of mine alive far beyond any normal man's lifetime. I've seen generations live and die from this perch of mine. I've watched history unfold, seen wars fought and lost, seen technological progress and the devastation it leaves behind. My life is what I grow weary of. I'm old, too old... No more."

He sat back in his chair and wheeled it around to the bar. "Would you join me for a drink? How about a well-aged scotch?"

"I'm not really a scotch man."

"Nonsense. Every man is a scotch man. One thing I have learned. You must always take the time to enjoy the true pleasures of life."

He poured the drinks with shaking hands, spilling not a drop. "Here. A swig of this will change your perspective."

Cruez took a drink and carefully exhaled, slowly.

"Typical. You can't even enjoy a drink without you invoking your training. Are you always in control, Mr. Montigue?"

"I try."

"Of course you do, but you're not always successful, are you? Don't worry, no one ever is. You're probably wondering why I called you here."

"Yes, Sir. I am a bit curious."

"Drop the Sir bullshit. I've known you since you were a baby, Cruez. I raised you like my son. I'm sick of being called Sir, it's a damn curse."

Cruez nodded. "Alright, fair enough, Tiberious."

The Old Man smiled. "Thank you." But the smile quickly vanished.

"I've a story to tell you, son. Something I'm not particularly proud of. I hope you can find it in your heart to forgive my mistake."

Cruez knew the Old Man very well. Old Tiberious was a tiger, but not tonight. Something was bothering him. Something showing in his eyes looked like defeat.

"Anard, God rest his soul, and I made a very poor decision which left others to pay a hefty fee. Have you heard the story of Ishaida?"

"Yes, of course. It was a failed terra-forming project, mid-way to Cauputain."

The Old Man nodded, took a large gulp of scotch. "'Twas back in my earlier years. I had big plans, big ambitions. I didn't understand the cost of my mistakes, really. I've learned much since then, you understand?"

Cruez nodded, not knowing where this was going but listening respectfully.

"You must understand failure was far from expected. Ishaida was a goldmine, that was a surety, but Anard-Bueller was going through a rough spot at the time. We had overextended ourselves by an order of magnitude that left us exposed. To put it bluntly, the company needed a significant influx of cash or it was going to be absorbed. So Jim Anard and I made a pact with the devil.

Soho-Beher was heavily invested in Jefferson. The planet had the resources but was just outside the main shipping lanes. All they needed was a reason for the superluminals to adjust their routes on their way to Cauputain. Anard-Bueller gave them that reason. The deal was a windfall for them. Jefferson became the new stop-off for the liners, and the promise of a developed Ishaida was effectively abandoned.

It wasn't an accident or a mistake. It was relatively easy to sabotage the TFPs. But I – we – never anticipated nor considered the true cost to the population. The number of lives lost and ruined turns in my heart like a molten blade. I've carried this with me for centuries now, centuries burdened with this guilt."

He took the last gulp of scotch and eased the glass down on the table. A speck of water fell on the glossy surface. He wiped it away with his twisted aged hand. The firelight reflected off the table's smooth finish. A gray, molted face stared back at him. On his cheek, a single tear crept down.

Cruez watched quietly, slightly astonished. He'd never seen the Old Man so vulnerable.

To some, he was a legend of the business world, an icon of industry, but they don't know him like I do. He was merely a man, a fragile old man who had centuries to lead, and the equivalent time to make mistakes, and then to contemplate them.

"I need you to help me, Cruez. I need you to fix this, somehow."

Cruez reached over, handed the Old Man a tissue. "Name it, Tiberious, and consider it done."

* * *

"Caleco TFP is the last one," April announced to the trio accompanying her. "You guys remember your training, don't you?"

"Don't you worry about us, April," replied Ron. He was the youngest, only 15, but probably the quickest study yet, and he had a reputation for being thorough.

"Good." April slammed the button on the elevator. "Let's get to the control center and start this baby up." Luckily, every TFP was virtually identical, subtract a few minor variations. The directions to the control center were no exception. They all knew exactly what to do.

April made it there in record time. She flipped over to the security feed and was able to monitor everything from the primary station.

The computer sequences fired through prestaging identical to the others. At the right time, she fed in the antivirus and watched the virtual battle commence.

The others stood at their stations monitoring various programs and systems executing their respective routines. They had found through searching the old libraries, a few ways to shorten the whole startup process, which shaved hours off the critical prestaging time but required manual intervention and multiple bodies. By now, the team had it down to a science.

"Bring the main reactor bank online now," she announced. "Looks like we'll be ahead of schedule on this one. The 'bots have very little repair work to do."

"Maybe, if we have time, we can go down to the engineering level and watch the furnace 'bots."

"Once we get to level two. Just remember, Ron, stay out of their way, they can crush you in a second."

"Don't worry about me." He laughed.

April smiled. He was a good-natured kid. *I need to laugh more.*

The monitors danced with activity. "Alright, looks like we have level two coming up already. Wow, this one is quick."

"April?"

"Yeah."

"I got a security alarm going off."

"Probably a malfunction."

"Well if it is, it's moving."

She walked over to Wendy's monitor, to peer over her shoulder. "Pull up the video feed in that section."

"Here," Wendy pointed out. "Look, see that?" It was hard to see, similar to a dark blur.

"Can't make it out. Engage security protocol, Wendy."

"Won't do any good. Whoever, or whatever it is, it's already reached core level. No security 'bots allowed in those levels."

"Alarms are off now."

"'Cause it's in the core, like I said, no security checks." Wendy's voice carried a high-pitched tenor.

April did not like this at all. "Ron, lock the doors – all of them. Everyone, just keep calm. Wendy, switch everything over to automatic. We may have to leave in a hurry."

April pulled her sidearm and switched off the safety.

"It could be a brother Porter. Maybe some kind of emergency," offered Ron.

"Oh yeah, then what's that?"

Sparks flew out from the door. "That's a plasma torch. Time to go!" April yelled.

"Where?"

"Back door, to the lower level. And yes, we're going to see those 'bots up close, Ron."

She grabbed the setup mods and pushed everyone to the back door. "Put it in gear, guys." She slammed the access switch to open the engineering door and ushered them through. A quick glance back revealed whoever was coming was almost through. She slammed the door shut and fused the panel with her blaster.

Turning, she almost tripped over Wendy. "What the hell are you waiting for?"

She was crying and visibly shaking. "I can't."

They were on an open gridwork walkway, suspended thousands of meters from the foundation floor level.

"Just don't look down."

"I can't. I can't move."

Something banged in the control room.

"They're through. Keep going, you guys." She waved the others on. "I'll stay with Wendy."

The cutter started again, sparks flew at them. April readied her blaster. The door flew open, a black image screamed out firing as it came.

April shot a barrage, but it was too quick.

Wendy flew up in the air, savagely pushed by some unseen force, her body went over the railing and down into the dark chasm below.

"And look who we have here."

April wanted to move but couldn't, it seemed as if her feet were welded to the deck-way.

"April McThurn, you have stirred up some trouble for such a little girl."

The sensation of suspension gave slightly, enough to pull the trigger, tilt her arm. Perhaps it was desperation, a realization of death, something. The blasts melted through the decking, and it gave and twisted, knocking the aggressor back through the doorway.

She was free. Without hesitating, she turned and ran, not looking back.

"April!"

Ron was calling for her.

"Over here!"

She turned right, grabbing the rail to keep from flying over the side. They were at the freight elevators.

"Hurry!" They waved to her desperately. Their voices seemed small, far away. All she could hear was her heart pounding in her ears and feel her lungs burning.

She slid into the elevator and Ron pounded on the controls.

Blasts shot through the opening as the doors pushed closed.

April raised to her knees, fighting to regain her breath. "Don't worry," she rasped, "we're headed to the lower level. Lots of places... to hide."

"April, who was that?" asked Ron. "He killed Wendy, he killed her, April!"

"I know. I saw." April said, straightening up. "He was an enhanced. A professional."

"But why? Why would somebody do that?" Ron's face was pale, taut.

"He's probably the same one who killed my family, Ron. I think he's come to finish the job. We have to split up. Maybe if he finds me, he won't go after you."

"Forget it. We stick together," Ron said.

She laughed. How the hell could she laugh at a time like this?

"What's so damned funny?"

"I don't know," she said, the feelings churning inside her as she fought back the tears. "Wendy's dead, and I don't know what to do."

The elevator stopped. "We get out," stated Jerry.

They stepped onto a blackened concrete floor. Ahead machines the size of small mountains raced back and forth, feeding atomic furnaces and hauling loads of ore from the surface strip mines.

April took a few seconds to assess their options. "Up there, near the furnaces. There's enough air generated from the ion converters to keep us alive and enough heat from the blast doors to stay warm when the night comes. We need to find somewhere dark to hide."

"OK. Good idea. But how do we get past these monsters?"

"We run," stated Jerry.

"Oh you're just full of good ideas, aren't you, Jerry," Ron said sarcastically.

A familiar sound of a descending elevator echoed from above.

"No time. Let's go."

They ran. A 'bot to the right was coming up on them fast, so they turned and ran perpendicular to its course. The massive mountain of steel loomed over them, its gigantic alloy wheels crushing pebbles to dust upon the hardened floor as it approached. "Move, damn it!" yelled Jerry.

The 'bot passed behind them, blowing a torrent of hot air in its wake.

"Stop!" Jerry yelled again.

They waited, huddled together in the middle of a chaos of moving monsters.

Jerry was silently calculating the time intervals between the machines. April took a quick look back. The elevator had not touched down yet.

They still had time.

"Go!"

Again they ran, this time straight through the path of two machines rolling at their feverish pace. The small group never stopped. One machine passed behind them and the other beside them, each roaring on with murderous indifference.

They reached the other side of the staging area out of breath and shaking. April checked the elevator. It had just stopped and the doors were starting to open. A large pipeline dropped down to ground level ahead.

"Get behind here, quickly!"

A figure came out and surveyed the area. He was slightly hunched over and moved like he was favoring his side, possibly wounded by April's shot. He turned around and headed back toward the main compound, away from them.

"Good, that bought us some time. Let's find the stairs and get across to the furnaces."

Far above the dusk sky was visible, through churning gray clouds.

"Night's coming. If we don't reach those furnaces, we'll be dead by morning."

* * *

Cruez brought the flier down in a gradual descent, careful to maintain altitude. He liked flying, traveling between the stars. It was exhilarating and liberating. He felt more at home in the cold emptiness of space than in any crowded room of an Anard-Bueller gathering.

The local spaceport was just to the east. His ship wouldn't even register on their tracking devices. It had the latest in camouflage technology; the most expensive money could buy.

He started the scans, carefully synchronizing the search matrix programs to overlap 5% in case his targets were moving.

What the Old Man had told him was terrible. But he didn't think any less of him. He was a great man just the same, a great man, just imperfect. In a way, he understood why Tiberious had done what he had done. It was true, what had happened to this planet, and its people was tragic, but he had seen the power of big business first hand. He watched them string along the public with their puppet politicians, seen them buy their way to whatever goal the Companies were aiming for. There were five companies left on planet Earth, five companies that ran the world, five companies that compete with each other mercilessly, leaving behind broken lives and ravaged lands – and people.

There was no such thing as war any longer. There was no profit in war. There was only control, control, and ownership. And of these five great companies, only one had remained constant over the centuries. As others lost and gained, ebbed and flowed with success, only one remained solid. Anard-Bueller was that exception, ruled by the firm hand of an aging ghost of a legend.

One day, probably soon, Tiberious Bueller will die, and the corporation of Anard-Bueller will gradually fade back to the same level as the other four. There were many rumors about who would run the company, and how it would be run, but all of that was still conjecture. Only one man knew, and Tiberious had a penchant for maintaining secrecy on such matters.

"In due time," he would say. The board hated that. They probably hated him, whether it was jealousy or just hunger for power, but they all feared him. The fear, possibly, was based in some way because of people like himself – Tiberious Bueller's personal guard. Every one of them was trained from an early age on the finer aspects of combat, stealth, technology, and survival. He was the Captain of the guard and a true friend of a frail and dying old man.

And as a friend, Tiberious had asked him for a favor. He would take care of this.

* * *

Time seemed to stand still as they waited, huddled on a concrete floor, camouflaged in a maze of metal pipes. Heat rose off the furnace doors in golden waves, distorting the lights of the TFP in shimmering waves. The heat kept them alive, abating the cold which threatened to sink down upon them from above. Each time one of the monstrous 'bots fed an oven, the heat would radiate out enough to scorch a man to powder if too close. The long line of ovens stretched into the darkness, 24 in all. Less than a quarter were active as more were to come online as the systems ramped up. April peered out past the reddish plumes emanating from the ovens. Somewhere, beyond the light, a man was out there, the killer of Wendy, and possibly of her family. He had been sent by someone, Anard-Bueller, Soho-Beher, or one of the other Companies.

Ron shifted in his sleep, moving closer to April, wrapping his arm around her breasts. She pushed his arm away, annoyed.

Typical male. Probably faking sleep. All they want is sex.

Once dawn came, they would move. They had no more than two hours before the winds would pick up and the heat would become unbearable. Within three hours, unprotected and exposed, they would be dead. They needed time to reach the tank. Would there be enough time?

Maybe the stranger had already thought of that, perhaps he already destroyed their only hope of getting back safely. She had no way of knowing until they made their way around to the front, where it was parked.

Again, another grab. This time it was Jerry.

Damn it! Bloody letches! She grabbed his arm and threw it down hard.

"Hey," he yelped.

"Just keep your hands to yourself – the both of you. You, teenagers, let your hormones run unchecked. HANDS OFF! You got it! Both of you. I mean it! And I know you're awake, Ron. I know you can hear me."

Ron only shifted, mumbling slightly.

Not fooling anybody.

She pulled away to sit across from them. From this vantage point, she was able to look up to the sky. The clouds kept it a murky black, for the most part, save a sparse and random moment when a star would shine through.

The pipe beside her was warm. She huddled close to it. In the time between, when the oven doors remained shut for more than a minute, the night air from above would descend. It was a sharp, biting cold, the kind of cold that if left to permeate, would freeze your lungs in a breath. A killing cold.

Ishaida had to be saved. They all had to be saved.

She moved closer and rested her cheek on the pipe, felt a comforting warmth fill her lungs. She fell asleep dreaming of better times, of her SeaClear, of her family.

* * *

Marcus struggled with the last stitch. His shoulder burned in agony, but he had been trained to ignore such pain. The needle went through the supple torn flesh easily. He tied it with a secondary knot under the last stitch, cursing under his breath.

The girl had done a number on him alright. She was quick, that was for sure. He had not expected that, not in a million years.

He eased back into his chair and watched the readouts as his ship's scanners reported their findings. The passes were calibrated in a meter by meter matrix. It would take hours to go through the whole complex, but he would find them. He adjusted the ship's environmental controls, raising the heat up slightly. It was cold out there now, really cold. Anyone unprotected would be dead in minutes.

They could already be dead.

But he was patient, and he was thorough. Life's lessons had taught him well.

He would find them either way.

* * *

Morning came with a dismal light rain. It had started to snow during the night, but the updrafts from the ovens abated most of the precipitation. The rain was much heavier above, but it was a mere light drizzle down at the bottom of the strip mine.

The Caleco TFP was built at the base of a mountain range, making it a difficult passage to reach by land when one needed to approach from the westward direction, of which April's group had. The tank had handled the rough terrain easily, but even it had its limits. April had calculated the time they had to get back through the pass before precipitation created by the TFP would accumulate a barrier of snow in the upper elevations.

Unfortunately, the planned departing time already came and went.

The pass would be blocked soon if it wasn't already. Getting back to GhenghisPrime may be impossible.

April wiped the drizzle from her face, squinting through a heavy blanket of fog that had settled onto the field ahead. The machines never stopped, guided by radio or whatever means the engineers deemed was most efficient, bad weather had little effect on their purpose. They rolled out of the mist, dark shadows of unstoppable steel, grinding anything flat that was in their way.

"What now?" asked Ron. "We can't even see them moving out there. We'll be killed trying to get across."

"We can't wait for the fog to lift. By that time, it will be a sauna down here. We'll be steamed alive." Jerry shook visibly. "Look, let's take another way. I'm freezing, and I'm a long way from thinking about how hot it's going to get."

"Yeah, would have helped if we had stayed together for the body heat. I swear I have frostbite on my nose," complained Ron.

"Stop your bitching," blurted April. "Maybe if you had stopped groping me I would have – too late now. Come over here, this pipe will warm you up. Listen, I have an idea on how to get to the tank."

"Yeah? Well this should be good," commented a doubtful Ron.

April shot him a menacing glance back. Ron checked his shoes.

"You guys watch the next miner 'bot as it approaches the oven. You should see a maintenance gangway leading up its side. I think it wraps around its back where it reaches the ground."

"Here comes one now," stated Ron, unceremoniously.

They moved up to the edge of the deck-way and peered through the fog. The basting heat from the furnaces kept the area in close proximity relatively clear of the soupy white fog.

Jerry spoke up first. "Yeah, I can see the gangway now. But it looks like that maintenance ladder is suspended at least three meters from the ground. I don't know about you, but I'm not that tall."

"I doubt even I could jump that," added Ron.

"Look down there. You guys see that waste bin the maintenance 'bots are using. There's some cabling in there, mixed in with all that junk."

"Barely. You sure? From this height, it could be anything. The fog is too thick."

"Trust me," asserted April confidently. "We use that garbage to make a grappling hook and the cable for a rope."

"And?" added Ron.

"And we run up to one of the miner 'bots, lasso the gangway and pull ourselves up," April stated as a matter-of-factly.

"Yeah, April, you have been watching these things move, haven't you? So you are saying we need to get out there, wait for one to pass us, and run behind it before the oven opens, otherwise, we're toast."

"More like piles of ash," stated Jerry glumly.

"Then we have, what, maybe 20 or 30 seconds once the furnace door closes to hoist ourselves up onto that gangway before the bot starts rolling back?" Ron was not impressed.

April realized the challenge but wasn't deterred. "Technically, we just need to get up the line as fast as possible."

"And the last guy on the bottom gets pulled under and crushed, right?" Ron said, but not without a hint of fear.

"You got a better idea?" asked April, openly annoyed at their glum reaction.

"What about taking this deck-way to the end and looping around back in?" Jerry offered.

"That will take us half-a-day. Our shoes will be melting to the deck before we reach the entrance into the controlled climate section," April countered.

"Then we make a dash for it. Take our chances. What is it, 100-200 meters? We did it before," Ron shot back, desperately not wanting to attempt this.

"Just in case you guys didn't notice, there's something called fog out there. We need to stay close to the ovens to see them. Too far out and we can't see them big bastards coming until they're practically on top of us. We'll be crushed for sure."

"Says you," huffed Jerry. "We can make it."

"You think so? Look down to your right, what do you see?" They both looked where she pointed. The fog, too thick beyond four or five meters, gave away little.

"What?"

"Keep looking," she insisted.

The orange glow of open oven doors pierced through the fog. Spots of light, blinking on and off, stretching smaller in the distance.

"Notice any difference?"

They both looked back at her dumbly.

"For crying out loud! There's at least a dozen more ovens running since yesterday. The plant's ramping up to full power. I bet you there are at least twice as many 'bots out there since we crossed last night. Hell, you can hear them if you just listen. You have to acclimate yourself to the noise."

They both looked out into the fog and looked back. By their faces, April knew they understood.

"So, any other ideas or are you willing to try my plan?"

They both shook their heads.

"We can't afford to lose any more time. Let's go."

They made their way to the maintenance dumpster quickly. Ron agreed to fish out the supplies and Jerry and April boosted him up. They had a makeshift grapple and cable fabricated within 10 minutes.

It was already growing noticeably warmer, especially down where they were, very close to the ovens. Ron wiped the sweat from his brow with a dirty sleeve. "Ok. I've tied up smaller cable knots every third meter or so, wrap your legs around the line and put your weight on it to hold you when you climb, OK?"

They both nodded.

"Good. Ron, you're taller than me so you toss," ordered April. "Jerry, you're up next. I'll take up the rear."

"Whoa there, I'm not stupid you know. The last one has the greatest chance of getting crushed. Who made you the hero?"

Ron was scared, his face white, but there was definite anger in his eyes. April admired that, if only for a moment. He would make a good man one day.

"No chance. I'm still the boss, remember?"

Ron turned away, grumbling something. One of the 'bots roared by, drowning him out. April decided it was better to ignore him.

"Alright, let's move out to the field, we need to start timing the 'bots, find a pattern, predict the next one, run out there to a safe position, wait for it to pass, and latch on. It's not too far. Simple, right?"

Jerry nodded, eyes darting back from Ron to her. His face was pale, so much so his lips seemed a shade of blue.

Maybe it was just the fog.

They watched the gargantuan machines approach, dump their loads and depart. They seemed to cycle in threes, a pause, then came the next set. It was orchestrated, she knew, from control systems far above. It was ironic really - these huge lumbering machines, all dancing with graceful efficiency.

"OK. I think I've got a pattern nailed down here. We wait for the next one to hit the oven to our left. As soon as it departs, we run out," April announced.

"And then?" asked Ron, apprehension in his voice, visibly shaking from excitement.

"Then we listen for the next one to come and get the hell out of its way before it crushes us."

"You ready?"

Both nodding and licking chapped lips, preparing to run.

The 'bot came in as expected, groaning like a monster. The oven door opened and a wall of flame blasted out, scouring the metallic beast. Impervious to the temperature, the monster deposited its load, paused, then reversed. The whole cycle took no more than 60 seconds. "Not much time," said Ron under his breath.

"It's moving," yelled April. "Go, go, go!"

They started out of their small recess of safety and chased after the retreating beast, only to stop about 10 meters out once April threw up her hand to signal. They waited but only briefly. The groaning and grinding of the approaching 'bot was unmistakable. It appeared out of the fog suddenly, a dark shadow of death. April grabbed Jerry by the back of the shirt and pulled, barely getting him out of the way of the whirring giant's metal tracks. "Get behind it! Go, Go, Go!"

They didn't need her encouragement as staying where they were meant sure death. Seconds later, the furnace door opened and a blast of heat surged past them, blocked by the body of the monstrous 'bot.

Ron didn't need prompting to launch the line. He knew he had only one chance and if he missed, they'd probably be dead within minutes. His throw was good. The makeshift grapple wrapped around the upper gangway and held. Ron started up with a leap. Jerry was right behind. For some reason, April hesitated. The 'bot didn't. It was already starting to move back.

Too early, she realized.

"Jump," yelled Ron.

April grabbed and pulled. She was in pretty good shape but lacked the upper body strength of the younger boys. Her feet were dragging on the ground. She grabbed the next knot in a panic. The thoughts of getting pulled under and crushed screamed at her from within. *Move damn it. Move!*

The boys were pulling the cable up from above. She climbed as fast as she could, her arms burning.

Suddenly, the cable went taut.

It was caught below.

A hand reached for her, she grabbed it. It was Ron. The cable let go with a 'zing'. A piece of it caught Ron's arm, wrapping around it for a mere second. He screamed in agony. She felt him lose his grip, and she crashed into the side of the 'bot, face first. She could feel the cartilage in her nose snap and the bleeding start. But she didn't let go and neither did Ron. Jerry reached over and grabbed her somehow, and they both pulled. She saw a rung and reached for it. In another second, she was up, laying on the gridwork, choking on her own blood.

She rolled over and spit, breathing hard, arms feeling limp. A quick look at the boys revealed Ron was a lot worse than her.

He had a glassy-eyed look of shock and pain. He was in agony.

She pulled herself over to him. The 'bot was bouncing and swaying as it gained speed.

A quick inspection revealed the cut was deep – almost to the bone.

"Jerry, rip your shirt for a tourniquet."

April grabbed the piece of cloth, twisting it tightly. "Hang on to him. I'll get this around his arm. Keep him steady." She managed to wrap the rag around the wound, although it was bleeding profusely.

"He's losing a lot of blood. If this doesn't work, he may go into shock."

She pulled it tight, used another as a dressing over the wound.

The air was getting thinner, and the sun was cutting through the fog with an unforgiving glare, even through the thick cloud.

"We're moving out to the mine pits – outside. Dunno if we can take the direct sunlight – or the thin atmosphere. I've got to get up there and open the maintenance hatch."

"You hear me, Ron?"

"I'm still here," stated Ron but weakly. "Get going, I'll be right behind you."

"Alright," she acknowledged, then bolted up the stairs keeping one hand on the handrail. The 'bot swayed dizzily, moving at a pace that made the ground pass by in blur beneath them. The gangway hung off the side of the great metallic monster, rising up in an alternating crisscross pattern to end at the 'bot's neck just below its 'head'.

What kind of locking mechanism the latching system used, April could only guess. She caught her hand on a sliver of rust protruding on the rail. It sliced into her palm with a searing burn.

"Damn it!"

It started bleeding. She had to stop and rip off a section of her top, to wrap it around her palm. It was already throbbing in pain. The gangway was showing the effect of centuries of exposure. No matter how ingenious man was in creating alloys, nature always seemed to win over time.

As long is holds and it doesn't collapse.

She was three-quarters of the way up now. The two boys were coming up but still far below.

She fought for breath. The atmosphere was thin and growing thinner as dawn turned to early morning. The fog had turned to a steady rain. Yet through the gray skies, April could feel the heat of the sun slowly cooking her with invisible UV radiation. It shone through the cloud cover in a bright orange-white glow.

To unprotected skin, Ishaida's sun was deadly.

She reached the top and stepped into the shade of a small enclave. The hatch leading into the 'bot stood before her, a circular wheel mounted in its middle.

She turned and peered over the railing to check on Ron and Jerry, and almost fell as the 'bot jumped over a protrusion. She caught herself on the railing, fighting down a momentary sensation of desperate fear. Taking deep breaths helped bring her heart rate down.

Damn, that's a long way down – she'd be dead for sure.

She turned to the task of opening a hatch. By the amount of oxidation, it seemed clear it hadn't been opened in centuries. She grabbed the rusty wheel and heaved with all of her strength.

Nothing. But they had to get in – or they were all dead.

She heaved again, this time pinning her legs for more leverage. Something shifted. A click. The wheel turned a full 60 degrees and then the door swung open.

The 'bots were designed for zero atmosphere. But they also had a built-in airlock system, with atmospheric generation and a life-support system. It was a costly measure to introduce such capabilities in an industrial 'bot, but it was mandatory since the space mining safety act of 2257. Any 'vehicle' beyond a certain dimensional size had to have this capability, regardless of its purpose.

April couldn't recall the exact specifications, but she remembered reading the history of why the act was amended – and the thousands of lives it had saved since it became law. Space miners on asteroids running equipment the size of small houses had died more than once because they simply had nowhere to go in the case of a minor accident. Spacesuits provided little reserve and few options. As always, such regulations had been written with the blood of the brave dead.

She entered the airlock, powered up the access console, and yanked the outside hatch shut. Cool air jets shot into the small space, raising the pressure and the oxygen level up to a more comfortable level. Breathing was a little easier now.

Entering into the main compartment, she could see they had just enough room for the three of them. As expected, no one had been in there in years. Everything was covered in a subtle layer of black soot. The cabin was dark and smelled of burnt ozone. Across the opposite wall, a spare maintenance suit swayed on a hook.

She dusted off the main control panel and triggered the displays. Three of the four came up, one with a dark line down the middle of it, another slightly out of focus. Too many years of bouncing around and this little area was low on the maintenance priority list.

Cameras mounted on the 'bot from many positions, scanned the horizon, and along all of its extremities, including one above the gangway. She could see Ron and Jerry still struggling, possibly at the three-quarter marker now.

She flipped to the outside sensor display. The temperature was steadily climbing, and the sun was hitting them directly now. Oxygen levels were dangerously low. She had to stop the 'bot, or at least turn it so they were out of direct sunlight.

She sat down at the control perch and scanned the instrumentation. With another a quick adjustment she was able to watch as the control logic flowed past in a steady stream. To the layman, it looked like hieroglyphics. To her, it was the thoughts of the machine.

Concentrate. The basics are the same as everything else. Apply what you know. Primary control override command - engagement – there. Command instruction set display – there.

She pressed the bypass controls, engaged the command console, and then entered the command.

The 'bot came to a halt, shifting slightly forward with the sudden change of inertia.

OK. So far so good. Now to turn it.

Alarms from primary control started up on the display. She killed them with a keystroke. Apparently, central control didn't like its unit being taken offline. She entered the command.

ERROR blinked back at her.

Shit. Old 3-Gen protocol. Remember the syntax, April.

She tried again. ERROR.

She glanced at the cam-monitor. Ron and Jerry were coming up, but it was already too hot. They were awkwardly trying to avoid touching their hands on the railing.

They were frying out there. Come on!

She typed in the command. The 'bot responded on her third try, slowly rotating 90 degrees clockwise, effectively moving the gangway and its climbing passengers, out of the sun's direct path and into the shadows.

She let out a breath, ignoring the alarms firing at her from central. Next to figure out how to put this on manual maintenance mode.

But first, need to find the medical supplies.

She queried the console, and it brought up the location for the supplies. Within a minute, she had them dug out of a dust-laden locker, including a skin conditioning cream for UV burn repair.

The boys struggled into the lock and collapsed.

April closed the outer lock remotely, pressurized and opened the inner.

"You took long enough," Jerry complained. His face was a deep red, singed from the sun's heat.

Ron's eyes were closed.

"He passed out the last few steps, you think he's OK?"

"Probably from the heat. Here, put this on your face." She handed him the cream, then she attended to Ron's arm and his burns.

"I have some antibiotic and an auto-stitcher for his arm, but he may have some nerve damage. We'll place an emergency call when we reach the tank."

She started applying the topical solution to Ron's red burns. "We'll make it. We're OK."

She smiled. Jerry smiled back.

He turned his attention to the monitor behind them, and his grin evaporated. "But what about the flier out there getting a bead on us?"

"What?"

"Behind you – the monitor."

"Oh shit. The bastard's found us."

"Can you get this thing to move?"

"Yeah," she scrambled to the control console. "Hang on."

She entered a second set of commands. The 'bot turned another 90 degrees and started back.

"I told it to go back the way it came, but I need to engage this control console."

"Well, stop talking about it and do it!"

She took a second to give him a menacing glare. "Not easy you know. This equipment is half-a-millennia old, it has separate heuristic algorithms that need to be overridden, and I don't have the keys."

"Whatever."

She pulled up the help libraries and started digging. "Gotcha." As soon as she entered the commands, the secondary control console lit up. She looked over at Jerry with a wide grin.

"There's not a machine I can't tame."

She grabbed the control stick and pushed it ahead. The 'bot picked up speed, leaving its lumbering pace for a quick stride. Inside the small cockpit, the once gentle ride turned to rough bouncing, causing everything to shake and vibrate insanely. "Whoa, gotta slow it down a bit."

"What about that flier?"

She checks the external camera feeds. "It's gone."

"No way."

"I can't find it."

Jerry crowded over the console, pressed a couple buttons. New alarms started.

"What the hell! Stop doing that." She reached over and quickly restored the settings. "Here, this is the external camera pan control."

"Thanks."

He scanned the horizon. "You're right, nothing."

"You sure?"

"He's gone."

She turned the 'bot off the main track. It slowed down noticeably as it struggled in the wet sand.

"What are you doing?"

"We're going around to the front. But it may take an hour at this rate."

"Can you lock it in, use autopilot or something?"

"Yeah. Why?"

"Do it."

She entered the command.

Jerry moved closer, taking a sohol-pad from the kit. "'Cause it looks like we're not the only ones who need first aid." He moved the pad over her face. It soaked up the blood and stung slightly as the solution permeated into numerous scratches.

"Your nose is swollen pretty bad."

"I think it's broke and while you're at it..." She put out her hand that she had wrapped with a dirty rag, now laden with dried blood.

He unwrapped it gingerly. "How the hell did you do this?"

"Caught it on the rail."

"If I tell you something, you promise not to laugh?" asked Jerry. He was looking at her somberly, face smeared with white gel.

"Sure, considering the circumstances."

He looked away.

"Well?" April pressed.

"Nevermind."

She reached over, touched his chin lightly, turning him to face her. "What?"

"I just. Well, I think you're beautiful. I think you're amazing. I like you a lot – I mean, I think I love you."

She laughed.

He turned away.

"Oh, look I'm sorry. I am. I really do not know how you could be saying that to me when I have a broken nose and a fat lip. How could you say that I'm beautiful?"

"You said you wouldn't laugh."

"Yeah, I know." She felt terrible inside.

Why did she have to do that – to hurt him?

"Thank you, Jerry. You took me by surprise, that's all. But I'm a lot older than you."

"Four years. That's it. That's nothing."

She looked away from him, feeling uncomfortable under his gaze. "I'm sorry. Now's just not a good time for me."

"Oh," he squirmed a bit. "Well, don't worry about it. I understand. I kind of expected that, actually."

It was his turn to look away. "It's OK, really. I shouldn't have said anything. I know I'm out of line."

She tried to smile, but the attempt was more of a grimace. "Let's just be friends."

"Right, friends." Jerry's eyes were glued to the floor.

Ron stirred, then moaned.

"Why don't you check on him? I've got to monitor the 'bot." She turned and switched control back to manual.

Machines were always easier to deal with.

They came up to the TFP main entrance within the hour and found what remained of their tank - a molten slug of twisted, melted metal.

Something dropped in April's stomach and began to tie it in knots, one turn at a time.

"Jerry. Look!"

"Oh shit," he said, staring out the window with a look of exasperation. "He destroyed it." He said, almost in tears. "Why? Why would he do that?"

"He wants to kill us," she replied, a matter-of-factly.

The com-link blinked. She flipped the switch over to the hailing channel. "Well now, aren't we resourceful?"

It was the familiar acidic voice from the control room.

"Here's your choices, April darling. You come down from that beast and I don't blast it to pieces, and for an added bonus, I'll let the boys go free. Or, you stay in there and I use the three of you for target practice. Take your pick, let me know, but don't take too long." The com-link closed off with a slight electronic hiss.

A long moment of silence followed. April got up.

"No way! You can't go out there!" Jerry proclaimed, face ashen, voice shaky.

"You heard him. I go, you guys are free. No decision."

"He'll kill you."

"Or he kills all of us."

He looked down. Tears fell to the floor. "I can't let you go."

"Not your choice, Jerry," she said, her throat scratchy. "You need to get Ron proper medical attention. This 'bot has enough power to churn around this planet 10 times. It should be able to get through the pass alright. Your air should hold out long enough for you to make it back to GhenghisPrime."

"Here," she transferred 'bot control to full manual. "Joystick controls it. Simple as it gets – just don't get going too fast, or attempt too steep an incline."

She pulled the maintenance suit from the hook. "You guys get back home and tell them everything that's happened. OK?"

He nodded, eyes red-rimmed.

She donned the suit quickly, then bent over and kissed Jerry on the cheek. "I'll be fine. He probably wants me as a hostage – to take me back to the Company for interrogation."

She twisted on the helmet and engaged the suit's systems. "Damn hot out there now." She smiled at him through the faceplate.

The walk down the gangway was slow and tedious. She was careful not to catch her suit on any snags on the rusty railing. At the bottom, she swung down from the lowest rail, holding herself up momentarily, then letting go to fall the last meter and land in a drift of wet sand with a squishy thud. She hit hard enough for her nose to start bleeding in a trickle. The coppery taste of blood made her heart race all the more. She headed for the TFP door.

Behind her, the 'bot's gigantic tracks started to move, and the monster machine crawled away slowly, plowing through the wet, soupy sand.

April didn't look back.

* * *

"Glad you could drop by," he said from the shadows. "Come on in, a little closer now, I won't bite."

April ventured away from the airlock door, watching the stranger warily.

"Take off your helmet, stay awhile." His eyes seemed to twinkle in time with his sarcastic wit.

She twisted her helmet off slowly, careful to keep him in sight.

"My, my, what happened to that sweet face? Had a little accident did you?"

He stepped in close, angry dark eyes, sharp features, a crooked grin. "Maybe one of those boys put you back in line?"

"Just tell me what you want," she said somberly.

He grabbed her and savagely twisted her arm around to her back, then pushed her down onto the floor. She hit the floor hard. Pain from her already broken nose was nauseating. She lay there, watching a small pool of blood grow in size.

He pressed his knee into her spine, jabbing down so sharply it paralyzed her. Her heart was racing, pounding in her ears. She sobbed under the pain, uncontrollably.

"Shut up you bitch!"

His hands traced up and down, padding her body from head to toe. He twisted her over, wrenching her arm so hard she thought it would break. His hands started from her chest and worked down.

She lay there, trembling and sobbing.

He's going to kill me now.

He stood back up, staring down at her, a satisfied look on his face. "Get up and stop your squawking, or you'll die as slowly as I can make it happen. And I have the skills."

She stood up shakily, legs feeling unsteady. He watched her with a satisfied, twisted look on his face.

Blood dripped down from her nose in a steady stream.

"Why don't you just get it over with!" she screamed at him. "Kill me, and get it over with!"

He only laughed at her.

"Who said I was going to kill you? Maybe I'm here to collect you, bring you back to the Company."

April wiped her nose with her sleeve, the bleeding now ebbing. "And which Company is that?"

His eyes narrowed a bit. "Nevermind." He walked around her, circling her like a predator. "Why don't you take off your suit."

She didn't move. *Fuck him. He's going to kill me anyway.*

"Defiant to the last, are we? Well, that can be easily cured. How about we make a deal? You do as I say and I don't blast the mech-monster your boys are riding in. They make it home safe and sound."

She nodded and slowly started pulling herself out of the suit. She unclipped the main seal and slid it down, letting the light silver suit drop to the floor.

His look suddenly changed. His face flushed red, and his eyes shifted nervously.

She had seen that look before - a ravenous look, like a wild animal. Too many times she'd seen that look.

"Not bad. Nevermind the face. Do the rest. Take it all off, now!"

Defiance melted away to fear. It raced through her in a shiver.

He wants me. He's going to rape me. She took a deep breath, fighting off the urge to turn and run. *Stay calm. Give him what he wants, buy them time. Maybe he'll make a mistake. He'll be vulnerable then...*

"Take it off, I said."

She nodded and proceeded to peel off her clothes, one garment at a time. She could feel his eyes on her, like a maggot-infested wolf, starving for its next meal.

Completely naked, she straightened and stared at him defiantly.

"Nice. Real nice." He came closer, a hand reached out and touched her, fingers traced down to her breast. She could feel her breath rasp into short bursts. Her chest felt heavy, and her legs quaked as the floor felt suddenly unsteady. A hand grabbed her by the throat and closed like a vice.

"Now listen princess, you do as I say, and maybe you make it out alive along with your boys?" He pulled her close. His breath stunk of burnt tobacco, his body of blood and sweat. He let her go, pushing her effortlessly. She flew back, tripped and went down.

He pulled something from a leg pocket, a large yellow pill, and gulped it down. "You see this?" He yelled viciously, cupping his shoulder wound. "You did this to me you little bitch. In all my days, I've never had a simple, weak, female get the best of me. You have a debt to pay out now, little lady. You know what this does to my reputation? You have any idea?"

She avoided looking directly at him. He was working himself into a frenzy. Spittle dripped down his chin.

She shivered, feeling her mouth go dry.

Something fell behind him. A dark blur moved in the shadows.

He turned quickly, pulling his blaster.

She pounced, grabbed his arm and tried to twist it back and force his wrist down. He glanced back at her with an annoyed look then hit her so hard she flew back and crashed into the wall. She scrambled back up, thinking he was coming for her, but he didn't.

He turned away, completely ignoring her, intent on what was hiding in the darkness. A moment later a figure slowly morphed out of the shadows.

"Well, now, I was wondering if you were going to show up. They warned me Bueller might send you."

"Marcus Delgany," said the other voice, slightly lower and softer. "Been awhile."

"How about we play with something a little more intimate instead of these blasters, what say you?"

"Take your pick," said the other man. "It's my preference. I think you tend to rely too much on those enhancements of yours."

Marcus tossed his blaster to the ground, reached around and pulled the other from his back holster, and tossed that one as well. "There." He held out his hands, palms facing. "You see? And, I think I'll go with knives. I hear you got a reputation."

"No problem, knives it is then."

The other man tossed his blaster down, and casually pulled a knife. It caught the light briefly, reflecting a long curved blade.

"You see this one here," Marcus said, pulling his own knife from his upper belt. He tossed it in the air and somehow caught it by the blade, swinging it by his fingers to show the hilt. "I notched her for every time I had a kill. Not marks mind you. Professionals like you and me. Twelve in all. You'll make thirteen. That's my lucky number."

"You talk too much," the man said.

They met blades arching.

Marcus blocked, twisted to the side and jabbed, but the other man had already compensated, went down to the floor with a spinning kick. Marcus went down hard on his back. The other man was on top of him in a blur. His arm swung and the knife penetrated.

It had lasted mere seconds. Marcus lay dead on the floor.

The man pulled out the knife, wiped it clean on Marcus's corpse, and then carefully put the weapon back in his side scabbard. He turned his attention to April.

She watched him, fascinated. "Who are you?"

"I've come to get you."

"You mean like him, like Marcus?" she said, nodding to the corpse.

"No, I am the good guy." He walked in closer. Gray eyes, square chin, broad shoulders.

He looked her up and down, then reached into a pocket and pulled out a small cloth. "Looks like he broke your nose. Try to pinch off the blood flow. We need to get back to my ship. How do you feel?"

His words seemed far away, like through a tunnel underwater. She was sinking. Darkness overcame her.

* * *

Chapter 7

The world, spinning slowly, ground to a standstill. She lay prone on the floor looking up at the stranger.

"Glad to see you're back with the living. You collapsed," he said.

"I did?"

He smiled. "I repaired your nose and all the other wounds you've accumulated. You'll need to keep that regeneration splint on for another 12 hours or so."

She reached up and touched the small plastic device. At least she could breathe easier, but the pungent taste and smell of blood lingered. She was also clothed.

"Why did I faint?"

"You've been through a lot. Probably your body just crashed, a sudden drop in blood pressure, something like that. It happens."

"Who are you?"

"My name is unimportant. I'm just here to help, that's all you need to know."

"You saved my life. I can at least know your name."

He glanced away. "Fine, won't do any harm I guess. Call me Cruez."

She smiled, feeling her swollen lips tight on her teeth. "I probably look a mess. I feel like it."

"You survived an encounter with a very dangerous man, a trained killer. I'd say you came out very well, considering."

"Where am I?"

"My ship, orbiting Ishaida. I figured you'd want to say goodbye before we leave."

"What do you mean, before we leave?"

"We're going to Earth. Someone wants to meet you, someone very important."

"I don't want to go to Earth."

"Listen, I just saved your life. You owe me one so just do it. Don't worry, I'll bring you back. Besides, have you ever been off this godforsaken rock?"

He hit the controls, and a large image came up on the wall. It was Ishaida.

The clouds were already traversing along the horizontal plane, following longitudinal lines, hiding the majority of the planet's brown surface, but occasionally one could see glimpses of green. These patches were the last of the few protected valleys that remained seeded with oxygen-producing algae. The poles were hidden under a sky of clouds – moisture, already high in the atmosphere.

She turned her attention to space, to the low orbit around the poles, where the expansive mirror satellites floated. It was the Low Orbit Satellite Mirror Array. LOSMA consisted of 14 satellites, a pair for each TFP. Most of the satellite mirrors were still only half-deployed, but their effect was already evident on the planet below.

Each satellite was interconnected and tied to the TFP control systems. They were capable of turning their luminescent mirrors in a precise synchronized fashion focusing unrelenting beams sunlight onto the planet's surface below. The system was finely balanced. Too much heat and the sparse atmosphere would erupt into uncontrollable destructive power. The delicately calibrated operation was tied into atmospheric densities, moisture dissipation, wind speeds, and equatorial flows.

From their vantage point above, it was clear the planet was coming alive, emerging from a cold sleep.

"What do you find so fascinating about this damn rock, anyway?"

"Can't you see it? The terra-forming process is restarting. It's beautiful."

"Yeah. I heard you were some kind of idiot-savant with machines. You started this whole thing back up, didn't you?"

"I had some help."

"Well, you let the dog out now."

"What?"

"You know the phrase, you opened Pandora's Box, let the light in, sprung the hatch?" His eyes dashed around as he searched for more phrases.

"I don't know your slang, or what a Pandora's Box is, or what a dog is. Just say it in English."

"You started this thing, and now the secret is out."

"Oh, so what," she said, waving it off. "It's worth it."

"So what? You have made some powerful enemies. They don't like it when you mess with their profits."

"You think Ishaida will take over from Jefferson tomorrow? This will take years – possibly half-a-century before we have decent conditions down there."

"You do not understand. These enemies are not people – they're Corporations. Hell, they have financial plans that have lasted longer than this measly colony of yours."

"Thank you for your concern, now can you return me back to Ishaida? The domed city of GhenghisPrime would suffice."

He laughed, shaking his head simultaneously.

"Nope. Deal's a deal."

"I don't recall making a deal."

"Let's not and just say you did." He shut down the display. "Follow me to the cockpit. Need to strap down for the jump. I gather you have never experienced a quantum light-speed jump before? Ever been superluminal?"

"No," she said, trying to fight down a sudden feeling of fear. "Was on a miner shuttle when I was younger."

"Well, this ain't no miner's shuttle. My ship's the latest and the fastest you can find. So first time for everything. Sit down." He helped her strap in. "Don't worry. Most people make this jump without a problem."

"Most?"

"A small percentage go insane, but I don't think you need to worry."

"Why?"

"Call it genetics. Your ancestors managed to reach Ishaida in one piece, didn't they?" He gave her a quick smile and a wink, then strapped down himself.

"I'll put up the heads-up display so you can watch," he offered.

The holographic image appeared above her on the off-white, featureless ceiling. Bright stars fanned out it all directions, mixing into the distance, lost in clouds of red, purple, and green of stray nebulae. The planet Ishaida started to move away and in the process, become smaller. Other stars shifted, becoming blurred, reddish in color. Behind her, the ship's systems began to stage up to jump beyond standard space, past the physical limitation of light-speed. Vibrations carried through the air, up through the cushion of the chair.

Above the colors seemed to mix to liquid form, dots became blurs.

A sensation passed over her, crawling through every cell of her body, vibrating incessantly with an empty ringing, a wrenching loss of bearing, like a complete absence of gravity. Darkness passed over her.

This time it was welcome.

* * *

"Time to wake up there, sleeping beauty."

Blurry dark images formed shapes. Shapes became more defined, sharpening their edges with bright, unforgiving light. April closed her eyes tightly. Her ears rang, her head pounded at the temples with every beat of her heart. The sharp burning wall of pain seared into her brain, somewhere behind her eyes.

"Don't feel too good, do ya?" a low voice laughed with a tinge of sarcasm.

"You didn't tell me about the headache," April replied miserably. "Thanks."

"Don't worry, it'll pass. Everyone gets it the first time, and the second, and possibly a third."

"Until?"

"Until you adapt," he countered with a sharp reply.

April was able to open her eyes fully now. The pain had settled down, retreating to throb angrily in the back part of her brain. The image above her was gone, revealing a crisp white nothingness. "Where are we?"

"In between the stars. Will be for a number of weeks, six to be precise. Just feel lucky, the original pioneers were out here for nearly 75 years."

"As a Porter, I'm used to being cooped up in metal containers, but at least we have some room in our tanks. What do you do in this tiny cabin for all that time?"

"Sleep, dream for the most part. I have suspension chambers set up in the cargo bay for long trips, for this one, we'll use the latest tool for deep space travel. Our chairs will be fine for this."

"Sorry, I find it near impossible to sleep more than a few hours at a time. You must be real fun back on Earth. Didn't know you could sleep so much."

He laughed again, this time, with honest amusement. "You think I can sleep six weeks straight do ya? Even I can't do that on my own. You see that contraption to your left. It's called a statmon, puts you in a hibernation mode using drugs, then monitors your system for variances, basically keeps you under."

"And my body, what's to keep me from sitting on my hand, cutting off the circulation and killing it?"

"Pretty astute of you. Guess you're not such an idiot for an idiot-savant."

"Stop calling me names, jackass."

He laughed again. His brown eyes lit up, his usual hard look left him, but only for a moment.

"You probably don't even know what a jackass is."

"Do so. It's a hairy, four-legged mammal. Had one on Ishaida for a while, was in the history archives."

"What happened to it?"

"It was eaten. Fed a lot of starving people – after the company shut down the TFPs."

"Oh." His face was serious again. "Well, to answer your question, the statmon keeps your mind asleep and maintains your body functions by interfacing with your chair vitalization systems – send small radio waves, vibrations, electric charges through your body systems. It's not perfect, but it does a good job. It scans your body two or three times a minute. Sometimes you can wake up with a killer cramp, but that's it."

"And those suspension chambers?"

"Completely different. Puts you into stasis, basically kills you and then revives you."

That gave April a creepy feeling.

Kills you and then revives you.

She shook the feeling off.

Cruez noticed her silent reaction. "Yeah, it's a bit freaky, but most people that go into stasis feel great when they come back out, recharged even."

"Most?"

"Well, there have been a few cases where people have not been revived successfully or didn't come back with all their marbles. Doesn't happen much, though."

"You are just full of good news aren't you?"

"I'd rather stay awake if you don't mind."

Cruez looked away, swept a gaze up and the down the forward control indicators. He waved his hand deftly activating circuits in the process. The cabin lights died down to a low, comforting dimness. "Sorry, April McThurn, that's not in the plans. Don't worry though. Like I said, this is the latest in technology. No one has this stuff but us. And I guarantee you will not wake up with a headache."

He rotated the arm of the statmon over her chair. Restraints pulled her left arm down, and the statmon attachment settled down over it. The IV injection came with a sharp prick of a needle but faded quickly under a flood of euphoria. The pain in her head was gone, and she was floating, feeling nothing but a calm, soothing, quiet.

"Night beautiful." A voice echoed in the distance.

* * *

Alarms pierced her deep sleep with harsh intolerance. Accompanying the noise was an acrid smell of cooked electronics. She was awake in seconds, her heart rate climbing steadily as adrenaline rushed through her body in a heated wave.

"What's going on?" she said, still a bit off-centered.

Cruez glanced over at her, a grim look on his face. Green light reflected off shadows, giving him the appearance of a corpse.

"Small problem. We had an altercation. Everything's OK now, though."

"What do you mean, altercation?"

"Take it easy, there. Keep your heart rate low."

She leaned back into the copilot seat, and took a moment to give a wide inspecting gaze over the controls, and out into the starlit cockpit windows. To the right and up just a bit, the remains of a vessel turned lazily in the void. Pieces floated around, strewn about in a haphazard fashion.

"Another ship?"

"Yep. What's left of it. A welcoming party just for us. You certainly are a popular one."

"Me? How could they even know?"

He looked back with the familiar ashen face of his, emotionless, unreadable. "They have their ways."

"Are there any survivors?"

"No. Just finished my scans. I think there was one pilot, but there may have been two. Either way, they're both dead now."

"And if they weren't?"

He cut into her with a fierce gaze. "Hey, even I have a heart. I wouldn't leave them out here, it's against my code. And yes, even though they did try to kill us."

"Sorry." She said and turned away to stare out at the wreck again.

"Back in the old days on Earth, one ship would sink another and leave the survivors to perish in the water. It was the way of war."

"So. We aren't animals."

"Aren't you the bleeding heart? We haven't changed that much in all of these centuries."

"Yes we have, and it's called being civilized. Even us lowly Ishaidans have a code – like you don't leave another Porter out in the open to perish. It's not right."

"And what about your scrapies? You must not consider them human 'cause you left them out there to die."

April glared at him. "What do you know about Ishaida, Earthman? You've had it easy with your blue skies, your rain, your fertile lands."

"Oh, so you're the only ones who've suffered in this universe, have you? You obviously don't know much of the slums on Earth, the overcrowded mega-cities, the poverty and pestilence, a resounding lack of resources and food. Each day the equivalent population of your whole planet dies in Earth's gutters. Didn't know that did you?"

April looked away, reluctant to reveal her true thoughts to him.

"Thought so. You see, each one of us has our own version of hell. As a matter-of-fact, why don't you clear up something for me? I heard Porters would just as soon run over a scrapie than stop, that true?"

"They're cannibals." She shot back.

"Maybe, they are definitely on the lower end on the luck scale." He half-laughed at his dry remark.

"Not all Porters believe in that."

"What, you would stop and save a scrapie?"

She turned away again and huffed, "Nevermind."

He chuckled again. "When the shoe fits." He added dryly. In moments, he had adjusted the flier to a new course and left the wreckage behind.

An hour passed in silence.

"For your information, we're about 33 hours out from Earth. No need to go back under now. Why don't you go to the galley and make us some food."

April complied without saying a word. She found the food packages without much trouble, with a shot from the hydrator and a quick heating cycle from the microwave oven, she had two hot, steaming meals of steak, potatoes, and beans. The aroma filled the cabin, making her mouth water.

"I spared no expense on the rations!" Cruez yelled back.

April snorted, acting like the food was awful. Deep down her stomach was churning with hunger. She brought out the plates.

"Here. What is this, anyway?"

"Don't worry, it's not real steak, probably derived from some plant mixture. Tastes like the real thing though."

"What's steak?"

He only looked at her and then rammed a fork full of food into his mouth.

April followed suit, secretly enjoying every bite.

* * *

The ship descended on the night side of planet Earth. Lights dotted the planet's surface, outlining the continents below in a white cloak. As the small vessel sank down into the atmosphere, currents of clouds raced around its superheated hull, making it all but invisible from the surface, until it announced itself with one last final sonic boom. It shed its vapor-laden cloak and turned to align on standard approach vectors. The Earth Space Protection Division (ESPD) traffic control tracked it in at least one thousand different ways. Deviation from registered flight plan was not tolerated.

Cruez spotted a military guidance ship matching his flight path, less than 5 km away. The ESPD would follow procedure to the letter, including deploying a barrage of missiles against his ship's hull if he deviated without proper notification. He traced his fingers over the control panel, and with a light tap, brought up the central radio control.

"ESPD central, this is flight 101-50 Alpha-Zebra-Baker, registered under Anard-Bueller, now on approach for landing."

"101-50, we thank you for your confirmation."

Cruez nodded silently to himself. This was only a polite exercise. His ship's computers had already relayed the required information when they had initiated descent. His secondary protocol was expected, regardless.

He guided the ship down into the marked travel lanes. The tops of skyscrapers reached up from below in a tremendous gridwork of suspended steel and cement. Each tower provided a leg that reached down into the bedrock of the Earth's crust. Each leg tied to another, forming a massive layer of complexity of trusses and cabling that was designed to tighten and loosen as the interconnected towers adjusted to the changes within the earth. The population of billions would conduct their everyday business suspended between the worlds of the sun and the Earth. At the top levels, above the dredge of humanity, the rich and powerful resided. The poor would live out their lives far below. Some would never see the sun. Far below, beyond the contaminated foundations of the cities, past the containment walls, and carefully parceled out in unnatural perfection, mega-farms were continuously growing the planet's food supplies. It was all very precise, artificial and controlled. Access to Earth's natural beauty had been lost to the rich and privileged.

Cruez brought the ship down to a private port between three massive towers. The vessel touched down with a slight jar. He ran the post-flight check then powered down the engines.

Quiet settled into the cabin. Beside him, a wide-eyed young girl passed her hands over the monitor controls, scanning everything around them with an unnatural efficiency.

The port was empty, save for a small shuttle that was moored down in the northeast section. The small vessel was the property of one Anard-Bueller's high-ranking executives. It was rarely used.

"See anything out there?"

She glanced back at him, suddenly jerked back into reality.

"I never knew."

"What?"

"Earth, it's so – so populated. These suspended cities, it's unbelievable."

"Centuries of population growth. Billions and billions of people. It's amazing we don't starve to death, or choke on our own waste isn't it?"

She stared back at him with a sort of quirky look.

Cruez could not help think: what's going on in that mind of hers?

"I guess. Now what?" she asked.

"Now we see the Old Man. You get to meet one of, well actually, *the* most powerful man in this world – and any other one we currently populate."

"I can only wonder why. Lead the way," she said, with a full serving of sarcasm.

* * *

Walls of dark mahogany reached to plastered coffers of aging alabaster. Chandeliers hung in sparkling elegance at intervals along the hallways.

An aged butler approached them, head slightly downturned, shoulders in a permanent hunch. His graying face bore a mask of bored indifference.

April watched the old man carefully, seeing through his dark gray eyes, reading past the minor inflections in his body movement. Initial annoyance faded, his stiffened gaze gave way to a slight smile, very slight, but it warmed the space between them.

"I am very pleased to welcome you back, Sir." He bowed, and swept his eyes over her, inspecting yet polite. "My master welcomes you as well, April McThurn. During your stay, if you require anything, please feel free to call on me."

April smiled back. "You are a very gracious host, a considerable improvement over my previous company." She shot an annoyed look over at Cruez.

White lips upturned in a more pronounced smile, "Indeed... Please follow me."

The maze of corridors continued on, through rooms of plush carpeting, fireplaces, and priceless antique settings. She drew to a stop beside a large window. Peering out, into the darkness, the lights from towers in the distance flickered as rain clouds rushed by. She could hear the rain pounding against the glass and the muffled pitter-patter of intermittent hail.

"The weather is very active tonight. Storm's coming in from the east."

A shiver raced up her spine. As the terra-forming continued Ishaida would have such storms, but more fierce and many times more dangerous.

"Are you alright, Miss McThurn?"

"Yes, I'm fine, thanks," she pasted on her best empty smile.

"Our destination is immediately to the left." He guided her with an outstretched arm.

Another grandiose room, sprawling ancient furniture, a fire crackling quietly in the fireplace. Unlike many of the others, the light was dim, and the darkness floated in the corners giving the room a solemn, almost cozy atmosphere. Sunken into an enormous winged chair, just off-center from the hearth, sat the shadow of a man.

Cruez approached quietly, nodded and said something very softly. April stayed near the entrance. She jumped as the doors behind her closed with a thud, startled by the noise.

No escape now... Jeez, that was a strange thought.

The shadow revealed a bony arm that waved her over.

April complied, stepping cautiously, swallowing with intention. Her palms felt sweaty and she wiped them on her pants.

The Old Man watched her approach, trying his best to fight off that infamous grimace he always seemed to project. It worked all too well in the boardrooms, but not here, not in his home. His smile was as genuine as he could make it.

"Come closer, my dear. I'm afraid my eyes are not what they used to be. Let me see you."

April could feel the Old Man's eyes burning through her.

"It is uncanny." The Old Man said with a shaky voice, passing his fiery gaze back to Cruez.

"What do you want with me?" April blurted out, although already regretting it.

"Yes, yes, of course. Why you are here. I must say, your directness is not totally unexpected."

Tiberious Bueller sat back in his chair, a bit smugly, still smiling.

"Look, I appreciate your help – your invitation here, but I would rather be home."

"Yes you would, but would you be safe at home? You have my dear, in your possession, means, knowledge, and desire. And that is a problem." He waved a hand over to the bar, signaling Cruez. "Would you like a drink, my dear?"

"No thanks. I don't drink. I'm curious Mr. Bueller, how I could be such a problem for a corporation as large as yours?"

"Oh, do not misinterpret me, my dear. I appreciate your talents. This is not me but others that raise such concern. I am only concerned for you, for your extended family, for your home, for the citizens of Ishaida. They've suffered enough."

"OK. I'll bite. Who are the others you speak of?"

"Anard-Bueller has little to lose if the Ishaida terra-forming project is resurrected. In fact, we have much to gain. Certain agreements made in the past did little to anticipate what has transpired, and in fact, terms have since expired due to your actions. It is time, however, that you ask yourself who your enemies are."

"And you know? You can tell me who killed my family?"

Cruez returned with a drink. Bueller grabbed it with speckled hands. The ice cubes rang in the glass as the Old Man's hands shook slightly. He noticed the look on her face. "Yes, age is an ugly thing. Your eyes give you away, my dear."

She looked away, into the fire. "I'm sorry."

"And you have a heart as well. A rare combination, I must say. Jones!" the Old Man yelled.

The butler appeared through the large wood-carved doors. "You called, Sir."

"Take care of our young guest, make sure she is comfortable."

"Do not worry. You are indeed safe here, my dear, I will absolutely guarantee it."

"I'm not interested in being safe, I am not hungry, and I am not tired. Tell me what you want with me!" She could feel her anger welling up inside her. She felt like exploding. The Old Man glanced over to Cruez, still maintaining that crooked smile.

"She does have spunk," added Cruez.

"Enough!" she yelled. "I don't care who or what you are Mr. Bueller, but I know that Anard-Bueller has a lot of explaining to do – to all of Ishaida. And if you know who killed my family, you can at least tell me."

"Very, well." The Old Man took a long gulp from his glass and set it down, hands shaking, ice tinkling.

A strange image of the most powerful man on Earth, April could not help but reflect.

"My lineage is long, Miss McThurn. Through the employment of advanced medicine and some black witchcraft, I've managed to keep this husk of a body alive. Centuries have passed and I have outlived my great-great-great-grandchildren. Can you imagine outliving your children, your children's children? To see all of those lives pass on, yet to remain to live on in this wretched world, it is, sometimes, very challenging." He paused to look into the fire.

"And yes, I remember Ishaida well. I've been carrying that burden for so many years that I cannot remember a time I have not felt guilt in one form or another. Do not be so impudent to me, you lady. I personally turned on Ishaida's terra-forming plants all those centuries ago. I know the price that has been paid. Your family is one of many that have perished in that harsh world."

"Why can't you just tell me what you know?"

"You need to think with a larger perspective, my dear. But perhaps, what I expect of you is unfair, not realistic."

"I can do whatever you need me to do."

He coughed out a laugh. "Can you now! Then tell me how easy it is to forgive? Are you able to walk away from something because it is the right thing to do, or to look past your nose and into the future? Can you consider the long term, not just the immediate present? Perhaps you are blinded by your own sense of morals, your code you live by, that Porter code is bred into you. It in itself is flawed. It restricts your mind, makes you blind."

"What the hell are you talking about?"

"You want to bring Ishaida's terra-forming plants back online, correct?"

"No, not exactly. I've already brought the plants back online. That part is done. And nothing and no one is going to turn them off again."

"And what of Jefferson, the economy of a developed world, what will happen if superluminal traffic is diverted back to Ishaida, and what of Soho-Beher's investments?"

"Who cares?"

"Exactly, my dear. Who? I can guarantee they do care, very much so. The question you must ask yourself is how much."

"I know how much they care. They care enough to kill my whole family, plus Branton, Wendy, and anyone else that gets in their way."

"Maybe Ishaida is in their way."

"What do you mean by that?"

Old Man Bueller took the last swig of his drink. "I'm tired. We'll talk in the morning. April, you need to sleep on this. You need to think about what I just told you."

Mr. Jones stepped in, holding out an arm. "Miss McThurn, it would be my pleasure to be your escort."

No sense pursuing this further. It was apparent the Old Man was not giving her any more. "Goodnight then, Mr. Bueller." She promptly turned and headed back out through the massive wooden doors.

Bueller called out to her as she stepped through the doorway. "Remember Miss McThurn, weigh the costs of your decisions."

Mr. Jones closed the doors after them, sealing away the crackling fire, and leaving them in the solemn quiet of the hall.

"Does he always talk in riddles?"

"It is his way of speaking, my dear. He is very old and equally as wise. Riddles they may seem to you, for now. Time will help, I assure you."

"You're almost as bad."

"Perhaps."

"Do you wish to rest? Are you hungry?"

"No. No to both. I've slept enough on the trip here."

"Yes, of course. May I suggest something that may be of interest to you?"

"Sure, what?"

"Would you appreciate a visit to my master's personal museum? It is a very impressive collection I assure you."

"And what is in this museum?"

"Monuments of our civilization, historic archives, technology, art."

"Earth history?"

"Indeed."

"Lead the way."

The walk took almost a half-hour, winding through the maze of corridors and rooms.

"We are here," announced Mr. Jones, slightly out of breath, standing just outside the museum's entrance.

"Wow, this place is huge," added April, quietly amazed at the scale of the Bueller residence.

He waved his hand over a small wall panel. The sizeable wood-paneled pocket doors slid apart quietly. Lights blinked on down the corridor beyond revealing uncountable treasures, paintings, sculptures, all forms of art and relics of history.

"Come," he waved at her eagerly, with a tinge of childlike excitement, "see over there?" He pointed to a large biplane supported by cables from the ceiling. "A flying machine from the 20th century – from the second world war."

"War?"

He stared back at her for a moment, eyebrows arched. "Child, you have not heard of war?"

"Well, yeah, I know the meaning. I just don't know Earth history. I have to say, this flying machine is crude, but it is fascinating. I can see how the basic principles of aerodynamics have been employed."

"I see you are well versed in engineering and physics."

She smiled back. "You don't know the half of it."

"You also notice the weaponry mounted on the fuselage, the guns?"

She appraised the vehicle once more, saw the black tubular machinery mounted on the top, just behind the propeller. It was hard to see from the angle as the plane was tilted slightly for dramatic effect.

"Guns you say?"

"Yes, to destroy the enemy's flying machines."

"I see."

"You are not familiar with the world wars?"

"No. Why fight amongst one another? Nobody wins in the end."

"Hmmm," he crinkled his gray eyebrows together. "Interesting. I find myself making assumptions, a victim of my own perspective."

"And what of these Earth wars?" she queried, unconsciously twirling her hair with her finger.

"There is a small booth to the right, with access to historical archives, perhaps you should reference these."

She saw something in his eyes, his hands trembled a bit. It was clearly upsetting him.

"Perhaps it is better we continue on. We need not worry about that past."

"No," she said somberly. "I think I need to know."

He nodded slowly, his smile fading. "I see. I'm sorry for this, please forgive me."

Shaking hands made minor adjustments to the view panel. She watched as the panel lit up with bright images and an extensive index.

"I have to admit, I've never taken the time to research Earth's history."

"Please, sit. This may take some time." He handed her a remote control. "You can also page me on this device when you are done."

"Thanks."

"And Miss McThurn."

She could see the concern in his eyes.

"Yes?"

"Some things you see may be disconcerting."

"That's OK. I'm sure I can handle it."

He nodded quietly.

She reviewed the menu and started at the eightieth century.

* * *

"Where is she?" Cruez asked.

"In the museum, Sir."

"The museum? Yeah, that makes sense. She's a smart one."

"A remarkable young lady."

"That she is," he chuckled, "that she is. Oh yeah, the Old Man will probably want to see her in the morning."

"Of course, Sir. Shall I retrieve her?"

"Why?"

"She showed no indications of retiring for the night."

"I'll go talk to her."

"The museum, Sir, is a distance from here."

"Oh. Well, I can certainly take a walk. Give your bones a rest, Jones."

"Thank you, Sir."

"The museum?"

"Down that corridor last door on your left."

Cruez peered down the hall. It seemed without end, fading into darkness in the distance. He gave a whistle.

"Long way."

"Yes, Sir. A long way."

He found her 30 minutes later. April was huddled in a small video room reviewing history mods.

"I finally found you."

She jumped, startled at his interruption. Her eyes were red-rimmed, evidence she was recently crying. Her features were drawn and seemed in many ways sad.

"I'm sorry, I really didn't mean to scare you."

"No that's alright. I ah... I just didn't know."

"Know what?"

"That we, I mean mankind, had such a violent past. We are such fools. This makes Ishaida's history look trivial."

"You OK?"

"Don't worry about me. I'm fine," she shot back defiantly. "What do you want?"

"Mr. Bueller would like to see you, in the morning."

"Fine. How long does he plan to keep me here?"

"Maybe you should talk to him about that."

She stared at him. "And?"

"Well, I can escort you back to your room if you'd like."

"No need. I've some research to complete before morning arrives, thanks." She turned her attention back to the history vids.

Cruez turned away, slightly perplexed. She's definitely not like any teenager he'd ever met.

* * *

The next morning the Old Man was waiting for them in the sunroom. The air was sticky and smelled of soil and plants. These were strange smells to April's sensitive senses, which had never been exposed to so much greenery before. "April, my dear, I hope you are enjoying your stay."

"No, I'm not." She glared over at Cruez.

The Old Man chuckled. "Tell me, my dear, the name of the dictator who instigated the Second World War?"

"His name was Adolf Hitler, a native of Germany, in Europe."

"And the Mars Treaty, when was it signed?"

"2115, after the Centari crisis."

"And the reason the Centari crisis started."

"A man named Gerald Agronti was murdered, brother-in-law to the Chief Magistrate."

"Remarkable." The Old Man commented, shifting eyes over to Cruez. "Just how much do you remember of your research?"

"All of it."

"All of it? Do you see the images, recall them visually?"

"Somewhat. There are some images I have committed to memory, but

I choose not to memorize everything that way. It's not useful."

"I see. April, has anyone tested your cognitive abilities?"

She laughed. "Of course not, and I would not be interested in performing any form of test."

"You are only 16 years of age, aren't you?"

"No, I'm 17 now. I don't know for sure."

"Yes. Your genetic mother and father were 'scrapies', the last of a very few surviving vagrants that managed to stay alive outside of the domed cities. They are both dead now, I understand."

April's could feel her insides twist in tightly. How could he know all this?

"I have my means to obtain information others cannot," he said, breaking the silence, seemingly reading her mind at the same time. "You are a product of evolution – mankind's evolution. We had stopped evolving for so many centuries, and here you come along, your full potential unknown even to you."

"What are you talking about?"

"Have you ever asked yourself why you see things so clearly and others do not? How you understand the very nature or behavior of your surroundings, yet others are so ignorant?"

"Yeah, so?" her bottom lip was quivering. She bit down on it.

"You are a genius, young lady. You are above average, the top percentile, the very tip of the Bell Curve of our population."

She let out her breath slowly.

Was the Old Man right? It kind of made sense. But so what? Did she really care about some IQ benchmark?

"I have a proposition for you," he said, interrupting her thoughts.

"I'm listening as you may consider me a captive audience."

Again, he chuckled. It died off in a weak chorus of coughs.

"I am dying, that much you can tell. I am a living fossil. I have been looking for you for many years now, so I can finally find my rest."

He moved his wheelchair up close. "I need a successor – not only to run Anard-Bueller but to do something more, to wield this power wisely."

"Me?" she half-laughed. "I don't know anything about running a company. Knowing what I do know about Anard-Bueller, I would rather cut off my right arm be part of it!" She spat out the words, letting them cut into the Old Man, making clear her disdain for him.

The Old Man's eyes softened a bit. "I do understand your anger. Do not misplace it. Things are not always as they seem."

"Either way, I have a debt to pay."

He nodded, wheeling back and away. "Yes, yes, an ax to grind, a score to settle, eye for an eye. Someone has to pay for the deaths of the McThurns. Revenge, it is ugly and reflects poorly on you. Do not hold it so dearly to your heart, for it will poison your soul in the end. I do know about this."

"And what would you have me do?"

"See to your justice. But make it measurable. Administer justice wrongly, and you will be the guilty one."

"Cruez!"

Cruez stepped in, handing April a small folder.

"Open it. Find the truth in there," Bueller said bluntly.

April flipped open the manila folder. Enclosed were a few digital images and a collection of papers. What they indicated was clear.

"You have enough information here to clearly implicate Soho-Beher in the murder of my family. Why haven't you notified the authorities?"

Cruez burst into laughter. "You really don't get it, do you?"

"What?"

"April, my dear, the influence of the Companies spread beyond any government, beyond any law. There are no authorities, only competition."

"And you're not about to move on this, are you?"

"On the contrary. The management of Anard-Bueller are very much appalled at this violent crime," interjected Bueller. "The course of action is not as yet clear, however."

"Then go after them!" she almost yelled. "Nail the sonsofbitches."

"Again, revenge from the lips of a child. Let's walk through this then, as you are so intent, who exactly would you seek revenge against? And what would you have me do? Shall I kill all of them? Perhaps I should have everyone even remotely connected to this crime quietly assassinated. What is your wish, my dear?"

With hands balled up into tight fists, she stood there, speechless. Just what should she do?

"You hesitate, April. You have all the resources of Anard-Bueller at your disposal, yet you refrain from taking advantage of this."

"You know why," she said quietly.

"Yes, such problems have a tendency to grow complicated over time. Simple vengeance is never, truly, simple. Is it?"

"I just want them to pay," she said quietly, a tear starting down her cheek. "They killed my family."

"The man who killed your family is dead. But the person or persons who gave the order are still very much alive. But it will not end there."

"What do you mean?"

"Now that the TFPs are online, Ishaida has potential. Soho-Beher has a considerable investment in Jefferson."

"If that's true, I have to go back. I have to warn them."

"What could you possibly do for them? After all, I can certainly arrange the transfer of this news."

"No. They wouldn't believe you. I have to do it."

"And what will you tell them?"

"The truth."

"And will they then deactivate the TFPs?"

Thoughts swam through April's mind in confusing storms. She reached for the arm of the closest chair and sank down into the plush cushion, burying her head in her hands.

"We are bringing the war to us," she said finally, tracing back through her recent memories of war strategy.

"Yes."

"I need to go home."

"Are you sure, April?"

"If anything, I am sure about this."

"Very well. I will have Cruez escort you back to Ishaida. I only ask that you consider my offer."

"Sure," she said, avoiding looking at the Old Man. "I'll meet you at the docking bay."

Cruez watched her leave, slightly bemused. "So, let her go back, Mr. Bueller?"

"Tiberious," he corrected.

He chuckled at the crotchety old man. "Tell me, are you serious about your offer to her?"

"My decision has been made. Take care of her. She is the future head of Anard-Bueller."

"So you say. Well, can't say she doesn't have her own way of doing things. She'd fit right in."

A smiled cracked over the Old Man's gray face. "Yes, I do enjoy that about her. That is what makes her the best choice."

* * *

Scars

Chapter 8

The white light seared into her eyes like razor blades. She reached up, tearing the IV tube from her arm in the process. "Ow! Damn it!"

"Here, let me help you." Cruez's shadow blocked the light. He disconnected the IV tube and cleared away the suspension gel around her face, winking at her in the process.

She ignored him, scooping away the green slime, wiping it off the bare skin of her arm, and then checked the HUD in the pod. It was still too early to be awakened.

"What's going on? Is there a problem?"

"Had an emergency message sent from HQ. Pulled us out of stasis early."

"How far out are we from Ishaida? What was the message?"

He smiled at her. "You always like this?"

"Like what?"

He only shook his head. "We're about four light-years away from Ishaida. Dunno about the message, haven't reviewed it yet. I decided to check on you first."

"Well, I am fine. I can use some privacy though." She was just barely buried under the green suspension goo and was not keen on the idea of presenting fully nude in front of him.

"Ah, right, sorry," he apologized and turned away. "I'll head up and give you a few minutes."

"Can we contact Ishaida from here?" she asked.

"Yes, we can, after I find out what the hell is going on," he yelled out while heading up the ladder. "Oh yeah – shower's over there. Try not to make a mess."

As soon as he left, she sat up. The gel squished up between her legs and gave her a strange sensation. She shivered from the cold.

It'll feel good to get out of this goop.

The warm shower relaxed her cramped muscles. She had spent far too many days cocooned in that stasis pod. She touched the air rinse control and warm air rushed over her, pulling the moisture down into the drainage ducts near her feet. Within a minute she felt dry. As she slid open the door and groped for her housecoat, she failed to notice Cruez standing there.

He reached over and handed her the garment, averting his eyes out of politeness.

With a surprised yelp, she ducked back into the shower and hastily put on the garment.

"Always sneak up on your women passengers do you?" she yelled out. No response.

She stepped out. He was still there. His face a dark mask.

"My apologies, April. But I need to talk with you."

"About the message?"

"Yes, it's about Ishaida."

He took hold of her arm, gently. "This will be difficult for you." Cruez's solemn expression was a giveaway. Something was dreadfully wrong.

"Approximately two hours ago an asteroid collided with one of Ishaida's domed cities – Monsoona, 30 minutes later a second hit AlphaRosetta. Given the specific nature of the strikes, my sources do not consider this to be a natural disaster."

April leaned back against the wall, suddenly feeling overcome with nausea.

"We can't be sure at this time, but estimate at least 300,000 dead."

Cruez reached for her, but she pushed him away. "No. Don't touch me. Just let me be."

He jerked back, checking himself.

"Sorry," she realized her intense reaction. "I just need a minute to process this. I just... just need a minute."

"Yes, of course. I'll ah... I'll be in the cockpit."

He left quickly. The small hatch door clicked down shut in his wake, leaving only the whirring of the air jets emanating from the shower enclave.

So many lives gone, but why? Why would they kill them? Tiberious had warned her. She was bringing war upon them just like he'd predicted.

She slid down onto the floor and buried her head in her hands. The tears wrenched from her in spasms leaving little more than emptiness behind.

He had asked her what she would have him do. But that was before it was just her family. They have to pay for this. They will pay - all of them.

This was war.

* * *

"How's she standing up?"

"She wanted to be left alone."

"Understandable."

"Your orders, Sir?"

"Just stay with her, keep her safe. I'm going to look into this myself. Report back in 24 hours."

"Will do, out."

"I see you're keeping the Old Man informed," said April, surprising Cruez from behind.

"Didn't know you were there."

"'Course you didn't."

"How long?"

"Long enough. I appreciate your protection, but that's not important right now. I need to go in. There are people down there that need my help."

"I will go with you."

"You're not obligated. These aren't your people."

"Works against my moral code not to do something so I'll be there with you."

She peered into those gray eyes of his. It was clear he was more than just a bodyguard, a lot more complicated. "Thanks."

He nodded, his eyes a penetrating gaze. "And once we're done there, what next?" he asked, somewhat pointedly.

"Then we trace the trajectory of these asteroids and find out who launched them. Then we hunt whoever did this and find out what company is behind it."

"We're still a little over a day out. I suspect when we arrive they'll be long gone."

"Then I may ask you for help."

"Of course, Anard-Bueller will put its considerable resources on this. We will find those responsible both directly and indirectly. But then you'll need to ask yourself how far you want to bring this. How far are you willing to go?"

She only looked at him. *That was a strange question for a trained killer to ask. Perhaps it was better to divert the conversation.*

"I'll not be going back into that pod."

He grinned. "No, neither am I."

The short time flew by. April stayed busy getting all available medical supplies together. The small medical bay was limited, but it did have a genetic incubator capable of producing unlimited quantities of antibiotics and other complex medicinal compounds. Cruez helped out by showing her how to work the control systems and calibrate the equipment. He worked through the details with her with amazing patience, teaching her in his own quiet way. It gave her some comfort until they came into visible range of the planet, and they both witnessed the extent of the carnage.

When cloud cover shifted in the winds, one could see the surface and two large craters, their centers still glowing red. Their perimeters were marked by fire, still burning.

"My God, I never thought it would be so bad."

"It looks like Monsoona may not have suffered a direct hit. Some of the city still stands. There may be survivors. We'll set down there."

As they moved in closer, she checked for any sign of help, but there was nothing. "I don't see anyone out here yet. No emergency relief."

"They're probably on their way. Would take some time to retrofit mobile help I would guess."

Cruez brought the ship in low, scanning the landscape for recognizable signatures, as the cloud cover was thick, and smoke of numerous fires flooded the lower skies in dark plumes. It was night now, but even with the TFPs running, the daily temperature swings could kill anyone who had not found adequate shelter. What they were looking for was anything that would pass as some form of protection.

"There are a few signatures over there."

"Looks like a pipe, probably thrown up from the explosion, a portion of the city's plumbing infrastructure, no doubt."

"It looks like it's been sealed up. Do you think someone's surviving in that thing?"

"It's big enough to house quite a few survivors if it is. I'm bringing her down, grab hold of something."

They hit hard, tilting slightly to the side, almost knocking April off her feet.

"Jeez," April complained. "Where did you learn to pilot?"

"Hey, we're in one piece, so good enough."

"Whatever landing you can walk away from I guess." Her words muffled as she twisted on her helmet. She proceeded to activate the suit radio by the wrist path panel. "Ready."

They both grabbed a pack which they had previously stuffed full of emergency gear, medicines, and supplies. Cruez grabbed the heavier one, lifting it easily. April could not help but notice, impressed by his strength.

The Ishaida night was a turbulent confusion of starlight and alternating darkness as cloud and smoke streamers raced above. Winds, gusting irregularly, would attain enough force to push them to the ground, only then to subside once again to a gentle breeze. It took them far longer than either would have guessed to reach the ramshackle entrance to the scarred, dented, and rusting remnant of the great city. The pipe itself was about 10 meters in diameter, with an exposed length of at least 50 meters. The one end descended into the ground at about a 25 degree slope. One could only guess the titanic forces that would have dislodged this chunk of metal and shot it out from the impact area with enough speed and momentum to bury it back into the hardened surface.

April turned to face Cruez. "What do we do now?"

"Judging by the looks of this they welded up the end and fitted up a makeshift door. I would suggest we knock."

Cruez bent down to grab a shard of bent metal bar lying on the ground. Using it, he pounded the door three times, each time the bar would vibrate with a high-pitched ring.

Another set of bangs came from inside.

"Sounds like they just welcomed us in," he said dryly. He stepped up and pried open the slab door. It did not move easily. He managed to get it cracked open with enough space for them to slide through. He turned back to face her, sweat visibly rolling down his face

"You first." He panted.

She stepped into darkness, fumbling for her helmet light with her left hand. With a click, light flooded into the chamber. There was barely enough room for the two of them. Cruez then pulled the door shut, heaving and cussing under his breath. Once done, he pounded on the inner door of the hastily constructed airlock.

The inside door began to open with a high-pitched squeal of metal on metal. In a moment, the second door not much different from the first, was open enough to let them through.

They stepped into the interior, careful to adjust their stance to compensate for the tilting floor. April glanced at her armband.

Breathable air.

They both eased off their helmets. It took a moment for their eyes to adjust to the gloom and register the scene before them.

Men, women, and children were all packed tightly in this metal coffin, some sat, some lay, a few moved about attending to the wounded. A strong, square-jawed man, no more than 20, was closest to them. He was busily tucking rags into the seam of the inner door to seal it. A large bandage was wrapped around his skull and covered his left eye. It was soaked in a dark crimson red.

"It's good to see others have made it," he said quietly, then turned away to cough. The sound was a loose chortling. The fluid was building up in his lungs.

"You do this?" asked Cruez.

"Yeah, me and my mates at the back. We had a portable welder on one of the maintenance trucks. It took us some time, but it holds enough of a seal and keeps us from freezing to death. But the heat during the day is killing us and we've little water left."

"We've supplies outside. I'll need to bring them in: food, water, medicine."

"Sit down," April said with authority. "Let me look at your injuries."

"Don't mind me, there are others..." he coughed again. This time small spatters of blood were evident on the hand he used to cover his mouth.

"You are in no shape to be moving," she said with a hint of anger. "I'm April, and this is Cruez. We've brought supplies. It's not enough, but it's a start."

"April, April McThurn?" It was the voice of an older lady who was lying on the floor wrapped in scraps of clothing to act as a blanket.

"Yes?"

"I know of you April, you turned on the TFPs. I'm proud of you, girl. You showed that damned Company."

April noticed an open gash in the old woman's left leg. It showed signs of sepsis and gave off an offensive odor.

"This is not good. We'll need all the medical supplies." Her look over at Cruez was directive if not urgent.

He put his helmet back on, preparing to make multiple trips.

"Don't worry Ma'am, we're going to help you," she said, attempting some reassurance.

"You already have, April." The old woman said. "And it don't matter if we all die here. You turnin' on those TFPs was all worth it." She pointed to the hatch. "We're going to be able to walk out there again. It's just a matter of time."

But is it worth the price? She finally realized what the Old Man Bueller had meant. She had a lot more to lose than she had ever imagined.

The hours passed. They both helped as best they could. Many needed much more than what their meager supplies could offer. They needed a proper medical trauma center. Cruez had locked eyes with her more than once – each time it was his signal - someone was not going to make it through the night.

The cold was sinking in. The makeshift heaters assembled from the welding gear managed to ward off its intensity. For a handful of survivors with little to nothing, it was amazing what they had hobbled together.

The morning came with a marked increase in temperature. The frost on the inside walls turned to water, then to tiny streams of steam.

"How hot will it get in here?"

"Depends," offered a grizzled dome-dweller. He shifted in the dark, revealing severe burns on his legs which were now swollen so thick his skin had cracked. "It gets like a sauna in here, but we can survive it alright, as long as the sun stays under those clouds."

"Cruez, is there any way we can use the ship's cooling systems?"

"I'm not sure, April, you're the mechanical genius."

"I don't know everything, least of all starship specifications."

"Maybe we should be focusing more on how we can get these people out of here," he suggested.

"That's a better approach," agreed April. "We need to get back to the ship, get on the com and tell the Porters where we are. How many at a time can we fly to the nearest city?"

"I don't think that we can carry any more than three at a time," Cruez said.

"No, four. I'll be staying here."

"Ah, no. I've been assigned to protect you. I'm not leaving you here alone."

"Look around you, Cruez. Where's the danger? Get real."

Cruez opened his mouth to say something but caught himself. One glance around was enough. *She was right.*

"I'll get survival bags from the ship."

April only nodded, busily tending to the dressings of an injured woman.

She seems a helluva lot older than 17, Cruez thought. He gave one last look at the suffering group before twisting on his helmet, then proceeded to wrestle with each door, only to step out into a sweltering wall of heat. His ship, less than 30 meters away, shimmered in the mid-day sun. He checked the horizon. The sky was a burnt red, full of angry churning clouds of light and dark striations that skimmed along at high-speed. Fires, still burning in the distance from the remnants of the city, glowed eerily off the lower clouds. He saw the rim of the crater, a dark silhouette jutting impossibly high, once a populated city now a scar on the face of Ishaida.

The place has gone to hell.

He reached the ship quickly and powered up its systems in a quick sequence. A warning signal blipped in red. Vehicles on approach – Porter transports.

"April," he signaled her on her suit radio. "Looks like we may have some help coming. Three Porter transports are headed our way, possibly three hours out by the rate of travel. This changes things. We need to rethink our approach."

He took a second to assess the situation. With help on the way, the trick would be to buy them time. The heat was almost unbearable in there before he had left. They needed to rig some sort of cooling system. He searched his memory for an answer. The portable enviro-tents had life-support systems – but one unit wouldn't do it. Maybe they could be connected in series somehow.

"April, do you think you can you rig a cooling system up from a portable enviro-tent life-support system?"

A long hesitation before her answer. "Yes," her voice crackled on the other end. "Just bring what you can, and your tools."

It took him another 30 minutes to haul everything out from the compact storage on the ship and drag it all to the door. Sheet lightning was now flashing in the skies, reflecting momentary shadows of darkened clouds and whirling sands across the horizon. The orange glow of the sun was a faint piercing shadow as black clouds rolled in blotting out its presence. The storm was coming in fast from the east.

"Cruez, what's keeping you?"

"Could use some help with the door," he puffed.

Extra hands joined from the inside. They managed to pull the equipment in quickly, but not without letting in some hot, poisonous air from the outside. Many of the survivors that were too weak to move gasped for breath. April tossed her supplies down and ran over the sprawled bodies to crank open the valve in the oxygen tank. It took a moment for the fresh supply to calm the cacophony of coughing. But the hot, dry air did little to quell their discomfort.

She had to cool this area down rapidly or they would be losing people.

"Quick, Cruez, get these lines pulled out along the floor," she ordered.

He moved as fast as possible, carrying the majority of the load as they spread out the cooling lines along the floor.

April grabbed the toolbox and got to work, ignoring everything around her. The heat was incapacitating, with every movement, sweat poured off her in torrents, some trickled down her forehead, eventually reaching and stinging her eyes. She wiped it away and continued on, pulling apart the last of the units into a mass of bare wires and circuitry.

"April."

"April."

She turned her head. It was Cruez. "What?" she yelled, openly irritated.

He was cradling a small boy in his arms, moving back and forth slowly.

April stopped. Something was different about him, difficult to see in the dim glow of the emergency lanterns.

"I, ah, I don't think this little one's going to make it."

April moved closer, trying not to step on any of the people lying on the floor around her.

Cruez's usually hard features had softened to point where she barely recognized him. He was on the fringe of breaking down.

"Here, let me see."

He handed the small bundle to her, reluctantly. The little boy was no more than two, his face covered in grime. She searched for a pulse on his neck, holding her breath in the process.

It was there, faint but there.

"He's still with us," she said, avoiding looking into Cruez's eyes. She ripped away the blanket. "Give him some water. It's just getting too hot in here. I need to get these cooling units working, OK?"

Cruez nodded.

She handed the child back reluctantly. "Look, I have to do this. I just need a few more minutes."

"Hurry," he said quietly.

She turned away, feeling the emotion welling up inside her. She fought it down with a few deep breaths. She had to stay in control and not let it take over. *Keep it together, April.*

Each passing minute seemed to last an hour. She made the last few adjustments and entered the startup sequence on each unit. They started up with a low, audible hum. Currents of cool air emanated out, engulfing those closer to the units in an immediate and soothing relief.

"Way to go," complimented Cruez.

"These units are pretty effective. Work through sound waves, by slowing down molecular vibration, and dropping the thermal potential."

"OK, but how long will it take?"

"A few minutes. Don't know how long they'll last though as I'm pushing them at least 400% over their design capacity."

She could already feel the temperature dropping.

Cruez held the boy close to the cooling unit.

"How's he doing?"

"OK, I guess. I can't tell."

"Did you give him water?"

"Yeah, yeah I did."

"Good." She smiled. "They're coming, aren't they? The Porters, I mean."

"A couple more hours."

"We'll make it, then. All of us."

"Yeah, we will." Cruez smiled back at her.

"You did it," announced a man to her right, his voice gravelly with exhaustion. "Damn if you aren't driving that blasted heat away."

"Just you hang on, more help is on the way."

She grabbed her medical bag and moved closer to the man, noticed that his face was covered in a dark crust of dried blood. She could see just above his hairline the ugly evidence of a large gash.

"Can I take a look at that?"

"Be my guest."

She dabbed the wound gingerly. He winced.

"We are almost through everyone now. I have some rations in my bag. I bet you're hungry."

He nodded and quickly grabbed some rations and water.

April noticed the Monsoona maintenance insignia on his shirt. It was possible he knew something more.

"You remember what happened here?"

"Yeah, boom. Then chaos. Fire, death all over. It was hell."

"How did you make it out – to here?"

"The sun was setting. My crew and I were outside in the truck on a maintenance run. You know the domes, they're practically falling apart. Guess we don't need to worry about that anymore."

She gave him a shot for the pain and cleared away the crusted blood.

"It's deep."

"Well, the truck, you know, it rolled. I don't know how many times. The whole truck. That thing weighs tons, and we were thrown around like a, like a..."

"Child's toy."

"Yeah. When I came to, there were only three of us left alive. The truck was mangled pretty bad, but it had rolled back on its wheels and was still drivable."

"This might hurt," she said, tightening her grip on the stitcher. "Don't move. You know, you never told me your name."

"Thomas."

"My name is April."

"Yeah I heard, April McThurn, I know who you are – we all know who you are, girl. You're a bit of a celebrity, you know. We heard about that killer chasing y'all. We all but gave you up for dead."

"Well, I'm not – dead that is."

He chuckled, but it was cut off quickly with a sharp intake of breath.

"Sorry."

"Sokay."

"So what happened, after the impact?"

"We collected our wits, managed to get the truck started, and headed back into that last piece of the dome still standing. It was terrible, the destruction would make ya cry. But we found survivors and loaded'em on. When the sun was settling, we realized we'd all be dead from exposure if we didn't find some shelter and some denser atmosphere. That's when we come across this pipe. I had the bloody damn crazy idea to weld it up. The other boys rounded up what they could for supplies – some water, a few oxygen tanks. Now we're here. And then you came."

"More help is on the way. They're coming – three Porter transports spotted, just hours out now."

"Well, that's good." He said quietly under his breath, eyes looking somewhere beyond.

"Hey, you saved these people, you and your friends. You are the real heroes here, not us."

"Ha," he scoffed. "We did what we could do. Just survivin'. Say, what was it? Was it a bomb?"

"Whatever it was, it was intentional. AlphaRosetta was hit too. Nothing was left there, absolutely nothing."

"Are you sure?"

"We surveyed it from above, total devastation."

"Why would they do this to us?"

"We don't know, not yet, anyway."

"It's because we fired up those TFPs ain't it?"

She finished the stitching and wrapped the dressing. *How could she tell him it was all because of her?*

"I know what you're thinking, girl. You're thinking it's your fault, don't you?"

"Yeah," she choked it out, barely containing her tears. "It is. It's all my fault."

"No 'taint. We all want those TFPs back online. The Porters voted it in. It is what it is."

"This would never have happened…"

"Don't fret, my dear. We all gotta die sometime. My family and many others lay in this Ishaidan dirt already, including my Elana, God bless her soul. Ishaida has always demanded her payment in blood. I know she will take me too, one day, probably sooner than later. Those TFPs have to stay on, the down payment has already been made."

"There," she said, with a final fastening of the last wrapping.

"April McThurn, remember this is not your fault. They did it – those damned companies. I know that much."

"It is still my fault," she said, carefully avoiding his eyes as she put away the medical gear.

"If you plan to carry that guilt around, and let it slowly eat away at you day in and day out, you better make sure you're guilty first."

April looked into the eyes of the injured man, feeling annoyed by his rashness. *What did he know, anyway?*

"Thanks, but I'll be my own judge on just how I should feel."

"April." It was Cruez. He had on an uncharacteristically silly grin.

The boy he had helped had his eyes open. "It's really cooling off in here – the units are working great. The little one is awake." He was barely able to contain his joy.

In his own way, once you get past the rough exterior, he was kind of cute.

"Looks like everyone has been stabilized for now, but these people need proper attention, they need a trauma center."

"I suspect your Porter friends should have some equipment for this."

"I hope so."

"I would have thought they would have been here by now. I think I told you a storm is coming in."

"Yeah, I can hear it already," acknowledged April. The wind was whistling eerily through the makeshift locks. "It's picking up out there. Maybe I should go out before it gets worse."

"Why the hell do you need to go out there?"

"They aren't here yet. They should be. Someone needs to check."

He thought about it for a second, knowing her response was perfectly sound. "Fine, I'll go."

"No, it's my turn. Besides, the Porter's know me."

"Just be careful. The winds can get hold of you out there."

She nodded. "I will."

By the time she twisted on her helmet, she had already navigated back to the airlock. The wind was shrieking through the cracks of the fabricated doors. It took all of her strength just to push open the interior door.

The outer door moved a bit easier.

The skies were undoubtedly angry. Swirls of dark grays and blacks mixed in with oranges and reds. She held up her hand in reflex, although she knew there was absolutely no chance of the sand getting in her eyes. The wind was blowing so hard she had to lean into it just to move forward. She reached the ship in tortured relief, legs and back muscles on fire from the strain.

Inside the ship, it was cool and quiet. She had watched Cruez power up the ship's systems multiple times now. It was easy for her to recall the proper sequences. But that kind of thing had always been easy for her.

Inter-transport Porter chatter was instantly picked up on the scanners. The closest transport was still at least a half-hour away at its current speed. Probably slowed down due to the storm.

She pulled the navigation controls up, momentarily tempted to fire up the ship's engines, fly over and meet the Porter tanks.

But why waste the time? Cruez would be pissed if he knew.

Instead, she initiated a hail over the com.

"Calling the Porter vessels on approach to Monsoona, this is April McThurn, formally of the SeaClear."

"April McThurn, this is the TerraGrande. I am Captain Buchannon. Where are you?"

"In the ship that you should have picked up on your scanners by now."

"No, we don't have a signature."

April fired off a ping beacon.

"Confirmed, we got you now."

"We've a number of survivors. Many injured."

"How many?"

"Thirty-three."

"Have you searched the whole area?"

"No."

"What about the matrices?"

She knew he was asking about the tunnel system underneath Monsoona. It spreads out for kilometers in all directions. "We didn't calibrate the scanners for that depth. I'm not sure..."

"That's OK. We have special equipment with us. We'll find them if there are any left alive."

"Do you know what caused this?"

"Either a projectile or bomb."

"Then this is an act of war. Tell me, how did you obtain a starship?"

"It is the Company's - an Anard-Bueller vessel. I am here with a Company Rep. He's been helping me."

"What the hell are you doing bringing Anard-Bueller into this?"

"Listen, Captain, it's not what you think. He was bringing me back from Earth. At the TFP, it was Soho-Beher that was trying to kill me. This man saved me."

"How can you be sure it wasn't them that did this?"

"I met Tiberious Bueller himself. He assured me he didn't have anything to do with this."

"April, you're young. It's not unusual for people to project an image, to manipulate others."

"That's not the case, Captain. I can judge people just fine."

She hit the console, shutting down the com-link.

She knew what the hell she was talking about. She did.

A telltale blinking light sprung up on the console.

Buchannon again.

She pressed the controls, reopening the link.

"We should be there within 20 minutes."

"Good."

"April, just be careful. Don't misunderstand me, we're behind you."

She could think of little to say back, leaving a long awkward silence. "I have to head back. We're all in the pipe. I need a check on the survivors. Hurry will you?"

"A pipe?"

"You'll know what I mean when you get here."

"Just tell them to hold on, help is on its way."

"I will."

As she exited the ship, the ferocity of the winds immediately took her off-guard, throwing her down to the ground. She landed on her side, her arm bent underneath her body. A sharp pain shot through her arm as she rolled over to free it. The sand was already starting to build up around her.

She fought down a rising panic. *Cruez had told her to be careful.*

She had to get her bearings. The ship's ramp was at her left foot. She could feel it. The direction of the pipe was about five degrees to her right. She started crawling, cupping the sand in each hand. She had to keep low, otherwise, the wind would get under her and throw her over. Then she would be in real trouble.

She had no idea how much time had passed before she reached the metal sill of the pipe. Two hands suddenly grabbed her wrists and pulled her up. She was utterly exhausted and welcomed the help. It had to be Cruez, as she could feel his raw strength. She had no idea how he had managed to open the door in the wind, or how they were going to get back in, she could only hope he had it figured out.

He pulled her up to her feet, hugging close to the inside wall. She could feel his iron muscles through the thick material of the suit, her breasts pressed tightly against him. Suppressed feelings urged themselves out. She could feel her face flush. At least their helmets were opaque from the dimmed sunlight.

"We need to slide to our right." Cruez's voice buzzed in her ear. "We have some help inside to pry the door open. What kept you?"

"Isn't it obvious," she responded, as sarcastically as possible.

They slid over, stepping carefully as mounds of sand were building up at their feet. She slipped a couple times, but Cruez held onto her, keeping her tight to him. It took a bit of time to get the door open. The men inside struggled to get them in, without the benefit of an enviro-suit. They fought further still to get the door sealed shut. In the end, most of them retreated inside, choking and fighting for breath. But they all ended up inside, safe, out of breath and overheating. April happily shed her suit, feeling a relieving coolness of inside, although stagnant, air.

"The coolers are working well."

"Yeah, almost too well. You need to adjust them. It's starting to get too cool in here."

"I had to bypass the control system. No feedback system in place."

She rubbed her arm, still raw from her lousy landing. She was not keen on sharing the details with Cruez.

"What did you do out there?" She could feel his eyes on her. "You alright, what's wrong with your arm?"

"Nothing. I'm fine. I called the Porters. They're coming. They should be here any minute."

"The sandstorm's probably slowing them down," commented Cruez.

A few coughs echoed through the air. She scanned the room, found the boy in the arms of an older woman. "And how's he doing?"

Cruez's voice softened, "He's sleeping now. I gave him some more water. But I think there's something wrong with him, still."

A series of loud bangs echoed with sharp intensity along the walls. It wasn't a natural sequence, sounded more like a conventional string of recognizable raps.

"Finally they're here!" April announced with excitement. "OK everyone, help is here, but you need to make room down the center if you can. They'll need to get in."

After a collection of loud thuds, the inner airlock door opened to reveal three sand-covered figures in enviro-suits. The lead figure twisted off his helmet and nodded to April. The others spread out to assess the survivors.

"Hello, April, I'm Captain Jerod Buchannon. Good to see you."

"Hello, Captain."

"I see what you mean now. Would not have believed it if I hadn't seen with my own eyes. We have a trauma center ready. We'll need to get everybody into enviro-bags so we can move them to the tank. The storm is not letting up out there, so we've rigged a line up between the tank and here."

"We can help."

"You already have. I want you and your acquaintance in the tank, stat. The Porter Council wants to debrief you."

"But these people?"

"Don't worry," he said, more softly. "My team is ready to handle this. And once you're done with the Council, you can help us more – with your ship that is."

"Whatever you need."

"That's a good lass, now head on out. My emergency staff needs as much room to work as possible."

April wriggled her suit back on, conflicting feelings racing through her mind.

She could still help here, damn it! But the Captain was right, the professionals were here now. She'd only get in the way.

The old woman grabbed her hand as she started out. "April, thank you. You saved us, you really did."

April smiled back. "Everything will work out. You'll be OK now."

She didn't let go of her hand. There was something in the old woman's eyes, she just couldn't place it.

"You just keep doing what you think is right, no matter what."

"I will."

She twisted on her helmet. Cruez grabbed her hand, not able to see her through the tinted faceplate, unable to tell how torn up inside she felt.

They stepped outside. The storm was upon them now, and the wind was gusting much faster than before. They started across to the TerraGrande holding onto the line tightly. She winced each time she pulled with her injured arm.

Maybe it was poetic justice for her. She should suffer for her mistakes. She toyed with the idea of just letting go, letting the wind take her.

A small rock caught her boot, and she tripped. Her hand slipped. The wind had her. Images of her life screamed through her mind but it all stopped just as suddenly. The iron grip of Cruez had her by the leg, and he pulled her in, hand over hand. He was yelling something at her, but she couldn't make it out.

She locked both hands back onto the rope and started again, Cruez close behind her. Through the swirling sand, she saw the shadow of the huge vehicle before them, noticed the anti-skid plates had been dropped. As they stepped in between the wheels, the wind died down dramatically. Other helping hands were already there to pull them up the stairs. She saw warm, caring faces, the familiar faces of family, of home.

"April, my dear." It was Mrs. Buchannon, a kindly woman, portly with a round face and soft eyes. "We are so glad to see you again. After word got through about the assassin, we thought you were lost."

"I would have been, if not for this man here," she grabbed Cruez by the arm and pulled him close, exposing an unusual fondness.

"Oh, and what is the name of this brave soul, my dear?"

"Cruez Montigue, ma'am." He bowed graciously, took her hand and gave it a light kiss. "Truly a pleasure."

Mrs. Buchannon's eyes lit up. "I see," she said knowingly. "'Tis a pleasure to meet an off-worlder of such extraordinary kindness."

"Thank you, but the pleasure is mine," he said with a dry smile. "With the exception of a certain company, I must also thank you for such kind disposition."

April gave him a push, irritated by his obvious slam.

"April, the Council has requested you. We have an uplink, and they're waiting on you, dear."

"Of course, Mrs. Buchannon."

"I promise I will be more of a host after your meeting," she smiled, feeling a bit guilty for ushering her into the lion's den.

"Please, follow me."

Cruez took a step, but Mrs. Buchannon held up a hand. "I'm sorry, Mr. Montigue, but this is strictly Porter business, you understand?"

"I see. I'll just help the crews, then."

April shot a quick look at Cruez. His face was of stone, emotionless, impossible to read.

So typical.

Mrs. Buchannon led her through the corridors to a small room reserved for com sessions.

"Please, have a seat. Ishbar Sequin has been waiting for you."

"April!"

An all-too-familiar face looked back at her through the large monitor. He was grinning from ear-to-ear. "I am relieved, lass."

"I'm here alright." She smiled back, equally glad to see him. Emotion flooded over her, just for a second. "And it's really good to see you too," she said, her voice cracking a bit.

"We'll be talkin' a bit, after, that is. I did have a chat with Ron and Jerry. Seems one of them has a bit of a shine for ya."

"Um, yeah. I'm glad they're OK though."

"And you?" he was peering at her through the monitor. It made her feel like he was right there. That old, appraising look he had.

"I'm fine."

"'Course you are..."

A long pause.

"They'll want to know what you know. How did this happen?"

"I think I have an idea, but no clear proof just yet."

Ishbar nodded. "Better tell this to the Porter council directly." He looked down. Suddenly the image was from a different angle, facing a table of council members, all looking back with faces of mixed emotions.

"I think it was Soho-Beher," she said flatly. "They stand to lose the most from the resurrection of the Ishaida. It's what makes the most sense."

"What about Anard-Bueller?"

"As I told Captain Buchannon, I've been to Earth, and I've met face-to-face with Tiberious Bueller. I doubt he has anything to do with this."

"You met him?" asked another, incredulously. "*The* Tiberious Bueller, CEO of Anard-Bueller?"

"Yeah, a dying old fossil as he is, still a charming but deadly predator as I've met. He showed me evidence that connected my family's murderer with the Soho-Beher Corporation."

The small group stayed quiet for a moment, taken aback by the news that had come from a 17 year-old girl. April could not tell if it was surprise or confusion.

"Why, what did Bueller want with you?" asked another.

"He had wanted to meet me face-to-face," April replied, debating whether to say more.

"And Ishaida, what about Ishaida and the TFPs?"

"What do you expect him to admit to? Even if he caused the great reversal, would it change anything now?"

"What about the fact that it was you who led the activation of them?"

"Maybe that's why he wanted to meet me. Regardless, he doesn't care. He just told me..." she stopped suddenly, fearful of telling too much, knowing what she was about to admit led to this disaster.

"What?"

April looked away, unable to stop the tears.

"April."

It was the soft voice of Ishbar this time. "What did he tell you?"

"He warned me there could be repercussions. He cautioned me to be careful. But I didn't understand. I never thought someone would go to this level."

Quiet overtook the group once again.

"It's alright, April," Ishbar said, interrupting the awkward silence, attempting to comfort her.

The Chair spoke up next. "Ms. McThurn, we have been issued a notice that this was caused by an onboard accident on an ore carrier passing within our system. Apparently, the ship was forced to drop their payload. The ESPD has already boarded the ship and begun their investigation."

"The ESPD is a puppet of the Corporations. Don't you think it strange that they are close enough to intercept and board this vessel? It is clear they are here to dilute the truth," stated April venomously.

"Yes, we realize that. This is clearly being staged as a tragic accident and nothing more. It is plausible enough."

"Aye, they don' want a war on their hands," added another councilor.

"And what would we fight them with, a couple missile launchers and a laser cannon refitted from miner equipment?" Ishbar laughed. "Soho-Beher's executive yachts are better armed than us."

"I'm sorry," April stated quietly, "I didn't want any of this. I never wanted anyone to get hurt."

"Ms. McThurn, this is beyond any of your doing. We certainly appreciate all the help you have provided so far. If you learn any more information, please let us know as soon as possible."

"I will," she promised.

The view switched back over to focus on Ishbar only. "April, if'n you need to discuss this more?"

"No. No, I'm fine. Just need some rest."

"'Course. We are delighted you made it. My family sends you their best."

"Tell them all thank you."

She reached up and terminated the connection. Ishbar may have wanted to talk more, but she didn't. She just wanted to be alone.

* * *

Chapter 9

The Buchannon Clan's second lieutenant reported in. "Captain, we have a signal. 30 meters northeast of your position."

"I can't see anything but rubble down here. The wind's getting up again, too."

"It's there. You're almost on top of it," reported the officer, peering through the scanner results.

Captain Buchannon grabbed a sheet of steel that was stuck in the sand and pulled. It flew up into the wind, twisting and rippling as it disappeared into sand-filled air.

"Yeah, got it. Looks like the remains of an emergency bulkhead. The door's pretty much melted, with about a half a meter of glass on top. We'll need a cutting crew down here immediately."

"You need to hurry, Captain," urged the dispatcher. "Your suit is not rated for the levels of radiation so close to ground zero."

"How much time?"

"Sixty minutes tops. The team's already in the lock. Will be out there in less than five min."

"Good. I want through this thing. Get Tig and McKenzie to grab the portable airlock and the pressure tanks. I don't want to siphon any remaining air out of this tunnel."

"Aye, Sir."

The cutting crew was already coming up in the rover. The vehicle's lights barely cut through the driving sands.

"We're running out of time boys. Wind's going to get too high pretty soon."

"We'll be through this in less than 10 minutes, Captain."

"I need one of you to weld up a seam for the portable airlock we have coming. Don't cut through until we have it ready."

"Aye."

Jerod watched the men work. They were professionals, knew how to get things done, even under these conditions. McKenzie showed up shortly after with the portable.

"Tig's charging the tanks. Up in a sec. Figured you were waiting for this." He pulled on a large bag containing the portable airlock.

"You figured right. I'll give you a hand."

They struggled with the sheet of mavron material, fighting with the wind to keep it from sailing away into the nothingness. The other man from the cutting crew fabricated up a metal anchoring grid for them. Tig showed up with the tanks and they pressurized the skeleton. The air-filled ribs raised the tent up in mere moments. The cutting crew went to work on the one end, welding the temporary seam onto the now exposed metal of the bulkhead.

"Got'er, Captain."

"Good, let's test it."

Tig connected the tanks and pressurized the lock. The external panel registered a steady pressure. No leaks.

"Let's finish the job, gentlemen. Tig, you run a cable-net over the lock and stud it down with one of the air-rams. I don't want this thing blowing off."

"Aye, Captain. When I'm done, it'll take a full-on twister to take it away."

They entered the lock, sealed it and took off their helmets.

"OK boys." He nodded at the cutters. "Cut through."

A short two minutes later, the bulkhead door was cut out, it fell inward with a heavy bang. Inside it was dark. The smells came first. Gut-wrenching enough to make one gag. They put their helmets back on.

Burnt remains of what were once living humans were curled up against the walls, and lay prone on the floor. They stepped over them gingerly.

"Must've got hotter than hell in here for a few seconds, at least by the door, I reckon," stated Tig. "Maybe we'll find some more deeper in."

"My map says this one runs about half-a-kilometer out. There's a curve up ahead and then a straight run. It branches about 10 meters after the curve."

"How many you figure's down here?"

"My radiation readings are maxed out right now. I don't know…"

The Captain's silence was clear enough for his men. Not many possibly, none likely.

They found a cave-in 50 meters down. It was a blessing and a curse. It might just have saved the lives of anyone beyond it, but it may also cost them if they take took too long to get through.

"How fast can we cut through this?" he asked.

McKenzie pulled the sound probe out of the rubble. "Looks like six meters, maybe, no more. Should be able to burn through it with our cutters in a few minutes. Just don't know how unstable it is, may cause another cave-in."

"No choice. Do it."

They all moved back. The crew adjusted their plasma torches to wide-angle and started on the pile. The rubble began to glow red, then a deep orange, then blue and white, to a point where it was blinding.

Once done, a glowing tunnel, with walls of fused glass, lay before them. Wind was rushing toward them, hot, dry and acrid. Beyond were glimmers of light and noise. There were survivors.

The crews from the three tanks worked well through the night and the next day, shuttling survivors and caring for the injured. Almost on the hour, they found another cave-in, another secluded corner holding wide-eyed, dirty, and grateful Ishaidans. Everyone worked to help, including Cruez and April.

April preferred searching through the catacombs. It reminded her of her childhood, of times spent in underground caves and rubble-filled corridors of building basements.

"Found another one," she announced. She checked the walls and the ceilings for severe cracks – which would indicate a possible further collapse. The sonar probe revealed the thickness to be at least 10 meters.

The cutters scrambled up, deployed the membrane and sealed it to the walls, less the other side of the cave-in had a poisonous atmosphere. They had to ensure they contained the whole system.

"Well, you comin' in or staying out, girl?" asked the one called Farev.

April stepped over the last piece of membrane before he sealed it up behind her. "In, of course."

The cutter bit into the rock, then promptly quit. "Shit." He systematically checked it. "Sonofabitch, bloody battery's cooked," Farev complained. "Will need to go back to get one. I can probably burn through with my small backup unit. Can we get through it though?"

"No," laughed his coworker, a particularly large man. "Doubt we can get through a hole that size."

"She can," Farev nodded to April. "She can go in and check it out."

"Sure," offered April, a bit nervously. "I can go in there."

"We don't know what's on the other end. Might not be pretty. And it'll be pretty close in there," stated Farev, grimly.

"I can do it."

He nodded, then started up the small torch. They burned through in a matter of minutes. The tremor came just after they finished. The shaking wasn't that bad, but some pieces came loose from the ceiling.

"Oh shit, Ishaida's up to her tricks again."

April peered into the small tunnel. It was barely wide enough for her small frame and was dark to boot.

"You sure you're up to this?" Farev asked her again.

"Not if we keep getting these tremors."

"Just be quick. In and out."

"OK, in and out." She nodded and started in, crawling on her hands and knees in a slow shuffle. All she could hear was her heavy breathing and her own heart pounding in her ears.

When the other tremor came, she froze. She could feel the pebbles and rocks falling above her.

I'm going to die in here, in this hole. Stop it! Just like her dad always said, being brave is when you're scared, but you still push on. If you're not scared, you got a screw loose.

"April, you OK in there?" Farev called out behind her.

"Yeah, OK," she said, shakily.

She pressed on, pushing loose rocks and gravel ahead of her with her hands.

Ages later, she was finally out, on the other side where she had room to stand and stretch. She shone her light around. Ahead, no more than five meters was another cave-in.

"Great, guys. We've another cave-in."

"Do your sonar test. Set it to max, you might get a signature," ordered Farev.

April did as she was told. She put it on a continuous loop and watched the small display. After a few moments, an image came through, it wasn't big, but it was moving.

"Got something, can't make it out, though."

"Does it look like a blurry dot with small wings?"

"Yeah, something like that. Multiples from what I see."

Silence on the other end. "Well?"

"I'm going to shoot you a line, you pull through the torch. It'll be tied to the other end."

"Why?"

"You got somebody on the other side – those wings are human hearts beating."

"Oh."

The image was strange, but it made sense to her now.

"Shooting now."

A small whistle and then a thud. April saw the line settle to the floor, attached to a grappling hook. She grabbed the line and pulled up the portable torch.

"I don't know how to run this thing."

"I thought you were a whiz."

"Holy crap, does everyone think I've worked with every damn machine ever invented!" she cussed brazenly.

Farev only laughed. "It's easy. Stream's already adjusted. Just press the orange button. Aim it well away from the signal. Watch the photonic feedback. It'll jump to 100% as soon as you're through."

"Fine. Fine."

She fired up the torch and started cutting. A third tremor was building to a crescendo, intense and long, with a nasty vibration. "Swear I could feel the S waves on that one," she muttered to herself.

The torch lit up the gloomy darkness with a blinding brilliance. She refocused her attention on the small LED panel, watching for the telltale sign. It came suddenly. She tripped off the power, hoping she had been fast enough.

"OK, am through. Headin' in," she reported.

She bumped her helmet on the still warm walls, filling her ears with a loud ringing.

This tunnel was not as long.

They watched her crawl through; a little boy, about four and a girl no more than a year older. Tear stains had created clear streaks down their dirty faces. Both of them ran to her with open arms. April pulled them close, trying not to cry herself.

"Are you OK?"

"No, I gotta hurt arm," answered the boy, holding up his right arm, exposing an angry scabbed gash.

"Can you crawl? Can you go back through this hole with me?"

"I'm scared," said the little girl.

"What's your name?"

"Sammy and this is Bobby, my brother. We got stuck in here after the ground shook."

"OK, Sammy, I'm April. I've come to get you out of here. But you got to go through the hole first."

Another tremor started.

They both started crying.

"We've got to move. We've got to go, now."

She ushered them into the tunnel, "Hurry, quick, as fast as you can."

The shaking wasn't letting up. She could only hope their makeshift tunnels would hold. She could feel the walls begin to shift around her. Then it stopped.

They were out a moment later. "OK. We gotta go through another one."

"I don't want to," cried Bobby. "I want my mommy. Where's mommy?"

"Listen, Bobby. Your mommy wants you out of here. She wants you to be brave. Can you be brave?"

He sniffled. "Yes."

"Next one, hurry, just like we did the last one."

"Last one was scary," added Sammy.

"Sure was," agreed Bobby.

"Shh. Go, quick kids. Go as fast as you can."

When they emerged out the other end, April was physically shaking. It took her a second before she realized that something was very wrong. The ceiling had collapsed. Two of the men lay half-buried in rubble, the other heavyset one was pinned under the main pile. She checked him for a pulse. Nothing.

She tried the other two. Farev had taken a hard hit to the head, although unconscious, his pulse was steady. The other man had a lacerated arm and a heavy rock on his chest.

"Kids, can you help me with this."

They pushed off the rock. She checked his pulse. It was there but weak. The man felt cold, clammy.

"I thought we was gettin' out," complained Bobby.

"I thought so too. Listen, I need to go back there and get a machine."

"No!" They grabbed onto her and cried. "You can't go away."

She pulled them close. Another tremor came and went. She just kept hugging them.

"Ok. Ok. Here." She grabbed Farev's flashlight. "This is yours. You hold onto this and shine it down the tunnel. You can watch me go down."

"What if it shakes again?" asked Sammy.

"I'll be fast."

"What if it falls on you?"

"It won't."

"Why?"

"Because I'm lucky."

"Ready? Shine the light down there."

She started down the tunnel again, tasting the dirt in her mouth.

Again, another tremor. She ignored it, focused only on moving as fast as she could. She could hear the kids crying out for her.

"Almost there!" she yelled back, then proceeded to fall off the edge. She wasted no time locating the torch and started back down the tunnel.

"I'm coming. You kids OK down there?"

"Yes, hurry April!"

That sounded like Sammy.

It was tougher on her way back. The torch was heavy, and pushing it ahead of her wasn't easy. She kept kneeling on the rope, thought of untying it but then thought better of it. She might need it later.

"Hurry!" came another cry.

Halfway now.

Another tremor. This time a small one. They seemed to be diminishing in strength. Some rocks fell ahead, but she pushed them out of the way. By the time she reached the end, she was exhausted.

"April, you made it!" announced Bobby with a wide smile.

"Told ya," stated Sammy with confident authority. "He thought you wasn't coming back. I said you were too."

"See, like I told you. I am lucky."

"That man is moaning," stated Bobby, pointing to the one with the bad arm. "He needs help."

"Yes I know, but first you need to get out of here, and then find them that help, right?"

They both nodded.

She fired up the torch. "Stand back, we're burning through."

Again a brilliant flash. She watched the LED readout, noticed the batteries were getting dangerously low. Another second and she was through.

"We have a way out. We have to wait for it to cool." She tested the walls. They were still hot.

There were shreds of mevlar membrane hanging from the walls, what remained of the previous temporary airlock. She used her knife to cut a few pieces off. "Here, you guys wrap these around your hands."

She noticed Bobby's arm was dripping blood and was full of gravel and dirt. "You are a tough little guy, Bobby." She cut off some of the mevlar pieces and wrapped his arm. He didn't even flinch, although his whole body was trembling.

The two were probably running on adrenaline.

She finished the dressings. "There, this will help."

Four large eyes watched her with frightened wonder.

"You two have to go now. You have to be brave."

They nodded obediently.

She ushered them into the tunnel, pulled the man with the bad arm to the entrance, wrapped him in a rope, and backed in, feet first. She could hear the kids scrambling ahead.

She heaved. At first, she didn't think she could do it, but he started to move. That was all she needed. She started down, systematically stopping to dig in and then pull as hard as she could. The tunnel seemed to last forever. She found herself hoping for the end to come, fear mounting in the back of her mind like the growing pain of a rotting tooth.

No, she was not going to die in this hole.

Another tremor came and went.

She kept pulling, ignoring everything around her, pulling as hard and fast as she was able. It felt like hours had passed before she could feel little hands grabbing at her to help her out the last meter. She finally reached the opening and out into fresher air.

"Kids, grab the rope and help me pull him the rest of the way out."

They did as she asked. A little at a time, but they managed to pull the unconscious man out. She sat for a moment with him cradled in her arms, catching her breath.

"OK. You guys have to go and get help down that tunnel there. Here, take this man's helmet light. He won't need it. I'm going back in."

They looked at her worriedly. "You can't, what if it falls in?"

"I can't leave that man in there. You get help. That way if it falls, they can pull me out. OK?"

They nodded, not really agreeing, but knowing enough they should do what they're told. "Hurry, now. This man needs a doctor."

They turned and started at a slow run, too tired to go too fast, and constantly checking behind them, fearful they might be doing the wrong thing.

She headed back in, rope in hand. Farev was where she had left him, still unconscious. She lugged him over to the opening, cussing at her aching, weakened muscles. Her sore arm was throbbing with a sharp pain that reached all the way through to her shoulder.

Again, starting back through the tunnel was the toughest, and getting Farev started seemed to be impossible. He was heavier than the other man, and she was tired.

Regardless, she kept trying, anchoring her knees into the sides of the tunnel to give her enough leverage. He started moving, and she kept pulling until she was out of breath, and he was at her feet. She wormed her way down, then started another round of pulling. Another tremor came, this time very light. Unhindered, she kept pulling. Her hands were raw, her legs and arms were burning, to a point where she could feel them trembling, ready to give out.

The opening came as a surprise, she practically fell out onto the rubble-filled floor.

She struggled to her feet and locked her legs against the opening. Farev had about a meter before he'd be out. She kept at it, hand over hand with the rope, ignoring the blisters, red and bleeding upon her palms. She managed to break him free of the tunnel, and he came out quickly, his weight pushing her back onto the floor. She had little strength left to move him. She lay there, feeling his breath, shallow but steady, and she waited.

Footsteps echoed off the rock walls in the distance. They were coming, late, but they were coming.

Cruez was first. He helped move Farev onto a gurney then proceeded to pick her up and carry her back to the tank. He never uttered a word, but she saw the relief in his eyes.

Was it all because of his assigned job, or was it something else?

She didn't want to be carried, but she lacked the energy to argue. She found it, at least partially, to be enjoyable.

After they reached the tank, he set her down.

"You should get some rest," he said gently.

"I will after I get cleaned up. How are the children?"

"Medical car. They're fine. You saved their lives."

"Nothing you wouldn't have done."

He smiled back. "You just keep surprising me. You sure you're only 17?"

"Well, I think I am. Either way, I'm old enough."

She smiled back at him. There was that old familiar look in his eyes, just for a moment. She had seen that look before, from others. This time though, it didn't make her feel uncomfortable. It made her feel good.

She turned and walked away, feeling his eyes following her, knowing he liked what he saw. She also knew he would be back to his old ways next time they met. That was a surety. He was expected, after all, to always be in control.

Just not in control of her.

* * *

"April, you's making quite a name for yourself."

"Thank you, Captain Sequin, I think."

Ishbar walked around the small metal desk that served as the Captain's station. "More'n more you are becoming a point of discussin'. The young girl who found the flaw, who cranked on the TFPs, fought assassins and rescued the last of the Monsoona survivors."

"Well. I think they're tending to exaggerate."

"Maybe, but you got a followin'."

"It won't bring them all back, though, will it?"

Ishbar reached out, pulled her close. "Hun, you 'ave to let this go. If your dad was alive now, I'd know what ol' Oranis would be sayin' to ya. You are responsible for what you do only."

"But I caused this, didn't I?"

Ishbar looked down into her tear-filled eyes. "Ishaida's been dyin' a long time, my dear, and with it, we've all been dyin' too. You caused everyone to start hopin' again is all you did. That's a priceless gift. There ain't no stoppin' now. Nothin's gonna bring back those people, neither your guilt nor you givin' up."

"That Soho-Beher company did this, I'm sure. This was a warning. They'll do it again if we keep going."

"Will they? You think everyone 'ill stand by and watch us get pummeled into dust, do ya? You think they can keep 'xplanin' away these bombings as tragic accidents?"

"I've seen what happened in the past. I've seen the atrocities our so-called civilization is capable of. I've read how whole counties and governments had ignored mass murders, genocide, and criminalization of the innocent. It turns my stomach."

"Then so be it. Ishaida dies off, and they finally win. It is much better than living in a frozen wasteland where we all slowly starve to death. Just how many generations do you think we could've held out if you hadn't turned on those TFPs? Why do you think the Council decided so quickly to let you keep going? You ever recall them to make a decision that didn't take them a half-year of deliberation?"

April sat down on the chair and thought it over.

Of course, he's right. The Council has never been known to make a quick decision.

"How long?"

"What?"

"How long were the projections?"

"Less than a century. Our seed reserves are almost depleted now. Our population level is dropping. Our economy is slowly but surely grinding to a halt. When that happens, with no foreign investment, no capital coming in, food production drops as well, and people starve. Now with the TFPs fired up, this changes everything. Like I said, we needed this. As for the cost, we all gotta die some time."

"I don't accept that."

"'Course," he laughed, "you're young yet."

"I think I should go back to Earth. I should talk to Tiberious Bueller and find out what his spies are telling him, find out for sure who's behind this."

"And then?"

"And then, kill them. Just kill them all off."

"If it does turn out to be coming out of Soho-Beher, what then? Maybe you should kill everyone that works for them? Maybe throw in the senior management team as well. Hell, you could kill off their families too; make sure no one tries to get back at you."

"Just what do you want from me then? Damn it! I've already paid in my own blood. How easy you seem to forget the thousands of dead out there. The dome-dwellers are Ishaidans just like us, or maybe you don't consider them the same."

"Now hold it there, Missy. Been around a long time you know. Seen death up, nice, close, and personal. Don't be preaching to me about Ishaida. I know we have two craters sitting out there where our cities used to be. I know it."

April turned away, her anger quickly deflated. "I'm sorry."

"Sokay. You just need to understand what you're talkin' here. Killin' to get even rarely works. Usually starts something that doesn't like to stop."

"No, we eliminate the threat is what I say. Otherwise, what should I do, leave this whole thing alone? Let the bureaucrats bury it like they did four centuries ago?"

Ishbar leaned up against the wall. Light glinted off his graying hair. He had a worn-down look about him, showing his true age. "I'm sorry. I honestly don't know."

"Neither do I, Captain. But I've been told I have Anard-Bueller's resources available to me. I will use that to my advantage."

"All I can tell ya, just before you go out there'n wage your own personal war. Ya better think the whole thing through, first."

"I have already. I will eliminate the threat," she stated with quiet, menacing intention.

Ishbar cracked a tired smile. "This ain't easy, I know. God help ya. Just don't do anything that you can't live with yourself after."

She nodded back. "Alright, I can do that."

A painful minute passed where neither could bear to say another word. Footsteps echoed from down the corridor.

"Probably Cruez coming to collect me," she said quietly.

"Just you be careful, girl. Sometimes things are not as they seem."

"I will. I'll contact you as soon as I find out something."

"Of course."

Cruez appeared, his sharp eyes passing over them in one glance. "Time's come, April. We're scheduled to launch."

"I'm ready."

"Captain Sequin," acknowledged Cruez. "Pleasure to meet you."

"Likewise, Mr. Montigue. You've helped April multiple times. We are truly indebted."

"Merely doing my job, Captain. And I do take my responsibilities seriously."

"Things may get more difficult in the near future, Mr. Montigue. I can only hope you are consistent."

"Persistent as much as consistent, Captain. That much I can promise."

Ishbar shook his hand, watching him carefully, smiling only slightly.

April observed in the shadows.

Doesn't seem to like him too much.

"Let's be on our way," ordered Cruez casually.

Within the hour Ishaida had become a mere pinpoint in the distance, another spec of light from April's point of view.

The expanses involved with space were incredible. It was truly amazing they were able to travel through this cold emptiness for such distances, able to locate another spec so far away, another green world teeming with life.

She shivered.

"You OK?"

"Fine. Just fine."

"You keep staring at that monitor like you can't bear to leave."

"It's my home, what do you expect?" she replied acidly.

"Yes, of course."

"Plus relativity is unforgiving. Months here turn to years there. When I come back how much will have changed by then?"

"I'm not sure. Guess it depends on when you get back."

"Well, I'm not going back in those stasis pods."

"Have to, too soon for statmon stasis. Plus we'll be pushing acceleration to maximum, best to be in the pods."

"Why don't you have the anti-grav generators like the big cruisers? Then we wouldn't need these damn stasis pods." April did little to hide her disdain for the 'latest in technology' this ship was supposed to have.

Cruez was ready to counter. "You may know that is a matter of mass and energy, and this little starship has neither. It's to the stasis pods at least during maximum acceleration or we take a lot longer to get there. Take your pick."

"Alright, we stay in stasis only during acceleration."

Cruez eyed her for a second. "OK, we have a deal."

Their small ship jumped up through the quantum instability level, phasing its matter into a new super-excited state. On board two humans lay embalmed in a green suspension gel, cocooned within tiny coffin-like pods. The ship's computers continued to monitor their vitals through quad-redundant systems.

And time passed.

Alarms fired, systems initiated. The humans, held near a deathlike state, were systematically resuscitated.

April came to first, feeling her senses flood back with an all too familiar cold pain. She gagged, went to sit up and banged her head on the pod. She would have cussed if she could. She quickly reached for the internal controls and pressed all the buttons. Air streams raced over her body, tiny fans started up, sucking the gel toward her feet.

Cruez had failed to tell her previously, of the automated suspension gel reclaim system built into the pods. Something to do with his twisted sense of humor she imagined.

The pod rotated up, righting itself to allow her to step out.

Yet another little fact Cruez had failed to mention.

She stepped onto the cold floor, completely naked. The air was cool on her skin, giving her goosebumps.

Faint lights blinked across the corridor from a nearby console, other than that the room was dark. She walked over to Cruez's pod. His sequence had already started, but he wasn't awake yet. She ran her eyes over the length of his body, unable to resist the temptation. Although still submersed in the green gel, it was apparent Cruez was in excellent condition.

Yes, he was a real heartthrob.

She fingered the controls, switching the pod systems over to manual, then reversed the resuscitation sequencing. *He would not be waking up anytime soon. Sure, he would be pissed at her, but that didn't matter. She needed some time to think, time to be alone.*

The weeks passed by slowly. She scanned through the ship's computer archives, looking for any and every detail she could find. Cruez was not sloppy. Almost everything worth looking at had security encryption at multiple levels. She had some luck breaking through some of the locked files but little else.

Undaunted she continued to dig around, eventually discovering other information: logged activity of landings and launches, ship scanner logs, tracing initiation histories. It was all there if you had the time and the patience to look, and related events.

Cruez had been monitoring Soho-Beher for months before any of this started. She had managed to rummage up a few addresses and names. It was enough to get her started.

* * *

Earth came up as a blue-green marble against a background of cold light and even colder darkness. It was a welcome sight to April, even though it wasn't her home.

She had waited until the absolute last minute before resuscitating Cruez and was glad she had. He was not too happy with her. He uttered curses under his breath and glared at her through the transparent panels of his pod while the last of the suspension fluid seeped down.

April just smiled back, giving a coy wave. His heads-up display had already exposed the little secret of time – and that he was being awakened as the ship was already on descent.

"Why didn't you wake me?" He scanned the pod's logs, rushed past her completely naked, and pressed another sequence into a panel on the facing wall. She watched him with interest, noting how his muscles moved, unabashedly giving careful attention to his buttocks.

He ignored her, still dripping and glistening from the clinging gel. Another swarm of figures raced across the console display before him.

"So, you've been up all this time. What have you been doing?"

"Reading stuff." She smiled back, feeling a bit flushed, a bit hot. Cruez was too close, smelled of something too alluring. Possibilities raced through her mind. She bit down on her lip, turned away, and started down the small corridor to the galley.

"Learned a lot, too," she said. "Oh yeah, we're on auto-descent so you might want to get to the cockpit and keep an eye on things," she yelled back, giggling slightly.

Time for some food. Maybe something chocolate.

She had just finished off a rich pudding desert she had found in the hydrator when the floor jerked slightly.

They were down.

Cruez's glare had not yielded an inch when he appeared next. This time, however, he was fully dressed.

"Nice," he said. "Our friends at the ESPD almost turned us to ash because of your little trick."

She tossed the dish into the segregator. It would be chewed down to basic molecules and rolled back into another dish at the press of a button.

"But they didn't. Besides, I just needed some time alone. No big deal."

"Noticed you were trying to get into my logs," he said accusingly.

"Trying? Is that what you think?" She giggled, licking the spoon slowly, with unusual attention.

"Stop your bloody teasing, girl."

"Who's teasing?"

He moved in close, pulling her to him, his hands like iron around each of her wrists. She dropped the spoon onto the floor.

Her chest heaved against him, nervously. She took deep breaths, trying to maintain her calm.

"Take your hands off me."

He stared down at her, the stern anger now melted away to something unmistakable. He let go and stepped back. "You shouldn't do that."

"What? Act like a woman? I am one you know."

"Oh yes, I know. And a very young one at that. Barely..."

"Had my 18th birthday, I think, on the trip here. I made myself a cake and everything."

He furrowed his brow. *Was she kidding or serious? He could never tell with this one.*

"I mean it. Check my records that you so meticulously keep. You'll notice my so-called birthday."

He reached to miniature console beside him and typed in a few symbols. "Well, I guess I owe you a happy birthday. Or maybe a birthday spanking is more in order." He laughed at his hollow threat.

She merely stared back, refusing to acknowledge his dry humor.

"See, I don't know my birthday for sure. My birth mother died when I was little. So the McThurns just gave me one. It's a good date for sure, one I'll remember since it's the date they picked me up. That night I would have frozen to death, I'm sure."

Cruez's grin slowly disappeared, losing the humor with the grim tale of reality.

"So Cruez, shall we go see Tiberious?"

"Why are you in such a rush? I need to eat first."

"You can eat when we get there."

"We are there, dearie. Just take a look outside," he pointed to a small hull portal. "Bueller's private dock."

"I know, but he's downtown. I already checked with the residence system."

"Oh. So you are thinking one step ahead of me now. Be careful with that."

"Being one step ahead of you is easy. Just need to think of the most predictable thing to do next."

He laughed again, shrugging off her witty comments with a broad smile and a casual grab of his jacket. He reached into a drawer and pulled out some energy bars.

"Want one?"

"No. But you wait for me," April warned with a glare.

"Why, I'm so bloody predictable you should know where I'm going."

She decided what she was wearing would have to do and grabbed a second over-jacket. It was a bit too large, fit quite loose, but at least it would keep the rain off.

They stepped down the ramp and out from the shadow of the ship, only to be pelted heavily by a driving rain.

"Why does it always seem to be raining up here?"

"'Cause it does!" Cruez yelled back. "Something to do with their weather control systems. Cumulative error or something."

April smiled. *The brightest minds on Earth, still can't control the weather.*

They stepped into an alcove and through an oversized doorway. A bank of elevators stretched to their right and left, some were freight units with expanded openings, others far smaller for personal use.

"We'll need to take this one," he pointed, "to go down to the main streets. You need to stick close to me though. It can be very dangerous down there."

She could tell there was genuine concern showing in his eyes. "No problem."

"You know I'm not kidding. This is not Ishaida."

"I got it."

"Hold on to your stomach," he warned, as he pressed the button.

The elevator accelerated down, and for the moment they turned almost weightless.

"The more expensive ones have grav plates. We're on the econo ride," commented Cruez with a wink.

"How fast are we going?"

"Less than 9.8 meters per second – you still have some weight."

"Thanks," she said, trying to color her reply with as much displeasure as she could convey.

"What? I gave you an answer. Cripes, I don't know. Fast. We're miles up and we're headed down. You are such a damn techie."

"So what? I just like to know how things work."

He let out his breath slowly and looked out the small portal window. Every once in a while, you could almost make something out, but it was quickly lost in the constant blur.

Their full weight returned rudely as the elevator slowed. April could feel the blood rush to her feet. It made her slightly dizzy.

"We're here." He announced. "Remember, stick close."

Doors opened to a street of streaming bodies. Unlike the drabness above, these streets were filled with colors, sounds, music, and voices of all kinds.

Cruez grabbed her and pulled, keeping a tight locking grip on the waist of her jacket.

Faces passed by her, appraising, watching. Some talked to her in languages she could not place.

"We are heading to the tram causeway, up there," he pointed above.

April's gaze swept above them taking in the vertical structures brimming with conduits, tubes rising into the sky. At their peaks, lightning streaks reached across in alternating bridges, filling the sky in a blinding luminescence. The light silhouetted between the structures in flashes, reflecting surreal images.

"We're on one of the highest streets in Toronto. People come here to look up – to see the sky."

"Not much of a view."

"They seem to think it is. Look over there. See those fliers racing above us down that other street, barely a meter apart?"

She looked. She could see them. Sky taxis. But they were moving far too fast, and far too close for her comfort. "We're going to ride in one of them? I'm not sure..."

He laughed. "Don't worry. They've been running like that for centuries."

"What if one breaks down? They'll collide."

"They all have fail-safes, redundant systems, failure reaction systems. Besides, everything is tied together. One goes down, everything stops, adjusts, restarts."

"Really?"

He laughed again, as he pulled her close to him. They shot up the open-faced elevator with a rush of air. For a moment, she thought she was going to fall, but Cruez pulled her tightly to him. *A little too tightly.*

A second later, he stepped forward onto a suspended corridor with a floor of richly detailed faux marble which flowed into walls of glass. A steady stream of sky trams slid in and out from a moving sidewalk.

"Let's take this one."

They stepped lightly, as the trams tended to allow one just enough time to get on board. Each car had an inner and outer oval of seats, allowing 10 adults to sit comfortably. Displays lined the ceiling, and holographic images played out through the enlarged windows, suspended; scenarios of native Earth life, commonplace yet so alien to her.

"What are these pictures referring to?"

"Oh, just commercials. Selling to the masses, I suspect."

"Capitalism. Fascinating."

"Definitely a step ahead of Ishaida, isn't it?" asked Cruez.

Another man with a pasty complexion and sharp beak of a nose moved in closer and took a quick inspecting glance directly at her.

"You are from Ishaida? You poor thing. It is truly a dreadful accident that has happened."

Cruez eyed the man with cautious disdain.

"You think so?" April asked candidly. "I didn't know anyone from here was the least bit interested."

"On the contrary. We are all very well connected." He waved over to the displays actively playing. "Communication is not a problem, here. If it's virtual, it's easy. It's the physical things we have trouble with. I'm sure you can relate."

She shook her head. The man seemed to be talking from another realm.

His eyes grew a bit wider. "I'm sorry, I'm not being clear. I am talking about goods, perishables, you know - food. That can be hard to come by in this world."

"I see. I can understand that very well. And you, what do you know of Ishaida?"

"The recent accident, the tragic and freak release of ore chunks from that intergalactic hauler. It is truly a shame."

"Who said it was an accident?" She said, squinting her eyes. "Perhaps you accept the validity of this communication network of yours far too easily."

Again, even wider eyes. "Indeed. Not an accident. Very intriguing."

Cruez pushed the man back gently but firmly. "Man, give us our space. We paid for it."

He bowed nervously, shifting a look from side to side. "Of course. My apologies. No intention to intrude." He faded back to the other end of the car.

"Why are you being so rude?" she asked, irritated.

"We paid for this space. It's ours outright."

"So."

"You've got to understand, this is the upper-class mode of transportation here. If anything is valued in this accursed city, it is personal space. As a matter of fact, your personal space is protected by law, and the law can get a bit strict around here on transgressions."

"Seems a bit over the top."

"That's because you've never been down below, down near the bottom. An hour down there and you'll understand."

"If this is the upper-class transportation than I guess a private flier is out of the question."

"Only the very, very privileged can move about in this city on their own accord. Even the emergency workers use public transit."

"Where are we going, by the way?"

"Well you checked the residence system," he mocked.

"So. Didn't mean anything to me."

"There."

He pointed toward a tower ahead. It rose out from an open square below, tied into the surrounding walls with mazes of horizontal connections. The outside skin of the tower seemed bronze in the bleak light.

"The Chrysler Tower."

"This whole city is a tower."

"Yeah, well we have towers within towers here."

"And what of this Chrysler Tower?"

"Hosts the Anard-Bueller world headquarters, my dear, arguably the control center of the Earth's economy according to some."

"Oh, that sounds pleasant."

The tram slowed and slid into its berth with quiet precision and nothing more than a slight jostle.

"Let's go."

They stepped out into a room of immense proportions. The ceiling was so high its peak was a mere blur. Painting of all sizes covered the walls, plastering the room with a rich palette of colors.

"Oh yeah, this is also a museum. See those people up there?"

She craned her neck and strained her eyes. She could see them, floating high above, small figurines lost in a sea of dancing light.

"You can rent a hover-board and coast along, go all the way to the peak if you wish."

"Maybe I will one day. The artwork here looks truly amazing."

"The lower ones are by the greats. The higher you go, the more obscure, and somewhat more modern."

He grabbed her arm and tugged her along. "Let's take this conveyor. We need to get to reception."

They stepped onto a moving sidewalk. April's legs felt like lead. At the same time, she could feel herself pushing through the air, enough to jostle her hair back.

"How fast are we going?"

"Pretty quick, 50 kmh maybe. Grav plating under the walk holds you down like an anchor. It'll lighten up in a sec once we slow down."

They got off near an extensive wooden desk which housed at least a dozen clerical personnel.

"Can I help you?" asked a primed smiling face. The blond woman seemed extremely pleasant, her voice hauntingly relaxing.

"Mr. Tiberious Bueller, please. Mr. Cruez and Ms. McThurn are here to see him."

The woman's pleasant features changed for just a split second. She had not expected his request, revealing for just a moment a shade of nervousness, a temporary loss of confidence.

"Just a..." She cleared her throat. "Just a moment, Mr. Cruez. I will see if he is available."

He had already turned his attention away from her and was casually eyeing everyone around with a trained assessing gaze.

"Mr. Cruez, I am sorry, but Mr. Bueller has just left."

"Where?"

"I'm not at liberty to say at this moment, Sir. This is highly unusual."

"Well find out – give me the scanner." He snatched it up and scanned his eye, then pressed his finger onto the sampler. "You'll find I have the highest clearance. Expedite please."

The clerk seemed a little harried, but she was efficient. A short call to another secretary and a small note was passed over the counter.

"Do you require anything else, Sir?"

"No thanks."

"It was a pleasure helping you, Sir," she said, with a broad smile.

Cruez just ignored her, pocketing the note with a grimace.

"Thank you for your help," April said, irritated at Cruez's distinct lack of manners.

The lady smiled and nodded back to her, sharing a brief moment of eye contact.

Damn men.

"OK. So. Let's just go back to the residence," he stated.

"No. We're out here now. Let's go to him. Just what is your problem, anyway? Maybe you don't want me to talk to the Old Man? Maybe you know something you're not telling me?"

He scoffed. "No. Not at all."

"Well, let's go. You have that note, I know that much."

"Fine. Time for another tram ride."

"Fine."

He marched out, paying little attention to whether she was following or not. April hung back just far enough to ensure he stayed pissed off.

They ended up on another crowded street. This time inclusive of two and three-wheeled vehicles, both manual and powered, which intimidated their way through the streams of flowing humanity.

Cruez momentarily forgave April's previous comments. He kept her close, often an arm wrapped around her protectively.

Given the rough looking faces of the crowd, April did not complain.

They stopped at what seemed to be a wall of red brick.

"Here we are."

"What?"

"The entrance is right in front of you. It's a holographic image."

He checked his wrist pad, pressed some buttons and gave a satisfied look. "Yep, Tiberious is in there all right – with all of his cronies no doubt. Sure you want in?"

April looked at him. *What wasn't he telling her now?*

"Sure."

"OK." They stepped through the wall and were met immediately by two very large men in black suits. They stepped back as soon as they recognized Cruez, following up with a lazy salute.

"Perimeter is solid, Sir."

"Of course it is," Cruez said quietly. "Location?"

"Eleven o'clock, facing wall near the end."

"Thanks."

He glanced back at April. "She's with me."

One of them raised an eyebrow but said nothing. It was hard to read their faces in the murky room. The lighting was poor in every part, except for the stage.

April immediately realized what Cruez had meant, and her mistake.

"Oh, shit," was all she could muster.

Cruez was watching her. A broad smile spanned across his face. "They're over there."

The music started up, blaring loudly, literally pounding against her chest. He led her by the arm, pulling her past a mass of seedy looking characters. The strippers eyed them with indifference, bearing their attention on future patrons. Their shreds of clothing left little to the imagination.

Tiberious was sitting with a number of his business associates. His old, gray face gleaned strangely in the dim lights. He was the first to notice them coming, the first to look straight at her. His leathery face gave away little emotion. He raised his crooked arm, signaling them to join him.

A stripper, who had previously joined the group, faded back into the crowd.

"Cruez, I am not sure I approve of your decision to bring her down here."

"You know as well as I, Mr. Bueller, our guest has a mind of her own. She insisted."

"So this is how you spend your free time, Mr. Bueller," April spoke up, tired of being ignored.

Tiberious leaned in close, speaking quietly into her ear. "My dear Ms. McThurn, there are methods of transacting business. This is merely one of them. Perhaps it is a bit distasteful, but it can be effective, after all, I own this place."

"I see. You'll have to forgive my assumptions," April replied with a forced smile. *Business my ass.*

"Exactly why are you here, Ms. McThurn?"

A roar of laughter came from across the table. A very young looking female had joined their group. April, noticing their momentary distraction, quickly inspected each of the men. Everyone was well groomed, wearing the highest quality clothing. Wolfish grins faded quickly as they turned to look back at her. She had no doubt these men were the elite, the powerful. Some of them were momentarily entranced by her, like flies caught in the light. She caught their appraising glances but quickly turned her attention back to the Old Man.

There was something behind their eyes that made her uncomfortable. Something akin to hate or possibly, fear.

The flickering candle in the center of the table caught her attention. The tiny flame danced erratically, seeming to fight every second to remain alight.

Not much different than her, or any other Ishaidan really, victims of the winds of greed and corruption. They were the innocent bystanders caught in the middle of an unstoppable power struggle.

"Ms. McThurn?"

Tiberious's voice brought her back from her thoughts. She refocused on the Old Man. The noise, the shuffling of humanity around her faded to nothing.

"The price you spoke of, Mr. Bueller, of activating our TFPs, has now been paid in full. Ishaida has paid in blood. These fabricated stories of unfortunate accidents need to be corrected. The truth needs to be told."

Tiberious shifted in his seat. "The truth is as much perception as it is fact, my dear." He suddenly clapped his hands together. Henchmen appeared around them, no longer confined to the shadows. They were all ushered out, Tiberious in the lead. A long, sleek, black personal flier was parked outside awaiting them.

April was next, Cruez following behind. He gently pushed down on her head as she ducked into the flier, as always watching over her.

The doors shut, drowning out all sound but the soft purring of music coming from a small microwave receiver unit.

"Please, have a drink," offered Tiberious, now seated across from them in a plush oval couch. He was offering a glass of wine of deep crimson red.

April accepted, taking a moment to breathe in the strong scents.

"Yes, it was a good year. Direct from my personal cellars. I'm glad you approve."

"I don't know much about this drink. It just smells good."

"It's called wine and it certainly does." He grinned widely. "A luxury not enjoyed on Ishaida, yet. As we are all merely struggling to survive."

She gulped the drink down. It burned slightly, forcing her to cough.

Cruez chuckled. "Ishaidans have little room for luxuries."

Tiberious nodded thoughtfully. "You'll have to forgive me. It was not the appropriate place to discuss such matters, nor the appropriate company. Certain gentlemen of the type best for you to avoid, my dear."

He leaned back on the couch, his previous vigorous image now fading to a familiar frailty.

"I tell you Cruez, these pills sap everything out of me, and for what? I leave them with the illusion of the shadow of my old self, and I am drained for the whole next day, and possibly more."

Cruez nodded quietly.

"And you little lady, you will find I do have an opinion on the Ishaidan situation. I do think that it is unlikely they will attempt such an act of aggression again."

"Why? Because it is too obvious? They've already gotten away with it. They've spouted out lies which the rest of the civilized worlds swallowed all too readily. What's next, a plague of some sort, maybe some sort of internal nuclear accident? A few more lies, a few more thousand dead. Kill us off a little at a time. It's simple."

The Old Man responded only by taking an extended gulp of his drink.

"April has taken the liberty of investigating during the trip," added Cruez solemnly.

The two men exchanged glances. A hint of a smile crossed the Old Man's gray lips.

"Oh? I see. Have you discovered the guilty party?" he asked, openly amused by April's initiative.

"I have my suspicions."

"And what will be the price to levy, once you find the guilty party – or parties?"

"Things have changed since our last discussion, by thousands of lives."

He nodded, the smile disappearing. "Yes, truly a grave situation we have. We are heading up directly to Arious Space Port, perhaps we'll get some answers for you. I know of some persons of interest that may provide some information with the proper incentives."

"And then?"

"We make our plans accordingly."

"Have any more of that wine?"

Tiberious smiled and reached for the bottle.

What happened next was initiated with a deafening explosion then an incredibly violent tossing of the group as the flier sought to stabilize. Thin, cold air shrieked into the small cabin, and April's lungs hurt breathing it in.

Cruez yelled at her, but she couldn't hear him, she couldn't hear anything. She reached up to cup her ears, and quickly pulled them away, warm and wet and covered in blood. She fought down the panic, mentally running a self-check. They were dropping fast and rotating, that much she could tell. She had to get to the cockpit.

Their cabin was separated from it by a large barrier overtop the inner seat. Cruez was pounding on its control panel, probably attempting to pull it down, but it wasn't moving. April crawled over to check the connections underneath, knowing there was little chance the interface would work in its partially shattered state. She yanked the access panel and reached in systematically feeling for the emergency release.

It had to be there.

Her fingers caught the small trip switch. The panel started down, opening up to a ghoulish scene. The two pilots were dead, their blood splayed over the controls in crimson trails. More troubling, however, was the scene through the primary viewing shield. They were falling, and fast.

Cruez dived into the cockpit, grabbing the main control wheel. Nothing responded. The console was shattered. Lights flickered crazily, cycling through mutated variations of displays. He fought with it a few more seconds and looked back at April, desperation in his eyes.

They were running out of time.

She jumped over the seat and wiggled down under the flight control panel, pushing the dead pilots' feet out of the way. The panels released easily with a push exposing a complicated assortment of carbon cables.

How was she going to do this? She could feel the panic building up within her, utter desperation. *They were going to die. And she wasn't ready for this.*

Think, damn it. Think.

This ship had to have the multiple controls hardwired, even with the primary control system offline, redundant backups should be active. But why weren't they? She needed to find and reroute power to the primary controls. She just needed to find the right circuits.

Over to her right, she could see a carbon conduit running from the outer hull. Judging by its gauge, it was significantly higher amperage. Most of the lines converged above her into the console, which was most likely the primary control center. There were two thick gauge lines running to it. Would it be as simple as switching to two?

She yanked at the pairs of cables, pulling them out of their connectors. The old supply pair gave way easily, but the possible new supply set didn't move. She twisted her body around, jamming her knees against the bulkhead, fighting to gain leverage, then extended her right hand up as far as she could, searching with her fingers for the release clip.

How many seconds had passed? How close were they to crashing now?

She felt the clip and twisted. The line gave way and the exposed carbon ends sparked against the bulkhead. She caught the line, careful not touch them against anything else.

Well, here goes. With any luck, she won't short out the whole system. She jammed the cables into the control connectors, and clicked in the clips, then yelled up at Cruez. She couldn't hear herself, but she knew she was screaming.

Something shifted. She became so heavy she could hardly breathe. She tensed up her diagram like she had read about, fighting to stay conscious. They were either leveling out or crashing.

Precious seconds passed.

The weight lifted.

No, they weren't crashing, at least not yet.

She wiggled out and looked up. Cruez's features were locked in intense concentration, but for just a second he glanced down and gave her a wink.

They were going to make it.

The wind was howling in from a hole blasted on the starboard side, whipping her hair into her face. Wiping it from her eyes, she could see the ground below passing by in a blur. They had to be less than 100 meters from the surface.

The flier rocked side to side as Cruez masterfully timed the rhythm with the compromised controls, just able to keep them on the edge of control, keeping them aloft. He pointed to the port side through the cockpit window. The wing-mounted engine was smoking badly.

He was yelling something at her, but she couldn't understand a word.

With a free hand, he grabbed at the pilot behind him. April caught on, unclipped the dead pilot's safety harness and pulled him off the seat. Cruez lowered into it and tied himself down, simultaneously fighting to keep the ship steady.

The ground was coming up closer. He waved at her to go to the back, eyes wide and intense. April took a second to process. *Chances to survive were probably higher in the passenger section than the front. But she had to secure the Old Man, too.*

She locked eyes with Cruez for just a second. Enough time to say goodbye. Then she jumped into the passenger compartment. She found Tiberious on the floor and managed to pull him onto the passenger seat. The Old Man shuddered in pain.

Her heart was pounding, and every movement seemed to be in slow motion. With her left hand, she reached over to hit the emergency harness deploy. The harnesses shot out and automatically pulled them both tight into the plush seats. Ceiling panels glowed yellow indicating imminent deployment of airbags.

Through the corner of her eye, she could just catch the dark edge of the oncoming surface, and Cruez's hands flying deftly across the panel, coolly maintaining an optimum descent angle.

Seconds later, they hit.

* * *

She awoke aside Tiberious, a sharp pain in her left side, and an overwhelming throb in her head. She struggled with the harness release to move closer to the Old Man. His arm had a compound fracture that was bleeding, and his complexion was pale. She used his tie as a tourniquet and adjusted him to a more comfortable position.

The airbags were still settling. The ship was upright, at least.

She pushed her way to the front to check on Cruez to find him slumped against the console, unconscious. Reaching over, hands shaking, she felt for a pulse at his neck.

Weak but present, thank God.

Something inside her gave out, and tears flooded out. She ignored them, wiping them away as she scanned the remainder of the ship. It was a total wreck. She could see outside through a hole in the fuselage and noticed the whole starboard wing had been clipped off. The port wing was still there, and the port engine was burning.

Fire, they had to get out, to get clear of the ship. "Move!" said a familiar voice. It was Oranis.

She staggered to the hatch, pressed the automatic and then the manual release. Neither would budge. Standard design protocol was to incorporate explosive bolts into the main hatch. She cracked open the plastic casing of the door panel and pressed the red timer.

At least they followed specifications.

She fell protectively onto Tiberious, waiting for the explosion. When the hatch blew, she could feel it through the floor and looked back to see blue skies and green fields.

Luckily, the Old Man was light enough that she could carry him through the hatch. She propped him up against an irrigation culvert far enough away to keep him safe, and then returned for Cruez.

The fire was creeping into the main fuselage area filling the inside with thick, acrid smoke. She choked on the fumes and kept as low as possible so she could breathe. She found Cruez in the same condition as before. Being dead weight and solid muscle, she was only able to drag him a meter before before yielding, her arms weakened and shaky. She yelled at him, trying to wake him, but to no avail.

The heat from the fire was building, the smoke black and hot churning around them. She lay with him on the floor sobbing. She couldn't get him out. She just didn't have the strength. *Maybe it's better this way. Just stay here, die along with him, the last of her family. Just another smear of Ishaidan humanity.*

Cruez stirred, moving his head back and forth. His eyes opened.

April stared at him still half-sobbing. "It's about time." She said, though not quite sure her words came out right. He said something back, but she couldn't hear him.

"We have to get out, or we'll die here."

He nodded, understanding.

They struggled together, pulling themselves out the hatch and away from the lethal smoke. Between the two of them, they managed to rise to their feet, with him leaning heavily upon her, shaky and unsteady. They made their way to the culvert to collapse beside the Old Man, out of breath and exhausted.

The wind was blowing lightly, moving the tops of the wheat in rustling waves. It was beautiful out here if one chose to ignore the smoking wreck lying in the middle of the field.

They waited there for what seemed a lifetime, until the emergency response ships descended from above, accompanied by a gunship with the block letters of ESPD stretched across its side. It was not long before they were strapped to gurneys and dispatched to a trauma center in the closest city of Calgary-Edmonton.

* * *

Chapter 10

April awoke to a ringing in her ears and a coppery taste in her mouth. "Ah, I see you are awake," exclaimed a nurse. Her jolly temperament fit her portly body and broad smile. She put the temperature gauge to her ear.

"Looking good. How's your hearing?"

"Good. I mean, I can hear. My ears don't even hurt. I thought they were ruptured?"

"You have the best doctors at your disposal, my dear. It's a simple restorative procedure. I understand you were quite brave."

April turned away to stare out a small window. A large metal column loomed in the distance, lights flickered upon its surface intermittently. Video holographic images danced upon catwalks and suspended bridges. Fog breathed through the openings obscuring the ugly scars of chipping paint and rust, a flowing river of white and gray.

What a strange world this is.

The nurse had already busied herself with other things, carting equipment into a small locker adjacent to the room, checking inventory.

"How is Mr. Bueller doing?" April called out.

"He had undergone extensive rehabilitative surgery on his left arm. He is doing very well, thanks to you," she replied, not missing a beat.

"And Mr. Montigue?"

"Who?"

"Mr. Bueller's security man, Cruez Montigue."

She turned back for a brief moment. "Oh, I'm afraid I don't know about him, my dear."

"I need to find out." She threw down her feet to the floor, but her head pounded all the worse.

"What are you doing?" the nurse exclaimed rushing over.

"I need to find out about Cruez."

"But you really shouldn't be on your feet dear, you've had a concussion."

"Sorry, need to go. Where are my clothes?" She had just realized she was wearing only a flimsy hospital gown.

"I'm afraid your clothes were discarded. You can ask one of your servants to obtain a new outfit for you, I'm sure."

"Servants?"

"Yes, they are waiting outside. Would you like to have one come in?"

April struggled with the gown. She could feel it was open in the back but couldn't seem to close it. Frustrated, she lay back down.

"Yes, please."

A woman walked in. She was about as old as the nurse, possibly in her mid-forties. Her brown hair was done up in a tight bun, and she wore a gray dress that looked more like a uniform than any fashion item.

"Good afternoon, Ms. McThurn. What can I do for you?"

"I need clothes."

"Certainly, I will see to it immediately. Do you have any preferences?"

"Anything that covers me. Maybe something similar to my old outfit?"

"I see," she said flatly, emphasizing her distaste.

April ignored her reply. "I also want you to find out about Mr. Cruez Montigue, right away."

"Anything else, Ms. McThurn?"

"What's your name?"

"Florence Tenoise, Ms. McThurn."

"Just call me April, Florence," she said with a smile. "And please hurry."

Florence bowed slightly and rushed out.

April noticed a vid-mod suspended from the ceiling. "This thing work?" She asked the nurse.

"Oh yes, and you certainly have all the options with this room."

She yanked it down and started through the interactive menu, eventually pulling up the ESPD Emergency desk.

"This is April McThurn, I was on board Mr. Bueller's personal flier when it was attacked. Can I talk with the investigator in charge?"

"One moment please," replied the virtual attendant.

A second later, a grizzled looking man appeared on the vid-feed. His hard-square features were amplified by his manner and dress. It looked like he had just slept in his clothes.

"April McThurn. Very good to meet you. Was a close call. I do have some questions for you on what occurred."

"If you could answer mine first, I'd appreciate it."

"I'll provide what I can, April."

"Who attacked us?"

"The ESPD has not been able to identify source vector of the attack. It seems we've had some untimely failures of certain surveillance systems."

"How unusual," April said as sarcastically as possible.

"No, not unusual at all, not when the parties involved have the means. This is corporation interference, quite clearly. The only question is, which one?"

"How about Soho-Beher?"

"You have reason to suspect them?"

"Yes." April did not like tipping her hand. He was supposed to have the answers for her.

"What exactly?"

"How about you start producing something first? I would think the ESPD has some non-civilly operated assets that are out of reach of these damned corporations."

He laughed, openly amused at April's demanding manner. "I can see why they failed their strike on you. My name is Bob – Bob Farelane."

"Well, OK Bob, let me know what you find," April said, trying to hold back her disdain. She disconnected, not bothering to say goodbye. *What kind of operation were they running anyway?*

She switched over to multiple news feeds, noticed their story on constant replay. She caught an overshot of their downed flier, a trailing cloud of black smoke, and the deep scar left behind in the wheat field. *Would that mean someone would be going hungry in the future?*

A knock on the door. It was Florence.

"I've arranged some outfits for you to choose from, Ms. McThurn – I mean, April," she said excitedly.

"Thank you, Florence and Mr. Cruez?"

"Oh, he's doing very well, dear. He's a strong young man. I'm sure he'll be on his feet shortly."

April tried to keep from grinning at the news but failed.

Florence watched her coyly. "Yes, and he certainly is a handsome specimen of a man."

"Yeah. Well, I'm just glad he's OK, and of course, Mr. Bueller, as well."

"Yes, of course," acknowledged Florence, smiling herself. "April, if you need to talk about it... I mean it must have been terrifying."

April searched inside herself. *Was it? Funny, it really didn't seem that way. It should have been.*

"I was kind of caught up in working the problem. Didn't have time to get scared."

"I would have been. You are very brave. And to think you pulled both men from the crash."

"Wasn't anything you wouldn't do, Florence, I'm sure. You know the stories you hear after are always exaggerated. They aren't nothing at all like the truth."

"I understand," she said. But her eyes told otherwise.

"Anything else I can help you with, perhaps some refreshments?"

"I just need to know how Mr. Bueller is doing. I'd like to see him as soon as he is able."

"Oh. Why I do believe his procedure is complete. I will make arrangements to take you to him, April. Please excuse me."

She disappeared then returned a few minutes later with a wheelchair.

"Oh no. Protocol or not. I'm not getting into that thing."

"A concussion is a serious injury, April. We simply won't be able to see him otherwise."

April grudgingly sat down in the chair. It was autoguiding and quiet. Deep down she didn't mind the rest.

Tiberious smiled when April entered the room. "April, my dear. It is good to see that you are alright." He held out his arms, offering an uncharacteristic hug. His left arm was bandaged from the shoulder to the wrist.

April stepped up and hugged him back. He may be a frail old man, but for a moment, he felt to her like family.

"How is your arm?" she asked.

"Seems to be working fine, my dear. They had a replacement graft ready to install before we even landed. It's very sore, of course, but will be as good as new in a few weeks."

"I've also heard that Cruez is doing alright."

"Yes, thanks to you. We both owe you our lives. You are an amazing young lady. Without your quick thinking, we would have crashed. Doubtful we would have survived."

"Well, we did. Now we need to find out who did this and why."

"I've made some calls already, April. I expect some answers shortly."

"Well, I hope they're more help than the ESPD was."

"Oh, the ESPD?" Tiberious chuckled.

"Yes, already had the pleasure. Talked with this Farelane character who didn't know much."

"Bob Farelane? They're pulling in the big guns on this. Now don't be fooled by their claims. They always know more than they're letting on. Regardless, I'm sure you can handle them. I've been told you and Cruez can check out now. But I won't be leaving with you. I'm afraid these pain-in-the-ass doctors are not allowing me to leave. Something about my age, apparently. Seems my body needs more time to heal."

"Oh? Surprise to me. They kept telling me I'm concussed."

"Ah. They addressed that the moment you arrived. Just protocol. I have you on my tab, my dear. The very best care, period."

"I see. A perquisite of the very rich."

"Yes, it is true of some things."

"Where should we go now?"

"I'll continue research on my side. You continue with Cruez and see what more you can uncover. Pick him up on the way out."

"Ok, so I'll see you later then?"

"Like I said, dear, I'm just a wee bit older than the two of you, and they want to keep an eye on me. I'll be fine."

She hesitated. Something in his eyes. It was just a flicker but something.

"OK. I'll let you know what we find."

"Good, and as for Cruez," he led the conversation carefully. "Just try to listen to him. He's very, very good at what he does. And what he does is protect people, but only if they work with him."

"Of course. I'll listen to him, as long as he listens to me."

Tiberious' smile grew even wider. "That's my girl."

He closed his eyes and winced.

Someone else may have missed the small inflection, but she didn't.

* * *

Cruez was waiting at the elevator, his head wrapped in bandages, eyes black and blue.

"Don't worry, looks worse than it is," he said softly.

April reached up and cupped his cheek in her hand. "Good going there, pilot. You got us down in one piece."

"You weren't so bad yourself, techie."

A quick wink, and then he was back to his old business-as-usual self. "We have to go back to Anard-Bueller Headquarters. Some accounts have to be settled on this matter."

"Do you know who did this?"

"Not yet. But by the time we get there, I will."

They left the hospital, April's two servants falling in behind, a mass of personal bodyguards surrounding them, pushing away the flowing streams of humanity. She looked back at the servants, realizing she hadn't even bothered to learn the other woman's name.

They boarded a second, heavier flier. Two armed escorts launched in tandem with theirs. The trip did not seem to take as long as before and shortly they were landing on the Chrysler Tower's private tarmac.

April peered through the glass portal. Security had been noticeably tightened up. Armed guards were openly visible throughout.

They marched out with an escort. Cruez saluted one of the officers as they approached the main elevators.

"We're heading all the way up, April. We'll be talking to the top brass."

"And then?"

"Decisions get made," he said, offering little else.

The elevator's acceleration was barely noticeable. It finally came to rest at the very top floor of the tower.

"We're here," announced Cruez, for April's benefit.

They walked down a wooden paneled corridor, through intermittent open-space offices, by hushed whispers and stolen glimpses from staff who were avoiding direct eye contact.

The 'top brass' as Cruez had referred to them, were all waiting in the boardroom. And what a boardroom it was. Three of the four walls were glass, standing at least five meters tall, exposing a view over a massive mechanical city. The sun intermittently shone through onto a facing wall hung with portraits of Anard-Bueller CEOs. Each portrayed a previous father of the Anard-Bueller Corporation, down through enough generations that April did not care to count.

The executive officers stood around the massive table of polished wood, like a collection of military leaders, waiting on cue to act with detailed precision. Their faces were masks, exposing little, but April could read their eyes. She sensed something there, and it made her uncomfortable.

Cruez escorted her to the head of the table, to Tiberious's station.

"If you don't mind, I'd be more comfortable to the side," she said quietly.

"Sorry, the Captain's always at the helm," said Cruez with a wide smile. "You're in charge. The Old Man's orders. And he was very clear about where he wanted you to sit." He pulled the chair out and gestured her forward.

Great. What the hell does the Old Man want her to do now?

She sat down, her throat a bit too dry, a jittering unsettledness stirring in her stomach. The others sat down with her, a cacophony of sound in perfect unison.

Military precision. She could not help but reflect.

She reached for a glass of water that sat waiting for her, and took a gulp, feeling its coolness soothe her raw throat. As she sat the glass down, it jiggled slightly, revealing unsteady nerves.

Get a hold of yourself.

"Hello, everyone," she said, her voice much too soft for her liking. "I need an update on this attack, as soon as possible."

"Ms. McThurn." A younger looking exec cleared his throat, arm half-poised in the air. "I have that information."

Eyes finally averted from her.

"We have a woman in custody from the Saturn moon system. She had launched the missile from the upper troposphere on descent in a single-person flitter. ESPD was notified immediately on dispatch and was able to intercept her before she was able to escape. Upon interviewing her, we have ascertained she is an independent working on a retainer with Soho-Beher. Her orders were to assassinate you and Mr. Bueller."

"I'd like to talk with her myself, can that be arranged?"

The exec shifted uncomfortably in his chair. "Um, not really. She ah, she died during questioning, unfortunately."

Even from the distance at the head of the table, April could see the man was sweating, his forehead glistening.

"Died? From questioning? I thought we had less harsh means at our disposal."

"Yes, Ms. McThurn, my apologies. It was an unfortunate happenstance."

"Nothing just happens. I want a name. This assassin was just the weapon, not the killer."

"It was an unexpected but engineered response to our administered treatment. I – ah – we've discovered some more information along another stream. It is not verified, however."

"And?"

"Well, we suspect this could have come from the top, from Carrigan himself."

"Who's this Carrigan?"

"CEO of Soho-Beher," interjected Cruez.

"I see."

"The Old Man wanted you to have this." Cruez slid a folder over to her. "Said it will help you out. He stressed to me that you read what's in it before you make any decisions on what to do."

She opened the folder, read the short letter attached. A thin-wafer mod was attached to the letter with a clip.

"Tiberious recommends we have the option to enact the trades contained in this mod." She held the thin strip of smooth material between her fingers. "Anyone object?"

"Ms. McThurn, we do support any decisions which Tiberious has tabled," said the gray-haired executive to her right. The man was old, but he had the eyes of a caged tiger.

Must be the Right-Hand of Tiberious. Funny, he didn't pick him to be his successor. I wonder why?

"But you haven't even seen them," she queried. She scanned the room for a contrary voice. No one else seemed the least concerned. "Well, I guess it's decided then. I'm sure Tiberious thanks you for his support," she said with a fake smile.

A clerk rose and snatched the mod from her fingers. "I will send these through immediately." He reached over her shoulder, typed in a command on the arm of her chair. A three-dimensional holograph appeared above the table. The windows automatically darkened, obliterating the streaming sunlight.

"You can monitor the effect through this. It will be a moment."

He disappeared behind her. Streams of characters whipped through the graphics, icons, numbers, and letters all dancing in the air.

"What is this?"

"The market, Ms. McThurn. Those particular figures in blue – they are Soho-Beher's equity/share value," replied the Right-Hand.

She saw the figures he was pointing to. They were dropping, slowly at first, and then faster. The tension in the room seemed to have increased exponentially.

She leaned over to Cruez. "What's happening?"

"War," stated Cruez, "Corporation style. See those numbers, each one means millions of dollars. The master is at work. He's picking apart Soho-Beher a piece at a time, anticipating the next shifts, the next demand, the next sell."

"How long?"

"Almost finished. There, it's done."

The Right-Hand gulped down his water, pale-faced and shaken.

April hit the switch on the arm of the chair. The image disappeared in a blink. "In my version of war, people die. They lose everything they have, including their future, not just some bloody savings they stashed away.

Maybe this bothers some of you," she scanned the room in disgust. "I guarantee you it's not enough. Just how much did they lose?"

"I would estimate about 4.5 trillion, but that's my estimate only."

"Their stock, can it start climbing again?"

"Yes, it should."

"What options do we have right now?"

"We can stage a hostile takeover," said a voice from across the room. It was a dark-haired woman with piercing green eyes. "But we have to move fast."

"What are all of you standing around for? Let's do it."

"When – I mean, what are your timelines here?" asked the Right-Hand.

"Tomorrow. Get it ready by tomorrow."

"And Soho-Beher's management? Do you propose to meet them?"

"Tomorrow at 9:00 am – our time."

Cruez cleared his throat. "Their head office is in Pinnacle-Vera, on Cauputain."

"Proceed with the takeover regardless."

They all merely stared back at her, possibly in disbelief.

"Well, what are you waiting for, get busy!" she yelled.

The execs jumped to their feet and filed out of the office at a hurried pace, leaving just her and Cruez, who continued to rock slowly back and forth in his chair, an oversized grin stamped on his face.

"What's so damned funny?"

"You. You just initiated the first hostile takeover in three centuries and expect your team to pull it off in an impossible timeline."

"So what? Ask me if I care."

He leaned in over the table. "Oh, you care alright, just a little too much."

"Is that ore carrier still in the Cauputain Cluster?"

He frowned. "What?"

"The bloody ore carrier, the one that bombed my planet."

Cruez pulled up a holographic keyboard at his station and scanned the records. "Yep. Actually in orbit around Cauputain right now, believe it or not."

"You contact those Soho-Beher bastards. Tell them I want to meet the senior team via a remote vid-feed tomorrow. Have them send everyone else home. Tomorrow's a holiday for all their employees."

The realization came over his face. "Hey listen, you can't..."

"I can," she cut him off. "And get your contacts to clear out any nearby buildings."

"They'll notice something is up. You can't just go killing the top execs of a competing company. There are rules you need to follow."

"And patch me a feed to that bastard Captain," she ordered, ignoring his protests.

"No way."

"Do it," she said quietly. "Time's up for them. They made the first move, I'm making the last."

"I don't think Tiberious would condone this. Not so sure you want to tie Anard-Bueller assets directly to this crime."

"He's not here. If he was, he would tell me I have to be sure. I am sure he would not stop me. I am sure this is not a crime. This is war. Do you see any specific retaliation for Ishaida's dead? You were there – you saw our cost in blood."

Cruez stood up, grin long lost. "Fine. I'll need about a half-hour to make some calls."

"As per your own advice: keep it quiet," she said, not bothering to look at him.

He left her alone to her thoughts.

She stared at the half-empty glass of water in front her, tapping her fingers quickly on the table's glossy surface.

Was she ready for this? There was a cost to this. But did she understand the cost?

* * *

Chapter 11

Tiberious adjusted his com-link. The image on April's watch projector shook slightly.

"This war will have victims."

"What victims? The Ishaidan population, maybe. I don't see anyone else suffering."

"No matter how good we perfect these damned devices, they are always a pain in the you-know-where." He laughed weakly at his own joke, ending in a short series of sharp coughs. "And yes, people do die in this war. People lose their fortunes, their way of life, everything. Their friends do little to help them, they are shunned. It can lead to suicide. In this culture, when they say you are on the way down, they also mean literally. Perhaps you should visit the lower levels before you make it back home."

"Oh, you mean where the poverty is. Yes, I've already seen it – in Ishaida."

"No, you haven't seen it like this, I assure you."

"Regardless, this is not about Earth. A few Soho-Beher employees lose their fat way of life. Big deal."

Tiberious shook his head slowly. "Sometimes you seem so old, and other times I am reminded of how young you really are. I understand you have made other plans, more insidious in nature than a financial takeover."

"What of it?"

"Are you sure you want to go through with it?"

"No... No, I'm not sure. But then I think of the thousands of lives murdered senselessly on Ishaida. That makes the decision much easier."

"You need to be sure."

"What would you do?"

The Old Man cackled. "A wise man once told me to forge a path of my own, for my perception of my life is that of my own life's lessons, nothing more."

"Yeah, well my dad used to say that if you ask for advice, you should consider taking it."

The Old Man laughed again.

April broke into a smile herself.

"I like to see that on you. You have to remember to live life, my dear. You can only carry the weight of your world for so long. You need to give yourself a break."

"I will after it's done."

Tiberious closed his eyes and nodded. "I'll not talk you out of it, for I know what you feel inside. But I would, however, advise against it."

"I don't feel I have a choice."

"Everyone has a choice. Every day you make thousands of them. A choice to be late one day may save you from a terrible wreck. A choice to procrastinate on a report at work may cost you a promotion. But sometimes it's the little choices that make a difference, like not making a call before letting it ferment in your mind for a time. That's all I ask. Wait – just wait for a time and know that I will provide you with any resources you require to support that choice."

"Why do I always end up confused by the time I'm done talking with you?"

"It's a gift. I will confer with you later, my dear. Be well."

She pressed the tiny button on her armband, and the image disappeared into nothing.

Be well? Far from it. She was in her own little hell.

A knock on the door.

"Yes?"

"It's Cruez." He walked in, sullen and stone-faced. He had changed his mood since the meeting. He looked at her like she was just another obstacle in his path. She felt like running up to him and slapping him across the face as hard as she could.

"Is it arranged?"

"I have what you asked for, including the link code, and the modified control program."

"Traceability?"

"It'll all be encrypted, and it's almost impossible to break. But nothing's a sure thing. The voice modulator is already configured. Here."

She took it, along with mod. "What about clearing out the other buildings?"

"I have notified some of my colleagues. They can move some, but there will be residuals. They have some sort of chemical leak scenario planned out. Remember launching must be incredibly precise. He could miss."

"There's always risk."

He looked back with angry, cold eyes.

Why was he so mad at her? She was no worse than him. What a damned hypocrite.

"I'll be leaving then." He announced.

"Where?"

"ESPD. I want to verify their findings."

"We didn't get our information from them, did we?"

"Yes, some of it. Most of it was through our own corporate resources."

"That's what I thought. Give my regards to Bob Farelane."

"I will. Goodbye," he said, stressing the finality in his tone like he would never see her again.

Maybe he wouldn't. Who's to say? But she doubted that. They were stuck with each other, at least as long as Tiberious dictates.

As soon as the door closed, she launched the com and entered the link code. The rogue Captain's image appeared almost immediately.

The bastard was ready for her, alright.

"This is Captain Abakas."

"I know who you are, Captain. A shared contact has already discussed the terms of our agreement with you."

"Oh, it's you." His demeanor switched, confidence lost, his color turned slightly pale.

"I understand you will have another serious accident occur on your ship."

"I've already rectified all source issues identified in the inquiry. It would be difficult to defend a second occurrence of such an event."

"You must have lost count. This would be a third such occurrence."

"I have been cleared of any wrongdoing." His eyes squinted tighter into a malformed suspicious gaze.

"Of course you have," April said, acidly, not sparing her disdain for him.

She adjusted the modulator slightly to vary her inflections. The device she was using made her voice an identical match to a local terrorist leader known to operate on Cauputain. It would serve as another dead-end for a capable investigator.

"We need a job completed, similar in nature to the first one."

"Negative. Undoable. Just like I told your companion, before. Too suspicious, and won't pass any credibility this time."

"And what did my companion say to you after your reply?"

The Captain gulped. A stream of sweat was beading on his temple, just starting to edge down. "He was clear there are others ways to compel me to cooperate."

"Exactly. Our terms are generous enough, that much I assure you. The scenario is simple: It's a bug in the cargo door control system. Extremely hard to find. Missed on the first scans, so it was not unreasonable for it to happen again. I have a modified version of the control system for you to download. All the license ID markers match."

A long silence on the other end. He was thinking about it at least.

"Fine. Target?"

"Soho-Beher Headquarters."

Another long silence.

"I can't be that precise. It's right in the city center. Look, this is getting out of hand. There is no way…"

"You do as I say," she interrupted, "or the authorities will find a little more on their next trip than you can explain away. Consider this just cleaning up the evidence of who paid you. That is good for you, just in case you do not fathom the finer subtleties of the situation. Besides, Soho-Beher's in the middle of a hostile takeover. Anard-Bueller is already destroying them from within."

"I didn't hear about that."

"Check the market news, you'll see."

"I will."

"They'll be squealing like pigs as soon as Anard-Bueller is done with them. You really should worry about this. A full government inquisition on a takeover as big as this may uncover some dirty deals. You need credits and a fast shuttle off that ore carrier or you'll be looking at a hard time within, let's say, a week?"

Abakus eyes dropped to the floor. He had already resigned to the fact that he was in way over his head. "What's the offer?"

"Three million credits."

"That's half of what the Ishaidan job paid. I want 10 million, in advance, or no deal."

This was her chance to stretch the silence out. *She had him now.*

"Too much," she finally announced. "Good luck surviving prison." She hesitated slightly before signing off.

"Wait! You know I'll need to disappear. There's no way they'd swallow this story again. No way at all. I need more. I need at least seven."

She could hardly contain herself. *Stay calm, play it cool.*

"Alright, four. But I need it done tomorrow, 24.03.123 galactic time."

"Just four? That's it?"

April just eyed him steadily. He'll take it.

"Fine. Fine, four. I should be able to arrange for that time without a problem."

"I must impress upon you, do not miss: the window or the target."

"I won't."

"Give me the account," she ordered.

He spouted out the long list of numbers.

He would be watching it, waiting for the transfer to occur. No payment, no job.

April cut the link, not bothering to say goodbye. She then pulled up the account transfer menu at the desk console and moved over the money Tiberious had loaned her.

She had arranged for 10 million, just in case, so she had some left over. What she could do with just one million credits, nevermind six million.

The image blinked complete. It was done, just like that, arranged. At 9:10 am EST here, Earth time, it would be all over for them.

She leaned back in the chair. What was it the Old Man had said – Forge your own path? Well, she was forging it alright. People were going to die.

Anard-Bueller headquarters had its perquisites, including executive suites available to those workaholics that worked into the early hours. Tiberious had his own suite, of course, which he had extended to her. She had accepted the offer graciously. She needed a shower, some time to relax, to contemplate.

The servants would be there already. It would be nice to talk to someone if only menial conversation.

Florence had already settled her things into the suite upon her arrival. A small golden box was on the bed. She opened it up and found a collection of chocolates. Eagerly she tossed one in her mouth. It was unbearably delicious.

The shower was next. The bathroom was immense, with marble floors and walls, and antique polished golden faucets. She had never seen anything quite like it. The water was hot and it washed over her sore muscles forgivingly. Not so many hours ago she had been struggling for her life. But now it all seemed a dream.

She was enjoying herself so much she did not recognize the soft ringing beyond the sound of the falling water. But it kept on, and she suddenly realized it was the doorbell. A visitor!

She got out and toweled off quickly, one of the towels was large and bulky enough to wrap around her. She tucked it in over her breasts and headed out.

The visitor was patient – and still there.

"Open," she said to the house computer, with still a few steps to go.

The door slid open allowing Cruez to step in.

Her heart jumped a bit. She bit down on her lower lip.

"Oh, it's you."

"I ah, I'm sorry, did I come at a bad time?"

"It's fine. I thought I was not going to see you again?"

"I just wanted to report in. Let you know what I found out."

He looked a little haggard and sore himself. Definitely a bit tired. He still had that aloofness about him. He was still mad at her.

The bloody nerve.

"Why don't you sit down, relax, have something to eat."

"No, I'm not hungry."

"'Course not," she said sarcastically. She walked over to the desk, bent over and grabbed the voice modulator. Her towel loosened a bit. She tucked it back in and glanced back. He was sitting in the chair and eyeing her closely. Their eyes met, and he turned away.

She smiled.

"Here," she walked over and handed it to him. "It worked well."

"Of course it did." He was carrying that similar glare from before.

"What do you want of me?" She frowned. "What's your problem anyway?"

"You. You are my problem," he stated sternly.

"I don't get it." She turned away, heading to the bathroom. "I don't get you." She could feel it welling up inside her, the rejection, the self-pity. *Stop it.*

"You just don't get it. Let me spell it out for you then," he called after her. "You just sentenced at least a dozen people to their death – if not more."

"So, and how many have you killed?" she yelled back, already regretting her words as the last syllable died out. As she struggled to pull on her silken sleepwear, she heard the soft swish and click of a closing door.

He's gone. Why did she always go too far?

She returned to an empty room and gazed over an unruffled bed.

Maybe she was wrong. Maybe this was all wrong. But there was no way out now.

* * *

The morning came, marking the end of a troubled sleep. She dressed quickly and waited impatiently for her escort.

Cruez came to collect her, quiet and somber. "It's time," he said, his voice flat, emotionless. "Let's go."

She took the lead.

"You know where you're going?" he queried.

"HQ, of course."

They walked in silence, slipped into the elevator with an older woman wearing a black dress and hair of bright gray. Cruez stepped in behind her soundlessly.

The floors blipped by as the elevator headed down. It stopped on the 152nd floor, where the older woman stepped off, leaving only the two of them.

"Call it off."

She turned to face him. "I can't."

"Just walk away from this, you can you know."

"No, I can't. How can you ask that of me?"

"When you step over this line, you're no different than I am."

"And that is so bad?" She stared into his dark eyes. "Being like you?"

"Yeah, it is."

"And what of my duty, my obligation to Ishaida? I'm a soldier, too. I just don't have the training like you, nor the scars."

"Not yet." He visibly resigned from the debate, stepping back a bit, averting his gaze.

"Fine." She turned about sharply, anxious for the elevator to stop.

Tiberious's personal secretary was waiting for them when the doors opened. She guided them through the maze of hallways to the boardroom. Massive polished wooden doors swung open to a sea of concerned and very nervous faces. Other faces hovered in the air, suspended at the very center of the circular ring of the main table - the Soho-Beher executives along with its CEO, Jake Carrigan. Their holographic images crackled and jerked intermittently, but their faces indicated all too clearly their anger.

"Where's Tiberious?" demanded Carrigan. "This is outrageous!"

April systematically swept her gaze across all the executives in the boardroom. Most of them had a weary, tired look about them. Few if any, had slept at all in the past 24 hours.

She diverted her attention back to the Soho-Beher executives.

"I am taking Tiberious's place."

"You." He sneered. "A mere child. This must be a joke."

"No joke. I represent Anard-Bueller in these proceedings."

She glanced over to the Right-Hand, cueing him to speak. The sharp-faced man cleared his throat, bringing the attention of all on him.

"With her authorization, we will have your stock," he stated bluntly. "It will be done. We will own you."

That was all that needed to be said.

April gave it only a moment to sink in. Anger shifted to a quiet desperation. It was sinking in now. Soho-Beher was no more.

"Did you follow our agreement?" April asked, breaking the silence.

Soho-Beher's CEO replied softly. "Yes, for the most part, just my executive staff and their administrative support. Everyone else has been allowed the day off."

He kept the administrative staff there. Innocents are involved now.

She averted her gaze to Cruez, their eyes locked only for a moment, but it was enough.

His meaning all too clear: *Told you so.*

"I understand you have your own network of intelligence gathering, Mr. Carrigan," April stated, quite loudly for everyone to hear. "Tell me, what do you know of me?"

Carrigan sneered. "You are an ignorant girl, most likely the latest harlot of Tiberious's. He's lent you the reins to wreak havoc on my company, adding only to our insult."

"You call me ignorant, yet I've taken everything from you. And I did this because I could, just a game for me you see."

"You're simple Ishaidan filth. Perhaps Tiberious enjoys your favors, but he has a short attention span. You will soon join your station along with the rest of your rotting population. When that happens, I'll be glad to buy you a return ticket home, economy class, of course."

"You are too kind," replied April acidly. "Although things may not always be as they seem. Just out of curiosity, what do you know of this alleged accident on Ishaida?"

"What now? Are you implying I had anything to do with that accident? What evidence do you have to support such an accusation?"

"I've posed a question, not placed an accusation. Perhaps your conscience is exposing your guilt."

"My conscience leaves me with no issue. I acknowledge what happened to

Ishaida was truly a shame, considering the lives lost, but then again, accidents do happen."

Right-Hand cleared his throat, urging April to commence the merger. April ignored him, knowing full well the majority of the executive team were eager to push through the agenda as aggressively as possible.

"My executives are indicating their desire to get down to business."

"Excellent idea," Carrigan said boldly.

April turned her attention to the Right-Hand. "Discuss terms. Hold off on any and all stock procurement until I say." She proceeded to fade to the back of the room and watch.

No more than five minutes into the negotiations the signal from Soho-Beher was lost. The technicians scrambled in, making feverish attempts to regain the connection.

A long 20 minutes passed before the news reached the boardroom. Eyes turned to her in stolen glances, accusing eyes, but fearful as well.

She moved to the front of the table. "Cancel all pending stock procurement orders for Soho-Beher stock. Terminate any and all merger plans and contracts. The merger is effectively canceled."

The staff filed out silently, none dared to speak their thoughts, lest they endanger their own future.

April had made a bold move in the takeover but had stepped into the unthinkable with the destruction of the Soho-Beher's headquarters.

At that moment there was no doubt she was indeed Tiberious's successor.

* * *

"They think I'm a murderer." She fought to remain composed.

"You are," replied Cruez flatly.

His words stung. No, she didn't want to hear it, not yet anyway, not like that. It was much more complex than that, that truth much too oversimplified.

"They do not know the whole truth."

"And they will never know it."

"Are you enjoying this?" she tried to mask her anger, but it came out with a ragged edge.

"Why should I? Do I look like I am enjoying this? I told you not to do it."

"But I..."

"Had no choice, yeah, I know." His voice softened a bit. "You don't think I know what you're feeling? You can find comfort that it can be much, much, worse. This was antiseptic, not up close and personal. You didn't kill them with your bare hands. You didn't look into their eyes as they died."

She could tell his words were coming from somewhere beyond that methodical, disciplined mind. It was from experience. "My dad once said to me, no matter how bad it gets, there's always someone out there who has it worse. It's a hollow comfort, I know. So I do understand what you are saying, at least I think I do."

"No, you don't, at least not yet. The worse hasn't yet begun. If you have a conscience at all, you'll see. You've let the flame out of the box, and it will consume you. And when it happens, you will need to find peace within yourself, somehow. If you can't you'll self-destruct, take it from me."

She nodded, staring out the window, not bothering to answer.

He left then. The door clicked behind him, leaving her in a comforting peace.

"Dad, if you're out there, help me through this," she said in a shaky voice.

* * *

Tiberious helped himself to the glass, his arm shaking more than ever.

"How is she dealing with it?"

"As well as can be expected. She won't do anything stupid if that's your concern."

"Ah, to anticipate my concerns. Even I have difficulty with that."

Cruez shuffled uneasily. The Old Man had a way of putting you in your place if you spoke out of turn. One had to be careful with him.

"I don't expect to be around that much longer, Cruez."

"What do you mean? The docs aren't what they used to be?" he joked sarcastically.

Tiberious turned his gray eyes to him. They stared through him as much as at him.

"There are limits, and I've managed to exceed all of them. I have a virus – something my artificial immune responses are incapable of dealing with. It is affecting all my organs, my sight, my liver, my heart, my mind. I am dying, and there is nothing they can do about it. It is just a matter of time now."

"Is that why you chose her?"

He sipped on the clear water, careful not to drink too much lest he choke.

He was tired of being old.

"I chose her for many reasons. Most of all, she reminds me of my first wife. I so loved that woman. Even after all these centuries, I can still feel her, even now, in here." He covered his heart with his free hand. "She could be a reincarnation of her if one were to believe in that kind of thing."

"After all these centuries you still believe in that?"

"Cruez, you are so predictable, always wishing to glean a spark of wisdom from a decaying old man. There are some things that are left to opinion, his, hers, or your opinion, none based on fact or science. What I believe is irrelevant – at least about this. Feel free to make up your own mind."

He moved his wheelchair closer to the fire, grabbed the steel poker and pushed the logs closer.

"But then again, I have seen some things," he muttered under his breath, more to the fire than his companion.

It was harder to stay warm now like his very limbs had already died off and atrophied. He needed to stop thinking that way. It was utter bullshit.

"Can you bring her to me? It's time we had an exchanging of the minds, a passing on of knowledge."

"I'll get her."

"It will need to be tonight, I think."

Cruez disappeared like a shadow.

Tiberious jabbed at the logs again, exposing hot coals. The wood crackled and spat. New flames took hold and grew higher.

Tonight he would not be cold.

* * *

A knock on the door. The doorbell remained silent.

Could only be one person.

"Yes?" April fussed with her hair a bit more. She wanted to look her best. She needed to look her best.

"It's Cruez."

She could feel her heart jump but fought down the sudden apprehension. "And?"

"Well, can I come in?"

"One moment." She fought with the last bang, then smoothed the ruffles on her dress. "Come."

He stepped in and stopped in midstride, caught off guard, possibly by what she was wearing. "I, ah, you look very nice."

"Thank you," she smiled.

His stone face cracked a bit – almost to a smile.

"What do you want anyway?"

His smile vanished. "Tiberious needs to talk with you. It's serious."

"Ishaida?"

"Ishaida is fine, as far as I know. It's something else. Better if he explains."

"I've finished here anyway."

He escorted her out, drinking in every inch of her with his eyes. "I never knew."

She shot him a disapproving frown.

"Well, I knew."

They walked for a moment, neither uttering a word.

She stopped suddenly, pulled him close and kissed him passionately. After a long delicious moment, she pushed away. "I wore this for you."

Something in her voice made his blood boil.

She continued on, leaving him standing there. Ten steps and she turned. "Well, are you coming along, or not?"

They walked in on the Old Man as he was adjusting some holo-image projection above his desk.

"Hello, my dear," he said, not bothering to turn around. "I'll be just a moment."

He reached into a tree of colored shapes, extracted a green rectangle, then reinserted it into another location. The tree glowed yellow for a moment, then shifted back to multiple colors.

"The ultimate user interface into a virtual world," he commented.

"What is it?" she asked, genuinely curious.

"A program, of my own design."

"What does it do?"

"Ah, yes the question: What does it do, or possibly what does it not do?"

"There you go again, talking in riddles." She said with a smile, sliding down into a heavily cushioned chair.

"It does not work miracles, but it is a miracle in its own right, a truly incredible piece of technology."

"Well, when you are done admiring this thing, whatever it is, perhaps you could describe its function, in laymen's terms, of course."

"April, my dear, you are so inquisitive." He hit a button on the desk, and the image disappeared. "Tell me, you must also be insanely curious about certain other matters. Ask me a question, perhaps I can help."

She frowned, wondering what he was up to now. "OK, tell me why I'm here. Why did you pick me, of all these people?"

"Ah, a deeper question than one would expect. Excellent. But truly, I had anticipated a question more about this device," he responded gleefully.

"Well?" she crossed her arms, attempting to emphasize her impatience.

"Yes, of course...I picked you for some reasons. You are a very bright young lady for one. And if I must be brutally honest with you, you remind me of my first wife."

"Oh." Her features gave away a hint of surprise.

The Old Man smiled broadly. "Regardless of the reason, I chose you, you must wonder just how I expect you to run this monolithic machine we call Anard-Bueller."

"Well, to tell you the truth, I was wondering."

"That is where my little magic machine comes into play. It allows one to transfer one's memories to another."

"You have to be kidding." April couldn't believe what he was proposing. Did she really want this dusty old man's memories clogging up her brain?

"No, I am not. As a matter of fact, it is a requirement of the position. Consider it a gift from me to you."

She shifted a bit, suddenly finding the chair too soft. "So does this transfer pose any risks?"

"Only to your sanity, my dear." He chuckled dryly. "Minimally - it will affect you."

"How?"

"You will have my memories as well as yours. It may, at times, be difficult to differentiate. But only at times. You will know, upon reflection."

"I see." She re-crossed her legs, "I'm not sure."

What else could it do to her?

"I assure you, the benefits of this procedure will outweigh any possible negative side-effects."

"But how can I possibly cram all of your memories into my mind? You've been alive for centuries, Tiberious."

"Only the relevant ones, my dear. I have been downloading my memories for years, organizing them, refining them. They are edited for clarity."

"And if I refuse this procedure?"

"I'm sorry, my dear, but this is the only way I know how to ensure this corporation lives on."

"I see, so this is about the company."

"It's always about the company. This company is the lifeblood of this civilization. When Anard-Bueller has a bad fiscal year, economies of seven worlds are affected."

"Factoring Ishaida into the count is a bit of a stretch."

"Not if Ishaida does not receive her annual supplies." He pressed a button on his wrist. The facing wall literally descended revealing a panoramic view of the top of the city. The clouds hung dark in the sky, menacing in a way. Below, lights of all colors shone and blinked, reflecting strangely against the bottom of the clouds. Sharp glints of sheet lighting flashed intermittently, providing an eerie combination.

"It is like the rain. You see, everyone is affected."

"So what are your conditions, exactly?"

"You inherit everything, but you also, in turn, agree to manage Anard-Bueller to the best of your abilities."

"And what of Ishaida, my home?"

"What of it? I am not asking you to give up your lineage, only to assume mine."

"And what if I can't do this? What if I can't run this company?"

"Really? And with that demonstration today? What was that?" he sighed, "I know the timing may not be right."

"Look, I don't know anything about running a company, nothing. You want to pass on your memories, that's one thing but expecting me to run the largest company on this planet. I don't get it, really."

"I'm rarely wrong about people, April. I chose you, not the other way around."

"How can you be so sure? I'm not ready for this. I – I don't think I can handle it. What happens if I say no? What would you do?"

"I would send you back home. You will be free to live the remainder of your life on that desolate rock. You've already seen to ensuring Ishaida's longer-term safety with Soho-Beher decimated. You have seen to that. Ishaida's transformation will continue, with no more accidents."

April got up from the chair, looked over at Cruez, then at Tiberious.

"Then that's what I want. I want to go home."

The Old Man nodded slowly. "I see." He guided his wheelchair back toward the fire, now a mere pile of hot coals. He grabbed the poker and jabbed it into the coals, stirring up a tongue of flame. "That, I did not anticipate."

A familiar figure appeared behind them.

"Jones will see you out. Good night, April." He didn't look up.

"I'm sorry, Tiberious. I really am. I'm just not ready. Not now."

She turned away from the awkward silence and was relieved once she stepped out from the dark room.

Was she doing the right thing?

"Shall I escort you directly to the ship, Ms. McThurn?"

"Yes, I suppose so, Mr. Jones. Thank you."

The walk seemed to last forever. It had started raining outside. The skies had opened up, again. Mr. Jones had produced an umbrella from somewhere. He stayed close to her on the walk outside. Short gusts of wind pasted them with warm droplets, salty and bitter to the taste.

"Tell me, Mr. Jones, am I making a mistake, walking away from all of this?"

"I'm sorry, Ms. McThurn, but I do not know what you are referring to."

"I was offered a job, Mr. Jones, here, on Earth."

"And you do not feel it is right for you?"

"I don't think it is."

"Ms. McThurn, your life is a reflection of every decision you have made, every right choice, and every wrong."

"How do I know if I'm making the wrong one?"

He smiled at her, holding out a pale speckled hand to help her up the ramp. "I am a lowly servant, Ms. McThurn. I doubt my advice could be of little value to you."

"Don't sell yourself short, Mr. Jones. I wouldn't have asked if I didn't value your opinion."

He shook off the water from the umbrella, closing it with one smooth swing of his arm.

"I can stay with you, here, until Mr. Cruez arrives."

"Yes, that would be nice."

They sat together on the suiting bench, watching the rain pelt against the bottom of the ramp.

"Well?"

He rested his arms upon the end of the umbrella, balancing its tip upon the floor. "I always consider two sources in every decision: my head and my heart. When the answer from either is in contradiction, well that usually means the final decision will be the toughest. Is that your situation, Ms. McThurn?"

"Sort of, I guess."

"Where is your heart?"

"Ishaida, it's my home. I belong there, not here, under these strange skies." She looked longingly out into the stormy night.

"And what does your head tell you?"

"With the power and authority promised, I can easily protect my home from anything and anyone. At least I think I can. But I'm just not sure. I'm scared, I know that much."

"Fear is not a reason. It's a feeling. You need to weigh this decision with the facts, cut it down to the basics."

"I don't want to. I don't want to break it down."

He patted her leg. "Then you haven't really decided to make a decision."

He got up, carefully straightening a stiff leg.

"Where are you going?"

"It's time for me to leave, Ms. McThurn."

"Why? I thought you were going to stay with me."

"You don't need any company right now, Ms. McThurn. You need to find peace. I can't help you with that."

He hobbled down the ramp. "It was a pleasure meeting you, Ms. McThurn. I know you will do something great, one day."

"Why?" she yelled after him, but he had already disappeared into the darkness.

Something great. She hadn't done anything great. It had all gone wrong. It had all ended in death.

* * *

"She's carrying a burden. She's just overwhelmed. I'm sure she'll change her mind."

Tiberious ignored him.

"Are you alright?" Cruez stepped in closer to the Old Man.

"No Cruez, I'm not. Time is moving far too fast now. I've had centuries to arrange this, and I have failed in just the last of minutes. I do not like to fail."

He looked up, the soft light of the dying fire reflecting a tear-filled eye.

"Don't be so hard on yourself, Old Man. You still have time."

"Time has passed Cruez, with it my children's children. My legacy is more of things, and things rust and wear, they never truly last. Speak of Tiberious but nothing of lost ideals or protected morality, especially few are any fond memories from those who have known me."

"Did you expect all that from her?"

He shook his head. "Expectations? To what value do you weigh the expectations of a dying man?"

Cruez shook his head. "I have trouble enough understanding you, least of all when you speak in riddles."

"I close my eyes and see her. I turn a corner and smell that fading wisp of her perfume. To this day I am haunted by her."

"Who are you referring to - your wife?"

"Did I ever tell you how she died, Cruez?"

"Who died?"

"She did, undeservedly alone. I was late, held up in a meeting. She had left for the function without me, not knowing whether I'd attend or not. I was a damn fool back then, had little sense to understand what was really important."

"An accident?"

"She drove herself as she always insisted. Lost control in a downpour. The sky car was crushed beyond recognition. I can still remember the dresses strewn about on the bed, where she had rushed to get ready, that same perfume lingering in the hall. But for the life of me, I cannot remember what the meeting was about. I cannot remember why I wasn't there for her."

"I've made more than my share of mistakes. People, however, are the most painful. My great granddaughter was no different. You would think I would have learned by now."

"You're only human, Tiberious."

"What do you know of the human soul? There are things that are grander than the world we build around us. You certainly cannot see it with your eyes. There is but one way, through unshakeable faith."

"I had no idea you had such strong religious beliefs."

"Religion? After all these centuries, have you seen me package it up so neatly and label it as such? I've seen more than most men and still find this difficult at best."

Cruez shrugged, not knowing what to say.

Tiberious waved him away. "I shall not make another mistake with this one. She wants to go home. Then you shall take her."

"We can always force her to stay."

"And would you be truly comfortable with such an action?" The Old Man's sharp old eyes pierced into him.

"No, of course not," Cruez said, averting his gaze.

"I guarantee you, such measures would only drive her farther away. I'm sure that is not your desire. Besides, I have an alternate plan."

Cruez stood there silently, avoiding responding to the Old Man's obvious nudging.

"You have feelings for her, do you not?"

"Yes."

"Perhaps my heart is not the only one broken."

A long, uncomfortable silence ensued.

"Take her home."

* * *

Chapter 12

Ap200 pril watched Cruez run toward the ship, hunched over against the driving rain. He appeared in the lock thoroughly soaked despite his efforts.

April giggled. "You're all wet."

He looked at her strangely, a faraway look, almost like she wasn't there.

"Well, at least I'll keep this dress." She twirled teasingly, showing off her assets.

"Why did you do it?" he demanded.

She avoided looking back at him. Obviously, he had no time for her girlish playfulness, and she no longer had any lenience to be a girl anymore, at least not in his eyes. She stared out into the rain, ignoring his appraising regard.

"Just think about it Cruez. Just think for one bloody minute. I'm not ready."

"You have just been handed the world on a silver platter. Others would simply consider you insane for turning him down."

"No, I don't expect you to understand. I don't expect anyone to. You stand there and judge me, but you don't know me, who I am, or what I've been through. I don't need to answer to you!"

She swung around and marched up the corridor to her quarters, leaving Cruez standing alone, even more frustrated.

"Fine then, act like a damned child." He yelled after her. "It's obvious how old you really are!"

She shot him an obscene gesture before disappearing behind the hatch.

Damn that woman! He turned and hit the bulkhead, hard. The pain brought him back, helped him regain his composure. He shook his hand, noted the blood on his knuckles.

He had seen blood too many times. Not his own. Maybe she was carrying some of this familiar guilt now.

He made his way to the cockpit, ran the pre-staging sequence and set a channel up to the ESPD. It took only a moment to obtain clearance.

Someone signaled in just before they were going to jump. Cruez acknowledged, more out of curiosity then obligation. He didn't recognize the signal, and he could have easily ignored it.

"This is 762-mark-victor-able, acknowledging incoming."

The band locked into full video mode. "Hello, Cruez."

It was the unforgettable face of Bob Farelane.

"Bob, haven't seen you for a bit."

"It's good to see you. Last time we talked it was over that torrid affair on Ganymede."

"Now, I was absolved of all of that. Was merely corporate protection, nothing more." Cruez tried to maintain a friendly smile, but it was difficult. He had little liking for this man.

"Yes, far be it to think I could consider someone with your connections touchable. But that is not what I am contacting you about, this is in regard to something quite different."

"Yes? And what would that be?"

"There was an unfortunate matter on Cauputain a day ago. Truly a tragedy. Many lives lost."

"Yes, I've heard about the Soho-Beher incident. A shame."

"There are always so many questions when such things occur. Clearly, there are winners and losers."

"Get to the point, Farelane. I'm just about to jump, and my window is shrinking."

"I'm interested in your passenger."

"My passenger? Now I haven't registered another on this trip."

"Come now, Cruez. ESPD has resources at its disposal. Besides April McThurn is a bit of a celebrity."

"Oh yes, April. Must've forgotten. She is such a quiet girl, you know."

"My understanding, not so quiet. We had an interesting conversation not so long ago. It illuminates matters, introduces a broader perspective."

"Oh, you mean you've finally captured that rogue who tried to shoot us down. Good show. I was beginning to think the ESPD was totally incompetent."

"I am not interested in your opinion of the ESPD. And there are a few more facts that do not add up on this Cauputain accident."

"Funny, I've heard you have a solid case against that rogue Captain, don't you?"

"So you are implying he worked alone? No, someone was pulling his strings, we both know that."

"I find your insinuations feeble at best, Bob. Perhaps this is just more wishful thinking on your part. Tell me what gives you such creative license to stray from the facts?"

"I am only following where the facts lead me."

"We all know the ESPD has consistently manufactured the facts, twisted them around to fit into whatever scenario that has been hatched at the time."

"Now, Cruez, we don't fabricate. We discover. We interpret."

"Unless you have a writ from a Judge, I believe I've listened long enough to your interpretations."

"I've reviewed your flight plan. I understand you are headed to Ishaida."

"You know I literally just filed that. So, if you want to talk to me further, you know where I'll be." He signed off, cutting Farelane short.

Something caught the corner of his eye, in the shadows. He turned and saw her there. She had changed into pants and a shirt of heavy, durable material, more suitable to Ishaida's harsh conditions.

"How long have you been there?"

"Long enough. He suspects, doesn't he?"

"Of course he does – it's his job. Suspect everyone, find the motive, connect the dots, and you my dear, are their suspect number one."

He peered back into the darkness. It was hard to see her, even with the starlight trickling in through the cockpit's transparent ceramic ports.

"They'll have to take me by force. This is war. The fools down there just don't realize it."

"Oh, they realize it alright. You may also note that they are letting us go. See over there. He pointed to a small speck near the red dot of Jupiter. ESPD deep space launch center. We're passing right by it. They'd have a swarm of class one destroyers on us in a minute if they had anything concrete."

"Why don't they?"

"Things are not always what they seem. The ESPD is careful enough to move with subtlety. Implicating Tiberious in this comes with the allegation. They know enough to tread very carefully."

"They're all the same. Every last puppet government in the civilized world is nothing more than a servant to the Companies."

Cruez turned his attention back to the controls. "Come here, and sit. We're going to pull some G's soon."

She moved out of the shadows, and closer.

The mere smell of her caught his attention. He inspected her closely. Red-rimmed eyes, splotchy face, all hints of the turmoil she was feeling.

"You OK?"

She nodded, hair half-covering her face. "Yeah, I'm fine, just fine."

"Sit back and let the chair adjust to your contours. Pressure wraps will come around your abdomen, your neck and legs - let them."

"I know, been through it before." She took a deep breath, just in time for the ship to lurch ahead in a literal bone crushing acceleration. The chairs did their bit, kept them alive at least. But it was damned uncomfortable.

"Bring it on baby," Cruez grunted under mashed teeth.

The ship vibrated violently for a second, then smoothed out, five seconds passed.

April was already seeing bright circles sinking into a dark blue-black background, her peripheral vision gone. She could feel her insides being pushed into the chair, the blood being pulled to the back of her head.

Everything faded to blackness.

She awoke seconds later. The incredible pressure had stopped. The giant hand that reached down to crush her was gone. She couldn't see Cruez, as she had sunk too far down into her chair, and the side braces had risen out to lock her head into position.

"Cruez." She said weakly.

"Still here, my dear. Everything is A-OK so far."

"Definitely more comfortable in the green goo," she said with a scratchy voice, her throat extra dry.

"Cruez, are you going to stay with me?"

"Well, I'm not going anywhere if that's what you mean." He chuckled.

"No, I mean, when we reach Ishaida. Will you stay?"

She pushed herself up to look at him. He scanned the controls, actively avoiding her eyes, now suddenly very busy inspecting the ship's vitals.

"Cruez?"

"I can't. You know I can't. I have a job to do."

"You can stay. The Porters will welcome you in like family."

"Why? Why should I stay on that barren rock?"

"Because…"

He turned to her. "I don't know what you want from me. I have obligations. I can't just walk away from them. Why can't you understand that?"

"Don't talk to me about obligations. It's a choice. A choice you're not willing to make." Her voice cut into him acidly.

"What about your choice? You just walked out of there, after all of that, you just walked out on that old man like it was nothing. He needs you."

"I had to."

"Bullshit. You're running away. Tell me the truth at least."

"I'm not. It's not for me. You know it's not for me."

"What do I know?" he scoffed. "I'm just a bodyguard."

She yanked at the restraints and jumped out of the seat, irritated and hurt. "You don't understand me. You never will. Do me a favor – keep to yourself the rest of the trip. I'm going into stasis."

She marched out angrily.

He watched her slam the hatch shut and laughed.

She did have a temper. He liked that about her. He liked a lot of things about her. It is very tempting to walk away from everything, join her on Ishaida. Tempting but not practical. It didn't matter what he felt for her. Sometime in the future, he would have to walk away from her.

That was his job.

And she would surely hate him then.

* * *

"They want us to set down at NewLondon, our capital."

"Who are you talking to, anyway?" asked Cruez, openly annoyed at April's commandment of the channel.

The last few days, since they had exited their stasis pods, things had been getting worse and worse between them. Arguments had receded to long bouts of complete silence, leaving things unsaid to both their benefit. April could not help but feel smothered by his incessant questions.

"Why does it matter to you? You don't want anything more to do with me, anyway."

"That's not true," he argued weakly.

"Whatever you say. Just set down and I'll get off."

"I was planning to stay for a short time."

"Don't bother sticking around on my behalf. I'll be fine."

"Will you, now? Maybe I'm just interested in seeing how your homeworld is adjusting."

Alarms started to ring, accompanied by the sudden appearance of a holographic image. Cruez ran his hands over the console in a blur.

"We got incoming, five ships, G-class."

"It can't be Soho-Beher. Maybe it's the ESPD." She issued a notification to Ishaida. A reply came back quickly. She smiled and let out a breath. "Don't worry, they're friendly."

"What?" asked Cruez.

"They're friendly. Ishaida's new fleet of small gunships. A gift, apparently, from Tiberious, along with some security satellites."

"I see." He ran an orbital scan, saw the new signatures in orbit. "New eyes in the sky. No more surprise attacks - with any luck, no more. Looks like the Old Man has already forgiven you."

"Beginning our descent, now," he announced.

The ship began shaking violently. "Wow, we've got an active atmosphere. The TFPs are changing things."

The shaking settled down to intermittent shifts and shoves as the ship bounced within buffeting winds.

"We're lined up with the landing beacon, but there's no way to fly by sight through this mess."

"Let me know if you need help," April shot back dryly.

"I'm up to it."

They came in fast, Cruez wrestling the controls against crosswinds. The landing was sudden and jarring.

"Nice," April commented sullenly.

"Any landing that you come out of in one piece is a good landing."

She unstrapped her harness, trying not to smile.

"Time to go."

A small group was waiting for them. A few of the leaders of Ishaida, three women, and five men, all veterans of tragedy and experienced at the diversity of suffering. Of the eight, seven were Mayors, of them, two being Mayors-Elect from the destroyed cities Monsoona and AlphaRosetta, and the last of the leaders representing the 'elected' leader of the Porter community.

They met them at the airlock with drawn faces, solemn and quiet.

An older woman, hair drawn back into a gray bun, wrinkles under her eyes, was the first to speak.

"Very good to see you, Ms. April McThurn, Mr. Cruez Montigue, please give our regards to Mr. Bueller."

April thought she recognized her. An old friend of her dad's perhaps.

"I'm Annette Theron, I knew your parents, April. I remember when you were only this high," she held a speckled hand above the ground a little more than a half a meter.

April smiled. "Hello, Ms. Theron. I thought I recognized you."

Annette moved in and gave an extra-tight hug. "You were so small last time we met. And things, well things have not been so easy for you lately, have they?"

April dropped her eyes to the floor. A soft, wrinkled hand raised her chin up. "I know about the decisions you've had to make. I want you to know we were behind you. You were very brave."

The others nodded in agreement.

"Thank you," was all she could say.

"Please, we have an upper-level room ready for you for debriefing. You will have to excuse the crowded conditions, many of our lower levels have collapsed or have been flooded by recent geological shifts."

A couple large gentlemen grabbed her by her arms and started out the lock entrance, in the process pushing through a mass of humanity. Eyes turned to her in multitude, questioning eyes, yet they yielded to the bodyguards pressing.

"So many people now," April said quietly, speaking more her thoughts than to anyone.

"Many are here to see you," commented the bodyguard on her left.

"What do you mean?" She tripped over someone's foot, but he caught her. "Steady. We're almost there."

Doors slammed shut, blocking out the noise, the stares, and in turn, opened up to a bursting splendor of space. Her bodyguards faded back to the entrance, leaving her with the small group of Ishaidan leaders.

"Please, sit down," coaxed Annette. "We need to talk."

April was directed to a soft cushioned chair, at the center of the group. She was offered a liquor drink, which she would have normally turned down.

Not this time, however.

"We need you to go through what happened. All the evidence you were able to obtain, what you learned, actions you've taken, everything."

An older man with white hair handed her the drink. His scarred and hardened features left little room for doubt. He was Terrant Meg, Mayor of

GhenghisPrime. She accepted it with a crooked smile and gulped it down, feeling the burn all the way to her stomach.

"You want to hear all of it? I can try, but I may miss something..." She looked for Cruez, but he wasn't there. "What about..."

"Mr. Montigue, I'm sure, is very comfortable in his room."

"But he can help corroborate."

"Nonsense," Annette held up her hand. "We'd rather hear it from you."

"Yes, it's better if it came directly from you," interjected another. The man's voice was much softer, much kinder. It came from the Porter Ambassador, Kam Heathrow. He was a quiet-mannered man, with a large muscular frame and gray hair. His eyes were soft and non-judgmental.

"Ok. I'll try."

She proceeded to walk them through everything, that was, everything that she thought was relevant. After all, certain events she would never divulge.

The small group remained politely quiet until she had finished, then started in with their questions. She answered as much as she could, some not as successfully as others.

"What made you so sure it was Soho-Beher? You had predominantly circumstantial evidence."

The question came from Mayor Elias Talbot, from a long line of Talbots dating back to the original colonies. He was well respected, being Mayor of the Capital of NewLondon, and he was known to carry his authority wisely. His question hushed the room to silence. They were all waiting for her answer.

April licked her lips nervously, feeling like this was becoming more of an inquisition than a debriefing. *What were they thinking? It was obvious enough. She hadn't made a mistake. She hadn't been careless.*

"I had the evidence about Soho-Beher from Tiberious himself."

"Yes, you did state that. The folder of pictures, logs, miscellaneous evidence, all pointing to Soho-Beher's link to the hitman."

"That's right. I also had the reference from Captain Abakas – making a definitive link to the Corporation of Soho-Beher."

"You see, April, that's where I'm a bit fuzzy. Yes, the Captain did admit his guilt with that statement, but the link to Soho-Beher is still unclear and unproven."

"The evidence was compelling enough for me."

They glanced at one another. A few whispers emanated from behind her.

"It is a bold step, April. I'm not sure that all of us here would have taken such a leap of faith."

"Let us not forget it was Anard-Bueller that drove Ishaida into rubble!" interrupted Annette Theron, loudly. "For all we know, this was a long, drawn-out plot to bring down Soho-Beher."

The thought burned through her mind like a jolt of electricity. *Had she been played?*

"This never occurred to you April? You need to think through things, consider the big picture."

"Wait a minute. You can think what you want. I acted. I did what I thought was right. Why are you giving me this third degree? I thought you supported me!"

"We do, dear. We do support you."

But Annette Theron's words echoed flatly, leaving something evident in its wake.

Like hell they support her. This stinks.

"Things are not always so clear," stated a brawny dark-haired man in the corner. He was leaning against the wall casually, dressed in a loose-fitting suit, and shiny black shoes. The man's hair was perfectly trimmed, fingers manicured – too neat to be native Ishaidan.

"Who are you?"

Dark green eyes turned to her. "Now why does that matter, Ms. McThurn?"

He said it carefully, stressing each syllable unnaturally. It was a strange, freakish, unnatural accent.

"It matters because I asked."

"Now, April, I think you've provided us with enough information," interjected Annette Theron, who eased her way in between them, blocking off April's view of the stranger.

"We have a room reserved for you, for you to rest."

"I'm not tired. I'd like to get back to my family if you don't mind."

"Of course."

Elias Talbot cleared his throat. "I have a question for you, regarding the TFPs. Perhaps you could help me."

"Maybe..."

"We have something strange going on..."

"I don't believe this requires April's attention, Elias," interrupted Annette Theron.

"Why don't you just sit down, Annette, I don't recall asking for your opinion."

Annette's face turned red, she sat down quickly, letting a noisy breath out in the process.

"Now, April, as I said, something strange is going on with one of the Northern TFPs – Alvilla Valley to be exact. Seems it is behaving somewhat erratically, deviating from the standard program."

"And that is why I am here," announced the green-eyed stranger, stepping forward.

Elias looked over at him, his features clearly exposing his annoyance. "Yes, so I understand. You consider yourself an expert on these TFP systems, do you? We have not, however, seen you in action."

"I can assure you, Mr. Talbot, that I can and will find whatever is wrong with that particular TFP."

"What makes you think there is something wrong?" challenged April.

Eyes turned back to her.

She had their attention this time. *Discount her as some kid, will they?*

"I'm sorry, Ms. McThurn," laughed the stranger. "Did you not hear what was being said a few moments ago, surely?"

She hated that laugh. Fake and hollow, just like this character. A typical high-priced consultant.

"Yes, I did. The TFP control systems, as you should know, are adaptive systems. They react to feedback on the surface and from their dedicated satellites in the sky. This behavior may be completely normal."

Elias beamed.

The consultant merely slumped back up against the wall with a twisted grin. "And, what Ms. McThurn, would cause this reaction?" he asked, trying to keep the edge from his voice.

"I have no idea. I'd have to go there and check. I know the security protocols have been engaged because I triggered them. No getting through from the outside. No remote connectivity. No external influence. I believe we should leave it that way."

"I'm afraid we are a bit too late with that, April. We have already sent a transport to investigate," stated Elias. "Mr. Green's business associate is on board."

"I see."

"Would you also consider going?"

"Really, Elias. I believe you are overstepping your bounds here. You do not have the authority to..."

"Enough, Annette. I'm not sure about everyone else here but I believe April has demonstrated impressive judgment under incredibly difficult circumstances."

Support came with silent nods.

"It's decided then." He slapped his hand on his knee. "You can intercept the TriggerFix. It is on the Pacifica ice shelf currently headed to Alvilla Valley."

"We fly in, meet them there."

"We?"

"Cruez Montigue and I."

"Oh yes, the Anard-Bueller man. I was under the impression he was leaving."

April glanced around at the appraising faces. *It would not do to let them know how she felt about him.*

"Oh. Well, maybe he would entertain helping me out one last time," she said quietly.

"It would not hurt to ensure you are adequately protected. I think that is an excellent idea," Elias said, barely containing his smile.

"We'll bring him up." He clicked his fingers. One of the bodyguards disappeared behind a door.

"Are you up to this, April? I realize I may be asking a bit much of you after such a long trip. I assure you, I am certainly comfortable with you rescinding your offer."

"You said the transport was the TriggerFix?"

"Yes."

"Well, Captain Sequin and I are old friends. It will be good to see him."

Shuffling sounds came from behind the group. The door opened and a familiar face appeared. He did not seem any different than the last time they talked. He avoided her eyes with all too clear intent.

"Welcome, Mr. Montigue. I trust you are enjoying your stay," announced Elias.

"Yes. Excellent. You have been more than kind."

"We require some help. It involves Ms. McThurn, as well."

He didn't even turn to look at her.

"And what do you need?"

"A ride," April interjected. "Need you to drop me off at a Northern TFP, that's all."

Still, he refused to look at her.

"No problem. Can do that on my way back."

"You're heading back already?"

He turned to her. "Yes," he said, "have to." Gray eyes looked into hers. "Had a message. Need to get back asap."

"Tiberious?"

"Oh, he's alright. He's made of salt and leather."

"Good. Then I guess we better get moving."

"It was nice meeting all of you," Cruez said, nodding politely.

"We'll have the guards escort both of you back to your ship," Elias instructed. "April, please keep us informed of what you find."

"Of course, Mr. Talbot."

* * *

"Well now. Out of the frying pan, into the fire with you." Cruez clicked over the diagnostics overrides, his hands busy on the overhead console.

"And what do you mean by that?" April asked, irritated. She shifted uncomfortably in the co-pilot's chair.

"Nothing."

"Ok, I have a lock on the TriggerFix. At least 125 km out from the TFP, I would estimate. Judging by the atmospheric distortions around the TFP, I'm not setting down even close to there. Safest bet is a transfer to the transport."

"That's not the plan. We're to go directly to the TFP."

"Can't. Too rough. Judging by that storm, we'll be lucky to land close to the TriggerFix. You want me to go with you?"

"I thought you were in a hurry."

"I am."

"Sure. I wouldn't mind the company."

He scoffed. "Typical. Here we go."

The ship jerked as it rose off the tarmac. "We have some wicked cross-winds. Seems your bloody TFPs are stirring things up."

"Things will get worse before they get better."

They shot upwards at a dizzying rate. Cruez did a masterful job fighting through the turbulent winds.

"Proceeding north, my dear. I'll stay in the lower troposphere. Seems fairly calm in this strata. Up or down 500 meters and it all goes to hell. Weird."

"Atmospheric dynamics are not my specialty," April stated.

"Coming up on your transport. I think they've slowed a bit."

"I want to get them on the com," she said, a little too excitedly.

"TriggerFix, this is April McThurn."

"TriggerFix?"

"Strange. No answer. Loop around, Cruez."

"Holy shit, woman. I'm driving this bus in the eye of a hurricane. Give me a second."

They dipped a little too low, and the ship shook violently, but only for a moment.

"We should be right above them now."

"TriggerFix, can you respond?"

She waited for a crackle, anything, but nothing. The transport continued on, crawling along the ice shelf below, silent.

"Try HQ," Cruez suggested.

"We need to set down."

"What? It's a bloody white-out down there!"

"Something's wrong."

"And how do you suggest we get on board?"

"Fly up alongside, drop me on the roof. I know how to get in. I grew up on these machines."

He laughed. "Look, the winds are getting up to 160 kph. You'll be blown off in a second."

"Then set me down ahead of it. You have a grappling hook?"

"What are you going to do, hook onto it and let it drag you to your death? Those wheels make for excellent meat grinders."

"Pretty much. I'm going to lay down in front of it."

He laughed. "You're kidding, right?"

"No. Just get me down there. Hell, they might stop. Maybe their radio's out."

"And when they don't stop, you'll lie in front of it and let it run over you?"

"There's a lower service hatch on the tank for maintenance on the axles."

"You can get in from there?"

"Yeah, I'll just grapple on and pull myself up. Simple."

"And you mess up, a simple slip, and you're dead. No way."

"I'm going down there."

"No, you're not."

"Yes, I am. You don't have any say here. Not anymore. You're leaving remember? You don't have any say in what I do."

"You want down there, fine. We'll both go."

April was already unbuckling from her seat. "And the ship?"

"Autopilot. I'll have it ascend to orbit."

"Then we better be able to get on. We won't survive out there for long."

"Don't worry, I can always recall the ship."

"Then let's go."

It took a few minutes to suit up. Cruez pulled a grappler and a launcher from the storage bin.

"You sure you want to do this?" he asked.

April nodded. He lowered her helmet on and gave it a twist.

"This better work."

She descended the ramp into a white hurricane. Cruez followed up behind her.

"Get low. Wind is too strong." He yelled through the com.

Lights faded to darkness as the ship ascended leaving both of them alone.

April tried to gauge where the transport was, but it was difficult in a crawling position. The ship had set them down in the projected path, but it was possible the transport would drift. The massive metal machine was bearing down upon them, she knew, not from its obscured lights, but from the vibration through the ground.

"It's getting close. Need to make sure we're lined up in the middle," she said, her voice tinny over the helmet's radio.

"This is insane. This is the most insane plan of yours yet."

Its lights were almost on top of them now.

At least she could tell if they were lined up.

"A meter to the left. Quick!" she yelled. "And lie down!"

It came over them in a sudden rush of monstrous metal. Light switched to darkness. The vibration and the rumbling were overpowering.

April fought the sensation of panic, swallowing in deep breaths.

Keep calm. Keep your head.

"One more second I think," she said shakily.

The door came up and passed over them.

"That's it."

Cruez fired the launcher. It hit its target with remarkable precision. With a sudden jerk, they were both being dragged. Luckily, between the snow and their thick suits, they were not feeling every last rock.

"Retracting now."

They pulled ahead closing in on the opening.

"Fuck, this is dangerous. Grab that line above you and pull yourself up. I see rocks are coming."

She grabbed for the large steel line and caught it on the second try, then pulled herself up with all her strength, leaving her legs dangling.

"Lock your midsection up and get your legs off the ground."

She struggled but managed. It was incredibly difficult to hold on with one hand and lock yourself in with the other.

"Ok, got it."

"Get your legs up, dammit!"

She glanced ahead, seeing only shadows whizzing by beside her.

Rock outcroppings, less than a meter high could easily kill her. Adrenaline kicked in, and she threw her legs up enough to get them twisted up around the protruding line.

"Ok. I'm good," she yelled, out of breath but relieved.

"Ok. I'm going first. Hand over hand. Once I'm in, I'll pull on the line and you just wriggle down."

He started pulling himself ahead, quickly disappearing past her field of vision.

She stared up the rope, the line dangling into darkness, with snow pelting her helmet.

She had no choice but to hang there and wait. Her arms and legs were burning from the strain. He seemed to be taking forever.

"Ok. I'm in. Feeding in the rope. Just free up your harness and walk it down the line."

She moved like a pregnant spider, stopping to catch her breath only once. A faint light ahead revealed the open hatch. Cruez's arms were outstretched ready to grab her. She had to reach over now.

"Grab my hands."

His hands clasped onto hers like steel. In a moment, she was being hoisted up.

It was over.

Cruez pulled on the rope and rolled it into a tight circle. He slammed a fist on the hatch control, and it slid shut, locking the cold out.

"Let's not do that again, OK?"

Sweat was dripping down his temples, and he was breathing hard.

"Little tougher than anticipated," she acknowledged.

"So where to now? I want out of this tiny little crawl space."

"Up, of course. There is an airlock at the end of this maintenance shaft. Once there we can get these suits off."

"Good. Maybe we can find someone and find out what's happening."

April led the way, crawling effortlessly through the maze of small maintenance tubes. Cruez was on her heels, finding the space much too cramped, and banging his helmet on each and every cross-member. April laughed the first time. The second and third wasn't as funny.

"I'll go through first."

"Whoa. I should go first. How do you know who's at the other end?"

"You are too damned paranoid, Cruez. We are on a transport running along an ice shelf. Just what do you expect could be up there waiting for us? Besides, you couldn't pass by me even if you tried." She pulled the hatch shut behind her, leaving a few expletives behind.

A few moments later it was his turn. He was relieved to finally get out of the tight space and achieve some elbow room.

They twisted off their helmets and breathed in the stale air, tinged with oil and ozone.

"I never you knew you were claustrophobic," she teased him.

"I'm not. Just don't like tight spaces."

"I've already tried to contact the crew on the intercom. Nothing. Maybe the whole com system is down."

"Let's head to the control area, wherever that is."

"It's called the bridge, and it's that way." She pointed down the corridor.

"Would you mind if I went first?"

"No problem, Mr. Paranoid Delusion."

He gave her an annoyed glance and started down the corridor. Every once in a while, they would pass by an external porthole with a view outside to the frozen wasteland and howling winds.

"It's damn cold out there. Wouldn't last more than an hour without an enviro-suit."

"Yeah." April agreed, watching the twirling winds of white ice. "Nasty."

When they reached the bridge, they found it empty. Further down in the galley, the dinner table still held a spread of food, as if someone was about to return for a meal.

"Where is everyone? This is crazy." April said.

"Look – the com system."

What was left of it lay on the floor charred in black soot, melted and twisted into tentacles of misshapen globs.

Cruez pulled out a large barrelled blaster that he'd hidden within some crevice of his suit. "Only thing that can do that is a blaster, close range. This doesn't look good."

April fell behind him as they advanced through to the adjoining rooms. They continued to find more evidence of violence, including splattered blood across the walls. April could only hope it didn't belong to her friends.

The bridge was in disarray, chairs tilted over, their bases sliced into parts by some unknown force. Remains of monitors and instruments lay strewn across the decking and pieces crunched underfoot loudly. April checked the console. The autopilot was locked on, headed directly for the TFP. The scanners and the navigation controls were offline.

How long would this ice sheet last? It wouldn't be a straight run forever.

"We have to get this back online."

"Why?"

"Because we can't see where we're going, and we can't control where we're going," she said with annoyance.

"Well, get them online then."

She started into the maze of broken conduit and fiber, managing, in a few minutes, to bypass the console control and route to an intact secondary unit. A few more adjustments and she had the diagnostics online and engaged the autopilot.

"Whoever did this was in a hurry, was sloppy, thank God."

"The tank's reactor has been shut down – control panel's damaged enough that it wouldn't be safe to restart it. The secondary reactor is still up, but it looks like the main power conduits for the controls are disconnected. Hard breakers. I can't reroute from here."

"There's no way you can fix it?"

She bit down on her lip as she used the computer to scan through the mechanical archives. "Here. Yeah. We need to get to the reactor core where the main breaker relays are. It's in the tail-runner, though - the last car."

"Whoever did this is probably still on board. I believe the tank is secure, but I will need to inspect each of the other cars as I go. You stay here. I'll tell you when I'm done."

"No way. I'm coming with you."

"No, you're staying here. Somebody's gotta drive this thing."

"It's on autopilot. If it encounters something bad, it'll stop."

"Look, something happened here, something bad."

"And you know how to power this beast back up? There's a sequence you know. You can't just throw every breaker. I know these transports. I grew up on them, remember? Besides, what happens if you get back there and there's more damage? I highly doubt if I could talk you through a repair."

Cruez peered down the hallway and back, split between leaving her here and taking her with him.

Would she be safe if he left her here? What if he missed something?

"Do you think they're still on board?" she asked brazenly.

"They?" He grunted. "Could be more than one I guess. Not enough evidence either way."

She stared down his pensive features. "Well?"

"Ah, no I don't think so. Seems doubtful at this point. If they were still on board, this is where they should be. They would have commandeered the deck and retained control here."

"Then stop worrying about it. Let's go."

He reached out and stopped her as she went to exit. "Whoa. Me first. You stay behind. I don't know for sure."

They headed out, cautiously. The majority of the cars had switched over to backup power with minimal lighting. The first car had some blaster damage on the control console. A high power conduit was sparking against the bulkhead causing the lights to flicker. The hydraulic control systems were also offline, and the car was rocking back and forth erratically.

"Be careful. That power line is swinging." April said.

"And if it hits this metal railing?"

"We're probably dead."

They quickened their pace, watching the sparking cable warily. As he cracked open the hatch to the next car, April noticed a light draft.

"I think we have a breach."

"More firefight evidence. Have to hand it to them. They must've put up a fight."

"You don't know Ishbar. The Sequins are tough people. They're Porters through and through."

"How many more cars?"

"Ten, if I remember right. They must have been diverted from their run. The Captain was always first to step up when someone needed help."

"What do think they are hauling?"

"Anything from perishables to equipment, possibly some passengers."

"Really?"

The hatch squealed as he yanked it fully open. This car was completely devoid of any light. It was emanating cold and the air seemed very thin.

Cruez produced a small flashlight from his suit. "Never know when you need it. We'd better seal the hatch behind. No sense in letting the whole transport lose nice warm air."

"I would imagine we are getting close enough to the TFP that the outside pressure will probably be close to three-quarter atmosphere. Say, do you think a passenger could have done this?" asked April.

"Could be. Someone could have landed from above. Who knows? What about the cargo?"

"I couldn't check the manifest, but I highly doubt someone would do this for the cargo."

"Why? Isn't that what scrapies do?"

The question caught April off-guard. *Why did he say that?*

"No, and the nearest surface city is about 100 km to the east and probably buried under 10 meters of ice by now. Doubtful there are any scrapies out here."

The next hatch came up. Cruez opened it up, peered down the corridor. This one was much warmer and had battery lights. But no signs of anyone, again.

They pushed on through the cars, not finding anyone alive - or dead. Bulkhead walls revealed long black scars – evidence of sustained blaster fire.

"The tail-runner's next."

"If it's empty, we're in the clear."

"Yeah, except for all the cargo holds."

"What?" He yelled. "What did you say?"

April stepped back, startled at his sudden change. "The cargo holds. We didn't check any of them."

"Why didn't you say anything?"

"Why? This is a damned cargo hauler. It has holds. I thought you were only interested in getting to the tail-runner."

"Sonofabitch! Don't you realize we could have passed right by them?"

"Yeah, could have, I guess. But getting to the tail-runner is more important. If I don't get these primary navigation systems online we're going to eventually run off this shelf, and either down a crevice or straight into a meltwater lake. I have to get this thing back under control."

Cruez shot her an angry look and cranked the last hatch open. The tail-runner was a larger cavernous car, three decks high of open scaffolding with dimly lit emergency lighting. If anyone was in there, it would be very easy to hide in the shadows.

"Great. They could be anywhere in here. Stay close."

April glared back. "Just get going."

He moved in slowly, panning his light past the maze of mechanical and electrical systems.

"Damn!" April cursed.

"What?" Cruez asked, startled.

"Hydraulics leaking." She rushed past him. The leak was on the main line of the car stabilization system. If the reservoir were to run dry, some of the cars could collapse under their own weight.

Cruez shouted at her, but she ignored him. There was no one here, anyway. She had been so intent on the problem, she hadn't recognized how wrong she was.

They were there, five shapes moving through the dark like cats, swift and sure-footed, diving down from high up, jumping out from the shadows. They hit them from different directions, knocking the blaster from Cruez's hand in a blur. But Cruez was quick, a reflection of too many years of combat training. He had a brief moment to move, and he took it, grabbing and swinging a piece of broken railing down on one of them while he jumped ahead, knocking April to the floor in just enough time to miss a whizzing blade.

"Run!"

She looked up to see a black figure standing over her, swinging high a whip of some kind, a thin line glowing of gold. It slashed down at her. She rolled instinctively, just in time. It cut down through the deck plating with a hissing snap so close she could feel the heat from the deadly thread.

Snaggers. Charged lines vibrating at an atomic level. Able to cut through almost any alloy, even the toughest of hull plating. In close quarters, the perfect weapon, and the preferred choice for assassins.

Everything seemed to be moving in slow motion. She saw the coolant pressure relief valve at her feet, watched herself kick at it once, twice, saw it fracture. Somehow she rolled clear, under a maze of suspended pipes and lines.

A superheated needle-thin spray of fluid shot out and sliced through her attacker's legs. She knew he screamed, but in this car, it all seemed loud, a wall of noise was thundering in her ears in an unrelenting blast.

The man fell, and the spray shifted, pushing out through a widening wound in a pulsating stream of high pressure. He was dead before hitting the deck.

She looked for Cruez. He was high above on a suspended walkway. The others were swarming up around him, swinging between the pipes and decking with the skill of acrobats. The first man activated his snagger. The golden loop swung out, snapping through the railing where Cruez stood with a loud pop. Cruez anticipated the move, grabbing the rail and throwing himself high, kicking deftly. The man's head clipped back with a snap. He fell backward, slumping into a heap on the lower walk. But another shadow came up behind him, and a sharp golden glow flashed again.

April watched desperately. The noise in her ears was familiar. She realized she was screaming.

The snagger swept through the air, and through Cruez's arm. He toppled onto the decking, managing somehow to somersault over and kick the other square in the chest. The assassin flew back, twisting over the rail, but still managing to catch himself before falling off.

The last two assassins were wasting no more time moving in on the injured Cruez, their snaggers already in motion.

April watched helplessly from below with tear-filled eyes.

Cruez, battle-hardened and angry, had not given up. He jumped over the rail, landing on the lower floor with an unsteady roll.

He was close enough now that April could stare into his eyes, could see his pain.

"Get out!" he yelled hoarsely, desperately.

They came down around him. He reacted quickly, striking at the first. But flesh and bone were no match for the snaggers. It was over in seconds, the last strike fatal.

"No!" April cried.

They turned to her, and fear replaced grief. Her heart was pounding in her ears, counting down the remainder of her life.

She had to find safety.

The realization came to her in a cold surety. She had seconds, only seconds. They were moving in close, getting ready to strike. She rolled out and jumped toward the maintenance hatch.

The console was just to her right, as she expected. She slammed the hatch release with one hand and felt for the protected switch plate with the other. One final look behind her revealed they were still at least 10 steps away. They could have had her, but they were taking their time.

Without hesitation she pressed the switch and dived into the maintenance tube, managing to catch the hatch control with her foot on the way in. It slammed shut with a loud bang. She moved quickly, pulling herself up into the tube, to find herself alongside the battery packs, and in between a set of auto-deploy airbags strategically designed to secure the batteries in the event of an accident.

It was hard to see through the meager light, but the sudden frosting on the hatch door was apparent. The switch had worked. The upper maintenance doors had opened, letting in the cold Ishaidan air. It was doubtful her pursuers would survive the cold for very long. With any luck, their lungs would freeze and they'd drown in their own fluids. It would be a painful death if she was right.

She huddled closer against the warmth of the battery bank, feeling the cold start to seep in around her.

They deserved it. They deserved to die painfully. *Cruez was gone. Her sweet Cruez.*

She cried for a while, her tears dropping on pipes below, the moisture slowly turning to a film of ice.

There was no way out for her now. Not until mid-day, when it warmed up. She wasn't able to trip the control systems breakers. The ice shelf would not last. The batteries would wind down, and the navigation system would simply die. But the transport would keep going.

She would ride the TriggerFix until it topples over the edge and slips under the water. She would ride it to her death.

At least then, she would see her family.

* * *

Chapter 13

The newly formed Ishaidan defense team had watched April and Cruez board the TriggerFix. They had also attempted, numerous times, to raise Captain Sequin. Their boarding was predictable. The lengthened delay was not.

The TriggerFix had not stopped, nor had it modified its course. It was moving directly for a pressure crack. At its current rate of speed, the transport would reach it within two-and-a-half hours.

At this point, it was clear to everyone something was definitely wrong.

The team had been busy planning, but unfortunately, there was little they could do to control the unpredictable weather. The storm was moving closer, the tendrils of its outermost spiral arms were just beginning to sweep over the TriggerFix. Time was of the essence.

"Can we get on board in time?" asked Elias Talbot. He watched the image of the tiny dark line move slowly against the bright white of the ice field. He switched his gaze over to the young Captain. The man's face was pasty white against the dark room, a reflection of the image projected from the Ishaidan satellites far above.

"No, Sir, we can't."

"I thought so. And the TriggerFix?"

"The tank will surely be wrecked. The transport has considerable momentum."

He noticed the look in Elias's eyes. "But I expect there could be survivors."

"Of course," he patted the young man's shoulder. "Thank you," he said softly.

The young man turned to leave but stopped at the open door. "We will have a team ready to move in as soon as the weather breaks."

"But will it be soon enough?"

"I don't know, Sir."

Elias only nodded. He watched as the feeds from the multiple satellites cycled through every sector of the sphere he called home.

Ishaida was in turmoil: storms, quakes, volcanoes, heaving seas. She is at her worst now - at least, that's what they told him. It would only last two, maybe three years max, but some thought it was closer to two to three decades.

Regardless, all they have to do now is survive it.

But that was before the irregularities appeared. First, it was Alvilla Valley, now it was all of them.

This wasn't caused by some glitch in the programming of the TFP control systems. He had reviewed the archives of terra-forming thoroughly. This was something else.

* * *

It happened suddenly, brutally. April smashed against the opposite wall, knocking the wind from her lungs. The battery bank's mounting pins sheared off, and the three-tonne mass heaved toward her. Just as suddenly, everything rotated, twisted in the other direction and they were in freefall. The airbags deployed in an instant. It all stopped with a deafening crash. She crumpled against the battery bank, her head slammed against the hard metal with an audible crack.

Pain surged throughout her body. She fought for breath, twisting around. Thankfully she was caught in the crevice between the airbags. But then they fell again, only this time she could hear the car grinding against something as it descended, slowing it from an outright freefall. The car finally hit something solid and came to rest. She lay there, in absolute darkness, fighting to catch her breath, momentarily disoriented. As her senses returned, they brought with it the sharp throbbing pain where she had hit her head.

They had crashed, that much she was sure of, and they had fallen. But it didn't make sense, she should be facing the other way, the car should be pointed down, not up. What had happened?

She had to get out. That much she knew. She had to get out.

The bags had deflated enough that she could crawl up the maintenance tube, grabbing onto anything that would work for a hand or foothold. The pain had crept throughout her body now, every muscle, every joint screamed at her, her arms felt weak and shaky. When she reached the hatch she paused, taking time to open her suit and yank off her over shirt. She wrapped it around her head, keeping a slot for her eyes. She could have used her helmet, but that was lost. What she had done was not much for protection, but it would have to do.

With a shiver, she pushed on the door. It didn't budge. She fought for footing, jamming her left foot into a space between some pipes, and then heaved with every last bit of energy she had left. The door gave, swinging up, subsequently bathing her in a cloud of extreme cold. She could feel it burn into her nostrils and seep into her lungs.

With any luck, her suit would keep her from freezing to death. Minus 60 degrees maybe? Maybe colder. But it's still warmer than it should be. They had to be close to the TFP now. She could get through this if she could climb up, and get to the other car, back into the warmth.

She pushed herself to move from the tube and out into the unforgiving cold. A slight breeze was blowing through the open doors instantly numbing. From her position, she could see bluish-white walls of ice, and further down a dark expansive blue.

She breathed slowly, careful to draw in the air through her nose, not her mouth. Air, Ishaidan air, fresh and clear, slightly thin but still breathable, and very, very cold. Dangerously cold.

She checked her orientation. The TriggerFix had fallen into a crevice, but not all the way down, luckily not into the frigid lake below. Its cars dangled over the edge like a sleepy tail of some monstrous beast. Most of the transport had to be anchored onto the ice shelf or it would have slid all the way down by now. She could feel the cars swaying in the wind, hanging only by their coupling hitches.

That much she could feel. But not much else. Everything was growing numb. Her lungs ached. *Not much time.*

She struggled up, past the hydraulics array, and up to the second hatch, grabbing hold of everything that looked solid enough to hold her weight. The next hatch was wide open, its large metal door banging routinely against some other twisted wreckage. She would have to reach for it. There was nothing else to grab. She would have to time it just right.

She looked down. If she slipped, she'd probably fall – and break something. But in this cold, it would probably kill her outright.

Her hands were already numb. Her gloves were not thick enough to keep out the cold. Without her helmet, her suit's enviro-systems could not engage.

She had to be careful. The makeshift scarf that covered her face barely touched the cold metal, but she could feel the burn through the thin fabric. She shuddered.

I can do this.

She jumped, hands stretching for the hatch-wheel. She had it, but her grip was poor. Her hands started to slide.

Grab dammit! She commanded reluctant fingers.

Her feet were dangling in nothingness. She could see her fingers held, just could not actually feel them. She took a deep breath and pulled. A few more centimeters and her feet found a small ledge on the door.

Handhold after handhold she pulled, desperate fear fuelling tired, strained muscles. One last heave and then she was in.

It *seemed* warmer in the car. She lay for a moment, just enough to catch her breath. The swaying motion was slight but enough to make her feel dizzy. The hatch controls were poking into her back through the suit. She rolled over and noticed the panel lights were still on.

Enough power to close it? She entered the sequence. The motors whined, but nothing happened. It should have closed. The hydraulic system must be damaged. It was on only electrical now, whatever the batteries could supply.

She felt around near the hatch, found a large pipe from a walkway railing. By working it back and forth a few times, it broke off. She gave the door another attempt, this time aided with a little human muscle to pry it, and the hatch came up and locked with a click.

Warmth.

She took a moment to let her hands and fingers warm up, ignoring the pins and needles sensation, then started up the car. This one was not so bad, as it was at a more gradual angle. The other hatch opened easily.

Only eight more to go.

The cars soon leveled off, although they were still difficult to navigate through since they were now lying on their side. She passed over open cargo hold doors, still wary of a surviving assassin jumping out to kill her.

Why did they attack? Where did they come from? What had they done with the Sequins? Too many questions and not enough answers.

She knew where the survival gear was kept. She could probably find a replacement helmet, additional rations, battery packs for the suit control systems. That would not be hard.

But how far down had they fallen? She was sure the TriggerFix had some onboard J-bugs. The little rovers could get her to the TFP, but they couldn't fly, or climb up a cliff of sheer ice.

On the third car from the tank, the damage to the transport was becoming apparent. The car had literally buckled in multiple places, folding up upon itself. The cargo door was ripped off its hinges and cold air was streaming in, snaking through with leaders of ice and snow. April had to duck through the twisted hatch entranceway.

Streams of light were coming in from above - a thousand tiny holes, rips and tears letting in the Ishaidan sun. Ice crystals glinted by her feet. Snow had broken through from underneath. The TriggerFix had hit hard.

What was left of the tank?

She felt it through her feet first. Vibrations that quickly grew to a violent shaking. The whole car started moving, groaning in protest. It lasted only a few moments, enough time for the wreckage to find a new hold on its precarious balance. As it settled, it continued to creak and groan, like a dying beast searching out its final resting place, ultimately at the bottom of the lake.

There was a constant banging down below now, echoing up from one of the cars. Something broke loose, probably swinging in the wind. Regardless, she had to search the tank, find what she could and get back to the top of the ice shelf.

The entrance to the tank was full of snow. She tried a maintenance tube and found it inaccessible, then tried another. This smaller hatch door opened easily. She slithered in, carefully negotiating past some sharp edges, and pushed through the inner door and into a dark storage room. It took a moment to get her bearings. It was good she knew these transports so intimately. She didn't need light.

Starting down the corridor she wriggled through a tight spot, turning left then right, mentally compensating for the tank lying on its side. She had to twist around and kick at the next hatch to get it open.

The extra activity was making her head hurt all the worse. Every heartbeat pounded in her brain, each triggering a wave of pain.

She entered a small room. A single emergency light flickered under some fallen equipment, feeble yet sufficient. Suits, helmets, all types of gear were there, strewn about as it had fallen out of the multiple lockers in the room. With any luck, she would find everything she needed. She loaded a pack with what looked useful, a collapsible enviro-tent, a tiny portable heater unit, an ultra-thin, moisture regulating sleeping bag, and a helmet that matched her suit.

She didn't forget the food rations nor the water, carefully cramming extra packages into every pocket she could find, from helmet bins to her inner suit pockets. Realizing how hungry she was, she ripped open one of the packages and pulled out a yellowish strip.

Didn't look very good.

She took a bite and chewed hastily, ignoring the metallic taste. She was starving. It may not be good but at least it would settle her stomach and give her some energy.

Systematically, one by one, she opened each locker, searching for anything she could use, hoping for climbing gear. That type of equipment would have been used very little on a transport. She would have to do with any odds and ends she could find. Two shackles, one locking pin, a 100 meter length of thin – but very strong rope. It wasn't much, but it was enough.

She headed back out, carefully wiggling past sharpened ragged edges of torn metal, then guided her pack of gear just as carefully. She knew the rover bays were at the rear of the tank. The J-bugs would be perched on their noses, or flipped over on their roofs if their locking clamps had broken. She entered the bay and noticed snow had infiltrated the room, covering everything with a layer of loose, compact ice crystals. The door above was cracked open, possibly sprung from the force of the impact. She cleared the white fluff off the control console with a wide swipe of her arm. Small lights flickered through the wisps of remaining snow, revealing the good news.

It still had power at least. But did the doors work? She toggled the control. The upper door jerked, rattled, then moved. At least the hydraulics were still working. But it was too good to be true. No more than half-open and the door bound up on one side and stuck. *Damn it.*

She played with the control, jogging the door's hydraulic arms up, then down, then back up, then down again and again. Snow fell down hitting her square in the face. She tossed her head side to side and continued on, all but ignoring the light blanket of cold.

If she did get the door open, any remaining heat in here would flash out in a second. It would get real cold in a hurry. Reluctantly, she grabbed her helmet and twisted it on. One last little bit of jogging and something gave with a crack. The door swung up, and bright white light glared down at her. The helmet compensated, by automatically dimming and hampering the bright light from penetrating the shield. Details appeared out of the glaring white high above - a looming wall of jutting ice.

She navigated her way up to the edge of the open door, pushing off of the rear of a J-bug. She could see everything from here.

Below, at least a kilometer down, was the cold, dark water of an ice-melt lake. It spread out with glassy calm to the horizon. Approximately 500 meters up above them, was the top of the ice cliff, a jagged edge, a crack between two immense ice shelves. Spanning across the crack were a collection of ice bridges, each casting shadows down into the crevice. Some of the bridges were enormous, easily thick enough to hold the weight of a transport. If only they had managed to pass over one of them, instead...

Her eyes followed the remains of the transport, a massive metal snake with a tail that slung down over the edge of the ice shelf. The end cars were swinging in the breeze, emanating a host of noises with every movement. A lazy rattler.

She had been down there.

In time, eventually, the whole transport would slide off and fall once again, this time ending up in the cold dark waters.

It was clear she would have to go up. The ice cliff faced her with unforgiving height. How could she scale that thing without falling? She'd never make it. She wasn't a climber.

Maybe she should just give up. She would join her Cruez. She missed him already. He would have thought of something by now. She was sure of it.

The remote control for the ship - he had it on his arm!

She scanned her memory. She had inspected the tail-car on her way up. He was no longer there. No other bodies either. They must have all fallen out. The control armband had gone with him. *But there had to be another way.*

She scanned the tank and the adjoining cars. Something was there, just at the tip of her mind. Then it came to her. It had been staring her in the face - the anchoring guns. If she pulled apart a few, she would have at least 1,000 meters of the superfine tethering cable. A well-placed shot could launch the anchoring missile high enough to reach one of those bridges. No, better yet, up and over a bridge.

She could collect the end when it fell back down, tie it to... she could wrap it to the J-bug wheel! Use it to pull her up – make an elevator!

This could work.

She scrambled over the slippery hull, checking each gun by line-of-sight, collecting up the fine line from those that had no promise. With a little bit of patience, she found the particular gun that was at the right angle for the job. One shot could put an anchor over a large ice bridge above.

She pulled apart its control base, tied the necessary circuits together by brute force, then began the tedious work of linking the cables.

The sun's glare moved across the ice shelf, marking the passing of time, and in its wake, it morphed into shadows. Every once in a while, the transport upon which she sat would shake, and in the distance, thousands of tons of ice would fracture and fall into the waters below.

Soon all of this ice would be gone. All that would be left would be the lakes – actual freshwater oceans – and the pockmark trail of islands that span across the pole, remnants of dead volcanoes.

The TFP was safe, however. Alvilla Valley was more accurately a small plateau on the top of a mountain. It wasn't really a valley at all. She laughed out loud. It was an odd sound to her ears. How could she laugh at a time like this?

She yanked on the last wire. It was time.

Here goes nothing.

Leaning back as far as she could, she crossed the wires. The anchor shot out with a loud bang. She watched it fly up, turn to a dot in the glare of the sun. The ice bridge glinted above, casting a shadow against the cliff wall. It was now too high to see.

Finally, a glint, a spec, falling… She predicted where it would hit the cliff-side and glance off, and watched where it should come crashing down. It disappeared into the snow with barely a whisper. Its tether left behind, suspended from far above, a dark thread reaching up to the heavens.

It had worked.

She slid down the hull into the snow, quickly finding herself buried up to her hips. She pushed through it with all of her strength. It made her nervous, not knowing whether her next step would be into another crevice, and possibly her death. The loose snow could hide too much.

She finally reached the cable, overheated and out of breath. The first tug or two revealed how deep the metal projectile had buried itself. She wrenched at it, pulling with all of her strength. It refused to budge. Not giving up, she kicked her feet in for a better stance, bent her knees and heaved.

It moved, again and again. She heaved and pulled. The anchor came up slowly, sometimes catching temporarily. It was a relief when the metallic pointed wing-shaped anchor came up and glinted in the sunlight. But did she have enough slack?

The trip back was a bit easier, as she followed her own tracks through the hip-deep snow. She kept a firm grip on the line, being careful not to lose it. It took a few minutes to find a decent handhold on the TriggerFix's hull.

The cable drew taut. She jammed it into a handhold and struggled the rest of the way up the hull. Her plan was simple. Simple, dangerous and foolhardy. But she had no other way. She couldn't stay here.

She grabbed the rest of the loose coil of cable at the bottom of the launch base and headed back into the opened bay door. She wasted no time negotiating down along the rover.

The toolkits were usually kept in the bay. She found one half-open in the snow, its contents strewn out. But what she was looking for was there - a small portable laser torch. With the tool in hand, she climbed back up, braced her footing, and began to cut into the rover's rear tire. It made quick work of it, leaving an exposed rim. She jammed the cutter into a leg pocket. Such tools can be useful.

She edged back down and swung open the rover's hatch. It took some looking but she found it - the remote control for the rover. Whether it would have enough range was anybody's guess. She climbed back out, started back up to the opening, grabbed the coil and pulled it down. A minute later she had the cable neatly wrapped around the inside of the wheel hub.

She fingered the remote. The rover's wheels started to turn. The speed was set to a slow crawl, just enough so it systematically pulled in the slack and wrapped up and around the rim, just enough to draw the line tight.

OK, no better time than now. It was time to go.

She grabbed her sack, heaved it up to the opening, and pulled herself up alongside it. A quick glance up left her with a feeling of dread. Was she ready for this? It was a very long way up. If the cable broke and she fell...

A chill ran up her spine.

Stop it. Stop thinking that way or you'll die.

She stood up and hoisted the sack to her back, fastening it with clips. The new weight on her back was taxing the muscles in her legs. She stepped carefully, she did not want to slip.

The cable was there where she had jammed it into the handhold. She worked it out, moving it from side-to-side. The anchor disconnected with a pull of a pin. She looped the end through her suit harness and reconnected.

Luckily, it was a standard design practice to integrate a body harness on enviro-suits like hers. They were designed to be a working man's suit: many pockets, extra tough material, redundant systems, with an embedded harness for latching onto safety cables.

She took one last look at the remains of the TriggerFix before she pressed the button, and drew in a deep breath. *Whatever you do, don't look down.*

She pressed the remote's button and waited. With a rough tug, she started up, leaving the wreck of the TriggerFix below her dangling feet. She tried to gauge her speed of ascent. Too slow. A small adjustment with the remote and the distance between her and the wreck below started to grow noticeably.

God, don't let me fall. What happens if the rover quits halfway up? She'd be hanging there, stranded. Stop it! Stop thinking!

She bit down on her lip and looked out. From here she could see the lake reaching out to the horizon. Gigantic icebergs littered the placid water, but from her height, each seemed no more than tiny silver slivers.

The cable was rotating, with her on it, ever so slightly, back and forth. Each time she would turn to face the ice wall, then over to the opening of the crevice. She scrutinized the cliff-side. The ice was sheer gray, so smooth in some places it seemed polished.

I could never have climbed that.

Above, in a black shadow, was the ice bridge.

How long before she would get there? A quick check of her suit's chronometer, a rough gauge on the distance the cable traveled, and she had an approximate answer: 35 maybe 40 minutes max.

Intermittently, the line would slow, then jerk up. Each time April's heart missed a beat. The cable would surely be cutting through the ice bridge above, digging a furrow as it traveled. If the cable hit something hard and it bound up, she would be in trouble. The rover's clamps might hold it in place, but something would have to give, sooner or later.

No. No, I'll make it. I will. But when I get to the top, what then? She hadn't really thought it through. Would she have time to disconnect before getting pulled over the opposite edge? What would it be like on top? Hopefully, the ice was smooth or she could be cut up pretty bad. She'd find out soon enough.

As if on cue the side of the ice bridge came up like a dark shadow. In no more than a moment, she was being pulled up along its side. She hit hard enough to jar her bones.

She yelled in pain. It hurt like hell.

The cable kept pulling her up mercilessly. She struggled to keep from getting pulled onto her back. The side of the ice bridge stretched high above. She would bounce and grind against it, then swing away, only to plow into it again. A helpless puppet on a string.

Soon the line drew tight against the ice and started to slope up against her. Although she slid along it easily, she had to struggle with both hands to hold out the cable which by now had cut a deep furrow into the ice. Luckily, it was not long until the ice started to slope back and began to level out horizontally. The cable pulled her up and over onto the flat surface.

At the top. Time to disconnect.

She struggled at the loop connecting the line to her harness, but she couldn't gain enough slack to pull the pin. Her arms were too weak. She just didn't have the strength.

Panic was welling up within her, climbing to a numbing terror. A few minutes at most and she'd be pulled over the other edge. She kicked at the ice, trying to jump ahead, and yanked at the pin desperately. But it wasn't enough.

Then she remembered the laser-cutter in her leg pocket. Her hands were numb and stiff, making it hard to search through her pockets.

Damn it! Which one?

She craned her neck trying to see ahead but wasn't able to gauge where it was.

She wasn't going to make it!

Her hands moved frantically. She found it. A quick tug and it was out.

A flick of her thumb and it was activated. The cutter glowed in her hand. She swung it down onto the cable. Molten pieces fell off and burnt onto her suit, but she ignored it, working it back and forth through the tough alloy.

She could feel her head dropping down. The edge was coming up.

It gave with a sharp 'ping' and the cable shot away from her. It took her a moment to realize she had stopped sliding.

She was safe. Tears welled in her eyes. *She had made it.*

She lay there for a long time, listening as her heart slowed from pounding in her chest. A light mist that had formed on the inside of her visor began to clear. She sat up slowly and checked her surroundings. The top of the ice bridge was worn smooth from the wind, and only a few rounded outcroppings remained.

Snow-laden winds left little range for visibility. It didn't take long for the white flakes to build up on her visor, which she had to wipe constantly with her hand. She checked the sat-link signal on her armband. It was coming in strong up here.

With a gentle nudge of a finger, she had the navigation display up. Alvilla Valley was 73 km bearing Polar North. She peered into blurry whiteness, trying to see beyond. Somewhere out there the ice bridge merged back onto the main glacier. Once she reached it, she would have to adjust her course about 30 degrees to the right to point due North.

She struggled to her feet, fighting the wind and nausea brought on by a new pounding headache. When she got off this bridge she'd have to eat and drink, maybe that would settle this headache.

The snow tapered off slightly. Streamers of it traced across the ice, leaving alternating dark and light patches. April stepped cautiously. It wasn't slippery, amazingly. Maybe it was just too cold.

The weight of the pack on her back might be giving her the extra mass she needed, but it also managed to catch the wind. She started at a slow pace, near doubled over into the wind. She had to be careful with every step. It would be too easy to get turned around and walk off the edge. At least it should not be long and she would be off this damn bridge. She would breathe a little easier then.

The sun, a mere dim whitish glob in the white horizon, seemed to already be sinking away. Soon it would be dark.

No. No that's not right. There's no darkness here. Up so close to the poles, this was an everlasting dusk. It was getting dark for another reason.

Another storm was coming. A big one.

She watched the cliff edge come and go. She was on the main ice sheet.

Her headache was only a dull throb. *No use stopping now. Keep walking. As long as it remained clear enough.*

Hours passed. Her limbs were now aching, her arms mere lead weights at her side. She found an outcropping of ice which provided some shelter out of the wind. The snow had circled around it leaving a slight depression behind.

She pulled out the tent from her survival pack and depressed a small button on the side. A trickle of an electric charge crept along the tent's membrane, activating its skeleton's memory. The white and yellow dome self-erected in seconds. She moved fast making sure to pound stakes into the ice to anchor it down from the wind. Another moment and she was stepping into the airlock.

The tiny environmental control panel was a bit difficult to manage with gloved fingers. She adjusted the controls, engaged the power cells, and started the rebreathers and heaters. She waited patiently as the inside air pressurized and warmed.

It would be nice to finally get out of this suit.

A light came on indicating it was ready. She checked the outer seals one last time, then opened the inner. Fans whirred to compensate for displaced air. April stepped in quickly and then sealed the lock behind her. The tent lighting built into the seams was just bright enough to provide a comforting glow. She set the pack down with relief and thankfully twisted off her helmet. The air was fresh in the tent, though cold. She could see her breath. The damn heaters were too small.

After some careful rummaging through her pack, she dug out an extra heater, a sleeping bag, and a few rations of food. She stripped off her suit, feeling the cold chill on her skin. The heaters, although very efficient on power, were slow in this extreme.

She touched her head gingerly. Her hair was matted with dried blood, and the gash in her skull was raw and throbbing. *Should she sleep? She could have a concussion, possibly. But there was no way she could stay awake, not now.*

The medical kit – why hadn't she thought of that? She unzipped a pocket in the pack and pulled out the small case. It was well stocked with all kinds of gauzes, sprays, medical tools, and medicines. She squinted her eyes to read the fine print on each bottle. Her vision seemed blurry. *Was it exhaustion or concussion?*

She had to eat. She found the rations had not improved in taste since the last time she had eaten them. She chewed on them mechanically, staring at nothing, until they were gone entirely. The sleeping bag was warm and inviting, and her sore, tired muscles welcomed the rest. But she found her mind was not as exhausted. Instead, it ran through the previous day's events, looping through the scene of the last minutes of Cruez's life, and the group of assassins.

None of it made sense. None of it. Why? Why did they kill him? What did they do with the Sequins? Were they all dead as well?

She eventually fell into a long, troubled sleep.

* * *

"We have a signal."

"A survival habitat has been activated."

"Do you have a location?"

"Yes, but it's near the heart of the storm. Can't get a visual from the geo-sats."

"What are you waiting for? Deploy an S.A.R and pick up whoever it is."

"All of our available S.A.R units are at NewLondon, Sir. A flood surge has ripped into a section of the dome."

"Damn it! Is there anyone else?"

"Possibly, here." He placed a finger on a small dot on the wall-sized display. "An arterial road maintenance team. But they've also locked down for the night in anticipation of the storm."

"How much time before the front reaches them?"

"A few hours, no more."

"Do they have a ground unit they can deploy?"

"Contacting them now, Sir."

A snowy image appeared, accompanied by a fuzzy hissing and popping.

"I apologize for the signal, Sir – the storm."

A haggard, drawn face filled the screen. "What you want?"

"This is Councillor Elias Talbot..."

"I know who you are," grunted the other man. "And I'm Jed MacErod, lead-hand. Now that we've met, what d'ya want?"

Elias smiled politely, although he would have rather reached into the display and pummelled the rude stranger. "We have a transport that has crashed in the Northern Hemisphere, near Alvilla Valley. They need your help."

"No can do, there, Councillor. They'll have to fare for themselves until this storm passes."

"You have time. You can deploy a rover, I'm sure."

"Nope. Winds are already getting up out here. I have a crane left to lock down. Can't afford any more time, nor any men right now."

"But the people on that transport!"

"Cannot be saved by rescuers who will need rescuing themselves. We wait, Elias. We have to. Check your readings."

Of course, he was right. The geo-sat feeds were revealing angry red cyclonic patterns throughout the entire area.

"We gotta lock down. As soon as it's safe, we'll git over there. Send me the info."

Elias nodded at the young officer at his side, who proceeded to enter some commands into the console.

"Relaying now, Sir," he said with efficient confidence.

"Got it. OK. Will proceed to this area as soon as we can. Over."

"My appreciation, Mr. MacErod."

The man only nodded, grunted out something and broke the link, the image suddenly died to black.

"They'll have to hold on until then," Elias said solemnly.

* * *

To Fade Away

Chapter 14

Apre pril woke to sounds of screaming winds and fabric walls folding in upon her. She pushed out at the material and could feel the wind, strong as iron, racing over her palms. The cold permeated through the thin material with enough energy to burn at her exposed skin.

She rolled over slowly, carefully, attempting to reach her suit. It was possible under such extreme conditions the tent could rip, and if that occurred, it would simply be torn to pieces within seconds. She needed to move quickly, time, she had learned long ago, had little forgiveness. To say it was difficult to wiggle into the suit with the tent smothering her every move would have been understating her effort. But she managed it. Inside it was warmer, and more importantly, safe.

She pulled on the helmet and ran the diagnostics: air reclamation tanks at 100% percent, rebreathers online, suit power already fully restored. She had not forgotten to stuff the chem-bladders with her ration wrappers. The tidbits of matter once dissolved in the bladders would power up the suit's systems for at least another 48 hours. The status display, multicolored and bright, reflected back at her from the faceplate.

She checked health stats. Her heart rate was elevated but within normal range. Core temp was fine. Everything fine but one very important item: communications. Signal strength at zero. Nothing getting through this. Nothing at all.

Now what?

She glanced over at the airlock, as with the rest of the tent, it was bent over, collapsed and useless. No way she could get out now – not until the wind died down, or the tent ripped open.

Getting out and trying to walk in this wind would be suicide anyway.

She was safe here. Nothing to do but wait. The winds, muffled by the suit to low reverberations provided a hypnotic background. Sleep returned easily.

The quiet was the first thing she noticed after she woke the second time. She checked the stat display - five hours had passed. Amazingly, her tent had almost resumed its normal form, somehow it had managed to withstand the storm's incessant raging. A look out the small, flexible window revealed only white, and her spirits dropped.

At least two more days of trudging through this snow, possibly as many as four. Would she make it?

She fought the sudden urge to cry, as the feeling of loneliness crept into the corners of her mind and twisted around it like a snake.

She took a deep breath.

If she had taken that job, she wouldn't be here now and most importantly, Cruez would still be alive.

Gloved hands worked clumsily as she entered the armband sequence to activate the cranium interface. An image appeared inside her visor – a vector to the valley, approach degrees and total distance in kilometers. But this wasn't coming from the satellite above – not now. This was calculated by her suit's computers, using Ishaida's weak magnetic pole as a guide. No, the signal to the satellite was only marginally better than last time. The storm was still churning above her, up in the higher levels of the atmosphere, a mass of swirling vapor and dust.

It was the TFPs causing this, of course, pushing the gases so high upwards, almost to the upper ceiling of the troposphere. The continuous streams above each plant, accelerated by temperature and electrical charge rose so fast they created low pressure at the surface, but then subsequently cooled and dissipated at the higher levels, churning back over and over, spiraling down once again. The planet's natural spin then took over, causing the whole turning mass of gas to revolve even more as it settled, increasing in energy as it sank, breeding continuous storms of tremendous strength and duration. They would cycle down in energy over time, eventually diminishing into buffeting winds as the pressures equalized. But this peaceful interval would only be temporary, and it would start once again. She had some time, hours probably, but no more than a day.

The closer she moved to the TFP the less chance she would have of raising anyone on her suit's com-link. But she was sure she would be able to use the tight beam sat-link at the plant. The system was designed to cut through this murky soup with ease. She could piggyback from the TFP satellite onto the primary communications geo-sat and then connect to the Porter network. It would be easy. All she had to do was get there.

After double checking the outside pressure and temperature inside the tent, she unscrewed her helmet, gulped down her rations and water, and started packing. A few minutes and she was outside, collapsing her tent in a swirling white of ice-laden wind. It crackled against her helmet like a thousand tiny insects had set upon her.

Her heads-up display would keep her course true. All she had to do was walk. Walk and keep an eye ahead. She walked without thought until her legs were merely mechanical extensions burdened with leaden feet. But she didn't stop. She had to keep going. Maybe it was the 15th hour, maybe the 20th. It didn't matter, she had lost count now.

And *IT* had decided to join her then. *IT* was a shape, dark and undefined, just outside of her suit's lights, traveling alongside her, matching her pace. Sometimes it was on her left, sometimes on her right. *IT* would call to her, shrieking at her, then fade away as soon as she turned, lost in the swirling white. *IT* would always remain just out of visual range, hidden in a blanket of dark dancing snow.

For a time, the fear of *IT* drove her heart into her throat, forced her tired legs to step quicker, infected her body with a fading adrenaline. But that was only for a time, as her strength eventually waned under the sustained stress, leaving limbs shaking and frail. She didn't care anymore, let *IT* come. Let *IT* tear her apart.

But *IT* never did come closer. Eventually, even *IT* left her to face the barren white alone.

She would fall now and then, trip on something unseen and topple onto the coarse ice. And each time it became more difficult to rise up, to start putting one foot ahead of the other. She was a robot, a mechanical being, obsessed with a single focus, to follow the destination on her helmet display.

Exhaustion would not stop her, but her last fall did. It was her knee hitting the outcrop of ice that stopped her. As the pain fired through her knee and set a cold fire that burned through her nerves, she could only sit on the ice and rock her leg in agony. The tears came this time. *I can't do this anymore. I'll never make it.*

Ultimately the pain lessened, allowing her some form of motion. It was perhaps good that she couldn't see the damage through the suit, but she could feel it bleeding, and dared not touch it directly.

Streamers of snow wrapped over her and deposited around her where she sat. Above the skies darkened, pushing out the last of the stars and bathing the area in a murky darkness her helmet light seemed feeble to cut through.

The storm was coming back down. In a few minutes, it would be upon her again.

The realization shot through her body like an electric shock, bouncing through her internals, and racing along her compromised limbs. It provided one final surge of adrenaline fueled by fear. She had to find cover, or a low area, something close. She caught a shadow of something out there in the white murk, no more than 50 meters away. In a quick, desperate trot, she hopped as fast as she could. The dark shape revealed itself as a large ice mound, its leeward side already full of light drifting snow. She dived in, pulling her body out of the growing deadly current, and into safety. Huddling her body into a fetal position, and shaking with fear and exhaustion, she could only watch the icy laden wind start to surge around her. Under her suit's light, the ice and snow pallets danced in a mesmerizing conjoining, flowing around and away. A low moan slowly morphed into a high-pitched shriek and the winds blurred into a deadly wall of death. But the mound of ice and rock held, and she had more than ample room to set up camp behind it, in relative safety.

She checked her chronometer. It had been 18 hours since she had started. She somehow gathered the strength to wrestle out the tent, once again. She erected it quickly, only to crawl within and collapse. She didn't even bother to take off her suit. It was easier to let the darkness take her.

* * *

The shrieking was louder, pulling her from a dream of a colorful, warm night and lively music of a Porter dance. She was just about to ask Jerod MacCallum to join her...

She flew upwards, then around and around. The sudden motion was nauseating, and she fought to keep from vomiting, simultaneously trying to get her bearings. The tent was turning with her, dizzyingly, with each turn she crashed down upon the hard ground with a sickening thud.

No! She hadn't tied down!

Something caught near the airlock, and the tent disintegrated into a maelstrom of shards of material, snow, and ice. Parts of it sailed off into the white, disappearing from view. A savage tug threw her over onto the hardened ice, her visor hitting so hard it cracked with an unmistakable click. She lay there and watched as the remaining fragments of tent danced away into the darkness, disappearing along with her backpack.

Gone. It was all gone.

But that wasn't the worst. She was in serious trouble now. She had to stay low, for as long as she hugged the ground the furious wind wouldn't be able to get underneath and lift her.

If it did get hold of her... No. Stop it. It's not getting hold of me. I'm not moving. I'm safe.

So she lay prone daring not to move and watched as the snow built up against her visor. The hours passed slowly, with each minute seeming to last forever. The snow drifted over her completely, leaving her in a cold, dark comfort, encrusting her in a tomb of ice. *She would survive this.*

Hours passed before the storm finally receded. When April could no longer hear the throbbing thunder emanating from the ground into her helmet, she pushed herself up and broke through the sarcophagus of ice and snow. Bright light made her squint as morning skies bathed her in alternating layers of yellow and red sunlight.

She turned her attention above and could see the dark layers where the winds still raged and cast mutating shadows on the horizon. The beast was still alive, swirling and screaming in an angry dance, twisted and misshapen, dispersing brief patches that would allow streams of sunlight to hit the surface. The storm was caught again in the upper atmosphere, a wild animal trapped in a cage, driven mad to escape. And it would. She knew it would. This was only another reprieve, another opportunity.

Getting to her feet she found her leg muscles taught and sore, and her knee throbbing in pain. Too little sleep with not enough time to recover. To top it off the loss of her pack meant her rations were down to what remained crammed within the multiple pockets of her suit, that is, what was accessible.

It was clear now that it was not just Ishaida against her now. It was time.

She checked her armband, verified her bearings and started walking, this time with a pronounced limp. She had at least another two days of traveling, possibly one more depending on the terrain and the weather.

Fear settled deep in her gut. It was a known fear, but she dared not think it, dared not give it form. But it was there, and it drove her to walk more quickly, to reach what lay beyond the horizon.

The day passed quickly. Her feet ached with every step, and her shoulders had developed sharp pains from carrying the weight of the suit. Those aches paled to her knee which now burned in a bath of fire. But she pushed on, attempting to keep up her pace, watching the skies warily. The storms swirled and danced in a range of hues, dark grays to ominous browns, twisting layers upon layers. As long as they remain elevated, she had a chance. She would walk as long as she could.

She activated the satellite com-link and watched the heads-up display. Intermittently the signal would peak enough to establish a link, but then it would drop just as quickly. She'd stop and toggle the uplink, but it would only repeat the same pattern.

By now, hunger and thirst had replaced her aches and pains. Her suit readings indicated the water reservoir was less than a half-liter. She sipped on the tube, enough to quench her parched mouth.

Her suit was capable of H_2O reclamation, from sweat and urine, but the idea always turned her off. She had only to turn on the subsystems through her HUD controls. She wondered how Ishaida snow would taste. She'd have to pack it in through the external fill neck, it had to be better than the alternative. The suit's heat would melt it easily enough.

She'd have to stay hungry. There was no way she'd risk taking off her helmet in this cold to eat the last remaining rations she had pocketed. Her suit had the ability to provide ration pellets, but that reservoir was empty, and she hadn't found any supplies in the TriggerFix to charge it.

The horizon was dropping again. The sky was filling up with a fog of white sleet. April peered out into the snow, searching once again for anything to guard her against the high winds that she knew would be coming. The winds were already picking up speed, and she leaned into them as she moved.

Not yet. She still had time.

Hidden within the moaning winds something announced itself with a hollow, foreboding shriek, a familiar hallucination to haunt her while she walked. This time, however, the darkness had a shape, a form. Although still quite far away, it seemed to be moving closer. She hurried her pace, pushing herself as much as possible on her damaged leg.

Whatever this is, imagined or real, she wasn't sticking around to find out. Fighting the ever-strengthening winds was taking its toll. Her right calf had developed a muscle-spasm that burned with a constant pain. Her once hurried pace had now decreased to a slow, methodical walk, driven by sheer will.

At least she was getting closer to the TFP. The terrain was changing, as once smooth fields of ice gave way to sharp ridges and hard granules which poked up into the soles of her suit's boots, and bit sharply into her feet. Around her, a forest of pinnacles spiraled up into razor sharp points, churned and worn by the winds. None of which would provide the necessary cover from the storm.

April pulled up the most recent sat-map images of the area. All this was new, recently formed remnants of some form of glacial erosion. Probably the result of high-speed melting initiated from the heat radiation emanating from the TFP satellites, and the driving surface winds.

There must be an edge to this ice shelf somewhere ahead, and then another ice sheet, and possibly in between the two either a chasm or a massive pressure ridge. Her conclusions were verified by the consistent vibrations she could feel through her boots – like so many tiny earthquakes.

She discovered an ice-covered boulder that was large enough to provide cover and thankfully sunk down behind it. She closed her eyes for a moment. What she would give to be in her own cabin on the SeaClear. So many nights she had spent curled up in her cot, wrapped up in a book or scaling through some tech-manual she had found on the Porter net, letting the drone of the great machine lull her to sleep.

It seemed to be only yesterday. Vivid memories streamed through her conscience, playing chess with her brother Jim, or battling Ty on some Automated-Response-Controlled-Holographic Imaging (Archi) game. He had always managed to beat her on the last level – every time.

Something crashed near her, jarring her back to reality. Another thud. Through alternating gusts of light and heavy snow, she saw a dark silhouette push through the pinnacles toward her.

She sat there for a few seconds, more surprised than anything. In that brief time of hesitation, the thing, whatever it was, halved the distance between them.

She got up shakily, heart pounding. Alarms were sounding within her suit, but she ignored them. Their useless notifications that her heart and breathing rate were elevated served little purpose right now. The wind was growing in strength now. Moving back out into the wind would be suicide.

The dark shape was not slowing.

Nowhere to go. Run damn it!

She started hobbling out into the wind. In the brief moment of rest, her right leg muscles had tightened up so stiffly that they had little movement left. She swung her leg out like so much dead weight and clenched her teeth each time she bore her weight upon it.

IT was just behind her now. She could feel *IT* looming above her. *She knew she couldn't outrun IT.*

A bright light lit up the ground around her. Forming her shadow, tall and wavering, before her.

Light?

Realization came as she turned: A pattern of floodlights set at a distance from the ground that seemed all too familiar.

A transport. A transport had found her!

She waved at it with both arms held high, hoping that whoever was at the controls would see her. As if on cue, the gigantic machine slowed to a stop, no more than 20 meters away from her.

April moved in close, favoring her sore leg. The front hatch had already been lowered for her, invitingly. She hobbled under the belly of the massive vehicle, and out of the harsh wind, to look up. She found what she was looking for. It was only partially readable, obscured, scarred, and blackened where it was once shone as detailed polished brass. She couldn't help but notice the gashes that traced along the transport's belly, nor the blackened flakes of aged oxidation that hung loosely off the plating.

Strange. It's unusual for a Porter Captain to have his transport is such disrepair.

At the hatch, the lighting on the ramp was dim at best. A glance upward revealed only darkness.

Spooky.

She stepped gingerly up the ramp, bearing most of her weight on her good leg. She found the entry bay dark, with tools strewn about the floor haphazardly. A suit lay in the corner, crumpled up, helmet screwed on tight.

What the hell is going on?

Something was not right here, that much was clear. But it was either take her chances here or out there in the storm. No, she would choose a transport easily over that barren wasteland. She had to get to the deck. That's where the answers would be.

Without hesitation, she hit the switch and watched as the hatch slide across the ramp opening. Dust kicked up as the room pressurized. She started up the maintenance ladder, pulling herself up with fading strength, biting on her lip to counter the pain. At this point, she had only one good leg and had to use her upper body strength to pull herself up.

At the second level she stared down a darkened corridor, her helmet light shifted in the shadows. Looking down at the floor, she could plainly see the imprint of her boots through a fine layer of dust where she stepped. One set of prints, and no one else's. No one had been through here for a very long time.

It was all she could do to suppress the fear balling up inside her gut. The sound of her own breathing seemed unmistakably clear right now.

The hatch to the control deck was closed. With a quick pull of the lever, it swung open. But she wasn't prepared for the scene before her. The air rushed out of her lungs, her legs gave out, forcing her to crumple to the floor. It took a few minutes for her to gather herself, for her heart rate to slow.

What lay before her were corpses, mummified remains. Each one perched at its station, as if attentively manning the controls of the mechanical monster. The monitors danced with color, hues reflecting grotesquely off the blackened dried bodies.

She scanned the readouts with an assessing eye. It took her only a moment to drink in the information. The transport was alive alright, with all systems online. Some warning alarms were blinking, revealing minor hull damage on the tank and some of the trailing cars.

The tiny fusion reactors were fired up and generating within spec.

She fought back a momentary sensation of dizziness. To her left, mid-room, was the identi-plate for the transport. She focused on that small brass plate, reached and wiped away a layer of dust.

"LightningRod," she read out loud. Her own voice made her jump. She turned around suddenly, simultaneously raising the suit's external microphones to maximum power.

"Anybody here?"

Her voice just echoed hollowly in her helmet.

No one. Just corpses.

The LightningRod - and she had thought it was only a legend. She was standing on the deck of one of the first, and the oldest, transports. It had been lost centuries ago, and since then had been the source of many stories designed to scare young Porters who wouldn't settle down for their night's sleep-shift.

The LightningRod had disappeared in a storm during the first terra-forming stage. No debris, no sign of it was ever found. Her crew were mostly first-timers, little experience with what Ishaida could produce, and eager to prove something. It was said that her Captain was on his first run. This was back when the transports were not run by families but by military, and as such crews were highly volatile and prone to altercations.

April had very few actual facts about the transport, save the stories, and she suspected they were just stories. It was said that the whole crew had gone mad and ended up killing themselves. Again, embellished lore conjecture and no fact. Sure, it was unusual for an entire transport to disappear, but Ishaida was a big, dangerous world.

These corpses weren't driving this thing. Someone or something else was.

Not all the bodies were at their stations. The Captain's chair was empty, although it too was covered in the fine dust. She reached over and pressed the intercom. "Is anyone alive in here?"

A very long minute passed, filled with the white noise of fine static and flowing shadows. She reached over the corpse beside her, ignoring his features, and systematically engaged the hydraulics to slam the hatches shut throughout the transport. The metallic thuds echoed eerily from within the darkened corridors. She reached over and pressed the deck hatch control. It swung shut with a loud thud, locking pins sliding into place with a pronounced click. *Nothing would be getting in here to get her. Only the corpses to keep her company now.*

The thuds of the last closing doors were muffled behind the reinforced bulkheads of the main deck. It took a full minute before it ended, and silence once again prevailed.

Despite her tired body and her exhausted mind, her heart was still pumping vigorously, and her hands felt clammy within the suit's gloves. This was beyond creepy, it felt like every hair on her body was standing on end, and it took all she had to calm her churning stomach.

Where was the driver?

She fought down a sudden urge to throw up.

Stay calm, damn it! Keep it together.

Search, she needed to conduct a search. A frantic moment passed as she hunted through the control system for the internal camera array. She found it, letting out a held breath in the process. The graphical image indicated most units were functional. Starting with the tail car, she systematically checked each with a full cycle scan. More corpses, dried up and motionless, lay crumpled on the floors, in the corridors, some at their stations, some in their sleeping quarters. But nothing moved. Nothing.

Car after car, 15 in all, and then the tank itself. Still nothing.

OK. But the cameras didn't reach everywhere.

The last camera was out in the adjacent corridor, which was also clear. She confirmed all three hatches were closed and locked. Maybe something could get in here if was it the size of a microbe and able to withstand intense ultraviolet. Maybe. But what did they die of?

She mustered up the nerve to inspect the closest mummy. A strong jawbone revealed it was a man. His skin had drawn tight upon his bones like thin leather. No signs of trauma, or violence. By the position of his arms and hands, drawn up close to his throat, it seemed as if he was choking, gasping for breath. He was young, with fine brown hair, and judging by his features, somewhat handsome. His insignia, hanging as a dull memento on a crumpled threadbare uniform, gave away his junior rank.

There was a man on the floor, face down. She bent down, mustered up her nerve to roll him over. His body was unusually light, a dust-laden skeleton, mere fragments of a human being. The uniform was deteriorated, but the tarnished rack of medals glared back at her with recognized clarity.

The Captain. His hair was gray, and even in a mummified death, he seemed distinguished. *Didn't look incompetent.*

They all seemed to be gasping. Lack of air, maybe, or some kind of virus.

She had to get them out of here. Get them all out, seal the deck, get this transport headed to the TFP.

It was easy moving the bodies. The hard part was opening the door. It took everything she could to turn the handle. The feeling that something was out there, ready to attack wouldn't leave, like that creepy feeling when you know you are being watched, by someone, or something.

The hatch raised open into the gloom, squealing loudly on tracks that had not been lubricated for too many years. But the cameras had not lied, and nothing was out there. She glanced down the corridor to the other hatches. Both were closed and locked.

The bodies were light, but she had to be careful moving them. It was far too easy to break off a limb. It was good she was in her suit. She couldn't have done it otherwise. Once they were out of the control room, she could finally take it off. It would be a welcome relief. But what if something remained, a virus or some sample of whatever killed these men remained in the dust?

She would vent it. Create a vacuum in the corridor, open the hatch, decompress the control deck, fill it with outside air, then do it again for another cycle or two. The rebreathers would cycle up and do the rest, raise the oxygen levels up to the ideal level as they extracted it from outside. That should pull out the dust.

She'd have to activate the rebreather conditioners, preheat and filter the incoming air so it would be breathable. That's assuming the external air conditioners were not compromised. No way to be sure. Regardless, she wasn't staying in this suit much longer. She was starving.

She moved to the air system control panel and reopened the hatch with the hydraulics. The air raced out, along with streams of fine dust and anything else that wasn't heavy enough to resist the pull of the vacuum. She cycled it through another three times, each time pulling in fresh air produced by the conditioners and venting the stale internal air. Internal heaters fired up in a vibrating blast, warming the freezing external air to a more comfortable level.

After one final check with the instruments to confirm the atmosphere was alright, she twisted off her helmet and took a breath. It tasted cold, and only a bit stale but with something else. She shivered. Death. The smell of death still lingered. Just a wisp, but it was enough. Better to keep the tank completely sealed off from the other cars. Hell, why not vent them all? But what if the driver was in one of those cars, hiding from her?

No, better just to leave it for now. Whoever or whatever the driver was, he had just saved her life. She would focus on getting this transport moving. She stripped off her suit and cranked the HVAC heaters.

Currents of warm air drifted over her, bathing her body in comforting heat. Her knee throbbed a little less, now able to move more freely. Her pant leg at the knee was thick with dried blood.

She would have to attend to that, but the storm outside was growing even more fierce. The external cameras showed the snow was building up at a rapid pace against the transport's massive wheels.

She ran a full system diagnostic and watched carefully as the results streamed in. Outer hull damage registered on a number of the cars and a few locations on the tank. But the capacitors were at full charge and the fusion engines were well within spec. All the motors checked out fine – at least on the tank. A few of the cars had their primaries offline, some secondary motors were non-functional. Regardless, the tank would pull them with no trouble. They would have minimal effect, provided the winds did not get out of range.

Once seated at the helm, she engaged the motors and started the metallic monster in motion. Moans and creaks echoed along the bulkheads. The LightningRod was protesting but moving again. She kept a close eye on the monitors, watching the hydraulic pressures, the brake and transaxle temperatures. Everything stayed in tolerance.

She may be old but she's solid.

A flick of a few fingers brought up the navigation console. TFP northeast 13 degrees. Her other hand wisped over the console on her left. Multi-frequency horizon scans pulled up a myriad of images. A small model of the scanned terrain appeared on the plasma screen on the main deck display.

Looking out the window gave little information but a streaming wall of grays and whites, the instruments were much more precise. A compression ridge lay between her and the TFP. It was directly ahead, at least 30 meters high, unnavigable even with the LightningRod. She scanned further south and found a spot where the ridge dropped down, less than two meters at one point. She turned the tank to the new course, instinctively adjusting her speed and trimming down the suspension for oncoming winds.

It was not long to reach the ridge. She stopped just long enough to take some sonic readings, double-checking for chasms or faults underneath the snow. The two ice sheets were pressed tightly against one another, without a hint of a subsurface chasm.

She juiced up the motors and started across, carefully at first, giving the tank time for its wheels to bite into the snow and ice, then faster once she traversed the ridge. The cars followed behind, bouncing and creaking as they twisted up the slope.

April did not let up, her teeth jarring in her mouth as the transport climbed the icy ridge. She fought to stay in her seat, taking a brief second to tie herself down by the belt restraints.

The bouncing finally settled down. But the noises echoing through the bulkheads didn't, which did little to calm her. It was eerie at best, the groans and noise seemed more than complaints of long fatigued metal, haunting and fearful. She carefully avoided glancing at the internal security displays, lest she see something she wasn't ready for.

Outside the skies were darkening even more. The closer they moved toward the TFP, the angrier they looked. Swirling in the upper atmosphere, the cloudy turmoil was interrupted intermittently with flashes of white lightning, and tremendous cracks of booming thunder.

Wind speeds were picking up as well. The gauges were already registering in the danger zones on the console, their indicators dancing from yellow to red constantly. If this kept up, she'd have to jettison the rest of the cars. In their damaged state, they could easily flip and start a chain reaction.

April pushed her chair over to the coupling controls. But something caught her attention in the corner of her eye from the internal security monitors.

Was it her imagination?

She peered into the monitor, inspecting the scene carefully. It was the 3rd car, maintenance corridor. A few of the lights were flickering on and off, signs of an electrical short. A slight adjustment and she had the camera controls up. It jerked into motion, starting on a full rotation scan. Too many shadows to tell anything. There was nothing discernible.

A wind gust hit the tank hard, momentarily tipping the whole machine to one side. In a desperate frenzy, she flew through the controls, adjusting the hydraulics to drop the body as low as possible onto the axles, reducing her speed and systematically checking each car's integrity.

The cars had to go. Car 4 had lost its hydraulics and was rocking dangerously. The cars following were snaking about. If they were to get into a harmonic cycle, they could easily tip the whole transport over.

What if the driver was back there?

She depressed the transport's intercom and blurted out a shaky warning. "Ejecting the cars in 60 seconds – if you want to live, get to the tank immediately."

She waited.

The storm's power was growing dangerously, the creaking and groaning from the twisting cars grew louder, and yet the cameras gave no clues. No one ran down the corridor to the tank.

60 seconds passed, and she waited.

90 seconds. Car 4 was out of control.

120 seconds.

One last check on the cameras and she depressed the switch.

The coupler's blasting pins usually delayed firing by a few tenths of a second. When it did fire, the tank jerked ahead nearly throwing her to the floor. She watched the cars on the monitor, suddenly tracking to the side, decoupled to run free. The wind caught them underneath and rolled them over and over until they were lost in the white haze. If anyone was in them, they're gone now.

With no cars to slow it down, the tank was managing to pick up speed, even against this wind. April locked herself down into the seat in case they started over more uneven terrain. For now, the tires were still cutting through the top layer of ice, but that would soon stop – once the temperature froze it to a cement-like consistency.

She checked the outside temps. They were still dropping. That would continue as she moved closer toward the TFP. The wind was coming in from behind now, and the tank was accelerating even faster – 140 kmh and climbing. Ahead lay white crests of waves of snow, drifts battered and hardened by the wind. With each, the tank's wheels would lift off the ground, just enough to make the job of piloting more difficult. Jumbling about in the cockpit she had little time to do anything more than concentrate on the horizon, desperately struggling to keep the vessel in line with the navigation vectors.

Perhaps it was her uncanny ability to focus that kept her from hearing the sounds, from noticing the changes in the shadows proceeding up the corridor to the deck.

* * *

"A female of the species."

"Are you sure?"

"It is obvious. Note the mammary glands. They have distinct sexes."

"That is all you base your decision on? Perhaps they are omnigender, change sex mid-cycle in their lifespan."

"You ignore what you already know. It puzzles me."

"That I question your authority?"

"No, that you argue a point that has already been determined. You must, in some way, enjoy conflict."

"Not at all." She turned away, drifting to the other side of the corridor, tasting the decaying metal of the bulkhead.

"Yes, you do. And you are the one arguing."

She passed her tendrils through the slight crack in the hatch control plate, feeling for the copper and sharp bitterness of gold.

"Omni-gender - nonsense." He spat out the thought, literally in a slap.

He shifted around in the gloom, purple dots sparkling like so many tiny suns. His colors shifted to blue-green and then back again in a brilliant cacophony.

Laughing. Laughing at me. Such arrogance. It was, as most things with him, infuriating to her.

"You dislike me so, but ask yourself why."

She shifted over to anchor herself onto the bulkhead. Her tendrils felt the electricity surge through, tickling her slightly.

The hatch door clicked open.

"Please proceed," she cut his questioning short, ignoring stating his title, making it very clear of her true thoughts.

"Very well." He shimmered through, carefully avoiding intermingling with her outer aura.

"There is but one hatch left."

"I can open it," he stated confidently.

"Of course you can, but what happens when you do?"

"We enter, of course," he replied dismissively.

"And we frighten her, destroy our chance of establishing proper communication. Not effective. I assumed, your graciousness, you would have had a superior plan?"

"Of course. We wait..."

Alarms echoed throughout the car. A small red light blipped with an increasing frequency.

"She is decoupling the cars," the female informed.

"Yes. An intelligent effort. Increase her speed, reach her destination in a shorter time."

"Perhaps you should ensure the aft hatch is secure before the decoupling initiates," she quipped. "A suggestion only."

"Indeed. Excellent recommendation. Please, proceed."

She pushed by him, making sure to grate into his aura with as much disdain as she could muster. The hatch controls glowed red on the aft panel.

"THE HATCH IS AJAR."

With a soft tendril, she searched for the trigger, a button. It lacked the sharpness of metal, bitter, near tasteless. A quick thought, a firmness of shape and matter, and the button depressed. The panel glowed with new colors verifying it was now locked.

Not more than a second later the tank jerked ahead with enough force to have the wall bounce her against the ceiling. She melted into the deck plating, feeling the sudden inclusion of uncountable atoms in her body. Cell by cell she repelled back out, much like one would push away from viscous glue.

Again he laughed at her. His colors shifting so fast, they dazzled more in the hue of white than the multiple shades of blues, reds, purples, and yellows.

"The lead drive vessel has detached its trailing vessels," she stated, ignoring his rash impudence.

"Yes. And the time has come."

* * *

April slammed the port hydraulics booster control and steered sharply to starboard, narrowly missing the ragged ridge of rock, but momentum and poor traction worked against her. The tank's tires slammed hard and ground into the rock face nearly tipping it over. The vibration surged through the tank, shaking the deck plating. The noise was deafening, sounding like a wild animal in its death throws, howling insanely. Yet, the great wheels held, though pushed well beyond their designed limits. She whispered a prayer of thanks to the ancient engineers, knowing they had managed to over-spec on almost every system on these machines – despite a wall of uncaring bureaucracy at the time.

But that was then and this was now.

She found getting the gigantic vessel back under her control was not as easy as she had hoped. The rock face continued on to the horizon, growing ever taller. She was locked in an unclenching marriage of momentum, the hydraulics strained to the maximum but were unable to turn the massive wheels away.

She powered down quickly, and the tank dropped to a crawl in seconds, slowed as much by friction as by the brakes. The past screams of metallic chaos were replaced with an uncommon quiet. April glanced around, soaking in the readings from each monitor subconsciously, quickly assessing the status of the old vessel.

Not much worse for wear. Temps up on the starboard bank of wheels, but that was to be expected: no hydraulic lines broken, well actually nothing broken at all.

She engaged the motors and accelerated slowly. The axle lock transmissions whined. *Rock it, ease it back and forth, gently now.* She could hear her father's voice coaxing her.

She crawled out and away in reverse, careful not to force the wheels more than a few degrees at a time. In a moment, the tank was again free, crawling through two meters of snow but free.

April pulled up the navigation maps. First thing, as the satellite link was down, she'd have to use the computer to calculate her current position. It used the activity logs from the last time of confirmed location as a reference point – usually accurate within half-a-kilometer. The computer superimposed her current position onto the map, blipping a dark red.

She checked her destination – 30 km left, in ideal weather conditions, possibly one hour, but not now, and not this route. Two hours at least. She realized that she would never have made that on foot. She had made a serious error in judgment.

A shiver raced through her. The knowledge of her previous plight was all too real to recall.

She pulled up the latest satellite scans from the database – judging by the time tags they were a few days old - the time of the last workable sat uplink window, however brief. The images were stitched together by the computer and revealed a disturbing picture. Judging by where she was, that outcropping the tank had ground up against should be at least 20 meters tall. She checked out the starboard port – five meters showing at most. Simple math, the tank was upon not two meters of snow but 15. A denser layer must lie beneath this fluffy top layer, too windblown to pack properly.

There was a pass 5 km ahead – at least according to this map. Which had always been her original course but she had drifted 15 degrees away from it in the storm. She'd have to be more careful.

The turbulent weather developed too many inconsistencies, the striations of snow below the wheels of the LightningRod changed in various layers of density. In such conditions, it would not be unusual for bubbles – empty pockets – to form under the snow. Such pockets could easily collapse and swallow the tank whole. She activated the forward subsurface sonar and fed the alarms into the primary navigation monitoring system. Her knowledge of the ship's systems was invaluable at this point, a strict by-product of endless drilling by her father.

Speed would have to be adjusted to allow for sensor feedback time. It was going to be a long drive. She accelerated the tank, carefully watching the feedback peak, then slowly drop down enough to maintain an effective balance. At this speed, the systems would be able to keep up, and hopefully afford enough time for an emergency stop. She locked in the course and engaged the autopilot.

At worst, they would stop dead if the autopilot couldn't cope with the input stream. But it was always possible it could react too late if the scanner input feed dropped momentarily, the guidance system would interpolate data from unsuccessful scans to maintain speed – much like one does with one's own vision.

Regardless, it was a chance she was willing to take.

She pulled her legs up, rolling into a tight ball, and closed her eyes, too tired to care anymore.

The transport rolled on, pushing through the blizzard, navigating only with mechanical eyes.

* * *

"Time has elapsed. We shall move now."

"And what will you say?" she asked, genuinely curious.

"As we have been advised."

"A hollow threat based on supposition and theory."

"No, based on history."

"Merely conjecture. No one knows for sure what happened."

"The deaths of our brothers and sisters is evidence enough."

"They could have died for many reasons. Some anomaly perhaps."

"Anomaly, possibly. They were the initiating group. Many things could have happened. But we do have their memories."

"Yes, damaged and non-restorable. A poor rendition of history with little fact and less actual verifiable theory."

"Regardless, we approach with caution."

"And we will not kill her."

He rotated slowly, an amorphous mass of color, transparent yet opaque. Dots of blues and greens lit up through his midsection.

"Ah. Yes. The ultimate act of indecency. It was what we were trained to do, yet you still refuse to embrace your role."

"My role is to assess and report back."

"Of course." His thoughts rolled, hidden under grays and blacks.

"Let us proceed."

She reached through the hatch, intermingling with the metal, felt the latching mechanism and hardened her thoughts.

It sprung, clicked and whirred and the hatch swung open.

She floated back and waved a tendril to him.

He moved in cautiously, and she followed as closely as she would allow herself.

The air was moist and warm and carried with it strong tastes, some sweet, others rancid. She shuddered in spite of herself.

He shifted back, checking her.

"I am alright. It's very... different."

"Yes," he returned, barely hiding his annoyance. "The female is there, in the state of non-consciousness."

"I believe the female in a state of rest, perhaps reenergizing." She moved in closer, fascinated with the being's shape, her tastes, the chemistry emanating from her body. "A *tectutu*, most extraordinary."

"Do not move to close. The memories of the old ones demonstrate the danger. But you must awaken the subject."

"How am I to do that?"

"Sound perhaps. An alarm?"

She scanned the console before her, a collection of contained conduits of electricity and light. This time she refused to shudder, although the thoughts of containment seemed frightening. She had investigated this vessel many times, and understood the workings of the systems, although not always their purpose.

"The machine's guidance logic is activated. I will tell it to trigger an alarm."

She waved a tendril, causing a cascade of events through the guidance system. In seconds, the alarm was ringing and the tank was decelerating.

The female shifted, emanated sounds but did nothing more.

"Alarms have sounded. It has capability to process sound. Why is it not conscious?"

"I do not know."

"What strange beings these humans are."

* * *

"I'm coming in, Dad," she said, pressing the accelerator further. The utility rover flew over a dune, and she laughed.

"Take it easy."

She could hear his voice, firm yet gentle.

"What ya worrying over, I've got it…"

An alarm sounded. She looked over the controls. Nothing. Nothing was wrong.

The alarm wouldn't leave. Her father's voice faded as did the image of the desert landscape before her.

No, the alarm was real. She wasn't dreaming. Something was wrong.

She awoke with heart pounding and palms sweaty. *What is it?*

She searched the console, desperately looking for the cause. Nothing on the scanners but snow. Sonar feed showed solid underneath. But guidance had shut down the motors. The tank was stopped dead.

A few deft presses of controls and the logs were up. She read through it quickly. An anomaly – scanners had read something – but it wasn't there now. These systems were old, with no maintenance. It was possible there was a bug…

She slammed the button canceling the alarm, which left the small cabin in an eerie quiet. A few more adjustments and she had the tank back up to speed, the big wheels cutting through the snow with ease, each throwing a steady plume of white stuff at least 15 meters in the air. She checked the forward and aft camera feeds, and shifted them through a full spectrum check. Nothing abnormal.

But something was wrong.

Her realization came to her as a shock. The hatch had been swung open, all the way. She knew she had locked it. It couldn't have been that way long. During her sleep possibly?

She turned slowly, heart pounding in her ears, breathing too quickly. Her eyes could not lie. What she saw was strange, but also in a way, quite beautiful. They hovered, no more than two meters behind her, in the air, suspended by - nothing. They seemed like transparent nebulous clouds, with oddly firing tiny bursts of flickering color within them.

In a way, she felt like jumping out of the chair and running. But to where? And why? Were they dangerous? No, they would have attacked her by now, while she was asleep.

So she stayed put and watched them.

"Hello."

It was a voice, oddly female, but not audible, not from sound. It was in her head.

"You may refer to us as Trectilla. This planet is our home. Do not be afraid. We will not hurt you."

"You are instructed to turn over control of your environmental transformation devices immediately," came another voice, more forcefully than the last, and definitely more menacing.

Could it be a male voice. Did these things have a gender?

April took a moment to reply, letting their words sink in. "I didn't know there were other beings on this planet," she said as much as thought it, hoping they would understand.

"We have awakened," replied the female.

A strange response, ominous in its own way.

"Awakened?"

"We were in… stasis. But now we have awakened."

"As the transformation has begun," interjected the other. "By your machines."

"You mean the TFPs?"

"Yes. And we require control of those machines."

"Control? Why? I don't even have control of them," April stated, trying to hide her true thoughts.

If anyone had any control, it would be her.

"Why do you lie?" asked the male.

"I do not lie. The government of Ishaida only has such authority," she retorted.

"Then what is the purpose?" he challenged.

"I was sent here to monitor the Alvilla Valley TFP. It is not behaving as it should."

"That is because we are influencing it," came the reply.

April looked around the room. No escape without going through them. Their abilities were unknown, but for their gelatinous and cloudy shapes, they seem to be able to somehow manipulate matter – how else could they have opened the hatch?

"Your thoughts are jumbled. I feel your fear. We mean you no harm. We only wish to control what is transforming our home."

It was the female again, obviously more sensitive to April's concerns.

"You say you have been sleeping - how long?"

The question seemed to confuse them for a moment. They rotated, then bobbed slightly in the air. Their bodies raced with tiny lights which changed color so quickly it all seemed to blur.

"413 rotations, and previous to that 10,783 rotations."

Their reply was literal. The most logical definition of a rotation would be an Ishaidan year – and that would mean they were awake just before the Great Reversal?

"Four centuries ago – your people were awake then?"

"Only a small group, as that was their function, as this awakening is ours."

It was an answer, vague, without any definite numbers. April bit her lip debating whether to ask the next question. Maybe she shouldn't know.

"And what happened?"

"We know their life signatures have expired and they have moved on."

"How did they die?"

"We are not sure. It is our purpose to investigate this."

"And what do you want of me?"

"We require your help."

"And this transport, where did you get it?"

"This machine was buried in the ice. We set it free, in order to provide you protection, as we predicted you would have perished in the storm."

"And what of this vessel's crew?"

"Their deaths were not our doing."

April shifted in her chair. They had saved her, that much was clear. And they only meant to keep the TFPs running. But maybe their idea of transformation was far from human standard.

"And what are you doing to the TFPs?"

"Our purpose is to accelerate this process. Your original rejuvenation intentions can succeed, we know this from before."

"From before, when Ishaida's landscape was green with life, and one could breathe in the air?"

"Yes, from the time before."

"Did you shut the TFPs down?"

"We did not. We too had hopes that your technology would work successfully. We are very confident they will work correctly this time. We will be involved this time. We will ensure they will not fail."

The male's words seemed ominous. *What did they mean? What were they capable of?* "And how will you do this?"

"We will oversee this process, and accelerate activities where we are able. We will ensure this transformation will not take as long as it did prior."

"Do not fear the outcome. We will all gain from this transformation. We see the great distress of your people. We feel their suffering," interjected the kinder one – the female.

"I guess we have the same enemy, you could say," stated April, more a statement of fact than intent to ally forces. *Regardless if they could shorten the transformation time…*

"Yes we do," confirmed the male. "Your enemies are our enemies."

* * *

Chapter 15

M r. Green was concerned. "Has delta team reported in yet?"

"No, Sir. They haven't. We are assuming they did not survive the crash."

"I need confirmation on the target. What about the evidence?"

"The vessel is hanging over a ledge. The next few storms will most likely bring it down into the lake. It will be unrecoverable then."

"You will confirm the target, and ensure that wreck sinks to the bottom of that lake. Take a demolition detail down and see to it."

"The storm will make the mission very difficult. I may lose men."

"It is necessary."

"Very well, Sir."

A knock came on the door.

"Mr. Green, you have been requested by Mr. Talbot to meet him in council chambers."

Mr. Green slid the tiny communicator into his front jacket pocket, closing the link unceremoniously.

"Of course, please tell Mr. Talbot I will meet him in 10 minutes. I have an urgent call to make." He talked through the closed door, reluctant to let the man in.

"Very good, Sir."

He leaned close, putting an ear to the door, listening to confirm footsteps falling away.

Bloody nosey bastard.

He pulled out another device and did a secondary scan for bugs.

Cannot be too careful, even on this backward planet. He grunted with satisfaction. Nothing.

It took only a few seconds to set up a link with Earth and another few to plug in his security key into the encryption port. A familiar face appeared on the screen.

"General Aldridge, I have unconfirmed reports that the target has been terminated. I have dispatched a detail to verify."

"Very good. Secondary targets?"

"Yes, that operation is in progress. Expect to have this resolved within two hours."

"And the TFPs?"

"The weather is making this task a little more difficult. Would advise destruction from orbit."

The General leaned away from view, temporarily conversing with another. "No. We need to keep the units intact. I want each one *deactivated* within the next 24 hours."

"Unable to comply, General. I no longer have the forces at my disposal for that kind of mission."

"What the hell is going on over there, Green? What's your casualty at?"

"Eleven men, I've five remaining, and one in orbit."

"Shit. And I was informed you were the best."

"I am. I need replacements."

"I'll arrange it, but transport will take time. Just get the job done, Green."

"Of course, Sir."

He closed off communications and ran a link scan, checking the feedback loop in the process. No one was listening. Even if they were, they'd never break the encryption.

Mr. Elias Talbot was waiting.

He made it to the Councillor's chambers with a minute to spare. A guard standing in front of the doors let him in. To his surprise, only Elias was there to greet him.

"I was under the impression you had others of the council with you."

"Really, and what would give you such an impression, Mr. Green?"

"I am mistaken, obviously."

"Tell me, Mr. Green, what exactly is your specialty?"

Green sensed a problem immediately. He prided himself in assessing situations, looking for the signs. Wherever the line of questioning was going next, he was not interested in partaking. He glanced around, fingering a small pen in his inner jacket pocket. He had to keep to his story – for a little while longer.

"Programming the systems of the TFPs, of course. I was sent here from Anard-Bueller to ensure the TFPs continue their function as planned, and to work through some of our latest terra-forming challenges, given the latent condition of the previous effort."

"Yes, the letter says here you have the endorsement of the Old Man himself. Very difficult to get."

Mr. Green pulled the pen from his pocket and clicked it on and off. "Yes, Elias. Tell me, what is it you need?"

He moved in closer.

"I'd keep your position, Mr. Green. We've been wary of you ever since you stepped foot on our soil. In your own arrogant way, you've managed to keep your affairs to yourself. That all changed the minute we lost that transport."

Mr. Green laughed. "I had nothing to do with that."

"Yes, but your associate did or possibly, his associates." Elias raised an arm, and guards stepped in from every doorway.

"You are working for someone, now who could that be?"

Damn. Green looked around in a frantic half-turn. *No way out.*

"Well, Elias, you could proceed with the questioning, but I'm afraid if I let go of this pen, well, NewLondon, flooding problem and all, will be just a big'ol mud hole."

"I'm not amused."

"And I've no sense of humor. Not one shred. I've never, ever, laughed. At least, not that I can remember."

"Who did you confer with on Earth?"

"My, my, how industrious you are. For such a backward hole, it truly amazes me you have any level of intelligence."

"You forget these are our satellites. Our ancestors were a bit paranoid. Why don't we take a look?"

The central screen lit up with the face of a familiar General.

"How did you break the encryption?"

"We didn't. Dual overlays, little more complicated for me to explain, as a layman, but suffice to say, it works. So we have incoming now, and the target, I'm assuming that's April?"

"Assumptions are merely that."

"Perhaps, but I'm not done digging. I have friends on Earth, they'll help me put this puzzle together. Why don't you put your pen away, Mr. Green, or whatever your name is."

"And why would I do that?"

"As much as I'd like to kill you myself, that would not show so well Earthside. So, we intend to escort you off to the tarmac, you, in turn, recall your team, order your ship to land, get in and leave Ishaida once and for all."

"That all sounds so very simple. Perhaps I should mention the Garmic Treaty?"

"Waste of time, Mr. Green. Just you and your men leave. These gentlemen will escort you out. And by the way, Mr. Green, April's not dead. But you'll find that out when you debrief your men."

Green held his composure and carefully walked through the line of armed escorts.

"Elias," he called over his shoulder. "You're dealing with something far larger than you can handle. You'd be wise to let the professionals do their work."

Elias ignored his advice with a wave, letting the door shut as his final reply. He took a moment to reflect, inspecting the frozen image of General Aldridge - a general - three times decorated, a national hero no less. Aldridge had personally shut down the Quanta-al terrorist party, squelched the uprising on Cauputain, and cleared the pirates out of the Mirian belt. Not a man of shadowy conspiracies or questionable morals.

What was behind all of this suppression?

* * *

The knocking seemed to be encoded. It was clearly not the wind.

Billy Sequin grabbed the steel bar and proceeded with a series of raps on the hull. Ishbar jumped a bit initially but faded back to his unconscious state. Billy's mother looked back at him with worried eyes.

She did not want him to have false hope.

But the reply came back twice as strong and twice as fast.

"They're coming in!" he yelled.

Sparks flew from the hatch door as cutting torches sliced into metal. In a few minutes, the locks were cut clean through. One last bang and light and cold coursed in. A dark silhouette stooped through the hatch, and quickly behind him a tarp covered the opening.

"Well now, figured the Sequins would never leave their TriggerFix. Glad I found 'ya. 'Bin gettin' a bit messy out there."

"Who are you?" asked Mog.

"Jed MacErod, your old man knows me. Where is he?"

"Over here, he's hurt bad. Needs some attention, quite critical," stated Maureen. "And I do know you Jed. You are a sight for us folk."

"What happened here, anyway?"

"We were jacked, but not by no scrapies. These guys were pros."

"I figured something smelled awful on this. I'm a thinkin' we have maybe only a few minutes to get you outta here. There's a winch line with an s-bag hooked onto it. Will hold two at a time. We need to get movin'.'"

"We all accounted for?"

A tearful look was all Jed needed to see from Maureen. "Tensen's gone. He was brave 'till the last minute."

"Sorry for your loss, Maureen. Let's make sure'n save the rest of 'em now. Clock's a tickin'. Here, throw these bags over yer' heads and stay low in the snow. Whatever you do, keep outta the wind. And don't let go of the rope."

The trek up to the winch line was no picnic. Shoulder deep in snow with a wind frigid enough to kill. The tiny clear survival pouches kept the heat in just enough to keep them from freezing. It was seemed warmer down in the snow. Jed had Ishbar with him, Maureen had Mary, Billy, Mog, and Taron were in the lead. They followed the trail Jed had created.

Jed grabbed the transmitter. "Tim, we got'em. First load ready to come up. Injured man and son."

"Bag comin' down," came a reply riddled in static.

The large bag with plastic see-through portals descended down the cliff at a rapid rate.

"I still cannot believe you survived the fall," he said while they waited.

"We were hauling fruit in that hold. Crushes easy, and kept us fed and hydrated," replied Maureen.

"Lucky."

They watched the bag as it descended. The wind caught it and smashed it against the facing cliff wall.

"Yeah, you better be ready for that. Might break some bones if that happens on the way up," Jed said quietly.

Ishbar and Billy were the first. Systematically they went up in couples. Each ascent seemed a little rougher. It was Jed that had the roughest ride. He was thrown into the opposite cliff face not once but twice. He came up bruised and miserable.

"What in the sam hell you doin' to me, Tim!"

His red face calmed when he caught the concern on his crew member's face. "Don' worry. I'm still alive."

When they were all safely huddled in the snow tracker, Jed took the controls. "I expect this may be a rough ride. How's Ishbar holding out?"

"He's breathing steady, wincin' and cussin under his breath," replied Maureen.

"Aye, leave it to that tough old bugger."

"By the way," Tim said, the boys got through while you were down there, "They said they got a ship on the scope headin' down."

"How long?"

"No more'n five minutes, seven outside. They said it wasn't runnin' legal."

"That ain't right, then. It ain't none of our boys. We still got those zipper-cannon on this baby?"

"Sure, loaded and primed." He glanced back at the group. "We use'em for triggering avalanches, clearing vegetation, clearing passes, whatever."

"What you got'em packed with?"

"Fifteen-pounders I think."

Jeb had the snow-tracker moving at a pretty good clip now. They were far from the cliff edge and away from the wrecked train. He kept the speed up hoping to gain some distance, ignoring the rough ride.

The unidentified ship came in range starting with an audible blip on the scope.

"Here they come. Might not see us if they've got their scanners on tight enough to cut through this soup."

"Hang on, they've stopped," Tim announced. "Looks like they're just hoverin'."

"You got anything more?"

"Well, can't be real sure. I think I got small signals, scattered. I figure it's men. Hell, just too shitty out there. We'll need to take our best guess and drop both them zippers on'em."

Maureen spoke up, her voice cracking a bit. "We can save her yet, just don't get those zipper loads too close, OK?"

Tim nodded, fully knowing that it wasn't possible to be sure.

"Look, Maureen, whoever pushed her over the edge has come back to finish the job, you're sure you want to want to let them go do you?"

Maureen's face grew a little more pale with the realization. "No, No I don't." *She knew full well chances of recovering the TriggerFix had now dropped to zero. But her son had not died for nothing.*

"Do it."

Tim shifted over to the cannon controls and pressed a few buttons. In seconds the cannon shot off into the blizzard with two loud pops. By that time the scanners had lost all hint of any useful detail.

They didn't see what happened, if anything, to the mysterious men.

* * *

"Jed, when God made you they broke the mold!"

"Listen, Elias, I made it absolutely clear - no one else had to come with me. I wasn't about to put another man's life in jeopardy because of my lack of good sense. Either way, Tim Durango joined me on this ride, as well. He deserves just as much credit or blame."

"You didn't find her?"

"You mean April don't you? I ran outta time. I could'a looked some more, but I had the whole Sequin Clan with me and the weather wasn't getting any better. I'm sorry Elias, she's gone."

"Are you sure? She could still be down there, trapped in a car."

"No, I don't think so. You ain't gettin' me. I figure she's as alive as the both of us. I found something strange in the tank – a J-bug had been set up to coil a cable around its wheel. Took me a sec to figure it out, but I know what it was now. All I had to do is look up."

"What do you mean?"

"I mean a cable had been sent up and over the ice bridge above. The end had been wrapped in the wheel to make an elevator. Only one person I know could have thought a way to do that."

"April."

"Yep. Now I only had the pleasure of meeting her once. She had my whole track-layer machine reengineered for me in about 20 minutes. We're still workin' to implement some of her ideas. Smart one, that little lass."

"But the others? Why would she leave them?"

"We found them locked in a hold. I'm a guessin' she didn't even know they were there."

"So she survived. Thank God."

"Well, I'm just guessin' here. Did find some depressions in the snow. Suspect someone had been moving around out there."

"Only one? She had that Anard-Bueller man with her."

"Near as I can figure, that cable was rigged for only one."

"Well, he was a professional. May account why you didn't meet up with any of those marauders down on the wreck."

"Yes, or they may have jumped ship before she went over. Just so you know, we think a group of men looped down to the wreck. It takes special forces types to repel down in those conditions."

"Special forces?"

"Yeah, but we didn't make it easy for them. We lobbed a couple zippers down on'em to keep'em on their toes. Figure it's good payback."

"That was Green's men no doubt."

"Green who?"

"No matter. They're gone now. Let's just pray our April managed to find a way to shelter in this storm."

"I'm thinkin' she's got only one way to go – to the TFP – if she can make it. And all I can do for her now is wish her good luck. We're all locked down here. Ain't goin' nowhere now. Storm's moving in too fast."

"I know I've been watching the sat feeds. We are projecting another 15 hours before it lifts."

"Well, as soon as it breaks, I'll get down there. Old Ishbar is on the mend and he'll be his usual pain-in-the-ass self not long from now."

"Can't say how much I appreciate this, Jed."

"No. No. Don't be making a big deal outta Porter code now. I did what I could. You get a transport or something over here as soon as you can before this Sequin Clan eats up all our good rations."

"Will do. In the meantime, I think it's time I talk to the one behind all of this."

* * *

April kept one eye on the controls and tried to keep the other on the Trectilla – at least that's what she thought they called themselves.

"We are getting close to the Alvilla Valley TFP."

"Yes, we know."

"The winds are getting worse, though. I don't think we'll be able to reach it."

"Please proceed on your course."

She engaged the brakes bringing the tank to a full stop. The winds were buffeting the hull with enough force to cause a constant swaying on the deck.

"I don't think you understand, it is too dangerous to proceed, even in this tank."

Colors shifted in turbulent flashes within the male. He was not saying anything to her, but she could feel it – and it was not warm, nor kind, not like before.

"Do not mind him," the female interjected. "We will make preparations. Please continue on your course."

April turned cautiously. The male had moved back into the corner by now, glowing with a snobbish intent.

She didn't like him. Not one bit.

"OK then. Engaging drive. You guys get ready for a bumpy ride."

She edged the speed up slowly, trying to keep the massive tires from spinning and digging in. The loose snow was at least 10 meters deep now, with multiple striations of hard and soft layers. They were sinking in enough to have the belly of the tank riding over the top of the snowpack. Much deeper and they wouldn't be going anywhere.

She cursed herself. Of course, the engineers had anticipated this type of terrain, she just hadn't remembered until now. She rushed across the cabin and kicked open a panel. Dust flew up as she reached in and pulled out an old-fashioned crank dial connected to an extendable arm.

"It's a skimmer," she explained, starting to crank the wheel clockwise. "It's designed to displace the snow under our belly so we don't get hung up. It's a simple device really, multiple blades splay out, shoots the snow past the tread path."

"You won't need it."

"What do you mean – the snow's too soft. We're digging in too much."

They only hovered in silence, neither attempted to respond.

"Fine." April pushed in the crank and slammed the panel shut. She returned to her chair, inspecting the instrument panels. Sure enough, there was something very different outside. It was a trench, wide enough to fit the tank, deep enough to cut through to ground level. She ran a scan. A perfectly straight line, stretching out far enough to go beyond the scanner's limit. This was impossible.

"How did you do that?"

"Please direct your vehicle to the cleared path ahead. We will not encounter any more difficulty reaching our destination."

"Yes, but how?"

Hovering in silence, neither chose to answer her question.

If they could do this how much more were they capable of? What kind of creatures were they? What kind of powers did they possess?

"Please, tell me how you did this."

The female seemed to glint with hues of red and orange, showing signs as if she was to respond, only to quickly return to a more standard silver and black.

"Be like that then," she said, not withholding exasperation. "Re-engaging the drives." She slammed the controls to full power, and the giant wheels spun angrily. The tank lurched ahead and down into the trench. Once they leveled out the ride became much smoother. She engaged the third and fourth drives, pouring on the power, winding them out to maximum. The kilometers screamed by as the walls on both sides blurred into a continuous white. Meters above the winds howled over the top of the trench. A light dusting of snow traced downward, just enough to create a slight fog.

April watched the instruments, trusting them to expose the road ahead.

"Based on the computer's imaging we do not have far to go. What happens when we reach the TFP?" April tried to hide the fear in her voice.

She had no idea what they intended for her.

"You are in no danger." The female replied, clearly reading April's thoughts.

"You're just saying that. Once I get you past the security, you are going to kill me."

"No, not at all. And we have already circumvented the security systems. We do not need your help with this task, and we have no intention to harm you."

"From what I can see, you are capable of doing whatever you want, already. Why do you need me at all?"

"These machines, they operate by a form of coded instruction you refer to as programs. These programs must be modified, and in turn, each TFP must be synchronized."

"And you can't do that by yourself?"

"It would take us time. Machines are quite difficult for us. Your help... simplifies our task."

"Tell me then. How many more of you are there?"

It took them a moment to answer. Strange purples and yellows danced in their midsections. *Were they perplexed or simply trying to hide something from her?*

"There are two of us."

"Not what I mean. How many others of your kind out there?"

Again they turned toward one another, continuing their private conversation. She noticed how the colors in their transparent bodies not only winked in and out of existence but also how they shifted into a variety of hues and brightness.

What a strange lifeform. So... alien.

"The others will be awakened in due time," came a firm reply from the male.

Alarms sounded behind her. The scanners had picked up a new signal – a massive signature.

"Well, that would be our TFP," April stated as much to herself as to them.

"Looks like surface winds are up to 380 kmh. Can you tell me why this trench is not filling in? I mean, those winds should be dumping in the snow by the ton."

"Please begin to decelerate."

Again, no answer and no further clues.

She dropped down the revs, letting the transmissions freewheel down. "We've a ways to go, yet. I'll drop her down gradually."

By now she could see the dark shape on the horizon. Flashes of sheet lightning burned through scouring winds, defining a towering structure. The scanners revealed peaks of a mountain range of steel in the distance, shadows of the sheer size of the monstrous machine which lay ahead.

The tank followed the trench through and under the maze of pipes and conduits, eventually leading up to the maintenance bays. One of the lower maintenance gates stood conveniently open, possibly stuck ajar over the years. April masterfully guided the huge machine through the entrance into the bay, finally bringing the vehicle to a halt adjacent to a loading ramp.

"End of the road."

"In response to your queries," stated the female. "Ishaida is not home to only one form of life. You do realize this do you not? Single-celled creatures live throughout the mass of the crust of this planet, throughout the air you breathe, the waters of which you drink, including this crystalline matrices you call snow. We are all connected."

"Ok, sure, but how did you dig that trench in seconds flat?"

"We simply asked for help. We have a bond with our brethren. Do you understand?"

"No, not really. But I think you would scare a lot of my people with this type of power."

"Yes... that could be a possible response. Yet, you are not frightened."

"Maybe I am very frightened, and you are misreading me."

"You are not exhibiting indications of such behavior. You are not attempting to escape from our presence."

The statement was factual and based on pure logic. No arguing that. Fight or flight seems to apply everywhere. "Right, so let's just say I am curious and leave it at that. Where to now?"

"We must relocate to the command center."

"Of course, but before we go on a trek, I need some supplies. My food stores are all but exhausted. I don't suppose either of you have anything that would pass for food with you?"

They flickered tiny bursts of light in silence.

"Forget it. Maybe there's some four-hundred-year-old supplies that are still digestible around here, however improbable that sounds." She eased back onto her feet. Her sore knee was feeling much better now, but it was still quite stiff, and it left her with a pronounced limp on her way to the tank's galley. "Stay here. I'll be a minute."

The ancient kitchen was stocked with some interesting possibilities, most that would be far too dangerous to consider, excepting for a few promising packages of sealed rations. She wiped dust from the labels. Energy shakes, guaranteed to last forever, but not very filling. They were probably brought over from the freighters which ran under standard light-speed between the stars. With these types of food packs all she had to do was add water, and poof, a hot and ready drink.

She came back sipping on a straw from one of the silver pouch rations, another half-dozen crammed into her pockets along with a few bottles of water. She found the aliens just where she had left them.

"Well, let's go." And she pressed the buttons to open the hatch doors.

The creatures had little trouble keeping up with her, yet still managed to maintain a comfortable distance, even during the elevator ride up.

"15th floor, that's the main command center," she offered, breaking the silence.

The elevator finished its high-speed ascent, momentarily giving a slight sensation of weightlessness. The creatures shifted upwards slightly but corrected quickly.

How do they maintain their position? She wondered.

Doors slid open to a minimally lit control room. April wasted no time, heading directly to a connected galley kitchen. Her previous meal only made her feel even more hungry. To her delight, there were dozens of ration packs available. Rummaging through, she checked the ingredients of each, a couple interesting ones caught her eye - steak and eggs of all things. Water bottles were lined up in the upper cupboard.

Following directions, she cracked open the chemical packets and felt the heat surge through them. In a minute, the food was fully cooked. She ripped open the packet, lost in a delicious aroma.

They drifted in through the entrance, curious where she had gone. Their bodies instantly lit up with a shifting and firing of color.

The noise inside her head left little doubt they were distressed.

"What's the matter? Can't stand my food? I didn't think you guys could smell."

"I find this sensation revolting," he commented with open disdain.

"Live with it. I'm hungry, and to me, this is delicious, alright?" she fired back, licking her fingers. "What do you want me to do here, anyway?"

"Modify the program."

"Whoa now, do you know how many lines of code are executing in these systems? You just don't go and make a change. You have no idea of the complexity."

"We have... understanding. I will guide you," the female countered.

"These changes must be synchronized in order to work correctly," stated the male, authoritatively.

"You can change parameters and such, but tweaking the code is dangerous, much less modifying all the TFP systems at once. Besides, there's only one way to do that. You need to hack into the sat-link. Not an easy thing to do. Maybe I should remind you that security protection has been activated. We have seven layers of encrypted protocols to dig through. This is beyond impossible."

"We will show you what to change, how, and when."

"Really? So you interface directly with the computers now? I thought you said you have trouble with machines? So you've adapted new abilities? You never cease to amaze me. So tell me again, why don't you do this yourself?"

"You must shut down the security protocols."

"Right. That's what I thought. So that's why we've been seeing this TFP going radical. You've been attempting to screw with the system and it's been counter adjusting each time. Pretty smart, isn't it?"

"Yes."

"So remember the questions I had from before, maybe you can answer some of them now."

The female moved closer. "Your people have been attacked from above. They are suffering. We can help you."

April held her ground. "Heard that all before. Like I said, just looking for some answers to some questions."

"We intend to raise the target mean temperature by 15 degrees centigrade. That is all."

"Go on."

"These machines your people have built, they will give us back our world."

"And what about us – the human colonists of Ishaida?"

"We can live with you and your people, in harmony. We have seen how your people have been treated. You will be under our protection. You will have nothing to fear from us."

The creatures hovered quietly, giving no hint of their true motives.

What if they were lying? There's no way she could tell.

"Believe me," the female pressed on. "This is the truth. This is a minor adjustment we are requesting."

"OK, then let's verify this with the TFP modeling system."

April knew her way around most of the systems in the control room, the modeling system being the most important. She pressed a few commands on the console, and the model of Ishaida appeared above the round projection in the center of the room. The planet slowly rotated, revealing green fields and dark blue seas.

April took in a sharp breathe. It was truly beautiful. This was the vision of Ishaida, the planned result. The goal of the TFPs extensive labors.

The aliens moved around the image, marveling themselves. "This is what our home looked like so long ago," stated the female. "It leaves me..." The words disappeared into colors.

The male ignored the other's reaction. "Human female, adjust the settings to the following, and you will see the effect of which we ask."

The numbers flowed into April's head at lightning speed. She worked quickly at the modeler to make the appropriate adjustments. "There!"

As if on cue, the green along the equator dissolved to a light brown, and spread to a thick line along the line of latitude. The Northern and Southern ice caps dissolved by roughly two third's their modeled size and certain small islands disappeared under the blue water, some shorelines receded slightly along the mainland coast.

"As you witness, this change will create desert along the equator. This will be very suitable for our people. The Northern and Southern hemispheres will prove to be very comfortable for your people. We can live together, each within our own environments."

"I need something more than your word. I need a guarantee of some kind."

"We cannot provide you this. We cannot guarantee what your machines are capable or incapable of. This is only a model."

"And if I refuse?"

"This is a matter of time. We will succeed in breaking through these security measures. But time is quite precious in this exercise. We require trust from you."

"We have rescued you from a most certain death, promised you that we would aide your people in their struggle, and asked for one small action in return. Perhaps we are disillusioned in our hopes. Perhaps we should not pursue any agreement between our peoples. Perhaps we should avoid developing a partnership."

"Is that a threat? Would you turn against us, as well?"

"No, we have no desire to harm you or your people. We only wish to live in peace. Ours is a decision of trust, and with this, faith in fulfillment of our agreement."

April laughed. "Faith, now that is funny. You may be able to read my mind and have that advantage. I have no such ability."

"It is much simpler than that. We are only asking for your help. And in return, we offer ours."

"Fine. What can you give me?"

"Protection. The past will not be repeated."

"OK, but I'm not so sure what you can do there, or if we ever need protection again. What else?"

"Some of your cities are in great distress with the recent changes in the atmosphere and the geological shifts. We can help rectify this."

"Really? Then I want to see it. I want you to prove to me you can help."

The male moved forward dominantly. "We shall consider your city of GhenghisPrime."

Monitors sprang to life to her right, images obviously fed from the satellite system above.

"As you may witness, it is a city under severe duress. The recent geological shifts and the increased precipitation have raised the adjacent lake's water level, which is in turn rapidly flooding the city. Given the current rate of the rising water levels, we have projected the majority of this city will be flooded within a number of days."

"And what can you do about this?"

"We will redirect this body of water."

April moved in close to the alien, fighting her own inside voice urging her to stay clear. The male shifted away from her, obviously uncomfortable with her directness.

"Then do it."

"And in return?"

"Do it first. Build my faith."

The aliens moved toward one another, colors flashed and ebbed.

"It is done."

* * *

Zack Bridges had been working through the catacombs for all of his life. He had seen fires ravage through the tunnels, dug out bodies after cave-ins, and struggled to seal off leaks. He had never been prepared for this.

"Drop it down some more," he yelled to the crane operator, waving his arms in a downward arc.

The metal pump was already two meters under the surface of the black water. He reached over and touched the cavern walls, felt the steady flow of water ooze over his fingers. It was already over his boots. And it was cold. Hours – two maybe three – no more. If the pumps could only keep up. The lower levels were already submerged. This was the last evacuated level and then what?

The cable went slack.

"Start it up!" he yelled, arms circling.

Circles emanated from the slack cable in the water, and Zack felt the telltale vibration through the soles of his boots. It was working. The last pump was in place and running. All they could do now was wait and watch. He peered down into the water, could see the dim light from the lower levels. Five levels, once home to his friends, his family, now gone. He adjusted the water meter and mentally recorded the reading.

"Ok boys, let's get up where it's dry."

"What do we do now?"

Zack searched out the face of the one who asked the question. Young Bill Gower, no older than 16, shivering and soaked from head to foot.

"We wait, son. We wait and watch."

"And if it's not enough? If it can't keep up?"

"We keep ascending."

"The walls of the dome are under water by at least 20 meters on the southeast side. We can't move up enough, you know we can't."

Zack reached over and grabbed his shoulder. "Don't bother frettin' 'bout something what ain't happened yet. Go. Git outta this water and warm up."

"Jerry – you and Emead keep an eye on the level. I'll come back down in an hour."

"Boss, look."

Jerry's finger was pointed at the water level. "It's going down."

Zack looked the checked again, he squatted down close to the floor, eyeing it carefully. "Can't be. It's dropping too fast."

The top of the pump was already visible and still dropping.

"No. This can't be the pump doing this."

As if on cue, the pump started snarling and gurgling, protesting as it ran dry.

"Shut it down, boys. Move it!"

The crew scrambled to turn it off before it burned its seals. The water was receding down the shaft at a phenomenal rate.

"Holy shit."

"Billy – hustle up to the control room and get those other pumps switched off." He glanced over – the kid was frozen in place, watching. "Now, Billy!" The tone of his voice left little for interpretation.

"What's goin' on?" asked Jerry softly.

"I dunno. Underground fault maybe."

"I don't recall a quake, do you? Not even a tremor. And if it is a fault, I'm not so sure that's a good thing."

"What do ya mean?"

"Well, I'm not a geologist," stated Jerry calmly. "But I'm thinking steam and lots of it."

"Oh shit," acknowledged Zack under his breath.

"Boys, we gotta get outta here, now. Move it!"

Zack took up the rear as they ran, making sure to seal the hatches behind them. Two levels up and he was fighting to keep his breath. He wasn't used to running.

"How much time we got?" Jerry yelled back at him.

"Dunno," Zack replied hoarsely. "Maybe once we get to the security station."

A small group was waiting for them, huddled around the monitors in the cramped room. Billy was among them.

"I told'em," Billy announced as if he were in trouble.

"Zack," acknowledged a co-foreman. "All pumps are down. And it's still receding. What the hell is going on?"

"Any sign of steam coming up yet?"

"Steam? Hell, no man. What are you talking about?"

"It's a fissure. Only explanation. Water will hit magma and she'll blow back."

"Level five's almost dry. If that's true, the hatches won't hold. We're as good as dead."

Zack moved in close, inspecting the images from the fifth level. The camera feeds were set to a 10 second rotation, some of them a little more blurry than others. From the looks of it, all the water had drained.

"Check everything, I want to know where that water went," ordered Zack.

* * *

April pulled up the sat images over GhenghisPrime. The encroaching lake had submerged a significant portion of the southern edge of the dome, but now the water was clearly receding, escaping down a newly created river which had somehow just formed, its waters now racing in an angry torrent to drain out to sea.

"How did you do that?" April said incredulously. "That's impossible!"

"We have demonstrated our abilities. As you can see, the new tributary is diverting the water very quickly."

"How?"

"We have informed you of our symbiont relationships."

"Right, symbionts. I'll need to look that one up. So, tell me again, where are all of your people?"

"As I have previously stated, the others are to be awakened in due time."

"Right. So if we hadn't arrived, Ishaida would be mostly a snowball by now. Exactly how long did you plan on sleeping?"

"You are correct. We were awakened early. Observe."

A milky fog spread above their heads. The fog receded from the center, swirling in a clockwise fashion, exposing a dark image of light and color. It was a celestial map.

"This is our home, our system. It is signified by the color of red. A small, insignificant point afloat in the stars. Observe the celestial tides of which we travel, and as time passes our system drifts, there, into the future."

Pinpoints of light shifted and swirled, marking the passing of time.

"And as our system approaches this cluster, our sun merges into the orbit with this young gaseous giant. Our planet again warms to a state of which we are comfortable, Ishaida will become a planet with two stars and no night to speak of. But this will take at least three billion cycles."

"As I have indicated, we awakened early."

Three billion cycles? Three billion years? You were planning to stay in stasis that long? Incredible.

"Time is of different perception to us."

"But you have all these abilities, why not just 'terra-form' Ishaida yourselves?"

"We do not have this capability. These wonderful machines of yours. We do not build such devices, such sophisticated tools, yet you manage to create them with such grand intelligence." The male commented with unusual vigor.

"I see, and this comes from one who has just adjusted the planet's crust to create a river."

"Yes, our power is somewhat different than yours. This world is full of life, both simple and complex forms. Such life flourishes in every river, within every meadow, and deep within the mantle of this planet. Life as a single entity, may be considered insignificant, but take a minuscule lifeform and combine it with millions and billions of others, they can no longer be dismissed as nothing. As a combined force - they are powerful."

"And you are telepathic?"

"That is a somewhat accurate description of our ability."

"Are you influencing me now, mentally?"

"No. We have never attempted to merge with you."

"Merge – you mean control. If you can do that, why don't you compel me to give you the codes?"

"No, we do not control sentient life. Life must choose. We may provide, perhaps, a subtle suggestion if we feel that is needed," stated the female.

"So you can't directly control us. But you can subliminally influence us."

"It is possible," she acknowledged.

"Over large distances?"

"We have the capability of reaching far beyond this planet."

"Really? How far is that?"

The creature shifted her position slightly.

Maybe she's giving away too much information, April wondered.

"Enough banter," barked the male.

"Really, enough banter?" April retorted. "I'm not done asking questions just yet. I recall a certain Captain that ordered an attack on us not too long ago, and now I learn you could have stopped him. How many lives did that inaction cost? Did you know – did you?"

The male moved away, choosing to de-escalate the conflict.

"You must understand, this was not our issue, not our affair." The female spoke so quietly and softly in her mind it was no more than a whisper.

April sunk into her chair, glanced up to watch the milky fog of the universal model fade into a drab gray ceiling. "But you could have warned us, couldn't you?"

The aliens shimmered quietly, neither daring to respond.

April felt a tear well up in her eye. "And then you watched us die. Possibly felt us die."

"We did feel your pain. This was not our – conflict. Life is precious, we know. It was why we approached you, to help you."

April stared at them but could tell very little from their amorphous shapes.

"Of course." She wiped the tear away, "you only want to help us."

"Yes, it is our desire."

April rose and walked around the projected 3D model of the planet once more.

"And you plan to live here, along the equator?"

"We require warmer conditions than you. We will build our own habitats. We will not interfere with your people."

"We will need a passage from North to South."

"We will agree upon designated routes, this will ensure little or no interaction between our races, if that is what is desired," stated the Trectilla male. Colors shifted within his body, reds to browns, oranges to blues.

There was no way of knowing what it was thinking. No way to tell at all.

She glanced back at the model of Ishaida, full of green and blue, alive and beautiful.

They only wanted their home back and they are willing to share it with us.

She couldn't help but think she was making a deal with the devil. But considering what's happened so far, did she really have a choice? These aliens, no correction, natives - as it was their home - have proven themselves two times now, first by saving her life, and second by saving GhenghisPrime.

"I will help you."

* * *

She typed in the override codes solemnly.

"It's done. You have temporary access."

"What I think you need to do can be done through the parameters update interface. There is no need to change the programs."

The aliens floated toward her. "This will need to be done to each of your machines."

"There is a synchronous download capability through the satellite network." April offered. "You can make your changes, and I can trigger the update to all of them."

"I will proceed." The male produced a small device from within its body. It floated up and over the console. The display began flashing busily.

"Our changes are complete. Please proceed with your download."

"I'll need to review the delta logs, and download them to the RPI engines."

The alien floated back. "You may proceed."

She moved in and settled into the chair. A few key entries brought up the delta logs. She scanned through them with quickly, noting the subtle changes. "With these changes, you'll increase the mean temp by approximately 15 degrees."

That was consistent with the model, with what they had stated. There was no other significant marker, no other large effect. Truthful so far.

April hesitated a moment, holding her finger over the command key. *Why not?* With one press she authorized the parameters transfer to the remaining TFPs.

She pushed back from the console, positioning herself to face the beings. "It's done."

"Then we shall leave you. You may also return to your home."

"I have no home. It was destroyed."

The female moved close. "If we understand correctly, you are a Porter. Your transport is your home. We award you the LightningRod."

"Thank you." April took a moment to let it sink in. Her own Porter tank. Her own transport.

"Can you tell me where you found it?"

"It was buried within the ice of a glacier. The forces of time had not destroyed it. We knew we could use it to save you. And now it is yours."

"Thank you. But as per our agreement, I mean, between our races, shouldn't we have something documented?"

"It has been recorded and archived in our collective memory. We will not forget."

"But we may – I mean, not myself but others, the representatives of our government for instance."

"You represent your people, can you confirm this?"

"Some may argue I do not."

"But they do not have your knowledge or access. They do not have the ability or authority to make such an agreement with us, now at this time. It is only you."

"And if someone else does not honor our agreement?"

"We have far more to give you than you have to lose. That would simply be foolish," countered the male.

They shimmered out through the hatch and into the corridor.

"It was a pleasure, dear April," came a soft whisper, fading slightly as they continued to move away.

April brought up the internal scanner arrays, hoping to track them, but most of them were offline, stuck in a diagnostic pre-check.

"Damn it!"

The odd one would come on in just enough time to catch a glimpse of the traveling pair. She checked their location - they were already at the lower level. A number of lights turned green on the display, cheerily announcing an additional scanner leaping to life. She switched over to the control console and triggered a sequential scan, but by this time there was no trace of the aliens, no hint of their passage, and no signature of any sort. She ran through each level of the monolithic maze, shifting the frequencies, searching for a sign, any sign at all.

Nothing. But where could they have gone?

She checked the outer bay. The LightningRod was still there, just as they had promised. Were they on it? She ran a history log search and it came up negative. Security protocol dictated that the outside arrays were the first to come online by design after a system reset. None of the outer history logs revealed any movement. Nobody – or to be more accurate – nothing, had come out of the TFP.

To Fade Away

They had simply disappeared.
It tightened a knot in her stomach, made her mouth turn dry.
Had she done the right thing?

* * *

Chapter 16

Billy's grin spread so wide it exposed the extra wide gap between his two front teeth.

"We found it!"

"Well, stop standing there grinning and tell me," ordered Zack.

"It showed up on our last satellite sonar scan, a fault running to the south – very deep – a natural drain to a lower elevation."

"So, it's really gone?"

"Yes, Ishaida pulled a fast one on us. The fault must have just formed. Wasn't there before."

"Are you sure?"

"Yeah." He nodded. "Yeah, we think so. We're in the clear."

"Bloody hell. I don't get it. No earthquakes, nothing. How's that happen?"

"Umm, I dunno. Just happened I guess," replied Billy, not particularly strongly.

"Yeah... just happened." Zack leaned back in his chair, contemplating. "Seems strange, don't ya think?"

"Hell no, Zack! We have underground faults all over. We're just lucky this one had formed here. You know, the shifts are happening."

"The shifts? So you think this was just dumb luck, like some kind of magic coincidence?" Zack's words dripped sarcasm.

Billy's mouth gaped open, "What?"

"Forget it. Just get your ass back down to level six. We got a failed air handler in corridor 45E and it's critical."

Billy mumbled something not so nice.

"Stop standing there and get your ass down there," Zack ordered, as he scanned his eyes over the maps Billy had given him.

What the hell did this?

* * *

"Alvilla Valley calling."

She clicked the receiver, temporarily interrupting the static, chewing on her nails with a deeper apprehension than she'd care to admit.

Damn it, why don't they answer?

"This is Alvilla Valley sending a general broadcast to... anyone?"

More static. April made a few more adjustments. It was a clear carrier signal to the other TFPs, as well as the primary receiver stations in every city, should be getting through with no problem. She switched from digital to analog.

"Hello, to anyone, this is Alvilla Valley calling, please acknowledge."

"Hello, Alvilla Valley, this is NewLondon. Who do we have on the line? We haven't had anyone on this frequency, well, for centuries."

"April McThurn, of the McThurn Clan, Daughter of Oranis."

Silence on the other side.

"Did you get that? Hello?"

"Yeah, sorry, April. We ah..." some rustling sounds. "We have the Mayor coming online, please hold."

Elias Talbot's rustic voice replaced the apprehensive operator's. "April, you made it?"

April laughed, as the statement was posed more of a question than a fact.

"Yeah, made it all the way to the TFP, but not without casualties. We lost the Sequins, Elias, all of them."

"And Mr. Montigue?"

"Dead, killed by a group of professional mercenaries. I think they killed the Sequins too."

"No, they didn't, April. The Sequins survived, most of them, that is. An emergency team pulled them from the wreck."

"What?"

"They were locked in a cargo hold."

"Couldn't be, I mean, I didn't see them..." She searched her memory, why hadn't she noticed? What had she missed?

"Are you OK, April?"

There seemed to be actual concern in his voice. But she didn't hear him. She was stuck in the past, lost replaying her memories.

"I didn't see them. I didn't... or I would have," she stumbled over her words.

"Yes, I know you would have. I know. Don't you worry about that now. They're safe. How did you survive the wreck or the storm for that matter? Truthfully, we didn't think you made it."

April hesitated. Should she say anything?

"April, please acknowledge. How did you get to Alvilla Valley?"

"I ah, I figured a way up from the wreck, and then I walked."

"You walked all the way to the valley, but how?"

"Well, not exactly, I mean, I had help." She let her last words sit on dead air for a few extended seconds. "I can't talk on an unsecured channel. I figure I'm 30-40 hours out if I start for NewLondon now."

"April, how are you planning to reach us? Can we dispatch a transport to you?"

"No need. I'll be piloting the LightningRod. I have full salvage claim on her. She's all mine."

"Just to confirm, you stated you have laid claim to the transport called the LightningRod?"

"Confirmed. I'll see you in a few days, Elias. When I arrive, I will need to address the Ishaidan council directly. What I have to tell you all is very, very important."

* * *

The trip back to NewLondon didn't seem to be taking near as long as she had anticipated. The LightningRod, though old, was responsive to her touch. Even though half-a-millennia had passed since the tank had been manufactured, it worked without fail, a testament to the workmanship and design of previous generations.

In a way, this was one of the reasons April liked machines. She could see the skill and thought invested in each component, could sense the interconnectivity of every system. Sometimes it seemed that only she alone could appreciate what it took to create such amazing machines, granted the one exception being the original designers. For her it was a form of purity, designing and manufacturing to pursue perfection, a form of sanity in the face of chaos.

Forward scanners blipped a warning. The LightningRod was coming up to a collapsed bridge which once traversed a deep gorge. She checked the video feed. The center span was missing. She spun the cameras. Severed suspension cables hung limp like so many dangling spider webs now broken free of their anchors. The lower deck was simply gone.

She brought down the cycles on the powerful motors. The low throbbing through the floor plates dropped in frequency as the gigantic tank slowed. For the last 200 km or so she had been making good time, rolling along at an average speed of 300 kmh, so now the landscape around her seemed to move in slow motion. Her mind needed to adjust back to normalcy.

The scanners swept over the lanes ahead. She had to be careful on approach, check for faults, not get too close, make sure nothing would give under the weight of the wheels.

But how to get across?

The feeds confirmed the integrity of the other ramp jutting out from the opposite bank. Most of the bridge remained intact, just the center span gone. She laughed at her own analysis.

Only the center span.

It had to be a 300 meter sheer drop to the gorge below.

She pulled up on the controls, bringing the Porter relic to rest with its wheels resting on the foot of the bridge's deck. A quick minute and she was out, sticking her head up through the LightningRod's roof hatch, smelling the warm freshness of a newly generated atmosphere. The air was rich and humid, thickened by the sprays of water from the rushing gorge below. She could hear its angry thunder and feel the river's power through vibrations that crept all the way up to the roof deck of the tank.

No wonder the bridge had failed.

Getting across could be done. She knew how. It was a simple, textbook maneuver perfected by a Porter a long time ago. The difference, as compared to then versus now, however, was that this Porter had little choice at the time – it was jump or fall victim to a horde of scrapies.

They called it the KeLeary jump, she remembered. It had made their clan infamous.

Why did she insist on remembering all the trivial details?

This was basic physics really: trim up your mass, make yourself lighter by counteracting the pull of gravity, get up enough speed. Then, rotate the secondary boost thrusters all the way to point downward for vertical lift, and fire them up just at the precise moment to maximize lift.

It would all be easy, assuming the boosters fired evenly, and timing was synchronized just right, had enough inertia, and the anti-grav plates had stripped off enough of the weight.

Too many assumptions, and far too many variables. Trying this would be foolhardy at best.

She looked out over the mist-filled gorge to the opposite bridge deck. At this distance, even the wind made a difference. She can always go around. Another 20 to 30 hours at least, but it would be safer.

She climbed down the tank's exterior ladder and started toward the river. The closer to the edge she walked, the more she could sense the sway in the structure. It was small, but it was there. The whole mass of steel and concrete was moving like a leaf in the breeze.

She grabbed a stone and threw it over the edge, feeling her arm snap with as much recoil as she could muster. The stone fell pitifully short of ever making it to the other side, disappearing into the white fog which emanated up from below.

"Shit!" she cursed loudly.

One last look revealed an interesting perspective. Judging from where she stood, the other side seemed lower - and that could work to her advantage.

She'd have to work the numbers, take the measurements, but she knew to cross such a distance the tank would need to be traveling pretty close to its maximum speed, and at that speed, anything could happen.

Inside the LightningRod, the tank's computers ran the simulations no less than a hundred thousand times. Each time it recalculated probabilistic failure scenarios, bringing up an overall estimate of no better than a 63% chance of success. She ignored the fatalistic projections. The modelers were conservative at best, biased toward safety.

Factor that into the calculations and the numbers would be at least 75%, she thought smugly.

She proceeded to switch the feeds to the anti-grav plating, then to boost up the power to put them to maximum excitation, with full reverse flow. She knew a few tricks the old Porters would never have known.

Temps were stable, power fluctuations minimal, but the plates were vibrating severely. Given their age, it was a wonder they were holding together at all. Their primary design was to increase mass, to pull the tank down and maximize traction at high speed, at the same time cancel out inertial forces on its occupants when maneuvering. Their primary function was inverted now, much the same as the tank's boosters that were not intended to point down. The boosters were often used to build initial thrust when pulling many cars, a simple, yet effective tool. It was a last-minute thought by some engineer who incorporated them into the design. It turned into an idea that worked so well it was requested on every build order the Porter clans placed, to the puzzlement of the original manufacturers.

Her father, Oranis, had passed on a few other little tricks to April as well. She remembered their what-if discussions. How they had sat on-deck for hours, passing the time with stories of the past, of how the Porter tanks had been pushed beyond their design so many times. They would debate out crazy scenarios and what would one do if...

Yes, she remembered his ideas. Fill the tires with helium, tighten the hydraulics to maximum and make the tank as rigid as possible, lock the motor synchronization and disable the slip differential drives to ensure even thrust on every wheel.

It would all help.

It took another hour to circulate helium into the tires. It was easy enough to refine the helium from the atmospheric filters. Just getting enough of it was the trick. Making the hydraulic adjustments was easy too, except for the seven different leaks that sprung up along the lines and the not so easy repairs of those leaks.

The hours passed by, and the sun moved down to the horizon.

She checked the readouts and blew the dust off the lower monitor so she could see the figures: 45% mass decrease, drain on the fusion system was 105%. *The batteries were making up for the deficit and the boosters were all set to the proper angle.*

She test fired each pair.

Green light on all systems.

She blew out a long breath. *Guess it was time to go. What the hell, you only live once.*

She activated the motors, decoupled the brakes and rolled the LightningRod back at a slow crawl. She needed distance to accelerate and that was the easiest part to calculate.

She had it all worked out in her head to the last figure. No mistakes.

One more glance at the enviro-scans. Winds westward at 5 kmh – a gentle breeze. Intermittent gusts registering 20-25 kmh fairly consistent. They came once every three seconds which was approximately the total time needed to complete the jump. She would start as a gust ended...

She adjusted the navigation controls one more degree to port, locking in the steering attitude. She could override manually at any time, but why should she? This had to be precise.

Forward monitors all focused on the bridge deck on the opposite bank - her ultimate destination.

She buckled herself into the seat.

The wind speed meters climbed and then started to drop. With a deep breath, she pressed the button to initiate the launch.

The tank's wheels screamed to a thunder, and April was slammed back into the cushion of her seat. She fought to hold onto the steering controls. Though essentially disconnected now, control would be returned to her as soon as they set down on the other side.

Only seven seconds to the bridge. A glance to the side revealed girders and cables passing by in a blur.

Boosters engaged, pushing her head down with enough force to knock the wind from her.

She fought for a breath and watched as the other side of the bridge came closer.

Everything seemed to be moving in slow motion. She watched the displays, saw the alarm indicating that the port booster number five had failed, saw the upcoming bridge tilt to the right.

Touchdown jarred her to her bones. Her jaws clamped shut chipping a tooth.

The computer guidance was ready. An automatic drop of hydraulic pressure compensated, allowing the tank to absorb the force of the first hit.

Then the first bounce.

April had tenths of a second to regain control. She wrenched to starboard, dropped all the suspension hydraulics down, felt the wheels bite once again. Another bounce, and more traction. She had both feet pressed on the brakes.

Alarms seared her ears with warnings of overheating rotors, but she kept the pressure on.

They were snaking from one side to another, barely managing to keep from crashing into the bridge's superstructure. The squealing of tires drowned out all the other noise.

She slammed the decompression button, and the tire pressure dropped. The snaking stopped, and the tank straightened, decelerating finally into a nice straight line.

It took a moment for April to relax her calves and ease up on the brake pedals, even though the Porter tank had, by that time, come to a full stop. Her palms were slick, and her shirt was wet enough to wring out.

She checked the main display, then checked the time. A little over two seconds airborne, less than the expected three.

She started the diagnostics and got up, stretching out quickly to fight a sudden cramping in her legs.

Something warm and coppery was running into her mouth. She reached up – her nose was bleeding.

OK, nothing to worry about considering you just jumped a chasm.

She wiped at the blood, spit out a tiny piece of tooth, then proceeded to scramble up the exit ladder, conceding to a sudden undeniable urge to get outside.

The air seemed to smell a bit sweeter, the thunder of the river a little softer. She took a deep breath and closed her eyes for a moment.

But she knew she had to see it, and she looked back into the misty distance. Her eyes adjusted focus onto the bridge deck, saw the snaking black trails her tank's wheels had left. One side over to the other and back again, five, no six times.

That was close. No one ever talked about the landing.

It took a moment for her to register the horn blasting madly behind her, further down the road. It was coming from a small amphibious rover racing up to meet her. In typical Porter fashion, she assessed her situation quickly. Although the vehicle was close enough that she hadn't time to duck back in and get a gun, the LightningRod's hatch would give enough cover if the driver was inclined to shoot.

So, she waited.

The little rover came to a halt within the tank's shadow. The driver, clad in brown and khaki, wasted no time jumping out through his roof hatch. It was a male, of that much she was certain, too stocky, too brawny to be female.

He stood for a moment and simply stared at her. And then, of all things, he raised his hands and started clapping in a slow, methodical applause.

"Thought I'd never live to see it," he yelled. "Not this bridge. No one would be crazy enough to do it. No one."

April smiled, wiped her nose again, and noticed with relief, the bleeding had subsided. "Crazy is not the way I'd put it," she shot back.

"By Jezuz, you just jumped that thing with a full-fledged tank. If I hadn't seen it with mine own eyes, I'd say that was impossible."

"Listen, Porter," she said, knowing that he was, just by his manner. "Everyone's heard of the KeLeary jump."

"Ha! That was just legend, just a story. Wait 'till I tell the Clan. They won't believe it! And what pray tell was so damned important that you couldn't go around?"

"I've a port to land and a charter to fill," April replied.

He laughed, "By God, ye are truly a Porter through and through. You have Elroy Talbot at your service, my dear." He bowed ceremoniously.

"And this little rover is what passes for a transport nowadays?" she teased.

"Ah, no, my dear. I'm on a bit of an excursion."

"Oh?"

"Yes. Looking for a woman, matches your description, pretty much."

"And why would you be looking for such a woman?"

"Orders from NewLondon."

April nodded. "Well, that explains it. You wouldn't be looking for April of the Clan McThurn, would you?"

His gaze was suddenly sharp, body stiff. "Aye. And it be my guess that who ya be, The April McThurn. 'Tis no wonder."

April smiled and nodded, but his strange reaction irked her slightly.

"Well, I hope what you've heard isn't all bad."

"What I've heard I was thinkin' was embellished with exaggeration, but now I know better. 'Tis the truth that is harder to comprehend than the stories downplayed in order to be believed."

"You are a Talbot? Then you know of Elias of NewLondon?"

"Aye, my father 'tis. He instructed me to search you out. I was 'bout to turn around when I saw this monster come up the t'other side. Didn't know 'twas you, ya realize."

He shook his head again. "By Jezuz, I cannot fathom, 'truly amazing."

"No, just a calculated risk. My father, Oranis, told me this was doable. He knew what these machines could do."

"Oranis. He was a good man your father, truly."

"So, I figure I'm three to five hours away from NewLondon."

"Well, ya figure? I guess if it's based on that infernal tank of yours. It'd be a day's ride in this little beast."

April studied him for a moment.

"Ok then, I'll open up the bay. You can drive her up and join my crew."

"Be honored, Captain McThurn."

She smiled. She liked the sound of that - '*Captain*'.

* * *

"Bring her about," yelled the bay controller.

A crowd had gathered at the port bay waiting for her to dock. So many questioning faces, apprehensive and excited they seemed like she was one of the traveling circus transports. Kids lined up tight against the containment ropes to see the creatures, the colorful characters, and the wide assortment of glittering rides and if one were lucky, free bags of cotton candy.

But that was a long time ago. So long in her mind's eye, it left but a few blurry images. Her father had brought them into NewLondon when the show came in. It had been a grand occasion. She was six, maybe seven - not long after they had found her.

The bay controller swung his flags furiously. April slammed the brakes, suddenly realizing she was about to overrun the dock. The mechanical monster slid to a stop with synthetic rubber squealing over concrete.

Elroy piped up. He had been quiet for the last part of the ride, content to watch the systems, but not now.

"April, with what I'd seen ya do with this monster, I'd've sworn you could manage a routine docking." He laughed at his own joke.

April shot him the nastiest look she could muster. It only made his cockeyed grin that much wider.

"We be home, so 'tis time to address the masses."

"Why do you think they're all out here?"

"To see you, me dear, why else?" He shot it out like a question that needed no answer.

April couldn't fathom why, in all honesty. No, it was to see the LightningRod, that to be sure. A Porter transport that had been lost for centuries is sure to draw a crowd.

She disengaged the motors and dropped the fusion reactor to standby, keeping a close eye on the gravitational containment vessel temps as the power output dropped down, uniformly, without a single spike.

One helluva machine.

"Don't dally too much, lassie, your admirin' fans are a waitin'."

"Will you drop it," April scoffed. "There, the ramp's down. You go first."

"Why, you afeared they'll bite?" He laughed again. She ignored him.

She kept pace behind him as they walked out, staying close. The crowd was there, many faces, hushed whispers, too many eyes watching her. It made her uncomfortable.

The familiar face of Elias appeared from within the crowd. He pushed forward to greet them, a few of the council members trailing behind him.

"'Tis good to see you made it without incident."

"Aye, not near as exciting as on the way in," Elroy commented giving an implicating wink to April.

"Did you assemble the council?" April asked, quick to avoid wasting time on more stories and chatter.

"Yes, April, however, I thought you may want to rest first."

She rejected the suggestion with a wave. Yes, she was really tired. That much was true, but she was wired on adrenaline now, and there was no way she could sleep.

"I'm fine, let's get to this."

The crowd parted as the small party started into to the city.

"Ms. McThurn, are the TFPs going to work this time?" The question came from an older woman. Her ragged clothes were clean but threadbare, and her features revealed the hard lines of one who had spent a life in the mines.

"Yes, they will, that much I can give you, a Porter pledge if nothin' else. We'll see those blue skies over Ishaida. The changes will stay. Not like before."

Hands reached for her if only to touch her, no more than a silent thank you.

They waded through the crowd, leaving April even more perplexed than before.

Elroy seemed to pick up on her reaction. "Why so surprised? You're a hero to them. Think about what you've done. Not only did you start up the TFPs but you've taken down Soho-Beher single-handedly, and there's rumors you were offered the throne of Anard-Bueller, nevermind you've just come back from the dead in a transport that's been lost for centuries. And don't forget, April, that blasted jump! It's unbelievable. Just thinking about it gives me chills." He honestly shook a bit, closing with an uneven laugh. "Hell, they haven't even heard that one yet. And I got it recorded."

"What did you say?" She stopped and the whole progression followed. April studied him for a second, enough to read that he had not been mocking her. "Delete it."

"Oh no, lass." He chuckled. "You are a might too late for that. I made sure to upload it to the vid feed already. We cannot rob your admirers of the truth, you know."

She resigned to his explanation, knowing full he was not lying. "Great."

He grinned his cockeyed grin and turned away. "And I will see you again."

"Hey, Elroy," she called after him. "I'm not done yet."

Elroy smiled.

They arrived at the city's administration tower and quickly made their way to the Councillor's chamber. Others filed in through adjoining doors, administrators and mayors alike. Elias escorted April to a podium near the center.

"You have your audience as requested, April," he waved across to the surrounding faces. "Please, feel free to start anytime."

April swallowed, and rubbed wet palms on her pants. She had spent hours going over this in her head, planning carefully just how she was going to do this, but for some reason, she could recall nothing.

"I'm ah... thank you for meeting with me," she choked out the words. "I am... I mean. I appreciate your time."

Quiet gazes fell upon her. No one said anything.

"Please, we know something has happened," came the soft voice of Annette Theron. "Just tell us in your words."

"OK, the first thing you need to know."

The words of her speech streamed out of her fractured memory and dropped away. She had such an eloquent delivery and now it's gone.

"The first thing is, we're not alone here on Ishaida. There are others here, other beings I mean, that are not human. They are sentient like ourselves but very different."

Eyes darted, a ruffling of voices started to grow to a loud throb.

"I've seen them, at the Alvilla Valley TFP. It was them that triggered the geological shift that saved GhenghisPrime."

Again, more raised voices and questions started to fly from all directions.

"Hold it!" Elias growled. "Let her finish."

April nodded. "OK." She proceeded to review the events to the group, attempting to follow it in chronological order, summarizing as best she could: the boarding the Sequin trader, the mercenaries, the wreck, her march out, finding the LightningRod, and finally meeting the aliens.

"We made an agreement."

"But on what authority!" yelled out GhenghisPrime's Mayor.

"On mine!" she shot back angrily. "As I have done before and as I will continue to do. As an Ishaidan civilian, I decide. You were not there, you could have been there, you could have joined me on this trip, but you did not, did you? As many times before, I stood alone to make my own decision. As before, I acted on the pretense of what is best for Ishaida."

"Enough of this," retorted the Mayor of NewBerlin. "If anything is to be decided, it is to be done by this council. Go and fetch these beings, child, and bring them forward to this council."

April did not miss the special emphasis he had put on 'child'.

"You want to talk with them? You go out there and find them yourself. Either way, it's done. The agreement's been made and there ain't any recalling it."

"Maybe so, April," replied Elias, "but don't you think it best for this group to set the terms?"

"It's too late," she said feeling the weariness creep into her bones. "The codes have been given, they've adjusted the TFPs, the terms have already been set."

"To what end? We don't understand. What have you agreed to?"

"I need to sit down." Her legs felt shaky now like her body was getting ready to shut down. "I need a drink."

Annette's concerned face appeared through the sea of others. "Here let me help, dear." She guided her to sit, handed her a glass. She gulped it down.

"It's not so bad you know. When it's done, it's really only a few degrees warmer than the planned mean average, with a slightly hotter equator. That's pretty much it."

"And what do we get in return?"

"Their protection."

A hush moved across the group like a shadow of a cloud moving across the sun.

April eased back in her chair, resting her now weary body. She had said enough.

The debate raged on well past April's retirement to a soft bed, and well beyond her refreshing shower, and a welcomed breakfast.

A sharp knock on the door interrupted her quiet, peaceful bliss.

"Ms. McThurn, your presence is requested by the Council."

"I'll be down in a few moments." She dreaded her own words the very second after she had said them. What will they want now?

Faces seemed friendlier, at least more so than before. Elias was gracious, as usual.

"Thank you for your promptness, my dear. We only have a few more questions."

"Certainly. I'll try to answer them as best as I can."

"We need to know what their intentions are, to sum it up." He cleared his throat a bit as if he was nervous about the answer. "The longer term intentions."

She took a moment to pass a gaze across the room. It seemed that no one was in any state to pounce and attack her. Of course, they were politicians, the masters of deception.

"I really don't know. They just want to live. It's more than a little difficult to read them. But I don't believe they're trying to harm us."

"And are they willing to talk to others? To representatives of the government perhaps?"

"Sure, if you can find them."

"You do not want to be involved?"

"No, not at all. I guess if you need my help I will."

"And what are your plans then, April?"

"Well, that leads to my question. As I have full salvage rights on the LightningRod, has any clan laid claim to her?"

"No, it was under military ownership back then. No one can contest your claim," confirmed Elias.

"So I then claim her under the Clan McThurn."

Elias chuckled, "So you want to fade back into the Porter life, disappear into the Ishaidan landscape, is that it?"

"I do. It's a big world. I'll be happy to fade away."

"And this rumor we've heard about Anard-Bueller and the offer for you to be the next executive officer?"

"That's not going to happen. I don't expect you to understand my motives, just know I am Porter in every respect, and as one, I have the right to choose my own path."

"But, April," Elias pleaded.

"No, this is not up for your discussion. I've laid my claim, honor it."

"Yes, yes, of course. No one will contest your claim on that museum piece. Go about your way and shuttle cargo between the cities. If that is the life you choose, so be it. But why April? Why choose such a hard life over such opportunity?"

"Yes, to have every *thing* one could want. And those things will then own you. I've no desire to lead a cold, empty life."

A few looked away shaking their heads in open disgust. To give up the riches one could only dream of. She must be insane.

April wasted no time pushing her way out. As the door closed behind her, it seemed like a vast weight had been lifted off her chest, and she was free to breathe again.

She started down the crowded path, her mind busy with the details of the coming days. She had a crew to assemble, cars to lease, repairs to make, trade manifests to arrange. She could only hope the McThurn Clan's insurance and bank funds would be enough.

The LightningRod was as she had left it. A few people were hovering around it, inspecting its scars, talking back and forth of rumors and legends. She ignored them as she passed by, moving quickly to avoid being intercepted. The ramp dropped, but not quite as fast as she desired.

"Ms. McThurn!" came a voice behind her. "I mean, Captain McThurn, do you have a minute?"

April turned, reluctantly. "Yeah, sure."

The woman she faced was probably no older than her. Her hair was blonde, eyes brown, attractive if not for the scar stretching across her left cheek and onto her exposed shoulder. But to April, that scar gave her that much more credibility.

"Name's Jasimine. I heard you're looking for a crew."

"How'd you hear that already? I mean, I just left..."

She smiled coyly. "Well, it was more of an educated guess. I've been waiting here awhile."

"And your clan?"

She looked down, kicking out at a loose pebble. "So that's the way it is, then? Clan only?"

The ramp clicked fully down, momentarily drawing April's attention away. Secretly she considered darting into the safety of her tank.

"Um, no. Not really. I'm not sure."

"Fine. I understand." Jasmine turned, already resigned against any further discussion.

"Look, I just haven't thought about it is all," April said, the pitch of her voice just a little higher than normal.

Jasimine turned. "Oh?"

"So, you have no clan?"

"I'm last of the line, as they say. My uncle's transport was lost in the bombing. No clan members left."

"You have experience running?"

"Well, no. I've been in the city most of my life. I was finally on the short list for the crew when the city was hit. I've been preparing, working in hydroponics mostly, and I have a degree in communications and electronics."

"You know how to set up a skip-link?"

"Yeah. Sure. Basic stuff."

"This rig I have, she's old. The com-link equipment needs a complete rebuild. Can you do that?"

"Yeah. Sure I can."

April gave her one good eye up and then down. She stuck her hand out. "Welcome to your new Clan – the Clan McThurn."

Jasimine smiled broadly, not hesitating to take her hand. "And when do I start?"

"Right now. The work is in there." April nodded to the lowered ramp. "If you have any friends that you'd vouch for, I'll consider them too. As of right now, you are the first member of the crew."

"Then I have to also ask... about the pay."

"I can pay board only until I firm up some contracts."

Jasimine drank it all in, and her eyes gave away her understanding, but she didn't change her stance. She just kept looking at April in that small knowing smile.

"That's all I need, then. 'Tis good enough for me."

"Don't worry about the pay. That will be coming, soon, too. I'm sure," assured April, a little less confidently.

The next few days were crazy. The word had spread – the LightningRod needed a crew. April did not stop with just Jasimine. One could not run an outfit like this alone. She needed help. She spent considerable attention compiling a list of who she needed. Mechanical systems, hydraulic, electrical and nuclear, cooling and thermal controls, navigation – they were all critical, all stations were key, and all had to be filled with the right people.

Jimmy Mayhew was here - an old friend of the family's. He'd been working at the docks forever. He had wandered down not too long after Jasimine, calling for April from the base of the ramp. After a brief discussion, Jimmy had been the second to join the crew. It wasn't long after that April had a lineup outside stretching all the way through the bay doors.

"For cryin' out loud, where's everybody coming from?" April threw her hands up in exasperation.

Jasimine just shrugged and went back to work on a circuit board.

They streamed in, all manners of Porters, and some city dwellers too. Some were looking for work, others a way out, some wishing for excitement. They had all heard of April McThurn, they all wanted to be part of something bigger.

April asked the tough questions, watched for cues: a quick aversion of the eyes, a swallow, nervous lick of the lips, how they carried themselves. More importantly to consider was what experience they had.

Oranis had taught her lots on reading others.

She had to pick seven in all, with two already chosen, there was only five to go. She could've added more – hell, many of the Porters had generations of their families all tightly squeezed into those mechanical houses. But seven would work right now. Not too many, just enough.

Given time, the clan would grow and so would the transport. She thought of too many unattainable comforts, but only for a moment. A mate, a husband. Someone to hold onto, to be close to.

No, her hormones would not own her, she was young yet. She had time, and she would be selective. But one day, to have a family, and have children, that was the ideal dream.

Jimmy sat beside her, taking down the personal information of the applicants of which a select few she would eventually refer to as clan members. Keeping accurate records was important, for they would have to submit a complete crew roster, with at least three descendant levels back, to the Porter council upon official registration.

Without a registration, the LightningRod could never pull registered cargo. It was a required step, more than just a formality. She would remain critical of the Porter Authority until that registration was in her hands.

Jimmy shook the hand of the last crew member brought on – a tall, slight fellow named Withers. He was a nuclear specialist. His name suited him somehow.

"OK, that's it. We're done for now." April waved off the rest of the lineup. "I may be looking for others down the road. Thank you."

They dispersed, some grumbling disappointment, others quiet and withdrawn.

"OK, let's do a roll call, Jimmy."

They all lined up, a ragtag mismatch of souls with nary a relation amongst them. And they were now to be a family.

This was like it was back in the day, before the family generations. Every one of them assumed the Clan name McThurn, and they would carry that name to their grave. Everyone would be joined by that clan name forever. Being a Porter was not a job, it was a lifestyle. Once in, there's no getting out.

Jasimine stood straight, beaming a smile so wide it must have hurt.

April stared down the line, giving each of them a thorough inspection. She then pulled the pledge form out of her pocket.

"Raise your right hand and repeat after me, please."

"I - say your full name now." Following a cacophony of different syllables and long-phrased names, April then continued.

"Will honor the Porter code of Ishaida, be it until my injury or my death, be it until the last Ishaidan city falls."

"As a Porter, I will perform my role without bias or favoritism, to protect my civilization, and all the people of Ishaida."

"No matter the danger, the hardship, or the cost, I will remain honorable and loyal to the clan of McThurn."

"And will hereby assume and carry the name of McThurn."

"And as long as I live, I and to my death, shall bear Ishaida within my heart."

April looked across the line. Each finished with a look of defiance on their faces. Each had pledged with honest determination. Jasimine's scar was stained with tears.

"You are now the proud members of the Clan McThurn, and the crew of The LightningRod, congratulations."

And a cheer came up, followed by a whoop and laughter, and hugs all around.

"Alright, let's get to order here," urged April quietly, fighting back her own tears – driven by pride possibly, but maybe something more, like she had somehow regained her family back.

They lined up in their haphazard way and waited for her.

"Jasimine, you have 12 hours to have the com system up, can you make it?"

"Half done already, we will be ready to go," she stated enthusiastically.

Immediately to her left stood Bobby Elias, an expert in hydraulics and the car systems. He had just pulled himself away from polishing the tank's outer hull, removing the scale of oxidation and erosion from the aging outer skin. His face was smeared in black, and he was filthy. She was sure he was still dressed in yesterday's clothes.

"Bobby, you need to clean yourself up. We Porters pride ourselves on our appearance even when we're neck high in dirt, and we don't smell. Are we clear?"

He nodded, grimacing a bit, uncomfortable that his lack of cleanliness was pointed out for all of them to hear.

"And I need to know where the best cars are out there for lease, and in what port they are. I don't want any junk, right?"

"I'll get on it, Captain. The LightningRod will have a good train on her before we pull out."

April moved her attention to Karen, whose dark eyes were barely visible behind the bushel of midnight black hair which hid a slight, delicate face. She was, undoubtedly, the most attractive woman in the crew, more so than April, if only she would expose her face from behind that mass of bangs. She was the navigation specialist, and she would need to spend most hours spewing over sat-feed data and images, sorting through the most recent changes in the Ishaidan topography. It was probably the toughest job on the transport. If she made a mistake, they were all in trouble. But April could tell, behind those dark eyes there was a flicker of genius buried there. Answers came all too quickly to April's unforgiving, probing questions.

Next in line was Quinn. He was a bulk of a man, with shoulders as broad as the LightningRod's corridors. He was the resident cook, and naturally, April had assigned him security detail.

The LightningRod was unique in many ways from the later generation transports. As one of the first of its kind, it was constructed with extra heavy military grade components, including a set of fore and aft gun turrets, which April had full intent to restore to functioning order.

"I want those turret systems pulled apart and rebuilt. You up for that?"

"Yes'm, I mean, ma'am, err... Captain."

April smiled a bit, enjoying how this mountain of a man seemed to quiver in front of her.

"I heard you have a talent for making good food. You think you can keep us healthy and looking forward to our next meal?"

Quinn grinned back. "Oh yeah, I knows a bit on how to prepare a dish or two. You'll not regret bringing me on board, Captain."

"We'll see. That galley is a bloody mess. You've a lot of work to do to get it into shape."

The next in line was Withers. He stayed quiet, watching the others, and never looked directly into anyone's eyes, least of which April's. But he was an exceptional engineer and had extensive experience in fusion reactors of all types.

"Withers, we'll do a full check of the reactor cooling system before we run the X-ray inspection on the reactor vessel, OK?"

"No problem, got it," he mumbled quietly.

"I don't want a square centimeter missed on that reactor. Be meticulous, Withers."

"You can count on it, Captain." He shuffled his feet, seemingly fascinated by something on the ground.

April moved to Tracey. She was an older woman, a bit plump, with attractive soft features and a warm manner. She was brought on as the resident medical officer, but also had heavy machinery operator experience, although you would never guess by first look. She didn't seem to carry that aloof calmness and confidence of an operator, but it was all there behind that easy smile. One just had to look.

"Tracey, I'll be assigning you primary pilot along with medical. You'll need to work with Bobby on hooking up the cars. I want you to double-check every connection. Weather out there can get real nasty. We can't afford any mistakes."

She smiled back. "No problem there. I'll also need to restock the medical bay. That may get expensive but a lot of those supplies are beyond expired."

April nodded, knowing she spoke the truth, and this was a necessary expense. She wasn't going out without the right medicines or equipment.

"Whatever you need."

"And I want to inspect and clean the environmental systems as well. I think maybe Quinn can help me if you don't mind before he tackles the weapons system. I think I know what killed the original crew and I am concerned there's residual in the HVAC filters. We've got to sanitize those scrubbers ASAP."

"What was it?" April asked, surprised that she already found the cause.

"A fungus. Some of the dome-dwellers had perished from exposure to the same thing in the earlier years. We've since adapted our HVAC systems to kill it off, but it's never really left. You and everyone here are quite immune to low-level toxicity as our immune systems have adapted over the generations. But it's wise to not expose anyone to high, toxic levels at any time, of course."

"Thank you, Tracy. I am already feeling better about our transport."

Jimmy was the last in line, chief mechanical systems, and second mate. He was the closest relation to her by blood, just a few generations and cousins removed. He would work with April, and he was quick, if not just as quirky in his mannerisms. He had a bit of a tick, a nervous habit, a constant shrugging, and shifting of his feet. But he was a good mechanic and prided himself on his machinist and creation skills.

"Jimmy, you and I have the driveline. We need to inspect the undercarriage and suspension. I fear I may have jarred or bent something in my efforts to get here."

"Ya. Saw the vid feed. Was a good one. I'm ready when you are." He shrugged, then leaned over and spat on the ground.

"Last but not least, so all of you are aware, we're not leaving this bay without a worthwhile payload. We'll wait if we have to."

April stepped back, looking at her new family.

All in all, it was an unlikely mix of a crew.

* * *

"A few more centimeters and we're there," yelled Bobby. He wiped his forehead, keeping the sweat out of his eyes.

The last 15 days had been anything but smooth, and his Captain hadn't let up. This was, at least, the last car. The car coupling clicked into place. He thumbed the neck mike signaling Tracey to stop.

"Good driving, Tracey. We're all good here. I'll be a few minutes to finish the hookups."

Tracey leaned back in her chair. "Finally," she said, letting out a long sigh. She checked the systems link to car 27 via the video feed, then rotated the chair back to the main heads-up display.

Each car can be driven via its wireless uplink, their wheel drive motors were not very powerful, but given one for each of their monster sized wheels, combined they were able to pull the car along with a full payload at a half-a-kilometer an hour. Given each wheel had its own ability to pivot a few degrees, it wasn't much, but it was enough to line up each car to the main train of cars.

She reached out to the heads-up display and touched the last car. A 3D hologram launched, projected a schematic of the car and its systems. The hydraulic system displayed red, and then suddenly switched to green.

Tracey smiled. Little Bobby was working his 18th hour straight, but he had not complained nor had he slowed down. He had something to prove to his new Captain, possibly to himself as well.

God knows she hadn't been easy on him, or anyone else for that matter. But they didn't mind, none of them challenged their Captain. They had all been given a rare chance, assigned elite stations of which only a few of this world would be part of. They were all Porters now. And they were ready for their first run.

April glanced down the long line of cars. Bobby's chubby figure was creeping along the port side of the last car, on the upper catwalk.

"You all clear, Bobby?"

"Yes, Cap'n. I mean, got one last check here."

"Jim, can you double-check that last car. Make sure Bobby didn't miss anything."

"Geez, April," He slammed the lower hatch of car 3 closed. "He's new. It's easy to miss a hydraulic – and he only did it once."

April kept her gaze steady on him. Jimmy, half covered in grease and hydraulic fluid shrugged, irritated by her directness. He turned and headed down the transport, saying nothing more.

Only Jimmy would call her April. Everyone else referred to her as Captain. She didn't mind, but it seemed to distance her from them. She wasn't sure that was a good thing. One thing for sure, Jimmy was irritated that she was not giving Bobby any latitude. She had her reasons.

Out there, there was little forgiveness for errors.

It would take a half-hour before they were ready to pull out. April watched from the main deck.

The primary airlock opened up, and Tracey edged the LightningRod ahead in a slow but steady speed.

April reached over the management console and ran a full scan on the car diagnostics. A few warnings came up, but nothing drastic.

"Jimmy, you got that pump on car 4?" she clicked on the com-link.

"Headin' up there now, Captain."

"Bring Bobby with you – he needs to learn those systems."

She clicked over to Quinn. "Quinn, you have those starboard rail guns refitted yet?"

"Well, kinda. I need your help I think. Need you to make a small pin. I'll bring up the original."

"Sure, bring it up. By the way, we need a special kick-off meal, something memorable."

Quinn chuckled, "that I can do."

"Captain," prompted Karen. "I have the latest weather forecast. We need to make it to that ridge in the East in the next four hours. A nasty front is moving in from the South."

April scanned over the navigation relief map which projected up from the central inspection table. Karen pointed at the ridge, pressed a few virtual controls, and played out the projected front's travel.

"It'll stay Southeast of the ridge as far as I can tell."

"I hope you are right, Karen. But we can't avoid them all. It's a long way to GhenghisPrime."

She opened up the com to all channels. "Crew, we have a change in plans. Will have to hold off on that special meal we have planned because of weather. We are about to expedite. Say goodbye to NewLondon."

A good-sized crowd had gathered at the port docks to wave as they passed. April muttered under her breath. It would be good to leave, and be away from being idolized. She was tired of the presents, the strangers asking for her signature, the constant invitations by the well-to-dos to dinner.

It was time to go.

As the transport left NewLondon in the horizon, a short message came over the com.

Jasimine announced the news over the open com. "A message from NewLondon: Crew of the LightningRod, Clan McThurn, congratulations and good luck."

Tracey let out a hoot. "We'll show'em we have Porter blood."

April laughed.

* * *

Chapter 17

I shaida was waking up. Her skin shifted and adjusted as her icy coating melted into oceans and lakes. Her atmosphere changed from red to greenish-blue and grew dense with moisture, and above, her skies turned angry.

In the past, windstorms had potential to be dangerous, but they lacked the density and moisture of the atmosphere of today. The sheer driving energy which these new storms possessed produced a lethal combination to the Porters.

The LionsPride was the first transport to find out just what Ishaida was now able to serve up. They might have made it if the storm had not stalled over them for those few extra minutes. The word spread through the Porter network in hours. The loss of the LionsPride was shocking, as she had done everything right, by the book, without fault, but all of it had simply not been enough.

April was on deck when the call came through. Jasimine announced the somber news from the co-pilot's chair. Her ashen face was all April needed to see.

"Get me NewLondon, Jasimine. Bounce it off a satellite or skip it off NewBerlin, but get me NewLondon. I need to talk with Elias."

April waited patiently on deck as Jasimine scrambled with the controls attempting countless variations. It took a while to get a clear signal, but she managed it, somehow. "Link established, Captain."

"Hello, Captain McThurn," Elias's familiar and tired voice resonated from the com.

"No need to be so formal, Elias. You look tired. I know why. Tell me, how many transports are dispatched right now?"

"Let me see, fifty-four give or take one or two."

"I heard the news. The LionsPride's lockdown protocol wasn't enough."

It took a moment for the reply. Elias tended to choose his words carefully. "Yes, I have the report here. We have evidence of bursts over 500 kmh. That is a tremendous amount of force considering the rising density of the atmosphere. The transports were simply not built to handle that much cross-lateral pressure, even tethered. I am afraid, based on this month's tracking, these superstorms seem to be becoming the norm."

"And if another transport, like the LightningRod, meets up with such a storm and we can't get out of its way?"

"Our engineers are looking at options. But we don't have any ideas yet. At this point, we are seriously considering a planet-wide docking of all transports."

April scoffed. "Forget it, Elias, no self-respecting captain will dock on a weather risk."

"If we do not grant cargo manifests they have no reason to leave."

"Yes, but that approach is not sustainable. You need the trade routes open. The cities need the cargo, nevermind any critical shipments. You can't lock us Porters down completely, and more than a few captains will be ready and willing to chance a run."

Elias nodded. "Aye, such as you, I suppose. But tell me what about your crew? Are they willing to chance it? Are they with you on this?"

"We'll see." April bit down on her lip. "Either way, if we see a storm we'll have the good sense to run for cover. I'll let you know if we have any other ideas. Meanwhile, keep Porter lines open and the sat feeds accurate."

Elias chuckled. "Yes, we will, that I can assure. Be safe, Captain McThurn."

Needless to say, the tension was noticeable on deck. Karen was assigned the job of monitoring the storm systems and recording their maximum wind forces. The trend confirmed what NewLondon had feared: Ishaida's atmosphere had hit a critical shifting point.

April experimented on the computer with varying designs attempting to find an improved profile for the transports. But nothing short of a massive hull restructure would work.

In the evenings as she walked her inspections through the decks, she felt her crew's eyes on her. They were all counting on her, the great April McThurn. What could she do about this?

Strangely the solution came to her in a dream. It was a strange dream at that.

She was on board a Soho-Beher starship heading through a band of meteoric debris. The shields were holding, but just barely. An asteroid was coming up at 15 degrees, and she kept yelling at Cruez to veer to port. But everyone was ignoring her. She kept yelling, and the crew only looked back at her blankly, like she was crazy. The shadow of the asteroid loomed closer in the viewport, and still, no one responded.

She awoke in a cold sweat. It took a moment to get her bearings back. Then she realized the answer had been right there all the time. All she needed was power and a lot of it.

"Jimmy, you awake? Jimmy?"

"Yeah, Captain. I'm up."

"Get the night shift up. We've some work to do. And wake up Withers."

When April walked through the hatch to the main deck, she knew something was wrong. Karen's face, at least what was visible, was paler than usual. Tracey didn't even acknowledge April's arrival, her eyes glued to the horizon ahead.

"How did you know?"

"Know what? What's our situation?"

"The storm. It formed incredibly fast. Its northeastern front is pushing a trough into this high pressure area, and we're on the edge of it. We're predicting F6 on the EDDF, but that I believe, is being conservative. We've switched over to route 65. Tracey's trying to outrun it. But I don't think we have a chance."

F6 on the enhanced-dynamic-density-fujita scale was incredible. She was right, they wouldn't have a chance against a storm of that force – locked down or not.

"How long?"

"Three hours max, maybe much less. Just dunno." Karen brushed her hair back with a nervous whip of her hand.

"Any close cover?"

"Nothing for about two hours until we hit an old mining settlement. I'd rather steer clear of there, though. It will create nothing but shrapnel."

"Lowlands, natural abutments, caves?"

"Here," she pointed to a darkened line on the navigation display. "We'd need to get off the highway, though. We'd lose time. The Jerico Abutment – remains of a crater wall. No more than 10 meters high but it's enough. If we can maneuver close to the west bank, it could block the wind."

"Good. Let's do it."

"We don't turn off for 45 minutes. Then it's an hour out. No telling what we could hit out there."

Getting stuck is always a possibility. In the worst case, they would have to ditch the cars.

April bit her lip, she had every last credit from what was left of the McThurn savings wrapped up in this transport. Financially this could ruin them.

"Stay on course, advise me when we are to make that turn."

She turned to the other crew members who were now crowding into the cramped deck. "Well, you heard her, we are now on the clock. I have an idea, but it will require moving cargo out of car 12 and redistributing it. Can we make some room?"

"All of it?" asked Bobby.

"Yes, I think we'll need most of it. I checked the cargo manifest. We have those fusion reactors in car 17. We'll need those moved to 12. That will free up some room."

"What are you thinking of, Captain?"

"We're going to construct a shield array along the length of the transport. Create a bubble profile over the ground. It will be completely aerodynamic when we are done."

Wither's eyes lit up, then shifted dark. "Too much mass hitting the shields, Captain, we'd overheat."

"Car 17 doesn't just have the reactors, it has a dozen capacitors packed away, as well. We've all the raw materials we need."

"And who's going outside to mount the projectors?"

April looked over to Quinn.

"Don't ya worry there, Captain. I can handle a bit a wind. You just tell me what I gotta do."

"Alright then, we have a plan. Karen and Tracey, you have the deck. Everyone else – let's get this cargo moved."

It wasn't as simple as April let on. Withers had to weld up mounts for the fusion reactors, and Jasimine had to play a complicated game of shifting cargo around to redistribute the load. Bobby kept up with her, securing each car as she finished, then tightening up the hydraulics and dropping the car's suspension profile as low as it would go. Quinn did the heavy lifting, moving things where the lift truck couldn't go.

In the lower decks of the tank, Jimmy and April were busy fabricating the projection disks. The overall design wasn't pretty but it would work, hopefully. They had to move fast, as they had 28 to make in total.

April directed Quinn back to the tank to pick up lines they'd need to run through to each car. Luckily the engineers of long ago had anticipated emergency runs and had built extra flexible conduit lines between the cars. If not for them, they'd have to run the lines through the hatches – and assume the risk of a decompression blowout if one of the cars were compromised.

The drilling into the car roofs from within was the most arduous and time-consuming of all the work. At first, it was just April and Jimmy running the drill, but Bobby and Jasimine came up to help, which ultimately sped up the process.

Quinn had the worst of all the jobs, moving from car to car on their upper decks, tying off as he went. Jimmy would feed the projection disks to Quinn by hanging out of the roof hatch enough to watch as he fed out the disk on a cable.

The wind would knock it around a bit, but the transport's overall speed kept it pointing in the proper direction. Quinn would snag the line, pull it in, then spend another five minutes or so to fasten it down and wire it up.

April watched their progress from the deck using the external cams. It was slow at best. She glanced over at the navigation display, saw the image of the storm creeping up on them. They were not going to make it. They needed more time.

"Turn off ahead, Captain," announced Tracy. "Do we take it?"

"Don't have much choice. Do we have a course verified from sat feed?"

"Looks like we can manage it," stated Karen. "But we'll need to keep an eye out for hazards."

April slid into the co-pilot's chair and flipped on the forward scanners to maximum. "Tracy, it's about time we see just how good a pilot you really are."

"I'll get us there, Captain. You just let me know if'n you catch something ahead. I've little time to react."

Their speed dropped dramatically, running as low as 130 kmh in some stretches. Jimmy had to walk the disks halfway as feeding them out by line no longer worked. April checked their progress intermittently. They were only on car 14.

"Tracy, see the ridge up ahead?"

"Aye, I do, finally."

"Let's bring her up nice and tight on the west side, OK?"

"Aye, we'll tuck her in there, nicely outta the wind."

Bobby had ensured they were secured properly by following a full lockdown procedure, including launching the side anchors into the neighboring granite and shale as soon as the transport came to rest.

Meanwhile, the storm front continued to build in power, and move toward them. Karen kept the crew informed as it progressed. Poor Quinn was being knocked around up top like a rag doll. But he kept working.

Jimmy and Withers locked down the two reactors in car 12 and wired up the distribution lines one by one. As they brought them online, April would run shield projection tests from the co-pilot seat. Every time they ran a test, the air would smell of ozone as the capacitors lit up under load.

"Can we lock half the transport down, then the other half?" asked April.

"We can keep the power distribution separate, but that means no load fault tolerance, a reactor goes down, so does half the transport," answered Withers.

'Let's do it."

April could hear the wind pounding and shrieking on the hull. "And this is supposed to get worse?"

"OK, we've isolated from the tank to car 14. Is Quinn clear?"

"I'm clear," came a garbled reply buried in static.

"Activating."

Suddenly the shrieking died away to silence.

April checked the feeds via the remote instrumentation connection display. The capacitors were holding without a problem. Reactor one was at 65%.

"We're looking good here, guys."

Cheers rang down through the length of the LightningRod.

The timing could not have been better, as the storm was on top of them now. They still had half the transport unprotected. The ridge was protecting them from the worst of it, which kept Quinn from being blown off the car. The genuinely high winds wouldn't reach them until the rear of the storm.

But they had no way to gauge how it was traveling now, as they had lost the sat feed due to interference. Quinn had some time yet, just no way to know for sure. Not until the wind shifted, and the ridge would no longer protect them.

A grueling hour later and he finally announced he finished the last car. He sounded utterly exhausted.

"Good job, Quinn," Jimmy stated, just as tired but unwilling to leave his post until Quinn was in and safe. "Captain, we're all clear."

"Activate the second array," she ordered. Jasimine who was waiting in car 12, tripped the relays. In the cockpit, monitors danced with colors on the heads-up display. April watched as they redlined, then subsided, eventually settling into the green. The second shield was up. And it was holding.

Quinn didn't waste any time getting back in. It was easier now that he was under the shield. The crew headed back to the tank sealing each car hatch closed behind them.

Jasimine helped Quinn peel off his enviro-suit. He was caked with a layer of sand and fine dust, but as his suit peeled off, she could see the massive bruises covering his arms and legs.

"Rough ride out there," she said, admiringly.

Quinn half smiled, too tired and too sore for any of his famous witty comments. "Yeah."

April took one look at her weary crew and could barely contain her pride.

"Good work everybody, we did it."

"What now, Captain?"

"Now? Now we wait. According to Karen, this storm is so big it will be at least a day before we are out of lockdown. In the meantime, I think everyone can get some rest."

"What about you, Captain?" asked Jimmy.

"I'll take the first watch. All of you hit the bunks, you deserve it."

They nodded in agreement and headed back to general quarters, leaving only Karen in their wake.

"Don't worry about me," April reassured her, "I'm fine."

"Well, I think I should be taking the first watch."

"No, it's OK. I couldn't sleep anyway. But don't worry, you can take the second watch." April gave a protective smile.

"Thanks, April, I mean... Captain. I knew you'd figure a way out of this." With that, she faded into the dark corridor.

April went back to the pilot's chair and eased down into the plush seat enjoying the quiet solitude. Peering out the windows, she watched as the winds rushed over the top of the ridge above. Streamers of dust and sand fired off the top and then danced in a chaos of churning winds. Intermittently reddish hues of light would glow through the haze, only to be eclipsed by a flash of white sheet lightning, to fade again to the darkness of blacks and browns.

Will Ishaida ever stop trying to kill her?

When will her skies be blue and quiet?

She leaned back in the chair, feeling the hum of the systems protecting them from the war zone around them. How long they would be in lockdown was anybody's guess.

* * *

The LightningRod had been traveling from NewLondon to GhenghisPrime, then onto NewBerlin. Porter navigation crews from both cities had watched as the encroaching storm put the Porter transport into its crosshairs. They had watched as it disappeared under that spiraling monster, and most had feared it was the end. Just like the LionsPride, they assumed it lost. No one expected to receive the sat-feed once the storm waned. But the infamous April McThurn and her crew managed to survive against all odds. The dispatch deck slowly filled up with curious eavesdroppers, everyone wanting to hear the LightningRod's story. On the other end, Jasimine spared no expense on supplying the details, and given her unique position, she had rights to embellish certain truths.

The story shot from city to city, eventually reaching Elias in NewLondon. He wasted no time contacting April.

"Looks like your legend continues to grow, April. Despite all this talk about fading away! I, of all people, should have known better."

"It's just another problem solved. Nothing I would relate to legendary behavior. I mean, really, Elias."

"It's not me. I hear it out there – in the streets of these cities. You are more famous than you realize."

"I don't want it. Don't need it. Don't want nothing to do with it."

Elias chuckled. "Well, you keep trying to run away from it, then."

"Is that all?"

"Actually, no. This force field of yours, can we retrofit all the transports?"

"Sure, it'll take time to refit every one. Need the Porter engineers to agree on some standards though. Every car needs to be part of the array – need standard connections so we can interchange any and all cars at any time. I'd suggest a dedicated reactor car for power supply instead of pulling the load from each tank, probably safer."

"I'll connect you with the chief of engineering here. Can you help move this along?"

"Of course, Porter code, remember?"

"Thank you, Captain McThurn. I look forward to hearing about your next feat."

April smiled. "No, I'm fading into the Ishaidan wilderness again, like I said."

* * *

The LightningRod and her crew kept busy running between the cities. Its new shield kept it safe from the most dangerous storms, along with every other retrofitted transport. Trade between cities was brisk and profitable. April became a shrewd trader, and her crew grew very efficient at their roles. She was finally content, what she had always wanted to be – Captain of her own transport.

But on Ishaida nothing ever stayed the same for long.

The storms waned as the planet's temperament continued morphing. The TFPs continued to run their programs, shifting focus from the mechanical means of generating Ishaida's atmosphere to a more adaptive and ultimately more effective way. Hidden deep within the bowels of the machinery incubators grew the next generation of biological machines which would turn Ishaida's now rocky terrain to a broad swath of colors, evolving the horizon into reds, greens, and yellows.

Biological life graduated from the simple fungi and bacteria to more complex plants, and then to stunted trees, which were the first of many new evolved strains. Each had been introduced as part of the master schedule dictated by the adaptive programs which directed small computer-controlled rovers to take samples, and satellites to scan the surface using everything from microwaves to tachyon bursts. The TFPs were enabled with multiple feedback systems, allowing them to be aware of what was happening to the planet, and ultimately where they were in the master schedule.

From behind the protective domes of the cities, a new generation of botanists studied the landscape with growing excitement. No one knew exactly how long it would all take, but they knew that one day they would not be confined to the walls of their cities, that they would walk amongst a planet covered with life, and the air would be dense and breathable.

As time passed, discussion of aliens was soon forgotten, now eclipsed by the Ishaida's multicolored sunrises and lavish life-filled landscapes. So much attention was focused on the planet that little time was spent monitoring the heavens.

A new storm was arriving.

The first battle group from Earth entered Ishaidan orbit at the beginning of the Ishaidan summer. The ships arranged themselves in a unique and deadly configuration around the planet, and they awaited the order.

The Ishaidan government's small collection of aged warships and smaller, but newer, gunships could do little against the modern, massive fleet. It was wise that they did not provoke them.

They relied upon a political solution, but the invaders ignored any and all requests for any ambassadorial meetings or discussions. Instead, they scanned the surface with every known device and monitored the planet intensively.

And through this inspection period, they were waiting patiently for the order.

* * *

A special ambassadorial committee was put together to meet with the Fleet Admiral. It was all done as quietly as possible, but the word soon spread to everyone, including the crew of the LightningRod.

The route LightningRod had taken, under the direction of its Captain, involved a small layover at a particularly pristine area adjacent to the newly indoctrinated Monsoona Sea.

April stood quietly at the edge of its shore, on a cliff high above, watching as the water hundreds of meters below heaved and sighed in slow progression. Waves crashed against the cliffs echoing upwards as distant thunder.

The grasses at her feet bent in a soft, warm wind that also buffeted against her face. She took off her small rebreather for a moment to taste the sweet air.

Ishaida was becoming what she had once dreamed.

Jasimine came up in time to catch her Captain wiping a tear from her cheek. It surprised her. April McThurn rarely exhibited such emotion, at least not at that level. She was different than most women she had ever met, so strong, so determined. She admired her Captain.

"Oh, I'm sorry, Captain."

"That's OK, Jasimine." She wiped her cheek with her sleeve. "You know, she's 40 fathoms below these waves. Just out there." She stepped a little closer to the edge.

"Captain!" Jasimine yelled, which startled April who turned and gave her an appraising look. The communications officer averted her gaze. Even with red-rimmed eyes her Captain still managed to make her feel small.

"It's just so close to the edge, you know."

April smiled. "I'm not planning to jump or anything. The TriggerFix is at the bottom of this lake. My Cruez is down there, under those waves." *She had to say it, had to tell somebody.*

"Cruez?"

"He's down there, in that cold, dark grave. He didn't deserve it, you know. Didn't deserve to die. Not like that."

"The TriggerFix? The Sequin Clan's lost transport. Yes, I remember that. But who was Cruez?"

April stood staring down the cliff, into the dark waters below, withdrawn and silent, lost in thought.

A moment later she turned away.

"It doesn't matter anymore. He's gone."

"So what's the issue, Jasimine?" Her features returned to a familiar stern, attentive look. The Captain was back to her usual self.

"I'm sorry for bothering you, but I just received word from another transport. I think maybe you should contact NewLondon. Something big is happening."

* * *

A New Identity

Chapter 18

April could feel her anger building. "What do they want? What gives them the right?"

"Power, they have it, we do not, and that is their right. As for why, I guess we need to sort this out," replied Elias with controlled calm.

"We'll see about that. We'll see how much power they have."

"Now, don't do anything stupid, April. We've just started negotiations."

"They have their ships positioned to deploy their planet killer, Elias. I saw this type of maneuver when I was on Earth searching their archives. Those ships fire that thing and we're all dead."

Elias's face turned a shade grayer through the screen. "You're sure about this? We should reposition our gunships."

"To do what? You know they're no match for those cruisers." April spoke her next words carefully. "I think it's time for our new tenants to hold up their end of the agreement."

"What you are talking about is a very difficult point to return from. If your friends destroy those military ships out there - that's war, pure and simple."

"If our survival is at stake, it's necessary. They made the first move by threatening us."

"History is written by the victorious, and in their perspective only. It does not matter if they initiated the aggression. Make no mistake, April, in the long run, they would win at that game. No, we need to find a peaceful means here. Anything else is a failure."

"Fine, you negotiate. I'll see if the Trectilla will help."

"But you haven't talked to them since Alvilla Valley."

"I know, and that's where I'm going. I'll need to borrow the Mayor's flitter to get out there in time. Don't worry – I'll find them. Elias, if you fail..."

"If I fail, April, you cannot."

* * *

"What is your desire?"

"You told me before that you have the ability. You can stop this, correct?"

"There are many ways to eliminate this threat. You must be more specific."

"Eliminate the threat, then. Disable their weapons. But if you cannot stop them, you must destroy them."

A brief pause and they replied in unison. "We are unable to disable the threat without inflicting harm on the occupants."

April stepped back into the safety of the shadows, eyeing the creatures warily. They seemed so delicate suspended in mid-air, how could they possibly be dangerous?

But she knew better. There was *something* to be feared here.

"How much time – I mean notice – do you need?"

"It will take only a moment."

"It? What exactly is *it*? What do you plan to do?"

"You will be the witness to what we will do."

April looked away, staring down the corridor into the darkness. "I've done this before, you know. I've made the call. I'm not afraid to do what needs to be done."

One alien briefly glowed with hues of purple, as if it understood her, as if it empathized.

"I don't need to make the call yet. We will wait. I've been instructed by my government to give them time."

"Perhaps... but you should advise them. We sense that something is changing upon the vessels. We feel power building. These machines of your design, they are capable of so much destruction."

"What do you mean, exactly? What is changing?"

She noticed the leader – the speaker – seemed to tremble. In a way one could say, he seemed frightened.

"We believe they are preparing to activate a weapon."

April grabbed the mobile sat-link and attempted to get a channel to Elias. "Elias. Need to talk to you, now!"

"Yes?" His drawn face appeared in the mobile vid. He looked tired and very old.

"Listen, they are powering the weapons right now! We are out of time!"

"Impossible – we have already arrived at terms..."

"That's not what I am being told." April cut him off and shot a glance at the aliens. "Are you sure? You have to be *absolutely* sure!"

"Yes. We can feel the power exchange grid forming between the ships, as they synchronize the weapon. Time is of the essence, April."

"Elias, the aliens know. They are lying to you. They are going to do it. It doesn't matter what they said. They're lying, damn it! Get them on the line. Tell them to stop."

"April, you must realize the situation is delicate, they told us..."

The aliens interrupted Elias. "The weapon is ready. You must advise us of your course of action. We fear the capability of this weapon."

April knew what she had to do. She knew they were not going to stop. Just like before, when they bombed the cities and left so many dead.

She had to protect their home.

"I'm sorry, Elias." She could see the grim ashen look on his face. "But we can't afford to be wrong."

"Do it," she told them, her voice flat with defiant confidence.

From Ishaida's surface, tendrils of light raced upward like flashes of lightning to briefly touch the starships, and in so doing, they initiated an effect that was immediate and terrifying. If one were at the right vantage point, one would have seen the ships systematically disappear, or more accurately, dissolve, into the dark emptiness. In space, there is no sound, and the screams of the dying were silenced all too quickly.

Perhaps April could feel what was happening thousands of kilometers above her, could feel the tendrils of darkness like the cold chills that now raced up her spine. In that moment, she knew something had happened. Something bad.

"Is it done?"

"We are no longer in danger."

"And if I hadn't told you, would you have done it anyway?"

The aliens hovered unwaveringly, replying with only silence, unreadable.

"Well, would you?"

"It is not our way."

April turned away, exasperated at the response. "Typical. So it was my call again, you say? You would've watched them destroy this planet, kill everyone and everything?"

Neither alien responded. It infuriated her even more.

"We need to work on this communications thing if we are to live successfully together, that much I know."

The aliens lowered themselves toward the floor, slowly, as if to bow, then they successively faded back into the wall from which they arrived. In only a brief moment, they were gone.

April waited quietly for her escort, finding solace in the utter silence under the white light. She wiped her forehead with her sleeve, lest the salty sweat reach her eyes.

These Trectilla keep it too damn hot in here.

"I understand that a major event has occurred," Evelyn said, as they slowly headed back to the entrance.

April glanced over at the alien curiously. Strange it seems, Evelyn had already become familiar to her. She could not put a reason to it, but in some way, she felt she could trust her. It was probably their telepathic connection, no doubt.

"Tell me, do you know what happened? What they did?"

"I am not authorized to discuss. We both have hierarchical entities to contend with."

April thought of the reprisals that she'd be expecting upon her return. "That we do. I think they destroyed the fleet."

"Yes, they did," she confirmed flatly. "However, I would have thought that you would feel relieved. The visitors were a significant threat to our safety."

Relieved? Yes, she did feel that way, like a weight had been lifted. Again, this ability to read her moods. It was uncanny.

"I may feel relieved, but I am not a fool. There are many more ships where they come from. You cannot destroy them fast enough. And they will come back with 10 times the number. We will not win this fight."

"Then how will we survive?"

"I need to go back to Earth, I think. I need to find out what is going on there - to stop it at its source."

"Then perhaps you need to be informed of the past. This may help you and us in the future."

"What do you mean by that? What happened in the past?"

"This event you call the great reversal. Tell me, do you believe the TFPs truly failed the first time?"

April did not need to think about the answer. She knew the answer deep down. "No. I know the TFPs were tampered with." She felt suddenly weak, energy draining as waves rushed out of her body.

"I need to sit down, just for a moment."

Instantly a white block rose up from the floor, stopping at a just the right height.

April folded down onto the perch, expecting it to be hard and unforgiving, but it wasn't. The mystery was lost to her, as in this moment she had to focus, to gather herself. *Breathe. Calm yourself, April.* She did a quick steadiness check with her hand. *Shaking is under control.*

"Are you alright?"

"Yes. Just give me a second. I just realized. I mean, I should have seen all this before. Should have figured this out a long time ago. I don't know why I couldn't see it."

Evelyn responded almost mechanically, "Please elaborate."

"No, maybe you should elaborate. Exactly what happened, before? When you met us? When you met my kind?"

Evelyn glowed red and orange, then transformed to a purple translucent hue. "You have failed to elaborate on your position. My powers are limited in my understanding of you. Your thoughts are quite jumbled, and it is difficult for me. I am quite sure I am unable to answer your question. I will make appropriate arrangements."

"For what?"

"There are those of us who believe in alternatives to dealing with alien life-forms such as your people. We believe we need to shift our paradigm of understanding in order to be able to relate to you, and that we should not apply our more rigid logical... approach... to arrive at solutions to our relationships."

"OK, so your people don't always agree, welcome to my world."

"You do not understand. We are *always* connected with one another. We *must* come to an agreement. We do not have the individuality that you experience. When some of us disagree, it is very significant. We are in conflict."

"Fine, I won't pretend I can understand your issues. I just need to know what happened, before. I'm a pretty good guesser so why don't you fill in the empty spots for me?"

Evelyn paused a moment as if she was contemplating. April knew better. She - they - were talking together on this network of theirs. Certain 'arrangements' were being made.

"Very well," Evelyn broke from her stupor. "I have been granted permission. I will attempt to answer where I am able."

April was pleased. It was time to confirm her suspicions. "Let's go back roughly four centuries ago, immediately prior to the great reversal. The TFPs where chugging along nicely, the world was warming up. I am thinking a group of you woke to investigate the situation, and found us colonizing your home. Your team attempted to contact us, but things didn't go so well, did they? Next thing you know, the TFPs go on a downward spiral to eventually shut down, and this lets Ishaida and your people slide back into hibernation. How am I doing so far?"

"Yes, a workable summation."

"So we, I mean, I, start up the TFPs again, fix the original problem that caused them to fail, and again the next scout team is dispatched - comprised of you and your other belligerent copy, whoever he is."

"His name is irrelevant, but that is largely correct, also."

"And you assess the situation more carefully this time, as you have no intent to repeat previous mistakes. You use the information from your predecessors and do things a little differently, avoiding direct engagement – at least to the larger population. So now the players are different and I am involved. Things seem to be transitioning to schedule. The TFPs keep moving the planetary climate along, but you were ready just in case. No mistakes this time. You stand ready on the offensive if needed."

"Yes, we are always prepared to survive. This is our home."

"Right, and if we had only left you sleeping all would have been A-OK. But we Ishaidans have a dream, you see. We want to be able to walk outside, to breathe the air, to feel the sun shine on our face. At least that is my dream, and I know it's shared by many others."

"Yes, we also wish to see Ishaida warm once again. Your machines are making this happen. We are confident in the process. We are awakening."

"How many of you?"

"Our population."

"How many?"

"As expressed within your mathematics, there are 1.35 billion of us."

April put her face in her hands. It all made sense now. "Tell me, as I do not believe you and your sidekick were truthful with me before. How can your whole population live just within the equatorial region?"

"We are fabricating vertical habitats. High-density living constructs. They are adequate for this duration."

"When – how? I didn't notice any changes."

"Close your eyes. I will attempt to show you."

April complied. She could feel something similar to a tickle, taste something sour, smell something dry, dusty – and then the image came: massive black towers jutting out of the Ishaidan sandy plains. Black shadows reached over to them, so dark it was difficult to differentiate from the foundation of the massive buildings. The image angled up to the skies, tracing along the face of the building, which seemed to lack detail, just a smooth black, shiny surface. The image faded quickly, and she opened her eyes to a semi-dark non-distinctive hall wall.

"That was incredible. You building these? How?"

She ignored her question. "We will leave this place now. It is too cold here. In the future, you know where we will be."

"Really, and that's it? See you later and all that? There is something you are not telling me, isn't there?" She looked at the Trectilla as closely as possible. "I can feel it, you know. What else are you holding back?" "This is all I can say, I am not authorized..."

"Not authorized to tell me what? This is much bigger than the two of us and it's real simple rules, you see. If you and I can't trust one another how will two different races do it?"

"There is truth in your words. I must convene with my people."

She pulled up rigidly, and all the colors of the spectrum flickered in an unending barrage within her translucent body. It was entrancing to watch, like staring into the night sky to peer deep into nebulae of swirling stars, as she had done so many times when she was young.

And in a moment, it was gone, leaving only silver and gray within a more silent opaqueness.

"I am sorry, I was not completely open to you."

"OK, so what is it?"

She paused. Something a human would consider a hesitation – a significant hesitation.

"We have decided that we must propagate to other planets in order to survive as a species. Our home has taught us this, and you have taught us this."

"Sure, makes sense. We moved from Earth centuries ago because we had to spread out to ensure mankind would survive. So you intend to move a large portion of your population to another planet?"

"Yes. And we require your help to achieve this – help through your machines. We cannot do this on our own. Such an arrangement will benefit both of our peoples."

April laughed. "You shift this planet's surface and weather around like it's your toy, make an enemy fleet disappear in a blink of an eye, communicate telepathically with one another and us, yet you can't build a spaceship?"

Evelyn did not recognize April's ironic tone, nor acknowledge the statement. "I will escort you to your transport, April."

Perhaps they misinterpreted her incredulous response, or something more, April would never know. Her walk back was quiet. Evelyn refrained from her usual prodding of questions. Sitting in the flitter's cockpit, April found her mind reeling with many profound realities. More importantly, she knew things had changed drastically now. She could no longer be a Porter and live a Porter's life.

* * *

The distinguished mayors of the great cities of Ishaida sat in the immediate rows, along with their aides and special communications officers. Some had taken the time to bring along their own media-cubes and were reviewing their contents as they waited.

April approached the podium nervously. Although this had not been the first time she had addressed such a crowd, it was the first time they would hear what she had to say. Most were very curious, some extremely angry, and of those, she knew a few were preparing to attack her yet again.

"Honorable Mayors, ladies and gentlemen, and members of the Porter council."

A few shifted about and one cleared his throat, retorting in a way to April's official recognition of the Porters. Some dirty looks were passed, but quiet was maintained.

"We are at an impasse at this time, as you know. The Earth fleet initiated action to destroy our population."

"According to who? Your friends?" Angry eyes burned into April. "Do we have any evidence they were about to attack? We had just left them with an agreement of truce." A few other vicious comments followed, but they were hard to decipher through the noise.

Elias stood up and addressed the crowd, hands in the air as if defensively warding off more attacks. "Not all of you are aware of this," he cleared his throat, "but we do have a few ships in orbit. They were able to corroborate this claim. Their planet killer was being primed. We have compelling video through our analysis of the recordings after the fact, as we did not recognize it at the time. Let me be very clear. The Trectilla were correct. They had full intention to destroy Ishaida."

He quickly turned, straightened his suit and sat back down, leaving the crowd in an empty and shocked silence.

April took the opportunity to restart. "And so the expectation is that we will have another wave of Earth fleet ships heading our way, although we do not have a definite timeline."

"But why?" one asked from the audience. "Why would they do such a thing?"

"It's those damn aliens."

"Yes, it is," April stated. "That's exactly why. That's why they sabotaged the TFPs before, why they were here to finish the job the second time. They're afraid of them. And by the way, we are the aliens here. This is their home. We are the invaders. Yet, in spite of all this, they want to be our allies. They have welcomed us."

"Well where have they all been then?" came a question from the crowd.

"They've been asleep. As Ishaida has come to life, so have they awakened. And they are many."

It took a moment for the last message to sink in. A number of faces grew a touch paler.

"How many?"

"Well, more than us to be sure. And they are very powerful. You've seen how powerful."

"April, my dear," interjected Elias, "why do you think they will remain on our side. Why are they tolerating us?"

"That would be the most important question tonight. They have chosen to become our allies because of what we can do for them. They have impressive abilities, but they do not have our technology. And they wish to go out to the stars."

That started an active discussion. April stopped speaking and allowed the debate to rage. The Mayors' egos would not recognize her as officially holding the floor for long, and that was fine by her. She stood at the podium patiently and waited to be addressed.

"April McThurn, are you able to meet with the Trectilla? Can we form an ambassadorial committee to meet and discuss these issues with them?"

"Yes, you can. Point your satellites to the equator, and you will see some very tall structures which look like black granite, standing where there was nothing before. Feel free to assemble your ambassadors to visit them. But it is not where I wish to go at this point."

This exposed a few perplexed looks, and one of them asked the question "Why not?"

"Because I plan to return to Earth, to meet with our allies at Anard-Bueller and convince the Earth government to stop this madness. Will any of you join me?"

Silence moved in a wave across the room, interrupted only by the odd mutter or indecipherable comment.

"What makes you think you can properly represent us?" The question came from one of her many critics. "What gives you the right to grant yourself such authority?"

April stared at the crowd with a defiant gaze. "It was I who settled the score with Soho-Beher. It was I who ordered the Earth fleet destroyed. I gave the order. I am the one to carry their blood on my hands. Where were you when this was happening? I tried to step away from all this, I did. I was happy just being a Porter." She paused, fighting back a surge of raw emotion. *Best not to lose composure now. Fight it back.*

"None of that matters now. I cannot escape what I've become. Besides, who of you will have the ear of the CEO of Anard-Bueller?"

The silence was absolute this time. There were no side conversations, no grumbling or off-color comments. They all waited, digesting her words, none ready or willing to break the silence.

"So let me ask again, who will join me?"

Eyes darted to and fro across the room.

Who will be brave enough now? She thought as she scanned their faces. Many looked away, uncomfortable under her gaze.

"I will, April. I would be honored to be at your side," Elias announced, standing up slowly with the obvious effort of an aging man. He seemed more frail looking than ever before, but he also had this image of pride upon his face which was unmistakable.

"I don't believe we need a significant number of people to represent us, but two is better than one."

"Thank you, Elias," she said softly. For some reason, she had a sudden compulsion to run over and hug him, but a smile and a nod was all she could allow. "I will need a ship, of course. You will need to provide me one. And it can't be a gunship. We will need to ensure it has the ambassadorial markings and carries the insignia of Ishaida."

"And when do you plan to leave, April?"

"As soon as possible. You must all know by now, we are already running out of time."

"Yes," agreed Elias, nodding simultaneously. "And those who control the medium, control the message. It's time we also deploy our messengers, while we have this brief reprieve of hostile sentinels."

"To where, Elias?"

"To Cauputain and to Jefferson. They need to know what Earth is doing to us. The message does not need to include all the details. Just that we are not in agreement with Earth's policy, and because of this, they have sent their death dealers. That should wake up the local governments. The Corporations believe their power extends out here, but they perceive inaccurately. It's time our sister planets woke up and recognized they could be next. All of us extranists need to join together. We need allies, and they're our best option."

* * *

Preparation of an old Ishaidan survey ship took some time. It had already been retrofitted with four plasma cannon, repurposed from deep field mining equipment, so it was not without some protection. The proper hull identifications were lacking, and given the ship was to represent Ishaida inbound to Earth, the council - as well as and most other Ishaidans - thought it important to ensure the image was 'proper'. This included repairing any hull damage and the removal of some of the old survey antenna relays to streamline its image. New paint required the ship to dry-dock planet-side, and the extended delay was beginning to irritate April.

Every time she thought the ship was ready, the dry-dock crew found one more item to address. She finally put her foot down, voicing in no ambiguous terms, that enough was enough. The head of the refit crew was a no-nonsense old Porter, known for his short temper and high demands, yet surprisingly, he responded with a somewhat sheepish nod of acceptance giving the official approval to pull the teams off.

It was time to go.

The council had selected the best crew they could muster to accompany her and Elias. Many of the chosen were previous Porters, some carried intersystem travel experience, a few had been on interstellar flights, noting one very important exception – the Captain. He had the look of a distinguished and aged officer and carried himself as such. But he also possessed a sharp tongue and had little patience for sloppiness, laziness, or general incompetence.

April met him for the first time as they boarded to leave. She had him sized up quickly, being very familiar with his type. The crew was in for an interesting voyage.

"Ambassador April McThurn, this is Captain Verage Isaac," Elias said, his tone carrying an embedded respect which April did not fail to pick up on. "Captain, thank you for assuming this mission. I must warn you it may not go our way, completely."

"Ms. McThurn, we may be blown from the skies, but it will not be without our best intentions to keep you and Elias safe. I feel very confident that you can make a difference where others may not be as effective. I thank you."

April smiled. For an old man, he had some suave.

"I do expect we'll be approximately six months relative time before we reach Earth. But from the perspective here, by the time we make it back, it could be in the neighborhood of a few years. Our ship is not as fast as those Earth built cruisers. I assume you have made personal arrangements for your leave."

"I have, Captain. My transport is in good hands with my second in command, and I have faith in my crew to ensure they maintain their charters in my absence."

Captain Isaac laughed. "Always the Porter I see. I only hope you have that kind of confidence in the Ishaidan Ambassadorial team who are meeting with those, ah... natives."

"I'm sure they'll fare just as well without me, Captain. They are the least of my concerns at this point."

"Let's hope it remains that way, especially upon our return."

"Exactly, Verage," said Elias patting the Captain on the shoulder. "We will return successfully."

The Captain seemed to tolerate Elias's friendliness to a point, as there was a sour tinge on his look which resulted in Elias providing a bit more space between them.

"Ms. McThurn, I have a request of you, given your years of experience as a Porter Captain, I believe your talents would be wasted as a mere passenger on this flight. I am in need of a second in command, and I believe you would perform this role very well."

April was taken aback by the sudden offer. She was not at all prepared for this. She knew little about navigating the stars or what was required to command a starship. She was looking forward to a restful time to contemplate her next steps and do some research on the ship's systems.

"Ah. Well, thank you, Captain. I don't see how I could be effective..."

"Nonsense, you'll pick things up quickly, and I understand you have a gift for mechanical and electrical systems – and this old can needs lots of attention. Besides, lass, it's best you don't get bored on these trips, as they can be arduous in that manner. Don't you worry, I'll help you out where needed."

What could she say? Outright refusal would not go well at this point. The Captain had already made up his mind. She could only hope to meet his expectations.

"Very well." She gave her most convincing smile. "I would enjoy giving this a try, Captain, under a condition, of course."

"Certainly, what would that be?"

"If I do not make the grade, you demote me back to Ambassador. I do not want to be in the position where my incompetence will cost a crew member's life."

He laughed. "Yes, you and I are cut from the same mold. You waste no time in being very precise in your meaning. Accepted!" He swung a powerful hand out and grabbed hers with a bit more intention than she was used to.

Now with a sealed agreement, she withdrew a sore hand and proceeded to rub it under the cover of her coat.

Men are so typical, she thought, grinding her teeth.

The Captain hit the com and issued the assembly order in the front cargo bay, stressing the expectation of immediacy. In a few minutes, the full accompaniment stood in two lines for inspection in full uniform. They looked suitably smart in the aged and slightly faded uniforms.

"Ladies and gentlemen," addressed the Captain casually, "As you know we have on board two very special guests."

"I would like to introduce your new second officer, recently designated Lieutenant McThurn. As she is new at this type of vessel, I would expect that you provide her your vast knowledge and guidance when needed, and in between that, listen and follow her every order. Is that clear enough?"

April scanned the group's reaction. A few shocked looks from some, quirky smiles from others, and unreadable masks from the remainder.

Yes, this will be interesting, she mused.

He turned his attention back to her. "As my second, you'll catch onto protocol soon enough, just follow my lead. Our formality will rarely get in the way of the work." He nodded. "You can relieve them."

Eyes moved from the Captain to her. It was time for her first order.

"Very well, Sir. To your posts, prepare for launch."

They saluted smartly. She did her best to match in return. An "Aye, Sir," in unison and they were away.

"Well, I think I'll need a primer on understanding protocol, Captain."

"Like I said, doing fine," he waved her concern off with a hand.

"Ensign, take their luggage. Elias, Lieutenant, please accompany me to the deck."

The ship was named the Overseer, a fitting name for a survey vessel. It was a class-M hybrid, with an eight penta-watt reactor and the old multi-stream style gluon disruptor feeds that traced along the hall like so many lateral splines. The ship was capable of generating a 1.8 warp signature (a warp bubble at 180% the footprint of the ship). Most newer ships are well over a 5.0 rating by this time, but every percentage increase cost energy to maintain. The more the buffer, the more the insulation against energy spikes from matter collisions. This ship was the epitome of older technology. It was, after all, over five centuries old. Then again, it had character befitting a well-used ship – and the crew maintained her with the fondness and attention of an old friend.

By the time the first 60 days had passed, April had learned the names and ranks of all her crew and even managed to get to know a few of the more outspoken and friendly ones. But she also learned the ship and most importantly, every small nook and cranny where one could escape to find a temporary peace from everyone else. It was in these chosen areas where she would disappear briefly and pull herself together. She listened all so closely to the sounds of the ship and the wide range of noises, groans, grinds and ticks that the Overseer was capable of generating as she flew through warped space-time.

A few of these hiding areas included the upper and lower weapons turrets. She would sit in the inverted bubble for hours on her off-shifts and stare out into the abyss of stars. Out here, beyond the atmosphere of a planet, their previous color of white was tinged with all the hues of all the visible frequencies. If one could stare at a star long enough, its core surrendered hidden reds, greens, and blues, all swirling and dancing. Perhaps it was all similar to the Doppler Effect, presented visually, it was entrancing.

She was in one of these moments of peaceful escape when she first heard the navigation alarms. The Overseer had many audible alarms, each with unique and specific meaning. It took her a moment to recognize this one. It warranted a prompt visit to the bridge. She dashed down the corridor, just missing a few startled crew members.

Captain Isaac was on station and only gave her a brief passing look on her arrival, his attention spent more on contemplation than anything.

"Let's see if they hold trajectory." He stated to the helmsman.

April scanned the nav projection, immediately absorbing their situation. Five ships just on the outside of their scanner range - Earth fleet signature. They couldn't trust the transponders, however, as pirates have been known to fake their identity. A moment later scans verified the shape, mass, and picked up transponder insignia. All doubts were removed.

"They are heading to intercept us," April recognized, aloud.

"Aye," acknowledged Isaac. "They've been on this course long before we could see them as their equipment is superior to ours. Lieutenant McThurn, looks like we are to meet with some very dangerous vessels. We are outmatched in all aspects. Shall we attempt to run?"

"Captain, I would suggest we hold course. This was inevitable."

"Agreed. Battle stations!" he ordered almost routinely. Secondary alarms sounded, and the noise in the ship grew by tenfold as the crew ran to their stations, some only half-dressed as they had been caught on their sleep shift.

A bleary-eyed Elias stumbled onto the deck, carefully steering past a few rushing crew. "This didn't take long now, did it, Captain?"

"Aye, seems they were already on their way to Ishaida."

"How far are we?"

"About a third of the way to Earth," offered April. "This is a small contingent. Could be a routine security enforcement group."

"Agreed, although these vessels seem a little overpowered for such a mission. Helm, I suggest we initiate deceleration down to 2.5 but no lower. This will be a flyby."

"Standby for 180 degree flip."

The helmsman performed the maneuver with a masterful touch, the massive ship reorienting itself for negative acceleration with only a minor discomfort to the crew. April swallowed hard and popped her ears as the gravity plates shifted slightly adjusting to the acceleration changes.

"Helm, ETA for minimum distance between us."

The officer announced after a quick glance of his navigation monitor with a routine confidence. "Approximately five standard hours, should be able to communicate within three hours."

Captain Isaac acknowledged with a nod. "Lieutenant McThurn and

Elias, time to put on your Ambassador hats," the Captain said with a sigh, "but until then we wait."

And they waited. Tension on board exposed itself through silence. None of the crew made their usual humorous banter, and few even talked throughout the time. As the ships drew ever closer April could feel the tension – and the fear increase.

A quick glance at the navigation officer's eyes, a brief nod at the com officer. Their faces all but revealed their thoughts - visions of disaster played through their minds in a twisted plague of fearful addiction. Few if any, predicted a positive end to this dangerous liaison. April waited patiently on the bridge, often pacing, carefully avoiding searching eyes, only to periodically check the navigation holo-projection, and play with the perception angles. After three hours Elias was also on the bridge, along with the Captain who had arrived from what April guessed, was a brief rest. How he could rest at this time was a wonder.

"Communications, attempt to hail the Earth fleet," he barked.

"We have a communications link, Sir."

The Captain glanced over to April. She took the cue. "I'll initiate. Open link please," she ordered quietly. "This is Ambassador McThurn, of the Ishaidan vessel the Overseer. We have come to discuss Earth's aggression to the Ishaidan world."

"This is Captain Terga of the Battleship ESS Lincoln, of the Earth Space Protection Divisional Fleet. Your planet and your people have initiated an act of war against our sovereignty and are, therefore, ordered to stand down and prepare to be boarded."

"You misunderstand our intentions, Captain. You may accompany us to a suitable meeting place, however, we fully intend to proceed in a peaceful manner to meet with your ambassadors to discuss this conflict. You are not permitted to have your trained soldiers board this vessel. We are a vessel of goodwill and peace."

"Ambassador, we are under orders to seize all vessels of Ishaidan ownership, regardless of function, under force if necessary."

"And with this order, you intend to simply overrun the terms of the Oort Treaty? We have clearly stated we are an ambassadorial vessel. I would suggest you contact your commander, Captain."

"Very well, Ambassador McThurn. We will re-establish this link shortly."

April took a moment to realize she was squeezing ever so tightly the back of a bridge chair. She let go, letting out a deep breath.

"Good work," acknowledged the Captain with a smile. "You did well."

"We'll see."

"Aye, I see why you have a reputation."

April smiled slightly. She did like the old man.

Captain Terga wasted no time. The link request startled the com officer. "Sir, I mean Lieutenant McThurn?"

"I'll take it. Open the com-link for bridge address."

"This is the Battleship ESS Lincoln addressing the Ishaidan vessel Overseer. We wish to converse with Ambassador McThurn."

"This is the Ambassador. Captain Terga, I presume?"

"Correct. We have verified your credentials with your home world government, and we have also discussed your request with Earth Command. We will accompany your ship to a destination to be provided. You will then disembark to meet with dignitaries of appropriate influence to discuss terms further. This will be allowed on the condition that you allow a boarding of your ship by myself and a small escort to perform a routine inspection for weapons of large-scale destruction capability."

April glanced over to Captain Isaac, who merely nodded back. His face looked as if it was frozen in wax, lending little clue to his actual thoughts. The brief delay in response quickly brought out a probe by Terga.

"I assume, you have no objection to this?"

"You assume correctly, Captain, we would be pleased to entertain you and your guests. You may perform your inspection, as we clearly have nothing to hide. We carry no secrets, and our intentions are transparent," stated April.

"I would also be pleased to meet with you as well. We will perform the necessary course corrections, please remain on your current trajectory, at your current velocity. Any deviation will be considered a breach of intent, and we will respond as per our original mandate. Is this understood?"

His last comment had not been missed by anyone on the bridge, that much April was sure. "We will maintain course and speed and await your escort."

"Upon completion of stated maneuvers, we will send over a shuttle. Please be prepared to receive the inspection party."

"We will await your arrival, Captain. Thank you."

A brief hesitation followed, was it possibly a sigh?

"Very good, ESS Lincoln out."

April scanned the eyes in the room. The fear had momentarily abated, giving way to what could only be discerned as hope. It was far from over.

"That was very good, April," Elias complimented quietly.

He had remained quiet all through the discussion but had remained at her side, although she had barely registered his movements. Regardless, it was good to have him there. She would need him yet, only a matter of time.

"Let's see if Terga plays this straight."

* * *

The ESS Lincoln's shuttle locked onto the outer main airlock and tethered over without incident. Captain Isaac had the crew in full dress uniform, each holding a full complement of weapons, cleaned to shine. There was no doubt the uniforms were to impress, as were the weapons, which would serve to be effective if needed.

April and Elias stood beside the Captain in the center of the corridor, although set back and adjacent to a shield projector. If the computer scanners suspected the slightest aggressive action, they would automatically raise.

Six security escorts filed out first, followed by the Captain and two of his officers. The compliment noted the positioning of the receiving party and their precautionary positions as a matter of routine. The security team stepped back and allowed Captain Terga to close the distance between the two parties. The two facing Captains saluted one another.

"Welcome aboard, Captain Terga," growled Isaac formally. "I've made arrangements for you and your officers to join us in the survey room for discussion of terms. I will also have a small security escort accompany your inspection team. We can make all areas accessible to your team with the exception of the bridge."

"Thank you, Captain. Yes, my inspection officer will also have an escort." He waved the team to assemble.

"I trust your escort can answer any questions he may have."

"Of course," Isaac nodded at his second lieutenant, "Lieutenant Govrage knows this ship very well."

Govrage signaled his team into formation in front of and following the inspection team.

"Lieutenant, please escort the inspection team to the aft engine rooms and move systematically up from there."

The team filed out quietly, the Overseer's crew systematically adjusting their weapons as they squeezed through and past some overhead pipes and conduit runs.

"And this must be Ambassador McThurn," stated Terga with a smile, extending his hand. April took it, although uncomfortable with this formality. "Captain," she acknowledged. "This is Ambassador Elias Talbot, Mayor of NewLondon, and member of the Ishaidan senate."

"A pleasure," he commented again, shaking hands stiffly.

"Let us retire to this meeting area. I would like to get started as soon as possible."

The trip to the forward Survey Room lacked any discussion and did little to smooth out the tension between the teams. With the security personnel positioned in the corridors, April found herself across the table from the Captain and his second officer, adjacent to Elias and Isaac.

"Let's get right to it, shall we? Our navigation control will transmit your assigned destination to your bridge officer."

"And where are we headed?" asked Isaac.

"Sol system, Jupiter's moon, Ganymede. We have a colony on the surface where an ambassador will meet with you. A shuttle will be waiting for you in orbit to take you to the surface. The Overseer will remain in geostationary orbit under the watch of our fleet. Regarding your negotiations, I have little help to give you, I'm afraid."

"Noted," commented the Captain, bending slightly over to issue an order through his wrist communicator.

"I assume you have something more to discuss?" queried April.

"Why yes, we do require inspection of your bridge, as well. We must ensure we abide the representation of our authorities, of course."

"Your inspection officer may enter the bridge, without your security monkeys in tow," stated Isaac in a warning tone.

Terga raised an eyebrow.

"You'll need to accept I've little trust in you and your commanders, Terga," warned Isaac acidly. "You'll not want to put your men in any danger, would you now?"

Terga was smart enough to know how far he could push his agenda. "Very well, Captain, I find this acceptable. Bearing in mind, the Lincoln has the firepower to destroy this ship a hundred times over, if once."

"Aye," laughed Isaac, "but would she do it with her Captain aboard her?"

"I'm afraid so," stated Terga dryly. "Precautions made upon my leaving. All scenarios of possibility you understand." He nodded to his officer who in turn passed on the orders to the inspection team.

April thought it was time to step in lest things get heated. "You must understand it is Earth that has declared war on us, or do we have this all wrong? Perhaps this has all been commissioned by one of the Corporations?"

Terga responded with a tight smile. "To my knowledge, none of the Corporations are behind this, although Anard-Bueller has made some enemies with its Soho-Beher takeover tactics. That corporation is under investigation under very grievous accusations. Ironically, Ishaida is a known Anard-Bueller asset."

"The tail can do little but wag on the lion," April replied, smiling inwardly with her knowledge of the Old Earth metaphor coming to mind.

"But are you the tail? I must impress upon you the Earth Space Protection Divisional Fleet does not report to any Corporation, nor do we operate at their whim. We are a discrete entity."

"Perhaps this is true, however on my past visit to the Anard-Bueller office certain realities exposed other possible arrangements."

Terga sat back in his chair, smile gone, face reddened. "Yes, your last visit to Earth," he acknowledged. "It's been brought to my attention that the timing of your last visit was the exact time Soho-Beher experienced a very egregious catastrophe. Do you have any knowledge of that event?"

April scrambled to maintain her calm expression, careful not to provide any clues. *Did he know? He couldn't have anything solid. Tiberious would have seen to that.*

"If you are referring to the Soho-Beher headquarters destruction on Cauputain, that was a very unfortunate event."

Terga shifted in his chair, eyes drilling into her. "I was and it was. I am curious to what knowledge you may have of this event."

"This is outside of your mandate, Captain," interrupted Elias. "Your questions have little bearing on our current Ishaida-Earth relations."

"Really? I do find it strange that two Ishaidan cities suffered the same type of calamity just prior to the remarkably similar event on Cauputain. It would be a fitting, if not an ironic message."

"Need I remind you, Sir, that we lost a significant number of our people in these calamities you are referring to."

"Yes," he acknowledged, "and we have seemed to have lost a small fleet that was dispatched to monitor Ishaida."

"Monitor!" retorted April, fighting hard to control her temper. "They were in formation and preparing to fire their planet killer!"

Terga attempted to project a look of injured surprise. "That would be counter to their mandate. Tell me, in any case, how could you even know their intentions?"

This time Captain Isaac interrupted. "We'll be reviewing all such pertinent details with the Ambassadorial contingent on Ganymede. I believe we have discussed everything that requires discussion, Captain."

Terga nodded, but his eyes revealed he was not nearly satisfied. As a conditioned statesman, he was wise enough to know when to stop. "Very well." He stood up, Elias, April, and Captain Isaac followed his lead.

"Captain," stated Isaac almost casually. "I'll have my ensign escort you back to the airlock. Please feel free to wait there until your team has completed their inspection."

"Of course. It is unfortunate we have these areas of conflict between us. Perhaps we'll meet under better circumstances in the future."

Terga turned on his heel and headed out. Upon his exit, Isaac broke the silence.

"I see from the direction of this discussion there are some prior events we must consider. I also assume either one or both of you are aware of all these events."

April nodded, but refrained from offering more.

"Very well. Nothing is simple, but I expected this. You are dismissed."

Outside in the corridor, April found herself taking a number of very deep breaths, slowly pulling her emotions back into check. Elias glanced at her knowingly.

"This won't be easy. Terga is a pushover in comparison to those vultures we're going to meet on Ganymede. Are you up for this?"

Up for this? She has seen too much, done too much already.

Memories flooded over her, and she fought to squelch them down, they would not stop. Images of the cities burning, the bodies strewn about. She recalled the feeling the moment she gave the order to kill the Soho-Beher executives. The guilt and remorse for the lives lost. *These were her sins to carry. She only wished she would not have to carry much more.*

She leaned up against the wall, closed her eyes.

Breathe. Just breathe.

She felt his hand on her shoulder. "Don't worry. I'm OK. I can do this."

"You're sure? We can't afford to lose this one, April."

"Yes," she said, although deep down she couldn't help but feel the burning doubt within her. "Yes, I just need some time to collect myself. I'll be ready."

Elias was obviously worried but didn't press it. "We have some time before we reach the Sol system. Let me know if you need anything." He left quietly.

April nodded, glad to be left alone with her thoughts. She wandered down the corridor, avoiding the crew. It was easier when she was alone. She navigated down the lower corridors through the engine room and found a dark recessed corner, away from everyone, close to the humming machinery. She sat down and pulled her knees tight to her face, huddled into a tight ball. Through the floor, she could feel the throb of the engines as they fused atoms into high energy plasma. The pumps and containment fields sang together in tandem, vibrating the ship ever so slightly, not unlike the engine room of a transport. It was almost like home on her LightningRod. It was enough to allow her to fade into a troubled sleep.

* * *

Where is she?

Captain Verage Isaac was clearly irritated. The crew avoided his eyes as he paced the deck. Yes, he was irritated that his first officer was missing, he exemplified his point by slamming on the ship's intercom control.

The female com officer jumped in pure surprise and quickly shied away from her senior officer.

The Captain's voice growled over the ship-wide intercom. "Will the first officer please report to the bridge, immediately!"

Most of the crew were wise enough to stay out of his way when he was like this, but not Elias, he was neither intimidated nor vexed. "I think she just needs some time alone to work on her next strategy."

"Not on my ship she doesn't," he snarled back.

"I'm sure she's just...." Elias stopped in mid-sentence as April stepped through the bridge lock.

"Lieutenant McThurn reporting, Sir."

"Where the hell have you been? I've this damn battleship hailing us for the last parsec. Terga wants to talk directly to you, and we're all losing our patience."

April passed an assessing gaze over the bridge. Pale and nervous looks revealed things were again very tense. Something had changed.

"Com, acknowledge and open link, please," she ordered. "Engineering, scan the Lincoln for power signatures. I want to know their current weapons state."

The Captain sat down in his command chair, letting out a long breath, and pointedly avoided countermanding his second officer's orders.

"They have changed their armament, Sir. Looks like all systems are charged from what we can tell. I believe they are in full battle readiness."

"Believe?"

The engineering officer looked away from her intense gaze and quickly rechecked his scans. "Yes, they are." He stated back, licking his lips, his mouth a bit too dry.

"I have the Lincoln." The com officer announced.

"Full bridge address," she ordered.

"This is Captain Terga of the ESS Lincoln, requesting direct council with your Ambassador McThurn."

"This is Ambassador McThurn, Captain."

"You may note we have moved to battle readiness, Ambassador."

"We have made that observation. May I inquire why?"

"I have received reports from the Ishaidan sector that we have lost communications with two more battleships dispatched there. It was the Earth Space Protectorate Division's understanding is that we are under a momentary truce, Ambassador."

"Issuance of further threats to our home world during our ambassadorial functions will not be tolerated, Captain. Please inform the ESPD headquarters to retract all vessels enroute to Ishaida."

April gave the signal to close the link.

"Have you lost your mind?" Elias yelled. "We can't play this posturing game with the ESPD."

"Those particular game pieces have already been moved, Elias. Keep in mind we do not control the Trectilla, they obviously perceived a threat and acted on their own. We cannot EVER lead the ESPD to think that we are not moving forward without full control of them. Do you understand?"

Elias nodded mutely.

"We are being hailed to reopen the link, Sir."

Captain Isaac dryly gave a quick nod and the link was open again, this time with full video over the bridge display.

"I've reviewed your request with ESPD and we will, for the moment, retract to Three Parsecs from Ishaida."

"You must appreciate, Captain Terga, that certain orders have been given and response actions anticipated ahead of time. These events will occur with or without what we discuss here, regardless how good or strained our relationship becomes. I would suggest that you also stand down on your own offensive stance as we both know accidents have been known to occur."

Terga's face did not flinch, but he did turn slightly off camera to issue a command.

"Agreed. We'll stand down for now."

"I will impress upon you, Ambassadors. The ESPD will not tolerate any further losses of any vessels under its protection. I have been issued orders to immediately cease diplomatic relations if we lose contact with any more ships. In addition, I have not been authorized to take prisoners. Are we clear?"

"Yes, very, Captain. It is very clear the ESPD is, in all aspects, the aggressor in this situation. I only hope there are some decision makers remaining in the Sol system who are willing to listen to reason. It would be unfortunate to have more lives lost over a simple misunderstanding."

"Very well, Ambassador." With a curt nod, his image faded to black.

For a minute, no one bothered to say anything. The Captain swatted at something on the arm of his chair, avoiding looking in April's direction.

"Engineering, please confirm lowered battle readiness."

"I have confirmed, Sir."

"Good, if I may be excused, Captain, I'd like to retire to the mess."

"Of course, please do."

After she left, Verage Isaac glanced over to Elias and chuckled. "She's some steel that lass, a bit of 'Porter blood in her alright."

"Aye, she has that alright." Elias agreed quietly.

The greasy food did little to quench the feeling of butterflies dancing in her stomach. No one made a move to sit with her, possibly they were intimidated by her, or maybe they just were not comfortable with her yet. Regardless, she had not achieved a real bond with any of the crew and she regretted that. It would have been good to have a friend right about now.

"May I sit with you?"

She looked up to see Elias.

"Well, good timing."

"Oh, why is that?"

"Nevermind. Did you have a follow-up discussion with the old bear?"

Elias chuckled. "Verage is not that bad, just short on patience. And no, not much of a chat at all. Guess we all know where things are. No use commenting on the obvious."

"No, guess not. It's a shame about those two other ships, though."

"Yes. But it does make one wonder. They must have been stationed close, or they came in from Cauputain in a hurry."

"A second line, possibly, in case the first didn't succeed."

Elias nodded. "They are intent upon our destruction. That is most clear at this point."

"They are afraid of them, you know. So afraid they would risk a second line of ships. Incredible."

"Makes one wonder exactly what took place four centuries ago."

"Yes, it does. There may be someone who still knows if he'll see me."

"You mean the great Tiberious Bueller?"

She nodded between slurps of her soup. "He may not want to see me since I turned him down, and after Cruez died."

"I'll send out some feelers. Still, have a few contacts on Earth that could be of some help. Old Tiberious is a known recluse. But it's been said his health is fading."

"Between you and me, it is. That's why he offered me the position that he did. Even though I don't understand why."

"Well, I do," Elias stated as a matter-of-factly.

His confident response was an unanticipated surprise. "Really?"

"Yes, he had a granddaughter, born of his son from his first wife. His son passed long ago, a tragic accident, but something happened with his granddaughter, believe she just disappeared. I remember seeing her image all over the vids. You could have been her identical twin."

"I must have missed that in my research. So I just look like her, is all?"

"Well, I wouldn't say just that," his look of dismay was too obvious.

April continued. "It's more than just looks to the Old Man. He's shrewder than you think. If it was just a look alike, there is probably one born each year on Earth. No there's something more, but I just can't figure why."

"Maybe he's going senile," chuckled Elias. "He's getting pretty old."

April laughed at the idea.

Yeah, senile. Now that was hard to picture.

* * *

The remainder of the trip was uneventful, with the exception of the slow accumulation of Earth vessel escorts as they moved in closer to the Sol system. Apparently, they were somewhat of a news item.

Once past the planet Pluto, the ESS Lincoln fired a warning shot to ward off some nosy escorts, as they were moving a little too far into the restricted path of the two ships.

The Overseer ran dutifully behind, adhering to the constant stream of navigational adjustments as the two ships moved into orbit around the Jovian moon Ganymede.

"Well, we are now safely in orbit above the planet," announced Captain Isaac. "Lieutenant McThurn, I now relieve you of your second officer duties in order for you to perform your ambassadorial function, and may God provide you aid."

"Thank you, Captain."

"My Porter days are well behind me now, girl, but I do remember some of the old chants. So in honor of you, lass, and to your continued success." He winked over to the navigator in an obvious cue. The others joined in.

To the blue skies of Ishaida, lost now in a dream,

A New Identity

We Porters will fare the storms, and travel the dark roads, upon her broken back,
And we will wait for the day when we will breathe in her soft winds,
And look upon what was lost, for our faith shall not diminish,
To look upon her blue skies, once again.

April felt a tear in her eye. It had been a long time since she had heard those words. Her father had sung them to her when she was young. She remembered all too well.

It was meant as a small parting gift from an old grizzly of a Captain. But it meant more to her than he could have imagined. She moved in close and gave him a huge hug, ignoring a tear running down her cheek.

"Thank you, Captain, I won't let you down."

"Aye, lass. You never will."

* * *

Chapter 19

The descent to the moon was unsettling. Ganymede's newly created atmosphere behaved more actively than its designers had intended. The shuttle lurched as it adjusted to the turbulent winds. Its passengers strained against their restraints, collectively breathing a sigh of relief when the shuttle finally set down at the spaceport.

A small escort, accompanied by a few armed soldiers, received them. A dark-haired, gray-eyed, conservatively attired man stepped forward introducing himself as Ambassador of Earth Extra-Spatial Affairs, Davies Smith. Following him, a blonde haired woman with hazel eyes and a square chin was introduced as ESPD Secretary of Affairs. She didn't seem military but there was something about her, the way she carried herself, moving with trained ease. She was dangerous, no doubt.

"This is Secretary Debiane Nord, and she'll be the other acting Ambassador during these meetings. We understand you've been on a very long trip, we've made arrangements for you to rest and make yourself comfortable before we start."

"Thank you, Ambassador, but as you said, Elias and I have been on a very long trip to reach here and we, therefore, are very eager to get started immediately. Lives may hang in the balance, and time is precious."

"Oh, I see," a nervous glance to the ESPD Secretary. "Well, perhaps you can check into your rooms and then we can meet within the hour?"

"Perhaps we can start immediately. Please escort us to your meeting room and we'll get started."

"Ah, very well, is it just the two of you? Do you not have any legal counsel?"

April hadn't missed the multiple suits surrounding them, all without any names, all remaining just outside of direct contact.

"You mean, similar to your small army here? No, but then I don't believe you understand the full extent of our situation, Ambassador Davies. There is no court external to Ishaida that will be recognized by the Ishaidan government, and no court order that will be honored."

"Ishaida and all of its assets belong to the sovereign government of Ishaida. Your government, your corporations, your business representatives, no longer have any jurisdiction over my home. Earth has declared war upon us and in response, all previous contracts, treaties and business agreements with outside parties have been proclaimed null and void. Since all assets are under the ownership of the Ishaidan government, of which Elias and I are representatives, perhaps you wish to modify your original strategy of corporate assertions and bring in your military and government representatives instead."

Davies was dancing now. His eyes darted back and forth, his hands visibly shaking. This was clearly not what he was expecting. He was expecting to intimidate the hicks from a backward planet and straighten this mess less the corporations pull out their interests. He had been misinformed. He had not realized they had pulled out long ago.

"We may need some time to revisit this and ensure we have the appropriate members available. We will need an hour or so."

All this time the square-jawed blonde merely smiled in a friendly but dishonest sort of way. *Just like a psychopath would as the knife goes in.*

"Then we shall progress on the original offer I guess, please ensure Elias and I are in adjoining rooms." A short, portly fellow stepped forward to help them with their bags. "Our belongings are modest, and they are not to be searched," April instructed.

Ganymede may only be a moon colony but it has significant financial backing. To say the hotel was opulent was an understatement. The rooms were decorated in old Earth style, with actual wood trim, and large crystal lights.

April walked through the expansive room, past the marble floors, and a sprawling stone fireplace. A grand piano, with its dark glazed-mirror lid, threw a gloomy reflection of her troubled face back at her. She ignored looking into it, stepping past to toss the large drapes of the bay window open. Jupiter shone through the three meter high windows in all of its magnificence, casting an array of colors which danced over the polished silver and crystal throughout the room.

Ganymede suddenly made sense.

"Amazing, isn't it?"

Elias had come in from his adjoining room. "It's an incredible view of a remarkable planet."

"Yes, words don't do it justice, do they?"

She fought down her amazement and looked over to Elias. "I'll distribute the anti-bugs, hopefully, they stay active for long enough."

"I'll give you a hand."

April handed him a handful of the small pin shaped devices. "Cover the perimeter, every four to five meters or so."

She checked her wrist comp she had obtained from the tech bay on the Overseer. The tiny devices created an overlapping bubble of protection. "Well, I do hope these work. Don't know what Earth's tech is capable of."

"Well, nothing we say here will be a surprise to them, I suppose."

"Like how I suspect they'll try to waste some more of our time."

"They'll have a hard time of it with you." He chuckled. "So far I've not had to do anything of note."

"Don't worry, you will, Elias – and you'll know when I need you soon enough."

* * *

They lined up on each side of a massive dark walnut table. There were 12 of them in all, seated along the expansive wood-grain surface: aides, advisors, council and the like. Directly across from April and Elias sat Davies and Debiane, clearly the defined leaders in this masquerade.

April nodded to the group, passing an inspecting gaze to each of them.

"We officially recognize the start of these negotiations," Davies noted the date and time and systematically went through all the attending parties, etc., etc., etc. April sat back, arms crossed and waited for the minutia to end.

And finally, it did.

"Quite the crowd," April commented flatly. "I assume they're all here to ensure the minutes are taken accurately."

Davies chuckled. Debiane kept a poker face. "Yes, of course. We do need to ensure we have all the needed representative parties here."

"And well you should consider the seriousness of the situation, Ambassador. Earth has proclaimed war upon Ishaida through its aggressive actions. It dispatched the ESPD to attack our planet and its people with the intent of complete destruction. These measures were instigated without cause or motive. The fleet's intent was clear - to destroy our planet and every citizen living upon it. We are at this meeting today because your war machine failed. Our retaliation was in self-defense, was remarkably effective, and obviously wholly unexpected by your strategists. We will proceed to act in the same manner again until you either run out of ships or you decide to negotiate a truce."

"Your actions were unprovoked, and you killed hundreds of our ESPD officers and troops. It is you who are on trial here," Debiane retorted with an even, yet somehow very clear disdain in her tone.

"Ah, yes, Ambassador McThurn, perhaps your records are not accurate..." Davies cleared his throat. "I do have the official recordings of your Ambassador's meeting with the Fleet Admiral Tonoch, the previous commanding officer of the destroyed fleet."

He tossed the transcripts on the table with a measured defiance. "This clearly indicates that we had arrived at a credible position of terms only minutes before you instigated your attack."

"Minutes before is an exaggeration, more accurately hours before. The Commander needed time to return to his fleet. Those transcripts do not provide any record of the measured rise of energy level signatures within your weapons systems, do they?" April retaliated. "Your Admiral was not operating with transparency and trust."

"Then kindly produce the evidence of these measurements you have," directed Davies.

"We will, as soon as you provide a clear reason for the positioning of your fleet around our planet with clear intent to fire your planet-killer weapon. What is the acronym you give it, HELL or something along that line?"

"How is it you have access?"

Davies cut Debiane off with a sharp warning wave of his hand.

"Perhaps a short recess is in order. We'll need to prepare a proper response."

"Fine." April pushed herself back from the table. "Get whatever story together you'd like. You'll manipulate the message easily enough. That's why we are here on Ganymede, isn't it? Didn't want to be in the limelight on Earth, did you? This home of the opulent and rich has the fringe benefit of controlling the news feeds."

"No Ambassador I do think..."

This time it was April's turn to cut off the conversation. "No, you don't think. No matter what is said here today, it does not change the fact we are now at war. All this posturing is wasting valuable time. More ESPD ships will be destroyed and with them your troops' lives. Ishaida's real story is already racing across the news-feeds at Cauputain and Jefferson. Our government has already seen to ensure the truth is told. With that, you have a much bigger problem as this sets a precedent for how extranists can expect to be treated. You better pull in more members to join you across this table, Davies, as the firms don't have hold of our colonies like they do here in the Solar system. Your actions are about to initiate a civil war, and all hell is about to break loose."

With that, April left turning her back to them in defiance, Elias in tow. No one attempted to stop them.

* * *

April ran a scan of the dispatched anti-bugs. They confirmed back positive on her wrist-comp unit. "Apparently, we are still clear."

"Well, that's good if not temporary. I do believe you have them sufficiently concerned at this point, although I had wished we had maintained the extranist card until a little later. We could have used the extra time to position certain parties."

"More political positioning, I assume."

"Well, yes, a necessary evil. Earth will be working on a spin on this story asap, I'm sure. All they need to do is raise enough reasonable doubt."

"That will do little to quell old hatred. You know this is the spark that starts the fire. The extranist colonies are sick and tired of their treatment by the Earth system coalition."

"I expect you are correct there. Competitors or not, Cauputain, Jefferson and Ishaida are more alike than we'd care to admit."

"Either way, we'll not be discussing who started what again."

"Like you said, no wasting time," Elias said following up with a chuckle. "Let's see how far they go."

"I doubt it will be raised here. The Trectilla will not be recognized at this stage. It's too much to lose, implicates too many firms. They'll need to invent another reason to kill us."

"Well, you'd better get that noggin thinking on just what that is or we'll be in trouble tomorrow. In the meantime, I've a few calls to make."

"I wouldn't trust these communications lines," warned April.

"No, I'll request a shuttle up to the Overseer. Will be back shortly."

"I'll stay here and prepare for the next wave."

* * *

April did not expect the knock on her door. It had been a few hours since Elias had left, and not enough time for him to return.

A squat man, impeccably dressed to match Earth's current fashion standard, with brown hair, sporting a part along the middle, stood staunchly at the doorstep.

"Ambassador April McThurn?"

April nodded wearily. "And you?"

"Gerald Lewis. I represent the firm of Osbort, Gilliam, and Lewis. We are a legal practitioner, and a representative of our client, and an affiliate of yours."

"Why don't you come in, Mr. Lewis. It is a little more private than this doorway, I suppose."

"Thank you." The man moved with a strange preciseness, passed by her quickly, taking but a moment to open his briefcase and produce his own 'privacy insurance' devices. These particular models took flight immediately, inspecting the room and placing themselves in key areas.

"You'll need to excuse the added precautions, Ms. McThurn. We cannot be too careful this day and age."

"Not a problem, Mr. Lewis. Appreciate the extra measures. I would assume your firm is quite old. Are you a descendant of the original Lewis family designated in the title?"

"No, but you can assume I am *the Lewis* part of the partnership."

"Oh. My apologies."

"No issues," he waved her concerns away. "Just the miracle of biotechnology available to those who can afford it. It is rare I do fieldwork these days, but I do make an exception for my most important customers – such as Tiberious."

"Yes, he does have that effect on people, doesn't he? How is he doing if I may ask?"

"Not well. I've been informed you are aware of his long-term prognosis. Things have taken the turn for the worst, I'm afraid. He doesn't have much time left. He asked me to personally make the trip to see you. For some reason, which no one else can fathom, he felt compelled to provide you with the keys to the house if you understand my antiquated term."

"I told him I was not comfortable with his offer, that there were others I was sure were more qualified."

"Yes, yes, perfectly understandable, my dear. But you must understand, this is not the first time I've been involved in the strange and utter genius decisions of Tiberious's twisted mind. And he does, for all intents and purposes, succeed every time. I've given up advising him against things many years ago. He's proven me wrong too many times."

"Well, you must understand my position then?"

"Just don't doubt him. The Old Man plays chess at an elevated level beyond us normal human beings. You cannot run a leviathan like Anard-Bueller for all these centuries without a special gift. I do believe he sees that same ability within you."

April sat down, feeling deflated and beaten. "Which is precisely my point."

"Here, allow me to get you a drink." He proceeded to the bar to mix two, one for himself. "Do you appreciate brandy?"

"I'm not sure."

"Try this, it has a burn, but it's quite smooth. They stock these rooms with some quality vintages."

It did burn a bit. The taste was remarkable, a mix of darkened smoke and sweetened fruit off some kind of Earth tree.

"Well, it does have a bite," she said, clearing her throat.

"We need to perform certain tasks with a level of ceremony, you understand? You are about to inherit control and ownership shares in one of the most powerful companies of all the civilized planets."

"By civilized you are also including Ishaida, I presume?"

"Of course," confirmed Mr. Lewis, "how about I just leave it simply as *the* most powerful company?"

"Can I refuse?"

Mr. Lewis took a nervous swallow of his drink. "Yes, I suppose you could. But I would advise against it. Tiberious informed me that your home is in need of resources, and you are in a precarious position. This will provide the help you need."

"I'm not so sure this agreement can make the war go away."

"Do not be so sure about that. This is true power: the power of commerce, trade, assets, and many, many lives. Most situations can be solved with proper reallocation of certain assets."

"I never really understood why Tiberious wanted to do this."

"Wants to do this you mean. He's still very much alive but in a weakened state."

"Can I see him?"

"Oh, I will have to..." he darted his eyes around the room, looking for where he left his briefcase. "I'll have to see, this situation is far from resolved. Certain level of discretion to exercise you must understand."

"I do. It's just that I'd prefer to talk to him face to face before I decide.

I need to understand why he has chosen me."

Mr. Lewis walked over to his briefcase, systematically removed a number of thick files and produced a small handkerchief, which he then used to wipe his face.

"My dear, you – and he - simply do not have the time required. I'll see what I can arrange at this short notice, but I do implore you to reconsider your approach. If this is not done today," he hesitated. "I am certain the sharks are circling, and after his death, certain things may no longer be feasible."

April took a long look at the small, unassuming man. Strange he would represent Anard-Bueller. More than likely this inconspicuous man was one of the best corporate lawyers – anywhere. His message was quietly delivered but was quite definitive and clear.

She turned and walked quietly to the window. Jupiter's great red spot was just coming into view. A storm so large it could engulf multiples of Earths, and from this vantage point, it was truly monstrous.

"They say that Jupiter's red spot strengthens and weakens on a cycle of six-hundred-and-fifty years. It's even been known to disappear for a time, but it always seems to come back. Did you realize this Mr. Lewis?"

"I cannot profess too much knowledge on the Jovian system, Ms. McThurn."

She could make out separate intricate layers, distinct currents moving at different velocities, piled one upon another, yet each in synch with the overall ebb and flow.

"We tend to view time in such small granularity, do we not? Regardless, we are like that storm, Mr. Lewis. All of us all moving somewhat in the same direction, sometimes in perfect harmony, other times in violent discordance, yet we all end up moving in the same direction in the end."

"Yes, I would suppose so." Gerald Lewis took advantage of the brief time not to admire the planet but the face of his new perspective primary client. It took but that moment for him realize the something that Tiberious had recognized so quickly. This was no ordinary woman, no ordinary person for that matter. There was something about her that drew you close but also held you away at a respectful distance. She projected naturally what has taken previous presidents of countries and CEOs of firms, their lifetime to achieve. Yet, she is still only a child.

"Ms. McThurn, I've known Tiberious well over a century now. I consider him a personal friend, and I've learned to trust him with whatever seemingly insane logic he applies to a situation. I will state that in this case, I have no concern about his decision to choose you."

April turned, her eyes meeting the smaller man's. Her face bathed in the multicolor maelstrom of the tremendous planet behind her.

"Why, thank you, Mr. Lewis."

"Yes, I think you will do just fine, my dear."

She smiled. She liked this little man. Perhaps this was not so bad – there are ways to solve problems no matter how big – if one has the resources.

"One proviso, if I may? As long as Tiberious is able, he retains control. I'll have control only on his assignment, or his death. I expect that will buy some time to get some of our affairs in order."

"Of course, Ms. McThurn." He handed her a pen ordained with a collection of lavish carvings and seemed to be made of gold. "Please sign here, here, and here," he instructed, moving quickly through a thick list of papers.

"These are master copies, but the digital signatures are being sent real time over an encrypted private line back to our office. I do expect some communications delay, but it would be of minimal concern. When we are done here, the legal documents will be complete in accordance with Earth, International, and Extra-national policy."

He shuffled more papers toward her. "Sign here, initialize here."

"Tiberious did anticipate your response already. His living will is presenting time limitations, however."

He could see the emotion project through her. It was an actual genuine concern. Again, proving to him Tiberious had not gone completely mad in his failing health. She actually cared for the dusty old bugger.

"But I thought you said..."

"He is alive and stable but not conscious. The terms of his living will are already enacted. Please sign here, and here, initialize here."

April followed along, only skimming the documents he passed to her. They were documents of ownership, awarding of shares, the assumption of directorship, and the variations went on.

"I thought I'd be able to see him again."

"I am sorry if it seems I mislead you. But I will attempt for you to see him as I stated, please be prepared he may not be conscious, or worse, he may not be lucid. There, the last of the required signatures. Please, if you don't mind, prick your finger on the end of the pen. Signatures are such an outdated medium, DNA is not."

She pressed her finger on the top of the golden instrument. A small blot of blood disappeared within the device.

Gerald Lewis handed her a small handkerchief. "Congratulations, you are now Chief Executive Officer of Anard-Bueller. Perhaps we should mark this occasion in a toast?"

As they clinked glasses, the pen gave out a quiet chirp. Mr. Lewis looked down to check a small halo-readout projecting from his watch.

"Well, that explains a lot. So he hasn't completely lost it, I see."

"What?" queried April.

"Ah, it's not important," he dismissed it with a wave. "Suffice it to say, you have what it takes."

April offered the pen back, but he just held up his hand. "Keep it. It's already analyzed the sample and relayed the results. You can consider it a token of my appreciation." He laughed, but then hesitated, noticing the look on her face.

"My dear, we are never in control of the terms or the exact circumstances of some changes, but we are in control of what we do to manage them. Perhaps we should also make a toast to our mutual friend."

April held up her glass. She wiped away a tear with her free hand.

"To the Old Man then?"

"Yes," agreed Gerald Lewis with added vigor, "To Tiberious Churchill McDonald Bueller, long may his legacy live."

* * *

Hours later April was busy watching a drop of water slowly creep down the side of her glass, ignoring the latest argument between Elias and Davies, only slightly interested in the small army of otherwise distracted parties across the table. It had been a long day, and they were no closer to meeting an agreement.

She finally had enough.

"Is there no end to this ongoing posturing?"

Davies stopped mid-sentence, and all eyes turned to focus on her, everyone suddenly all too awake, all too aware.

She stood up, Elias followed her lead. "I am tired of this constant, useless drone. It is time we recess from this exercise permanently. When and if you wish to reconvene, it will be on Earth. I have a friend that I need to see. The Earth delegation can meet us at the Anard-Bueller headquarters. I'm sure that location will provide both parties an acceptable stage for more useful discussions."

She turned to leave.

"Wait!" demanded Davies. "We didn't agree to this change. We can't possibly..."

"Ambassador, I do appreciate the quiet calmness of this location and the excellent patronage you have provided, but enough of this. Too many have already died, and possibly more will as precious time is burned within this cozy little hideaway you've stashed us away in. So the rules have now changed. Inform your reports I wish to address the representatives of the United Nations directly. Consider that I am formally presenting a grievance to you, about this process you've subjected us to, that we are being controlled and contained, and that the truth is being repressed. The people of Earth deserve to hear the truth."

The resounding meaning of her words left everyone momentarily quiet. As they had once before, she turned and promptly started out, Elias at her heels.

"Ambassador McThurn." Debiane Nord called after them, "We do not recognize this request, nor will we allow this change in venue to occur."

April returned her answer with the solid thud of a closing door.

A quick glance to her side revealed Elias' face had lost all color. "They're not going to let us break orbit for Earth you realize!"

"Remember that time when I said I'll need your support?"

"Yes. I do - but this is insane, April. They will blow us out of the sky! We're talking about the crew of the Overseer here as well, not just us."

"Let's give them some time to digest this. Then we'll see. If they push back, we'll make alternate plans."

"What alternate plans? We've got no leverage here."

April only glanced back, fighting the urge to tell him more. "We should wait for a more secure location before we discuss any further. I'd like you to shuttle up to the Overseer and fill in the Captain of our plans. He'll need time to prepare. I'll stay here so they do not think we've decided to move too quickly. I do expect a personal visit from Davies shortly."

"Will you be OK?"

She smiled at him. "Are you really asking me that?"

Elias smiled back. "We'll play it your way, of course, even though I am scared out of my wits. I agree we're getting nowhere here. They're just playing a game with us, letting time burn our story away until it's no longer anyone's interest, and we truly will be the news of yesterday. I'm not sure of this, but maybe this is the right move, this is what is needed, I am just not sure what they will do. Don't worry, my dear April, I have your back as always."

They embraced for only a moment. "Good luck," she whispered, "and be ready."

* * *

Debiane Nord announced herself with a soft knock on the door.

April had expected Davies, not her, so her surprise may have exposed itself a moment before she contained it.

Debiane smiled crookedly, catching the subtle expression and the meaning behind it all too well. "So you didn't expect me, Ambassador?"

"No, but I did expect someone. Please, come in."

She slipped in like a cat, in a dress that hugged her features, pronouncing it in an alluring manner. April noticed the muscle tone of uncovered legs, the soft whiff of perfume, and her flowing blonde hair.

"I'd like a drink," she stated, turning smartly, moving quite teasingly. April watched her with appraising and slightly jealous eyes.

"Well, you know where the bar is, help yourself."

She proceeded to pour herself a glass of the dark rum. "You?"

"No, Johnnie B for me, thanks."

"Johnnie B?" she laughed softly, "first time I heard that one, how quaint."

She moved in close to April, cradling her drink in her hand, moving her finger along the top of the glass. "I do like you, you know. I find the way you handle the ah... debate refreshing."

She dipped her finger in her drink, pulled it out to suck on it with luscious red lips.

April finally clued in. She understood machines far better than people. "Sorry, not interested."

Debiane only smiled back. "Interested? In what per se?"

April turned away, not entirely comfortable with the way this was going. The room was growing steadily darker as the great red spot slowly eclipsed the view. She gravitated toward the window, moving away from this strange exotic woman.

"I see you like the view. It is lovely, isn't it? That storm is moving ever so closer."

She could feel her gliding up behind her, could feel her breath on her bare shoulder.

"It is so powerful, yet it remains imprisoned along the lateral streams of the upper and lower bands, never really able to push its way toward either pole, a beast of incredible power and yet incredible weakness. Somewhat like you, my dear."

Her voice sounded low and husky, dangerous yet alluring.

"We are so very much alike."

April turned quickly, repositioning her back toward the window. "No, we're not."

What a weak response, damn it! And this woman was a bit too close into her personal space.

Debiane reached up to touch April's hair. "You do realize, my dear, I could have killed you at least a dozen ways by now. You have such a lovely skin tone, I imagine it is all natural, yes?"

Her green eyes felt like they burned into and through her. April felt numb, unable to move, hesitating on what she should do next.

"Don't you worry little one." She laughed, gentling guiding a long strand of April's hair out and to the side. "I've been advised, shall we say, to stay within the lateral streams."

The woman took a long drink, passing her gaze over April. "That would be a waste, as there are other things I'd rather do to you."

April could feel her heart pounding in her ears. "I'm not interested."

"Yes, I heard you before." Her eyes turned hard, only for a second, and then her features softened once again. She leaned in close, touching cheeks, and whispered: "But one may change one's mind, anytime."

With that, she stepped back and turned with graceful ease, taking the time to move in a most suggestive sway but never looking back. The door closed with a click. She was gone, but her perfume still lingered.

April let out a long breath, put a hand up to inspect a visible shaking. *Damn it. She was not ready for that at all.*

That woman was as dangerous as a mad scrapie. She could have either killed her or seduced her, she was sure of it. But her leash had been pulled tight for some reason. Either way, she had not been ready. Of course, she knew about such things, just never been so directly exposed to it. In a way, she could understand it. She remembered the electricity of the moment as she had moved in to touch cheeks. It reminded her of Cruez.

She shook it off.

Enough!

If her visit was meant to shake her up, it succeeded. She had to get focused.

The Overseer's encrypted com whistled.

"April?"

"Hang on, Elias."

April tapped on her wrist controller. A warning instantly came up.

Sure enough, she'd replanted bugs. Luckily, the tech was able to sense them.

"I had a visitor, and she dropped off some presents. Need to neutralize them."

April pulled out her small traveling case and tossed a couple of the countermeasure pins in the air. They buzzed about the room, locating the offending signal, and moved in for the kill. The red alarms faded to green on her wrist scanner.

"Ok, looks good."

"What visitor?"

"Doesn't matter. The Captain ready? Dispatch the shuttle, I'm coming up."

"I thought you said you were going to wait there."

"Let's just say I've had enough of Ganymede."

"We have some interesting news. Seems we have an escort on their way. Should be here within the hour. Some Anard-Bueller security ships. They have some impressive firepower, enough to match these ESSP monsters floating around us."

"Good. Time for round two, Elias. This one may get rough."

"Rough?"

"Well, don't expect this to be easy, and this time we'll need to contend with the news feeds."

"News feeds? Oh yes, I forgot about them."

April laughed. "You are getting too old and too soft."

Elias chuckled, eyes twinkling in the small com-link projection. "Well, I am kind of looking forward to this. It's a dream of mine to see where we all came from."

"Probably not where our descendants came from, we'll be up in the clouds, and from that vantage point it will all seem beautiful. But lower down, it's not. Too many people, overcrowded cities, overloaded infrastructure. They live like rats."

Elias' forehead wrinkled in his look of concern. An expression all too familiar to April.

"I see. It is not the utopia that is touted to the extranists is it? Hopefully, on the shuttle descent, we'll see some of the country from the air. They do say the undeveloped view is absolutely beautiful."

"It is, but I don't know how much we'll see. They'll keep our descent vectors very tight."

Elias's excitement sapped from him. April felt suddenly guilty.

"Look, we'll be able to feed up real sights from the planet directly to our rooms, I'm sure. It's a pretty popular thing – seeing actual nature feeds. You can almost feel like you are right there."

"Really?" a small smile came back. "Can we control where we want to see?"

"Sure – but I warn you there's so many places – you won't be able to sample them all."

Elias's mood turned to eager joy, and he was practically beaming with apprehension. His wrist communicator signaled. "Oh, looks like the shuttle has been dispatched. We're also at emergency stations, April, and we have trackers and drones running alongside the shuttle. Anyone tries anything, we'll take them out."

"I think we'll be OK. Don't forget our escort will be here by the time I get up there. Besides, I think they've decided to let us visit."

"How do you know?"

"Let's just say certain rules have changed."

* * *

The Anard-Bueller Destroyer class escorts arrived on cue. April was able to run an inspection pass by them on her ascent. The ships were, in all practicality, new, just out of dry-dock, and sporting all the bright colors and icons of the Anard-Bueller signature. They lacked the scars produced from the odd pirate scuffle, the many dents, and scrapes of too close for comfort collisions, the marks earned of a ship that has spent too many years within the great expanse of the Milky Way. Just the same, being official 'security' vessels, they were also quite elegant in design, with long lines, a smooth outer hull, and wings for atmospheric engagements.

Whoever captained them wasted no time moving in close to the shuttle, providing a protective guard for their small ascending vessel.

Although she was reasonably sure they would not encounter any form of resistance, she did breathe a relieving sigh when she stepped foot upon the Overseer.

Captain Isaac Verage stood at attention as they stepped on board, accompanied by Elias and a smattering of his officers. "Ambassador, I do believe you are sufficiently providing them with a kick in their collective asses."

April laughed. "Permission to come aboard, Captain?"

"Granted. But this time, we'll be transporting you in full ambassadorial status, I'll not burden you with duty when you need every moment possible to prepare."

"Thank you, Captain, but it's really not a burden."

"Nonsense. A trip to Earth is merely a hop and a skip from here. No need to worry. Elias here has filled me in with all the gory deals." Isaac cracked a smile. "And I did enjoy his reports. I trust you'll join the Captain this evening for dinner?"

"I would be honored."

Verage Isaac grunted on that response. "Let's not overemphasize the obvious. I look forward to your interpretation of these – these scrapie pickers."

April smiled at the Ishaidan reference. Scrapie pickers, those who would snipe from a distance to kill off the scrapies, versus a full – and more honorable – combat engagement.

"Pass the order to fasten down, prepare for superluminal," ordered the Captain to his officers. "We'll waste no time here. Also, let's ensure we convey our flight nav plan to our escorts out there so they don't worry too much."

"Aye, Captain."

He gave a second to wink back at April. "Ya got'em whipped into shape nicely, my girl."

"Thank you, Sir."

* * *

The trip to Earth was unremarkable and quick. The growing collection of escort ships as they moved closer to the planet was not anticipated. The Anard-Bueller escorts were quite effective at dissuading the numerous newsfeed vessels from interfering with their course. April could tell from scans on the world net that they were big news. At least for now – and timing was important.

As they prepared to shuttle down, April was surprised to see that Elias seemed to have a pronounced nervousness about it. She thought best not to say anything and kept their discussion to light chatter on what she had learned about Earth on her last visit.

"You do realize we will be staying as a guest at the Anard-Bueller headquarters? We may actually see the Old Man himself," Elias announced with enthusiasm.

April looked away, avoiding eye contact, lest she see something she rather not have to explain.

"I doubt you will see Tiberious, Elias."

"What do you mean? We'll be staying at *the* headquarters. I've no doubt he'll drop in to wish us well. Don't you think?"

She could feel his eyes burning into her.

"April, tell me, do you know something? Has something happened that I should be aware of? Please look at me."

April did, ensuring to present a mask for her emotions. "Nothing you need to know, Elias. It doesn't affect you at all."

"But it does affect you, doesn't it?"

She looked away again, feeling a sudden upwelling of sadness. *Why couldn't she just keep it together?*

"What's going on, April? Can I help you?"

"No. I just won't be coming home with you. It's OK though."

"What do you mean?"

She looked at him squarely, eyes red-rimmed but resolute. "It will be alright, trust me. I thought I could spend my days as a Porter, live out my life like my parents did. But that was a dream I've already let go of. Just know I've put Ishaida above all else."

"Of course."

The shuttle launched with a jerk. It would not be long now. The news ships kept a respectful distance as short-range flitters from the Anard-Bueller destroyers kept pace with their small ship as it descended through the clouds.

"Elias, don't forget to look out the port. You should be able to see something from up here."

And sure enough, they both did. Expanses of green fading into a blurry horizon of mist. From this height, the surface looked like a patchwork quilt of differing shades of greens and yellows.

"There are the fields, and over there, the darker areas, are the preserved forests."

"Ah, I see, and beautiful they are. One day, April. One day our Ishaida will look like this as well."

April smiled at that. A green Ishaida. Not just moss and wisps of grasses, but mature trees reaching up meters into the sky.

Elias smiled back.

"That'll be the home we make all these sacrifices for: for our children, and their children."

"I can imagine it now, Elias. I know it will be beautiful. And it won't look like it does below, not like that exactly, because it will be our planet, it will be our Ishaida."

He nodded quietly, peering down through the portals beside them, watching the green fields slowly disappear into the harsh lines of steel and concrete.

The shuttle landed at the Anard-Bueller home residence.

"Welcome, Ambassador McThurn, Ambassador Talbot, we are looking forward to your stay."

Mr. Jones gave a slight bow and smile, just enough to ensure they felt comfortable. "I'll have a porter bring your belongings." He signaled to a younger man behind him with a slight flick of his wrist.

"Ms. McThurn, we have made special arrangements. I trust you will find the West Wing to be quite comfortable. We have set aside the penthouse suite for you."

Elias propped up an eyebrow. "Nothing like rolling out the red carpet, is there?" He chuckled at his dry humor.

"Perhaps you would also like to meet your house staff?" he prompted.

"Not tonight, Mr. Jones, thank you," she replied.

They stepped off the Shuttle's ramp onto wet pavement. The skies had turned gray, and the wind was blowing briskly from the North. The rain had already started. April shivered slightly.

Mr. Jones raised a large umbrella, quickly adjusting it to guard them against the pelting drops. "I'm afraid fall has begun. Temperatures have already started to drop."

They hurried into the building, but not before April glanced overhead and saw the hundreds of news flitters bouncing about in the winds above, although everyone was staying respectfully out of the Anard-Bueller controlled airspace. She checked the net feed on her wrist and could watch herself rushing into the building. *What a strange vantage point to see yourself.*

The staff was lined up to meet them - or more accurately her - as they stepped in, but Mr. Jones shooed them away. I'll escort you directly to your room. Do you wish Mr. Talbot to stay in the apartment?"

"He'll have his own room?"

"Of course, Ms. McThurn, the penthouse has many rooms."

"I need to see Tiberious."

"I understand. I will need to check on his situation. I will return shortly, please make yourselves comfortable." He left in a prompt shuffling gait.

"A pleasant fellow," Elias commented.

He didn't seem to notice anything was off. Perhaps it was better that way.

She took a moment to let her eyes drink in her new quarters. Mr. Jones was right about it being spacious, at least as opulent as her hotel room on Ganymede, incredibly ornate fixtures, glossy wood panels, and most notable the fragrances of all numerous bouquets of fresh cut flowers located in every room. Their scents flooded April's nostrils, and she fought down the urge to sneeze. They tickled her nose with smells so sweet it seemed to her to be indescribable. She had never smelled such rich scents.

"This is amazing," stated Elias from behind her. She quickly turned to see her pale yet wide-eyed cohort passing his gaze down the long hallways through to the adjoining rooms. He was in obvious awe. "I mean the hotel on Ganymede was truly something, but this..."

"Yes, Elias, it is a bit over the top. I'm sure this is an example of the finest spaces on the planet, no doubt," commented April, containing her sarcasm only slightly.

"Why it is, of course, you do understand even the mere space involved here..."

"Yes, the benefits of knowing the right people, regardless of whether you are a reluctant benefactor."

He looked at her in partial confusion. "I don't understand you, sometimes. You'll need to explain to me just how you managed this one."

"It's a long story, Elias. Not tonight, I've some things to do first. We can discuss this in the morning. I want to get to my room."

They navigated around a large fountain and directly facing was the entrance to the main penthouse bedrooms. "I'm thinking we just pick one." She nodded over at a room with an ancient looking wooden four-post bed. "And I think this one will be my stop."

She stepped into the room, grabbing a large brass-figurine which furnished as a door handle. "Goodnight, Elias."

"I'll see you in the morning, April."

She wasted no time getting settled. Mr. Jones appeared as a holographic image before her. A quick study of his face revealed more than the uniform calm he had demonstrated previously, a tell-tale look of distress.

"Hello, Ms. McThurn."

"Hello, Mr. Jones."

"I'm afraid Tiberious is not doing well. He desires to see you, immediately if possible. I will be there in a moment to escort you to the North Wing hospital area."

* * *

The most powerful man of earth's civilization lay on a bed, a mere wisp of his former self, a frail shape, attached to a web of multiple life support systems, each sub-system monitored full time by a staff of doctors.

"Who is in charge here?" she asked.

A senior, thin bend of a man with a gray, serious face approached her. "I am Doctor Teranne, Ms. McThurn. I am in charge of his care."

"How long does he have?"

"Not long I am afraid, anytime now. At this point, we cannot do anything more for him."

She nodded, watched as a nurse fussed over one of the various machines.

"Tell me, Doctor Teranne, if you were him, is this how you would choose your last moments?"

He stumbled a moment on his reply, taken aback by her question. "Well, I would guess not. I would ask for my family, but he has outlived all of his immediate descendants and has not fared well with the current generation."

"So he has no one?"

"Well, not exactly. He has you."

It took a second for it to sink in. *So many years and no one to leave*

Page 309

behind and he chose her. She would look out for him, that much she could do.

"Drop the lights, bring up a background he would find peaceful, and please clear the room. Your team can monitor remotely. I want to talk to him, privately."

"As you wish, Ms. McThurn." He clapped his hands and directed his team out. Lights darkened, and the hue of blues and greens flooded over them as a full spatial holograph of an island beach scene appeared, included with it the soft lapping of ocean waves, and the distant cries of some unknown type of birds.

April took a moment to survey the scene around her. It made sense. A place away from everyone and everything, in the middle of an ocean with nothing on the horizon. It was an enthralling vision, utterly alien to her.

So much water.

She bent over the bed, passed her hand over his forehead ever so lightly.

"Tiberious, I'm here. Can you hear me?"

A slight shift of his head was the only response. Was she too late?

"I'm sorry I wasn't here sooner. I made arrangements as soon as I heard. I've signed the papers, everything's taken care of."

The Old Man's eyes opened slowly, the hint of a smile came on blueish lips. "You're a good girl, that's why I picked you."

His voice was a mere whisper. He coughed weakly, his whole body shaking.

"I knew I could count on you."

She took his hand and squeezed it. It felt limp and heavy.

"I need to tell you," she said, tears welling up her eyes, "I'm sorry that Cruez isn't here. It was my fault you know. I didn't mean for him to die."

His gray eyes only smiled back. "Now, that was not your fault. He was looking out for you. He was doing what I asked."

"I know he meant a lot to you," she said softly.

"Too much regret. Don't cry for me, dear. I've lived a long, full life. It's your turn to shine."

He winced in pain and let out a proclamation. "It's time."

"But wait," pleaded April. "I don't know what to do. I need your help."

He smiled and closed his hand on hers with a shaky grip. "Do the right thing. Make a difference," he mouthed the words more than said them. "Goodbye, my dear."

She felt his grip lessen, and heard a soft rush of his last breath escape...

The small army of medical staff rushed in, only to scan the readings and solemnly step back.

"I'm sorry, Ms. McThurn," Dr. Teranne stated. "He was very clear about what he wanted. He stipulated not to resuscitate him once you arrived. He was holding on for you, and he was in a significant amount of pain. He had refused the medication that would have made things easier. He wanted to be clear when he saw you... Are you religious, Ms. McThurn?"

She only shook her head.

"If it brings you any comfort, I believe he's gone to a better place, where his soul can find peace."

"I hope so."

She leaned forward and kissed him on his forehead, then stepped back, letting go of his hand.

"Goodbye, Tiberious."

* * *

Chapter 20

Elias was nervous. The past 72 hours had not been anything like it was on Ganymede. He glanced over to April. Her complexion seemed a little paler than normal, and she was jittering her left leg in obvious apprehension.

The Earth party filed into the courtroom in their normal morose and cold attitude, with only a curt nod from the Ambassador.

April acknowledged with her own subtle nod. "Gentlemen, we are running short on time. We are at an impasse, and I do not see a way through this."

"Surely you can, Ambassador McThurn. We require a simple gesture of recognition that Ishaida does acknowledge crimes against Earth have been committed. Surrender your weapon you used to destroy our ships, and we will cease all hostilities."

"Again, not going to happen. No, I will not in good conscience, give up our people's capability to protect ourselves, and no, I will not surrender those that initiated the strike on your ships. We have established, beyond any doubt, these ships were intending to fire a weapon of mass destruction."

More than a few retorts shot across the table, but the Ambassador quieted the room with a rising of his hand. "We've been arguing this point for hours, shall we move on? Perhaps you will provide us some background information on your weapon?"

April shot Elias another glance. It was time to raise the stakes, she knew. The question was whether this group represented the ones calling the shots.

"I know exactly why you sent your planet killers to Ishaida. I know why you arranged to bomb our cities and tried to stop our TFPs from starting up. It's too late now. Your secret is no longer suppressed. They are under our protection now."

April watched their ashen faces for signs. Most had no idea what she was alluding to; actually, it seemed to be only one – the Ambassador.

"I suggest we clear the room," he stated quite evenly. "Admiral," he glanced over to an older gentleman, clothed in a dark uniform ordained with far too many medals, "please stay."

The others filed out, somewhat grudgingly. Most had already realized certain facts had come to light that were game changers.

The Ambassador waited patiently for everyone to leave, waited for the pronounced audible click of the door latch. He enunciated his words carefully, and precisely. "They are dangerous."

April sat back in her chair, giving the slightest of sighs. *Now we have a chance to end these talks.*

"They are our allies."

"News of this must not come out."

"Too late for that, citizens of Jefferson and Cauputain are already well informed. It's only a matter of time."

He shifted in his chair and cleared his throat. The Admiral interjected, his face slightly red, not totally hiding his suppressed anger.

"You do not know what you are doing," he stated, not hiding the irritation in his voice.

"The government of Ishaida can choose when and who to establish agreements with. Your assumptions and your opinions are simply not relevant."

"Not relevant? We will ensure your world is left a barren rock."

"At the cost of starting a war with Cauputain and Jefferson and the rest of the extranists? Where do you think Mars and Titan will side? Maybe Ganymede is Earth-allied, but are IO and Europa? Are you so sure they'll not consider themselves aligned more closely with the extranists? Do you think you will be able to justify the destruction of Ishaida to our brethren and convince them to just turn the other cheek?"

April was standing now, body trembling, attempting her best to hold in her absolute fury. "Do you intend to kill us as well? How do you think the mob of news reporters out there will absorb the story of our death at the hands of the Ambassador of Earth? I will guarantee you when I leave this room I will embrace your mob. It will become very clear how Earth attempted to suppress the most significant discovery in our history, and how they literally attempted to kill off a world to do it, and are about to try it again."

The Ambassador leaned back and gave a long sigh. The Admiral was about to retort but caught himself and stopped.

"Yes, we knew this was inevitable one day, Ms. McThurn," added the Ambassador dryly. "Our contacts have already confirmed your information envoys have been somewhat successful. I still think we could suppress all of this. A well-placed bomb, some disinformation, we make a few people disappear, encourage the rest that it's best to stay quiet. This has been done before. You'd be surprised."

"Recall your fleet."

"Or what? You've nothing to leverage."

"We do. We have their knowledge. We have their technology. Something you were too scared of to obtain."

The two men glanced at one another.

Perhaps this was a bargaining chip. April sat back down. It was their turn to squirm a bit.

"Alright, we'll bite. What do they want?"

"Simple. To be left in peace."

"Of course. Don't we all? And what will you grant in return?"

"You want to talk to them. We'll let you."

"Technology, science?"

"Whatever they're willing to share, they will."

The Ambassador nodded over to the Admiral, who promptly stood, nodded and left. Focus turned back to the Ambassador.

"I can only assume you achieved this level of relations with them. This may be of interest. I can't tell you with any degree of certainty, however. We'll need to recess for a time."

April scoffed. "What is the term you say? I think the correct response is 'bullshit'. You're wired, I'm sure. Tell them to back off or you will regret you ever started this war. This is not like before. You're not dealing with a small scout party this time. They're all awake now, and that weapon that wiped out your ships so efficiently– that was them."

"Yes, that was anticipated. We did not believe Ishaida had developed a technology of that capability."

He paused as if receiving a message. His facial features softened, and a small grin appeared. "You desire a ceasefire, a truce? You will have your reprieve – for a time," said the Ambassador.

"And your fleet?"

"As of now, we are recalling. However, we will position our defenses a few parsecs out of your system. We'll be establishing a controlled access arc. Nothing will go to or from your planet without a full inspection."

"Ishaidan ships will not submit to inspection."

"Of course. Your small contingent of vessels will not be approached."

"Not so small. This includes all Anard-Bueller vessels."

Eyebrows raised. "Under what authority?"

"That would be mine, as Chief Executive Officer of Anard-Bueller."

This time jaws dropped – including Elias's.

"You'll find all of this is in order. A recent change. The Anard-Bueller fleet will be hosting Ishaida's banner."

"I seemed to have underestimated your influence, Ambassador McThurn. Regardless of this announcement, we must ensure that what you are offering is not without substance. We will be sending a contingent to Ishaida. We... I... expect that they will be treated well."

"Most assuredly, Ambassador. But you will have a limit on your stay, three Ishaidan months, no more."

"I really can't estimate what such an effort could involve. I could hazard a guess it could take years to convey information of any value."

"It's probably best that you do not extend your stay beyond the deadline. News of who was really behind the domed city destructions would not play well with the population, I assure you."

The Ambassador clenched his jaw. "That was Soho-Beher's doing."

But April just glared back. He was about to impress his point but changed his mind, knowing enough it was better to stop. "Very well, that timeline will suffice, as long as we have Ishaidan support for relations. We have an agreement then?"

Both April and Elias nodded. "We do." They said in unison.

"I'll inform the reporters of our successful treaty." The Ambassador nodded curtly and promptly left the room to allow Elias and April to reflect.

"You don't suppose he'd follow through on a bombing response now, would you?" Elias asked, ever so cautiously.

"No. Too costly, they can't afford the upheaval. The corporations would not sign on. But let's get out of here just in case."

They found the mob at the gates had dissipated a bit, as most had been allowed in and diverted to the press release chambers where the Earth Ambassador was already threading his intricate story of a successful truce. A few stood outside with cameras, waiting to catch the Ishaidan Ambassadors. April took the time to give a smile and wave, under the urging of Elias.

"Look at that, they love you," he urged her.

"Yes, just another dirt pusher of a backward planet," April retorted.

"No. Don't understate your image, my dear. You are the beautiful, brave Ambassador making a desperate appeal to the Earth government to stop hostilities. Your image plays well in their news feeds."

"Yes, I can see that from here," April commented, retaining a forced smile, as she watched her picture projected up onto a tremendous sized video feed splaying over the side of the adjoining massive city tower. The headlines were clear enough along the bottom. News was already out about her new CEO appointment.

It had started raining again, and they both rushed to the Anard-Bueller shuttle. April could only wonder if the sun ever came out. A sudden pang of homesickness shifted through her, a reminder of the bright morning sunrises on Ishaida, the skies filled with multicolored rainbows as the morning mists settled down from the TFP gas ejectors.

Will she ever see her home again?

Elias broke her from her thoughts. "I didn't know about this CEO appointment. How? When?"

"It was a few nights ago. Tiberious passed away, Elias. I was with him when it happened. That's what he wanted. Earlier, on Ganymede, his lawyer had visited and appointed me the position. Tiberious would not take no for an answer."

"Yes, I've heard that before. My condolences about Tiberious."

April passed a troubled glance to her friend. "I did get to know him a little. You would have liked him."

The shuttle rambled through the crowded streets as its pilots negotiated clearance to go airborne. In a few moments, the vehicle jerked and launched, pressing them down into their cushions under the moderate G's.

April watched the multicolored lights as the signs danced away, only to give way to the extensive projections of the framework of sky rises. The higher they rose, the light and the noise all faded into a fog below. April sighed, allowing herself to relax.

"Elias, you'll need to head back home, and inform the others the results of our negotiations. I want you to personally oversee this Earth party visit. And don't give away anything more than we said. They are on the clock."

"What about the Trectilla?"

"Hopefully your ambassador compliment has had some success meeting with them. I can't help you with that. I have to stay here."

"When will you come back?"

"I don't know," April responded, suddenly realizing her situation more fully. "I may be awhile," she added.

Elias did not miss the sadness in her voice. "I'm not surprised after Tiberious met you that he could see you were special. I'm sure you will excel here."

"Thanks, Elias," she stated, with a bit more flatness in her voice than she was able to avoid. "Elias, you may not realize it, I know you don't know all Earth politics or the latest corporate information, but Anard-Bueller is by far the largest, and most powerful, corporation on Earth. Its former CEO has left control of his empire to a mere teenager who is not even a native of Earth."

Elias's features seemed to draw a bit tighter. "We may not know why he chose you, but he did. Whatever the challenges that may lie ahead for you, I'm sure he had taken that into account."

She knew Elias was attempting to comfort her, but his words just seemed hollow.

The shuttle settled down onto the landing area, with only the slightest jar.

"Elias, you stay on the shuttle. I'll instruct the pilots to fly you to the Overseer. Get back home as fast as you can push it. I'll make sure you have an escort all the way."

"April," he called to her as she went to step out. He extended his arms and gave a warm hug. "It'll all work out, my dear. If you need me, I'm at your disposal."

She could feel the genuine warmth in his hug. She prompted her best smile. "Take care of our home."

* * *

Tiberious did not leave her completely without help. He had left her a few valuable tools, along with an advisor – an artificial intelligence that seemed all too similar to Tiberious himself. She knew he had downloaded his conscience into the estate system before he had died. This was technology not wholly held legal, nor refined enough to work properly, at least that was a common belief.

But to her, AI Tiberious was just like her old familiar friend only with a 3D projection that looked just slightly off. Strangely, the image often appeared a bit grainy, and it shuddered and jumped sometimes.

April suspected there was nothing really wrong with the technology. This imperfect image could have been implemented on purpose, but she didn't know that for sure. What she did know was there was enough technology under Anard-Bueller's estate coffers to merge Tiberious's likeness. This likeness could, in fact, be downloaded into a very lifelike android, but in this case, he would not be considered a legal person, therefore, Tiberious had not proceeded. In any case, his legacy would remain tied into the mansion's computer systems which could also extend into the Anard-Bueller systems as well. Just how powerful this new entity of Tiberious was, was truly unknown.

Regardless, April knew his decision to avoid the android route also avoided blurring the lines too much for his new protégé, her. His executives must learn to adapt to the new authority, which he needed to support, not undermine.

Anard-Bueller's enterprises were extensive, and the simple act of becoming familiar with them proved to be challenging for April, much less defining strategy and direction.

"How do you expect me to sort all of this out?" she asked AI Tiberious.

"This will just take time. Remember that I had centuries to build this intricate web of corporations and holding companies. You'll catch on. Consider them cogs in a machine. That's what Anard-Bueller is, April - a big machine."

April eased into the chair, soaking in his new analogy. *A big machine. She was good at machines.* But she just didn't understand what each component did, much less the principals of how each functioned.

"I guess I need to understand the basics. The rules of engagement, how each part works."

"That I can help you with," smiled the image, grinning in a fluorescent shimmer, seemingly pleased. "It's time we start with the basics of business 101 by Tiberious Bueller."

April smiled back.

She didn't leave the mansion for six weeks.

* * *

The news of the Ishaidan attacks had spread throughout the colonies during April's absence. Certain factions of resistance gained members and support over that time. They represented the believers of freedom, the fighters against the corporate oppressors, sworn enemies of Earth and her government. Hate spread like a flame racing along a line of fuel, rushing to an epicenter of explosive capacity. What was once a swaying stability of uneasy peace, was now relinquished to those who would consider themselves defenders of freedom, and rebels to the establishment. War was coming, and fear and hatred propelled its inevitability.

Despite Earth's announcements of a new peace accord and a cease of hostilities toward Ishaida, the flame had been lit. Extranists joined together against a common enemy – more so the Corporations that represented Earth than Earth itself.

April had monitored the situation through the news feeds as she studied. She moved from the mansion to Anard-Bueller's executive offices in order to immerse herself in the business's operations. She watched the reports flow in, recognized what was happening before many of the other more experienced executives even realized. Perhaps it was their arrogance that kept them blind, or it was merely their Earth-based perspective. Regardless, how things used to be was not how they would be in the future. She knew shipping operations were in jeopardy. But her executives were not as convinced. Who would have the audacity to seize a merchant ship? Or, freeze corporate transactions across the entangled Universal-Net?

"Pull them out." She directed, with a flat, unmoving firmness.

They responded back with looks of utter disbelief. In a room full of experienced, incredibly rich and upper society money spinners, she had few friends here. Strangely, they had yet to attempt to oust her through some warped legal debauchery, but she knew they would try. In the meantime, they would have to listen to her or resign.

"But Ms. McThurn, we have considerable assets on the line here. We've just recently leveraged…"

"Doesn't matter, you may not realize it just yet, but the charters with the colony worlds are no longer active. Agreements of the past are now forfeited."

"You predict this over a few acts of piracy? This did not even involve any of our fleet. A few criminal escapades do not add up to an eventual destabilization all of the colonies."

"You failed to mention the 300,000 that marched outside Cauputain's capital buildings yesterday. Are you all blind?"

They watched her sharply, eyes dark and piercing. It was apparent only a few agreed with her.

"Anard-Bueller will close its colony consulates, recall all Earthborn personnel, and will retract all non-essential merchant runs. All vessels will be restricted to primary routes only."

"So you think Anard-Bueller merchants will be hit by a few poorly outfitted rabble? Our ships, Ms. McThurn, are perfectly well outfitted to protect themselves."

"We have a very small window to act. Our employees deserve our consideration for their safety."

A few nonchalant shrugs conveyed an obvious message. "Then we'll send out more."

April had little patience to argue her point. Her latest updates revealed to her the rebellion's true intentions at work. They were getting organized, and they would mobilize in days, not weeks. Blood was going to spill.

"Would you have said that to Tiberious's face? This is not your call. It's mine. Suspend operations. Recall all employees, and give them proper leave compensation. Make it happen in the next 24 hours. If you won't, I'll get others in here that will."

Her last words cut through the side chatter and softened a few of their hard looks. Fear and coercion can also work effectively when applied in the proper way.

She disbanded the meeting, intentionally inspecting each of them as they filed out. How could the Old Man have trusted this lot?

"Ms. McThurn... Excuse me."

She turned around to face Anard-Bueller's Chief Financial Officer. He was a small man, quite slight, large nose and small eyes that seemed a bit magnified through his antiquated glasses. Of the lot of them, she did not mind him the most. He seemed almost likable in his mousy way. He was an unlikely character considering his position as one of the most powerful men on Earth.

"Tell me, Mr. Robson, if you don't mind my asking, why do you wear those artifacts?"

He gave a thin smile, "They are comfortable, I guess, but enough of me. We have a serious problem with our shipbuilding division. We are running up quite a deficit."

"I know. An interstellar war cannot be fought on the ground, Mr. Robson."

"The Mars port is not out of reach from Earth's fleet, Ms. McThurn."

"For every one ship we build there we put out four at Jefferson. This is merely a diversion, but an expensive diversion nonetheless. The Mars production line units are missing a few key components, in respect, most are just shells."

"Regardless, we can't keep this production rate up for long. Star going vessels are quite costly, regardless if they are missing primary drives, as you do realize."

"I do. And if things become more difficult over time, we may eventually finish those vessels. So we'll keep up with appearances. I need you to divert as much capital as you can to Jefferson without raising suspicion from the other divisions. I need those ships."

"And what are you going to do with those vessels, Ms. McThurn? I must warn you, you are walking on a very dangerous line. Anard-Bueller's history has been very consistent in its alliances with Earth."

"You are a businessman first and foremost are you not, Mr. Robson? I've reviewed your profile. The Old Man held your loyalty in high regard."

"Of course, Ms. McThurn, I just find this all very troubling."

"We are just balancing out the forces. It would not do to align Anard-Bueller with Earth's forces as they successfully exercise acts equivalent to genocide, would it? We need to ensure both sides of this conflict do not gain too much control."

"I will support you as I did Tiberious, but again, you are playing a very dangerous game. Earth's government may not have the resources at its disposal, but they can reposition alliances with other corporations. We would not be the first one to be brought down under the pretense of treason."

"Yes," April acknowledged, "I have not missed that consideration. I do remember reading about Magular Holdings. That corporation was quite powerful in its day. But it made the mistake of putting profit before the good of Earth's citizens. It was easy for a mob to align itself on common ground."

"And you feel you are not doing the same?"

"Oh no, Mr. Robson, my intent will be clear, although it will leave most of Earth's citizens in a conflicted state. After all, history will prove we are the good guys. Anard-Bueller will police known space. Our role as merchants for profit is about to evolve. We have a new business model to pursue. We will diffuse conflict when it arises, and we will shut down this war before it starts."

"To what end, Ms. McThurn?"

"It's time that we retract Earth's Space Protection Divisional Fleet's authority. They have overextended themselves and exercised clear immoral intent."

"What you are proposing..."

"This is quite achievable, Mr. Robson. Our ships may not be outfitted with as many offensive weapons as yet, but they are faster and much more plentiful. We'll start small initially – escort ships for our partner corporations – for which we charge a small fee. Not to mention they get a bump in cargo since our ships are dropping off routes to be refitted. But we still maintain our income stream in another way."

"There's no precedence for this. Our competitors won't buy these services."

"No, not yet. It may take a few piracy events before they entertain our offer, but they will. And Mr. Robson, you need to get this new income model sorted as soon as possible. We need to get the numbers right. Also, Anard-Bueller will be enforcing access tax on all shipping routes for all vessels within a year. This will include any and all Earth vessels – including the ships of the ESPD."

"I see. One question, Ms. McThurn, how do you intend to crew these police vessels?"

"What do you know of Ishaida, Mr. Robson? Have you by chance heard of Porters, and the Porter way of life?"

* * *

The Cold of Space

Chapter 21

The rebellion had begun.

If you were from Earth and unlucky enough to not to make it on the last of the emergency flights back home, chances were you were either killed or locked up in a makeshift jail.

The first few lives were lost with the burning of the Earth ambassador's residence on Jefferson, a tragedy which included the Ambassador's family. But the bloodshed did not stop there. Earth corporation ships were being intercepted and boarded. Cargo seized, crews killed or taken prisoner. Few, if any, actual Earth-side travelers were safe in the extranist colonies.

The ESPD responded in kind, dispatching as many ships available to hunt down the rebels. Extranist citizens where rounded up and questioned, some killed and tortured. Those extranists that attempted to stay neutral were quick to regret their decision as their ships were boarded and impounded under the ESPD banner.

It was ugly and tragic. Information was difficult to discern from misinformation. Like all conflicts, the lies of hate were being thrown about far too easily, and self-fulfilling excuses led to conflict and loss of life. It was an evolving cycle of grieving, more hate, more killing and so on. No one was exempt from its effects. The economies of all the worlds were devastated. Earth fed resources into the ESPD but desperately discovered their true ineffectiveness to maintain any degree of stability.

It would not be long now before any and all trade would cease completely.

* * *

April scanned all the reports from the extranist net with a heavy heart. She had been anchored to Anard-Bueller's operations for almost a full Earth year, frustrated at her inability to escape her newly assigned duties. Her escape came in the unexpected form of an invitation.

The newly elected president Charon of Earth has called upon the corporations to come to the table. To somehow find a solution that could stabilize the now tenuous and fractured relations with the outer colony systems.

"I do believe our time has come," she stated with some confidence to AI Tiberious.

"Be careful, my dear. Not all is what it seems. In war, there are always backroom deals and someone getting very rich off the misery of others."

"This opportunity will not come again."

"And how do you plan to manage this new fleet from Anard-Bueller headquarters?"

"Not from here, from out there."

"Ah, an opportunity to retain your Porter roots, you mean?"

April turned away. AI or not, Tiberious's gaze was not something she was always a fan of.

"So, what of it?"

"It may prove to be addictive. The lure of a nomad's life may override your desire to drive real change back here."

"Alright. I'll bite. Let's just say I do go. Is that so bad? I need to get out of here. I want to see Ishaida again. I need some freedom. I am young. I have to live you know."

AI Tiberious chuckled. "Of course, you are, and yes, you certainly do. How will you ever grow to understand life, to really know and appreciate the universe?"

"What, you are agreeing with me?"

"Earth needs you more than you realize. You just haven't realized it yet. Well, I can't stop you, after all. I'm just an AI."

She peered at the image, watching it jerk and darken, and slightly blur every so often. It was hard to judge a projection. She preferred a real Tiberious in these moments.

"And why don't you just fix yourself?" she asked flippantly.

AI Tiberious only laughed. "Just remember the big picture, April. There is work to be completed here. But for now, go. I have already started the construction of Anard-Bueller headquarters on Ishaida. You'll be impressed when you see it."

"What? Still up to your tricks, I see. I appreciate you initiating that. So then it's settled, I'll go. But first things first, however, I need to put the pieces in play. It's time to take down the ESPD once and for all."

AI Tiberious watched her leave with a new spring in her step. The image shook his head slowly as it sharpened the projected resolution to a lifelike quality. "Good luck, my dear."

He then vanished altogether.

* * *

"Respectfully, I do not agree with you." The Executive Admiral of ESPD sat back with his arms crossed, obviously frustrated.

"You don't agree that your resources are overextended or that you are simply outmatched in offensive capability?" chided April. "Just how prepared are you to leave Earth with minimal protection when you dispatch your ESPD fleet across the primary trading routes? I estimate that your best efforts would leave a significant percentage of travelers and merchants at risk. How do you think this will play out when a passenger liner carrying many of your upper society is robbed or worse – jettisoned?"

"Now let's be clear, Ms. McThurn," interrupted President Charon, "Earth's position in this conflict is to support the interests of our corporations and its citizens. This includes all colonies and even extranist organizations."

"Position? You pretend to justify your position? How long ago was it that the ESPD was willing to destroy the colony of Ishaida to keep the news of the Trectilla quiet? Don't you think you've lost some credibility on that statement, Madame President?"

She leaned back, her face a tight, grim mask. It took her a moment to compile her response. No one jumped in, nor interfered in the long pronounced pause. "Perhaps certain past decisions did not seem to encompass the good of the people, at the time."

"Your motives are clear. You are afraid of the Trectilla. Instead of looking to engage them with peace and understanding, you assessed their capabilities as superior to us and decided to leave them buried in the ice, regardless of the colonist lives you destroyed in the process."

"That was centuries ago. I cannot conjecture on the decisions of past administrations or other corporate representatives."

"Yes, but at least their decisions didn't involve attempted genocide."

"Of which the courts clearly acquitted the ESPD!" President Charon shot back, irritated that April had managed to steer the discussion so far.

"Let's all just bring it down a notch," interrupted Jeff Blackstone, the CEO of the sprawling conglomerate of Garth-Turing which specialized in mining operations throughout the established systems. He was a big stature of a man, even while sitting he could look clearly over many at the table – and it was a very large table. Attendees were representatives of every major corporation from Earth through to Cauputain, including some fringe outer colonies of the Sol system.

"No one is denying the ESPD stepped past their primary obligations, but we all know the Trectilla harbor potential threats, which are still at this point unknown. By basic defined protocols, they are very clearly categorized as a serious threat."

"Yes, they are seen as a threat, but they are also a people that have applied for amnesty and protection from the Ishaidan government, which the Ishaidan government has granted." April fired across, defensively.

He held up his hand, acknowledged with a slight smile and nod. "Yes, of course. And they are indeed safe from any further reprisals – of that we all can agree." Faces nodded across the table. "And we also all agree certain rebel contingents pose very serious risks not only to the lives of our law-abiding citizens across known space but to the financial health of our corporations as well. These self-proclaimed rebels are continuing to wreak havoc with our operations. If this continues, it will literally put a freeze on all normal business trading in all off-world sectors, including the fringe colonies. This untidy war is days away from shutting down the economies of multiple worlds."

He stood up, addressing the crowd with a fierce defiance. "With respect to all the members around this table; I will state this is a powder keg set to blow. I've already taken a big enough hit with production downtime. I say if Anard-Bueller is willing to step into this mess and commit resources and capital to help settle this down – let'em. I have my business to take care of."

"So you are willing to pay these outrageous fees?" shouted back the CEO of Soho-Beher, Arim Aysinov. "Did any of you bother to read the schedules in the back of this proposal? Every ship departing from any of the main shipping ports is required to pay. And all those credits are directed to Anard-Bueller's coffers. This is supposed to be free space."

"Read the subtext," countered April. "Waive the fee at your option then, and Anard-Bueller will not be obligated to provide you with protection services," countered April.

Aysinov ignored her, preferring to grandstand and sway the group. "I for one, am not interested in shelling out one credit to Anard-Bueller, with whom I am in direct competition with!"

"Then my friend, take your chances with the rest of them," stated Blackstone dryly. "To me what they are asking for is reasonable to cover their costs. It's cheap insurance, and I trust Anard-Bueller much further than the ESPD that they can get this done. No offense, of course, President Charon." He put out his best wide grin, showing just enough of his bright white teeth.

"I understand your family was originally out of Northern Texas," President Charon stated, smiling back. "It certainly shows you are straight and to the point, Mr. Blackstone."

April stood up, pulling the attention back to her. "I will indeed concede," she offered as a matter of fact. "That's our intent, of course, to cover our costs plus incur a small but reasonable profit margin. It is not our intention to hold any business hostage, regardless of your beliefs, Mr. Aysinov." She turned her attention directly to the Soho-Beher CEO. "Anard-Bueller is prepared to provide a quality support service here and not engage in corporate espionage activities."

"You are unable to discern your own conflict of interest," he fired back with a venomous look on his face.

"There is no conflict of interest. I did not incite this rebellion – it was the ESPD's attempt to destroy Ishaida. And now the independence rebellion is very real, and any outbound vessels from the Sol system are clear targets, regardless of your opinion of Anard-Bueller or my so-called agenda."

Aysinov stood up, muttering some profanity not legible. "You manufactured this mess somehow. Mark my words, you'll all realize this!

She's spinning this around to her benefit. You are all caught up in her lies now!" His voice was cracking, his attempts to point at her interrupted by a visible shaking.

April stared back into his wild, angry eyes. Deep within her, she could feel the seed of fear and guilt rising up into her stomach like a wretched acidic poison. She could feel her hands trembling, to the point where she clenched down as tight as she could on the arms of the chair.

He knew something, something from the past, something that could implicate her, somehow.

President Charon did not appreciate the outburst, and her attention remained focused on the Soho-Beher CEO. Perhaps she missed April's reaction, perhaps not, but the security team did not fail to react as Mr. Aysinov was promptly escorted out of the meeting, leaving in his wake a cloud of profanity and accusations.

"Mr. Aysinov certainly has a negative opinion about you, Ms. McThurn." She glanced with an inspecting eye over her. "I certainly hope none of his accusations turn out to be true."

April tried her best to pull herself back together, quell down the growing feelings of guilt, even though she could feel the countless eyes upon her now. She remembered a quote she had read in Tiberious's diary. *The sins of war will never leave you.*

"He's entitled to his opinion, Madame President. This does not change the reality that Anard-Bueller is willing to commit its resources to police and secure all travelers to and from the outer systems and provide armed escorts upon request. It is a very dangerous space out there. Opportunists are using this situation to their advantage. Thieves and criminals are hiding under the guise of political rebels."

"I am sure Anard-Bueller can bring calm to the storm and not fuel the fires of war that a direct intrusion by the ESPD would. The extranists know who I am, and they know what I stand for. No one really wants war, except the weapons dealers and the psychopaths."

Her last words carried some weight with President Charon, who leaned back in her chair and contemplated. It all made perfect sense.

"My conditions are simple," April continued. "The ESPD adheres to its mandate of protecting the systems of Sol only. In addition, any travel by ESPD vessels outside of the Sol system requires an Anard-Bueller escort."

Again, it was the Executive Admiral who decided to retort. "Earth will not concede to having escorts assigned to any of its starships."

"I am not requesting escorts for all vessels, Admiral, only ESPD vessels, as it is the ESPD that is seen as the catalyst for this upheaval."

Nods around the room by all the non-Earth parties revealed she had their support. The sullen faces of the Earth systems negotiation teams were not hard to miss. Blackstone did not miss the opportunity to comment. "I consider this a workable compromise. The ESPD continues its primary function, protecting Sol's systems. No more fanning the flames for the rebels. I think this has strong potential for success."

"And how long are we to sustain these oppressive conditions?" asked the Admiral, clearly not on board.

"As my proposal states, Admiral," responded April. "Anard-Bueller will retain this policing contract for a term of 50 years, at that point the contract will go up for bid. Our contract will be binding with the consortium present around this table."

"And what of performance and exit clauses? If you can't or don't meet your commitments, you surrender this contract?"

"I'll ensure our legal team will put together something amiable for all," responded April, dismissively. The last thing she wanted was to turn this into a discussion of legal details and liabilities.

"And how is Anard-Bueller going to provide enough ships? My source on Mars tells me your new fleet are lacking a number of key components. You are grounded."

April did not recognize the speaker, but she had a feeling it was a representative of one of the primary suppliers for the needed drive systems. Those same drive systems now earmarked for the next wave of an ESPD fleet build-out. Anard-Bueller had enemies throughout the systems. The speaker was vying to leverage a future negotiation.

"Yes, we are experiencing a few delays from some of our suppliers. I've outlined in the proposal the minimum number of vessels we must have operational before we will initiate this service. I have them. But I do desire the Martian vessels to be functioning as soon as possible – in consideration of the total space that must be protected. I do expect our vendors with back orders to fall in line, or I will obtain those components from extranist sources."

"Surely, revoking supplier contracts would pose financial hardship on many of Earth corporations, Ms. McThurn."

"If those contracts are not held in good faith, I've no problem with that. Holding back production on existing contracts in anticipation of an ESPD order inspires little confidence in future relationships."

"Now hold on, who said anything about ESPD fleet amendments?" interrupted the Admiral.

April just smiled. "Short of seizing Anard-Bueller property you have little hope of raising the number of ships needed. I guarantee you I will not make that easy."

"And if we recall our deployed ESPD vessels we have more than adequate assets to provide the needed protection services," president Charon interjected. "That reduces our costs considerably, Admiral, given our latest budget review."

The Admiral sat down, clearly irritated.

"I will iterate this to everyone," announced April. "If you choose not to consider my proposal so be it. Chaos shall reign as the merchant routes stall. Let's just clear the air on this, and ask the real question - does anyone else at this table have the resources or means to do this?"

No one offered to jump in, and April was not naive enough to think the Earth government did not already know about Anard-Bueller's massive buildup at Jefferson shipyards.

"I will also point out one specific provision in my proposal, that all ESPD vessels be recalled, including the Ishaidan blockade, and this be performed immediately. That is not negotiable."

The President sat back in her chair, took a deep breath. "As the Earth government representative, we'll support this proposal. I motion to bring this to a vote to move forward with a binding contract."

The announcement quieted the room. Possibly it was surprise or maybe it was shock, but it only took a moment for them to recover. "I'll second the motion," announced the big Texan. The voting process did not take long, with an old-fashioned show of hands.

And with that, Anard-Bueller was in the business of policing the extranist systems.

* * *

"Excuse me, Sir."

Del Amanto Stride looked up from his meal, a look of irritation on his face. He leaned back in his chair. "This better be good, Earl," he warned.

"You have a visitor," stated the butler flatly. "He is requesting to dock. He preferred not to provide any identification, only stated he was from the Consortium."

Del raised an eyebrow. "I know who it is. He's late. Open the bay doors, and escort him in here."

"Very well, Sir."

The visitor brought the small but powerful vessel into the landing bay of the asteroid. The ship carried the lines of a vessel constructed for speed and maneuverability, lacking the plethora of external equipment you would normally see hanging off the hull of a spacer. This machine was built to handle not only the vacuum of space but the atmosphere of a planet. One might miss the subtle swells where multiple cannon had been purposefully integrated into the design, hinting this ship was not built for pleasure, but something more.

Earl received the man at the airlock. His grim, tight-lipped face and stern jaw lacked any friendly features. Without a word, he handed the butler his helmet, disrobed his suit with the push of a button, which he also dumped into the butler's arms.

"Mr. Stride?" he inquired as gruffly as his manner imposed.

"This way, Sir. May I ask, was your trip enjoyable?"

The dark visitor only grunted, avoiding any small talk.

This was not the first time Earl had received visitors of such personality, as Stride had a tendency to invite more than a few of the rougher crowd into his company.

This man, Earl noted, was a slightly different breed. His tie clip alone must be worth his wages of a full year. No, this was one of the rich elite from Earth: very rich, very powerful, and notably, very dangerous.

Earl gave a slight knock on the faux wood door before announcing his visitor. The knock exposed the obvious density of printed plastics. The door was not so different than most things on this rock. They were constructed to provide the 'illusion' of the trappings of the very rich, but once one looked a little closer, it was easy to see the cheap veneers and coatings. To most belters, the illusion was close enough to result in the awe which Del had wanted.

The visitor tossed his black handbag onto the rich, glossy-finished fake cherry wood table, with little concern for the finish, of which Del was so attentive to.

Del's fake smile disappeared as quickly as it came.

The visitor did little to acknowledge anything at all.

"Fancy to see you again, Canon. Heard you and the consortium boys voted little Miss princess into policing our rebellious sectors. Couldn't stand to keep getting your hands dirty?"

"You lacking etiquette, Del? Where's my drink?"

Del turned and clapped his hands. A slim-looking woman wearing a gray maid uniform appeared from a side door. Her hair was tied tightly into a bun, and her features exposed her age to be mid-thirties or so.

"Two scotches with ice. From the good cupboard," he ordered.

The woman scurried around the massive table and quickly poured the drinks from the side bar.

Del watched with a smirk as Canon's interest lingered a bit longer than usual over the maid's prone figure.

"It is what it is," commented Canon, who slugged down his drink and gave out a sigh. "The Guild is none too pleased about it either. So now I am here. Too damn long a trip to get out here to the back-hole of the galaxy."

"I'd think you have more affinity for this sector given the amount of money it's made for you."

Del swigged down his drink, enjoying the burn at the back of his throat. He shook his glass in the air, indicating to the maid to refill.

"Yes, and those profits are now in danger, nevermind the slap in the face from the Ishaidan dirt-mongers that President Charon's bleeding heart was so quick to warm up to. That posturing bitch."

The maid poured Del's drink, but she did so with apprehension and managed to spill a small amount onto his cuff.

"Excuse me a moment."

In a savage fit of rage, Del leapt up and struck the poor woman in the face. She collapsed crying in pain. He grabbed her by the hair and pulled her across the room, tossing her into the door where she had arrived from.

"You will learn to be more careful," he warned her coldly.

Earl stepped forward to help, but Del's look was quite clear. The woman, now sobbing, pulled herself along the floor enough to open the door and drag herself out.

"My apologies. Quite difficult to find good help nowadays."

Canon squinted slightly. "I understood you to be a cold-hearted bastard. Now it's clear you are truly a psychopath."

"And what of it?"

"Makes no difference to me," Canon replied. "But I do require you to focus some of that attention on this new player – this April McThurn. She needs to be stopped."

"Look, I've already paid you the percentage from the last few liners we've hit. You want more, you need to cough up some additional credits."

"We did not ask you to space those passengers. I believe you owe us…"

"Hold on there, you weren't there. I was. Couldn't be helped."

"That's not my understanding."

"So you fly up here to spank me? My methods a little too brutal for you? You wanted a clear message, I sent it. Not my fault the response wasn't exactly what you expected."

"One of those you spaced was the daughter of a very prominent family."

"What can I say? Rebellions can be bloody."

Canon smirked and sat down, clearly not liking how the conversation was going. He decided to change the topic. "Yes, I do concede we expected the ESPD to win that contract. What we expected we did not get. Ishaida should be degrading back to an ice ball, and those alien things should be irradiated meat. These rebels should have all been rounded up and eliminated by now. But none of these things seem achievable at this time, at least not in the state things are in today."

"Such states have been known to change, bend like plastic if you will," offered Del, attempting to add some further enticement. "What is it you have against these Trectals or whatever you call them?"

Canon eyed him shrewdly. "You know perfectly well what they are called, Del. I've known your nature. It's arrogantly precise."

"Yes," he admitted, again with his crooked smile. "But what of it? The backstory on this?"

"I honestly don't know the details. Some Corporate family has a vendetta against these things. Apparently, some great relative was lost in the original negotiations," replied Canon.

"You mean some Tenth League member?"

"That's not for me to say."

"Oh, my mistake - as if I give a shit."

"I don't align myself with fools."

"Enough, already. Just tell me, who is so damned intent that they'd destroy Ishaida over this?"

"Can't help you there. Certain privileges of the oath you understand?"

"I see. That's enough to point me in the right direction."

"Look, Del, I would not advise you to start digging around. There's a limit to even what I can protect you from," he warned, voice lowered. "You are fond of this little plastic kingdom you built. You want to keep it, leave this alone."

Del acknowledged with a nod. It's rare he'd ever heard Canon speak so cautiously.

"So, onto a livelier topic. I've five ships worth any salt, a dozen other flying junks. Got the rebellion moving along hot and heavy, with some dedicated bitter lifers on my side."

"Yes, and we want you to take down this little princess McThurn, her armada of police ships, and find a way to turn the tide on this Trectilla situation."

"Oh, is that all? Hand over the extranist sectors to your corporate cronies yet again."

"We will pay handsomely."

Del walked over to face Canon eye to eye, "Don't believe you have enough credits in all those banks you front."

"What's your price, then?"

"Perhaps what you need out here in the wild sectors of space, is some form of governorship, a reporting tier to manage all the extranist colonies, plus a few extra ships."

Canon laughed, but then his amusement faded quickly. "You can't be serious."

"Do you have that ability or not?"

"Possibly, but that would take some work to pull off. Of course, I'll need to know you can do this before I start moving pawns all over the board, you see."

Del laughed. "This is great, I mean really. I love doing business with you guys. But I think you've outstayed your welcome."

Canon gave him an incredulous look. "Are you walking away from this?"

"No, just know you League types are too damned cheap to pay what it costs to get things done."

"On the contrary, we will honor our end. But the League families will be looking to you to inspire their confidence. Can you do what they are asking of you?"

"Yes, I guess that's possible. I think I can provide you with this little princess in short order. Would that do?"

Canon smiled crookedly. "If you make that happen, there'll be little room to doubt your abilities."

Del reached out his hand. "Deal then. I'm sure this has been a long trip. I'd be more than happy to extend my residence for you to rest prior to your departure."

"Thank you. And if I could trouble you..."

"Don't say another word. I'll have the maid dispatched to your room immediately. I've no more use for her in that capacity any longer. She can pay her debt to me in other ways."

"Debt?"

"Oh, you are under the impression I need to pay these poor souls. Well, unfortunately, working under my employment usually involves incurring debt; living expenses and the like. It's unfortunate for those who aspire to the dreams of wealth, however, for the most part, I do treat them well."

Canon left the room with relief, glad not to be one of his trapped servants. *Evil bastard.*

* * *

The new police fleet was ready ahead of schedule, mostly due to the fact that the Jefferson shipyards had been working overtime steadily since before the war. In addition, April was able to leverage her new found relationship with the Earth President to 'free up' more ship drives for the unfinished vessels in the Mars shipyards – much to the chagrin of certain ESPD friendly corporations. It seemed to April, President Charon had a vested interest in lowering the overall scope of influence of the ESPD, despite her embedded alliances. There was more at work behind the scenes than she originally assumed.

There was but one problem with the plan. Each and every ship was in need of a crew. To April the answers were simple – time and trust. It was also clear that in order for the new police fleet to be respected by the extranists, the crews had to be populated with extranists. Draft centers were established on every colony, including the outer mining belt regions.

The next critical piece was communications. The messaging would have to be very precise. The rebels need to feel they were not surrendering all they had fought for, that this was not yet another ploy by Earth to suppress them. They had to believe that the newly formed police force was there to protect not only the interests of every extranist but it was also able to ensure the ESPD were kept at bay.

April knew some would never buy it, that hate would never leave their hearts, but others would, and they would see it as a way out – a way back to prosperity. Few could be trusted to bring this all together, except possibly a native Ishaidan, recently appointed controlling interests of the largest corporation on Earth. One who would demonstrate the most transparent motivations towards peace on all sides? She knew her plan was not foolproof, but she had time to work out all the details on her trip back to Ishaida.

She boarded the Cruiser Tolomok, under Captain Jeremiah Uurgad, formally as the Grand Admiral of the Anard-Bueller fleet, and was quick to retire to her quarters. There she proceeded to spend tireless hours tied to a workstation, communicating with AI Tiberious, and directing the massive components of the Anard-Bueller machine. She would only pause for the scheduled interruptions from her assigned Ensign, who would bring her meals and quietly suggest that the time was getting late as the night cycles came and went within the ship.

A plan grew that would bring an end to the ongoing hostilities - from both sides.

* * *

During April's absence, Ishaida had continued its metamorphosis under the watchful eye of the TFP systems. The geostationary mirrors had long since unfurled in the southern hemisphere, turning night into extended day, their rays focusing the heat of its red giant sun back down onto the planet's surface.

The life-giving gases of the Ishaida's atmosphere had now been warmed into the golden zone, where the original extremophiles once seeded by the TFP's were now being crowded out by more 'normal' plants compatible with less severe temperatures, and a tendency to grow in abundance. And upon this, more complex plant forms continued to be introduced. Scrub bushes and trees were now dwarfed by large swaying trees which reached up to the skies with full canopies, large open tracts filled up with grasses and families of plants related to old Earth's corn. Tiny mechanical insects, abiding under the direction of the TFP computers, helped the process by pollinating the millions of growing plants, promoting the migration of seeds and gestation of seed pods into the Ishaidan soil. These nano-sized machines would, in time, be replaced with actual insects, all pulled from the TFPs' biological coffers.

Hills once strewn with bands of browns, reds, and yellows were now rich hues of greens and multiple colors of teeming life. And deep down in the soil, new plants rose up, not those so carefully bred and engineered by the TFPs but other, older, native plants of Ishaida. Waters which now filled ancient lakebeds, streams and rivers, washed ashore evidence of strange gifts of alien life.

Her warm air grew heavy with the scents of life and carried with it the compounds of Oxygen and Nitrogen. In lowland areas between the mountains, the air was rich and breathable.

Indeed, a native Ishaidan could stand over the land, fill his lungs, and proclaim his freedom.

Ishaida was prospering in many other ways. Travelers from every known edge of civilization converged on the small planet. Some were drawn there to see the first alien species, to meet the Trectilla, see them up close, relate to them some way, and face their own humanity. Others, more shallow and bent upon their desire of profit, sought to glean what knowledge or technology could be used or stolen.

And then there were the settlers. Those that were prepared to risk all, as they had little to nothing already. They were here to make Ishaida their home.

The Ishaidan government had been ready for the onslaught, somewhat due to a predictive warning from April. Infrastructure improvements were initiated throughout the cities but were experiencing difficulty keeping up. The inner cities bustled with activity and strained under a load of rising populations. Between these great cities, the Porter network did its best to keep up with the trade and transfer of materials, equipment, and people. The Mayors knew things were about to change for them. The centralized control they had enjoyed would disappear with each tract of land sold and distributed to those willing to take on the risk of starting homesteads and farms in the outer lands. It was time to break out of the confines of the once protective great cities, and the government had to quickly devise a method to enable this to occur as fairly as possible.

* * *

As the Anard-Bueller cruiser approached her old home, April could feel the excitement building, yet in a way, it seemed bittersweet. Would she be welcomed back? How many people would she recognize now? It's been such a long time. She doubted her own Porter family would remember her. How much had her world changed?

Perhaps her inner strife had kept her too preoccupied to pay much attention to her crew, but as she stepped out on the bridge, they all saluted sharply. She could feel their eyes upon her as she navigated through to her best vantage point on the bridge. It was strange being the center of attention and not entirely comfortable. Thankfully, she could appreciate the lines of her uniform, the way it pulled in at the right places, and the way it looked - professional yet quite attractive. She had caught more than once, through the corner of her eye, the odd crewman giving her a little more attention than usual. She had even toyed with the idea of pursuing an affair with one of the good-looking officers that saluted her every day. But she knew it was just a fantasy, nothing could really fill the void she had within her, could quell the guilt, or drive away her loneliness as no one could know her secrets. Maybe one day, but not yet, not today.

"Admiral on the bridge," the ensign announced.

April nodded to the Captain, giving a silent acknowledgment.

"We will be establishing orbit within the next few minutes, Admiral. Your yacht is being prepped for service to the planet. We will stay in orbit as long as needed. I will be handing you over to the attention of Captain Ed Zehrna."

"Thank you, Captain Uurgad. Please feel free to arrange for crew leaves as I assume this will take some time."

"Certainly, Admiral. We will await your orders."

April did her best to control the butterflies in her stomach as the yacht departed. As before she had found an ideal location on the yacht's deck so as not to interfere with the crew, yet view the incoming stream of video feeds of the plant's surface scans, and the surrounding orbital images.

First thing that caught her attention was a significantly sized asteroid in orbit, upon which there seemed a number of attached manufactured constructs, alight with obvious signs of habitation.

"Captain Zehrna, what is that over there?"

"I do believe that is Ishaida's space elevator project. Looks like they're progressing well. You may be able to see the glint of sunlight from the cable they are feeding down. Looks small from here, but believe me it's not."

As they initiated their descent, her experienced eye did not take long to notice the changes below.

The brown shadows of dust storms were now replaced by white billowing cloud formations, and spiraling storms infested the skies full of flashing instances of lighting. The great plains which were once exposed scorched scars of bare sand and rock were now covered in hues of greens, yellows, and reds. The low lying areas now glistened with deep blues of seas and lakes. The planet was awake, and life was again surging into every crevice.

She searched her memories of the TFP programming. Where should it be at this stage? What would be the next step? Right, she remembered now. All that lacked was the recharging the planet's dead core and awakening its geological heart.

She had plowed through those programming schedules so many years back with Branton when they had dug through the source code searching for the elusive failure points. She realized with an unparalleled certainty that Ishaida's transformation was well beyond the original schedules laid out in the programs. It is clear the Trectilla had modified the plan. The state of the planet was beyond anything she had ever expected. And this was not the only surprise in store for her. As her ship settled down on the tarmac of the ancient ship port of NewLondon, she had also never anticipated the scope of the reception party awaiting her arrival.

* * *

Apparently, she was, according to the average Ishaidan, nothing less than a native hero. Thousands were waiting on the blacktop, both young and old, everyone eager, cheering and waving.

To April it was simply unnerving.

"Would you look at that, Admiral. Your people are certainly glad to see you back home!"

"Captain, if you wouldn't mind, please have some of your men keep the crowd back some."

"Certainly, Admiral. Though I think your admirers may be slightly disappointed." His wide grin quickly disappeared when he caught the look on her face. "I'll ensure you have a full security detail."

The ramp lowered, and the noise from the cheers, whistles, and yells were deafening. As promised, the crowd was kept at bay by the escort.

April made sure to follow protocol, turned smartly to face the Captain. "Captain, I give you the ship."

She saluted, and he returned a crisp reply.

At the base of the ramp, a smaller official reception party stood in waiting, which included a collection of government officials – and the familiar face of Elias's, plus NewLondon's Mayor and a few prominent businessmen and representatives of the Porter guild.

Elias stood forward first, hand outstretched to welcome her. April grabbed him and pulled him close for a hug, which resulted in another cheer but also gave her a chance to speak a few choice words in his ear – something along the line of "What the hell!"

More outstretched hands, more smiling faces, and then she was whisked onto a rover and shuttled up into the main city entrance, the crowd in tow. April did her best to smile and wave, all the time internally hoping this would end soon enough, but not before a few words at a podium on the steps of city hall. Unprepared and slightly shocked, she could say little more than to extend her thanks and reinforce the fact to everyone how good it was to be home.

With the help of her security contingent, she was able to fade back to the safety of the hotel lobby, but not without quickly grabbing Elias in tow. They retreated to an open elevator, where she quickly directed the guards to hold back all others until the doors finally closed.

"You have a lot of explaining to do!" she said, a little more loudly than she should have, admittedly.

Elias just grinned. "They love you!"

"No. No. No. I do not want to be Ishaida's sweetheart. I am as far from that as I can be."

"I am truly sorry, but this was not in my control, my dear. I did my best to keep the situation to a minimum. Here…" he pressed a key. "Penthouse floor booked just for you only."

As soon as they arrived in the room, she looked for the bar, poured herself a drink with slightly shaking hands and slugged it down.

"I can handle welding a ship's hull in zero-G in the dead vacuum of space, drive a transport down a twisting mountain road in the middle of a sandstorm, and pretty much build any piece of equipment you can think of – but DO NOT put me through that again, Elias. I mean it."

He lowered his gaze, "Really, I am sorry, April. I really did try…"

"Enough!" She cut him off.

"You handle it. Dissipate that crowd. And no I will not sign autographs."

He stared. "How do you expect I do that?"

"Your problem, not mine. Why are you still here?"

He left, head hanging.

April took the time to slug down a few more shots until she felt it take effect, and practically stumbled into bed, uniform and all.

It had been a long day.

She awoke under the darkness of a cool, inviting night. The heat of the day was surrendering itself to dissipate along the massive plexiquartz slabs above the city, entropy driving energy to star-filled skies. She ripped off the outer jacket of her uniform, drew out her light white blouse, and stepped out onto the open balcony, where a slight breeze beckoned her. She paused and took a moment to take a long deep breath. Down below, the city was jostling with noises of vehicles and people, barely legible sounds of voices, a mirage of sounds and light.

But up here it was quiet. The stars shone through the plexiquartz, some splitting into separate wavelengths and colors as they passed through the crystalline structure. The sky above was clear but for a few upper strata clouds. It was truly a beautiful night.

The penthouse apartment was so high she could almost reach up to touch the massive girders that suspended the octagonal plexiquartz plates. They interlocked into each other to form the titanic dome network above the city.

Something caught her attention, a small set of markings she could just barely make out writing on the lower part of one of the girders. Hard to make out what it said exactly, but definitely a name and a date.

It was a common misconception the cities were built by armies of robots, but the truth was not spoken too often anymore. Few mentioned the first colonists, about the lives they had chosen to live, about real hardship, and unforgiving deadlines they had to meet to build these massive cities. Deadlines back then were not dates set in some corporate build schedule, they were days spelled out in containers of breathable air, drinkable water, and edible food. The work was dangerous and demanding. Each of the cities was constructed on ground soiled with the blood of many of its builders. The corporations did their best to control costs on such projects. Robots were in short supply back then and expensive. Human lives were expendable and cheap. If one colonist falls, there would be 10 to take his place.

How quickly we forget, she thought, reflecting upon the irony of their existence.

Such as were the days back then, when Earth itself was a cesspool of humanity, its support systems maxed to the limit. Go out to the stars. Live free, own your home, live like only the privileged rich class can. Just sign this contract, and leave it all behind.

And they came, by the thousands, and then hundreds of thousands. Ishaida's history was blotted with mass deaths and perilous stories of heroism against all odds. This may be the Trectilla's planet, but it was clear man had earned his place here as well.

A knock at the door redirected her thoughts.

"April, it is Elias, would you be available for a brief discussion?" His voice came as a low murmur from behind the door.

"It's late, but of course, come in," she replied, raising her voice just enough, "I'm on the balcony."

He walked with some difficulty and leaned on a cane made of spun carbon fibers. Perhaps he was attempting to incite some pity. Or maybe she just didn't realize he was growing very old.

"It's good to see you, Elias," she stated genuinely. "I'm sorry I didn't tell you that first. I was ... perturbed."

"That's alright," he said, waving his hand. "No harm done."

"Did you notice? The air smells much sweeter than I remember."

"That's because it is. We are pumping it in from the outside now, although we're still passing it through the atmospheric scrubbers, it can't hide the smells of the flora out there. Ishaida is greening up."

"I noticed that on the way down. Things seemed to have really changed since I was here last. Much further ahead of the TFP schedules that I can recall."

"Well there have been a few of us thinking the very same thing, but our Trectilla friends are not exactly known for providing direct answers. They control access to all the TFPs now, and have formally requested, or more accurately, told us, to stay away from them."

"So they have been making changes. You think there is a problem?"

"Perhaps. Our engineers conjecturing mostly. Some are concerned about them overtaxing the TFP systems. Others worry that the Trectilla may not know what they are doing and cause irrevocable damage. That contradicts the true success of the way things are out there though. The environment seems to be very stable. Weather's calmed down, plants are growing, the water table has settled, hell we even have a few forests starting up."

"Right," April pondered on his statements. "All is good, just one minor point: it is about half-a-century earlier than predicted."

"Precisely," Elias agreed. "And we don't know how that's possible."

"Well, you do. It's them. Don't be fooled into thinking it's all the TFPs. Funny thing is they seem to have trouble with machines, remember? They must be doing other things – whatever it is they are able to do. Have the temps stabilized yet?"

"Still seeing some swings in certain areas. You may have noticed the TFP satellites have deployed their mirrors, but you may not have noticed their surface area has tripled from the original designs. At least that's what our research is telling us. The 'bots up there are busy spinning more and more mirror surface."

"That's just the TFP programs reacting to the modified set points."

"We've been running predictive models with the changes. I do expect the temps to settle in at approximate ranges the Trectilla were looking for, but..."

He hesitated.

"But what?" April asked.

"Well, we're just not sure."

"As long as they keep to their agreement, we stick to ours. I've already drafted a contract for Anard-Bueller to provide them their generational interstellar traveler. One might consider it an Ark. But as per our initial plans, they are not getting it built until the TFPs go into maintenance phase. That may be a long time from now, may even be centuries."

"Or maybe not," offered Elias.

April nodded in understanding. "Or maybe not."

"You will be glad to know, April, that they are proving to be quite helpful. They are quite engaged in their ambassadorial duties. We are sending parties South every week to meet with them – that included your Earth representatives, by the way. We've even had a few of them tour our cities. Had a contingent of Trectilla travel, hover, walk, whatever the hell they do. They went through NewBerlin and then toured the remains of Monsoona just last month. That raised quite a crowd of onlookers. They are fascinating creatures, to say the least. Their colors are..."

"Amazing. Tantalizing. Mesmerizing. Yeah, I know and unmistakably, utterly, alien. Just remember to always keep control of the situation during the times we interface with them. One stupid human, add a little bit of fear, and a dumb action and we are in a deep well of trouble. We need to maintain exceptional relations with them. Earth is monitoring our situation very closely."

"Do you really think they would do something against us now?"

"They're afraid of them. I don't know what happened centuries ago, but someone on Earth has not forgotten. Tell me, can you think of anything that would result in Ishaida being completely destroyed?"

"You mean now? With all this going so well?"

She nodded. "Yes. Maybe some insane thing that would manage to position blame on someone or something else and be plausible enough to create suspicion? If you can, then don't rule it out. But I can't think of anything right now. Maybe I'm just not creative enough."

"We are monitoring all incoming vessels – nothing is landing on the planet that has not been cleared."

April laughed. "You think our advanced tech can stop a fully camouflaged spy ship? Give your head a shake, Elias, they are already here. Just be on your guard."

"Very well, I'll advise the council. In the meantime, April, I have a request of you, it's somewhat pressing – and no it doesn't involve any more crowds."

"OK..." she urged him on, but not really wanting to hear.

"We'd like you to convene with your Trectilla contacts. As per our engineers, the TFP systems should be about to move to the next stage of nitrogen seeding. We have a number of people ready to migrate out of the cities, we are about to parcel out lands to attempt farming."

"Nitrogen seeding?"

"Yes, we need you to confirm they are going to initiate the seeding. Has to be done soon, apparently."

"Certainly, I'll reach out to my friend Evelyn and see what I can learn. But Elias, I need your help too."

"Of course, I'd be glad to help."

"This may sound a bit crazy, but I need volunteers – a few thousand of them actually. I have a fleet of starships, of which I intend to crew – and I want to fill the executive officers' roles with Porters."

"I'm not sure you'll get that many volunteers, April. Not too many Porters would take the job. They aren't exactly the spacefaring type."

"I know. I just need you to get the council to convince them to meet me. I'll handle the Porters. The rest will be difficult because I need to find experienced spacers. I've set up draft centers on all the main extranist systems."

"We will do everything we can to help, of course, but Ishaida is not exactly the epicenter for this type of talent. Cauputain would be a better source."

"Yes, but neither Jefferson nor Cauputain has the Anard-Bueller's extranist headquarters."

"What?"

"You heard me. I'm building here. Actually, I should already have started. I just need to catch up to Tiberious."

"Tiberious? But he's dead."

April caught herself. "Just a figure of speech. So, back to our volunteers. Expect they'll all come here – because the jobs will be here. I need the council to recondition all their major spaceports. I don't care what it costs, get it done, and don't worry, you'll get it back in traffic fees."

"And when these people arrive, what then?"

"Let's just say Ishaida spaceports are going to become very busy in a very short amount of time."

"We are having a difficult enough time keeping up now."

"You always wanted that economic boost. Ishaida is getting it. If you hear any complaints tell them what my dad always said to me – when opportunity knocks, you listen, you act."

* * *

"It's been a long time," April said, fighting back the urge to be overcome with emotion.

She hugged Jasmine as the others of the McThurn Clan were fighting to get in. Jimmy, Quinn, Karen, Bobby, Tracey all of them were there, but everyone looked quite a bit older by at least 20 years.

"You look great, April, you've hardly aged at all."

"Far too many years traveling superluminal or in stasis," she acknowledged. "You never get used to it."

She scanned the group and realized one was missing. "Withers?"

Tracey shook her head. "We lost him. Went down with a fever a few years back. We couldn't place the virus. May have been something from Ishaida herself."

"Aye, she continues to demand her payment on our blood."

It took a moment for it to sink in. How does one respond to losing a brother?

"We saw him off well, April. Even had a drink in your honor," added Quinn, in his typical clumsy attempt to comfort. He put his big hand on her shoulder.

"Thanks for that. I'm sorry I couldn't be here."

"But you were in spirit," reinforced Jasimine. "And we have a bunch of new members, including some wives, husbands, and other smaller additions." She walked her through the crew lineup, listing out everyone's names, their lineage and posting on the clan's transport.

April took everyone's hand, welcomed them to the McThurn Clan, felt the genuine warmth in their eyes. She had not lost her family after all.

"OK, so where is the LightningRod?" April grinned, excited to see the ancient Porter transport.

"In Bay w13 – getting some retrofit work done. We needed to modify the tires, too many thorns and greenery out there now. You need to get out there, April. It's evolving, changing every day. We run wide open most days, air scrubbers off. It's one thing to see it from space, but you need to be here, on the land, to truly appreciate it."

April could feel the excitement building in her. The thoughts of getting out there, traveling the roads again, seeing what has changed.

Her wrist communicator signaled. She scanned the holographic projection of a 3D building plan. A memo from the engineering office. Problems with construction on the second tower.

Karen and Jasmine looked knowingly at each other. "April, why don't you take some time to take care of that. We'll still be here. We expect to be down for two days while the LightningRod is being refitted. I promise we'll check in with you before we head back out."

She swatted the image down. "Good, because I'm coming with you guys. I need a ride south."

"Sure, how far south?"

"The equator - to the Trectilla city." She caught the looks between them, realizing the problem. "You already have a charter run don't you?"

"Of course. With all the construction projects and the growing farmer homesteads, we can hardly keep up."

"Don't worry, I'll pay you whatever it costs."

Jasimine stepped ahead. "You are the CEO of Anard-Bueller. You can have flitters outfitted at your disposal to get you anywhere on this planet within an hour. You don't need to run in an old Porter transport. And we have people counting on this shipment."

April nodded, knowing all the truths she was speaking. But each word cut into her like a knife. With each plunge, her reality bit into her yet again, and again.

No time to be with her family.

"It's not fair, you know. This is all I ever wanted."

Jasmine responded by holding her tight.

* * *

Chapter 22

A pril piloted the flitter herself, despite the noise her staff put up. She wanted to get out on her own, travel Ishaida, and see for herself what her clan told her about. And to her, it was well worth it. The green hills, valleys of fledgling forests, rivers with waters of red clay, and broad expanses of grassy plains dotted with multicolored flowers. The closer to the equator, the more it reminded her of the old Ishaida. Greenery was replaced with cacti and brush, then eventually sand, and rock. It all looked so familiar now, at least until the tall black ridge appeared on the horizon, and slowly grew into a mammoth cluster of towers of dizzying heights.

She maneuvered the flitter into the cooler shadow of the buildings and scanned her geo-navigator for where the entrance was supposed to be. She landed just outside, the flitter's legs settling into hills of dry sand.

The walk in the shade was still incredibly hot, as the wind tended to draw all the moisture from one's body.

Evelyn waited at the opening for her, she did not look much different than before. April could only wonder how they aged – or even if they did age.

"Hello, Evelyn."

"My friend, April. It is very good to see you, again."

"You may notice I am slightly older, hopefully, a little wiser as well." She smiled at her own wit.

"I have. I am sure you are."

"You have some place a bit cooler where we can talk? I find this heat oppressive."

"Yes, follow me."

Nothing has changed with her. Evelyn still had not learned to chat.
April let her curiosity break the quiet.

"Tell me, Evelyn, what is a typical lifetime for your kind?"

"By this, I assume you are asking about how long the average Trectilla will live from birth to death?"

"Yes, you *were* born weren't you?"

"Not in the same fashion as humans, but we do have a moment of conscience – a moment of birth if you will. And what unit of time would you like this expressed in?"

A typical perfunctory response from these alien types, she thought. "Well since our universal standard is based on the Sol-Earth year unit. You are familiar with that time unit – it's buried within the TFP programming."

"Very well, an average lifetime is approximately five-hundred years, in consideration that one does not hibernate in that timespan, which we always do as we age. Some of our elders are approaching nine-hundred years, many have in the past, exceeded one-thousand."

"Oh," was all April could muster, caught by surprise. "That's a long time."

"Due to this, we have found our perspective may sometimes vary from your kind. It explains why you always seem to be in such a hurry."

"Maybe so, but your changes to the TFPs are pushing the limits on the schedule. So I would say you are the ones in a hurry."

"We have not adjusted your machines, but we have helped through compensation."

"Compensate how?"

"The methods are not important. I will state we have found other ways to accelerate the process. But we have discovered an unexpected variation. We have investigated this and have discovered a problem."

"What type of problem?"

"It is a matter of stability. We have calculated a net loss of the atmosphere. Over time it will be lost due to entropy, slowly bled off by the pressure of the sun's radiation."

"Oh, that." April ran through her memories of the TFP environmental cycles.

"Yes, the engineers had this accounted for this. The satellites are to deploy matrices of lower frequency radio emitters to create a negatively charged counterforce, the envelope created around the planet should be enough."

"Yes, your engineers have informed us. We believe this will be inadequate."

April's mind was spinning. She ran through the specs in her head, searching for the elusive information regarding the atmospheric bleed off. Could the original engineers have made a mistake? This was not Anard-Bueller's first terra-forming project. Maybe some baseline changes had occurred from half-a-millennia ago?

"Has our sun increased in output? I just don't understand how the engineers could have miscalculated. Can we increase the emitter levels to compensate?"

"We believe Ishaida's magnetic field must be strengthened."

Of course, the magnetic field has also decreased over time. Her realization came at the same moment of the scope of the actual problem.

"I don't know how we can fix this, Evelyn."

"It is a matter of gravity and magnetism. We simply need to reinvigorate Ishaida's core. Ishaida needs a moon."

April took a second to let the idea sink in. "Evelyn, we may be able to make some impressive machines and seem to have some incredible technology at our disposal but being able to move a moon – that's a little outside of our capabilities."

"I understand." The alien seemed untroubled by the news. "We must, nevertheless, work to achieve this in the very near future; if you are agreeable?"

"By all means, if you know of a way, I'd love to hear it."

"We do."

Again, April was taken aback. "Umm, OK. But ironically, I just came here to ask about something much more trivial - nitrogen seeding."

Evelyn paused for a moment, her colors shifted to yellow and blue hues, then returned to normal. "There is a fault in the TFP programs. But we have countered this. You can inform your people this has been initiated."

"Thank you." April was almost afraid to ask. "And moving a moon, how would we do that?"

"It is not time yet. We will inform you." She turned, preparing to float away.

"Hang on, Evelyn. I haven't seen you in how many years? And that's it?"

The alien bobbed slightly in the air, taking a moment to understand. "Yes, perhaps there is more to discuss?"

"Yes. Like how have you been? How are your people doing? What, exactly, are you doing with the TFPs? Where are we going to get a moon?"

"I have been well. We are doing well. The TFP machines are working as designed. We will use the moon from the second planet. We have noticed you are building a device in orbit."

April smiled, finding the dry response humorous. *Good comeback.*

"Yes, that device is what we call a space elevator. You may notice a cable slowly dropping down from the asteroid in orbit that we are busy hollowing out up there. An elevator will attach itself to that cable and essentially provide a means to go up and down from orbit in a quick, efficient, and safe manner."

"But your ships can land easily enough."

"Not the superluminal cruisers. Too big. Even the small ones prefer to stay in orbit to save fuel. All about saving energy."

"I understand."

"That asteroid will become a very big spaceport by the time we are done, capable of docking multiple starships at once."

"We have begun to plan our exodus. We believe this will require a number of vessels."

"The cost of building a significantly sized generational vessel can exceed billions of credits. I am not convinced you will need multiple vessels. We are capable of constructing one vessel large enough. Unfortunately, neither the Ishaidan government nor Anard-Bueller can afford to finance a venture of this scope. We will need your help."

"How can we help?"

"We need some knowledge, something that will have some demonstrable worth in time, like the means to relocate this moon. If you plan to do this with some telepathic magic of yours, that's not usable, but if you have some science behind it, something that we can take advantage of ..."

"It is a machine we require you to construct. We have the understanding. We need you to employ the technology."

"Are you able to provide us schematics, plans, engineering specifications? Do you know what we are looking for?"

"Show me."

April thought hard, recalling as many engineering diagrams she had reviewed over the years. Luckily, she had a knack for almost perfect recall of such things. She could feel Evelyn's probes, as they tended to interrupt her recall, and kept interfering with her stream of thinking, raising strange sensations of smells and colors.

"I see. We can provide this to you very easily."

"Good." April could barely control her excitement. "Then this may be the ticket for paying for your ships."

"We will send them to you when they are ready. Goodbye, April."

"Goodbye my friend, Evelyn."

* * *

The trip back to NewLondon gave April time to plan. This would take time, money and resources to pull off. She had to bring peace to a shattered collection of worlds through building a police fleet from a disparate collection of volunteers, complete the construction of her headquarters on her home planet, and in the process complete an incredibly challenging technological marvel of engineering – the space elevator. But she also had to, in short order, initiate construction of a super-vessel for the Trectilla race, and top it all off by successfully engineering one of the best magic tricks ever seen – moving a moon from one planet to another.

Her days of being a Porter were much easier.

First things first, in order to build her fleet she needed the Porters – and their leaders were now gathered in NewLondon, at her request. As she brought in the flitter, it was quite obvious they had arrived by the sheer number of Porter transport parked haphazardly about the bays and just outside the city. They were all here at least.

Elias had come out to meet her, a wide grin on his face, quite pleased with the turnout no doubt. "At your request, they came," he announced. "Unfortunately we are at such a capacity many have not been able to enter the city."

"Looks like you have your own temporary Porter city just outside the main entrance," April commented. She could not help but notice the children playing amongst the transports and the tents, hastily constructed to form a sprawling outside market. The steady stream of city dwellers had formed lanes coming to and from the main locks.

"When was the last time you'd seen Porters collect in such numbers?" she asked, unable to keep from smiling. "After we're done, let's you and I go out there. I bet you'll be able to procure things you've never seen before – and never thought you would ever need."

Elias's eyes twinkled. "That will be fun."

The quick trek through NewLondon was far too crowded for April's comfort. She kept her shawl wrapped tightly around her, and face covered, being careful to avoid being recognized. She only relaxed when she was inside the walls of city hall.

The Porter leaders, Captains, and Grand Captains had collected in the city's amphitheater, the only room big enough to hold their numbers. April came in through the back and managed to adjust the podium microphone and collect her thoughts before she was noticed. The high-level noise of talking and shuffling from so many seemed to die off into a mere whisper.

"My brothers and sisters, welcome, and thank you for coming." Her words seem to ring from every corner of the room. She adjusted the volume down slightly, clearing her throat in a nervous involuntary reaction.

"Some of you may know of me. I am April McThurn of the McThurn Clan."

A few whistles shot through the air, following along with a wave of laughter.

She scanned the crowd for her crew from the LightningRod, but there were so many faces.

"I have asked you here because I need your help. We all know the Porter code. We – you and I – live it every day. This is what matters. This is what brings meaning to what we do."

Many nodded in silent agreement, all respectfully listening.

"I am building a fleet that will bring peace to the extranists and an end to this rebellion. Even though I will have the ships, they alone are not enough. I need crews. I am not willing to settle. In order for this fleet to sail, I need Porters."

The background noise started, rising as a wave would as it approached the shore.

"April McThurn!" Boomed out a loud, deep voice above the others. "I am James McGalvin, we ran in tandem with your clan a number of times. Oranis was a good friend of mine."

"Yes, please Mr. McGalvin, I recognize you."

"April, you must realize we only know our Tanks, few of us, if any, know anything about space-going vessels."

"Yes, I understand your concerns. But more importantly, you know people. You know how to get things done. You understand the Code and Protectorate law, and you can teach it. I need you to be my officers."

"You are asking us to step out onto the deck of a battlecruiser, instruct a bunch of space monkeys to possibly fight against our own people – our own sympathizers?"

"Yes, but we can stop this war without killing anyone because they will trust us to protect them. The ones left that want to fight will be the real criminals. They were most likely pirates before this all started."

"We can't do this, we don't know starships, and this isn't our fight," yelled out another.

"I have negotiated a reprieve. But only if I can pull this off with enough ships and crew. Bottom line, we either step up now or let the ESPD step in later. Earth will not lose this war if it comes to that. This is how we win. We police ourselves and we keep the ESPD out."

"We're not military. We're not trained killers."

"No. Not killers. We start with the Code. And we bring it to space. We are nomads. Whether it be on a lonely Ishaidan road or in a shipping lane within the void of space, this is our calling. I cannot do this alone."

Men and women shifted uncomfortably in their chairs. Many began debating with one another.

April could tell all too well. *She had lost them.*

"Registration desks have been set up in the back. I need five-hundred officers to sign on for the next five years. I won't need you forever. You can return home and you'll be paid well while you are in service."

The crowd started to file out. Many stopped at the back to talk with the registration secretaries, many didn't.

She felt the burn of frustration. A glance over to Elias, but he simply nodded and avoided further eye contact. He knew it, he just didn't want to say it.

It wasn't enough.

He finally came forward, patted her on the shoulder. "They'll come around."

"I doubt it. I'm asking them to go way out of their comfort zone here."

They glanced over at the small group around the registry table. "Well not all of them – looks like you have a few interested parties."

April noted a familiar mop of black hair mixed up in the crowd. It was Karen, of course. Someone of the McThurn Clan had to sign up. They would always stand behind her. She made a mental note to ensure Karen had a command. She was a McThurn after all.

"Let's bring this meeting to an end. I think we have a market to visit."

They headed out, only this time being joined, quite stealthily, by a group of bodyguards. April did not bother to wave them off. It was futile anyway.

"Don't worry, Elias, they won't bite. You will barely notice they are with us. I picked them up Earth-side during my stay. I think I am their boss, but they won't do a damned thing I say. So I've learned to ignore them."

* * *

"Coabi has landed, Sir."

"Confirm with Captain Zehrna the point of hand off. No, better yet patch me through to him."

Commander Richard Nearson approached the projection table, pulled up the 3D image of the spaceport, including every human in the vicinity.

"Scan for heat signatures."

"Scanning" replied the AI. "No threats located."

"We have the Captain, Sir." The Sergeant nodded and flipped the com over to him.

"Captain, this is Commander Richard Nearson, Coabi protection detail. Do you wish to transfer?"

"No Commander, my men have this under control."

"We'll be on standby. Escort to the hotel and we'll pass off from there, thank you, Captain."

"My pleasure, Commander. Watch over her – she's a rare one."

"That she is." He flipped the channel. Always good catching up with old acquaintances, even if only briefly.

A red dot blipped up on the center image. It was moving quickly to the podium, in a zigzag pattern.

"We have a bogey, transmitting."

"Have him," came another voice from out in the field. "Confirmation on zero-grade firearms."

The man's holographic image popped up above the spaceport image. The computer had already matched the image to a records database, and the history files were in view.

Richard flicked a finger through the files. "Code 5, gentlemen."

Field agents moved in, in a deft almost imperceptible action, the man was injected, and instantly incapacitated. Two field agents escorted him away from the crowd.

The image settled back to a peaceful green.

Richard was curious, not at the fact this was a spacer from the Cauputain belt, known to have a temper and a poor sense of judgment, just where did he get a zero-grade firearm from anyway? Zero grade equipment was reserved for operatives, barely perceptible by most traditional scanners. There's more to this man than it seems. Some questioning was in order before they retired back to central.

Richard watched as Coabi addressed the crowd. She was clearly uncomfortable but did an admiral job of presenting herself. The Old Man would have been proud. He continued to monitor her until she was escorted to the hotel.

"Handoff," he stated succinctly.

"Handoff confirmed," the agent replied.

"I want all vantage points covered – including the balcony."

"Standby. Confirmed. All vantage points."

Satisfied, for now, Richard headed downstairs. As the elevators were not yet functional in the new Anard-Bueller headquarters, certain levels of comfort had to be sacrificed.

In how many basements had he questioned suspects?

The agents opened the door for him as he entered the small, dimly lit room, bare but for two chairs, one of which the suspect sat, bound tightly. A small amount of blood dripped from his mouth from a cracked lip, and a bruised cheek. His eyes were wild, darting back and forth to each of his captors.

One agent leaned over and whispered in Richard's ear.

"Blood test says he's I-positive. We'll need to do this the hard way."

Richard grabbed the other chair, flipped it around to rest his arms on the back of it as he sat.

"High tech gear for a grunt. Who gave it to you?"

The man spat blood on the floor. "Forget it. I ain't talking."

"Oh don't worry, we have ways for that. My boys tested your blood. Did you know, if we injected you with our standard truth serum it would stop your heart? Now, who would do that to you?"

That caught his attention. Eyes were a bit bigger now.

"Expendable, that's what they think of you, obviously."

"So, it was worth it," he mumbled back.

"Oh you mean the credits transferred to your ex-wife and kids – that was a tidy sum. Too bad it never arrived."

He fought to get loose. "You're a lying sack of shit."

"You think? I checked the transactions myself. The funny part is my boys didn't pull it. You know what that means right? It was your friends who took it back."

An agent opened the door behind them, came in with a black device.

"Ah... this thing is not any fun at all. Kind of bypasses all that chemical firewall stuff and gets to the center of things. May not leave you completely whole when we're done."

"You can't do this. You guys are..."

"Not ESPD. No, we are company men you see. A good chance you may not survive this."

Richard got up, swinging the chair over to the corner and went to step out.

"I don't know nothing."

He turned back. "Tell you what; we have ways to reverse certain digital transactions. Those credits can be redirected by us. Only difference is, when I say your family will get those credits, that's what will happen."

"And what about me?"

Richard looked up to the second agent in charge, who shook his head slowly.

"Sorry, bud. Talking can still work. Think on my offer, it goes away when that door closes behind me."

He really wasn't surprised to hear him yell out, "I'll do it," as he stepped out. The man wasn't a complete idiot.

He put on his earbud communicator and caught the last of the conversation.

Coabi was missing.

"What the hell, I wasn't out of touch for that long." He was absolutely pissed. How the hell had she managed to get past his agents this time?

"Tell me you have her, damn it."

"Confirmed. She's on an 82 degree vector heading south."

Richard walked over to the scanning console. The image came up showing the small flitter running at high-speed just above the ground, leaving a small trail of dust in its wake. From time to time Coabi would bounce it high and flip it 360 around, then come barreling back down to just meters above the surface.

"She can certainly fly that thing."

"Plotting intersection vector."

"No, hang back. Triangulate to the Trectilla towers, and scan for threats. We need to obfuscate from above. Get the Cruiser Captain on alert, and have her ready all cannon. I don't want any vertical hits on my watch."

"Confirmed, Sir."

"Captain hailing you, Sir."

"Told you she was a handful."

Richard smiled. "I know."

"We're good here. Nothing for a parsec at least."

"Thanks, Captain."

"No problem at all. Whatever Coabi needs."

Richard pulled the satellite image of the Trectilla and amplified the image.

"So this is the one she calls Evelyn." He mused out loud. "Strange creatures these – what are they Trectils or Trectillians?"

"Trectilla is the common reference," replied the monitoring system AI.

"All right. Looks like she is headed back. All you smartasses out there, make sure you don't lose her this time." He killed the com and cussed under his breath.

Once Coabi returned Richard would feel a little more at ease. At least here he could control the situation. Presented more variables but he had a higher degree of assets to respond.

"Commander, intelligence from our suspect has paid off. We have enemy activity confirmed."

Richard scanned the report. "Interesting. Guess now is just as good as any time." He started toward the stairs.

"Where are you headed, Sir?"

He paused to answer. "To see Coabi, of course."

* * *

April walked to match Elias's gait. She was in no hurry, and it was a good speed to inspect most of the wares displayed out on the market tables.

"How about these glass goblets, Elias, for all this wine you profess to drink?"

He chuckled heartily. "I'm slowing down nowadays."

April stopped to inspect a strange looking device on one of the tables. "Where did you find this?"

"A scrapie town, South of Monsoona."

"What is it?" asked Elias.

"Nothing. Old tech – original 'bot mechanism, tied to the TFPs – a leg off of a seeder. TFPs retired these old models."

"Really?" Elias picked up the unit, with some effort. It was heavier than it looked.

"Yes, the TFPs were dormant, but they kept updating their systems – and hardware on their own."

They both stopped to turn to the source of a shadow that appeared behind them. He was a tall man, sharp features, a long scar on his left cheek and dark eyes. Something was different about this man.

April could not help but feel that every glance assessed everything about her like there was something not quite human behind those eyes.

"Good afternoon, Ms. McThurn, Mayor Talbot."

April scanned the crowd for her guard shadows, none were to be seen. Strange.

"Can we help you?"

"Forgive my rudeness. I am Richard Nearness, under your employee Ms. McThurn, commander of your security detail." He bowed slightly.

April returned the bow, highly curious now.

"So you are the reason why I find it so hard to rid myself of my shadows."

"Your shadows are a necessity, Ms. McThurn. You are a target, at all times."

"So I guess you have a difficult job. Tell me why I am meeting you now, in the middle of a Porter market on an extranist planet."

"We have acquired some troubling information, which I feel you must be made aware of, given your future planned station."

"Which is?"

"Why Grand Fleet Admiral, of course." He smiled.

April scowled. This guy had too much knowledge about her. He probably had already profiled her a dozen different ways and could predict what she would do before she could herself.

"OK, what's your title, Captain, Lieutenant, what?"

"Commander."

April paused a second. *Seemed a bit of a high rank for this unassuming figure. How much power did he actually yield?*

"Alright, Commander. What is this information?"

Richard looked around, "Perhaps a quieter place would be more suitable."

"This is as good as any. Quiet places are often bugged."

"Very well. We may have the coordinates of your troublesome rebel leader's coordination center." He handed her a small tablet. "This will decrypt under your fingerprint."

"Thank you. Is that all?"

"Well no, Ms. McThurn. As you know, the dynamics of our relationship are about to change drastically. As a fleet Admiral, my duty to protect you becomes intrinsically more difficult. We will have to operate in a more visible manner moving forward."

"Or not at all. You can forfeit your role, move on."

Richard laughed. "I'm sorry, that's not possible. That's not going to happen."

"Am I not your boss?"

"Indirectly, yes. The position is more direct, however."

"So I cannot be rid of you even if I say go away."

"No, you cannot. But that is not all bad." Richard responded in a light-hearted manner.

"Ugh," April grunted in frustration. "Whatever."

"I for one, am very glad someone is watching over my dear friend," offered Elias. "Thank you."

"My pleasure," Richard responded, appreciatively.

"Fine. Come out of the shadows then. You may as well be integrated into my operation. At least I can watch you then."

Richard bowed in acknowledgment.

"And stop bowing," April insisted, feeling slightly irritated.

The sun was starting to set, and a few of the Porters had just finished laying down a temporary floor in the middle of the market. A few musicians were pulling instruments from cases, and plucking strings, testing for tune. A man walked past April's small group with a torch and lit the top of a tall gas-supplied post. It fired up with a large whoosh. A few of the crowd around applauded, enjoying the pyro-effects.

April was not overly impressed but stood close enjoying the warmth of the flame. The evening breeze felt cool, and she pulled her shawl close around her.

The music started up and the crowd moved in, many clapping to the time of the music, and more than a few taking the hand of their partners, or prospective ones, to join them on the dance floor.

April found herself keeping time by tapping her feet, smiling and laughing at the group. Elias beamed, hands clapping, thoroughly enjoying the moment. She glanced around for their new acquaintance, Richard, but he had faded somewhere back into the night.

Behind her, familiar voices called out. A dancing Jasmine grabbed her hands and pulled her toward the platform. Jimmy was beside her, and Quinn and even quiet Karen.

April jumped in, laughing and thoroughly enjoying herself.

From behind a display case, Richard pulled off his remote target finder and scanned the crowd in a quick circle. He could see April's face lit up by the flames of the torches.

"Coabi is enjoying herself. Let's make sure she doesn't have anyone interfere with all her fun, shall we?"

His new subtle approach took some getting used to by some of his junior agents, but it didn't take them long, as his meaning was clear.

He found himself tapping his own foot in time.

She would be safe here, with her own people. Time would come where it would not be this easy. May as well enjoy it now.

* * *

"Really dear, you are quite lovely. We need to see your face, please stop hiding it under that mane of yours." The makeup artist did one more pass with his brush.

Elias came up to the station, peering at her in the mirror. "Absolutely lovely."

"Elias, is this really necessary?"

"You know it is. It's the beginning of the end!"

"You can only hope. And why is it so important everyone see my face? Why can't we just send out propaganda or something?"

"You are more effective than any propaganda slogan."

April let out a sigh. "Did you see the length of this speech I have to get through?"

"It will reach them all. We'll make sure of it."

"Will it have the impact we are looking for though?"

"It's a start. If it ceases hostilities, just for the time being, it can save lives."

"Right, timing is everything. Make sure this doesn't play out until we're ready."

The director waved her over. "April dear, please, time is money."

April glared at Elias, who merely laughed.

"I feel like a dressed up clown."

"No, you look beautiful."

"Say's you," she replied with a small half-smile.

"Oh baby girl, you don't realize just what you got here. You are gorgeous." The makeup artist winked and threw her a kiss.

"April, if you could stand at the podium," instructed the director.

"You do realize you are talking to a Grand Admiral, mister... whatever your name is. Since when did we get on a first name basis?"

"Now April, no time for a hissy fit. Focus now darling," urged the makeup artist with a smile and a wink.

April glared into the camera. *She cannot stand these glitzy types, not at all.*

"Great, let's get the lighting over here boys, no more yellow tinge on the left."

"OK, April look at me, give me a smile, think nice thoughts. Good. You'll see the speech on the prompter, start anytime."

April cleared her throat.

"Hello, my fellow extranists. Some of you may know of me. My name is April McThurn, of the McThurn Clan, Porter Captain of the planet Ishaida, Grand Admiral and Commander of the Security Divisional Fleet, and Chief Executive Office of Anard-Bueller."

"I am reaching out to you today with news of peace..."

After about the 10th retake they had managed to get through the entire speech, and April was exhausted.

"I do think, dear, if we could just pull in some of the deep emotion," the director hinted.

"No. Enough. You have what you need. Edit it or do whatever you need to. I'm done."

She left the makeshift stage and headed back to her room through the great hall of the Anard-Bueller headquarters.

Richard intercepted her, but quickly rescinded whatever he was going to say when she raised her hand and gave him the thin-lipped glare.

He made the right call. Probably best to leave her alone.

* * *

The propaganda program was working. April, the savior of Ishaida, was now a common image on an extranist display. The word had got out amongst the colonies and the outer systems. Excited volunteers converged onto Ishaida from all the recesses of known space. Domed cities grew crowded by thousands of newcomers all looking to satisfy one need or another. Some were looking for refuge from a war, others employment in a collapsed economy, a few were there to answer the call and make a stand for the rights of all extranists, and a small few were there for more nefarious reasons. Regardless, they each brought able hands and capital, along with mouths to feed within an infrastructure stretched to its maximum.

April moved from NewLondon to the ever-evolving Anard-Bueller headquarters. Living quarters were part of the first projects of focus. April's 'apartment' adjoined the large halls where the main offices would be located. Gigantic quartz windows opened up to look down into the valley where the space elevator cable would eventually be locked, deep into the bedrock of the planet. The view was picturesque, even with the cranes and construction robots erecting the immense superstructure of the interconnecting maze of girders and cement.

Her living quarters were spacious and included multiple living areas that would rival her Earth counterpart. It also included library quarters which contained a sister computer system to the Earth's main system – another home for AI Tiberious. She would often spend hours in her library working with AI Tiberious and managing the multiple projects on both Ishaida and Earth.

When the stress became too much, she would steal away from the hustle of the HQ center and enjoy a walk out in the Ishaidan adjoining wildlands, often following a path through the sprawling forests and grassy meadows. Of course, her shadows were never too far away.

* * *

"I understand your recorded messages are an inspiration," AI Tiberious commented.

April stared at the holograph for a moment, still wondering why this version was just as blotchy and irregular as the one on Earth.

"Yes, fine, rather not talk about it."

"Good. I have a lot of work for you to authorize to keep this project going."

"I'm glad you are minding the store. I don't think I would be able to do this without you."

"This is all by design, April. You know that. I never intended to leave you all alone." AI Tiberious gave her a genuinely sincere look.

"And what happens if you get corrupted? How do I know someone else won't be able to affect you, reprogram you in the background somehow?"

"I have fail-safes in place, hashing algorithms, continuous system checks. I've had the best minds work on this project of myself for years. I already thought through every security issue. Yes, there are possible risks, but I've mitigated most vectors."

"The very best minds and this is all they could do for your display?" She reached out and wiped her hand through the image, slightly disrupting it.

AI Tiberious ignored her comments. "Elevator is progressing nicely. Cable should be down within the year, barring any problems, of course."

"Headquarters?"

"Will stretch into at least another six months after, as we've added the SPDF training center and the additional living quarters."

"I also need to add squadron fighters for my ships, light armored, powerful, maneuverable in and out of the atmosphere. Can you pull some specs together for me to review?"

"I can. I assume you, being the resident mechanical genius that you are, would like to see full plans and multiple models?"

"Yes, please. I also need to modify the existing cruisers to outfit these

Page 357

units."

"A landing bay is not exactly a post-manufacturing feature."

"You may have noted I selected the cruiser specs. I anticipated this requirement, just didn't add it in at the time."

She brought a 3D image of the Triple-A class cruiser up on the holographic adjacent to AI Tiberious.

"Look, see how sharp this image is? Why can't you be like that?"

He only twinkled a slight smile.

"Anyway, you see here in the belly of the beast?" She pointed to a where enormous metal ribs extended down. "We build the bay offsite, and then it will attach and lock it in here. No problem. I have already routed accessory power channels, and everything else to support them. We'll need to get these started right away. I think I'll need them when I go into the belt."

"Very well. These are the units I was able to find. Good starting point."

"Good going AI Tiberious! Let's get to work."

* * *

The HQ building was being constructed as a grand statement, imposing and domineering to all of its visitors. The Upper Hall housed the main planning levels and the logistics control center. It was from here that the elevator and the spaceport would be managed.

The Upper Hall overlooked the Great Hall, another intimidating building of massive proportions. Through here all traffic coming in and out of Ishaida would pass, whether it be by elevator or through the adjoining spaceport. The hall was built with its share of mythic statues and figures, carved out of Ishaidan white limestone which lined up in a band above the upper windows.

At April's insistence two transport tunnels and an aboveground highway to the closest Ishaidan City, NewLondon, were also under construction. She kept a close eye on the progress but did not allow it to take away from her primary goal of training the new crews for the growing police fleet.

Far above Ishaida, the collection of new, unnamed ships slowly grew from a few to tens of ships circling around the planet, each manned with a few trusted souls. The growing collection of battle-grade cruisers made for a ripe target for many of her enemies. April recognized the danger far before it became an issue, and quietly dispersed the ships to a secret location in deep space, far past the fringe of any traveled shipping lane, safe from being discovered. It was a better approach than leaving them at the spaceports upon completion. They were just as good a target there as anywhere else. A particularly non-descript part of space can be a very, very difficult place to find.

As newly completed ships left the Mars or Jefferson spaceports, they were dispatched to a specific set of coordinates in space, each time to a different location. There they would meet with another vessel, exchange crews, and the original ferried back. From there the new vessels were taxied to the location, the crew taking careful precautions to avoid acquiring any tails.

As the crews were assembled and trained, April then called upon them to assume their ship, but not without some ceremony, after all, this was a significant affair. Crew members lined up in The Great Hall, in full uniform. April would speak a few inspirational words and send them off via shuttles to board their new home.

She had some doubts that her speeches inspired anyone, but she worked to improve with each cycle.

The latest ship was the Tesla-Continuum, just arrived from the Mars shipyards. As with most ships, this one followed the standard Triple-A Cruiser specifications, and as with every ship, her construction deviated ever so slightly from the others. It was a reflection of what specific parts were available, small adjustments made in overall design improvements, and even subtle build-schedule changes. This particular cruiser carried two extra forward cannon, the first having this enhancement, and given the retrofit delays this change caused, possibly the last.

April appreciated the design, regardless, and decided to assign the ship to one of the newer faces of fledgling Captains – and a particular officer she felt a little drawn to. She had talked to him no more than a half-dozen times, but somehow she felt they made a connection. Maybe it was his sense of humor, or possibly the way he looked at her – with something more than fear, or desire to please.

April marched to the podium in full uniform, being careful to maintain a consistent gait as she had been coached. Her small entourage of administration staff followed her up the steps. At the podium, she systematically ran through the crew list of names. Each was presented a gold medal bearing the symbol of their assigned ship and a small scroll containing the oath of a guardian of the Anard-Bueller Security Divisional Fleet. She released each with a sharp salute.

Now through the full crew, she pulled her small tablet from her pocket and placed it on the podium.

Maybe this time she would make it through without a single mistake.

"Ladies and Gentlemen, Guardians of the Anard-Bueller Security Divisional Fleet. We stand at a difficult time in our history. The extranist conflict with Earth has cost lives and taken away the means of living for many. As we have learned from the past, war produces no winners, spares only the few and promotes unwanted suffering. As Guardians, I call upon you to put your personal desires aside, and instead, carry the burden of peace through enforcement of Protectorate Law, a law which supersedes all laws of place, citizenry, creed, culture, or religion. This is the Law you as a Guardian will stand for, and with the combined strength of your brothers and your sisters, you will stand against those who choose not to recognize what is right and what is truth."

"I call upon each of you to swear your allegiance not to any one person, nor any organization, but to an idea that remains above all else, applicable to all men and women, everywhere."

"As your Grand Admiral, Commander of the Anard-Bueller Security Divisional Fleet. I welcome you, and I am proud to present to you the starship Tesla-Continuum. May it protect you from the dangers you encounter, and forge the fires of retribution to strike your enemies down!"

With that, a cheer rose up from the crowd.

And with one last ceremonial action, April left the podium, marched slowly down the inspection line, and stopped to salute the newly assigned Captain.

He kept his eyes straightforward, and only once did she catch him diverting his gaze to her.

"Captain David Ironstrike, is your crew in order and complete?"

"It is Commander."

"Then I will turn the ship over to you."

She saluted him in earnest. "And may God protect you."

* * *

April watched the crew file out from the upper annex of the Anard-Bueller headquarters. From here they were mere stick figures, a stream of ants winding their way down to the shipyards.

"A very moving speech," stated Richard as he all but slid 'up' the stairs in some unnatural agility.

"And where do you come from?" She asked in earnest.

"Was here all along, never really left."

"You didn't like my speech?"

"On the contrary, felt it was truly inspirational."

April turned back to look out, irritated by his flippant responses.

"If I could ask a question, Commander?"

"That question infers I have the power to ignore you, doesn't it?"

He chuckled, "Well, you certainly could. But not sure that's wise."

"For all the sands on Ishaida, Richard, just blurt it out," she ordered exasperatedly.

"I noticed we've deployed the last of your trusted inner circle of Porter officers. I assume we have, for now, crewed our last ship."

"You assume correctly. No need to be concerned. The others have been disabled quite effectively. No one will be stealing them easily."

"Very well. Have you chosen your flagship – your preferred Captain?"

"Now that's a strange question," she stated quizzically, turning to focus her attention, once again, upon him.

What is he up to now?

"Not so strange, Commander. More security related than anything. I need to know who you've chosen as I intend to background check the lot of them."

"They've already been vetted."

"Not by me they've not." His voice carried that irritating self-confidence of which he had no lack of.

"Knock yourself out, as they say. But if you do find anything, tell me."

"Of course. And?"

"And what?"

"And... what is your choice, Commander? Or shall I hazard a guess?"

She decided to take the bait, as she was genuinely curious. "Let's hear your guess."

"I think it's no coincidence your last ship, your last Captain. I noticed something there, between you."

"That's laughable," she retorted, "You're way off."

"So who is it you are willing to put your life in the hands of? Perhaps I have it all wrong? You prefer more a father figure then, instead of a dashing young hero?"

"I've reviewed the files of every last one of my Captains. Every one of them has earned their position."

"Of course, they're all good, but I would suggest the dashing young hero, however."

"Why's that, Richard, since you seem so outrageously wise in such matters?"

"Simple, you have enough father figures. You are a young woman, you need something more."

He stepped a little closer, his dark gray eyes intent on hers.

She stepped back, slightly uncomfortable. "Very well, then. I'll take your advice. I choose our last Captain, and my flagship shall be the Tesla-Continuum. But not for all the reasons you suspect. I like the ship."

He half-smiled, moving back, quick to adjust to the non-spoken cues. "I'll advise you if there are any inconsistencies."

"Thank you." She turned back to watch the last shuttle launch upward into the reddish-yellow skies of late evening. Peering deep into the horizon, past the construction, the green valley, and the sandy shores of the waters of the newly named Lake Neprid, she noticed the skies were slowly churning darker as a storm was coming. She looked up and could just catch the shadow of the elevator cable as it glinted in the failing light of the setting sun.

Too bad she wouldn't be here when they reached the surface.

* * *

Chapter 23

The Anard-Bueller Security Divisional Fleet officially launched without ceremony days later, initiating the maiden voyage of its Flagship – the Tesla-Continuum.

On the day of departure, a Porter arrived with a package of scrolls. The delivery boy stated it was from Evelyn and that she wished her care in her travels.

April gave them a quick inspection. Each seemed to be made of some very fine woven silky cloth, which she would later find was made from a tiny caterpillar creature, to be more precise, the work of thousands of tiny insects. Each scroll bore upon it finite markings of symbols and drawings, oriented in such a strange manner, April had trouble determining the orientation of the pages. The illustrations were so meticulous in some areas that she had to pull a magnifier over them to appreciate the detail, which in turn would reveal even more detail. It was as if the woven material produced a third dimension when viewed at a certain angle. She quickly rolled them up knowing full well, deciphering these documents would take much more time than she had at the moment.

Her yacht, now captained by a younger, less seasoned officer, launched from the Anard-Bueller spaceport and met up with her flagship, the Tesla-Continuum. A temporary lifebridge was extended between to the ships to allow April to board.

Captain David Ironstrike, in full uniform dress, accompanied by his senior officers stood at attention to receive her as she struggled out of the flexible tube, and the zero gravity airlock. April appeared, red-faced, and a bit embarrassed, not so happy with her attempts to navigate in zero gravity. She had some more learning to do to get accustomed to space.

The Captain smiled.

"Grand Admiral on deck," he announced smartly and saluted. April responded as sharply.

At least she had started to become accustomed to all this military-like culture.

"At ease, all of you, and thank you, Captain."

"You are welcome. I assume you have luggage?"

"Well, I do." She peered back into the tube to see a young officer attempting to kick-off the sidewall only to lose grip on a suitcase. "Seems I'm not the only one that needs time to adjust. The ensign is having some trouble getting through."

David laughed. "I'm sure he'll manage. Grand Admiral, would you like to meet your senior officers?"

April nodded and they started through the lineup.

"Your Navigation Officer, Lieutenant Jeremy Black."

April could not help but notice how young he looked. "I've reviewed your records, Jeremy. Very impressive assessments."

"Helm Officer, Lieutenant Sharon Cross."

"It's good to see females in the officer ranks, Sharon. It is fitting you will be controlling our ship." April commented with a supportive smile.

"Communications Officer, Lieutenant Bran Edge."

"I know your father, Terrance. I'm expecting big things from you."

"And Monitoring and Science Officer, Lieutenant Terrance Ridgeline."

"I have some ideas to improve our equipment. Look forward to working with you on this."

"Yes, Commander, I'd love to hear your ideas."

"Weapons and Logistical Officer, Lieutenant Alfozo Das, or Daz as he likes to be referred to," offered David.

"You worked on the road building crews. I understand you are also genetically enhanced?"

"Yes, Commander, I can survive in a low oxygen environment for extended periods. Was helpful during those Ishaidan days in the Northern mountain regions. Spent a lot of time outside."

"I'm jealous." She winked.

"And last but not least, Engineering and Nuclear Officer Cameron Emeron: your second female senior officer."

"Your assessments are off the charts, Cameron, and I can certainly relate to your technical proficiency."

"It's an absolute honor to be working with you, Commander. This is a dream of mine, just to meet you much less work as part of your crew."

April felt taken aback. The idea of being some form of an idol never sat well with her. "Thank you," was all she could muster.

"I see all of you senior officers in front of me, and I know behind you there are multiple shifts that report to you, all of which you mentor and develop to become future senior officers. This makes you so essentially crucial to the success of this ship. Do not ever underrate the importance of your effect on others and the importance of your role. I look forward to working with all of you."

The Captain stepped in. "Commander, would you prefer to go to your quarters, or to the bridge?"

April smiled, appreciating that he knew enough to offer the correct choice. "The bridge, of course."

* * *

The SDF had enough ships to meet the minimum terms of the contract with Earth – and that was all that mattered. But despite all their preparation, they were untested, and only experience would bring them the confidence they needed. As Grand Admiral, Commander of the fleet, April knew more than anyone their fundamental flaw of self-confidence.

Regardless, their first action was the formal surrendering by the ESPD of its security roles and the dispatching of each and every one of the ESPD warships back to the Sol system. Few actually resisted April's directions, as the majority seemed more than eager to turn about and head home.

April's fleet spread itself thin spreading the word, but soon reformed to almost full strength in a final escort of the last few ships, including the ESPD flagship back to Sol's system. This was more than a 'symbolic' action, and the pullout of the primary aggressors in extranist space did not go unnoticed.

In a measure to sustain continued stability on the merchant trade routes, April systematically posted fleet ships to routine patrols in each sector. With each assignment she cut the force of her mobile response fleet, eventually draining its strength to only three cruisers - only three cruisers for which to respond to emergencies, and backup existing patrols. April had kept her most trusted and experienced Captains with her: Captain Alder of the Entrago, and Captain Isaac of the Aarcona - originally from the Overseer - and her own Captain David Ironstrike, all of Porter descent.

Ironically, known only to a trusted few, the potential remaining ships of the SDF floated empty and useless in space, all awaiting crews. Unassigned extra hands were put to work on Ishaida construction projects or had submitted to intense Guardian training. Some spacers who developed an aversion to labor found excuses to disappear back into the ether of extranist space. The stubborn held out hoping for a position.

April's second task was for her small spearhead fleet to visit each of the main extranist colonies. She needed to reach out to the rebel leaders, and with some luck inspire the jaded, incredulous, and bitter to lay down their weapons.

Jefferson was the first planet to visit. It was a smaller planet as planets go, but given there was no one leader, nor even a small few, the challenge would be difficult to address all of them. April networked out through her contacts and requested an audience with as many as was able. As expected, a small fleet of three cruisers did little to impress them, but they did agree to meet with her, in a nondescript old warehouse, in one of the oldest cities of Jefferson.

April thought it was a strange meeting place, but at least they were willing to listen to what she had to say.

Richard arranged the security measures. The other two Captains insisted on coming along with them, as well as assigned extra security crews that had multiple shuttles stationed around the meeting area, just in case.

* * *

"I do believe you all know who I am. I also believe you know that I've successfully escorted all ESPD ships from extranist space. My fleet is now assigned to police all non-Sol occupied areas."

"We know who you are," stated one of the local leaders. He looked more than a bit rough around the edges and carried a large ugly scar down the side of his face. "The real question is, what is it you want?"

"It's my desire to bring peace to this conflict," April responded, probably a bit too quickly.

"Using whatever means you have at your disposal as the CEO of Earth-based Anard-Bueller?" commented one of the audience.

"Yes, perhaps you would prefer I stand by on the sidelines and watch as the ESPD slowly and most assuredly dissects your rebellion."

"They would never..."

"Break your spirit? Overcome your beliefs? Beat you?"

"Are those the words you were looking for? Dreaming is a fool's errand. I'll be the first to call you on this, this shit of a belief. You recognize the old Earth term of shit, don't you? If you think you were going to beat back the ESPD, you are full of shit. Everyone knows it, just no one says it. The ESPD was already ramping up, getting ready to crank up that massive military machine of theirs. Would be good for the economy of Old Earth. Lots of jobs because of it."

"The rebellion was started because of you, Commander McThurn. It was the attack on Ishaida itself which spurned us into action, fearing we were next."

"And do you see the ESPD anywhere near us now? Where's the danger? The problem is already solved without anyone else dying."

They all looked at each other. What she said was the simple truth.

"And what would you ask of us now?"

"Cease all hostilities to the corporations. Open the trade routes. Return any prisoners you have."

"What about Ishaida?"

"What about it?"

"What of these Trectilla?"

"We reached an agreement with Earth. They're upholding their end. So we'll uphold ours."

A few sat back in their chairs, considering.

"Look, I know this is painful. Lots of people here have relatives that have been killed or hurt in this war. But I tell you again, the ESPD is gone, people are safe."

"Our people won't believe it. They'll think it's a trick. What if they refuse to put down their arms?"

"The Security Divisional Fleet is not interested in pursuing homesteaders. They can arm themselves until their arms tire. I don't care. But if they perform a criminal act, they'll be arrested and detained by the Guardians of the Security Divisional Fleet, then sent to Ishaida for trial. They'll be tried under the Court of Protectorate Law."

"What the hell is Protectorate Law? You making this shit up?"

April almost laughed at the choice of words but held back to maintain a straight face. "This Law was created centuries ago. It has been adopted by a few Earth countries in the past, but in the end, most failed to implement the full scope, as these laws are written contrary to the idealism of materialism and ownership."

"I've heard of this Law," stated one of the older men. "It counters corporate law structure. It flies in the face of corporate evolution."

"Yes, and best represents our current strife as extranists against the corporate machine."

"So you're willing to take on a corporation head-to-head under Protectorate Law? You being the CEO of the biggest out there?"

"That's the law we use. As for where it applies – anywhere in extranist regional space. I can't force you to adopt this legislation, but this Law supersedes any local laws."

"And what if we want to?"

"The SDF could consider constructing local bases here. We could provide policing forces at a reasonable fee."

"We can police ourselves," grumbled another.

"Can we? We can't even get agreement between the lot of us on water rights, much less local law enforcement. You know as well as I do, there are certain parts of Jefferson that no one goes – and it's only worse now with this damn war burning."

"We'll consider your proposal," announced the facilitator.

"Good, and in the meantime, I'll ask that you please surrender all your political prisoners."

"You'll take them home, I suppose."

"Part of the agreement. ESPD goes home. All prisoners of war are returned to Earth."

"Well good riddance to them, I say."

"Let me know where to deploy my shuttles to."

"And if the locals kick up a fuss?"

"As I stated prior, this may not be my jurisdiction, but if a citizen interferes with a Guardian's function, he'll be arrested."

"You can't do that!"

"Protectorate Law overrides all local jurisdictional law. Citizens committing crimes will be arrested and processed under one law. Any interference and Guardians are prepared to respond in force."

"That makes you worse than the ESPD."

"No. Far from it. They aren't governed by Protectorate Law. Besides, open fire on Guardians and you may be shooting at your own sons or daughters."

Her last words took a moment to sink in. It was true many of the younger idealistic had converged onto Ishaida to sign up.

"I know this may be a bit of a shock, but the rebellion is over. The enemy is gone. You have won. The extranists have their own police force. The only possible downside to this is that the Law must be, and will be, maintained. If you want to have some influence on how things turn out, get your lawyers trained up."

April left the meeting feeling like she had a qualified victory. It was possible they would consider adopting Protectorate Law as the overreaching model of 'Law in force' through the local planetary governments.

Cauputain was next. This was a much larger but more organized planet. Large sections of the planet had been seized by different corporations. With the pretense of war, most had fallen to the purview of local leaders. Some were no different than dictators, others tended to be closer to true statesmen.

April met with the ones that were willing to meet with her. The others she provided an ultimatum to surrender their prisoners or SDF would go in and take them by force.

Unfortunately, that's precisely what she had to do with two particularly troublesome leaders. The SDF ground troops were not completely successful. Guardians' lives were lost, along with some of the prisoners. It was the first blow to the new Guardian rank, a first cost paid in blood. To April, as much to her forces, it was a difficult cost for success.

News of the raids spread like wildfire. It became clear how far the new police force was ready to go. To some, this incited further anger, but to others it brought pause.

The outer Cauputain belts were the last holdouts of the rebels, according to Richard's intelligence. It was a haven of multiple hideouts, hidden within a maze of churning asteroids. Effectively routing out any specific group of spacers would be next to impossible. With the constant motion of the belt, navigation was especially tricky, and if you were not familiar with the area, returning to a specific location was a near impossibility.

April knew enough to avoid an actual invasion attempt into this last bastion of rebel strength, but she knew she had to try to reach them. The cost of doing nothing inferred they would eventually meet in conflict in the cold of space, and someone would lose.

While still on Cauputain, April reached out through her contacts to arrange a meeting. It took some time to arrange, as the scars left by the ESPD were easily transferred to the Security Divisional Fleet.

* * *

"Commander, this is quite dangerous. One ship can easily be overpowered."

"They see us come in with three cruisers, full armament, they scatter to the void. Then I will be meeting with a handful of miners, not the heart of the movement."

"We can at least escort you to the belt, perhaps stay out of range..."

"Halfway, possibly, no more. Standby just in case you are right. But you must understand, I have to try."

She broke off the three-way conversation with the other two Captains and nodded to her own. "It's time we broke orbit, Captain."

As directed, the other two cruisers decelerated approximately halfway out to the belt. Captain Ironstrike was not taking any chances, maintaining a tight frequency of scans along a 360 degree vector, at the cost of a large amount of power reserve.

April stayed on the upper deck walkway, high enough to be away from the main bridge action, but close enough to hear what was happening. It had the added benefit of spanning just under the large quartz panes, where one could watch the stars glowing in the distance. She glanced down to the Captain now and then, catching a look of worry in his eyes. The tension on the bridge was visible in everyone, save for Richard, who seemed more preoccupied with his palm device than anything else.

"Do you really think you need to be up here with me, Richard?"

"Well I could be down there, but I think, like you, the view is much nicer up here." He smiled calmly. "You are quite composed for one who has decided to step into the lion's den."

"So are you, as I do believe you would be bitten first."

He chuckled. "Your Captain seems a bit taken by you. I see you and him are still trading looks. Perhaps it is time to move to the next step?"

April looked away. "Do you think just maybe you could afford me a semblance of privacy?"

"Of course, Commander. But my intention is not to belittle. I think, perhaps, a friend is something you could use right now."

"And I thought you were my friend?" she returned, snidely.

"On the contrary, Commander, I have the distinct impression you just tolerate me."

"No, Richard. Don't think so poorly of me, please. I know you have a very difficult responsibility. If I lash out, it's more at the situation than at you or your fellow agents."

Richard could feel her gaze, eyes peering into him, reading his response. "Thank you. I do appreciate your honesty. I very much enjoy working for you, Madame Commander."

April laughed. "Madame? It sounds so old, although I do feel old enough sometimes, I guess that fits."

Richard smiled back, but his gaze was averted, and the smile faded quickly.

Alarms rang from below.

April turned, following Richard's attention. Moving in the darkness with no running lights or external ports, a shape was coming in closer, visible only as it blotted out the stars as it moved.

"Commander, it's a J-class, decelerating, looks like it'll loop past us. Armament is deployed."

"Hail them," April ordered.

"They responded with a data stream only - it's coordinates."

The Captain pulled up the holographic navigation display. Their scan data was partial at best, but the images were clear enough. Their destination was an asteroid, a large one. From this distance, it had the scars of mining and a significant amount of man-made modifications along the outside of it.

"I'll assemble our team," offered Richard. "This will be close quarters. They could vent the atmosphere. I suggest you wear an enviro-suit."

"No, they have to see my face."

"OK then. Carry the helmet at least. These suit models have a short-lived energy field – will hold enough air for you to get the helmet on."

"Fine." She submitted, knowing enough that arguing with him on this was not worth the effort.

They moved off the bridge and to the airlock, the small team readying themselves in the suits.

Captain Ironstrike was among them.

"Captain, I do not need you with me."

"Commander, I am not going to bring you into danger without clearing the area myself."

"No, but I will need you on the bridge, ready to respond if needed. My security forces will protect me in there, but I need someone to make the right calls if I'm to get back off this rock in one piece … please."

They locked eyes for a moment. He didn't like it, that much was clear, but what she said made a lot of sense.

"I'll be standing by." He nodded, handing his suit to a crew member. "Just be careful."

April smiled. "This is a truce meeting, not an assassination attempt."

In minutes, the small group was on its way through the airlock and into the maze of mined out corridors of the Asteroid. As they entered, just above, she was able to read the sign: 'Amaria's Sumblifare'.

What a strange name, she pondered…

* * *

They met up with a handful of rough looking miners. A few of them had side arms, a few others rifles, some of the weapons looked like they were built of spare parts.

"Admiral McThurn, I presume," asked a red-headed, gruff, slightly overweight man. He waved his arm and the group split apart.

He was obviously the leader, thought April. "You know why I am here?"

"The others are waiting for ya. Ya wanted an audience, they'll listen to what ya 'ave to say. Don' expect them to agree wit' ya though. They's are hard men – and women."

"That's all I can ask for."

"The others – they stay."

Richard glanced over at her. He did not like that suggestion.

"Ah. No, they come with me. All the way. They are my protection, you realize. Besides, I really don't think they pose much danger here."

The redhead grimaced a smile. "Guess not. Not really a concern as ya said. Just you boys keep them weapons cocked down. Some of my boys don't take threats too kindly out 'ere."

"Follow me. It's a bit of a maze."

And it was. Down through one corridor, a right, a left. April was losing track. She could only hope her escorts could remember – just in case.

They ended in a large anteroom. The walls, although still rock, were polished smooth and covered with ornate carvings. Some of the creatures seemed similar to ancient Greek legends, others were just symbols, possible family crests. The hall was circular, an interior of a sphere. At the top, a bright white light shot through multicolored valences that wavered ever so slightly. Bands of color razed down the walls, over the floor, and back up the other side. Around them, a semicircular row of seats was filled by a group of hard-looking men and women. Their faces seemed dark and angry, eyes appraising and unwavering.

"Tell me the meaning of Amaria's Sumblifare," she inquired.

A sharp-faced man with black cropped hair and a silver-gray streak down its center was the first to speak.

"You have the manner of an entitled one. First time we meet, and you ask us a silly question." He smiled back like a snake, not really smiling.

"No, I just want to understand those who constructed this place. Perhaps it will give me a hint on who they really are, what they value."

"What they value?" asked a portly man with a large black beard. A dark scar traced up his cheek and crossed over a gray-white pupil – what remained of an eye. "Was a little girl, and her father used to play a little game of sumblifare – something like hide and seek you see – only in zero gravity. This is her asteroid. We're just borrowing it for a time."

"It's a nice story."

"I'm not done, not just yet. Ya see the belters never get things too easily. The little dear and her dad died when they hit a gas pocket. 'Twas unfortunate an accident. They say her spirit wanders down here every so often. Often she wails at her loss and it echoes through the corridors. Scares the bejezuz out o' ya. And that's what it is, ya see, a tale of loss. So now you can see into the heart of a belter, just a tiny grain. Loss is a normal way of life here, ya understand."

"I do."

"So let's not get too acquainted 'ere. We don't need to share too much. Just say your piece."

April nodded. Her small escort spread out, most stepping back to the entrance. She officially had the floor.

"The rebellion is over. I ended it for you. No more need for bloodshed. I need you to give me your prisoners."

One of the men burst out into a short laugh. "You figure so do ya?" He kept laughing ever so slightly like there was something incredibly funny left unsaid.

"Aye, favoring to loss or not, they say the belts are the homes for the pirates, not rebels, just pirates."

The man stopped laughing and leered at her, quick to defend his honor. "Now lassie, them's words one would not call hospitable."

"No, hang on there, Sid, she didn't say that's what she thought, did you now, dear?"

April appraised the new speaker. He seemed laid back and an easy talker, but she did not like the way he said 'dear' to her. Like a word dripping in filth and disgust. Something deep down in her was ringing alarm bells.

"Precisely, that is the truth of it. I'm afraid I'm at a disadvantage. You know me, but who are you, Sir?"

"Sir!" he laughed and others followed. "I am, Del Amanto Stride, at your service." He bowed slightly.

She addressed all of them. "No one wins during war. All sides lose. I ask you all to cease hostilities with the corporations, with the Earth travelers."

Del spoke again. "Sure we will, as soon as Earth provides us compensation for our pain and suffering. As Sid had stated, 'tis loss that leaves us wanting. We've all lost someone to this conflict, but maybe not so much, eh dearie?" He passed a gaze across his brethren. "So the ESPD retreats back home and expects us to forgive them. Let's just forget about our families, our sons, and daughters, ya ask?"

April watched the others – too many nodding heads. This Del was clearly one of the main ringleaders. "It's not about forgiveness..." she started, but Del interrupted.

"Try again. 'Cause that's what it's about to us. They demand our forgiveness for our loss. Then they pull out and leave a wee girl to fight their battle. You have a nice innocent face, April McThurn. It's too bad you got taken for a ride."

"Taken? In no way was I mislead."

"Oh, you were complicit then? Well, are the rumors correct? You're Anard-Bueller's poster puppet then? Now it's all makin' sense."

She could feel the tension growing in the room. Richard gave her a warning glance. She knew what he meant. *Time to retreat.*

"I asked for an audience to appeal to your desire to return to a peaceful life, to abandon this never-ending circle of hate. Only you have the power to do this."

Another man chimed in, large and gruff looking, his hair greasy and matted. "Lassie, we truly thought you would have something more for us, something of interest you could relay from those bloodsucking scum. But you clearly don't. Leave us be. We mean no harm to you unless you come looking for trouble."

"Thanks, Berger," added Del. "You know he always leads with quite a statement he does, all those kind words and such. But I'm of the mind you're not so innocent now are you, lassie? You've a full-fledged cruiser parked outside there and two in the wings. Didn't think we know about those two did ya, now?"

April scanned the room, not liking the looks she was getting.

"I came here under a flag of truce."

"Ah yes, the pretense of no harm done. But maybe your Captain and his crony crew are busy scanning us now. Checking for all our little hideouts and weapons caches, looking for a reason to raid us in the near future. Takin' inventory if ya will. Would that be it then?"

"No. My intentions are true."

"Maybe, but maybe not so much. Maybe we should insist on you staying awhile? What d'ya think boys, should she stay?"

April licked her lips. She knew she was in trouble. Her escorts were on edge, ready.

"Well Del, seems you're a real big mouth in this group. Seems the others have no voice but to defer to yours. I have a whole fleet standing by. If I wanted to act against you, I would. I want a peaceful settlement to this conflict."

Del only smiled.

"No Del doesn't speak for us, lassie, but he's not so far off the mark, now is he?" replied Berger. "We'll manage our own affairs, including anything to do with these greedy, immoral corporations. So why don't you head back out, bring these boys of yours with you? They seem to have itchy fingers on those triggers. No need to raise this to the next level. You said your piece. You bent our ear. Now you will leave."

"I will ask you once again before I do leave: Please submit any prisoners you may have, and cease all hostilities against any and all non-extranists."

Del replied. "Don't you worry little missy. We do not keep any prisoners, ever."

April glared back, "You're a sonofabitch, Del Amanto Stride."

Del laughed and Berger waved her away.

Richard was at her side, his hand on her arm. April took the cue, and her small security escort formed a protective perimeter and wasted no further time making their way out of the maze to the dock. Richard wasted not a word, just the odd hand signal, and moved with intensity, making sure to check all angles throughout the journey, but no one intercepted.

They were all relieved to get through the airlock and back on the

Tesla-Continuum.

April wasted no time making way for the bridge.

"Captain Ironstrike, I suggest we return in haste. I do expect we may be intercepted, so battlestations may be wise."

The Captain looked from April to the just arriving Richard, appraising their manner, letting her words sink in for just a moment. "Battle stations!" he barked. "Navigation plot us out of here, straightest line you can find."

April climbed the stairs above the bridge to her favorite vantage point and scanned the dark starry skies for any possible attackers. Richard stood at the base of the steps, monitoring the hustling deck crew, talking quietly into his com. After a few moments, he focused his attention on April.

"You think your eyes are superior to all that technology below, Commander?"

April looked back, her features a bit pale. "I didn't know any of them, leastwise the bastard Del Stride. Get all the intelligence you can on the lot of them,"

"You were right. They didn't scare off like you said. They wanted to measure you up, get a chance to spook you. Did they?"

April nodded. "Evil men. I could read their eyes. Seen their type before."

"Where?" inquired Richard.

"Just have, is all."

"You walked into their lair that time. I don't suggest we do that again. You OK with that?"

She took a moment to reply, considering. *Would she ever do that again? No. Not the wisest thing to do.* "Am fine with that. But I really don't think we're out of their lair just yet."

The ship lurched as it accelerated.

"You see we're in a race right now, Richard. A mad, desperate dash through the darkness. It's the evil that follows us now that I have readied myself to destroy. I know if we don't get to the others in time, I expect we'll be overrun, and it will not be by old mining junkards, but by heavily armored well-equipped cruisers. I expect we'll be outnumbered and outgunned. They are out there right now receiving their orders and depending on where they are, they'll be moving to intercept."

She brushed past him to the stairs. He grabbed her by the arm. "Then I would suggest, Commander, that you retreat to the safety of the backup bridge, as we are about to engage the enemy."

"Not a chance, Richard. I'm staying here."

"Listen, my job is to protect you."

She wrenched off his arm. "These are dangerous times, Richard. I'm not going to hide in a hole fearing for my own life. That's not me, besides I'm not allergic to death." She shrugged. "We all have to die sometime, the lucky ones get to choose how."

Captain David Ironstrike missed very little from the bridge. Especially anything concerning April. He gave her an acknowledging nod as she descended the walkway.

"So far nothing on scans."

"They are coming in hot. Probably from behind, out of range of our normal scanners. Perform a 60 degree adjustment every now and then to close that blind spot. Make it random."

"Will slow us down."

"I know," she replied. "Everything has a cost."

On the third turn, the scans caught something coming in, too far out to discern the details. Fourth turn revealed multiples closing in fast.

"Drop a proximity torpedo out there," she ordered.

"We don't know for sure, Commander," contested the Captain. "Could be friendlies."

"Maybe you don't, but I do."

"If you're wrong, this could result in a substantial loss of life."

"We can't wait. My call. I'll take the risk." Her face was a sullen, grayish color.

She had been here before, ordering death.

"Dispatch a proximity torpedo," the Captain ordered.

"Stop the course adjustments. Maintain heading. Pull them into it."

"We'll be blind."

"We'll pick it up soon enough, the explosion that is."

As if on cue, something flared up behind them, big enough to catch on the rear sensors.

"Contact," reported the monitoring officer. "Dispatch another?"

"Negative," ordered April. "That will only work once."

"When will we be in com range to our other ships?"

"About 45 minutes, give or take."

"Captain, a 180 flip may be wise to better position ourselves."

He agreed and gave the order. As the ship flipped the enemy came into view. Three ships, all sporting more cannon than the Tesla-continuum, each getting ready to fire weapons.

"Not in range for laser cannon. Ready the torpedoes," ordered the Captain, amazingly calm and cool. "Seems they considered you a viable enough threat after all." He glanced over at her with a crooked grin.

"More than luck, I suppose," April smiled back. "I guess I made an impression."

Richard was not amused by the banter. "Captain, just tell me you will get us the hell out of this situation."

Ironstrike gave him a level gaze. "Three of them, but they don't have our superior technology weapons. We've about a 50-50 chance, I suppose."

"Weapons. Target and launch torpedoes on all three. Let's follow that up with cannon fire."

"Aye, Sir."

"And don't miss."

Torpedoes launched with a slight 'bang', followed by a crescendo of sharper thuds as the laser cannon lit up.

"Launch Second Salvo, then repeat until we are out or they are gone."

Daz initiated his count. "Second off... third off... forth off."

Navigation called out. "They're diverting."

"Won't do them any good. Torpedoes will follow them. Keep targeting their offensive cannon."

The scans picked up multiple explosions as some of the torpedoes went off prematurely. The holographic imaging played out the assault on the enemy ships.

One vessel veered sharply from its incoming vector, attempting to pull away from the incoming salvos. For the briefest of moments, it stopped firing, attempting to roll over and reposition itself, but that was a mistake. A torpedo found its hull and detonated, tearing it apart midship. A second collided into its stern, detonating near its engines. The ship disappeared from the holographic image.

The second kept coming in, providing a minimal profile to the torpedoes as they ineffectively shot by.

"Increase the proximity sensitivity, no more flybys."

"Yes sir, but the closer they get..."

"Let's not let them get too close, then, Lieutenant."

The second ship was pounding the torpedo salvos with a barrage from laser cannon. Unfortunately for that ship, it was also in the range of the Tesla-Continuum's main guns, which were raking across her hull, slowly raising the energy levels of the shielding to a critical overcharge. Its guns diverted to the Tesla-Continuum, desperately trying to avoid a shield shutdown.

The Tesla-Continuum rolled slightly as energy blasts pounded into its hull.

"Shielding holding," reported Daz.

"Just lost the communications array," reported Edge.

"Sonofabitch," cursed Ironstrike.

The incessant pounding of the energy plasma was short lived as another torpedo slipped past and into the second ship's hull, brutally tearing a gash from the bow through to its port side. Three more torpedoes tore into it, and then it was gone, adrift in flaming pieces.

A new salvo started up from the remaining enemy ship. The pounding was deafening, and the effect of the Tesla-Continuum was literally jarring.

April fought to remain standing, as the acrid smell of smoke and ozone filled the air.

"Navigation, swing the stern 30 degrees," yelled the Captain. "Weapons, activate the third bank."

The other bank of cannon came online, thudding in a resonating staccato.

They found their target quickly, matching, and outmatching shot for shot. The nose of the enemy ship, minimal target as it was, could not take the punishment. Its shields failed, allowing the pulsing plasma beams to tear into the innards of the vessel. The enemy's cannon ceased, dropping its curtain of defense against the incoming torrent of torpedoes. In a moment, it was gone, but not without launching its last desperate salvo of torpedoes.

Each was being tracked by the Tesla-Continuum's scanners. Onboard computers ignored the high probability hits by the defensive cannon, leaving two red dots on the image, beeping intermittently, and more frequently as they approached.

"Navigation, auto evasive please," ordered Ironstrike, evenly and coolly. Surrendering the ship's navigation controls to the computer guaranteed the fastest response to the inbound weapons, including launching deterrents to lure the torpedoes. It was a matter of seconds now.

The first torpedo passed by and exploded close enough to pound the outer hull with a tremendous crash, but the second was 30 seconds out and lined up for a direct hit.

The primary canon array was busy blasting away, chewing through the remaining incoming, and as predicted, the troublesome ship killer kept encroaching.

"Standby," stated Ironstrike, ever so calmly.

The ship lurched sideways, nearly knocking them all off their feet. And the torpedo was upon them, scraping along the hull as it passed. But it didn't explode.

In as many seconds, they were safe.

"Cease auto-control. Weapons, destroy that torpedo before it comes around again."

The scans revealed a silent perimeter.

"Execute a 180 degree flip," stated the Captain, not wasting a second. The ship maneuvered seamlessly, transparent to its passengers.

"Helm, accelerate."

"Accelerating, Captain."

The gravity plates fought to compensate, but this time the passengers could feel the press of the acceleration. "We are resuming our course," noted the Captain with a smile.

And at that moment, the ship died.

They hadn't seen the other enemy ship, just out of range, nor the salvo of torpedoes climbing up quickly behind the main burners as the ship accelerated away. The first of the torpedoes collided with the main burner casings, exploding with enough force to throw the ship forward, but inflicting minimal damage, the second wave hit with enough force to tear into the stern of the ship, disabling the main burners, and exposing the engineering section to vacuum, instantly killing the handful of crew stationed there. The torpedo blast continued up through to the top of the ship, thrashing into the stern shuttle bay, and wrenching the two reserve shuttles into twisted wrecks as it ripped off the top of the bay, throwing the ruins into the void.

Power instantly failed throughout the ship, leaving only emergency reserves, just enough to initiate automatic hatch closures. As the grav plates lost power, they did so with a sudden sickening shift. In time, the plates would lose all residual charge and everyone would become weightless, but for the time being they retained their effect.

The bridge remained lit from the backup circuits only, as all primary lighting systems failed.

April scanned the deck via the glow of the navigation holographic, one of the few systems that were given priority other than life support systems.

White and gray faces peering into the darkness. Eyes were all centered on the nav display, watching the enemy cruiser encroaching on their position. Alarms were sounding throughout, and the deck officers were desperately working to assess the damage.

"Engineering is down, Captain. We can't reach anyone."

"We have atmosphere venting on stern sectors one through six. Emergency portal closures throughout all corridors."

"Weapons?"

"Cannon offline, but torpedoes can launch under reserve power."

The Captain activated the intercom. "To all crew members, we are under attack, arm yourselves and prepare to be boarded." He looked to April. "Expect this is where it's going to get interesting."

"Enemy closing in... 10,000 km."

"He had to be hiding out of range. Weapons, standby to launch – three torpedoes per salvo."

"Enemy is veering away 200 degree vector, Sir."

"What? Hold deploying. What are they doing? Is somebody else coming to help?"

"Nothing on the scans, but we are on low power."

"Enemy continuing on vector, vessel is accelerating, moving out of firing solution range."

The Captain passed his bewildered gaze to his officers, then to April.

She only shrugged. "Believe there is some old saying about a gift horse, although I've never seen such as creature."

"We'll take it," agreed Ironstrike. "Cancel battlestations," he stated to Officer Edge. "Let's see how bad things really are."

It took hours. Maintenance ROVs were dispatched to survey the rear burner area. They were able to enter into the ship's interior via a gaping hole through the primary burner plates and fly directly into main engineering. The devastation was disheartening.

"Gluon disrupters are simply gone. We have no superluminal ability."

"Move in close to the reactor," directed April. She scanned the instruments. "Power output nominal. Emergency shutdown due to compromised secondary cooling circuit. The reactor remains viable if we can repair the leak."

"That's a big if," commented the Captain. "Even if we could, the main burners are offline, we can't even crawl home, nevermind jump to superluminal."

"We'll need to get to the shuttle bay from outside and secure a shuttle."

April had a bad feeling. "Rotate the ROV, head north, follow the blast damage."

The small robot moved through the darkness, weaving its way through a maze of twisted conduit and metal until it emerged into space.

"Whoa. Where's the shuttle bay?"

They panned the cameras and rotated the ROV for a full 360 degree picture.

"Captain, there are no shuttles in what's left of the shuttle bay."

"Well that settles it," conceded Ironstrike. "We have no superluminal drive, no plasma burners, and no short-range shuttles. Our communications array has been blown to pieces, so we have no ability for long-range communications. We have no power, but we may be able to restart the main reactor, but that's a big 'if'. Am I missing something?"

"Yes. The escape pods – but they have limited range. They are the last resort," commented navigation officer Black.

"I don't see a way out of this," the Captain stated.

"Don't count our ship out just yet," April stated, trying to project the positive.

"Battery banks are intact, critical life support systems are still working. Grav plates will hold their charge for at least 30 hours. We have air, water, food. Our ship is still structurally sound, and the port burner assembly is still intact."

"So," said Black, not so easily convinced.

"We can rebuild the feed systems to restrict the plasma flow to the intact burners."

"And how do you suggest we do that, Commander?" said Ironstrike, with a half-smile. "I know of your past, heard of the things you've done, but this is way beyond a Porter transport. Space is much more brutal than Ishaida's deserts."

"Alright, so we sit and wait? How long do you think we have, really?" shot back April. "20 maybe 25 hours on the battery reserves, no more. Then what?"

"Our escorts will come looking for us."

"Navigation, given our last point of reference, where are we, and where are we headed?"

He took a second to calculate, then brought it up the holographic. "This is us, drifting at a 59 degree vector from our desired course, approximately 40,000 km/s. In 20 hours we'll be here, a red dot showed on the display, in 40 hours here, a blue dot. We are drifting out into the abyss, away from anything of note, away from Cauputain and any standard shipping routes."

"Can the others find us?" asked another of the deck officers.

"It's possible, but not probable, and less probable the further out we go. You must take into account the distances involved here."

April passed her hand through the holograph, watched as it wavered ever so slightly from the movement. "We don't wait. Our attacker is also out there. I'd bet he's already plotted our trajectory and will be back to finish the job. The only option is to fight." She turned around, to face the crew. "And I don't mean against that enemy ship. We fight against time, against the impossible. We re-seal the hull back up. We restart the reactor, we re-plumb the plasma feeds, and we wake this cruiser back up."

Captain Ironstrike stepped forward. "Commander, it sounds plausible, but there are so many failure points."

April turned back to the nav console, entered a few keystrokes on the pad, and brought up a detailed schematic of the ship.

"Computer, show all compromised decks in red and all suspected compromised in yellow."

The image refreshed instantly, revealing the critical cut through the heart of the ship. The damage at the stern showed very clearly now, like that of a sword wound sliced from the stern and up through the shuttle bay.

"We establish priorities. First thing we restart is the reactor, regain power before our life support systems begin failing. We go out the airlock here, into engineering through this rupture here, reach the reactor console and run the diagnostics locally to find the leak. Once we find it, the portable welder kits should have enough charge in them to repair the problem or problems. Then we cycle up the reactor to full power. We may need to reroute some primary power circuits, but we should be able to get the main systems back up."

"Next step, seal the minor compromises to the hull, then recharge any lost atmosphere. We have enough ballast tank water to restart hydrolysis and rebuild oxygen levels. We'll restart the ships air filtering management systems and temperature conditioning so we don't freeze to death."

"Then we set up alternating shifts to begin rebuilding the stern hull at engineering, and the upper bay damage."

"Once that's done, we re-pressurize engineering, re-plumb any damaged life support systems, then work on the rear burner plasma routing."

"Once we've completed that, we fire it up and start heading back home. We won't have superluminal, but we should be able to get close enough in a few months to contact our fleet. I suspect by that time, we'll have the communications array working in some form or another."

"Months?" questioned Ironstrike.

"Well, if I may, Sir – Umm Commander," offered Nav Officer Black. "We could consider another way, and avoid costly deceleration."

"Please, go ahead."

The young man moved a bit uncomfortably to the nav console and brought up a schematic of their current position and all the major celestial bodies. "We could shave some time off. But this may seem a little crazy."

"Just let it out, Officer," ordered Ironstrike.

"Instead of decelerating, why not accelerate to the closest sun – here. System Oneon-756. M-Class, your typical red dwarf. We'll spin around it, then re-vector ourselves back to Cauputain. This way we don't go back through the belt, as I suspect they'll be waiting for us there, and we have the added benefit of extending our hydrogen scoops while we're around the sun and recharge our depleted systems."

He stood back with a grin. "We can build up speed all the way."

April stepped back, thoroughly impressed.

"Well Jeremy, I like it."

"Alright. I'll be heading down toward the stern, looks like this midship airlock is the most viable way out," stated Captain Ironstrike.

"Ah, no Captain. This is my plan. I'll be doing it."

"No, Commander, you are needed..."

"In Engineering. You don't understand systems like I do. I can get that reactor up on my own."

"Listen, Commander, you are not going out there," Captain Ironstrike ordered. "It's damn dangerous. You could tear your suit and depressurize in an instant."

"I am going out there. You have anyone else that understands reactor systems?" asked April openly challenging him.

"No," admitted the Captain. "Our specialists were in Engineering at the time we were hit. We lost Officer Cross."

"Right," proclaimed April. "So I go."

"Fine. I'll be going with you then," commented Ironstrike. "It'll be spooky in there. There'll be bodies of our crew. It won't be easy. You cannot vomit in your suit."

"I won't."

Captain Ironstrike moved closer, concern on his face. "This can get graphic. You can't unsee some things."

"I'll be fine."

Richard interceded. "I'll go in with you, too."

April shook her head. "No, this is not your element, Richard. You can take a raincheck.

"Again Commander, your safety is my responsibility."

"Too late to be safe now. If I don't pull this off, we're all dead."

Her words hit the room hard. She could see the fear in their eyes.

"I've wriggled myself out of much worse predicaments than this." She glanced over to the Captain. "OK, Captain Ironstrike, get your space legs on. Time to hop to it."

With this, the long task of reawakening the Tesla-Continuum from the dead began.

* * *

Chapter 24

A pril and Ironstrike were outside, on the hull. It wasn't the first time April had done a spacewalk, as she had a chance when she was younger with Oranis, during a short visit off-world to some relatives in the outer belt of Ishaida's system. She was nervous then, and this time was no different. The vacuum of space can be unforgiving.

At least David was here with her.

"Breathe deep and slow," he said. "We're coming up to the 90 degree turn, at the rear burner. We need to be very careful. Watch for sharp metal that can puncture your suit."

"Bring it," April said posing confidence, though falsely.

"Kneel, grab the edge, and use your other leg to magnetically seal against the other wall. Test it, make sure you're locked or you'll be pushing off into space."

She wriggled her foot. "Definitely locked in."

"Pick up with your leg slowly, drag your foot and slide it onto the wall and lock it in place."

"What happens if I go too fast?"

"Don't worry, I got you." He was close, ready to spot and grab her by the leg.

April followed the instruction precisely and slid her other foot over quickly to lock it in place.

"Good job. Now I'm coming over. Standby to grab me if I mess up."

In seconds, they were situated to look over the rear burner plating, scorched and blackened by plasma and looking like a vast sea of crevices and outcrops of snaking metal.

"Looks like a bomb went off here."

"Precisely."

"Let's find a spot that looks somewhat safe to enter."

It took some time to find, and as they searched, they could not help being anxious, as the metal shards reached out to them like beckoning claws from all angles.

"Alright, here's our spot. Lock in your cable on your suit. I'll pull you in once I'm secured."

April nodded, watching him disappear into the darkness, illuminated by only his helmet light.

She took a moment to view the starry skies. Above her a vast nebula shone down onto her, reds and oranges, blues and greens obscured the white light of the background stars, all dancing in utter silence, thousands to millions of light-years away.

"OK, step off the edge slowly, I'll feed you in, stay clear of any sharp edges."

April refocused back to her reality.

Careful, one mistake and you're dead. Stop thinking like that. Focus. Think it and it happens. Do you want to die, is that it?

She shook her head. "Stop!" she said out loud.

"What? You OK?"

"Yes. Keep reeling me in."

The engineering deck came into view, demolished, walls covered with a blanket of twisted metal, conduit, and decking, braided like a carpet.

"Looks like the force of the blast shot back out here, luckily."

April scanned the area in the murky darkness, the reactor was in the far corner, further away from the carnage.

"I see it."

"Hold. We have a crew member. Let him pass."

April tried to avoid looking directly at the body but could not help but see the twisted look of horror on his face.

"It's Lieutenant Joseph, I sent him down to Engineering during the battle."

"Not your fault, Captain," April stated, attempting some consolation.

"Yeah."

"Doesn't look like we have any visible problems with the reactor. Activating the console."

A few deft touches through her clumsy suit and she had the menu up.

"Running diagnostics."

"David – I mean Captain, can you get that portable plasma cutter over there," she asked, simultaneously shining the light on the equipment.

"No problem, April – I mean Commander," he jested back.

"That's OK by me. Considering we could die out here, feel free to address me by my name."

"Go it," he announced. "Now what?"

"Thought so. Diagnostic indicates cooling circuit open behind this bulkhead. Need you to cut a circle about here."

"No problem." He didn't take long, but it seemed to take forever. April could not help but think of what was beyond the flickering light emanating from the cutter. *All the carnage and death.* She shuddered.

"Done." He bent the plate back and exposed the black pipe.

April peered in. "Gotcha. This is good."

"Oh? Why?" asked David.

"We need to find a portable welder. We can fix this."

"Stores should be over here." He disappeared for a second. She went to follow. "No stay there, you don't need to see this."

April caught herself.

No, she did not want to see what was in that room.

"Here it is." He pulled it out. She noticed a dark stain covering it. It seemed almost black, though frosted with a thousand crystals.

Blood.

David looked a little pale, slightly shaken.

"You OK?"

"No," was all he said.

April felt compelled to reach over and hug him, but it was awkward in their bulky suits.

"April."

"Yes."

"I think I'll take you up on this hug once we get back. If that's alright."

"Yes, sure. I'm sorry," she backed away.

"No don't be sorry, I mean... Can you switch to local radio for a second?"

She did.

"You receiving?"

She nodded.

"Well, it's not befitting for an officer of yours to..."

"To what?" She asked, feeling her heart pounding in her chest.

"Forgive me, but I've been attracted to you for a long time. This is not exactly the place I planned to tell you. I understand if..."

April cut him off. "It's OK, really. I am truly flattered, but I don't know what to do with this."

"You don't have to say anything. If we get through this, I can certainly apply for another assignment."

"No."

"No?"

"No, and hand me the welder."

He gave her the unit, keeping his eyes averted from looking directly at her.

"When we get back, we can talk. You misread my reaction, I just didn't expect it. But I think I like it."

"You do?"

"Just no puppy dog eyes, alright. Not befitting a Captain."

He smiled and she smiled back.

"Switching back to standard channels," she announced. "Let's fix this."

Once April had the cooling grid repaired, she reran the diagnostics.

"Pass. Don't worry, this thing is designed to run in absolute zero. We fire this up, I expect we'll see a cascade of initial circuit failures, but the system will rebalance instantly. You ready?"

"If it doesn't start?"

"We're screwed. So it'll start." She triggered the sequence. Lights came on. The primary console display lit up showing the full schematic of the ship, and multiple red zones, with associated alarms, sounding off silently.

She canceled the alarms, closed off the damaged channels and ran through the configuration setup, patching full control back to the bridge.

"We're up. Bridge has control."

The trip back seemed much quicker, and the crew gave a cheer as they exited the lock.

April shot a look over to David, who returned a subtle smile.

"Phase I complete," she announced.

"Now we have power. We seal up the hull and re-plumb the stern burner assembly, and I initially forgot to mention, reprogram the ship's inertial systems to compensate for the changes."

"And bury our dead," interjected the Captain.

"Right," she said, realizing her excitement had gotten the best of her.

"How long?" asked Ridgeline. "How long will this take us?"

"Judging by the damage I've seen, at the earliest - two weeks, maybe three, if we work in shifts, to do the basic patching, and maybe get this ship moving again," April replied. "Once we get the burners fired up, we'll run at minimal speed until we're confident we have full containment."

"Then it may take us two to three months to reach Oneon-756," added Black.

"Worst part is we'll need to ration the water until we get there," replied the Captain.

"We can do this," urged April. "We may stink for a while though."

The crew laughed.

* * *

"It's been six months. We've expanded our search grid multiple times, we can't find her."

Verage nodded in agreement but was not convinced. "She's out there. We're just not looking in the right spot. Damn it, Kennaith, you know we haven't even made a dent in this hole of black space she could be in."

Captain Alder looked away in frustration. "I know we could spend the rest of our days searching and still not find her."

"So we keep looking - yes?" coaxed Verage.

"I just wish we hadn't broke formation. We killed her when we made that decision."

Captain Verage Isaac sat back in his chair, taking another swig of his whisky. "Yeah, maybe 'tis true. But we did what she'd 'ave us do. That liner was in peril. The passengers would have been dead today if we hadn't acted."

"Regardless, we moved out of range. She might've tried to reach us and we weren't there."

"Again a maybe, or maybe not."

"I say we move on the belt, regardless. We have the numbers."

"Agreed, her disappearance has done more to solidify the extranists than anything else. You can see solidarity in their eyes, more so than ever 'afore. But I'm afraid we'd 'ave some trouble controlling them, as in which way they go. An' we cannot allow things to get out of control."

"Would not be the worst thing to spill some of these troublemakers blood. Maybe a few of those dredges would no longer be able to endanger honest merchants."

"Regardless," resigned Verage. "We've been recalled to Ishaida by the government council."

Captain Kennaith Alder stood up, pulled a coin from his pocket. "Someone stays here and continues to coordinate the search."

"Fine, flip."

* * *

Del Stride stood at the edge of the bridge, peering out into the darkness, waiting for the enhanced magnification to come up.

"They're intercepting, Sir."

"What the hell's wrong with this thing? Get this sonofabitch up, will you?"

He glared at the technician who scrambled from one console to the next. A satisfied look finally came upon his face. "Go it, Captain."

"About damn time," Del grumbled, stepping back to assess the situation.

Three ships are closing in on the Tesla-Continuum. This should be a good show.

He watched and grew angrier by the minute. When the third ship disappeared in a fiery burst, Del marched up the steps and pulled up the navigation display.

"We're almost in range. Standby to deploy torpedoes."

"Standing by."

"We're in range, shall we fire?" asked his weapons officer.

"No. Hold. Wait until they resume course."

"Captain," interrupted the com officer.

"What now?"

"Anvil fleet has a bogey. They want to engage."

"What is it?"

"Liner enroute from Jefferson into Cauputain. Company insignia."

"Ah, a rich bogey, at that."

"They've flipped, Captain."

"Hit'em," he ordered, nonchalantly.

Torpedoes launched, sounding throughout the ship with a momentary rumble.

He watched the display, the distance meter clicked away along the bottom.

The first torpedo hit and exploded. The second one fell in behind and hit again.

"That one counted," Del announced a smile from ear-to-ear.

"She's dead, boys. Move in."

"Cap, she's still got batteries. Torpedoes could still be active."

Del considered it. It was true, the tech on these ships was definitely more advanced than most. But he had a fat target waiting to be plucked. They weren't going anywhere now.

"Change our vector, we're joining Anvil. Need to ensure my cut is accounted for."

"Aye, Captain." The helm officer turned the ship and accelerated to maximum.

"What about the bitch, Cap?" asked the weapons officer.

"You got their vectors? Know where they're drifting?"

"Yeah, straight out into the cold."

"Good. Plot it. We'll come back for them."

"Aye."

* * *

"Thank you for coming, Captain Isaac."

Verage took the open seat in the center of the room. The members of the Ishaidan government were seated around him in a semicircular fashion in multiple bands that rose up at a gradual slope. There was also an upper balcony, which seemed to be packed with others, standing room only. It would be intimidating for some, but Verage shrugged it off.

"I lost the toss," he explained.

Elias who sat at the apex said, "Excuse me?"

Verage chuckled. "Nevermind. Why don't you get to the point of it? I traveled far too many light-years to get here, and I am very busy, as you know."

"Very well," Elias responded, clearing his throat. "Captain Verage Isaac, can you confirm you are the acting admiral of the Anard-Bueller Security Divisional Fleet, at the moment?"

"Aye, I am, stressin' the term actin' that is."

"We've asked you here to report on the disappearance of the Tesla-Continuum."

"Aye, I expected. Understand now, we've been searching nonstop for her since we suspected her as lost. It's been a painstaking slow effort to scan through that many cubic AU's of space. It's taken a toll on my crews," Verage complained. "And we've not found anything to indicate where she may have gone."

"But you did find wreckage?"

"Aye, we found a site. Definite evidence of a fight. Found the remains of three wrecks and pieces of what we suspect were from the Tesla-Continuum. We've found some bodies as well, including three of her crew, we've even located what we believe is a section of her communications array – a very important piece – which explains why we have not been able to make contact with her. Unfortunately, we also found what remains of her shuttles. But in the end, what we did not find what was most important – we did not find the wreckage to signify, even remotely, that she was destroyed. No indeed, we know she not lay adrift in that graveyard of blackness. She took a hard hit, but she remains alive."

"Then where is she?" asked another.

"Hold it, now." Elias raised his hands. "I am facilitating the questioning."

"Verage, can you walk us through the first 48 hours prior to the moment you suspected the ship was lost."

The old ship Captain took a deep breath and began his story. It took some time and a host of probing questions to get through to the current status of their search effort. But the message was becoming very clear to all. The Tesla-Continuum was lost, along with their beloved April McThurn.

At the end of it all, the truly difficult questions came out.

"When, Admiral, would you say the search effort should be suspended?" was the last and very painful question for Elias to deliver.

"'Twas up to me, I'd not stop until I found her, or until I died of old age, but we all know it's not just up to me. Let's say I'd recommend at least another three months searchin', maybe six."

That started a round of murmurs and talking throughout the room.

"There are some that voiced concerns that the pirate fleet have you outgunned and outmaneuvered at every engagement. They say it is only a matter of time until the SDF fails to meet the obligations of their contract, and this will result in a forfeit and the return of the ESPD into extranist space."

Verage glared back at Elias. "Dare you say! I've seen the rats scuttle more'n once on a dying vessel, but this is truly putrifyin'. We have brave men and women on these patrols, puttin' their lives on the line every hour to keep these shippin' lines open."

Elias held up his hands. "Excuse me, Admiral. No disrespect. You must understand the fear out there. People are looking to you to regain confidence, with Admiral McThurn lost, the fears are real."

"Aye, fear is real alright. If anything survives the blackness of space, 'tis fear alone. I tell you all, I continue the search not because I think she is dead, 'tis because I know she is alive!"

"That is fine for you, Admiral Isaac, but we cannot continue to function on faith alone. There will need to be a time that we will need to make the hard decision, to face a possible eventuality she may be lost." A slightly portly, but very well dressed, gentleman stepped ahead from the crowd. His demeanor and accent gave him away to be a fresh one off Earth.

"And who might you be, Earthman?"

"Gerald Lewis, of Osbort, Gilliam, and Lewis, attorney on retainer for Anard-Bueller, and this man," he turned to introduce a slight and timid gentleman, "would be Mr. Robson, former CFO and acting CEO of Anard-Bueller."

The crowd murmured in background discussion. Elias signaled for quiet.

"I see, and I imagine Anard-Bueller has been through some difficulty since word has got out," Verage nodded understanding. "And you are here to get the truth of it?"

"Yes, Admiral. The truth will do."

"Then let me repeat. The Tesla-Continuum took a hard hit, but she is indeed out there. Her crew, including your CEO and our Admiral, is very much alive. We've not been able to locate her because she is adrift. Knowing April and her abilities, I'm more than confident they've managed to keep the ship alive enough to sustain them all. We just need to do our job, and find her."

"Very well, I pray you are correct," added Lewis. "And if not, how long is 'long enough' before you call off a search?"

Verage shook his head. "The crew can sustain on a crippled cruiser for years, 'tis true. But I will state, as I do understand the need for closure, if you must declare her lost, it must not be before one year from now. As acting Admiral, that is my declaration, so be it."

Mr. Lewis nodded. "Thank you. And I assume you would accept more help if we could offer?"

"I would take it readily. I must keep the wolves at bay as I search the abyss. "

"Then I can provide you ships, just let me know what else you may require, Admiral."

Verage inspected the men carefully, grateful they were there. "Aye, I'll take your offer then, Anard-Bueller. Anyone else?"

Another stepped up – a Porter of recognition, one of the Porter elders. "Aye. April McThurn our beloved lassie stood in front of us, nary a few months ago, and asked the lot of us to become more involved. Instead, we told her no. No, we were not ready for space, no, we would not abandon our families, no, we were needed at home. And now she is out there, in the cold of space. Lest we forget she was fighting for us, to make the extranist systems peaceful again, a place to raise our next generations."

Men nodded in agreement.

"I see what difference this wee lassie has made. And yet we all refused her. It is clear what we need to do now. If she truly is lost, we need to step up and fill her shoes. And it will take more than one man here to do that."

"Aye," raised the crowd, in a torrent of proclamations following raps and claps.

"It is time we were involved. We shall pull together every vessel we can find, space worthy or barely. Our April has shamed us, and rightly so. No one else carries that burden. No one else carries that right!"

The noise in the hall was deafening. Elias put down his hands in surrender, listening to them raise the chant as it was a holy cause. "McThurn! McThurn! McThurn!"

Verage stood up, charged to his very soul by their passion. He put his hand on his heart and waited for the old Porter to pull the crowd quiet again - which he did with a clench of his fist.

"You there, Anard-Bueller man, tell me how many ships you can add?" he demanded.

"Eight ships, I'll have them here within a few days – they are already inbound. Many have smaller shuttles that can also be used in the search."

"Then the Porters will join you in your search, and we will work shifts until we find her."

A cheer rose through the crowd.

Verage smiled. He was looking for some help. He did not expect this much.

* * *

"Bring her about," ordered Ironstrike, unable to hide the intensity of his order.

"Firing primary burner," announced Cross. "She's responding, Sir!"

April stood on deck, her hair matted and uniform filthy. Her tears cut through the grime on her face. She watched as the others laughed and cheered, danced and hugged one another.

David moved to her, a grin so wide it made her laugh. But there was something more in his eyes. She looked away, avoiding getting lost in her emotion.

He pulled her close and held tight.

The others only laughed, watching them knowingly.

"I'm a little ripe," she stated, pushing him away. "And so are you!"

They both laughed.

"Well, you said this could be done. You were right, of course."

"Navigation, plot the course to Oneon-756. Helm, set her true."

"Aye, Sir," they said in unison.

"Let's get her up to speed. Helm, maximum acceleration. We've a sun to pivot around!"

"How long?" asked April.

"Approximately three months. We will see once we crank this baby up. Lots of variables. Once we reach Oneon-756, we pivot around the sun, coming in low to harvest the hydrogen. Then we break orbit and head home, accelerating most of the way back," informed Black. "Just like this."

He pulled up the graphic on the navigation console. Their ship came up, with a dotted trajectory showing it loop around the sun, then shoot out back to Cauputain. "Estimate another five to six months if my assumptions are correct on achieving subluminal, and then we'll be in earshot of Cauputain."

"We'll have communications only if our resident genius can get a replacement array working," commented David. He gave April a playful push.

"With Officer Cameron's help, I'm sure we'll get something figured out. It won't be pretty though. And it won't have any range."

"Worst case if we can't arrange a tow to decelerate, then we'll need to start decelerating here," commented Black, pointing to a small yellow x on the trajectory line, "and then we pull into Cauputain's orbit. That'll take a little longer, of course."

"First things first," announced April. "We need to deploy the hydrogen collectors and get ready for our pass to the sun. Officer Cameron, do we have the converters ready to mix the carbon dioxide with the hydrogen to refill our water tanks? I'm not spending another month without taking a shower."

They all laughed. Nobody wanted that.

* * *

"Where the hell did she go?"

Del Amanto Stride marched back and forth on the deck. "You sure you have that vector right?"

"What do ya think Captain, I pulled these coordinates outta my ass?" shot back the nav officer.

Del just glared back. Few if any, could get away with talking to him like that. But the nav officer was different. The computers and star charts were only so good out here. Without him, they would be lost. Literally. And you did not want to get lost out here.

"So they managed to alter course somehow."

He pulled up the star charts, zoomed into to their current location. "OK, we plot a cone here, vectoring back to Cauputain. That's where we search. If they did get their burners firing by some miracle, they'll be running subliminal. We'll catch them."

They began their scans.

Del watched impatiently and time slipped away. Days turned to weeks. As the time passed, they started to encounter ships on the long-range. Others were looking for them. He kept his power signature reflecting back at a minimal impression. This cloaking tech had cost him dearly. More than a few jobs completed for the 'Guild of the Tenth Level' to pay for it. He was relying on it now.

Nothing. Scan after scan and nothing.

"Where could they have gone?"

He went back to the nav display and brought up the last known coordinates of the Tesla-Continuum and the vector they were on. He overlaid the star chart and zoomed the image back.

The solution revealed itself, sitting just far enough out to make things interesting.

Del laughed. They'd refuel there then slingshot back, of course.

"What's so damn funny, Cap?" asked his nav officer.

"We're looking in the wrong spot."

"We should be looking over here." He pointed to the tiny sun.

"You think they're mobile enough to vector in and sling back via that sun? That's a stretch."

"Well tell me smartass, why haven't we found'er as yet then? It's 'cause she ain't here!"

He slapped the controls, and the console went dark.

"Forget it. Getting too hot around here, with all this searchin' traffic. Time to head back home. If she manages to swing back to Cauputain, good chance it's a casket full of dead by now."

"Head home then?"

Del thought about a nice turkey meal, and that last little slaver girl he procured to work in the kitchen.

"Yeah. I'm hungry. And I'm tired of Jobe's crappy cooking."

All he had to think about was the cook's slop gumbo dish, and it was enough to make him gag.

He has to find a better cook.

He glanced at his chronometer. He ran out of time. His new ships would be arriving shortly.

Now that the bitch was out of the way, he had a war to fight.

* * *

"Damn, it's hot."

"We hobbled the environmental support as best we could, Captain," reported April. She could feel the sweat trickling down the back of her neck. Her uniform was drenched. It would be worth it. All they had to do was pull in enough hydrogen and they'd be set up with as much water as they needed.

"As long as we don't hit one of those CME's directly we're set." She noted the towering semicircle of raw plasma they were flying through. If it collapsed at that moment, it would kill them all. But she knew it wasn't likely. A new ejection was another story.

April checked the meters. "About half. We're going a bit too fast for optimum collection."

"Yeah, but we're also coming in a lot lower than normal to compensate," offered David.

She checked them again. The collector bands were hot, but still well within operating range.

"Just keep it coming," she ordered.

More sweat in her eyes. She wiped it with her sleeve and fought the urge to rip off her uniform. Would be so nice to be cool. She was sure David wouldn't mind.

"I'm going to the mess. The enviro-coolers are working the best there," she announced, no longer caring to monitor the collectors. She had to cool off.

"Good idea. Let's set up a rotating shift from the bridge. We've an hour of this left before we start pulling away."

April found the cool air vent just outside the mess – and stood in its outflow for at least 10 minutes, basking in its coolness. The funny thing was the AC was barely working, but it was an improvement of the stifling heat of the bridge.

A familiar voice sounded from behind her. It was Ensign Macovy. "Sir, Captain's looking for you."

April opened her eyes. The image of her lying on the cool beach of Lake Neprid was no longer.

"It's only been a couple minutes," she complained.

"He asks that you bring up some water before they all pass out. I think he was kidding though."

An hour passed already? Have the collectors maxed out? She grabbed some bottles of water from the mess and made her way up in a hurry.

Once on the bridge, she did a quick situational scan. Most of the crew were at their stations, weary from the heat and utterly drained. No one saluted, which was fine. The crew had grown accustomed to the slight lax of etiquette with her, especially since she had been working side by side on the ship's repairs for the last few months.

"I have some water for everyone." She dropped the bottles on the navigation table and handed one to the Captain.

"Thanks."

He wiped his forehead. "We're about to break orbit."

"Course plotted and transferred," announced Black.

"Course accepted, Navigation. Initiating plasma burn and accelerating," announced Cross.

Black was watching his scanners intently. "Breaking orbit."

"We're on trajectory. Burners pushing out nine G's. Anti-grav plates are compensating. Accelerating smoothly," reported the helm officer.

"I for one, will welcome getting out of this heat," stated the Captain in relief.

"We are out of the gravity well," stated Black, indicating the Tesla-Continuum was now far enough away and moving at a sufficient momentum to not be pulled back into the star.

"We're on our way home," April said, a little more to herself than to the others.

"Thank the stars," replied the Captain.

Satisfied that things were going to plan, April retired to the science station and pulled up the metrics on the H2O converters. "Our hydrogen tanks are fully charged," she announced.

"Captain, recommend we see if the rest of our repair work holds together."

He smiled at her. "You outrank me, Commander, plus... you are the one that fixed it."

She smiled, "Too bad Cameron's on sleep rotation. I'm sure she'd like to see this."

"Initiating H2o conversion," she announced, then activated the converters.

She checked the flow sensors. "Yes. Water tanks are filling and venting the excess heat to the plasma stream. Conversion steady at 800 liters per minute."

"This is good. We have water!"

Applause followed. It was a strange reaction for anyone else but them, who had spent the last few months under strict water conservation.

"Captain," stated April, "I am retiring to my quarters, you have the bridge."

He smiled and saluted. "Enjoy the shower, Commander."

She did. The feeling of warm water washing the dirt and grime off her body and out of her hair was heavenly. The acrid smells of welding permeated her nostrils, and she doused her hair with shampoo twice to drive the stench from it.

She was appreciating a cool, tall drink in her robe and scanning the ship's monitoring systems when someone knocked on her cabin door. The panel display revealed her caller. She opened the door, still running her comb through her hair, attempting to pull the last of the knots out.

"Hello, Captain. I am sorry, but I am not yet presentable."

"I think I'll stay out here for now," he stated. "I've not yet managed to get cleaned up, myself."

"Nonsense." She grabbed his hand and pulled him inside, being careful not to get too close.

He watched her, eyes wide, slightly uncomfortable, yet fully mesmerized by her enticing smell and alluring dress, or in this case, lack of.

"Something on your mind, Captain David Ironstrike?"

"I just wanted to check in on you, before I retired."

"Oh?" She tossed her hair to one side, running the comb through it again. "Or did you want to finish your conversation you started?"

She moved closer, teasingly close. Knowing she was driving him just a bit to the edge, barely in her robe, just out of the shower. Just the same, he seemed to be holding himself together well.

He shifted on his feet. "If you are referring..."

"Yes, I am. I am referring." She turned away, walked to the hull window. "You look out there and it does not take long to realize just how small we are, does it?"

"Commander? You mean April, don't you? I mean, you are in my quarters for heaven's sake."

He smiled. "Yes, April."

"Very good, David."

She turned about, met his eyes. "I've read your file. I had my security team investigate every last detail about you. I think I know you better than I know myself." She followed with a slight laugh.

"And what did you find?"

"You are the second born, of Jonias and Emily Ironstrike, of the Clan Ironstrike. Your family ran the Northern routes, through the mountains, undeniably the most dangerous roads on Ishaida. On your 15th birthday, you inherited command of the BearClaw because your father was killed in an avalanche. You served as Porter Captain until you reached 20 when you decided to step away from Porter life and supervise a Northern road crew, where you specialized in drilling through the mountains - hard, dangerous work. What made you do that, David? Why were you so intent on cutting through those mountains? Was that because of your father?"

"I needed to do something..."

"To make a difference, I imagine? At the age of 26, you stood there in that hall, carrying the scars of too many close calls, and you listened to my pathetic speech. You heard my call for help, and instead of going back to what you knew, you decided to leave everything behind, to put yourself in danger and become a spacer. Why? Did you think you could make a difference again?"

"No."

"No?"

"No, I left everything because *you* asked me to."

She smiled softly. "You are just enthralled with the idea of who I am, this mass-marketing image, half the stories you hear about me are exaggerations."

"You mean like the time when you saved those people in Monsoona?"

"Well I don't know exactly what you heard, but what I did exactly was..."

"Jump a raging river with a Porter tank?"

"Yes," she admitted with a small laugh. "That was fun but a little hair-raising."

"How about the time you ran the LightningRod into the eye of one of the worst storms in Ishaidan history and came out intact on the other side? I guess you'll downplay that too? April, you are the same age as me and have earned enough stories and lore about you that, yes, I am intimidated. I am also enthralled. I am captivated. But when I saw you working with the welding crew, putting your life in jeopardy with every step, shoulder to shoulder with everyone else, it proved to me what you really are. I watched you work to the point of exhaustion to seal this ship back up and then you pushed way past that. You didn't stop. When you rebuilt that burner assembly, nobody thought it could be done, not even your miracle-working engineer, Cameron, thought it possible. But you just started in, crawling under those conduits, ordering your teams around like some mad conductor. I've realized just how much more you are compared to those stories. The real you is so much beyond what they say."

"Did you know I'm also a killer, a murderer of many souls?" she blurted out painfully.

He stepped toward her, placed his hands softly on her shoulders.

"No. But I know you are a soldier. You are amazing. You are beautiful. This may sound corny, but you are my hero."

She wiped tears from her eyes. "Sorry, I have a bad habit of crying lately."

She stepped in closer, allowing him to hold her.

"I'm not a hero. I'm a soldier, and I'll do whatever it takes to win."

"So will I. And I've had to make those calls as well, sent men and women to their deaths. They were all friends of mine. I know the pain, and I know the guilt. It haunts me every day. You're not alone in this."

"So where do we go from here, Captain David Ironstrike?"

"If you want me, April, I'm here for you."

She looked into his brown eyes, wanting him more than ever.

She let her robe fall to the floor and pulled him to her.

* * *

Chapter 25

The Guild of the Tenth Level was not without resources. The new fleet arrived at Del Amanto Stride's asteroid station on time. Eight modified battlecruisers, outfitted with the latest weapons and technologies, and in some aspects, superior to the Anard-Bueller Security Division Fleet.

Del watched them come in from his quarters, through the massive triangular quartz window. He was so excited; he didn't even notice the girl scurrying from his bed, moving as quietly as possible as not to attract his attention.

He met the Fleet Captain and his group of officers in the shuttle bay. He could not fight the feeling of utter delight. The universe was compelled to give him what he wanted.

"Captain!"

"Commander?" he replied, not quite sure how to address him.

"Certainly, that will do."

"Tell me, Captain, would you consider yourself qualmish?"

"Excuse me?"

"Ah, you know. You have scruples, per se?"

"I do believe one should conduct himself with some fortitude."

"Fortitude? I see." His voice revealed his disappointment.

"You do realize why you are here, don't you?"

"We're here at your behest, to squash this rebellion."

"Yes!" he clapped. "Squashing. I do like that word. Like qualm only squishy. Captain, you really should have had qualms about coming here. I would think anyway."

"Tell me, your sidearm, is that ornamental or is that actually a Winchester plasma 540?"

"No, this is the real thing."

"May I?"

Del held the weapon in his hand. "Such a well-balanced weapon. Really, works of art these old blasters. Just slightly on the heavy side, would you agree?"

The Captain attempted to reply, but Del cut him off. "They're such a brutal weapon though. Guess that's why they pulled them out of use with the Mars-Titan peace accord."

"Look here."

And he shot the Captain, the plasma burned a dinner plate sized hole in his chest, and the remnants of its discharge crept up his body in yellow tendrils.

"Isn't that a painful way to go?"

The officers, initially in shock, all reached for their weapons, but Del's men were already around them, all armed and ready.

"Now calm down. Obviously, someone made a mistake here, and it wasn't me. I asked for a Fleet Captain that could help me destroy the enemy. I think this one here, he'd have qualms about my methods, you see?"

"Tell me, gentlemen. Do you have any reservations about you? You OK with killing women? Children? Would you beat a man to death in front of his family? Do you have that fortitude?"

The men nodded as the Fleet Captain wriggled on the floor in his death throes.

"I said these things are brutal, didn't I!" he yelled at the dead man.

He was about to chuck the weapon but then decided against it and clipped it on his belt.

"You do as I say, and we do A-OK, right?"

Again, nods.

"Good. Tell me, who knows the extranist sectors the best?"

Two raised their hands.

"Who knows the belts?"

Only one was left.

Del moved in close to the man holding up his arm. "So ya 'bin here before, have ya? What's your name?"

"Gerald Montgamery, Sir."

"Such a nice Earther's name. Assume you used to run with the ESPD then?"

The man nodded, lowering his arm.

"So you had a hand in hitting the Pritchard mining base, killed off those six families, did ya?"

"I wasn't in command…"

"Tut… Tut… Tut," Del wagged his pointer finger. "But you don't have qualms, do you? That I can see. You're my new Fleet Captain, then."

The man visibly relaxed, his pale complexion regaining color.

"We depart in an hour. Give you time enough to bury your previous Fleet Captain."

"And oh yes, my boys here will be accompanying ya on each of your shuttles. So they can get to know you and your crews."

"See y'all in one hour. I've a particular piece of tail owed to me. And it'll be a long patrol."

* * *

The call came in from a small merchant trader along the Jefferson route. By the time the SDF cruiser Aeronis-Telvus had reached the merchant, it had been all but emptied of cargo, her crew ejected to vacuum. The patrol was still tethered to the trader when they came out from behind an asteroid.

Multiple ships bore down upon the police cruiser with no hesitation or concern. It was a classic maneuver of hide and attack, and the SDF Captain had already calculated his odds. He did not waste a second, immediately firing all weapons, simultaneously broadcasting an emergency call for help.

But no one was getting out of this alive.

For Del Antonio Stride this was the first of many.

Strike. Lure. Strike again. All too easy. These luddites were all too gullible.

The reputation of the dark pirate fleet spread quickly.

* * *

No one on Cauputain was expecting the communications signal, at least not from that direction. The local security cruisers were the first to intercept the crippled SDF ship enroute. After a few active discussions with its crew, they tethered up and helped the ship decelerate.

News spread from Cauputain to Jefferson, to Ishaida, and ultimately to the inner Sol systems. The princess of Anard-Bueller was alive and well. A miracle some would say, having been lost almost a year in space. Word reached out to the belt quickly, and the SDF ships in the area swept in to converge on the colony.

Aboard the Tesla-Continuum, most of the crew were excited to arrive at Cauputain, with the exception of one couple, April and David. They knew it meant their short time together was now lost. The reality of the rebellion would swallow them up and leave little for anything else.

In the weeks leading up to their 'rescue' David had spent as much time as possible with her in her quarters – at least as much as he could get away with without raising too much suspicion. April knew, despite their efforts, everyone had already figured it out.

Richard had, of course, as his habit of being ever too close, caught her and the Captain sharing a kiss in the observation lounge. He was quick to smile, nod, and disappear, not saying a word. But she knew if word did get out, it would not be from him.

She had intensely enjoyed their time. David had proven to be much more compatible with her in ways that she had not anticipated. They had worked closely together building and installing a temporary contraption to replace the communications array. He had been genuinely interested and helpful with her pet project of redesigning the cruiser. It was a relief to have someone work at her level and to bounce ideas off of. She could talk to someone about almost anything, including venting her frustrations on how certain things irritated her beyond explanation, such as the placement of such a critical device as the communications array that would expose it to enemy fire. *What were these engineers thinking?*

None of her ships would carry an exposed array again. All her ships would be refitted – and soon. But the Tesla-Continuum would have a few more enhancements beyond any standard Cruiser. April would turn her flagship's past weaknesses into strengths.

She pulled her final set of specifications together and dropped the small cube onto David's lap.

He was reading some deck reports, draped over her favorite chair, legs dangling. He was startled and dropped his tablet as he scrambled to grab the small data cube only to have it bounce to the floor.

April laughed. "Nice reaction, Captain."

"What's this?"

"Plans for version 2.0 of the Tesla-Continuum."

He tapped the cube and tripped the holographic switches until a full schematic of the ship came up.

"Ah... OK.... You're moving the reactor further into the ship and it's twice the size! Cannon at the rear."

"And a scanning array – which connects through to the mid-line array."

"Yes, I see that. But what did you do to the reactor?"

"Oh, the anti-grav compensation plates? Extra power for the inertial dampeners, plus radiation containment. Best to keep the reactor core under zero gravity influence for maximum efficiency."

"And what's this?" he pointed to what looked like a tube under the reactor, which reached to the outer hull.

"Maintenance access tube also serves as a core dump facility in case of critical damage."

"Oh... Why?"

She looked at him perplexed. "You always need an ejection mechanism. I was surprised we didn't have one."

"Well, I just never thought of one I guess. When would you eject your reactor core?"

"Not sure. We always had them on our Porter transports. Seemed like a good idea in case a damaged reactor went out of control."

"Really? That would have left an environmental catastrophe."

"Yes it would, come to think of it," she admitted in realization. "But not out here."

"No, not out here."

"The communications array is inside the shuttle bay."

"What's this bay at the bottom?"

"That's for the squadron fighters."

"Oh... wow. And these tube's at the stern?"

"Torpedo conveyer and launch tubes."

"On the rear? And more cannon to boot."

"To ensure we have 360 degree coverage. One reason why we have the bigger reactor."

"A few compromises though. I had to move our gym to the lower bay – but it'll have a nice scenic view through this large observation port."

"Yeah, looks nice."

"OK, but I've heard that voice before, what's wrong?"

"How long do you think this will take?"

"The dock at Cauputain is limited somewhat – will be challenged to re-outfit a Triple-A class cruiser, but they can do it. Five, six months maximum."

"And what do you expect me to do in that time?"

April was taken aback. "Figured you'd enjoy some leave while the work was in progress as I expect you'll want to oversee it directly."

"And you?"

"I'm sure another Captain would invite me onto their ship for the time being."

"Ah... No!"

"What?"

"You're not pulling the Grand Admiral card on me in here. In here, we are friends – we are lovers."

April sat down facing him. He was obviously very upset.

"I've a lot to catch up on. I've heard some rumors, and none of them are good. Verage Isaac, who assumed fleet command in my absence, is on his way to Cauputain now. We'll meet with him and get the facts. Sounds like the Pirates have been slowly picking away at our undefended routes and have recently hit one of our cruisers. Seems they've recently 'found' some additional warships, and that sounds more like ESPD cruisers than recycled ships. I know it's that same sonofabitch that hit us from behind. If we are going to retain this policing contract, we have to root him out and destroy him."

"We both want that, but I don't want you to go out there without me. This is dangerous work."

April smiled softly. "I know. I feel the same. I don't want to be away from you, either. Let's you and I make a deal. You stay here and get this refit started so I have a proper flagship. Instead of heading back out, I'll head back to Ishaida. I can't imagine what things are like back home, anyway. I'm sure the management team of Anard-Bueller has already tried an all-out coup. Without control of that situation we've truly lost this war – none of it matters then. I'm sure that will take some time to sort out. I won't be heading out on patrol for a time. Once you have this project under control, you can come visit me."

"OK. But going back out with one refitted flagship is not enough. You do realize we need more numbers. We'll need more ships, and therefore more crew, to hunt these criminals down."

"Ah, but I do have other ships, Captain. You didn't think the SDF was done growing, did you? I'm not done just yet."

* * *

The Cold of Space

Richard was not pleased with the crowds. April could tell by the constant scowl on his face.

"It's just temporary, they thought we were dead."

"I think you underestimate your appeal," was his only reply.

The mayor of Pinnacle-Vera, Adrias Mao and grand senator Gegario Janz met them in the busy spaceport bay. A small crew of local police enforcers made quick work of pushing back the crowd.

"April, my dear. We thought you lost. You have come back to us."

Adrias seemed authentically concerned for them – well possibly it was just her.

"Thank you, Mayor. We appreciate your invitation to your beautiful city." She said, graciously.

"I understand we will be expecting a number of visitors very shortly, other members of your police fleet, and friends and relatives, all searching for you and your ship."

"I am looking forward to seeing them."

"You must tell me, what happened out there?"

"That, my dear Mayor, is a much longer story," April followed up with a smile, avoiding any details.

The Mayor paused for only a moment then grinned widely. "Of course, we must get you off this dusty tarmac and into comfortable lodging. I'd like to extend my humble estate if you are willing. I can guarantee this small matter of privacy and security will be much easier to manage there."

"Of course, we'd be happy and appreciative to accept your offer. I assume you can direct the others to our location?"

"Others? Oh, yes. Well, I can certainly see to it. We will have a place to meet. They'll need to resign to the local establishments, of course."

"Of course. Are you sure you have room for my full contingent?"

The Mayor scanned the faces of her escorts, crew and security alike. "I'm sure we can allow for all your party." He stated, a little less jovially.

April only smiled, knowing full well his intentions – obtain as much of her story as possible and sell it to the networks. At least he was harmless. She enjoyed the walk and the open trolley ride through the busy city. It was full of color and life, and far above, the skies gleamed a bright blue.

This will be Ishaida one day.

The Mayor's estate was grand – a massive building sprawling over the hills at the end of the city. He certainly had enough room for them, and probably her whole crew. But they were all either busy at the spaceport or at the dockyard working with the Captain.

"My master of the house will see to your needs, and direct you to your rooms."

"I dare say, Commander McThurn, we do wholly intend to have a grand feast and a ceremony with you, and your compliment, tonight. I certainly hope you will attend?"

April could hear the slightest twinge of desperation in his voice.

"I would not dream of missing such a ceremony, Mayor. Of course, especially as you are so gracious to host my meeting with our guests when they arrive."

He proactively beamed. "Most excellent. I will ask the House Master to collect you around 7:00 then. By the way, we can certainly provide you with more flamboyant clothes, if you so desire," he winked.

"Thank you for the offer, Mayor, however, I don't feel it would be befitting to not wear my formal uniform. This is my finest formal uniform, you understand?"

He smiled, realizing pushing further would not necessarily yield fruit. "I will retire, and please, make yourself comfortable."

As April went to enter her room, Richard slipped past and through, surprising the House Master.

"You'll have to excuse him. He's my security."

With that, she closed the door.

The room was despicably grand and over the top ornate. Richard was already systematically scanning the walls, floors, furnishing, and carpets, and successfully locating devices, all most likely bugs. He pulled a few from the small bag he carried and set them free to fly about.

"Well, he did have enough bugs in this place. Pretty sure I got them all."

"Pretty sure?"

"Well no, I'm sure. I got them all. You plan to stay here long?"

"Long enough to arrange a ride home."

He nodded. "Here," he said, handing her a small communications device. "Put this in your ear."

She did.

"Can you hear me," he asked talking softly.

She nodded. "Do you hear me?"

He confirmed and moved to the door. "Stay safe, Commander. We'll be available at your request."

"Thanks."

She was left with her thoughts. Outside there was a wonderful garden, full of plants of multiple shapes, sizes, and colors, and all emanating lovely smells. April spent her time there until she was prodded by Richard.

"Dinnertime."

The dinner hall was opulent, embellished with raised wood panels, walls plastered with rare works of art, garnished with placements of carvings and statues. April was seated near the head of the table beside the Mayor, of course.

Guests were already arriving, garbed in elaborate dresses of fine silks and cloth, and tailored suits of all colors.

Cauputainites certainly liked all shades and hues of color, April thought. Not so different from the Trectilla.

Each was brought forward and introduced to her, with a formal reading by the House Master of a litany of names and prefix titles for each, all which meant absolutely nothing to April, but she bowed acknowledgment to each as gracefully as she was able. The visitors seemed delighted with her genuine smiles, well wishes, and blessings and commented on how good it was that she had found her way home.

Someone rang a bell and they proceeded with multiple courses. The food was delicious, although she had no idea what she was eating most of the time. The wine was smooth and heavy with just a hint of sharpness to provide a bite.

Conversations were painfully shallow and with little meaning. April had first attempted to explain how they had survived, and the particular steps they had taken to modify the ships' systems, but then realized quite quickly she was wasting her time, and reset her conversation to light and witty banter, adding the odd laugh. She ensured it had just enough content to keep her sane.

"Richard, get me out of here."

"Sorry, Commander. Advise against it just yet. Would be considered offensive. Perhaps once the music starts."

"Music?"

As if on cue a small band started. The music reminded her of something of ancient classical and modern generational pop. The adjacent floors started to fill with dancers, some very agile and romantic as they waltzed tightly together as one.

April was able to navigate back through the sea of faces to the Mayor.

"I'm sorry, but I need to retire back to my room. I'm afraid I'm not feeling quite up to par."

The Mayor's features twisted with concern. "Of course, please. I certainly realize this whole experience must have been especially trying. Perhaps I can request my personal physician to attend to you?"

"No, thank you. I believe it is merely exhaustion."

Richard and his team eased into position by her side. In a moment, she was out of the oppressive crowds.

"You all right?"

"Yes. Just not comfortable with so many people. I'll be fine with a few hours rest. Thanks, Richard."

She entered her room, hit the soft bed and slept for uncounted hours.

* * *

Sun was streaming through the window, tracing along the floor, and exposing tiny suspended flecks of dust floating in the area. She followed the beam with her eyes until they met up with a leg and the sleeping person connected to that leg half-prone on an adjacent chair.

"Wake up sleepy head."

He stirred and opened his eyes.

"I thought you would be busy on your ship, David."

"I'm here to check on you, of course."

She slid off the bed and went to him. "Nice surprise, just the same. I did expect some visitors today, but not you."

"I know, they've been streaming in all morning."

"Really?" she asked, excitedly. "We need to get moving, then. Did Verage arrive yet?"

"Hold on. Maybe we should consider breakfast first?"

She smiled, pulling him closer. "Maybe we have a few minutes for something more."

* * *

She walked into a hall now full of familiar faces. They all stood, and a few started clapping. She waited, smiling, saying thank you, waiting for the applause to settle.

Captain Alder approached, taking her arm. "April, you are a sight for sore eyes," he said.

"Oh, I thought Verage was coming."

A look came across his features, dark and concerning. "Oh, I'm sorry. You may not have heard. I assume you've heard about the Aeronis-Telvus?"

She nodded. "They destroyed her."

"Yes, and since then they've become much more brazen. Just before I departed for here, a Corporate liner inbound to Cauputain was intercepted. The worst of it was they ejected some of the passengers, for no apparent reason. It's a horrendous, arbitrary killing of the innocents. Verage had to investigate this one personally."

"I see," April acknowledged, lost in thought. *How much longer can this go on? They would all be looking to her to stop this.*

"Please, allow me." Alder escorted her to the head of the expansive horseshoe-shaped table. A tiny microphone suspended in mid-air just within range.

All eyes turned toward her, and silence fell over the room.

OK April, make it count. Don't screw this up.

"Thank you, everyone. I appreciate the warm welcome. As you know, Captain Ironstrike and I, along with a brave crew, have survived a near-fatal encounter with multiple pirate vessels. As you know, we have not been the only victims. They leave a trail of death throughout the stars."

"But they are not without sympathizers. They would like to convince you, and everyone else, that they represent the true rebellion, the bringers of independence and self-governance, but what they really stand for is greed. And once they are done looting and pillaging the so-called corporate enemies, they will turn on everyone else. They will continue to take everything they can, including what you cannot replace – your very lives."

"Kill them bastards!" someone yelled.

"The SDF has one simple mandate – protection. In order to bring true peace to all extranists, we need to catch and incarcerate each and every one of these pirates, and if that is not possible, then we will terminate them!"

The crowd roared, but April raised her hands, requesting a temporary silence.

"These words are easy to say, but to do this – to defeat this enemy - is a much more difficult thing to accomplish. Their vessels bear the designs and the lines of the latest ESPD cruisers. They are being supplied by a much more devious enemy, one with intentions I can only guess at, although I'm sure it involves the eventual control and subjugation of all extranists. We must not allow this to continue. Regardless the viciousness of this enemy we must not abandon our resolve!"

"Here, here!" Applause rang throughout the room. April let it echo until it died.

"I recognize many of you here. You are my brothers and sisters of the Porter families of Ishaida. I once asked for your help, but you thought this was not your war. Yet here you stand, a long way from your home."

"Tell us what you need, April," stated one of the Elders.

"I need more ships. I cannot win this war with the numbers I have today."

"We can only provide a few to your fleet," stated another. "But they're yours."

"If I were to tell you I had the ships but lacked the crew? What would you say? Would you join me then? Would you put your lives on the line?"

A raucous of noise filled the room, radiating many proclamations to join her.

April smiled and raised her fist. "Then join me for Ishaida!" she said, loud and strong.

The Porters started to chant, "Clan McThurn! Clan McThurn!" The walls reverberated as the crystal light fixture swung in unison.

April would have her fleet, now. This time the Porters would make a stand.

* * *

A Debt Repaid

Chapter 26

Anard-Bueller headquarters was near complete. The massive towers of the main building cast long shadows over the now busy spaceport. The highways and tramways were crammed with busy vehicles, all rushing to move in one direction or another in an organized, yet chaotic dance. Shuttles and small ships raced overhead, and most importantly, a massive cable hung in the skies, no longer a distant glint, ominous and pending.

April saw this all from the upper hall, watched as tiny specks representing everyday people moved throughout the maze of interconnected buildings. She looked past the manufactured world of man, noted once bare lands were now thick, lush and green. The waters of Lake Neprid glinted with sharpened shards of a late afternoon sun. It was, in every sense of the word, beautiful.

"Things are moving amazingly fast," she stated, talking to her artificial friend AI Tiberious. "And you've performed exceptionally well on your own, especially hiding your influence from the executive."

AI Tiberious chuckled, and one could have said his eyes twinkled, but that was more than likely another choppy image artifact. "It was challenging, truthfully. Let's not disappear like that again, April. They were becoming suspicious, beginning to investigate, getting very close."

She nodded, acknowledging his struggle. "It wasn't intentional you realize, but I know that leaves you with little comfort. I assume you've averted their probes, after all, you still managed to finish the headquarters."

"Yes, we are almost complete. Your small army of engineers, builders, and tradesmen have been working without rest, three shifts around the clock."

"How long until the cable is down?"

"We have encountered delays. Many more months yet – well over a year. It is a very slow process now, as we've needed to start mining from other sources as the primary excavations of the asteroid are all but complete."

"I'll need to inspect that station soon. I'm sure it is something to behold."

"Ah, most importantly, I have had some time to digest and process those plans from the Trectilla. They are incredibly illuminating and thrice as complicated as one would consider on first analysis."

"So you have figured out their specifications?"

"No, but I have appointed the finest minds we have in Anard-Bueller on this challenge. There is much more encapsulated knowledge here than any of us realize."

"Such as?"

"To put it simply, the calculations that define space and time, and relate the forces of the universe, all working in unison to expose a single function – to fold space upon itself."

"A wormhole? Impossible."

"No. Absolutely possible. A way to fold space that will allow a body to move from one location to another in an instant, as long as the body's mass is accounted for in proportion to the power transfer invested."

"If this works, Anard-Bueller will be able to manufacture gates for instantaneous travel throughout known space."

"Yes, but I would not consider it advisable to operate gates on a planet's surface, too much radiation and temporal fields - not so friendly. At this point in time, these devices must be kept out in space to be operated safely."

"Manageable compromise. We create a network of gates to and from key points of travel, and subsequently, reduce the time of travel to a minimum."

"Almost, but there are limitations to these constructs."

"Like?"

"The power these gates will need. It is best we orbit these devices close to suns, to ensure we can properly source the energy needed. But before we move ahead with too many plans, we need these alien ones deciphered. This may take months or possibly years. There are some ideas conveyed here we have not mastered yet, plus they have provided us with a mathematical model of principals of which we still have to understand. Without this, it would be impossible to construct the devices."

"I see."

"So in the meantime, I have to subdivide the work, to compartmentalize you see. We must ensure no one has a full picture of the device if we are going to be able to control this."

"Do what you need to do. In the meantime, I'll do what I need to do," April stated.

"You mean hunt down this elusive pirate? I see not all the sins of war have yet been inflicted so long as the enemy remains. Vengeance has yet to be levied."

"Vengeance? You don't think retribution is due? How many have died so far? I've lost count, nevermind how many more will die if we do nothing. Besides, I have to protect my soldiers."

"No. There is something more at stake here. You must protect your soul, April McThurn. Few if any, remain unscarred by war. Fewer yet become stronger from it."

April nodded. *She understood him all too well.*

* * *

The remainder of the fleet was brought out of deep space storage. Ship by ship, crew by crew, the fleet increased in size and strength. More Porters joined the ranks, in the process leaving their families and their Porter transports to step into the unknown life of a spacefarer.

April rotated out the more senior, experienced ships with the replacement patrols, and dispatched, upon each launch, communications relays that would establish connections back to other relay stations and ultimately transmit data back to the Ishaida headquarters. They were systematically assembling a network that would monitor the shipping lanes throughout the extranist systems. In time, enough of the relays would be in place to ensure there would be no gaps from the Earth system to Ishaida, to Jefferson, and from both to the Cauputain system. As each additional patrol ship and communications relay node was added, they began transmitting their raw data to the centralized network. A detailed, real time picture of the main shipping routes developed. This was the new tool that would recognize the next strike from the dark fleet.

It did not take long to test the system.

The target was a merchant freighter, stocked with silver ore from the deep belts, heading to Earth with its precious cargo. The ship was attacked but allowed time to issue distress calls, which resulted in two SDF cruisers responding immediately.

This was a familiar pattern. Disable the prey, but don't kill it. Allow the SDF ships to come to its aid, and hit again, only this time with superior numbers. The SDF had already adopted alternative strategies in preparation for this scenario. The second ship would remain a farther distance out on a perimeter patrol, enough to double the range of external scanning and sound the alarm if a significantly larger force decided to encroach.

The pattern was familiar and accurate. Multiple pirate vessels had wasted little time starting in on the target cruisers and merchant.

At the time, April was the Commander on the fleet control deck at headquarters. The deck crew was monitoring the situation closely, and April wasted no time pulling up com-link to the perimeter ship, the Acronis.

The young Porter Captain appeared on the video feed, looking a bit pale but confident.

"Captain, you may be outnumbered, but unlike your companion, you still have the advantage of velocity, position, and trajectory. I need you to vector into the heart of that incoming fleet, countermeasures and offensive weapons maximized, and inflict maximum casualties. Are you prepared to bring your ship into harm's way?"

"Yes, Commander."

"And hold fast, Captain. You can get through this."

He only nodded, cutting the video feed.

"Hail the Pernagesion."

"Commander," responded the Captain. "We are about to be obliterated. Any ideas would be helpful."

"Can you extract the crew from the merchant?"

"We should have enough time."

"Can you rig the merchant for remote control?"

He leaned off screen for a second, then reappeared. "No, not in time, Commander."

"That ship is your advantage, Captain. I suggest you consider making it your Trojan horse. Stay tight behind it. They'll avoid damaging it if they can. They want its cargo. You vector out as soon as you are ready, and we will coordinate a pass through your tail with the Acronis. As you retreat, they will pursue, and that ore ship will get into the midst of their numbers. When it does, you destroy it."

"Not so sure they'll come in that tight, Commander. The resulting explosion may not inflict the damage we are hoping for. Regardless, it's worth a shot. I'll dispatch an officer over to it right now."

"Just... That's a one-way ticket for that man, Captain." April felt compelled to revoke the order. *She didn't want him to die.*

As if the Captain had sensed her thoughts through the thousands of light-years of distance between them. "Aye, Commander. We all know what we signed up for here. Standby."

He disappeared from view, then appeared again a minute later. "Commander, please make this worth it. I surely hope you have help coming?"

"I do." She checked the holographic tactical. "But as of now, we calculate they are 63 minutes out."

He took the news well, swallowing hard, and tightening his grip on the deck rail. "We have about 15 minutes to coordinate this before they're in range. If this works, I'll owe you a drink, Commander."

"Good luck, Captain."

The video feed dropped. The Captain's picture seemed to linger there in the gray afterimage, like a ghost.

Her eyes were playing tricks on her.

"Monitoring, I want a full image of the engagement. Can you do that?"

"Aye, Commander. Rendering will be a few seconds late, though."

April waited, impatiently tapping her fingers on the holographic console rail.

The image came up, showing the two SDF cruisers, the merchant ship, and the incoming dark pirate fleet.

The Acronis was moving fast, at nearly a right angle to their incoming trajectory. It hit first, moving through the pirate fleet with no mercy. Ships started disappearing off the image, others veered off at crazy angles. A few modified their course to engage the SDF cruiser.

April couldn't see the exchange of weapons, but she knew the Acronis was experiencing a harrowing flight into the eye of the storm. And as quickly as it started, it was done, and the Acronis was hurtling away from the engagement. She had possibly one more pass in her if she was able to expend the energy for an angular acceleration to loop back through them.

The merchant ship was already steaming back, directly into the oncoming enemy formation. As anticipated, they ignored it and flew right past. A moment later its profile disappeared on the holograph, just as it reached the very center of the mass of attacking ships - a perfectly timed weapon. More enemy signatures disappeared, and others exhibited signs of severe damage, veering off wildly, twisting and turning uncontrollably. The damage was more than any of them anticipated. It took a second for April to realize the ship's ore cargo was playing a major role here, introducing millions of tiny projectiles accelerated to a hull penetrating velocity.

The Pernagesion was running, doing its best to keep a safe distance from its aggressors and at the same time attempting a maneuver to allow the Acronis one more fatal pass into the wake of its attackers. The SDF cruiser was putting up an admirable fight, stopping acceleration long enough to rotate the ship, launch multiple warheads, realign and resume acceleration. With each deploy of ordnance, the enemy grew closer, but they were feeling the effectiveness of the SDF cruiser's tenacity as additional signatures dropped out of the chase.

The Acronis was ready for another raid, and it started into the remaining mass of the enemy. Its torpedoes found their targets, and between the Pernagesion's ordnance and the Acronis's mad blitz, the attacking ships were fading in numbers quickly. But this time the enemy was prepared, and the exchange of fire was remarkable. The Acronis was almost through the wake of enemy ships, but then its signal suddenly disappeared off the holograph.

"Hail the Acronis, we lost her on scans."

She hoped for a response, but she knew it down deep in her stomach. The ship and the crew were lost.

"Nothing. Commander, she's gone."

"Then we focus on the Pernagesion," she ordered. She checked the long-range. The SDF interception fleet was getting closer but not yet there.

"Raise the interception fleet's Captain."

Verage Isaac came up on the screen. "Grand Admiral," he acknowledged with a nod. "I do hope they get there in time."

"We're sending you our data. Intercept them bastards, Verage. They killed the Acronis."

"Our torpedoes will arrive there before we do, that you can be sure of. If this data of yours is right, it should ensure multiple kills."

"We have you 20 minutes away. Deceleration will be aggressive. Godspeed, Captain. Give'em hell."

"Enemy ships are converging on the Pernagesion, Commander," reported Ridgeline. "I expect they intend to board."

"Good. That should buy us the time we need."

"Open a channel to the Pernagesion," she ordered. "Captain, we are anticipating a boarding attempt. Please ready your crew."

He looked weary. "Our regrets to the crew of the Acronis, Commander. She was a good ship."

"Don't count yourself out yet, Captain. Interception fleet has launched ordnance."

"Maybe I will be joining you for a drink. My preference is scotch."

"Not a problem, I've a full bar," she smiled.

Alarms sounded on the Pernagesion's bridge. Officers were scrambling behind the Captain. "Looking forward to it, Commander, but right now we've a roach infestation to deal with now. Pernagesion, out."

April glanced over to the monitoring officer. "I can confirm, enemy vessel has attached to the Pernagesion."

April walked back and forth, repeating her steps, counting the minutes. Time dragged.

"We are deploying torpedoes," reported Verage. His voice shocked April out of her trance.

"Monitoring?"

"Too close to tell, Commander. My guess, they will reach their targets."

She checked the holographic. One ship was attached to the starboard side of the Pernagesion, another was coming to the port side. As she watched, other pirate fleet vessels started to blink out of existence.

Verage's torpedoes were hitting home.

"The pirate fleet is changing course, Commander. They are disengaging."

April felt the emotion well up within her, like a wave building as approached the shoreline. She stepped back, turned away from the officers, and gathered herself together.

"Instruct Verage to secure the Pernagesion." She ordered, quickly wiping her eyes, then turning back to the control deck.

The holograph told the story. The battle was over as quickly as it had begun. The pirates were spreading out and attempting to retreat. The influx of the secondary SDF interception fleet had surprised them, and they were no longer under a cohesive plan of attack.

"SDF cruiser Gandolf-Auricia decelerating to intercept the Pernagesion," announced Ridge.

April knew this was a difficult maneuver. If gauged incorrectly it would be extremely likely to miss the Pernagesion altogether. "Who's the Captain on the Gandolf?"

"That would be Captain Karen McThurn, Commander," replied Officer Ridge.

Karen. Be careful.

She watched as the other port side pirate attempted to disengage, only to meet with a volley from the Gandolf-Auricia. The ship lurched away, then began a lazy roll, its main drive disabled and hull venting an atmosphere of flame.

"Monitoring." She glanced over to the officer. "Maintain deep scans. I want to know where these rats are running to."

"Yes, Commander."

"The Gandolf-Auricia is docking onto the Pernagesion now," Officer Ridge reported. "They are confirming enemy contact on board."

Time passed. April waited, pacing the deck impatiently.

Verage brought the small fleet together and began the process of rescue and recovery. A second ship was dispatched to join the Pernagesion.

"Captain Karen McThurn from the Gandolf-Auricia reporting in, Commander."

Finally, April thought. She motioned to the officer to put her up on the display.

"Commander, we've secured the Pernagesion and the enemy vessel."

"Thank you, Captain - and the crew?"

"A number of casualties, including Captain Etheridge. He went down holding them off. I am sorry... April."

"Oh. I was hoping to..." She held back on her words. "Thank you, Karen – I mean Captain McThurn. Please attend to the deceased. We'll bring them all back home."

He wasn't supposed to die today.

"I will, Commander." She signed off giving April a moment to assess the situation. There was nothing left for her to do now. Verage had it under control.

She had to get out of here.

Quickly thanking everyone for their contributions, she excused herself from the fleet control deck and headed back to her apartment. She needed time to sort this out, to pull herself together.

Later that day came the door chime, then incessant knocks. The matters were not pressing, easily diverted to the officer on deck. She elected to stay in her quarters, finding some solace sitting in the dark, drinking the bottle of scotch she had promised a certain Captain. Besides, she didn't need to hear about anyone's concerns about her, or how she wasn't handling the pressure or evoking true leadership or some other bullshit. It was better she was alone.

The knocking returned and grew louder. Whoever it was, that person was persistent.

"Leave me alone!" she yelled.

Another swig should knock her out. She took it gratefully.

Damn it, no such luck.

The knocking had now turned to a loud thumping.

"Activate AI system, please."

The image of the Old Man filled the dark room. He peered over the edge of his projection perch, looking down at her. She was sitting on the floor, her back against the projection console, a ¾ empty bottle of scotch in her lap.

"Hello, April. Seems like you've encountered some demons today."

She tilted her head back. "You don't know the half of it, old boy. And if you weren't a damn projection, I'd insist you have a drink with me. Can you tell me who's at that door, maybe figure out what they want, and tell them to bugger off?"

"Certainly, will be but a moment."

The image reappeared two minutes later. "Was a personal visit request. I've sent them away. You have your privacy and peace now."

"Good job. They can all go to hell right now."

"Who? Your officers, your security detail, or maybe your new lover?"

"Ha! You've been spying on me!"

"No, not really. I've just reviewed Richard Nearson's logs. I am relieved you have found someone."

She took another drink and dragged herself over to the couch. "In the end, he'll just die as well. Not sure why I bother."

"Oh, is that what you think? You believe everyone you care about just dies off?"

"You silly questioning pile of bytes! Are you so damned unable to do the math here? To think of the irony that you are a member of that statistic. Crap, would you look at this bottle? Almost empty. I shouldn't be able to down this much, you know. But of course, I surprise myself yet again. Good work Grand Admiral April McThurn, you brave-assed drunken scrapie."

"Scrapie?"

"Oh, you didn't know that? I'm an orphan, really. Mom died when I was young so I never really knew her. After that, Oranis and Lavenue adopted me into their family. I loved them, you know. You can find the whole family in your database, right? Ty, Chancy, Jim, and Elsie all my brothers and sisters. All dead. Even my good friend from long ago, good ol' Branton. Gone. Dead. Every last one of them. Let's toast them all tonight."

She took a long drink. It had lost its burn long ago and didn't seem to even taste like anything anymore. It was the last of the bottle.

"But you cannot blame yourself for all their deaths."

"No? Let me see. Yes, yes, yes, yes to all of them, even Cruez, you remember him don't you? But maybe I should not blame myself for Captain

Gerald Etheridge's death, after all, they signed up for it didn't they? You know I didn't even know his full name, had to look him up. Etheridge is a fine Porter name you know. Their clan ran mostly the southern routes. I'm sure his family will thank me for his chance to join the almighty SDF." She broke down. Crying somehow helped with the pain.

"And time and again I call upon my people, my friends, and time and again they die, if not for a cause, then for me. I don't want that. I don't want them all to die. Not for me. I'm just a killer. They can't die for me."

She rolled herself tightly into a ball. "Just tell all of them to go away. Leave me alone. I don't want any of this anymore." She sobbed and sobbed, recalling visions of her close friends and family and could feel the love in their eyes, even at the moment when death came for them. Why couldn't she remember Cruez's face? Another drink might help. Was it wrong to hope for the pain to end?

Another drink. She tilted the bottle. Nothing left. She threw it down the hall, and it landed with a crash of splintering grass.

She lay down, drawing herself into a fetal position. The world was spinning images of faces, explosions, death. At last, the darkness came, like a black wall of comforting warmth, hiding everything.

AI Tiberious shimmered in the dark, unable to comfort her. Something processed at a lower level, a thought, a feeling once connected to emotion. Was it regret? For all his capabilities he could not hold her, could not comfort her.

"Sleep, my darling girl, sleep. Know that many more remain alive because of you."

* * *

Del Amanto Stride was livid.

Too many ships lost. All the gains over the last year, gone.

He knew he had to deal with this damned SDF full on. He knew there was only one way to kill the serpent - to cut off its head.

"Get hold of Canon." He ordered his com officer. "I need another strategy."

He retired to his quarters, feeling the weight of loss and failure. It was not something he was familiar with. Usually, he managed to move obstacles out of the way. If one way didn't work, he'd find another, but he'd succeed. And he'd rarely lose so much doing it.

Damn the cost! Twelve ships in all. Each worth millions of credits. Each now floating scrap. And now he had to come crawling back to the Guild, and that damn arrogant Canon. Upper-class waste.

They all needed to be taken down a notch.

He had plans for the Guild, and for the rest of the Earth systems. Why was this bitch McThurn getting in his way? He was working for her, for all of them in the end. Why couldn't they all see that now?

He had tried to reinvigorate the movement, but the pacifists in

Jefferson and Cauputain would rather sit and wait and hope it all works out. Only the belters really understood. They knew the cost that may have to be paid, the risks that they faced.

He needed more of their type.

That's probably why his ships were lost. It was infecting the crew as well. Too many weak pacifists doubting their true calling. Probably best the weak ones burned. It's best they were pruned and didn't weaken the others. This loss should strengthen their resolve.

"I have Canon on an encrypted channel, Captain."

"Good. Connect me up."

Canon's smug face lit up on-screen.

He's such an arrogant, ugly sonofabitch. And what is it with his fake hair? Who's he fooling anyway?

"Hello, old friend. It is good to hear from you," he stated, literally chewing down on each syllable.

"And you, Del Stride. I assume you've made some progress since we've last talked?"

"Some. But I have to say, it's a bit embarrassing really. I mean I have a hard time justifying my tiny fleet against the numbers under the Anard-Bueller banner. You'd think the Guild was expecting miracles."

"What are you implying Stride? We've given you everything you've asked for."

"Right, knowing everything I ask for is a bit limited insomuch I don't have access to the facts as you have them. Seems the Guild is just too cheap, looking to set me up for failure."

"What? Where the hell are you getting off?"

"Now. Now. Time you took a real hard look at the SDF numbers. Stop expecting me to pull all the weight and take all the chances for free. I don't have enough leverage, and definitely not enough ships anymore. But you know that don't you? You either get serious and deliver to me what I need or it simply will not happen, and you and your Guild members can sit around and scratch your heads all day long and ask yourselves why."

"Standby, Stride. I have to relay someone in..."

Del sat back and tapped his fingers on the console. What the hell was Canon up to now? Why was he taking so damned long?

He was about ready to close the channel when Canon's face appeared again.

"I have someone from the Guild who wants to talk with you. Be sure you stay on the respectful side, one slip of that foul mouth of yours and he'll end you, savvy?"

The piqued his interest. "And who is 'He'?"

"Chairman of the 10th League."

Del swallowed hard. This was not expected. The infamous chairman: few if any had the unique pleasure.

"Del Antonio Stride, I presume?"

The Chairman's face looked aged enough to be ground out of a pillar of chalk. Dark inset eyes glared back at him not indifferent to a blank stare of a corpse.

"Chairman," he acknowledged respectfully.

"I understand you are demanding more ships. Didn't we just fill an order for you?"

"Let's cut the bullshit, Chairman. You know what the situation is. I was taken apart by the SDF fleet. They've been bolstering up their numbers steady. I can't do this without ships. And no one out here can make this happen but me."

"True. I do believe you still have yet an integral part to play, Stride. Tell me that you can you take her out."

"Her? You mean that McThurn bitch? It's already done – just give me what I need and I'll see to it."

"Do believe you've said that before."

"I did my job. She got lucky. Won't happen again."

The old man stared at him through the vid channel for an uncomfortable amount of time. "Alright, Stride. I'll give you your ships, but if you don't succeed..."

"I'll succeed alright. She won't see it coming."

The old man closed the channel without another word.

Del leaned back with a broad smile. His time was coming. He'd have some preparation to do before the ships arrived. But when they did, it would be time to chop the head off the serpent.

* * *

"April, April you there?"

David hammered on the door until his knuckles were raw. He patched a text channel over to Nearson. "Hey, where is April?"

"She is in her quarters," came the reply.

"She's not opening up. Something's wrong."

He waited. Let it sink in for a sec. Her personal security detail would not like this. Nearson showed up five minutes later and opened her door. How he managed to unlock the encrypted set, he could only wonder.

They found her on the floor in the main living area. A near empty bottle lay beside her. "April!" David pulled her up to him and checked her pulse. "She's OK, but we need to give her some meds. I think her blood alcohol level is dangerously high."

She opened her eyes, then quickly turned and her body heaved as she vomited, some over David, some over Richard's shoes.

"Let's get her to the bathroom." Richard offered, wincing. "I've relayed a request for alcohol meds. Should be here shortly."

"No. Leave me alone. Don't want either of you here," she yelled. She fought them, but her efforts were weak and paltry. "Just leave me here.

I've had enough of all this." She heaved again, her whole body fighting to rid itself of the poison coursing through every vein.

"What happened?" David asked Richard.

"Lost an SDF Cruiser yesterday, plus severe damage and crew loss on the other. Think she blames herself."

"We all know what we signed up for. Not everyone is expecting to make it back."

"Don't tell her that. She feels every last one I think, poor thing."

"Stop talking about me and get the hell out! I don't want you here I told you. Why don't you listen to my orders?"

David just held her over the lavatory and ignored the angry outbursts. "Maybe better when she's back on the deck of a ship," he said. "It's a little different playing with lives on that chess board upstairs."

"Judging by yesterday, I think there are a few thankful souls she was there to coordinate it. She took a sure loss scenario and turned it into a save. Now she's trying to drink herself to death to forget the ones that died – when it could have been all of them."

"Hell of a woman," commented David.

"Hell of a leader," corrected Richard.

April moaned, lost in a world of pounding pain. Whatever the hell they were talking about, she wished they'd just shut up, leave her alone, and turn off the damned lights.

"Meds are here. Oh great, old-fashioned needles. I assume, David, you can proceed on slightly safer grounds than I with these."

David just grabbed the needles and went to work administered them, relying upon his medical emergency training. April slumped in his arms, asleep once again. "That should do it. I'll bring her to bed and let her sleep this one off."

"Of course, David, just do me one favor," pleaded Richard.

"What's that?"

"If she asks, I wasn't ever here, OK?"

× × ×

The morning came with its harsh light and painful, though blurry, memories. April's head throbbed and her body ached within every joint, every organ seemed to be retaliating against her with no remorse. She pulled herself out of bed and crawled to the washroom, to vomit once again. Her stomach heaved until it was dry of everything, only to keep heaving.

No, nothing had changed from the day before, she realized.

A hand rubbed her back, which was now covered in a light sweat.

"Why are you here?"

"I arranged a short leave. I thought I'd surprise you."

"Can't you see I'd rather be alone right now?"

"What happened? I heard about the battle yesterday. You handled the situation incredibly well."

"Just leave me alone, will you, damn it! I just want to be left alone."

"Whatever this is, I am here if you want to talk about it, it may help."

"No. I don't want to talk about it. I don't want you here. I want you to go. Just go."

"But I..."

"Get the hell out of my apartment! You are useless! Why can't you understand? I don't want you here!"

"Fine." David stepped away, offended and angry. "You want to be alone. I can help you with that. I'm out of here!"

She yelled out at his receding figure. "Good. Leave. You can't help me, no one can!"

The door slid shut.

April felt the tears come yet again, and angrily pulled herself into the shower, only to lay on its floor and watch the water swirl down the drain. Hours passed before she had assembled enough of herself to make a call to Richard via the vid-phone connection.

"Hello, Commander. You aren't looking so well."

"Glad to see you too, old man. I did not call to share pleasantries. I want to know who that sonofabitch is that's been coordinating all these hits. He's not your average thickheaded miner, and undeniably not the typical lazy contemptuous criminal type. Did you get anything more from the background on that crew of miscreants in the belt?"

"Yes, most of them pretty bad eggs. A few could be our guy, but..."

"But what?"

"His name keeps coming up constantly. Whether I run an investigation after the fact of some of these bastards that initiated an attack, or start into tracing illegal cargo, it all seems to head to one name."

"Who?"

"Del Amano Stride, that especially mouthy one at the meeting in the belts."

"Yeah, I remember him. That's what I expected. So you know for sure he's the one?"

"He's a strong contender. History of human trafficking, robbery, and allegations against him of murder. Bad enough dude. Did serve some time. But to tell you the truth, this one we are looking for could be anyone. We just don't know for sure exactly who it is."

"Keep digging. I need to know for sure."

"And when you find him?"

"He will not be going to jail. We are going to kill him."

"Not exactly a message you should be spreading about, Commander. And vengeance is not as satisfying as it seems."

"This is not vengeance. This is preservation. Whoever he is, he needs to be eliminated before he kills more of my people."

"Sounds like retribution to me. But what do I know? I'm just a security guard."

April pursed her lips, ready to lace into him for his lack of subordination. Instead, she slammed the disconnect link.

* * *

Evelyn floated up the vertical corridor, past the moss birthing floors, past the steam spore rooms, and the lichen baths. They had requested her direct presence, which was unusual to fathom. It was rare for any Trectilla to be within a physical distance of any of the elders, much less summoned.

It was extremely uncommon indeed.

But she was dutiful in her means, as dutiful in her beliefs to serve the greater of the Trectilla race. She found satisfaction in her humble capacity. Very few things would rival this intensity, save for possible submersion in the sound caverns, where the low frequencies would throb and hum into her very being and bring upon such peaceful bliss.

But alas, there are times for pleasure, and this was not one of them.

The corridor twisted and turned above, a seemingly random maze, but that was an illusionary maze, as the patterns and directions followed a mathematical precision. The great antechamber was doused in a yellow hue given off by the gel. It attached in a tight symbiosis with the porous walls, feeding the gelatin with sucrose-laden water pumped from the basins of the lower chambers.

The Elders broke free of the gelatin upon her arrival and slowly floated into a large mass.

As a dutiful daughter of the Strain of 'Angla, she hovered upon the visitation pad, daring not to touch the golden network of knowledge. Her lineage forbade such activity as the class of 'Angla does not consider itself pure enough.

Regardless, the tempestuous rebel in her thought of reaching down, with the smallest of protrusions, just to taste.

As if the group of Eldest recognized her thoughts, they called out their recognition of her in unison.

"Daughter of 'Angla, former the Strain of the first awakened. We call upon you."

"I am here," she replied, careful to maintain thoughts of purity and wholesomeness within her.

"You have provided the rational machine thinker with the data, have you not?"

Evelyn pondered upon their descriptive label they had bestowed on the one she called April. It was accurate, but also slightly humorous. This idea of humor, however, did not appeal to the Elders, nor did they understand it.

Evelyn pulled close her inner flanks, drawing her colors close so as not to be too obvious.

"We see the great cable fall from the sky, we see the flying machines swarm onto our home, yet nothing seems to have changed in the great migration. No one has noticed an alteration, not in mass or color, not in any quanta of time."

"She has promised us. She will deliver onto us."

"You are to find this human and determine the true nature of her machines. We feel a great impending; a pressure that cannot be withstood."

"A conflict? With whom, my Elders? The humans of their seed sun have detailed agreements of concern."

"They are a complicated collection of individuals. They have no appreciation for the symbiosis of mind. They are quick to conflict with one another. They are insane."

"Yes, I understand. How long, my Elders, shall I divulge?"

"The time of Ishaida is peaceful, but this probability of dissimilation erodes the deterministic randomly, and accelerates as their insanity quickens."

"The machine construction is not started. That much we know. And we must leave."

"Perhaps she will panic when I present her the truths."

"They are possible truths. You are well aware of that. You must speak with precision to her. Meaning must not be left in ambiguity."

"Am honored to serve."

"As we are honored for you to serve. Go to the new metal towers in the North. Bring our message of urgency, if not, then inform her of our impatience."

"Yes, my Elders."

Evelyn left the soaring black towers of the sands, floating quickly over the flowing dunes, for she must move in haste.

The essence of time can be unforgiving, as it is suddenly elapsing in a flash of occurrences. The Trectilla are beings of patience and observation. To rush is... uncomfortable.

* * *

April's door chime rang. For a fleeting moment, she thought it would be David.

"Yes?"

"Commander, it's Ensign Lannery. I've come to inform you that you have a visitor requesting to see you. It's a Trectilla," she stated with some hesitation.

"Please welcome her, or him, in."

Evelyn floated into the room with barely a whisper. April recognized her immediately and smiled. "Evelyn, it is good to see you."

April could not help but notice how she was covered in dust and lacked the luster of previous meetings.

"And I feel, gratified, to see you as well."

"Lannery, you can retire, I'll be fine. Thank you." April waited until the Ensign had left before resuming the discussion.

"And what can I presume is the purpose of your visit?" she asked, knowing all too well Trectilla did nothing without clear intent.

"I have been dispatched by our Elders. Time is of the essence, my dear April."

"It always is it seems, at least nowadays."

"It is the wish of the Elders to impress upon you the need to deliver that which you have promised."

"You mean the ships which your people wish to use to venture to another home? You do realize that such vessels require incredible effort. I've had my hands full bringing about peace in our home."

"This venture requires your immediate attention."

"Why? What can you tell me?"

"I have not the details. The Elders see many things, futures of many probabilities."

"And for all your powers, your capabilities, you are still unable to construct a starship. It seems so contrary."

"A contradiction in our abilities? I see no such conflict."

"Really? No contradiction?" April could not help but stare at the alien in disbelief.

How could she not see it? So much power, so much knowledge?

Evelyn was not compelled to repeat her statement, she hovered quietly, colors brief yet translucent.

"My projects are near complete here, you see above us the cable is growing close?"

"Yes, it is a strange device you are pursuing to construct."

April glanced up at the cable, now hanging so low it cast a shadow upon the enormous headquarters complex. The massive tether swayed ever so slightly in the upper skies, ominous in its very presence.

"This will open a doorway to the stars and make Ishaida the busiest spaceport of the galaxy, at least for a time until the other planets build their own." She realized she was rambling. Her vision was of no interest to her visitor.

"I will commence building your vessel very soon. Our army of engineers and tradespeople would value continued employment. I will oversee the plans for the vessel myself. But this cannot start until the cable reaches its anchor and the space elevator is operational. I will, however, start the building of components at both Jefferson and Cauputain." She turned her attention wholly to Evelyn. "This is what I can do. I will keep my word."

"Why do you use the singular instead of the plural form of the noun?"

"My intentions are to build one vessel, a very large one at that. Enough to house the population of your people."

"And when do your forecast this vessel will be ready?"

April shrugged. "I don't know. I've never built a ship of such magnitude. Anard-Bueller archives do have a variety of designs which I've reviewed to date. These vessels are incredibly complex in design, and so they are not easy to modify. We need to minimize any significant changes to the original plans. Therefore, I must choose correctly. Manufacturing is another problem. The volume of raw materials needed is staggering. I know Ishaida would be challenged to provide all that is needed, much less the other shipyards."

"Perhaps, the moon of Calandria would provide?"

April was surprised by the immediate response. *A planned anticipatory answer.*

"This moon can certainly provide the raw materials, to be sure. Having it in orbit would help with the schedule. I have already issued a build request for a container ship delivery of a portable robot factory from Earth. I expect the factory to arrive here in the next few months. If I can drop these containers on a raw material source like a moon, then set the robots to start replicating, we will have a workforce of enough breadth to begin the outer hull construction."

"You create machines en-masse to create another greater machine. And what of the device which we provided?"

"You mean the devices, Evelyn. We are still struggling to understand your calculations – or at least the meaning of your theorems. We are experiencing a problem – with meeting the power requirements."

"I see. I have been provided a key for you in this regard. It is a mere concept of implementation."

"OK, any ideas can help."

"You must build a third gateway, near to the sun, to harvest its energy and power the entangled gate devices to extend into the nether dimension."

"Nether dimension? Forget it, that detail's not important right now. I will pass the details of this onto our team."

"Very well. And I will ask you to convey the timelines of completion, once you are aware."

"Of course, I can arrange that. I also have a favor to ask..."

"A favor? A request with intent to repay in form?"

"Something like that. Evelyn, I have received multiple requests from Earth representatives for a visitation by one of your ambassadors, specifically to go to Earth. It is a request, you must understand, that may benefit human and Trectilla relations."

Colors fired within Evelyn's abdomen, and she seemed much less steady in her suspension.

"Evelyn?"

"I must apologize. Such thoughts are very troubling."

"You do understand the Trectilla are the first sentient race man has encountered. A visit by ambassadors of your people can raise awareness throughout the most influential members of the human race. It could even suppress those who instigated this aggression toward you. They will all see just how gentle and non-hostile your people are and that their fears are unfounded."

"I see. I do understand. I do not believe you understand what you are asking of this ambassador. What you ask, can introduce significant suffering. We have historic cases of incitation of madness."

"I don't get it. We'll ensure your people are safe. No one will be allowed to harass them."

"We are all connected, joined as one. To be apart from this state of being is very unsettling, but to do this for an extended period of time, at such as distance. It may not be possible."

"Can you not arrange for a group of your people to go? It will then be a small connection to others but a connection nonetheless. Like a pod. You must have done something like this before?"

"A pod? Perhaps. I will deliver your request to our Elders. Thank you for your consideration of our request."

With that, Evelyn promptly turned and exited, leaving April slightly exasperated.

Strange creatures.

She approached the AI console and activated it manually.

"Hello, AI Tiberious."

"Hello, April."

"I have news – we are starting a new project."

"Indeed? What would this new project entail?"

"We are starting construction on the Trectilla ship. I've already started some activities. You'll need to catch up to me. I've a file on it – you may access it under 'project ark'."

"Interesting, we about to construct something for the first time, yet again." AI Tiberious rubbed his hands together.

April chuckled. "Dramatic flair and everything. I'm sure the real Tiberious would have reacted the same way."

AI Tiberious grinned. "The game is afoot. The toys are coming out. You will also be happy to hear our progress on the 'project moongate' has moved to the next level."

"Next level?"

"Yes – we are beginning construction on some of the more rudimentary components. We'll have the remaining sorted soon I suspect. Such intrigue and excitement. It's sheer fun."

April looked perplexed. "Really, you, have fun?"

"Why not?"

She threw her hands up and walked to the window.

Why is it an AI can enjoy life better than her? What is she doing so wrong?

The opposite towers of the elevator buildings lit up a magnificent profile in a sky that was traced with wisps of clouds and flooded in hues of deep crimson and violet. A ship launched from the spaceport, momentarily flooding the skies with intense white. It bathed her apartment momentarily, exposing a disarray of clothing, and unkempt dishes. *You are a mess, April McThurn.*

The realization hit her hard, enough that she literally folded down onto the faux-wooden floors, feeling overwhelmingly weak as she sunk to her knees.

The shuttle grew dimmer, eventually fading to match the stars. As its last light faded, darkness overtook the unkempt corners of her apartment, hiding all of its ugliness from her eyes.

"Are you alright, dear?" asked her shimmering mentor.

She waited on her knees for a minute, finding solace by looking out at the night sky. "I think I need a drink."

"That didn't work very well for you last time," warned AI Tiberious. "Won't work now. What you really need is to talk to someone."

"Who? To you? A facsimile?"

"Sure, I'll listen. I can be very supportive, actually."

"Can you cure me, AI Tiberious? Can you heal me?"

"The pain you feel is self-inflicted."

"Pain." She laughed and rolled back onto the floor. "Every time I escape this feeling I do something to bring it back, twice as intense. There is no escape."

"You cannot continue to carry this burden of guilt. It weakens you, and will lead to other's deaths."

"Is that the best you can do? I mean really, Tiberious. I thought you had better programming at your disposal. Regardless, I'll be leaving soon."

"Leaving? May I hazard a guess?"

"Go ahead, Grand-Oracle. Your record remains untarnished to date."

"I shall then. You are planning to hunt down the leader of the dark pirate fleet."

She glanced over at him. At that very moment, his image blurred and then jumped slightly. *Was he doing that on purpose to annoy her?*

"You have it, Tiberious. I'm going once more into the abyss. But don't you worry, I do have some surprises ready for him this time."

"Why do you think you are ready to do this?"

"Who said I'm ready? I just want the sonofabitch dead, him and all his pirate psychopaths that have butchered all these innocent people."

"But why do you think you are ready?"

"I'm ready because I'll do whatever it takes."

"Yes, yes, you will, that much is true. You will enter into the breach where others would not dare. You will put yourself in harm's way where others would not have the courage. It will be unfortunate that you will be accompanied by your crew and your Captain."

April drank in his words, knowing full well she had no contrary argument. *Command the Tesla-Continuum to its ultimate doom, and she would be the killer of her own crew, of her ship, of David.*

"No, you're wrong. I won't take them with me. When my time comes, I'll be facing it alone."

"Perhaps, but will you have the good sense to pull back when the time comes? I just don't know. That's not how you're built."

"Good sense? Yes, I may be short on that, but I'll consider your words, AI Tiberious. It's good we talked."

"I am glad to be of service, April."

* * *

Another month passed. The details of the space elevator project, working on the 'project moongate' and 'project ark' did little to quench her desire to get back out into space.

The dark pirate fleet attack frequency had reduced down but had not stopped altogether. The pirate ships were quick to escape on arrival of SDF fleet ships, choosing to avoid conflict in favor of committing future crimes. Unescorted ships remained ripe targets and despite the SDF's best efforts, people continued to die.

The Tesla-Continuum was finally completed by the Cauputain shipyards, despite some significant cost overruns, which April found, through her Anard-Bueller resources, were instigated mainly by other competing corporations. She chose to overlook the situation in the interest of getting the final work complete.

The newly updated cruiser arrived at Ishaida's orbital spaceport with little fanfare, but not without the attention of a few SDF Captains who had heard about some interesting changes to the flagship. The Tesla-Continuum bore small resemblance to her original design, and her belly was expanded with a berth full of squadron fighters.

Captain David Ironstrike monitored the docking from the bridge, torn between the excitement of showing the completed ship to April and ensuring his newly repaired vessel was properly docked.

"Ship secured," reported the helm officer.

"Ready the shuttle. I'll be heading to the surface immediately."

"Aye, Sir."

Captain David Ironstrike gave the bridge one more pass with his eyes, a broad grin upon his face. The deck officers smiled back. "Our return flight was exceptional, excellent work to all of you."

Applause filled the bridge.

The newly refitted SDF flagship Tesla-Continuum had returned home.

* * *

A Debt Repaid

April stood quietly at the spaceport's receiving area, in full uniform dress, boots shone to gleam, cap tilted low to block out the streaming sun. The crowd split as it moved around her. Some recognized her and passed by with a murmur of whispers. Few if any, would dare approach her, seemingly imposing even without her officer guard, which seemed today to be missing. But that was only an illusion, as her private security ensured they were strategically positioned throughout the crowded lobby.

April ignored the others, busy with thoughts in her own head, careful to maintain her most rigid professional stance. Last time she had seen him she had not left him with kind words. She fought down the butterflies in her stomach and took long deep breaths.

This will work out. He'll forgive her.

She watched as a shuttle landed on the tarmac bearing the insignia of SDF and the designation of the flagship Tesla-Continuum in bright gold. A small group exited the side ramp and took the ground shuttle to the spaceport.

She suddenly felt nauseous but willed it to stop with every fiber of her being. *Hold yourself together.*

The group entered through the main doors laughing and joking amongst themselves. Captain David Ironstrike walked up to meet her with some of his deck officers in tow. They all saluted smartly, almost in perfect unison. April returned the salute.

"Grand Admiral," he nodded, his face wooden.

"Hello, Captain," she said, then tore her eyes away from him to focus on the others. "Please, consider yourselves relieved."

They all started away. "Not you, Captain. I mean, if you will stay for a moment?"

David waited until the others were around the corner, then grinned from ear-to-ear and grabbed her tight.

"You won't believe the Tesla-Continuum, even with the added weight she's more responsive than ever, all because of your enhanced burner redesign and the reactor upgrades!"

"Well, I am glad to see you too," she smiled back, letting out a long breath. "I didn't know what you would be like, I mean after you left. I didn't mean to be so cruel..."

"Don't worry about that. You have a lot of pressure on you. It's understandable, it may have taken me a couple days, but I let it go."

People around them were staring. David noticed and let go, stepping back. "Commander, perhaps it's best we assemble at the headquarters."

April cleared her throat, suddenly aware of the prying eyes. "Yes, good idea, Captain."

The trip back to her apartment seemed to last forever, as she was constantly barraged by officers, Anard-Bueller execs, and project managers. She did her best to fend them off and deferred one major issue after another.

As she opened the door to her apartment, David grabbed her and carried her in. They kissed, frantically pulling off each other's uniform in the process, to make love on the entry floor.

Afterward, April lay in his arms, feeling for the moment, at peace.

"You know, I'm not so sure we're doing a very good job keeping this quiet."

"Oh?" she teased "Why not?"

"For one, the Tesla-Continuum's crew all know, though no one ever says anything."

"Yes, but they're loyal," she countered.

"I'm sure someone may have suspected something at the spaceport."

"If they recorded it, maybe word would get out. I don't care," she rolled over. "I'm the damn boss, doesn't that account for anything?"

He laughed and watched as she trekked to the bathroom.

"You know, for a Grand Admiral, you have a beautiful body."

April laughed, enjoying the attention, and their brief intimacy. It never lasted long enough.

The next day they both readied themselves, yet again, in full uniform dress. This time they helped each other and packed bags for an extended stay.

"It's time to go hunting, David."

"Yes, Commander, I agree."

He pulled his sidearm and checked the safety. "Just in case. Where's yours?"

"I ah... I don't carry those things."

"You may need to if we ever get boarded."

"No, I don't need to, as I have no desire to live with the results. Besides, I have a full protection detail. What do you have?"

He laughed. "Fair enough. Let's go shut down some pirates."

* * *

The crew looked smart in formal uniform dress, and their numbers had increased - the additional squadron pilots and extra gunners, plus an additional nuclear engineer.

The ship also looked exceptional. The enhancements had made it more powerful and significantly more dangerous. April took the time to review each of the changes in detail, was given personal tours by each of the officers in charge. All this managed to burn away the quiet waiting time as they made their way to Cauputain's outer belts.

This time, however, they were not alone. Seven cruisers with handpicked battle-seasoned Captains were accompanying the flagship, and each with their own compelling reasons to settle the score. All the ships had holds and corridors filled with ordnance to launch into the belt region, as they fully expected a long and difficult engagement. April knew half the ammunition would be spent on ineffectual asteroid collisions and had planned for the excess waste.

She knew they would be waiting for them. This would not be an easy battle. They did not have the advantage.

"We are 150 million km from the outer edge of the belt, Commander."

"Open a channel to all ships, all crew."

"Aye, Sir."

"Today I will call upon you, the Guardians of the Security Divisional Fleet, to step into harm's way and destroy an enemy of the people: known killers, thieves, and criminals who are responsible for the deaths of our own brothers and sisters. This will be a dangerous incursion. They will be waiting for us. Do not hesitate, do not waiver from your purpose. I have confidence in your abilities, I believe in your courage."

She signaled to close the channel.

Probably not her best inspirational speech, but that was not her specialty.

"Deploy the scanning probes. I want to know what's out there."

Each ship was positioned as per their previous approach plan, and each launched their probes into the belt. The fast-moving robotic devices were easily capable of navigating through the maze of the pirate's realm while mapping crucial routes through the moving labyrinth.

April watched as the data streamed in, slowly building a 3D picture of the region in the holographic navigational display. This process would take hours.

That's OK. She was patient. No need to move in unprepared. No need to be reckless.

The fleet approached the belt, decelerated and stopped, forming a lethal wall of offensive force. She double-checked the scan images. No evidence of any adversarial presence. Soon the probes would be passing by the asteroid 'Amaria's Sumblifare', and what would they encounter there?

"Ready all battlestations," she ordered, offhandedly. It took her officers by surprise, and they scrambled to meet the command.

"Com, relay readiness state from all fleet ships."

"Aye, Sir."

"Excuse me, Commander," interrupted Captain Ironstrike.

"Yes?"

"I'm not sure why you just ordered the fleet to battle readiness."

"Neither am I," she admitted. "We came here with intent. Does it matter?"

"No, Commander."

"We've a positive from the 'Ameria' asteroid, small G and F class vessels, nothing more," reported Black.

"They've gone," commented the Captain.

"Our stern scanner readings picking up anything?"

"Negative, Commander," offered Ridgeline.

She gave David an extended look. *Read my mind, David. Just trust me.*

David took the hint and decided on the side of safety. "Com, relay to the Pernagesion and the Entrago to reverse-loop."

"Aye, Sir. Confirmed, they are flipping."

"Scanners are almost through the belt region and starting to thin out," reported monitoring officer.

"We have anything at all?" queried the Captain.

"Nothing of significance. Multiple inhabited asteroids and small class ships. No vessels matching pirate ship specifications. No sign of the enemy, Sir," replied the officer.

David stayed quiet. April gave him a quick look ready to debate but dropped it given his placid manner. She knew he thought this was a waste of time. They had escaped.

She started back into her inspection of the navigation display.

"Officer Ridgeline, I see this area here is becoming increasingly dense at that location. Redirect the probes to that area."

"And by the way, Captain Ironstrike. Here, we have positive contact, and here, and here. All mining asteroids, some actively mined, others serving as havens for the miners. These are all potential areas for hiding a larger vessel."

"Agreed. One vessel, possibly two at most. But they'd be spread out to the point of being ineffectual to engage. Not an ideal situation unless their intent is only to hide."

"No, this Commander of theirs is arrogant. He's not going to hide from a small fleet like us."

"Very well," offered the Captain, "We've just not found their lair as yet, then. Monitoring, pull up the Cauputain star maps from the archives, everything we have on record, no matter how old, transfer the files to the science station." David promptly stepped over to help the monitoring officer.

"Just find me those bastards," she directed, more annoyed than any of them of their current situation.

Hours passed with no results. The search team located three other possible areas, although April disliked each one. She was sure there would be no doubt when they found it.

"Captain Verage is hailing from the Aarcona, asking for you Commander."

"Put him on the main."

"Hello, Admiral April McThurn."

"Captain, what can I do for you?"

"Well, I'm just curious about your plans. We've been looking for some time now, to no avail."

"Agreed. We may not find them today, or tomorrow, but we will find them. I intend to stay out here until we do."

"This waiting is difficult on the crews, perhaps we could relax the battle readiness stance?"

"Captain, we shall maintain stations until I see a compelling reason to cancel our stance, no sooner. I do not have an answer for you on the when or where. Please ensure you are ready when I call upon you."

Verage nodded. "Of course, Admiral."

April dropped the channel unceremoniously.

Captain David Ironstrike moved in close. "Little hard on him, don't you think?"

"No... well, maybe," she admitted. "Regardless, we stand ready."

"I think you may want to see what we've found off some old navigation records. Interestingly enough they predate the colonization of Cauputain."

Ridgeline pulled up the ancient records. Maps this old lacked the high resolution and detail of the more modern ones, seemed crude in comparison. David panned over to an area nearer to the current belt region. "There happens to be another dense area of the belt here, undocumented in the later surveys for some reason. I suspect this area has been intentionally left out."

"By who?"

"Certain groups that may benefit from not publishing this information, of course; that is the who."

"How far?"

"Approximately, 60 million km – that-a-way," he pointed to the port side.

She searched the old map. Yes, there was definite potential here.

"We need to pull all the Captains together. We need a strategy. Captain, can you coordinate?"

"Aye, Commander, I'll request they convene here."

April called over to Black. "Lieutenant, it's time we started thinking in three dimensions."

"I'm already there, Commander, never really stopped," he quipped back with a smile.

The Captains all came on deck and met on the Tesla-Continuum's bridge. It was the best place where they could lay out a plan with a full display of their possible tactics.

April scanned their faces. The group represented the most experienced and effective Captains of the fleet. There were eight of them in all, Verage Isaac of the Aarcona, Captain Kennaith Alder of the Entrago, Captain Jericho Kanneshe of the Pernagesion, Captain Karen McThurn of the Gandolf-Auricia, Captain Nadir Fareside of the Maelstrom, Captain Nicolas Brittock of the Perthena's Bounty, Captain Jack Warlock of the FireHaven, and closing up the group to the rear was Captain David Ironstrike.

"We have a base plan," she announced. "But I want your opinions. Want to ensure we do this quickly and effectively. I don't want any ships to escape and wreak havoc later."

"Of course, there is always a possibility they are not docked there and are currently on the hunt somewhere," offered David.

"We do not know for sure the state of the situation, but I have a gut feeling we have them here, this time," April countered. "Here's the latest plan." She pulled up a holographic of the area and the proposed placement of the ships.

The Captains moved in closer. They were out here for a purpose and eager to engage.

"We'll need to swing way out and around that pile of rock. So I'll do it," offered Jack, who was usually the first to action.

"That's some tricky maneuvering. If'n you need to see da whites of dere eyes 'fore you blast'em into hell," said Nicolas. "'Tis probably best Jack and I overshoot and come back in. Will take some time an' am sure we want this simultaneous-like."

"Yes, I have the key positions signified in red," admitted April. "They are far enough out to allow for overlap on scans from one ship to the next. No gaps. As soon as you reach coordinates, you dispatch the deep scanners. I suspect some of them might be destroyed, but I want that whole system mapped out in minutes."

"They'll either cut and run or start shooting. I'd suspect the latter, as we're out in the middle of the vacuum with no cover, they'll have the advantage," warned Verage.

"So we get'em before they can return fire. That area's not that big, but plenty lethal for a ship to stray in unwelcomed," offered Zen. "I'll take my chances out there in that vacuum. No surprises out there. Suggest we also start with the big pounders right off. They'll have some asteroids outfitted through that mess. We'll not get through with the cannon. Will make some noise and bump about some of them there rocks, get them scrambling to adjust."

"I expect they'll have a number of asteroids hollowed out and impervious to cannon fire. If we can locate bay doors or any other openings that's where we'll hit'em." April commented. "We will also need to consider this mess of rocks will all be in motion."

Verage contemplated, then spoke out. "Tricky shooting from a distance. May take a few minutes to figure out a firing solution. I'd suggest initial salvo in any opening we consider an escape route. Then we do the sniper business. Bottom line, we are going in shooting and asking questions later. Do we really want to do that? You OK with this, Commander? In firing on these asteroids, there's a strong possibility there be families in there."

All eyes all turned to April. "Alright, let's measure this up first. Make sure we have a threat. We need to assess fast. But no warning hails. We recognize any of those ships, we start hitting – and yes, we continue to pound them until every last one of them is a twisted hunk of metal, or we run out of ammunition. I fully suspect this is where the pirates are. Just in case you are wondering, their track record of spacing crews and travelers leave them on the no mercy list."

"Officer Black, can you assign each ship positions, and Captains, please advise my officer on your preferences. We're moving in. I will personally give the green light to start dumping the pounders, so hold off unless... unless you are fired upon. We'll hit'em enough to knock out most of the problem areas, then I'll dispatch our fighter squadron. They'll be able to encroach where we can't. Our fighters are too maneuverable to lock in on."

"You got enough firepower on those little buggers to make a difference?" asked Jack.

April nodded. "They've enough. Good luck, gentlemen, let's secure this space for good."

* * *

Del Antonio Stride was in the ship bay of his asteroid when the first salvos hit. Alarms were firing off all over, and he had just managed to reach the locked door when a torpedo plowed into the bay gates. He scrambled through the labyrinth of plating and stairs to reach the control room, becoming angrier with each step he made.

Damn that bitch! Damn her to come into our backyard and try this shit.

His tactical team seemed to be wavering around in confusion. He yelled at them and slammed the intercom. "All ships, pull in and exchange fire. Don't engage out there. I want them to come see us. Where the hell did they come from, you falling asleep or screwing around out here?"

"No, Sir. They just came out of nowhere. I didn't even have a trace lock on them. They jumped right in from superluminal."

"Open up the damn perimeter turrets, will you? We should be hitting back already."

"Bringin' them up. Couple of em's been damaged."

"That's just great. And I can't get to the Deathstalker because the shuttle bay's been hit. Get a direct line to the bridge."

Guy Mercer answered, a deep scowl on his face. "Well, at least you are out there. Start returning fire for fuck's sake. You got a lock on anybody?"

"Too far out. Figure they are planning to keep pounding us from out there. Don't matter if they hit us, they just need to get close. No sign of them coming in."

"Shit. OK. If we can't draw them in, let's give'em a little taste of what we got. They'll run out of ammo before we do."

* * *

A barrage of torpedoes was coming toward them, and laser cannon were pelting their hulls from multiple sources throughout the belt.

"They have some firepower. Looks like turrets located on the asteroids all through the belt. Nice surprise. Some big guns," commented Captain Ironstrike.

April stayed calm, watching it all play out.

"Target all sources, including the ships. Captain, prepare to launch squadron fighters."

April started off the deck.

"Commander, where are you going?"

"You have the bridge, Captain." She headed down to the fighter squadron bay, passing a few confused crew in the process. She had made it to the entrance of the bay before Nearson intercepted her, out of breath.

"Look, Admiral, you can't fly one of these things."

"You'd be surprised what I can fly, Richard." She tried to push past.

"I'm responsible for your safety."

"I relieve you of that responsibility."

"Sorry, not that easy."

"I think it is. Get out of my way."

"Admiral, if you go out there and get yourself killed…"

She grabbed his face in her hands. "It's ok, Richard. This is war. Just do what you do when I get back."

He took a second to make up his mind, then stepped aside, and she moved through quickly, intent upon getting into her flight suit. The other squadron pilots were almost done. She ignored the uncomfortable stares and stripped down.

She was just about to twist on her helmet when David came in.

"What are you doing? We are in the middle of a battle."

"I can say the same thing to you, Captain. You need to be on the bridge. Just keep us under cover, hotshot. I'm flying."

A report came into David's earpiece. "Increase the proximity sensitivity on the torpedoes." He ordered, clearly irritated by the distraction.

"Look, you need to be on the bridge, with me."

"No, you need to be there, this is your ship. The fleet knows what to do. And I haven't rescinded my command by stepping off that bridge, Captain. My commands will just be coming from a different vantage point."

She said it, but she had no intention of making fleet strategy calls from out there. They didn't need her.

"April, it's still too hot out there. At least give us some time to shut down their offenses."

Engines blasted as the first of the squadron fighters launched, drowning out her last words, and shaking the deck. "We're already launching. Look, I gotta go."

"Just don't get yourself killed." He leaned over and kissed her.

"The same to you, Captain David Ironstrike."

She ducked into the corridor and ran for the launch bay. The ship sat idle but prepped, and the flight mechanic gave her the all clear with a thumbs up. She was in the seat and locked down in seconds. She ran through the launch sequence, and the engines throbbed in a deep vibration. In seconds, she was thrown back into the seat as the fighter roared out into space.

She had read somewhere the first few seconds after launch were the most dangerous. As the fighter broke free of the bay, the situation came into focus very quickly. Laser blasts were tracing along the cruiser's hull, the hot plasma just missing her starboard wings, and above her, return fire was being blasted in a staccato from the Tesla-Continuum's port cannon. She had to fight the controls to veer clear of the massive streams of plasma, or else be incinerated.

A quick adjustment via retinal controls and the flight navigation computer found their target. The squadron was going for the largest cruiser, deep in the belt. She pushed to maximum acceleration to meet up with the rest of the squadron, easing into the gap left for her.

Immediately on her right was the squadron leader. She could make out his profile in the cockpit.

"Good to see you could join us, Red 5."

She was Red 5. The intent was there alright. Nothing like being called out on a late launch. Should she respond? No. No use apologizing. Nobody was interested.

"Standby to receive my navigation plan, everyone. Broadcasting and locked," he announced.

Each ship announced receipt, April called out. "Red 5, confirmed."

Seven ships in all, each of them having something to prove.

On the bridge of the Tesla-Continuum, David watched the formation of fighters move closer to the enemy. "Captain," reported Officer Edge, "squadron leader transmitted tactical. They're moving in on the cruiser."

"That figures, take on the most dangerous target. Officer Daz, make sure we do NOT hit our own but we provide sufficient cover. Understand?"

"Understood, Sir. Sir, we are losing a high degree of ordnance against the asteroids."

"We need to move in closer, Helm. Officer Edge, pass on the order to the fleet. Everyone needs to stay in step."

"Officer Cross, coordinate in step with the others."

"Daz, I want some firing solutions on that big bastard to take out her torpedo launch bays. Can you do that?"

"Aye, Sir. Entering solution for the torpedoes."

"Did you pass that solution to the fighters?"

Daz shook his head. "Not yet."

"Well do it, damn it!"

Daz scrambled to relay the data to the squadron just as they launched.

* * *

April had the main ship in sight and her cannon locked on. It would be no use blasting her hull with their arbitrary fire, as it was fully reinforced and shielded. They had to get behind her main cannon and be very precise with their shots.

She ran the schematics of the target cruiser model via her flight computer, flipping through multiple specifications at a time, trying to locate any power feeds along the hull.

There had to be a weakness here.

Her ship suddenly shook as it took a minor hit. The cruiser was already attempting to realign its cannon to spray them. She readjusted course and ran the diagnostics. She cursed at the diversion and resumed searching.

An alarm sounded on the navigation display. She had to acknowledge. *Damn it. She was running out of time.*

She relayed the news to the other squadron ships, just in case someone didn't receive it. "Red Squadron 5 adjusting course 30 degrees. We have incoming from the Tesla-Continuum." They diverted just in time to watch a swarm of white blurs fire by.

"The boys are warming up the soup for us," she stated through the com. "Three minutes out. We've got their attention. It's going to get rough."

The plan was easy, move in close, destroy any and all offensive capabilities and if possible, destroy communications and/or disable the main drive. This would take multiple passes. It was possible some of them wouldn't make it.

The squadron entered into the maelstrom of enemy laser fire, all ships broke into auto response mode. Cannon blasted from all directions, the smaller pirate vessels were moving to engage.

April made multiple adjustments at once to avoid tracer fire from the gunship. The large vessel screamed by in a blur. For some reason that didn't scare her. She was in control of her own ship. No one else was in danger from her decisions, just her. Except that wasn't true either. She still had to support her squadron, be part of the team.

"Keep it tight, everyone," said the squadron leader. "Don't divert from our target."

They had reached the cruiser. Auto turrets were firing at them from all directions. A blast jarred her stern. As she fought to bring it back, another explosion came on her port side rocking her ship sideways. She pulled the yoke and hit the auxiliary boosters, struggling desperately to regain control and bring the fighter in close against the cruiser's hull. The fighter responded in time. The massive ship's cannon turret was firing just above them, so close she could feel the heat radiate through the cockpit window. If it tipped just a few degrees, it would obliterate the lot of them.

Focus on the objective.

Something came up in the previous spec image. It took a half-second to roll back and find it, but it was there. A quick transfer to navigation display allowed her to magnify a new target. And there it was - a small gap between the mounting plates and the rotating turret base.

"Red 5, I have a firing solution, transmitting," she announced to whoever was listening, just in case she didn't make it. She engaged the automatic laser cannon. The first few glanced off the base, but others found their target. In seconds, the massive turret shut down, but not before tipping ever so slightly, and instantly incinerating Red 7. The bluish-red-orange explosion lit up her cockpit, and it took a moment for her to realize what at happened.

Damn it. Why did he have to be there?

They swooped around the dead turret and ran another scan looking for secondary targets. Multiples came up. She ran the targeting solutions and locked them in.

"Red squadron, we have a gunship on our tail," announced the squadron leader. "Red 2 and 3 - break off and engage."

April remained focused on the next target - the hydrogen intakes for the plasma burners. Taking these out would disable the main burners, possible cause a chain reaction which would take out the superluminal drive as well.

"Red 5 you are in direct line of fire of the gunship. Pull up."

"Negative. I have my target in range."

She flipped to rear view just in time to see a flash of plasma from a laser cannon. It hit her rear burner plates and bounced off harmlessly.

She launched a missile to the stern.

"There, swallow that you sonofabitch," she said.

Another shot, this one blew out a corner piece of the burner deflector, and the fighter slammed against the hull, belly sliding with a deafening scraping squeal. She fought with the controls to pull up, managing to separate from the hull as she flew past an auto turret, and clipped the guns with a sickening crunch.

Then she was off into the void, the cruiser shooting well past her. Only it was her fighter that was moving, not the other way around. Alarms lit up her panel. A quick pass to acknowledge, and another few critical seconds to reroute power, and she was back up. But her ship was badly damaged. Maintaining her course now required considerable counter pressure on the controls, and the vibration was incredible.

"Red leader, this is Red 5. I've taken a hit but still have some control."

A gunship passed her and exploded, leaving a gaping hole in its starboard side. It crashed into, then slid along the cruiser's hull, ripping into it and tearing open sections.

"Red 3 - We've taken out the gunship!"

Targeting alarms rang out. She straightened the ship enough to fire two more missiles. Each found their target. But she realized a hair too late that she needed to adjust course.

Oh, shit.

The resulting explosion emanating from the cruiser forced tons of twisted metal and explosive plasma outward, catching April's fighter squarely underneath and repelling her away from the cruiser, careening and twisting. She fought to pull it back under control, but the damage to her burners had somehow increased with the hit, and it made the job all the more difficult.

"Red Leader: Red 5 has severely compromised navigational ability, unsure if I can be effective any longer."

"Red 5, disengage and return. Your last target disabled the big bitch. You did your job. Good work. Now go home."

April did not know whether she should feel relieved or angry. Maybe she could still do more, but with the burner plate damage, she may not even make back to the Tesla-Continuum. If it was bad enough, it could burn through and be the end of her.

She plotted a course back and attempted to maintain it, compensating with systematic shots from external boosters. It was tricky, took some precise timing, but doable.

A new alarm sounded, this time not related to battle but to the life support systems. The fighter had a leak, and she was venting from below. She sealed her helmet and diverted all life support to her suit. It was more an annoyance than a danger but revealed the explosion hit her ship harder than she thought.

OK. I can do this.

Bitter realization followed. This was the end of her independent escape. For a moment, she considered it, shutting down her systems and coasting on to oblivion. But that wouldn't happen either. They'd come and get her. There was only one real escape.

The fighter's tactical caught something in the belt. A fleeting image – another cruiser. *No. That would have to wait.*

* * *

Chapter 27

The monitoring officer reported in. "I have the Commander inbound, Sir. Her ship is badly damaged."

Captain Ironstrike checked the navigation holograph. "Navigation, please project her course."

A wavy, dotted line came up on the navigation display. "Her ship is demonstrating some erratic behavior, I've tried to take that into account."

"Does she really have to run through the hottest region of exchange of fire? She won't survive that. Helm, we're moving in. Navigation, plot me a solution."

"Captain," interrupted his weapons officer. "If we get the fleet any closer we'll be opening up the risk of infiltration of a torpedo."

"No. It will just be the Tesla, all other ships remain in position."

"Aye, Sir."

The Tesla-Continuum crept closer into the engagement, and with it, the intensity of the exchange of fire increased. This was counter to Captain Ironstrike's plan and in effect, was putting April's crippled fighter in more danger.

"Damn it. Weapons, focus your attention on those two gunships and find that other source inside the belt. We need to end their offensive capabilities."

The Tesla-Continuum brought into service its secondary turrets, doubling its intensity of fire at half the range. In moments, the two gunships were overwhelmed, succumbing to the relentless barrage of hot plasma.

"We have a lock on another cruiser."

"Firing salvo."

"Focus all cannon on that target," ordered the Captain, knowing full well, their increased reactor size allowed them to output more energy than any of the other ships, enemy or otherwise. "Helm, bring her about to cover the Commander's fighter."

David waited impatiently, pacing the deck.

"Com?" Officer Edge shook his head.

He glanced over to Richard. "Perhaps you should go down there, Mr. Nearson."

"The Commander acknowledged, Captain. Proceeding to dock."

He let out a long breath. "Get a medical officer to the bay."

"Sustain continuous salvos on that cruiser and Com, relay new target to Red Squadron."

"Captain, the other ships are also moving in."

"I did not request that."

"Incoming message from FireHaven, Captain."

"Open channel."

"Don't expect you to have all the fun, Ironstrike," came Captain Jack Warlock's gruff voice.

"Why is it I am catching transmissions from Red Squadron that are remarkably similar to our lassie. Where is she?"

"Why, she is on board, Captain. Just detained."

"Keep her safe, Captain. Feel free to pull back. We have this."

By now, all eight ships had now encroached into the belt region, sharing space with spinning hunks of rocks the size of mountains. Captain Ironstrike was very aware of this, probably more than any of them.

He stepped up closer to the display, watching what remained of the pirate fleet desperately struggle to escape.

"What's the latest enemy count, Officer Edge?"

"Seven or eight. Not sure on the last report. We have confirmation that four remain operational."

"We're nice and close now. Should be able to see them hiding in here. So what surprises do they have for us now?" he said aloud.

"Back out!" ordered April, marching up the bridge, still in her flight suit. "They have traps in here, I'm sure of it."

"It's good to see you've made it back in one piece," replied Captain Ironstrike, a little tersely.

April caught herself. "Yes, the ship took on some damage, had to pull out. How's Red Squadron?"

"Still inflicting damage as planned. Found another cruiser. They're finishing the job. We were watching you. Seems you kept up well on your piloting skills, Commander. You successfully disabled an A-class cruiser."

"It was educational," she replied, not wanting any more attention paid to that. The others were still out there risking their lives.

"Why's the fleet so close? I wanted them to stay back."

Captain Ironstrike scanned the navigation holographic. All the SDF cruisers were now engaged slightly within the belt. "Seems too late for that, Commander. We've already put our toes into the water."

"I don't like this at all. They're baiting us. If I was them, I'd be hiding ordnance throughout this maze. I'd have explosive charges behind every asteroid, and ensure they'd be able to take down a cruiser."

"We have to close this down sooner or later."

"We will. But no need to be in a rush. Stick to plan. We don't go in, yet. We have them surrounded. We pelt them with everything we have."

"And if we can't reach the targets?"

"We flush out whatever is left with the fighters."

"Look," he pointed to the navigational display. "We've crushed their offensive capabilities. All we need to do is trek in there and blow them to hell. We can do this quick."

"No, Captain. I was serious with that order. We stay outside. Hit them from all angles, wherever we can calculate a solution."

"It gets too dense in there, we can't reach them."

"Not true. When things shift in there, it opens up windows. Then we hit them with our most powerful ordnance."

"Our largest pounders have little effect in here against those hunks of rock. We need something much more deadly."

April thought on that for a moment. *If they were able to utilize some of that gate technology.* She took a mental note, more work for Tiberious.

"Inform our captains to back out to our planned coordinates and resume with our original plan."

Captain Ironstrike passed the order. The Captain's listened, although grudgingly. The SDF fleet eased its way clear and proceeded on their systematic circumnavigation of the belt, scanning, and firing as the opportunity provided. They were given a simple directive, if they find a shot, take it. Maximize the damage, minimize the risk.

The process was slow and cumbersome, but safe.

* * *

"Three days we've been at this, Commander. We're running low on ammunition. Most of us are out of our heaviest ordnance."

April felt annoyed as if Captain Fareside was blaming her for their position. "Are they destroyed, Nadir? Do you have evidence that we've eliminated their offensive capability?"

"No. I cannot ascertain what I cannot see. We need to get in there and confirm."

The open conference displayed all the captains on video on the primary display. April kept herself within camera shot but kept one eye on the navigation holographic. Nothing was moving in there, at least for now they were quiet.

What is he waiting for?

"Alright, we can suspend all fire, let Red Squadron run a pass. Monitor for any offensive attempts and locate the sources. In the meantime, we wait for more ammunition to be delivered. I'm not endangering our cruisers in that mess."

"No," returned Captain Warlock. "Not yet. Naddir is too eager. The dangers are the same as day one. I'd expect their counteroffensives are fully automated and active. We need to dump in more fire as yet."

"Agreed," added Captain Brittock. "We wait on resupply, and in the meantime, we ensure we maintain enough ordnance in the case they decide to make a run or an offensive move."

"Exactly," April commented. "It is possible they'll try something. They may make the mistake of thinking we are out of ammunition. But it is also possible they are too damaged to attempt anything. Either way, we remain on alert and prepared."

"We estimate there are at least three other cruisers deployed. Maybe they will make a run toward us," added Brittock.

"No, they'll not endanger any capability they have left. Whatever ships we've missed they'll turn up. They've nowhere to go. We'll take the rest of them down one by one."

The restock freighter arrived the following day, with the SDF AirCovner as an escort. Captain Johnathan Baresky hailed the Tesla-Continuum on their arrival. April was the officer on deck when they arrived.

"Commander, Captain Baresky is requesting an open channel with Captain Ironstrike. He stated they are old friends."

"Really? I'll talk with him."

"Hello, Commander, I'm a bit surprised. Was expecting David."

"Good to see you, Captain. I'm afraid David's off shift right now. So how do you know Captain Ironstrike?"

"Well, Commander, that's a loaded question. I've known David since he was a little guy. I'm his uncle you see. He's always been a go-getter. Doesn't surprise me he managed to land the sweet job of Flagship Captain, if you don't mind my sayin', Ma'am."

"'Course not. Always good to hear stories about David. Perhaps you have some time to come over. I do believe I have some very old scotch that I think may still be good. Have yet to crack that bottle open."

"Scotch? A fine drink. Of course, I can. I understand unloading is quite a slow process. I'd be glad to join you."

Captain David Ironstrike arrived four hours later to relieve April only to find Helm Officer Cross in command.

"Where's the Commander?"

"Meeting with Captain Baresky in the officer's forward lounge I believe," replied Cross.

"Johnathan Baresky?"

She nodded.

"You're not relieved until I return." David turned and headed to the lounge. He found them laughing and sharing a drink.

"Captain, did you have a good rest?" asked April.

"Yes, somewhat," he responded, eyes darting from one to the other.

"April and I have been talking a bit about you."

"About me?"

"Yes, been catching up on some stories of when you were younger. Some quite funny ones at that." She laughed along with Jonathan.

David's face turned a bit red. "What stories?"

April laughed all the harder. "What are you worried about? Maybe having some incriminating family tales is a good thing. At least you have some family. Sit, have a scotch. Let's enjoy some time as it's fleeting enough."

"Well, I have Cross in command right now. She may resent being kept on deck this long."

"Cross? She loves every minute. Sit down. Unloading is not scheduled to be complete for hours as yet."

She poured him a scotch. "Special batch, apparently."

"I'll attest to that," Johnathan stated with a laugh. "Let's talk about little Davy's first love." They all laughed at that.

* * *

"How many's left?"

"Four gunships. Everything else blown to shit. Their strikers are coming in every hour and wreaking havoc. At least Anvil is still on their run."

The small group of pirates sat around the immense table in Del Stride's great room.

"So what's the plan, Stride?" asked one of the group.

"Survival. Keep the gunships hidden. We need to get mobile once they leave."

"Ya mean if'n they leave. They keep peltin' us from outside, the damned cowards. Our traps were useless. Their strikers are too small and fast to be caught."

"What d'ya mean? I caught one!" corrected Peltier.

"Shut the hell up Peltier, you only got the one. It's a damned miracle ya was able to nail that one with that incindee-ary."

"Maybe I'll show you a miracle ya won't forget." Peltier had his hand on his blaster.

"What the fuck?" Interrupted Del. "We're down to a handful of men, more'n likely only a few out there still kicking in those derelicts we once called ships, and you want to fight amongst yourselves? The enemy is out there, in case you haven't noticed!"

Del pulled his antique blaster from its holster. "You know why I like this weapon? Because it's simple and it's effective. There's no doubting what it can do."

He swung the barrel back and forth, the others moved away slowly.

"Look Del, no harm done here. We've a lot of work to do once this is over. Ya need us." One could hear the desperation in Peltier's voice.

Del just laughed and holstered the violent weapon. "Ain't nothing wrong with simplicity, boys. So our plan is simple, we wait'em out. When they leave, we pull things together. Then we go back after that bitch and roast her alive in her tin can."

"Go after her with what? Ain't nothin' left."

"You leave that to good ol' Del. I'm expecting a shipment soon. When it arrives, we'll be set. In the meantime boys, let's drink."

He slammed a bottle on the table and the motley bunch roared.

* * *

The special pirate extermination group of the SDF arrived back at Ishaida with little fanfare. News of the destruction of the pirate fleet did not go unnoticed, however. Merchants and corporations alike intensified their cargo and passenger liner travel to near double the previous level. Over the next few months, a new stability was attained throughout the extranist systems, and the Security Divisional Fleet patrols became a common and relied upon entity.

Instead of destroying aggressors, SDF ships were in the business of rescuing vessels in distress, and settling disputes via a common law – of which Ishaida became the central facilitating entity to house the 'Law of the Protectorate.'

A larger shift presented itself for April. No longer was she required to travel on board the SDF Flagship, as her ability to coordinate fleet activities from on-planet via the fleet control deck enabled her to remain at the Anard-Bueller headquarters, and monitor an extended network of shipping lanes and travelers. The space between the planets became more traversable, and Ishaida became a critical stopover for travelers.

* * *

April had not been there to see the great anchoring of the space elevator cable, but the event was projected across the extranist systems. She had to witness it while on patrol with the Tesla-Continuum. Just the same, it was a joyous event on board. The whole tethering sequence was transmitted across the void to all the planets, and also throughout the Tesla-Continuum, including the various lounge areas and private quarters.

April chose to spend the time with her officers. David joined her in the lounge to witness the final connections and the initial rise of the first elevator into orbit. It did not go completely without issue, as a few delays occurred after the anchoring of the cable. The elevator stalled for a number of hours just 10 meters above the surface, but the problems were eventually resolved and as it resumed its rise, Ishaida officially became accessible to superluminal cruiser travelers.

What began as an engineering triumph became a national holiday, not unfamiliar to the celebrations of old Earth's New Year's events. It also set the stage for Anard-Bueller's new engineering projects, landing contracts for both Jefferson and Cauputain and in an unprecedented move, a very lucrative contract with Earth. This was not the end of the Anard-Bueller's profit shift. Years of constant investment had driven Anard-Bueller to its lowest profit margins in centuries, and April had fought to maintain a level of trust and integrity within the board and the executive offices. If it had not been for AI Tiberious, she would have lost her position the first year, however, now her critics had all but dissolved into the crevices where they belonged.

What they didn't know was this was just the beginning of April's reign of control. To her, the rules of conduct and limitations of possibilities were only suppressed by her own creativity. The elevator was an old idea, and moving forward she would be delivering on something not yet thought possible. The celebrations of the space-elevator would pale in comparison. But this took intensive planning, details, time, and unfortunately left little for Captain David Ironstrike.

April could sense they were in trouble. David's patrols were extending far too long, and when he managed to arrange furlough, April was lost in the depths of HQ engineering levels working on projects he did not have clearance to access.

They were moving apart.

As April worked herself closer to the point of exhaustion, she realized certain things were less important to her, and certain things should not be missed. She left work to call David from her quarters.

"Hello, April." David acknowledged, face wooden.

"David. I need you."

His response was more of a surprise than anything, "Hang on. I need to transfer this to my quarters. Give me a sec, OK?"

"Alright, what's the matter? What's going on?"

"Finally everything is falling into place. We are building Ishaida into a world we knew it could be. I am able to step away from the violence and the death, but I cannot step away from you. No matter what I accomplish, it leaves me empty without you with me. Do you understand?"

"I do. But every time I managed to get away, you were working. I thought you were ending us."

"No. I wasn't. I'm not like everyone else, you know that. When I dive in, I sometimes drown in my work. But when I come back up – I need you. You are my air, David."

David smiled. "I've been called a lot of things, but air?" He laughed, and so did she. She wiped away a tear. "I want to share special times with you, like the day the elevator was anchored."

"Yeah, we had a good time then."

"The Tesla-Continuum is scheduled to dock at Ishaida in a little over a week's time. I'll come by then. We can work this out, you know. I'll be your air, April."

Something distracted him. "Looks like we have a distress call. Need to check in later. I love you. See you soon, April."

She took a breath. A week.

And time did fly.

April worked through the specifics of what the moon would do to Ishaida with the gateway project's geophysicist. She had an idea why the Trectilla wanted the moon, but there was much more hidden below the surface on this, not so dissimilar to the scroll provided to them on the basics of the gateway.

The geophysicist's name was Helen Aurolia. She had been a native of Earth as a child and had relocated to Cauputain with her parents in her adolescent years. She had moved herself and her family to Ishaida to work on the elevator project and had then been reassigned to the gateway project. Initially, she had fought vehemently to stay on with the elevator project until she was brought up to speed on what her new project really was. Few of the team understood the full extent of the project and even fewer had the necessary security clearance.

Helen was somebody April could discuss in earnest the details of the project, and for all their interactions, she found a steadfast friend.

"So let me understand this, Helen. Because I will need to explain this to our members of government in a very precise manner. I'm not so sure they're going to appreciate the effect of this change. I do think they will fear it."

"Why not just do it? Blame the aliens or something."

April laughed. "If something goes wrong? A mess up of the proportions we are talking would not be an easy explanation, regardless if we blame the aliens."

"OK. Well, let's just break it down to the basics. Here's why we need to do this, why the Trectilla have requested us to do this: 1. We need to rebuild the magnetic field around Ishaida. This is critical to ensuring our atmosphere is not stripped away by the emanating coronal winds off Ishaida's sun. 2. We need to reinvigorate and expand the internal core, which will, in turn, warm the planet internally. This will drive moisture out to the crust, restart tectonic plate activity, and also introduce sources of more complex gases and minerals onto the surface, essentially supporting a higher degree of biodiversity on the surface. 3. We need to stabilize the polar axis swing. With this, we will, in turn, stabilize the seasons and ensure we have a long future of standard weather patterns. 4. We can use the moon's resources for future construction projects, and it can source a number of economic benefits of which I cannot foresee at the time."

Helen stopped her long explanation and took a long drink.

"OK, with you so far, but if I want to go a level deeper. How does the moon rebuild the magnetic field?"

"This is gravity 101. Take a body that is semi-liquid and has an iron core, synch it up with a significant gravitational influence, and kick-start a very massive magnet into a high-speed rotation. Do that and instant magnetic field."

"OK, Helen. Got it."

"Next question: Why the hell do we want to awaken the geological machine here? Why do we want volcanoes, earthquakes and plate tectonics alive and well?"

"All part and parcel of a healthy core. Like I said before, it promotes geo and bio and atmospheric diversity over time. A healthy planet needs a large degree of variance markers to support multiple systems."

"Yeah. What happens if one of those geo-variance markers start to force magma into the domes of one of our great cities?"

"Oh, that is always a possibility according to my data. For instance, Zeranius just happens to sit adjacent to a dormant volcano."

"That's great news. I'm sure that is going to play well."

"Well, it is dormant for now. In all probability, it will stay dormant. Who knows?"

April laughed and took a slug of wine. "Who knows?"

"Well, you have not sold me on number two."

"OK, let's put it this way: You can't have one without the other. Hot core equals warm planet. A warm planet supports life. You'll be able to shut down some of that TFP mirror array, in, well let's just say some time in the near future."

"Sure. Little better. As for number three, why do I even care? The small variance we see today..."

"Is pure luck. The rotation of Ishaida is at an all-time low since it was created 5.5 billion years ago. You know what a spinning top does once it slows down too much. It starts to wobble. Wobble is very bad for us, very, very bad."

"OK, no wobble. The moon keeps things spinning nice and uniform for a while longer."

"Alright, I have it now. All I gotta do is sell it. This should be fun. When will you have all three gateways operational?"

"We only need a few more weeks before we can initiate field testing."

"I have a half-dozen cruisers patrolling your test areas right now, just in case we encounter a problem. We cannot afford a mistake."

"You may want to bump that number up for the final procedure."

"What do you mean?"

"Just in case some radical decides to blow up a gateway node or something. I'm not sure what would happen to something the size of that moon if we were to pinch it off between dimensions. It's possible Ishaida may not survive an explosion of the energies involved."

"Oh. I thought we put in redundant nodes on all the gates."

"Sure we did, but I really can't predict what would happen with a catastrophic failure on multiple nodes. Let's just make sure we lock down our idiots that day, OK?"

"Agreed." They clinked wine glasses in a toast. "To our new moon, Calandria, or whatever we decide to call it."

* * *

"And what do you expect of us, to trust your word that all of this will work out just fine?" Garmon Keith, Mayor of AlphaRosetta, threw up his hands. "This can be disastrous."

"Yes, Sir. There are remote possibilities that something could go wrong. But we are doing everything in our power to mitigate these situations."

"Can you guarantee the safety of our citizens?" coaxed Annette Theron, in a slightly more gentle and calm tone. "Zeranius is nearest the equator. I suspect we'd be the first to be affected by any possible catastrophe."

"I need to reiterate to you the importance of what we are trying to achieve here," stated April, no longer willing to maintain a calm composure.

"This atmosphere you are enjoying will not last. The planet is losing gases every day due to the cosmic winds from the sun. With that sun being a K-Type - an Orange Dwarf, this process is accelerated. We are projecting the sun is moving into a very active stage over the next two years. Do you know what that means? Higher frequencies of CMEs. Every time this planet is bombarded, it is like we are being robbed of time. You want to ask the experts? They say 10 to 75 years and we'll be back to our thin and very unbreathable density. Do you realize what that means?"

She brought up the portable halo projector images of current Ishaida, with all of its lush greenery and blue oceans and lakes. "See all this green here, that all dies."

With a press of a button, the image of the later Ishaida came up, brown and dead.

"We can use the TFPs to adjust for this," offered Manuat Talbot, Mayer of NewBerlin. "It's how we got here in the first place."

"The TFPs will use up the oceans attempting to compensate. But they may not be able to work fast enough to respond to any particular savage onslaught. Besides, they cannot run indefinitely. They will fail."

"It is safer than what you are proposing," shot back Manuat.

"No, it is not. You are just afraid. Instead of treating this like a gift that has been given to us, you are hiding in the corner and shaking in fear."

That raised an outcry, the government representatives of Ishaida were by no means comfortable being challenged in that way. Elias Talbot raised his hands. "Now let's just calm down here folks. You too, Manuat. I know you have a big ego to tote around. I've had to put up with that since you were knee-high."

"April, tell us the odds of failure and the impact if it does."

"I've worked with a number of our scientists to come up with something that you can relate to on this. We feel we have a 99% chance of success, and a 1% chance of failure. That 1% can be considered 100% catastrophic. To put the odds of this into the frame, consider this: Ishaida has a better chance within the next three-thousand years to be hit by a planet killer."

"But that's three-thousand years from now, nobody here will be alive then," retorted Annette.

"No, not quite. What it means is that it could happen today, tomorrow, one-hundred years, or three-thousand years. That's what it really means."

"Well I guess we do need to start investing in our deep scan technology to protect this planet," added Elias. "But that's another discussion."

"We all take chances. The elevator could fail. You realize how massive that cable is, and how much it would damage if it ever came down?"

"Surely this is a managed risk. The engineers have thought of this, and anticipated, overbuilt."

"Yes, just like when you look above your glorious cities and even after half-a-century, the protective domes have not come crashing down on you. The gateway will work, and this world will remain vibrant and alive. And it all starts here with the moving of this moon from one planet to another. Think of what an amazing achievement we are discussing here. Can you imagine the incredible interest this will incite when it happens? Can you picture looking out at night to see the horizon bathed in moonlight?"

The councilors sat back in their chairs, emotions of anger dwindled as they envisioned the possibilities.

"And of course, the planet will warm internally, and become geologically active again. This is a good thing."

"Whoa now!" This perked Elias's interest. "Geologically active?"

"The core will be hotter like it was in Ishaida's younger years. It'll behave as a normal planet with an active core."

"You mean volcanism, earthquakes, plates shifting around?"

"Of course, part of the price of protecting our planet. We will have geo-diversity. Right now Ishaida is slipping away into a deep sleep. We need to revive her."

"And could this endanger any of our cities, April?" asked Annette.

"I had requested an in-depth geological survey of all the areas below and surrounding every city. Seems fitting you have asked this question, Annette, as there is only one city that has any remote chance of being affected, and that is Zeranius."

"Oh, this is just getting better by the minute," she proclaimed, her voice dripping with sarcasm.

"Now understand, Annette, this is classified as a remote chance. I must reinforce my meaning here."

"Zeranius fills up with lava, so be it, tell your people to come over to Languana," stated Emerson Trite, enjoying a show of sarcasm.

"We cannot predict anything of the sort," stated April, trying to keep the group from abandoning all the progress they've made so far. "We started this eventuality the day we set foot on this planet. Our intent was to revive her. This is what we are doing. You wanted green hills, to breathe fresh air, to swim in clear waters. Go outside. It's all there. That's what we're doing here, and we cannot afford to be timid about it. We need to close the deal to keep it stable and lasting. There are no shortcuts."

Elias brought up his hand. "April, thank you. We do appreciate your candor on such things. We've just not had the time to process the implications of which you've had the luxury of time to do."

"Agreed, I've had more time to think about this. However, we are on a schedule, you must realize. I have obligations to meet and I intend to move forward with this as soon as I am able."

"You can't do this of your own accord," responded Emerson. "You need our approval to perform anything of such grand scope."

"Did I ask you when I restarted the TFPs? Yet now you are appreciating a planet that all of you have dreamed about. Did I ask your permission to build the elevator? The spaceport? To arrange Ishaida's long-term security? This is my home too, and my home was dying. Look at it now."

"But April, if something goes wrong..."

"I may kill everything and everybody I care about? Don't you think I know that? Or should I take the conservative approach and do nothing, let things take care of themselves? You forget I was here when things were in that state. We were all dying. If you want to live – you fight your way with every step – you take chances."

April glared at each of them, irritated and ready to take any one of them on.

Crotchety, old, conservative and scared. What the hell kind of government electives were they?

"We can raise this to the people, you know," countered Elias. "Deliver a message that is counter to what you've said here. Raise the fear level to a state not even you can ignore. You won't be so loved then. Is that what you want?"

Elias just moved to checkmate.

He was supposed to be on her side, damn it!

"Fine. You want to discuss it. Do it. I'll throw my opinion in right now. None of you have the fortitude to make this call. You will all take the conservative route. Let's hope for the best, right? So before we go to war over this, and I do mean I will, because I can reach out to the average Ishaidan just as well as you can. I'll wait for your decision. You have 48 hours – let's see if you have the courage to make the right call."

She turned and left the hall. Half of her felt like telling them to stick it where the sun don't shine, just like her brother Ty used to say, but the other half had her twisted up so much in fear it hurt.

If she was wrong... But the Trectilla were never wrong, at least not that she'd ever seen. They were the tie breaker here. She trusted them more than even her own people. No. It was going to be OK.

Upon arrival at Anard-Bueller headquarters, she went directly to the fleet control deck to check on extranist systems, but also to check on a certain ship that should be arriving very soon.

"Commander," saluted the Commander on deck. "I wasn't expecting you."

April smiled. She liked the latest batch of officers, they had rotated off of some of the patrols and carried with them earned confidence. They knew what to do and when to do it. The Commander on deck was a young lady, came off of Verage's ship the Aarcona with glowing recommendations from Verage himself no less.

"Officer Tarid is it?"

"Yes, Sir."

"Status?"

"Nothing of significance. Few equipment breakdowns. Have a merchant vessel mid-way between Jefferson and Cauputain DITV - dead in the vacuum. Tesla has it in tow. Strayed quite a way off course. Should be at Cauputain by now. She'll be inbound to Ishaida following the drop-off."

"Oh, I see." She scanned the holographic, entered the region to amplify. "I don't see Tesla's transponder. Do you have a confirmed image scan from the last few hours?"

"No." She pulled up the logs. "But we do have communications log four hours ago. Strange we don't have a lock though." Her hands flew over the control panel deftly adjusting and enhancing the image.

"Monitoring, give me a deep scan of the area, immediately, please."

"Coordinating a deep scan, Commander."

"Sorry, Commander," Officer Tarid apologized. "This sometimes happens, we obtain a lock on a synch pass. Should only take a few more minutes."

"I'll wait," April stated, attempting not to let her mind go where it shouldn't. She stood at attention, as she had so many times before.

Tune out the world. Watch what matters. Observe carefully. Breathe.

She knew when the scan completed by the alarms on the monitoring station, before the monitoring officer announced the results, before the holograph cleared and reset.

Officer Tarid activated a silent alarm and the deck went alive. The communications officer started contact protocols with ships in the region. Monitoring officers began systematic diagnostic checks. An SDF patrol was dispatched.

She turned to look April in the eyes.

"I am sorry, Commander. We have a lost ship. We've initiated all necessary protocols."

"I see that, Commander. Please keep me apprised. I was expecting to see her dock here in a few days. I've close friends on that ship." She fought with every ounce of her inner strength to retain composure.

The walk up to her apartment was difficult. Smiling faces met her, but she could not return any cordiality. She locked the door behind her, and slid down against it to the cold floor, pulling her knees to her face. She rocked back and forth.

"No. No. No. He's OK. They're OK."

But deep down, she felt something was wrong. She knew something was wrong.

* * *

She waited for word, and time seemed to crawl. It really did not make any sense. It wasn't like she was flying too close to an intense gravity well. But it was true. Minutes felt like hours. Hours felt like days.

Distractions helped.

April stayed busy coordinating the first of many gateway tests. Test number one was a simple transfer of a small asteroid into a remote orbit. It failed. Adjustments were made. The second test completed with success.

All the while she maintained an open link to the fleet control deck.

Test three was a more significant chunk of rock.

Test four was a derelict from the pirate battles.

Test five was an empty drone ship.

Test six was a drone ship populated by test animals.

Every one completed without issue and she heard nothing back from the fleet control deck.

The SDF cruiser had already arrived at the last known coordinates of both ships and had found nothing. Next protocol was a sector search, and more patrols were dispatched.

Test six was repeated a dozen times. Variations were attempted on transfer speeds.

Test seven was scheduled for the next day.

The first evidence of foul play was located. Evidence of a battle. Debris from both the Tesla-Continuum and the merchant's vessel.

A manned test through the gateway was attempted – and successfully completed. The young Guardian pilot received applause at the atrium on the upper space elevator docking center. Pats on the back and drinks procured for a courageous young man for a feat never before attempted.

The merchant ship was located. Its crew was found huddled in a cargo bay, the rest of the ship void of atmosphere, most of the valuable cargo gone. At least they weren't killed. Not like the old days. It's possible this was a new pirate threat, from another source, or maybe some form of corporate deception game. But no Tesla-Continuum. The merchant's crew were attended to and debriefed.

A second manned test followed, and quickly on its heels a third. Variations attempted. Special controlled tests – safety was a consideration always.

April ducked into her temporary quarters at the space elevator docking center. There was little room for such pleasantries for most, but exceptions were made for the Commander. Even though the room was cramped and very basic, it was at least, private.

She reviewed the merchant Captain's statements. The SDF cruiser had arrived and commenced towing approximately a day-and-a-half of normal travel to Cauputain. He had been able to board and meet briefly with David. They had planned to bring in the ship at a much slower acceleration given she was hauling high gross tonnage of seeds which were now all spoiled because of flash freezing.

At least a dozen ships had appeared, coming from Cauputain's general direction. They had refused all hails, and once in range replied with full-on cannon fire. The Tesla took the brunt of the force but had refused to break the tow and risk losing the merchant, which severely limited the cruiser's offensive capabilities.

Regardless of the Tesla-Continuum's valiant efforts, the merchant ship was eventually boarded, its tow cable severed, cargo pillaged, and crew shunted into a cargo bay. That's all they knew.

At least 12 ships? Who would have that kind of firepower out here? Was this initiated from Earth?

She polled all her contacts at Anard-Bueller and missed the two manned tests and the following multiple ship tests of the gateway. Nothing. No new cruisers had been contracted at either Mars or Earth for at least a year, other than standard ESPD orders, or at least that is what was found on the surface. It took an intense investigation to uncover the truth: exposed one-off contracts for the ships, cruiser-class with separate retrofit contracts for weapons. It was all made to look like normal, standard, routine maintenance work, except it wasn't. *Some entity was bankrolling a replacement pirate fleet.*

All the questions did not help find the Tesla. She was lost and no one found her, not until the following day. A belter ship hauling ore reported her to the SDF – a floating derelict, battle damaged and dead.

April took the elevator down to the fleet control deck and waited for the intercepting SDF cruisers to arrive. She paced the deck the full day and into the night, refusing to leave the station.

Reports came in slowly. Systems scuttled but repairable. Crew unaccounted for as yet, but initiating a systematic deck-by-deck search.

They found Engineering Officer Sharon Cross locked in a torpedo bay tube, near death. She had a recording with her addressed to April McThurn.

April approved the activation and review of the media. They played the recording over the com-link. She had heard that voice before. He bragged about his skills in battle, about how he had forced the crew, one at a time, out the airlock, and how he had made the Captain watch it all to the end. He bragged about how he was going to wreak havoc. How he had left the Tesla intact to invite April to engage him. How he was going to destroy her and vent her just like he did her crew.

And April fell to her knees and cried. The crew on the fleet control deck were frozen, dumbfounded. It was Richard who carried her to her apartment and attended to her while she mourned. He reached out to Verage, who took control of the fleet and arranged to tow the Tesla back home, along with the collected bodies of her crew. Her crew would be buried in Ishaida soil, not left to float in the darkness.

The burial ceremony was a somber event. Citizens from many of the cities poured into NewLondon to pay their respects. Porter hearses traveled the streets of NewLondon, then out into the adjacent hills now covered in a blanket of grasses and wildflowers. A 21 gun salute echoed into the skies.

It was a service befitting a brave crew.

April attended, dropped a handful of wildflowers onto David's coffin, haunted by the thoughts of what could never be. How their children would never run through the grasses here. His last words echoed in her mind painfully, again and again.

She refused to leave long after everyone else had, not until the casket was lowered, and he was buried, deep into the Ishaida soil. She knelt in the grass and watched as the workers filled the hole.

A memory flashed back to her, from when she was younger. It was a just a brief memory.

"Kneel in here, baby," her mom instructed. "It's warmer in the furnace duct, as long as the furnaces keep working. You'll be safe."

She watched her raise the outer grate and lock it in place. "I have to go outside now."

"But Mommy!"

"No. Too dangerous for you baby. I'll be back soon. You're safe here, safe and warm. I love you. I'll be back soon."

She watched her shadow disappear. She had pulled her doll close to her. "Mommy is coming back, baby."

But she never came back.

"April, we have to go."

It was Richard.

"No, I can't."

"They're done, girl. We need to go home now."

"I don't think I can. I feel too weak."

Richard pulled her up and carried her to the tracker.

"Only time will make this easier, April."

* * *

Chapter 28

April's world shrunk to the walls of her bedroom, and the textured ceiling. She had counted the diamond patterns from left to right, top to bottom and she knew every scratch and imperfection. Within this mundane existence, she found tranquility. The thoughts of leaving her bed led to a racing heart and cold sweats, and a heaviness in her chest she just couldn't bear. Outright nausea followed by waves of depression. She had little comfort but for the mundane, and she began to count again...

Elias met with Richard just outside the Commander's apartment. "Not so sure she's ready for visitors, Elias. She's had a breakdown. It's not good."

"I've heard. Have you attempted to get her some help?"

Richard gave him a half-smile. "And you know how far I got with that, right?"

Elias nodded. "Yes, I most certainly do. This can't be healthy for her."

"Maybe it's just what she needs."

"I understand it was her flagship, and she knew everyone on it, I just don't understand why the severe reaction."

"It was the Captain."

"What?"

"David and April were lovers - not a fact that was broadcasted."

"I see. The pieces all fall into place now; first her mother, then the Sequins, then her previous friend, now this. Poor thing. That would be enough to tear apart anyone."

"Previous friend?"

"It's history now, Mr. Nearson. Would you mind if I attempt to reach her?"

"Not at all. Please do. Just duck if she throws something at you."

"What?"

"Nevermind. I'll announce you."

Elias caught on quickly, April was not her normal self. Tissues spread across the room, her eyes were red-rimmed and her cheeks shallow.

"My dear, when was the last time you ate?"

"Not hungry." She turned away from him. "Please leave me alone. I'm not interested in what you have to say."

"Certainly understandable. I don't think we parted on the best of terms, but that's alright you know. We shouldn't agree on everything."

She didn't respond.

"I do want to emphasize that we understand the sacrifices you've made and you continue to make, on behalf of our home. Some of us, we don't operate with the same unique perspective as you. We have trouble cutting through the chaff, as they say, to see what's really important. We had a very active discussion for a number of days after you left. I wanted to come here and tell you that you have our full support."

"I don't care about the gateway, or about the council, or about you or about Ishaida. Just leave me alone."

"I understand where you are. You are in a state of profound depression. These words I say to you are just hallow echoes in your mind. But I also know the pain will leave one day. It will go. You will be able to care again."

April did hear him, despite not wanting to listen. The old man had his ways of getting under her skin and prying out her emotion. But she had cried too long, and there were no tears left. The pain hadn't gone away at all.

"You are a liar, it will never leave me. Ever."

"It will, my dear. You will see."

His footsteps echoed loudly in the empty apartment. She heard the door slide open and then closed. She let out a long breath.

Alone is what she wanted to be.

* * *

Despite the Commander's absence, the world marched on. The SDF fleet formed a special response armada under Verage's guidance, which would be responsible for moving in on a suspected pirate attack. They returned to the distant belt region only to find it abandoned, with no sign of the aggressors.

Additional intermediate scanner relays were distributed with updated firmware to adjust for multiple levels of dispersion on a single scan. No fancy scanner deterrents were going to work with these updates.

The Tesla-Continuum was repaired and enhanced with long-range torpedoes and a third bank of cannon, making it the most dangerous ship in the fleet. With the refit, the engineers reviewed the archives on how the ship was captured and implemented automated internal cannon to dissuade any further boarding attempts. Its scanner systems were upgraded with the latest auto-searching capabilities and a bank of new squadron fighters added fresh out of Jefferson's shipyards.

Additional lower flight bays and squadron fighters were also added to three more cruisers, following April's original design amendments. The Entrago, the Pernagesion, and the FireHaven. They were all primed and ready to engage the criminals who had decimated their flagship and killed her crew.

Verage took over the Tesla and promoted his first officer, Lieutenant Commander Jerald Miner, to Captain of the Aarcona, then called upon the fleet Captains to help crew the new flagship with the most experienced crew members – onto the ship that had earned the reputation of refusing to be destroyed, despite the odds. He did not have difficulty obtaining volunteers –

all of them looking for a chance to work under the direction of the Commander herself.

The Anard-Bueller project team continued with their testing and modifications of the gateway systems. Plans began in earnest to arrange for the most significant engineering feat of the millennia – to move a moon from one planet to another. Details needed to be absolute in order to achieve this goal. The Trectilla had left little to chance, once the scientists managed to understand how to read the innocent looking document. It laid out the exact orbit and velocity of the new moon, the angles the gateways needed to be positioned, the duration of the power demand, the entry and closure dimensional opening timings.

It was all there.

Each and every calculation and fact provided by the Trectilla was not taken on faith. Every last detail was checked and double checked by the brightest minds under the employ of Anard-Bueller including both teams on Ishaida and Earth. No mistake was found. The precision of such a task was almost incomprehensible to comprehend, at least for the average human.

As the specifications and plans firmed up into a schedule, announcements were made to the council. The rest of the extranist systems and Earth would learn about it soon enough, but not until everything had already been initiated. Timing was sensitive. There would be no security deviations tolerated.

Upon Calandria's moon, a collection of containers had been deposited. Within these containers were automated beings, embedded with unique capabilities. Special bio-interfacing circuits and bio-support systems supported biological brains grown within a lab and installed into each. This hybrid technology was outlawed on Earth but developed on Mars and shipped to Ishaida upon the special request of the CEO of Anard-Bueller. These enhancements made the robots very expensive and bulky, however, the contract of development was very precise, and under extreme secrecy. It was not the first time this type of work had been completed, but it was the first time this regeneration technology was implemented within a self-contained auto-replicating factory, designed to turn out units on an exponential curve.

These passengers did not know they would be warped through space via a multidimensional gateway. If they had known, it would not have mattered. Their mission was to secure resources from the moon and replicate, and their mission was their focus.

Contracts were also put in place through Anard-Bueller, spanning multiple shipyards to start the fabrication of components of a ship of extraordinary dimensions. The vessel would be multiple kilometers across, with a central rotating cylinder suspended midship. Individual builders would construct to specification, each arc of this massive cylinder, of which its inner walls would suspend a unique and incredible world of land, plants and trees, lakes and rivers. Such a project should take decades to complete, but not under this projected schedule.

All of these things were in motion by a lonely, depressed woman who felt no significance in the universe, and at the time, would rather die than count the diamond pattern on her ceiling once again.

* * *

Richard brought the wheelchair and signaled the rover driver to pull up.

He knew there was a chance he would not succeed, but he had to try. He had to do this for her whether she thought he was looking out for her or not.

"Hello, April, I have a surprise for you."

"What do you want?"

"You're coming with me. You haven't been eating. You're wasting away. It's time for you to get out of here."

"No, I'm not going with you."

"Well, you don't really have a choice. You can fight me or you can just lay there. One way or another you're getting in this chair. I will remind you I am trained in handling uncooperative parties."

She just glared at him. "I'm not getting in that chair. I'm your boss. Turn around and get the hell out of here."

Richard laughed. "Since when has that ever worked for you?"

He reached over and collected her within the covers, effectively immobilizing her enough to pick her up and set her in the wheelchair.

April stopped struggling once she realized it was ineffective and chose to stare away blankly, avoiding his eyes.

"Just in case you care, we're going out the back. No one will see us."

He pushed her out the corridor where a small army of agents surrounded them.

April cursed under her breath.

Why can't they just leave her alone? Why's that so hard?

"Bring it in tight. Let's ensure the transition is seamless," directed Richard, coordinating his army of agents.

Outside, a slight, warm breeze drifted between the buildings. Although they were in the shadow of the tower, the sun shone brightly on the green gardens planted on the outside edge of the property. Gentle winds carried soft, sweet hints of the various flowers that were in bloom.

April remembered the Cauputain gardens, and with them, David. He had been waiting there for her while she slept. How long had he sat there?

The smells were rich and beckoning, catching her attention. She didn't notice these flowers before. How had she missed this?

The trip in the eight-person rover did not take long. It was only her and Richard seated across from each other, his eyes focused on a small tablet, hers out the large glass windows. They and the oversized sunroof allowed for an unfettered view of the areas passing by. The vehicle transitioned from developed areas to the undeveloped naturalized.

Roads turned to rough trails in the soil.

Eventually, the vehicle rolled to a stop. "We're here," Richard announced. The small army of agents poured out of multiple escort rovers and scattered across the region, disappearing into the landscape. Drones hovered high in the sky, visible only as mere specs from the ground.

April recognized the area. "Why did you bring me here?"

"You'll see." He dropped her in the chair and pushed her up the hill. It was bumpy ground, and he struggled intermittently enough to bring some sweat to his temples. The grounds smoothed out near the gravesite where the grasses were meticulously manicured. Richard rolled her up in front of a large white headstone and applied the brake. An agent handed him the large flower arrangement which he then placed on top of the headstone.

He reached into his pocket, unrolled a flexible tablet and handed it to April.

"Pulled from the archives on the Tesla, before she was seized. Take your time. I'll give you some space." He started back down the hill.

"Richard!"

He turned sensing something desperate in her voice.

"Don't... Don't go too far."

"Never do, Commander."

April flattened the tablet, leaned over slightly to cast a shadow from the sun.

"This is Captain David Ironstrike, I'm leaving this record as we are in severe distress. Enemy surprised us, probably used some variant of long-range scan dispersal technology that we haven't seen before. Last count was at least a dozen cruiser-class vessels, heavily armored with long and short-range weapons. Looks to me like Earth design, although they are flying a pirate banner. Possible they are ESPD but only conjecture at this point. I've encrypted the logs for analysis in case this core is found."

"We're outnumbered and in trouble. The Tesla's been critically damaged, we're immobilized. Could have, maybe should have, abandoned the merchant vessel in tow, but just could not go through with it. We've taken some serious hits, the main drive is down, we've had to shut down the reactor, and the last of our squadron ships succumbed to enemy fire just moments before I stepped in here. My crew has acted admirably. They have all given a valiant effort. The squadron, the crew, the officers, they died with courage. We took a number of them with us, but I'm not sure how many."

"I've locked records and initiated a systems wipe. I've ruled out self-destruct. Need to save what remains of the crew, too many unknowns at this time. But I have ensured this ship won't fly for them. I won't be the one to kill her. She has a heart of her own."

Alarms sounded. David looked off camera for a second. "They're moving closer, so I have only a few minutes. I've dispatched desk officers to slow their encroachment. We are literally down to hand to hand combat. We'll make sure they earn this."

"This message is for April McThurn, Commander of the Fleet, my best friend, my love. April, I'm sorry. I may not ever see you again. I know you lost others before, that you've blamed yourself. This one is on me. I let my guard down. Nothing you did. What you did do is give me a chance to make a difference, change things for the better. For that, I say thank you. I would do this again, no hesitation, and so would everyone else on this ship. Our mission is true but uncertain and sometimes it requires the ultimate sacrifice. I want to thank you for the time we had. The love we shared."

Blaster fire sounded behind him.

"April, I know you are just holding on, and I know if I die what this will do to you. But do not succumb. Take these bastards down. You're not alone, and we'll follow you into hell if you ask us. Remember we need you. We love you. I love you."

He stepped back, checked his weapon charge and started out the door. The recording kept on for a few seconds longer then went black.

April sobbed. He was so damned brave, such a good man. He couldn't severe the cable to save himself. That's why his crew loved him. That's why they died for him.

She looked at the new, bright white headstone. A small bee floated above the flowers, methodically landing on each. When did the bee's get added? She didn't recall them in the TFP inventory. Of course, it made sense, but maybe there was something more going on here. Further down the headstone, she noticed something else dressed out in the fine lettering.

David Lee Ironstrike.

Why didn't she know his middle name?

Inscribed upon it, at the very bottom, three words, "Make a Difference."

She laughed. *Sounded just like him to leave words on his gravestone like that. Must have been in his will. She didn't even have a will, but he did. He was meticulously detailed, always the planner, and prided himself on being a step ahead.*

And they had crept up on him like so many cowards. They killed him with no regard. They would pay the price.

Those fuckers need to die.

She stood up on shaky legs, tossing her blanket aside. The sun bathing her in an invigorating warmth.

"April?"

"I'll walk, Richard. But if you don't mind, I may need to lean on you some."

"Not a problem, Commander."

She grabbed the tablet, and they headed down the hill.

"I need full reports on everything we have on those bastards. If I have to bring this all the way to Earth I will, God damn them all, I will."

"Yes, Commander."

* * *

Elias stood beside April and waved to the crowd below. They all waited with anticipation. It would take hours yet before the great moon move, but people were already assembling, chanting and erecting banners. The main courtyard area to the Anard-Bueller headquarters was crammed with people, and one could feel the excitement emanating throughout. Fireworks were primed and ready.

It was a beautiful starry night. The sky was clear with all but the highest wisps of upper stratus clouds typical of a warm summer's evening. It could not have been a better night to do this.

April turned and re-entered her apartment. "I understand everybody's excited. It's something that will be amazing to see, I'm sure."

"You seem almost nonchalant about this, April. How can you underrate this task you are about to take on? This will be incredible."

April just shrugged. "I had hoped to share this with someone else, Elias. No offense, of course."

"No, I understand. I really do," he reached over and took her hand. "But you are making history here April, please don't miss out. I thought you would be on the elevator space dock, vying for the best seats in the galaxy."

April laughed. "No, I'll be on the fleet control deck. And it will be me and the deck officers who will have the best seats in the house, actually. I'll be able to see this thing occur from every angle, in multiple bandwidths, and will be talking directly with each team to ensure this unfolds as planned. So no, I'll not be missing out on anything. But feel free to stay here, invite your close friends if you like. My apartment provides a unique view. Oh yes, and all those tickets we sold to watch the big show from the space elevator – will be used for the Ishaida city reinvigoration fund, managed under my purview, of course. And I will ensure there will be no misallocation of monies."

Elias's eyes twinkled. "Keep'em honest my girl, that's fine by me, and thank you."

"Maybe after, I'll meet you up here to watch the fireworks."

She headed down to the fleet control deck, taking a moment to put on her earpiece and personal projector. The heads-up display allowed her to start through the queued list of approvals and status reports but made walking a slight challenge.

The first thing to check was security. All seemed normal. Every spare SDF cruiser available was on standby, plus additional ships were now pulled from patrols to ensure that there would be no situations. They had enough ships in the area to defeat an all-out attack of any number of pirate ships. Nothing was going to interfere with this today.

She literally bumped into Dr. Helen Aurolia at the control deck, who squealed in excitement and grabbed her tight. "Do you realize what we are about to do here, April? This is the most exciting thing to happen, since, well, forever!"

April laughed. It was good to see her friend so outrageously happy, if not so uncharacteristically out of character.

"Before you get too excited I still need to give the final OK to initiate. And Helen, just to recap, we have the magnetic field readings on this display here, but we are not expecting to see any change tonight, correct?"

"No. No. Not yet. I expect the moon's effect will build up slowly. We should start seeing some appreciable changes within the first five to seven days."

"And this talk of geological activity, what should we expect again?"

"We don't know. Most likely, we may experience some mild earthquakes in some unstable regions. Definitely will see some tidal effect in the seas."

"Right. Good. No surprises, same answers as before."

She gathered herself, and intentionally moved to a more central position on the deck to address the control crew, then nodded to the com officer to open a channel to all the teams.

"Officers, I know you were each hand-picked by your Captains and recommended for this position. For this, I have no doubt you are considered the best of the best. And also to our civilian teams, I know we have the best and the brightest on this project. I want each of you to know that what we are about to do here today is historic, and absolutely reliant on everyone playing their individual part. You will be my eyes, ears, and hands as we move through this journey of creating history. If you notice anything amiss, announce it. Nothing is too small. I fully expect something to go wrong today, and I expect we'll need to move fast to fix it. So let's stay calm, stay focused, and mind the details. Let's get started!"

Checklist after checklist was cleared. Team after team readied for a GO status.

April watched carefully, not overcome with the excitement that most of the others were feeling. It was as if she was totally detached, just an observer. Maybe it was because to her this was merely a step to move forward, to free up the fleet, and enable her to hunt down David's killers. Either way, her job was to be on point and clear. She could do that. All in all, she would just be glad when it was over.

"Gateway Red, are you in position? Our scheduled position is 20 minutes before moon contact."

"Gateway Red reporting: We are being towed into position now. I can confirm we will be 20 minutes from countdown starting as of... now. Synchronize all clocks."

"Gateway Orange, have not received your ready, we are now on the clock, what's the delay?"

"Gateway Orange reporting: We are having a problem with a heat deflector anchor, Commander. We have a drone adjusting it now. That should bring it down a few degrees in here in a minute or two."

"Would that be one or two minutes, Orange?" April asked. *They need to be specific and precise, no room for error on this one.*

"Gateway Orange reporting: Got it. We are a GO, Commander."

"Let's ensure we communicate timing very precisely moving forward, Orange. Understand?"

"Yes, Commander. My apologies."

April wasn't in the mood. She didn't have much patience today to tolerate incompetence. She checked the clock and they were already approaching zero minute.

"Gateway Red reporting: Moon on approach, all systems synchronized. First contact with gate event horizon in 60 seconds. Gateway Orange, please standby."

"Gateway Orange: Ready for power transfer."

"Gateway Violet: Ready. Standing by for activation."

"Here she comes, ladies and gentlemen," announced April. "Remember, Gateway Violet, do NOT open until the moon is completely through and passed to Gateway Orange."

"Where is it going, then Commander?"

April turned to see a young ensign watching from the side.

"To put it simply, the moon is traveling into another dimension. That's why we use Orange gate to power a temporal field around the moon, so it has time to travel completely through from our dimension. If we open up Violet gate too early, it will cause a tear in space-time, and that would not be good. This has to be timed precisely."

"What if we don't get it right?"

"The moon would be torn apart as it comes through the Violet gate. The resulting explosion would probably rip the atmosphere of Ishaida away and scorch this side of the planet, and we would all definitively die," she stated flatly.

"Oh. Good to know."

"Ensign, please feel free to join us on the control deck. It is the best place to learn."

"Yes, thank you, Commander." He jumped up to the deck literally skipping the three steps so eager to be involved.

April ignored him. Too many things to watch.

"Orange, why are we seeing a power fluctuation?"

"Sunspot. But we're within acceptable limits. Hydrogen collection is flowing nicely."

April waved her arm to the monitoring officer to kill the low threshold alarms.

"Gateway Red reporting: We are 60 seconds from full entry starting… now."

"Violet please confirm readiness for transfer from Orange, upon our signal."

"Gateway Violet confirming: Ready for transfer upon your signal."

April watched the timers dial down on the control deck monitors. So far, everything was working in unison, sunspot or no, this was moving along nicely.

"Violet you are 10 seconds from gate activation starting … now."

This was the countdown everyone was watching for. To the Ishaidans in the square, they were waiting to see the first appearance of their new moon.

"4.. 3.. 2.. 1."

A light sliver of a concave shape appeared above, and slowly began to grow larger. The control deck crew could hear the crowd outside cheering wildly.

"Gateway Violet reporting: All is nominal, moon transitioning to plan."

Alarms sounded once again. April approached the monitoring station and verified the displays. The monitoring officer's face was pasty white. "Orange, your power is continuing to fluctuate. Are you sure this is only a sunspot?"

"Negative, Commander. We have an anchor busted loose on the heat deflector. We are heating up, and it's essentially burning up our external power transmission lines."

"Is your drone able to correct?"

"We are trying, Commander. I think we may have no more than a minute before these lines start melting."

April checked the navigation display for the closest ship. "Communications, hail the FireHaven."

"Commander," acknowledged Captain Jack Warlock.

"Jack, you have about 60 seconds or less to position your ship strategically in front of Orange's heat deflector, can you do it?"

"We are maneuvering with haste, Commander."

April watched the clock and the power fluctuation readings. If they dropped below the required level, things would not go well.

"Counting on you, Jack."

"Sliding up into our slot. She is a bit warm, so we're tilting our aft burners to the sun."

The power reading steadied.

"Gateway Orange reporting: Looks like we have some static potential building up on the hull, Commander. Think we have a power short."

"How bad?"

No answer came.

"Orange, how long do you have?" April checked with the monitoring officer. He only shook his head. Levels remained steady on their display.

"Orange, I don't have eyes on your power leakage."

"Gateway Orange reporting: Would suggest that this will be close, Commander. The drone has confirmed one of the three main lines has sheathing melted and we're getting a trickle charge off it."

"I'd say," interjected Captain Warlock. "We've got some lightning shooting across to our ship, purty much a jumping here."

"Jack, can you rig up your ship's capacitors to soak those surges up?"

"Aye. I reckon you want this done asap?"

"Within the next few minutes would be good," replied April.

"Gateway Orange reporting: We are building up a charge then discharging to the FireHaven, looks like it's causing a stabilizing effect. As long as she can keep us at a positive charge, we're good."

"Gateway Orange, FireHaven is working on that solution for you."

"Gateway Orange reporting: That's good Commander, or else we will be firing up like our own little sun if this doesn't work."

"Gateway Violet reporting: We are at approximately 80% transfer. Estimate we are 30 seconds from full transfer starting... now."

Captain Warlock reported back in. "Capacitors are draining all excess charge from the hull, Commander. My engineer figures we can do this for maybe on the outside, 20 minutes tops."

"Only need 30 seconds, Captain, thanks."

"Gateway Violet reporting: We are anticipating full transfer in 10 seconds from... now."

The final countdown started. The crowd outside were notching up their cheering as a big clock in the square revealed the countdown. Thousands of voices yelled out the seconds.

"4.. 3.. 2.. 1."

And Ishaida had a moon.

The officer's on the control deck gave a cheer.

April sat down and pulled back her hair from her face, taking a long, slow breath, letting the stress drain from her body.

Not only was this event being broadcast to every major city on Ishaida, the whole thing was being recorded and relayed to all the other systems. Calls started coming into the control deck from every direction, all wanting to congratulate them.

April waved them off. "Follow our script as planned," she instructed the communications officer. He nodded with a wide grin.

"Gateway Orange, please confirm you are powering down," relayed April. "I would like both you and the FireHaven to remain intact for the near future."

She waited for the reply, which seemed to last forever.

"Gateway Orange reporting: We are powered down and fully stabilized. Please convey our thanks to the Captain of the FireHaven."

"Orange, tell him yourself. I'm sure Captain Jack Warlock would not pass on a drink if you offered."

"Very well Commander, grand idea."

"May as well arrange the FireHaven to tow you back home while you're at it. Sooner you get here the better. You're missing out on a big party."

"Will do. Orange out."

April went across the deck and shook hands with everyone but with one exception, Dr. Helen Aurolia, who just hugged her, tears in her eyes, a blubbering wreck. "We did it April! We moved a moon!"

April just smiled and ushered her off the deck. "You and I have some fireworks to watch."

* * *

Congratulations continued to stream in from all ends of the human-populated galaxy. The executive board of Anard-Bueller gave April a standing ovation. It was very clear to them what gateway technology meant to space travel. And it was the beginning of a new era.

April attended the functions and provided a limited number of speeches, but her heart was not in the celebration. Her attention remained on the fleet control deck, watching for a hint, the slightest indication of another attack. She was sure they were going to move the night of the moon transfer, as the patrols were recalled throughout the shipping lanes. Secretly she was hoping she'd be speeding off with her fleet to chase down and destroy this elusive enemy, but mysteriously it did not happen. A month passed with literally no activity, which left April irritable and miserable.

Where the hell were they?

"Captain Verage, please confirm the Tesla-Continuum is ready for service. I do expect we will need to react quickly."

"Aye, Commander. I can say the crew is now as ready as the ship. I have the dispatch plan in front of me now. We have 10 ships in all, ready to jump to superluminal at a moment's notice."

"Good. I half expected them to show their hand the night of the moon move." She tipped her hand on her expectations, just to assess where Verage was on it.

"I agree, we should have seen something occur then. But it didn't. That makes me think David did some damage to them when they attacked the Tesla, at least that's the only thing I can think of to explain it."

"So what are they waiting for?"

"Dunno. Don't you get blood in your eyes just yet. Anything can happen. Keep your cool there, lassie."

"It's hard."

"Aye. We'll know soon enough. Then we may not want to know - as these be dangerous times."

* * *

Chapter 29

Del Antonio Stride nursed his side as he walked into the large anteroom. Every Captain was there, including his old crew and that slimy bastard Canon Stalk. They shuffled about noisily, drinking his best vintages and arguing about trivial nonsense.

Del grabbed his blaster and rapped the table loudly with the hilt. "Gentlemen, gentlemen."

He started around the table, looking for the ones too stupid or careless to not stop their damned yapping. A couple kept on near the far end until he rotated his blaster to point directly at them. At least that got their intention.

"As you know, we've been waiting far too long now to resume our pillaging."

"Ya Del, when are you gonna give us the clearance to start making some money again?"

"Like I said before. I expect our next hit to be met with the full force of the SDF's vengeance. From what I've seen, when we hit their flagship a couple months ago, you boys weren't ready. We took too many losses and wasted ordnance on sheer damn misses. So don't go bitchin' to me about not makin' money when you aren't ready to earn it!"

That started some carrying on around the table, but Del chose to ignore versus confront it. He pounded the butt on the table again. "Don't expect this one to be easy, boys. Some of you ain't coming back from this if ya ain't listening!"

That quieted them down.

"So you've all been drilling on the simulators. I see the scores. Things are looking up, just like my wounds are healing up good."

"That Cap'n got a piece of ya, alright," reminded the mouthy sonofabitch Mitchell.

Del glared at him. "Anyone can get hit. Even you, ya jackass."

Mitchell glared back but held his tongue. He knew Del was crazy and preferred to live through the day today.

"So I asked my girls to pour y'all a drink when I came in here. I assume some of ya still have some left? Anyone empty?"

A few raised their hands and Del nodded to the servant girl to fill them up again. The girl walked with a slight limp and carried bruises on her face now turning a shade of golden yellow from the once original deep purple. She moved quickly and topped up the crew as they requested.

"Boys, I do think we should put together a toast now." He stood. "To the end of this bitch April McThurn, and the systematic decimation of their Security Divisional Fleet and all her weak-assed Guardians. May they all rot in hell!"

"Aye!" came the yells.

"I've picked out a special spot in the Jefferson system. We'll use the planets and moons to hide our numbers. We'll pick out a nice ripe target to lure in the SDF. Then we wait for the so-called saviors to arrive. But we'll have a surprise for'em. We'll do some preparation ahead of time – we'll mine the regions where we expect them to come in at, and where we'll box'em all in, and we'll set up some stationary auto-guns on some of the asteroids and moons, just to add some apples to the apple pie."

"How many of them will come ya figure?" came a question from the back.

"They can probably afford 10 to 15 ships altogether, as they are obligated to keep their patrols and escorts running. We'll outnumber them at least two to one and that's before our mines take'em out. Then we rip into the remaining ships. Probably be all done within the hour."

"What 'bout if'n they bypass our mines? What then?"

"Like I said. Some of us won't make it back. This ain't gonna be easy. I guarantee you this time the bitch will be leading'em. If you expect this bitch to roll over on her back and ask for it? No, she's gonna bite and scratch. You're gonna earn it if you want that piece of ass."

"So what then?"

"Then boys, we have the run of the extranist sectors as per our buddy Canon here. We just start printing the coin. We won't have enough room in our holds."

They all laughed.

"But one thing, boys. Ya pay attention to this. No one does the kill shot on the bitch's ship but me. Ya got that? She's mine. I'm boardin' her and I'm goin' ta learn that bitch, not just once but many times. She's gonna service me until she begs me to kill her. That's the way that little piece of treasure is gonna go. You got that?"

Nods from across the room.

"Then it's time to wreak some havoc."

* * *

There were times like this in the past that she could remember, at the precipice. But nothing like this. Nothing like today. She swallowed down her anxiety, held up her hand and willed it to stop shaking.

They were being lured in. She knew it. They all knew it.

"You all right?" asked Verage.

"Nerves is all. I don't like this."

"Me neither."

Jefferson's inner system was populated densely with four planets all with multiple moons, all in close quarters, along with a light region of loose asteroids and chunks of ice. The scanners alarms were pinging off like crazy. So much noise. And they were hiding in the midst of it. How many? At least enough to match her small interceptor fleet.

The miner ship's distress signal varied slightly as a large moon moved into position between them and the endangered vessel. The pirate's prey was a larger vessel as miners go. Typical miners in this region operated much like Porters on Ishaida, generational families, all working together as single units, instead of independent crew members. It was a natural evolution of time and reason. Who else would take on the constant risk, the loneliness of deep space, and battle with the challenges of living out in the void for so long?

No, this took special people. Their unique ships, often added to by derelicts they found in space, were outfitted with more than enough armament to make them very dangerous. Messing with a miner ship was like kicking a hornet's nest. Rarely does one get away without at least one painful sting. Ship's crew members were taught from the youngest of ages to defend what was theirs.

She knew these people, and she would not let them die out here. But she knew they would not leave their ship, either. She'd need to send in engineers to reseal their hull, rebuild critical systems. All this took time.

A perfect lure.

"I don't like this," added Verage, knowing full well the dangers from raw experience.

"What else would you do, Verage, if you had the time to plan this out?"

"I'm not a military mind, April, but if I was out here, and I had an enemy, I'd lay out some surprises for them."

"Surprises?"

"Mines, my girl. Lots of 'em. And they'd be hard to spot in this mess."

"Open a channel to all ship Captains," she instructed the com officer. "Everyone, we suspect this area to be laden with mines. Do not hesitate to destroy suspected ordnance."

She nodded to her weapon's officer as she talked.

He had already started targeting individual floating debris.

"Battle stations," ordered Verage. The alarms sounded throughout the system immediately after.

April glanced over with surprise. "And I thought you hated extending readiness protocols."

"Not when one of those wee little bastards could blow just a bit too close to us. I want our vessel sealed and our crew standin' ready."

April nodded. She trusted his judgment and it helped quell the twisting in her stomach.

"Perhaps we are close enough to launch the fighters," offered Verage.

"Really?"

"I think they're out there'n waiting. An' they are purty much getting what they're waiting for."

That was good enough reason for her.

"Launch the fighters. Com, please relay to the other ships as well."

Another blast of alarms. As each ship lurched away, a tremendous thud echoed throughout the corridors, sounding below decks.

"That was efficient," commended April to Verage.

"Aye, lot's a drills to keep'em sharp."

"Think I have multiple bogies on the deep scans. Working to resolve," announced the monitoring officer.

"More dispersal tech at work?"

"Aye, Earth tech for sure. These ships are not revived old derelicts are they?" asked Verage.

"Nope," confirmed April. "I expect the latest armored cruisers. No different than us fighting the ESPD."

"Helm, bring her about 15 degrees," ordered Verage. "Weapons?"

The short cannon burst resulted in a tremendous blast.

"There ya go. Proof positive for mines."

"Shit, that limits us in movement," April commented. "We need multiple egresses when they hit."

"Sure as I reckon, they'll drive us into their minefields."

"Or lure us into them."

"Full stop," ordered April.

"Full stop," confirmed the helm officer.

"Relayed and acknowledged from all ships," added the com officer.

"Ensure the squadrons remain inbound to the miner."

"Aye, Commander. They've acknowledged."

"What are you thinking, April?"

She smiled. "They sit in the shadows and wait for us to move to the optimum position for them to hit us. But I don't want to play their game. We stop and we make them wait. One thing I know is they are impatient. We wait. They'll come to us. In the meantime, let's launch some scanner probes. I want them to fill in these unknown areas where I suspect they could be hiding, such as here, here and here." She pointed to numerous empty areas on the navigation holograph that was still only partially completed.

"Aye, Commander," acknowledged the monitoring officer. "Prepping probes for launch."

* * *

"What are they doing?" asked Del to his second officer, Masgard.

"They hit our first mine. Maybe they're sorting out what they want to do now."

"Maybe. Fighters are still moving."

"What do you want to do, Cap?"

"We'll wait. I don't want to hit them until they get out to this spot here." He pointed to the holo-map image. "That's when we bring the other ships around from behind the moon. We'll move in from behind to close off their route. When they attempt to escape, they'll hit a wall of mines on all sides. Simple. A child could outmaneuver this bitch."

The time ticked by.

The SDF ships just hung there, not moving.

"Cap, the others are getting a bit edgy. They want to hit'em now."

"No, damn it!" yelled Del. "We want them boxed in. Just tell'em to hold. They gotta move some time. Better yet, Com, hook me up fleet-wide."

"Listen boys, I understand you are getting antsy, but we need them to move into our trap. No sense in hitting them now. We do that and it's to their advantage. Let them move into the minefield, then we'll hit'em. Anyone jump my orders I'll have his head, literally." He signaled to close off the channel.

"So we wait?" asked Masgard.

"Just how thick are you?" He glared at him. "Yes, we wait. They'll move."

And time dragged on. The SDF remained motionless. Ripe for the picking.

Del left the bridge, frustrated. "Masgard keep an eye on'em and let me know if you see any change." He headed off to the mess, hungry and pissed that this was not going to plan.

This bitch never made it easy for him.

He was chewing through the last remnants of imported Earth steak when his com went off. "Cap, the boys are movin' in."

"What?" He jumped up and choked a bit on his steak.

"Masgard, get on the com. Tell them to hold back before they break scanner range."

"Too late, Cap. They're closing in, and the ships have started in from behind the moon, too."

Del was already on the bridge, out of breath and on fire.

"Stupid sonofabitches! Nav, pull out the resolution to include the moon. Sonofabitch!" he cursed. "Look at this cluster-fuck now! Timing's all wrong."

"Battle stations!" ordered Masgard. "Navigation, plot a course."

"Whoa, whoa. What are you doing?" yelled Del. "Am I not on the bridge, Masgard? Am I not the Commander of this damned fleet?"

"Well, I thought you wanted to head in for the kill."

"No. You figured wrong. Fleet Commander needs to keep a big picture on this. Cancel battlestations. We'll see how this plays out."

"They're all engaging now, Cap," reported the monitoring officer.

Del only shook his head. It was all coming apart. Those dumbass idiots were going to blow it for him.

* * *

Alarms were sounding throughout the ship.

April watched the enemy streaming in from multiple angles. "Fire at will, all ships."

"Recall the squadron. No. Hold on that."

"Monitoring, what do we have from the moon probe, any more ships?"

"Aye, Commander. Six more cruiser class and they're coming in too."

April smiled. "I knew it. He couldn't hold'em off. His first mistake."

"Com, recall the squadrons, but leave a pair to reach the miner." She smiled. "I want them coming up behind those moon cruisers."

"Monitoring, divert that moon probe now. Get a detailed scan of this whole region. I want everything mapped out to a grain of sand. I'm sure that's a minefield. I need multiple solutions through it, understand?"

"Aye, Commander."

Verage was pitching orders out in streams, managing the Tesla's engagement. The cannon had started and torpedoes were not far behind.

April watched the holographic methodically refresh.

Her heart sunk.

"Final count of 28 cruiser-class vessels coming in from the fourth planet," announced the monitoring officer.

"We're outnumbered three to one. Let's make every hit count."

"Weapons."

"Little busy right now, Commander."

April was not phased. Sweat was pouring down the young officer's temples, and he was madly plotting solutions for the torpedoes.

"Captain Isaac, I suggest we deploy Bertha."

Verage gave her a short but meaningful look, it took a second to register what she said.

"They're damn close, April and moving closer by the second. If you think this thing does what you say it will do..."

"We'll push it out with enough ordnance to draw their fire. This one will look like a miss, so they'll let it fly past'em. We just need to make sure the epicenter is far enough away. They'll get caught on the edge."

Verage walked over to the weapons officer, briefly distracting him from the panel. "Can you do it?"

"What?"

"Can you deploy Bertha, fire it past the incoming, ignite, then catch them jackasses in the ripple?"

"Yes, Sir. Can be done, but..."

"But what?"

"I don't know the range for sure."

"Best guess, Ronny. That's all we have. Do it. Do it now before they get closer."

April ordered a channel to the fleet. "Issuing Bertha, standby to fire a simultaneous volley, then coordinate a 180 on my mark, full burner retreat."

"Monitoring, you coordinate with the others." He nodded back, face ashen.

"They're off," announced the weapons officer.

April watched the small volley advance, and one by one, they were picked off by the incoming fleet, disappearing from the display. But one specific green blip shot right past them. As predicted, their weapons defense systems had calculated it would be a miss, so they let it by without concern.

"Flipping now, increasing to full burner," announced the helm officer. The fleet reversed in unison, coordinated through the Tesla-Continuum.

Far beyond the approaching armada, Bertha ignited. The weapon was not like other nuclear ordnance. It utilized some of the new gateway technology, opening and closing two points of a dimensional portal in an overlapping fashion, causing a local, temporary, dimensional tear. If the engineers had done the math right, the SDF was out of range, but unfortunately, no one had even test fired such a device. No one was absolutely sure.

The dark point of space briefly lit up to the brightness of a star, then as quickly faded only to emanate multiple waves of disrupted dimensional space-time. It traveled in multiple rings of light, like ripples in a pond only in three dimensions, to form an imperfect sphere of milky white perturbations. The waves rolled with incredible ferocity, completely engulfing the outermost encroaching pirate vessels, only to tear them apart in another fraction of a moment.

April watched the scene unfold, praying they had enough time and enough distance between them.

"Amplitude is decreasing exponentially," announced the monitoring officer, letting out a breath. "We're out of range."

The first wave dissipated, and the second wave hit, this one reaching deeper into the enemy flanks. Its wave frequency was a longer amplitude but it was just as deadly. Another string of ships took the brunt of the wave, twisting and tearing within its crest.

"Full deceleration, turn to re-engage," ordered April, satisfied the effects of the new weapon were subsiding. She could feel a calm overtake her, her stomach was no longer in knots, her hands steady.

"Monitoring, get me a count."

"That hurt them. I have 16 still moving, Commander."

"Com, relay all ships, focus fire into the center of them."

The fleet rotated and started back into the breach, firing salvos ahead of them.

The Telsa-Continuum rocked with the pounding of the torpedo blasts and cannon fire. Shock waves struck the external hull, momentarily flexing the tremendously thick ship's skin, internally forming air pressure waves that screamed down sealed external corridors creating a strange collection of moans and shrieks. Torpedo bay systems fired successively, creating trace amounts of smoke and heat which leaked into the air supply system and permeated onto the bridge, bringing with it acrid smells of flame and ozone.

"Enemy ships are firing torpedoes at a higher rate than us, Captain," informed the monitoring officer.

"We can compensate with our extra cannon," replied Captain Verage.

An explosion blasted close to the main bridge's external port screen, instantaneously shooting a large crack diagonally through the quartz. Air whistled as it found a way to escape through miniature crevices. April calmly reached over to the controls and closed the main blast doors. The whistling quieted substantially but did not stop altogether.

Two ships were converging on them, and Verage had already brought up the third level of cannon, blasting away at both of the ships' forward plating.

"Place a torpedo between the two of them, Weapons," she stated quietly.

He complied, somehow hearing her in all the insane raucous.

The blast tore laterally into both ships, penetrating past their primary plating. The damage was substantial, but not enough to stop them.

"Again, if you will, Weapons," she ordered.

Another blast rocked the Tesla to starboard, attempting to throw April off her feet, temporarily sending a ripple through the anti-grav plating.

The weapons officer vomited onto the deck.

April reached over to the firing panel and pressed the launch trigger.

The bridge was filling with smoke as the second salvo reached between the two cruisers and ignited, effectively blasting both of them sideways.

"Between the two of them, Helm," ordered Verage.

"Com, relay to the squadron, one pass only on those six incoming and get back through to the main fleet. Tell FireHaven to pull back."

The Tesla-Continuum raked the two ships with its massive cannon, blasting through the light plating and into the inner decks. The enemy ships rocked with successive explosions, then detonated in a blast of white fury.

Not all the other SDF ships were doing as well.

Maelstrom was taking on critical fire from two cruisers and had suffered a close proximity mid-strike from a torpedo. The FireHaven was deep into the enemy fleet taking hits from all sides. It was only a matter time.

"Verage, we need to get to the FireHaven."

"Pernagesion, can you help the Maelstrom?"

"Negative, Commander, reported Captain Kannashe. I have lost aft burners."

Just then the Maelstrom lit up and came apart.

"Damn it!" April cursed.

"Com. Need a channel to squadron leader."

The Tesla-Continuum was inserting herself between the FireHaven and the multiple ships attacking her. Cannon fire obliterated incoming torpedoes at close range, resulting in a staccato of explosions that shocked the ship in her belly, knocking April off her feet. She hit the navigation console on the way down, which momentarily stunned her.

Black smoke started to flow in through the air circulation vents, and multiple alarms began to sound. The smell of apples and bitter ozone followed as the auto suppression reacted.

Fire in the squadron bay.

She stood up, blood now dripping from her nose and lips. She ignored it.

"Squadron leader, get your ass in here, now."

"Commander, we need a second pass on the incoming cruisers. The fleet can't take another wave from these cruisers."

"There won't be a fleet if you don't move it."

The FireHaven launched a proximity torpedo, the explosive force jamming the nose of the Tesla upward.

"What the hell is Jack doing?" she yelled over to Verage.

"Saving our asses more'n likely."

He slammed on the intercom "Auto-targeting is down on the belly cannon. Need a man down there to operate."

"Can't, Sir, the fire isn't out yet."

"Then close her off and vent her."

"But Sir, we still have men in the bay,"

Verage walked over to the internal sensors. "I know, son. But we won't have a ship if we don't put'er out. Seal and vent, now, Lieutenant."

April knew what it meant. It was Verage's call, but...

"Is there no other way?" she asked.

He only shook his head, then nodded to the officer.

"Opening main hatch doors. Full vacuum, venting successful, Captain. Heat sensors dropping."

"Keep it at full vacuum for at least six minutes, Lieutenant, then reseal and pump in atmosphere. Have a crew on standby to dispatch the lower cannon."

Another explosion blast came from above them, savagely wrenching the nose of the ship down, and throwing the bridge officers in the air. April landed flat on the floor, but Verage went down on top a railing, breaking something in the process.

"Tell me you got them, Weapons!" snarled April shaking off a wave of dizziness.

"Aye, they just took a direct hit port side, Commander."

"Verage!" she yelled.

The weapons officer was untying his belt. "No!" she ordered. "You keep focused." She crawled forward toward the Captain. The look of pain was evident on Verage's face.

"Broke my hip, I imagine. Get me in a chair before we have another one of those."

She pulled him close, attempting to carry as much weight as she could as they stood up. The deck was vibrating with the intensity of the cannon fire. She dropped Verage into the chair, and he let out a moan of pain.

"Tie me down, April. And wipe your face. You look like hell."

She laughed. "Good, that's the effect I'm looking for." She wrenched down the belt and Verage moaned again. "I'll call a medic."

"No. My crew needs them more than I do. I got this. You see to the fleet."

"Hard port 45 degrees," he belted out to the helm officer.

She scanned the nav panel. Pernagesion was disabled, Maelstrom and Perthena's Bounty were gone. Tolomok, AirCovner all showed signs of severe damage. Only the Entrago, Gandolf-Auricia, Aarcona and FireHaven seemed intact enough to fight and they were already turning into the six incoming cruisers.

The squadrons were focusing on the last of the enemy cruisers from the main fleet, with the FireHaven providing cannon fire cover. Except it wasn't the last of the cruisers. There was one exception, far off in the distance, near the cover of the planet.

"Com, open a channel to the fleet," ordered April.

"Gents you have six incoming cruisers with three squadrons at your disposal - correction you have five incoming." She noticed one just blinked out of existence. A torpedo no doubt. "The Tesla-Continuum has a remote target to pursue."

"Looking for our blessing, Commander?" asked Jack Warlock. "We've got these bastards."

"I'll keep Jack company, Commander. We'll take care of these others," Captain Karen McThurn added.

April closed the channel, taking a moment to make up her mind. The incoming cruisers may be damaged from the squadron passes, but they were still very dangerous.

"Get me Red Squadron Leader, Com."

"Red Squadron."

"I want two fighters to accompany me. We're going long range, so they'll need to dock immediately."

"Aye, Commander. Red 5 and Red 7 will be joining you, immediately. Good luck."

"Thank you. Give'em hell, Red Squadron."

"We've re-pressurized, Captain. Belly cannon is manned and operable," announced the monitoring officer.

Verage just winced, nodding weakly.

"Captain, we are in pursuit of that sonofabitch out there. Will you concur?"

"Aye, Commander, that's the ringleader. Need to seal this deal."

"Captain, we'll be pursuing this one with extreme prejudice. I've no intention of letting this one escape alive."

Verage barely nodded. April moved closer and could tell he was fading fast.

"Squadron fighters are docked, Captain," reported the monitoring officer.

"Captain Verage is not doing so well," April announced quietly. "Navigation, lock in a solution directly to that enemy ship. Monitoring, do we have any mines out there?"

"Aye, Commander, but we have multiple paths through," he stated as he merged the courses to one.

"Good, engage to maximum burner."

* * *

"Sonofabitch! Sonofabitch!" cursed Del Stride. "The damn squadron has the moon unit flanked."

"Cap, something just happened."

Something exploded and just took multiple cruisers with it. "What the fuck was that? What kind of weapons has the bitch got hold of now?"

"Main fleet down to 18, no 16 ships, Captain."

"Sixteen? Fuck. OK. No matter. They can't deploy that again, they're too close now. The additional torpedo launcher modifications should make up the difference. Tell'em to start launching everything they got. Kill'em all."

Del watched the battle progress. The extra torpedoes were either not enough or his captains were just too green in dealing with an enemy who fires back.

Ship after ship went down.

"Those incompetent bastards! The fleet from the moon hasn't even reached them yet! The timing was all wrong. Incompetent sonsabitches!"

He slammed his fist down on the console.

"Monitoring focus scans on the flagship."

He smiled at the image. The ship was venting fire and had multiple scars of cannon and torpedo hits. But it was still alive.

The moon fleet was engaging, but Del had little hope at this point. It was a perfect plan until that bitch messed it up.

"Sir, their flagship is heading our way, maximum acceleration."

"Battle stations! Helm, get us the hell around this planet and pointed to the sun. Time I gave this bitch the most serious ride of her life."

* * *

April wiped the blood from her face.

Multiple medics had arrived on the bridge. One was seeing to Verage while the others were checking the crew. Her lip kept bleeding. The medic gave her a quick freeze and ran a micro-stitch to seal it up.

"Any other problems, Commander?"

"No. How's the Captain?"

"He has a crushed hip and internal bleeding. He needs surgery, but he won't leave."

She crossed the bridge to Verage's side. "Verage, if you stay you will die. Don't worry, I have this."

He looked up at her, eyes a bit out of focus from the pain medicine. "Ya ever read Moby Dick, lassie?"

April shook her head. "Can't recall that one."

"This one you're chasing, he's your white whale. Don't make the same mistake Ahab made. OK?"

She looked at him quizzically. Ahab? Most likely the drugs are taking effect. What the hell was a whale?

She glanced at the medic. "You make sure to let me know his status pre and post."

"Yes, Commander."

They carried him off the bridge.

She turned her attention to the nav display. The pirate ship had already turned and started around the planet.

And where was he going?

"Fire a scanning probe, maximum acceleration. Monitoring, get on this, I want a trajectory of this bastard."

The Tesla-Continuum was shaking under the stress, creaking and shrieking, complaining about the damage it had endured. She reached over to the door frame and caressed it.

"Hold together, baby."

"Captain, this is Engineering. We've some plasma leakage. We need to dial it down."

"Internal?"

"Negative, mid-port burner plate."

"Then no, Engineering, we maintain."

"But Commander, this can digress into a serious situation quite quickly."

"Understood. Monitor it." She closed off the channel.

"Helm?"

"Closing in, but he has a significant lead, Sir."

"Can we maintain him on long range?"

"Possibly."

"We do have a trajectory, Commander."

"Have Navigation plot a pursuit course."

They swooped around the planet at maximum velocity, close enough to see the details of the planet's surface. The vibration increased.

"Picking up some atmosphere, Commander."

"Are we slowing down?"

"Not appreciably."

"Good."

They were out and pointing to the sun.

What the hell is he doing getting so close?

"We need to end this. You get within the maximum range you launch ordnance, understand, Weapons?"

"Aye. Closing in. Expect solution within 18 minutes."

Time ticked. The ship began a rhythm of deep to shallow vibrations and wavered slightly to port, which needed intermittent correction.

Engineering was busy patching and sealing the outer hulls. The damage from the fire in the squadron bay kept all the shifts working steadily.

"Get me Engineering."

"Commander?"

"Do a maintenance check on all three cannon banks."

"But Commander, we still haven't sealed the outer hull."

"Pull them off it. We can't afford a problem with our offensive systems."

The engineer didn't like it, but he acknowledged. "Aye, Commander."

"Getting in close to the sun, Commander."

"Flood the forward outer hulls with water, Helm."

"But Sir, we only do this for radioactive..."

"Just do it. Three-quarters volume capacity."

"We may have some leaks, Commander."

"They'll freeze closed."

"Have a solution, firing torpedoes," announced Weapons.

"We have only a slight acceleration advantage on their ship, Captain. They're running along the Sun's inner gravity well plane. If we lose acceleration capability in there, we'll be caught."

"Good place to exchange fire, then. We'll have the advantage. Dive in lower, Helm. We'll take him from the inside."

They dipped down into the plane of Jefferson's red dwarf star. A wall of burning flame as far as the sensors could read. The temps started to climb as the life support systems fought to compensate.

"Commander, be advised we are well within range of a CME. If we take a hit and lose altitude, we won't survive it."

"Agreed, Helm. Please do your best not to hit any CMEs."

"Monitoring?"

"Aye, Commander, monitoring the surface for CME's."

"Deploy the hydrogen collectors. May as well recharge while we're here. Let's refill the water tanks."

"Outer hull is nearing 650 Celsius, Commander. It's getting hot."

"She can take it."

"I have a second solution, Commander," reported Weapons.

"Fire at will, Weapons."

"We are closing in, slowly," reported Monitoring. "Shit, I have a salvo incoming."

First, then second forward cannon banks began firing.

"How? They can't have a solution."

"Maybe they're just hoisting them out a lock?"

"That's original. Where's our third bank?" demanded April.

"Still in maintenance, Commander."

"Suggest to engineering to complete their maintenance soon, Com."

"Salvo destroyed," reported the weapons officer.

"And ours, Monitoring?"

"Also destroyed."

"Commander, one good hit like this and we are done, you realize this?" offered Verage's second officer.

"Duly noted. I will state that it is the same situation for our enemy."

"But they don't have a plasma leak, Commander. You are endangering this ship."

April regarded him with a half-smile. "Your job is to engage the enemy, Lieutenant. Is this your attempt at humor?"

"Well, no, Commander, I was merely pointing out pursuit of this vessel is leading us into an area of risk we can avoid."

"At the price of losing our prey?"

"Incoming salvo," announced Monitoring.

The cannon turrets fired a staccato.

"Torpedoes destroyed," announced Weapons.

"We are closing in on cannon effectivity range."

"Fire at will, Weapons."

"Commander, the crew are abandoning lower cannon turret due to intense heat."

April nodded, watching the nav display intently as the ships moved within range of each other. Within a moment, the exchange would become intense. In this case, it was the Tesla that had the advantage of firing solutions.

"Increase forward angle to maximum."

"Firing multiple salvos, Commander."

The exchange began. April watched as three torpedoes flew by, while the others disappeared in fiery balls under their cannon barrage.

The pirate cruiser was not as lucky. "We have a hit," announced the weapons officer.

The Tesla blew past the pirate cruiser as it struggled to pull up and out. It had already sunk down to their altitude and was sinking further, under duress and struggling against the intense gravity.

"Pull us up, Helm."

"Engineering reporting in that we cannot increase the plasma flow, Commander. Our leak has become more intense."

"Suggest we do a gradual curve up, Commander," offered the helm officer. "We can do this but we'll lose tracking on the enemy."

April nodded. But just maybe *he* won't make it back up.

"Just get us out of this gravity hole," she conceded, sweat dripping into her eyes.

* * *

"She's on our ass, Cap."

"Yeah, drop in low, Helm. We'll roast her on some open flame."

He watched on the navigation holograph as the SDF cruiser surprisingly crept down even closer to the sun's surface. *So, she wasn't afraid to play his little game of chicken. Wait 'till they start trading ordnance. Then we'll see who has the balls.*

"SDF cruiser is dropping lowerin' us, Cap. They be in our blind spot, and have a better firing attitude 'cause of it."

"Crazy bitch trying to catch up to us. Gotta give her points on that."

He thought for a second. "We may not have a good launch angle but that don't matter. Better below than above us. Get some torpedoes set full proximity and heave'em out the belly as soon they're in range, and keep'em coming. We'll do some damage soon enough."

The ship was shaking, and the air was sweltering hot. It smelled of burnt dust. The view screen revealed a sea of white-hot plasma on a horizon that stretched on far past their field of vision.

"One mistake and we're in the drink alright," Del commented.

"Closing in, Cap. Think we're about to exchange."

"Stay on top of it, Weapons. I don't want to miss any firing solution," urged Del, transfixed as the image edged in closer.

"We have a window. Firing," he announced.

The exchange took all but a few seconds. Then a pause and a second wave. The third came later, followed by a massive bang and shaking. Alarms began to sound throughout warning of an environmental breach. The torpedo had penetrated the lower port side and ripped a gigantic hole in the hull.

A second set of alarms started across the bridge. Del scanned the instrument panel.

"Reactor's offline!" he yelled. The ship twisted and started a slow roll, burners momentarily suspended. They fell toward the sun, the roll churning into a spin. Del watched as they accelerated downward past the SDF cruiser.

"Failover. Failover. Fire those damn burners," he screamed. He could only see the sea of white-hot hell below rushing toward them. The ship shuddered and groaned, but it recovered and stabilized, and then started fighting its way back up, shaking and vibrating violently enough to affect Del's vision, making everything seem blurry.

"Come on baby," he muttered under his breath. The rest of the deck crew were white-faced and grim.

"We're pulling out," reported Helm. "But we got problems with the plasma supply, and the reactor's cooling is compromised. Engineering reports shrapnel damage and temps are climbing. We can't hold this up for long. We won't be able to pull outta this one."

True to his word, the ship was turning over slowly, and acceleration was slowing. In a few more minutes, they would start to sink again.

Del slammed the intercom. "Engineering, can you fix it?"

Tersen came on. He was one of his best engineers and the best on the reactor. "We got no time."

"Then we open it up to vacuum," stated Del, knowing it was a risky gamble at best.

"We'll need to expose to corridors to reach it. We've got gunners on those levels, Cap. They'd be good as dead if we do that."

"Helm, keep our belly pointed away from the sun. Seal all the stern hatches, Tersen. Masgard, you take the bridge. Keep us floatin'," he yelled as he ran out. His first stop was the armory, where he grabbed two bricks of explosive and timer heads.

He headed down the port corridor at a brisk pace. The closer he got to the damaged area, the more it filled with a white-hot haze of steam. He thought it was radioactive, but there was no way to know for sure. He picked up his pace, reaching the spot where a large steel pole had shot through the bulkhead and through to the reactor containment. Steam was billowing out of the breach in a deadly stream.

Del punched the timer in the brick and tossed it down the corridor near the outer wall. He could see someone on the other side waving at him, but he just ignored him, knowing he's as good as dead in the next few minutes. Turning and sprinting down to the cross-alley, he sealed the forward hatch shut behind him, letting out a long breath in the process. He started down the outer parallel corridor in a brisk walk. This one was full of debris, and at numerous places, large punctures in the wall had been temporarily patched by the auto-sealing sheets and the outer bulkhead was frosted up from exposure to the external cold.

The radioactive steam was taking its toll on him. He coughed wildly, spewing out white vapor in the insanely cold air. The bodies of a couple of gunners lay splayed out on the floor. He and kicked the one as he passed and the man groaned.

Still alive, but not for long.

He kept moving, reaching the spot where the steel pole had shot through. It took only a second to set the timer on the last brick, then he sprinted back, passing over the injured crewman again. In a few seconds, he had reached the forward hatch and closed it quickly. The intercom was immediately on the right of the hatch panel.

He broke into another coughing fit, his shirt now soaking wet in sweat. *This better be worth it.* He slammed the intercom. "Tersen, you have those stern hatches sealed? Tersen?"

"Aye, Captain, but we got a couple gunners locked in there, and they are banging on the door."

"Don't you open them, Tersen. She's about to blow."

"But Cap, it'll only take a second."

"No!"

The bricks exploded with a tremendous bang. The ship shuddered again. The corridor lights blinked off, but the hatches held. If it worked, the explosions had left behind two successive gaping holes through the outer bulkhead walls, exposing both corridors to full vacuum.

"Tersen, you still there?"

"Aye, Cap. Think it worked."

"Just tell me your temps are dropping."

"Readings getting there. But we won't get full power, maybe 60%."

He coughed. "Masgard, you hear me? Keep us belly up and put burners to the maximum we can handle. Get us the hell away from this sun."

His chest felt raw and sore. *Too many rads this time.* He popped a half-dozen radioactive suppressants down from the closest first aid box. *It would have to do for now. He had priorities. He had to find that bitch. The Deathstalker may be damaged, but it'll hold together long enough to blow a hole in that SDF cruiser's hull.*

The deck crew's grim faces had lifted somewhat when he stepped back on the bridge. Probably due to the fact that the sun was shrinking in the viewscreen as the ship blasted away from it.

Why the hell were they so concerned about their useless damned lives? None of them had the balls to do what he just did, damn it!

"Make for orbit around the first planet, Helm. We need to do some repairs. That bitch will be lookin' for us, and I want to be ready. And Masgard, get the hell outta my chair."

* * *

Hours had passed since the battle. The Tesla-Continuum was in a comfortable orbit around the sun. Maintenance work was being completed on the rear burner to address the plasma leak.

April dispatched multiple drones in hopes to relocate the pirate ship. They were going to find him, that much she was sure of. They had drawn blood. The enemy flagship had sustained severe damage.

"Bring them all online. I want to see all the feeds simultaneously."

"Commander, you've been at this for 16 hours. Perhaps you need a break. We'll stay vigilant in our search." The lieutenant's attempts were in earnest, but he knew they were futile. She would continue until she fell over in exhaustion.

"No. Not until we find the bastard. Channel the feeds to the console," April directed the monitoring officer.

The feeds came up from the probes. The second probe feed caught her attention. It was headed to the first planet and had picked up a radioactive trail.

Was their reactor venting?

The probe moved closer and the readings grew stronger. As it came around the small planet, the dark image of the pirate cruiser was all too obvious.

"Divert number two probe, maybe they'll miss it. We have him now. He's bleeding alright. We got the sonofabitch!"

"Relay to engineering, I need full burners. Are they done the repairs?"

"Not yet, Engineering needs another 90 minutes, Commander. They have dispatched a crew outside."

"Tell them I want it done in 60."

"Engineering says not possible. They need the full 90 minutes."

April paced the deck, 90 minutes and then at least 20 to reach the planet if they're still there.

"I'm retiring to the Captain's office. Let me know if the situation changes."

The door closed behind her, leaving her in quiet. The office chair was plush and comfortable. She leaned back.

Just a few minutes to rest.

She closed her eyes. Images of battle faded to the quiet greening hills of Ishaida. Sleep came over her.

She woke to a shaking ship, the air was acrid and full of smoke. It took her seconds to scramble to the bridge. The scene was utter chaos. The officers were working furiously, throwing desperate looks her way. She reached the navigation console and ran a pass on the ship's systems. The story became evident quickly.

They were in pursuit. Ship diagnosis revealed a hit on their starboard side had opened up some of the decks and fires were burning in the aft section.

"Why the hell didn't you wake me?" She yelled at the second officer.

"We thought we had him. His weapons systems were down."

"He was baiting you. You have no damned idea who you are dealing with! Go see to the damage," she ordered, unable to contain her anger. She didn't want to see his face on the bridge.

"Helm, fall back."

"But we're just about in range."

"Our trajectory's all wrong. We have no reaction time. If I were him, I'd drop ordnance out the stern bay and end us right now."

The helm officer nodded, and dropped down acceleration, easing away from their prey.

"Adjust out a 15 degree swath, but stay with him."

"I want a full damage report. Why are the temps so high on the reactor?"

"I have engineering, Commander," reported the com officer.

"Pass me the channel."

"Commander, we have a heat pump problem on the reactor. Under control but need a few more minutes to repair. Aft fires are almost contained.

Not sure on an estimate, possibly an hour for that. Starboard decks are all sealed, starboard stabilizers are offline, possibly unrepairable."

"Give the reactor full priority, Lieutenant. I need to bring these cannon back online."

She scanned the nav display. *Where was he headed to? His reactor's still compromised and he's trying to shake us.* Realization hit her with a sudden satisfaction. *He's headed toward the Jefferson belt.*

The Tesla was rocking. Starboard stabilizers were out, and the port stabilizers were overcompensating. The low-level vibration had increased in intensity and was modulating high to low much more quickly than before. April walked over to same door frame and laid her hand upon it.

She's dying, came her only thought. She could feel it deep inside. She scanned the diagnostics. They were venting atmosphere now more than ever. The hydrolysis conditioners couldn't keep up at this rate.

"Com, we're about as close as we can get to Jefferson. Raise flight control for me, please."

"We have them, Commander."

"This is Commander April McThurn of the Tesla-Continuum. We are in extreme distress. We are venting atmosphere, and most of our major systems are compromised. We are in pursuit of a pirate vessel. We will not break off pursuit. I repeat, we will stay on course. Please relay this to any SDF vessel that is in proximity. Support is required immediately. McThurn out."

The crew had all stopped what they were doing and were looking at her. The gravity of her words sinking in.

"We have maybe 10 minutes before we engage." She announced to the handful of deck crew. "All of you please ensure you take a moment to record a goodbye to your loved ones. You can use the Captain's office."

"Com, can you raise the squadron pilots? Are they still alive?"

"Aye, Commander, they are standing by. Channel open."

"We are about to engage. I need you out there. We can't take many more hits. Distract him as much as possible. Inflict as much damage as you can. Redline their cannon. Their reactor is damaged. If we can make it go critical, this could draw our fight to a quick end. Standby to launch."

"Raise the medical bay. I want to know Verage's condition," she ordered the com officer.

"Commander, we are overloaded here. No time for reports."

"What's Captain Isaac's condition?"

"Not good. He's been stabilized, was bleeding internally. He's sedated, but only time will tell."

"Can you revive him?"

"Not advisable, Commander. His state is too precarious."

She signed off. Alone again to make the calls. Typical. She glanced at the clock. Time was up.

A quick check on the reactor temps indicated they were returning to normal. Engineering had pulled it off. She gave a last look at her crew. They looked haggard and beaten.

"All of you, before we engage, I want to thank you for your dedication, to this vessel, to our cause, and to me. Our enemy out there is singlehandedly responsible for more deaths than we can count. He will not be brought to justice alive. He will continue fighting until his last breath. This ends today. We will end it."

"Com, signal the fighters to launch. Helm, accelerate. Weapons, prep a full salvo as soon as we're in range."

The ship groaned as it increased velocity. The vibration shook the deck noticeably now. April watched the cracks in the forward quartz creep along to form a spider web pattern.

Hold together, baby, just a little longer.

Torpedoes launched in quads, salvo after salvo.

The pirate's cannon started, blowing red plasma angrily at the oncoming rush of death. Two fighters accelerated past the Tesla, engaging with a retaliating torrent of white and yellow fire.

The two ships performed a rotating dance around the pirate vessel, somehow avoiding the ship's main cannon, but taking the odd hit from the multiple single gunner turrets.

Like the Tesla, the pirate ship was outfitted with multiples of turrets and even more single gunners. It easily outnumbered their offensive capability three to one, and her heavy plating was built in across her whole midship. It was dumping salvo after salvo at the Tesla.

"Almost in cannon range, Captain."

"Divert as you can. Rake her hull. Find her weak spot."

The pounding of the exploding ordnance turned the skies between them white hot. The computers and sensors worked overtime to calculate and anticipate the next ordnance solution.

It was only a matter of time until something got through.

The fighters were doing their job, however, and provided enough diversion to sneak the first torpedo past them. The blast pounded the port side, and pirate cruiser started venting atmosphere in a billowing flame.

A cheer was cut short as the first fighter disappeared in a shower of red plasma.

The second fighter took a hit and the pilot fought to keep it under control.

"Signal Red 5 to pull away, Com."

"He says 'nuts', Commander."

"Nuts? Tell him I am ordering him to break off."

They watched as he stubbornly wavered into a strike position again.

"Intensify cannon fire ahead of him if you can, Weapons."

"I have him, Commander."

His next volley took out a major turret, but it was a hollow victory as his ship took a direct hit and burst into pieces.

Simultaneously a second torpedo snuck through, again hitting the pirate's port side. This time it tore away plating and exposed decks.

"She's losing acceleration, Commander! We're closing in."

"Commander, we will be out of ordnance by the time we reach her," yelled out the weapons officer.

"No ordnance? No, I will not allow this ship to outgun us! I will not allow this ship to escape!" she yelled out the words vehemently.

"Helm, set a collision solution."

It took a second for her to realize the gravity of her order. *Were they ready? Were they willing?*

She scanned the deck crew, faces battle weary and frightened. The com officer was the first to nod, then the weapons officer, as she passed her gaze across each of them, each of them passed on his or her agreement with a silent nod.

Perhaps it was relief she saw on their faces, the thoughts to ending all of this.

"Com, open a ship-wide channel."

"To all crew. Abandon all forward bow compartments and brace for impact, you have 90 seconds."

She sat down in the Captain's chair and pulled across the restraints.

"Commander," offered the helm officer. "Standing by to accelerate on your mark."

She watched her chronometer countdown. "Helm, engage."

It all seemed to move in slow motion. Time is relative when you are close to death, at least that is what they say.

The Tesla-Continuum bore down, into and through the pirate vessel, streaming parts of both in a myriad of cannon fire and massive explosions. The pirate ship split in two, both ends aflame, exploding, twisting and turning crazily off into the darkness.

The Tesla's nose crunched in and twisted, ripping apart at the seams. The bridge, at three-quarter midship, survived, but all her critical systems went offline, and the ship rotated wildly, swinging madly with no propulsion, hemorrhaging atmosphere, and fires burning throughout.

* * *

Chapter 30

A pril awoke five days later on an SDF medical frigate.
Starlight was streaming through a port window and the beam razed a unbroken line through the medical bay. But unlike home, it was not filled with tiny dancing particles. It did not smell of sweet flowers. It was all too antiseptic.

The small portable monitor above her bed was beeping with regularity. Some orderlies rushed in.

"Commander, please remain calm. Don't move just yet."

She reached to touch her head, only to feel wads of bandages. Why can't I see out my right eye?

A doctor stepped in. "Glad to have you back, Commander. It was touch and go for a while there."

"You'll be feeling disoriented for a while, that's normal."

She nodded, still feeling drugged and hazy. Her head pounded and her insides felt twisted into bitter knots.

"You have experienced severe head trauma, and you've lost your right eye. Other than that, being bruised and battered over the remaining parts of your body, you're in stable condition."

How was it possible? The collision should have ripped them all apart.

"How?" she tried to say, but couldn't get it right.

"Not for me to say," she replied. "Maybe someone is looking out for you, and your crew."

"My ship?" again it came out all wrong, more like a mumble.

"Your ship? Is that what you asked? Well, I'd hazard a guess as a Captain, that's your question alright. What's left of the Tesla is being towed back to Ishaida. Your crew, however, let's just say we had quite a few heroes at work there too. Your security team managed to pull you off the bridge before it decompressed. We have quite a few stories. I'm not sure I can believe all of it. Abundance of bravery there."

"Verage?"

"You mean Captain Verage? Oh, he's giving the nurses a handful. Please take him with you. In the meantime, I'm going to sedate you until I see this cerebral edema gets down to where I want to see it. Goodnight, Commander April McThurn."

Everything faded back into the blackness.

* * *

Voices...

"When do you think she'll wake up?"

"Anytime now. This was a traumatic injury, should have killed her. Luckily she's young and strong."

"Can I stay with her for a bit?"

"Of course. I'm sure she'd like the company."

And the voices faded back to darkness.

"Why did Ishaida go to back to sleep, Daddy?"

"That is the big question, my dear. No one knows. But there are a few of us who believe she will awaken again."

"Do you?"

"Of course, what would life be without dreams, without faith?"

Her eyes opened to bright sunlight. A warm summer breeze ruffled her sheets. A window was cracked open and the muffled roar of a shuttle launch brought her senses back.

Home. She was home, in her bed.

Across the way, sleeping on the small loveseat which had been pulled out haphazardly, was a snoring Verage Isaac, still wrapped in a cast.

"Wake up old man," she said. Her words seemed a little off, like she was talking with marbles in her mouth.

She checked her clothes. Standard hospital dress. Kept her covered enough though.

She stuck out a bruised leg and gave Verage a push.

"Wake up."

He stirred then opened his eyes. A broad grin lit up his face.

"The mad Commander Ahab is alive!" he stated with some animation. "Am I glad to see you, lassie. Been waiting a while."

"How long? What's wrong with my mouth?"

"Nothing's wrong with your mouth, my dear, you are as beautiful as ever, just less a right eye, and a rebuilt portion of skull, but you are good. Doc says you'll get back to normal with some practice."

"Practice?"

"Yeah. Like talking practice. The more you use it, the sooner it'll come back. So keep talking to me. I can almost make you out." He laughed.

"Before you ask, most of our crew survived. We lost some though. They were there for you all the way to the end. I dunno where ya grew those pair of brass balls, lassie, but by God, what you did out there needed more than two of 'em. An' don't worry about Del Stride and his gang, they're gone. You wanted vengeance, you surely got it."

She nodded, feeling a tear flow down her cheek.

"Was it worth it all?" he asked earnestly.

April thought of David and how he died, watching his friends forced into the void one by one. Del Stride deserved to die.

"Yes, Verage. I'd do it again."

"That's why you're the boss, me-lady. Others couldn't stomach it. You're as hard as nails. But I know your insides are hurtin'. I know you are as soft as my daughter was so long ago."

This time it was his turn to well up in tears. "I'm glad you made it, my girl. I dunno if I could bear losing you, too."

She reached over and took his hand. They listened to the wind blowing through the window, and somewhere out there the sweet whistling of a solitary bird.

* * *

It was a long recovery. One does not just walk off severe trauma, nor the dark memories they carry.

April woke more than once, soaked in cold sweat, images playing through her mind that were less reality and more twisted possibilities of multiple ways the past had occurred. It left her troubled and exhausted.

The modern drugs helped. The long talks with AI Tiberious helped even more.

She buried herself in her work. A ship had to be built like no other, on a schedule that was impossible at best.

The Trectilla had formed a habit of sending ambassadors weekly to her office to remind her of the importance of constructing their ark. Strangely, Evelyn was not one of them.

In a way, she missed the quirky alien. Perhaps she felt hurt that the one Trectilla who she would more closely align to as a friend, did not feel the urge to come visit her, nevermind the fact she had very nearly been killed.

She visited the moon to inspect the robot army at work. Things were coming together as planned. The mining operations were moving well. The ore refining factories were busily churning out smelted alloys. More importantly, the robot factory was also running at peak capacity. The key factor in this plan was the ongoing creation of more synthetics until they reached a critical mass of capability. The machine world reminded her more of a beehive than a settlement.

Shipments arrived from Jefferson - components of the Trectilla's ark. They were deposited on the moon base where the skeleton of the ark was beginning to form. These shipments were the most intricate components, multiple reactors, drive engines, primary and secondary computers. Armies of robots assembled the constant stream of components and mounted them onto the evolving vessel's substructure.

April stayed for a number of weeks to oversee the construction. She found herself walking the gray silty sands of the moon each night, only to look back upon the now green and blue orb of Ishaida. The planet hung in the stars, a beautiful painting of life, traced with a thin blue line that protected what was so precious to her.

It had been not so long ago, she remembered, she had traveled the desert plains of Ishaida and had a dream. And now it lay before her. Yet she could only feel hollow inside.

On the horizon, a mountain glistened in the starlight. Tiny ants scuttled about it busily forming it layer by layer. In the end, they would create something never before constructed: a vessel of such magnificent dimensions that it would leave anyone in awe. But from here, it was merely a dark shape on the horizon, its bones glinting faint sunlight. Time would make the difference.

Just like her home.

Her walk was cut short by a familiar voice in her ear. Something moved in the shadows beyond, in the shape of a man.

"I'll be but a moment, just enjoying the view, Richard. Our next step will be where we are standing. We need to bring the shipbuilders here, to work amongst the synthetics. These creations of ours need inspiration. I have tasked them to stop the mining so they can refocus on creating a new world here. A new domed city in this crater. It will be a world green and lush just like home, a place where you would want to bring your family to build a life."

"Why go through the trouble?"

"And I thought you were finally catching onto thinking big picture. No, I see something more here, not just gray silt and black crater walls. Can't you see it? We are becoming the masters of our worlds. We are able to create an oasis in the desert, how could we not do this?"

"Why play God? Why must we be the all-powerful creator of all things? Maybe we should just learn to leave things alone."

"Leave it to you, Mr. Logical. With all our knowledge, our tools and technology, we'd be best to leave things alone. You know, Richard, I look back on the things I've done and it's not the times where I've created or repaired something that I regret. No, that's always given me joy. I'm not conflicted at all about this. I have no doubts. My times of deepest sorrow, of most pain and regret, are the times when I've destroyed. Out here I'm not playing God, I'm being who I want to be. I'm alive. I have the power, the capital, the influence to turn things into something better, and if I do this enough. If I make enough positive change, maybe, just maybe, I'll find some peace, I'll find some forgiveness."

She kicked at the fine sand, and it billowed up into a small cloud. *Yes, even on a cold, lifeless rock I can make a difference.*

"Forgive me, April. I didn't understand..."

"It's OK, really old man. Did you know that back on Earth Anard-Bueller is building multiple gateways out to the stars? Mankind will have its own dedicated highway of connected gateways."

"No, I didn't. So now they'll be flooding in from Earth like crazy. You see that as a good thing?"

"Yes, it is a great thing. And it won't be just the rich and well to do, you see. I've set up a lottery for the poor and the oppressed, the lower class, the caste of those with nothing. These are the people that live on scraps, in the filth of the lower cities with little to nothing. The price of a ticket is meager for most, but a week's wages for these souls."

"A lottery?"

"Not just a lottery. It's something more. They buy a ticket and they buy hope. Strangely enough, the odds are stacked in favor of the purchaser, who instantly has a 50-50 chance of winning – but it's not the cash award. Anard-Bueller exec's just haven't figured that out as yet, but Tiberious and I built this scheme a long time ago. Can you guess what you win?"

"No cash? Then a way out?"

"Yes! A ticket – all expenses paid. A ticket to Ishaida! Give us your sick, your poor, your uneducated, give us your dreamers! We have a world for you here, all shapes, all sizes, all colors and creeds. Do you see it yet, Richard? The rich and well-to-do will simply toss those winning tickets to the ground, and trample them into the dirt. They were looking for the big payoff, the mother lode and nothing came of it. But the poor will find those tickets and they will see their true value. They will come. They will be looking for something more, expecting anything better, looking for life itself."

She could not suppress her smile, but it was wasted under the darkened glass of the helmet faceplate. "And don't you worry. I won't upset the applecart too badly. Anard-Bueller will continue to rake in the credits, as it will own every gateway. It will charge a reasonable fee to give one instantaneous access to anywhere we've installed another gateway, anywhere. A trip that used to take months at incredible expenditure now lies mere seconds away. And one day these gateways will be perfected to a point where you will just walk into a booth and step out onto another planet, and all this for a small but reasonable fee."

She playfully spun around in the light gravity and settled to face the construction site.

"That's not the end either. That ship over there – these mini-floating worlds will also have gateways built within them. Generational travel ships would become destinations, a choice not a prison. And when these travelers find a new destination, they will build a gate, and off they will go to the next star."

"Tiberious tried to teach me when he was alive, but I was too naïve to understand. Anard-Bueller will be my hand, Richard. The poor and destitute will live with respect. They will build their own homes, grow their own food, have children, and their sons and daughters will know what it is to have self-respect and confidence."

"Sounds wonderful."

"It can be. But to succeed it requires a foundation. That thing I am talking about is the Porter Code. It's what I – what my family lived day in and day out. Can you see the big picture now? You understand why I fight so hard to keep this moving?"

Richard grabbed her shoulder. "Is your air mix OK?"

April pulled her arm free. "Yeah, it is."

He laughed.

"What's so damn funny?"

"You are, girl. You are so damned perfect, sometimes."

"What do you mean?" she asked, grinning.

"Nevermind."

They headed back, both laughing at no specific thing, but just to laugh.

* * *

As the months passed April found she had become attached to her eye patch. The medical team had offered multiple times to replace it with a donor, but the idea seemed to leave her with a strange revulsion. She had come to understand that deep down she felt she needed to carry this wound as payment for what was owed.

It helped her cope.

When the Anard-Bueller Executives and the Ishaida Mayors made the pact to build The McThurn Museum, it was outside April's knowledge. They brought the hulk of the Tesla-Continuum down to be housed in the new museum. The story of her life was laid out in detail for everyone to see. Pictures of the Sequins, the terra-forming plants, the SeaClear and the LightningRod; her life described in so many mini-stories.

It was much easier for her to look up at the larger than life photographs of herself before she wore the patch. She was not that beautiful girl anymore. That person enlarged upon the walls was no longer her, it was someone else. She carried the scars to prove it.

No, she never asked for such notoriety. She never set foot in the building again.

* * *

On the 18th month, Evelyn arrived at the Anard-Bueller headquarters. She seemed different, presented a hue of new and unique shades of pinks and violets.

"Hello, my old friend. It is good to see you. It has been a long time."

"Has it? I am sorry for that. It was my oversight, and I must extend my apologies. Tell me, is this a new type of clothing or are you damaged?"

April laughed. "It's an old injury. I'm OK. So I've heard your people will be streaming through here pretty soon. The Mayors are all converging at the headquarters, and a parade route has been set up. People are lining the streets to watch."

"Yes, I see the evidence of your ceremony. We are truly humbled."

"I told you I would deliver. And I think I told your ambassadors every month for the last eighteen that I would deliver. This ark of yours, she's up there, waiting for you."

"And that is why I have come. I must thank you personally."

"I am happy you did. I have one last gift for you and your people. I was hoping to have a chance to tell you, myself."

"And what is this gift? Shall I look?" she queried, awaiting permission to telepathically search.

"No," laughed April. "No need. I have given you hands, Evelyn."

"Hands?"

April smiled and held hers up, wiggling her fingers. "Yes, these little things, for the mastering of machines, the manipulating of tools."

"To be augmented would not be welcomed."

"No, my friend." She pointed above. "Up there in that vast machine, are other machines built to service it over its long life. Those machines have minds, somewhat like ours. You will learn to meld with these machines to become one and do what they can do. They will be your hands."

Evelyn rotated and bobbed ever so slightly.

Perhaps it was excitement or pleasure, April could not be sure.

"That is my present to you, you see, before you go."

"Then I thank you. It is a very thoughtful gift, although I am sure I do not foresee its true utilization at this time."

April laughed, but her smile died quickly. "You do realize Evelyn, this may be the last time we ever meet."

"Yes, your statement is correct. I will be departing as well. Many will join me, but some will stay, to keep the memories of Ishaida. It is their purpose to protect what was, and what will be. They will continue to interface with you."

"I had thought you were all leaving."

"No. We wish to ensure the survivability of our people. We must spread out amongst habitable planets. This is the best way to do this. I will join the others on the vessel you have constructed for us. We will create new memories, and when we locate a suitable planet, we will again segregate, and then a part will continue on to keep alive the memories of the vessel of travel."

April was a bit perplexed by her strange references to memories, and Evelyn seemed to pick up on this, more through her telepathy than her ability to understand humans.

"I must recall a previous conversation of ours. It is of my understanding that your home planet has based the measurement of time in quantifiable components, a year is a complete cycle around the sun, a day is a complete rotation of your planet Earth. Is this so?"

"Yes, approximately 365 days in a year, 24 hours in a day Earth Standard Time."

"And you carry this with you, this measurement, through the stars, but once you find another planet, and settle upon this new home, you find these measurements of time then differ. They are in conflict."

"Well, true, Ishaida's day is approximately 30 hours. Its rotation around its sun is approximately 388 days, but remarkably close. But what are you getting at?"

"You find comfort through affixing your understanding of time. Just as you see yourself within it. It is through these gauges you measure your accomplishments, plan your goals, tie together what has become."

"Certainly, that is all evident..."

"You must understand, April," she interjected. "You are a magnificent race. But your lives are so short, as a flame that burns so brightly only to exhaust all of its fuel. You do not see time for what it is. You remember so little of the past, it is a madness you carry with you. What you do remember represents what is most painful to you, what you have lost, what you have learned at a cost. These are the realities you carry with you, that which shapes your decisions for your future."

It was true. This alien knew her better than she did.

April poured herself a drink from her bar, slugged it down. It left her little comfort, but it would take effect soon enough.

Best to bury that pain yet again.

"Evelyn, you are quite a philosopher. I truly did not expect this kind of discussion on the eve of your departure."

"It is a framework, a context I am attempting to provide, to detail the method of how you process and understand your world. You know that we, as a people, live much longer than you. We, as a people, are joined mind to mind. We do not forget. Memories are not fading shadows of what had once been. They are clear and bright as the day they occurred. They are with us constantly, as is this day, as this moment."

"Talk about our madness. You can keep yours."

"Madness? We can recall the subtle details of our first days as children, to our last as the aged, and the memories of all who lived and died. All memories are precious to us. All are our learnings. It is why I am here, to give you this gift."

"A gift?"

"Of the days you no longer remember. I see by looking into your mind. The memories you carry are not conducive to your happiness."

She laughed, "Ya think? And what makes you the expert on this?"

"I have come to give you what you need. Please allow me to ease your pain. You are my friend."

April apprised this quiet glowing alien, who hovered in the air through no apparent means, yet seemed to master things that were far beyond her understanding. "I do consider you my friend, Evelyn. I know I will miss you."

"And I will miss the opportunity to create memories with you. Please, allow me to leave you, my friend, this gift."

"OK. What do I do?"

"I suggest you to sit, rest comfortably, and close your eyes."

April complied, eyes closed, mind wondering, until suddenly, feeling *something* new: *The fresh smells of a flower garden in Cauputain, the roasted garlic of a meal at Tiberious's – and then she was falling, down a deep well, into the darkness.*

She landed softly, blinded in bright light.

Something floated to her. Vivid in smells and sound. It was a day when she was a child. A warm breeze blew down the barren streets, yet everything was full of color, everything was full of wonder. And then she came. A gentle wisp of golden hair, dark eyes and a warm kiss. She pulled her up in her arms and could feel her love.

Mom.

"I love you, baby," she whispered.

And time shot ahead, her ninth birthday on the SeaClear. Oranis was clapping his hands and Lavenue carried the cake. Her brothers and sisters laughed and yelled the words, and the candles danced to the music.

Then she was being held by Cruez, never did she feel so safe.

Light twisted to yellow hues. Sunlight on a sandy beach, towering coconut trees swaying in the breeze. She held Tiberious's hand and watched him pass.

Then she was with David. They were in her cabin on the Tesla. They were arguing about how to make spaghetti and she threw the half-boiled noodles at him. He grabbed her and wrestled a kiss, all the time, laughing and feeling so much in love.

This love. It did not leave her. It had never left her.

As she opened her eyes, she knew she was back. But it was different. It was so very different.

"Of all the days gone by, I thought I lost them too," she said, tears welling up. "I've forgotten so much."

"You have so many more days ahead of you, my dear friend. May you remember them all."

"Thank you, Evelyn. This is truly a beautiful gift."

She wanted so badly to hug her friend before she left. To have actual contact.

Evelyn understood, carefully, hesitantly, she moved closer. April wrapped her arms around the soft, rippling alien. She could feel her warmth and hear the sounds of multiple hearts. She closed her eyes but for a moment.

Remember.

* * *

A day later the gigantic starship of the Trectilla started off on its maiden voyage.

A large crowd had assembled in the upper space-elevator observation foyer. For many, it was truly a sight to behold. The first generational ship of such incredible dimensions, engineered to operate not for hundreds, or thousands, but tens of thousands of years – a testament to the ingenuity of mankind and a promise kept to a people now enabled to reach out to the stars.

April stayed long after the last observer had left. The observation lounge was mostly empty and provided a breathtaking view of the surrounding galaxy, and a thriving, beckoning planet below. She stared out in the direction of where her friend had departed. The massive starship had all but faded into the background. One of a million tiny points of light.

She should be feeling sadness, but she didn't somehow. All she could still feel was the warm presence of her past. Memories of so many priceless moments of her life she had thought once lost.

She smiled, then headed back down to the main elevator. There was much work to be done on Ishaida, and her role as the CEO of Anard-Bueller and Grand Admiral of the Security Divisional Fleet left her little time for reflection.

Richard appeared from background shadows and quietly relayed a message for his team to prepare.

"Coabi's in motion."

The End

Acknowledgements

Thank you for reading "Of Days Gone By". Please feel free to post your feedback on Kindle/Amazon, or through your favorite social networking site.

I would also like to thank a fellow author and good friend of mine, Chris Campbell (aka Norman Christof) for his constant prodding to get my work out.

Most importantly, I would not have been able to publish this novel without the ongoing support and editing reviews by my wife. She is my favorite (and first) fan.

Moving forward, feel free to check my website at www.patrickmjlozon.com for new titles and other blog updates, and please sign up to receive news on upcoming novels.

www.ingramcontent.com/pod-product-compliance
Lightning Source LLC
Chambersburg PA
CBHW032135270626
47172CB00008B/13